BLACKWOOD FARM

BLACKWOOD FARM

THE VAMPIRE CHRONICLES

ANNE RICE

ALFRED A. KNOPF

New York • Toronto

2002

THIS IS A BORZOI BOOK
PUBLISHED BY ALFRED A. KNOPF
AND ALFRED A. KNOPF CANADA

Copyright © 2002 by Anne O'Brien Rice
All rights reserved under International and Pan-American Copyright
Conventions. Published in the United States by Alfred A. Knopf,
a division of Random House, Inc., New York, and distributed
by Random House, Inc., New York. Published simultaneously
in Canada by Alfred A. Knopf Canada, Toronto, and distributed
by Random House of Canada Limited, Toronto.

www.aaknopf.com
www.randomhouse.ca

Knopf, Borzoi Books and the colophon are registered trademarks
of Random House, Inc.

Knopf Canada and colophon are trademarks.

ISBN 0-375-41199-2 (U.S.)

National Library of Canada Cataloguing in Publication

Rice, Anne
Blackwood Farm / Anne Rice.

ISBN 0-676-97542-9

I. Title.

PS3568.I265B53 2002   813'.54   C2002-903083-8

Manufactured in the United States of America
First Edition

Dedicated

to

my son,

Christopher Rice

My days have passed away, my
  thoughts are dissipated, tormenting my
  heart.
They have turned night into day,
  and after darkness I hope for light again.
If I wait hell is my house, and I have
  made my bed in darkness.
I have said to rottenness: thou art
  my father; to worms, my mother and
  my sister.
Where is now then my expectation,
  and who considereth my patience?
All that I have shall go down into
  the deepest pit: thinkest thou that there
  at least I shall have rest?

JOB 17:11–16 DV.

BLACKWOOD
FARM

1

Lestat,

If you find this letter in your house in the Rue Royale, and I do sincerely think you will find it—you'll know at once that I've broken your rules.

I know that New Orleans is off limits to Blood Hunters, and that any found there will be destroyed by you. And unlike many a rogue invader whom you have already dispatched, I understand your reasons. You don't want us to be seen by members of the Talamasca. You don't want a war with the venerable Order of Psychic Detectives, both for their sake and ours.

But please, I beg you, before you come in search of me, read what I have to say.

My name is Quinn. I'm twenty-two years old, and have been a Blood Hunter, as my Maker called it, for slightly less than a year. I'm an orphan now, as I see it, and it is to you that I turn for help.

But before I make my case, please understand that I know the Talamasca, that I knew them before the Dark Blood was ever given to me, and I know of their inherent goodness and their legendary neutrality as regards things supernatural, and I will have taken great pains to elude them in placing this letter in your flat.

That you keep a telepathic watch over New Orleans is plain to me. That you'll find the letter I have no doubt.

If you do come to bring a swift justice to me for my disobedience, assure me please that you will do your utmost to destroy a spirit which has been my companion since I was a child. This creature, a duplicate of me who has grown with me since before I can remember, now poses a danger to humans as well as to myself.

Let me explain.

As a little boy I named this spirit Goblin, and that was well before anyone had told me nursery rhymes or fairy tales in which such a word might appear. Whether the name came from the spirit himself I don't know. However, at the mere mention of the name, I could always call him to me. Many a time he came of his own accord and wouldn't be banished. At others, he was the only friend I had. Over the years, he has been my constant familiar, maturing as I matured and becoming ever more skilled at making known to me his wishes. You could say I strengthened and shaped Goblin, unwittingly creating the monster that he is now.

The truth is, I can't imagine existence without Goblin. But I have to imagine it. I have to put an end to Goblin before he metamorphoses into something utterly beyond my control.

Why do I call him a monster—this creature who was once my only playmate? The answer is simple. In the months since my being made a Blood Hunter—and understand, I had no choice whatsoever in the matter—Goblin has acquired his own taste for blood. After every feeding, I am embraced by him, and blood is drawn from me into him by a thousand infinitesimal wounds, strengthening the image of him, and lending to his presence a soft fragrance which Goblin never had before. With each passing month, Goblin becomes stronger, and his assaults on me more prolonged.

I can no longer fight him off.

It won't surprise you, I don't think, that these assaults are vaguely pleasurable, not as pleasurable to me as feeding on a human victim, but they involve a vague orgasmic shimmer that I can't deny.

But it is not my vulnerability to Goblin that worries me now. It is the question of what Goblin may become.

Now, I have read your Vampire Chronicles through and through. They were bequeathed to me by my Maker, an ancient Blood Hunter who gave me, according to his own version of things, an enormous amount of strength as well.

In your stories you talk of the origins of the vampires, quoting an ancient Egyptian Elder Blood Drinker who told the tale to the wise one, Marius, who centuries ago passed it on to you.

Whether you and Marius made up some of what was written in your books I don't know. You and your comrades, the Coven of the Articulate, as you are now called, may well have a penchant for telling lies.

But I don't think so. I'm living proof that Blood Drinkers exist—whether they are called Blood Drinkers, vampires, Children of the Night or Children of the Millennia—and the manner in which I was made conforms to what you describe.

Indeed, though my Maker called us Blood Hunters rather than vampires, he used words which have appeared in your tales. The Cloud Gift he gave to me so that I can travel effortlessly by air; and also the Mind Gift to seek out telepathically the sins of my victims; as well as the Fire Gift to ignite the fire in the iron stove here that keeps me warm.

So I believe your stories. I believe in you.

I believe you when you say that Akasha, the first of the vampires, was created when an evil spirit invaded every fiber of her being, a spirit which had, before attacking her, acquired a taste for human blood.

I believe you when you say that this spirit, named Amel by the two witches who could see him and hear him—Maharet and Mekare—exists now in all of us, his mysterious body, if we may call it that, having grown like a rampant vine to blossom in every Blood Hunter who is made by another, right on up to the present time.

I know as well from your stories that when the witches Mekare and Maharet were made Blood Hunters, they lost the ability to see and talk to spirits. And indeed my Maker told me that I would lose mine.

But I assure you, I have not lost my powers as a seer of spirits. I am still their magnet. And it is perhaps this ability in me, this receptiveness, and my early refusal to spurn Goblin, that have given him the strength to be plaguing me for vampiric blood now.

Lestat, if this creature grows ever more strong, and it seems there is nothing I can do to stop him, is it possible that he can enter a human being, as Amel did in ancient times? Is it possible that yet another species of the vampiric root may be created, and from that root yet another vine?

I cannot imagine your being indifferent to this question, or to the possibility that Goblin will become a killer of humans, though he is far from that strength right now.

I think you will understand when I say that I'm frightened for those whom I love and cherish—my mortal family—as well as for any stranger whom Goblin might eventually attack.

It's hard to write these words. For all my life I have loved Goblin and scorned anyone who denigrated him as an "imaginary playmate" or a "foolish obsession." But he and I, for so long mysterious bedfellows, are now enemies, and I dread his attacks because I feel his increasing strength.

Goblin withdraws from me utterly when I am not hunting, only to reappear when the fresh blood is in my veins. We have no spiritual intercourse now, Goblin and I. He seems afire with jealousy that I've become a Blood Hunter. It's as though his childish mind has been wiped clean of all it once learned.

It is an agony for me, all of this.

But let me repeat: it is not on my account that I write to you. It is in fear of what Goblin may become.

Of course I want to lay eyes upon you. I want to talk to you. I want to be received, if such a thing is possible, into the Coven of the Articulate. I want you, the great breaker of rules, to forgive me that I have broken yours.

I want you who were kidnapped and made a vampire against your will to look kindly on me because the same thing happened to me.

I want you to forgive my trespass into your old flat in the Rue Royale, where I hope to hide this letter. I want you to know as well that I haven't hunted in New Orleans and never will.

And speaking of hunting, I too have been taught to hunt the Evil Doer, and though my record isn't perfect, I'm learning with each feast. I've also mastered the Little Drink, as you so elegantly call it, and I'm a visitor to noisy mortal parties who is never noticed as he feeds from one after another in quick and deft moves.

But in the main, my existence is lonely and bitter. If it weren't for my mortal family, it would be unendurable. As for my Maker, I shun him and his cohorts, and with reason.

That's a story I'd like to tell you. In fact, there are many stories I want to tell you. I pray that my stories might keep you from destroying me. You know, we could play a game. We meet and I start talking, and slap damn, you kill me when I take a verbal turn you don't like.

But seriously, Goblin is my concern.

Let me add before I close that during this last year of being a fledgling Blood Hunter, of reading your Chronicles and trying to learn from them, I have often been tempted to go to the Talamasca Motherhouse at Oak Haven, outside of New Orleans. I have often been tempted to ask the Talamasca for counsel and help.

When I was a boy—and I'm hardly more than that now—there was a member of the Talamasca who was able to see Goblin as clearly as I could—a gentle, nonjudgmental Englishman named Stirling Oliver, who advised me about my powers and how they could become too strong for me to control. I grew to love Stirling within a very short time.

I also fell deeply in love with a young girl who was in the company of Stirling when I met him, a red-haired beauty with considerable paranormal power who could also see Goblin—one to whom the Talamasca had opened its generous heart.

That young girl is beyond my reach now. Her name is Mayfair, a name that is not unfamiliar to you, though this young girl probably knows nothing of your friend and companion Merrick Mayfair, even to this day.

But she is most certainly from the same family of powerful psychics—they seem to delight in calling themselves witches—and I have sworn never to see her again. With her considerable powers she would realize at once that something catastrophic has happened to me. And I cannot let my evil touch her in any way.

When I read your Chronicles, I was mildly astonished to discover that the Talamasca had turned against the Blood Hunters. My Maker had told me this, but I didn't believe it until I read it in your books.

It's still hard for me to imagine that these gentle people have broken one thousand years of neutrality in a warning against all of our kind. They seemed so proud of their benevolent history, so psychologically dependent upon a secular and kindly definition of themselves.

Obviously, I can't go to the Talamasca now. They might become my sworn enemies if I do that. They *are* my sworn enemies! And on account of my past contact, they know exactly where I live. But more significantly, I can't seek their help because you don't want it.

You and the other members of the Coven of the Articulate do not want one of us to fall into the hands of an order of scholars who are only too eager to study us at close range.

As for my red-haired Mayfair love, let me repeat that I wouldn't dream of approaching her, though I've sometimes wondered if her extraordinary powers couldn't help me to somehow put an end to Goblin for all time. But this could not be done without my frightening her and confusing her, and I won't interrupt her human destiny as mine was interrupted for me. I feel even more cut off from her than I did in the past.

And so, except for my mortal connections, I'm alone.

I don't expect your pity on account of this. But maybe your understanding will prevent you from immediately annihilating me and Goblin without so much as a warning.

That you can find both of us I have no doubt. If even half the Chronicles are true, it's plain that your Mind Gift is without measure. Nevertheless, let me tell you where I am.

My true home is the wooden Hermitage on Sugar Devil Island, deep in Sugar Devil Swamp, in northeastern Louisiana, not far from the Mississippi border. Sugar Devil Swamp is fed by the West Ruby River, which branches off from the Ruby at Rubyville.

Acres of this deep cypress swamp have belonged to my family for generations, and no mortal ever accidentally finds his way in here to Sugar Devil Island, I'm certain of it, though my great-great-great-grandfather Manfred Blackwood did build the house in which I sit, writing to you now.

Our ancestral home is Blackwood Manor, an august if not overblown house in the grandest Greek Revival style, replete with enormous and dizzying Corinthian columns, an immense structure on high ground.

For all its huffing and puffing beauty, it lacks the grace and dignity of New Orleans homes, being a truly pretentious monument to Manfred Blackwood's greed and dreams. Constructed in the 1880s, without a plantation to justify it, it had no real purpose but to give delight to those who lived in it. The entire property—swamp, land and monstrous house—is known as Blackwood Farm.

That the house and land around it are haunted is not only legend but fact. Goblin is without a doubt the most potent of the spirits, but there are ghosts here as well.

Do they want the Dark Blood from me? For the most part, they seem far too weak for such a possibility, but who is to say that ghosts don't see and learn? God knows that I have some accursed capacity to draw their attention and to endow them with some crucial vitality. It's been happening all my life.

Have I tried your patience? I hope to God that I have not.

But this letter may be my one chance with you, Lestat. And so I've said the things that matter to me most.

And when I reach your flat in the Rue Royale, I'll use every bit of wit and skill at my command to place this letter where no one will find it but you.

Believing in that ability, I sign my name,

Tarquin Blackwood,
known always as
Quinn

Postscript.

Remember I'm only twenty-two and a bit clumsy. But I can't resist this small request. If you do mean to track me down and eradicate me, could you give me an hour's notice to say some sort of farewell to the one mortal relative I most love in all the world?

In the Vampire Chronicle called *Merrick*, you were described as wearing a coat with cameo buttons. Was that the truth or someone's fanciful embellishment?

If you wore those cameo buttons—indeed, if you chose them carefully and you loved them—then for the sake of those cameos, let me, before being destroyed, say farewell to an elderly woman of incredible charm and benevolence who loves each evening to spread out her hundreds of cameos on her marble table and examine them one by one in the light. She is my great-aunt and my teacher in all things, a woman who has sought to endow me with all I need to live an important life.

I'm not worthy of her love now. I'm not alive now. But she doesn't know this. My nightly visits to her are cautious but nevertheless crucial to her. And should I be taken from her without warning and without some explanation, it would be a cruelty she doesn't deserve.

Ah, there is much more that I could tell you about her cameos—about the role which they have played in my fate.

But for now, let me only plead with you. Let me live, and help me destroy Goblin. Or put an end to us both.

Sincerely,

Quinn

2

For a long time after I finished the letter, I didn't move.

I sat listening to the inevitable sounds of Sugar Devil Swamp, my eyes on the pages before me, noting against my will the boring regularity of the handwriting, the muted lamps around me reflected in the marble flooring, the glass windows open to the night breeze.

All was well in my little palazzo in the swampland.

No sign of Goblin. No sense of Goblin's thirst or enmity. Nothing but that which was natural, and faraway, keen to my vampiric ears, the faint stirrings from Blackwood Manor, where Aunt Queen was just rising, with the loving help of Jasmine, our housekeeper, for a mildly eventful night. Soon the television would be going with an enchanting old black-and-white movie. *Dragonwyck* or *Laura*, *Rebecca* or *Wuthering Heights*. In an hour perhaps Aunt Queen would be saying to Jasmine, "Where is my Little Boy?"

But for now there was time for courage. Time to follow through.

I took the cameo out of my pocket and looked at it. A year ago, when I was still mortal—still alive—I would have had to hold it to the lamp, but not now. I could see it clearly.

It was my own head, in semi-profile, carved skillfully from a fine piece of double-strata sardonyx so that the image was entirely white and remarkably detailed. The background was a pure and shining black.

It was a heavy cameo, and excellent as to the craft. I'd had it done to give to my beloved Aunt Queen, more of a little joke than anything else, but the Dark Blood had come before the perfect moment. And now that moment was forever past.

What did it show of me? A long oval face, with features that were too delicate—a nose too narrow, eyes round with round eyebrows and a full cupid's-bow mouth that made me look as if I were a twelve-year-old girl. No huge eyes, no high cheekbones, no rugged jaw. Just very pretty, yes, too pretty, which is why I'd scowled for most of the photographs taken for the portrait; but the artist hadn't carved that scowl into the face.

In fact, he'd given me a trace of a smile. My short curly hair he'd rendered in thick swirls as if it were an Apollonian halo. He'd carved my shirt collar, jacket lapel and tie with equal grace.

Of course the cameo said nothing of my height of six foot four inches, that my hair was jet black, my eyes blue, or of the fact that I was slight of build. I had the kind of long thin fingers which were very good for the piano, which I played now and then. And it was my height that told people that in spite of my all too precious face and feminine hands, I really was a young man.

And so there was this enigmatic creature in a good likeness. A creature asking for sympathy. A creature saying crassly:

"Well, think about it, Lestat. I'm young, I'm stupid. And I'm pretty. Look at the cameo. I'm pretty. Give me a chance."

I'd have engraved the back with those words in tiny script, but the back was an oval photo case, and there was my image again in dull color, verifying the accuracy of the portrait on the other side.

There was one engraved word on the gold frame, right beneath the cameo, however: the name Quinn, in a good imitation of that routine handwriting which I had always hated so much—the left-handed one trying to be normal, I imagine, the seer of ghosts saying, "I'm disciplined and not insane."

I gathered up the pages of the letter, reread them quickly, bristling again at my unimaginative handwriting, then folded the pages and put the cameo with them inside of a narrow brown envelope, which I then sealed.

I put this envelope in the inside breast pocket of my black blazer. I closed the top button of my white dress shirt and I adjusted my simple red silk tie. Quinn, the snappy dresser. Quinn, worthy to be a subject in the Vampire Chronicles. Quinn, dressed for begging to be allowed in.

I sat back again, listening. No Goblin. Where was Goblin? I felt an aching loneliness for him. I felt the emptiness of the night air. He was waiting for me to hunt, waiting for the fresh blood. But I had no intention of hunting tonight, even though I was faintly hungry. I was going into New Orleans. I was going, perhaps, to my death.

Goblin couldn't guess at what was happening. Goblin had never been more than a child. Goblin looked like me, yes, at every stage of my life, but he was forever the infant. Whenever he had grabbed my left hand with his right, the script had been a child's scrawl.

I leaned over and touched the remote control button on the marble desk. The torchères dimmed and slowly went out. The darkness came into the Hermitage. The sounds seemed to grow louder: the call of the night heron, the subtle movement of the rank dark waters, the scurrying of tiny creatures through the tops of the tangled cypress and gum. I could smell the alligators, who were as wary of the island as men. I could smell the fetid heat itself.

The moon was generous and gradually I made out a bit of the sky, which was a bright metallic blue.

The swamp was at its thickest here around the island—the cypresses, a thousand years old, their knobby roots surrounding the shore, their misshapen branches heavy with trailing Spanish moss. It was as if they meant to hide the Hermitage, and perhaps they did.

Only the lightning now and then attacked these old sentinels. Only the lightning was fearless of the legends that said some evil dwelt on Sugar Devil Island: go there and you might never come back.

I'd been told about those legends when I was fifteen. And at twenty-one I heard it all repeated, but vanity and fascination had drawn me to the Hermitage, to the pure mystery of it—this strong two-story house, and the nearby inexplicable mausolem—and now there was no real later. There was only this immortality, this brimming power which shut me off from actuality or time.

A man in a pirogue would take a good hour to navigate his way out of here, picking through the tree roots, and back to the landing at the foot of the high ground where Blackwood Manor stood so arrogant and aloof.

I didn't really love this Hermitage, though I needed it. I didn't love the grim gold-and-granite mausoleum with its strange Roman engravings, though I had to hide inside it from the sun by day.

But I did love Blackwood Manor, with the irrational and possessive love that only great houses can draw from us—houses that say, "I was here before you were born and I'll be here after you"; houses that seem a responsibility as much as a haven of dreams.

The history of Blackwood Manor had as much of a grip on me as its overweening beauty. I'd lived my whole life on Blackwood Farm and in the Manor, except for my wonderful adventures abroad.

How so many uncles and aunts had managed to leave Blackwood Manor over the years, I couldn't fathom, but they weren't important to me, those strangers who had gone North and only came home now and then for funerals. The house had me in thrall.

I was debating now. Do I go back, just to walk through the rooms again? Do I go back to seek out the large rear first-floor bedroom where my beloved Aunt Queen was just settling into her favorite chair? I did have another cameo in my jacket pocket, one expressly bought for her only nights before in New York, and I should give it to her, shouldn't I? It was a wonderful specimen, one of the finest—.

But no. I couldn't manage a partial farewell, could I? I couldn't hint that something might happen to me. I couldn't gleefully descend into mystery, into which I'd already sunk up to my eyeballs: Quinn, the night visitor, Quinn who likes dimly lighted rooms now and shies from lamps as though he suffers from an exotic disease. What good would a partial farewell do for my beloved and gentle Aunt Queen?

If I failed tonight, I would be another legend: "That incorrigible Quinn. He went deep into Sugar Devil Swamp, though everybody told him not to; he went to that accursed island Hermitage, and one night he just didn't come back."

The fact was, I didn't believe Lestat would blast me into infinity. I didn't believe he would do it without letting me tell him my story, all or at least in part. Maybe I was just too young to believe it. Maybe because I'd read the Chronicles so avidly, I felt Lestat was as close to me as I was to him.

Madness, most likely. But I was bound and determined to get as near to Lestat as I could. From where and how he kept watch over New Orleans I didn't know. When and how often he visited his French Quarter flat I didn't know either. But this letter and the gift of the onyx cameo of myself was to go to that flat tonight.

Finally I got up from the leather-and-gold chair.

I went out of the splendid marble-floored house, and with no more than thought to direct me I let myself rise from the warm earth slowly, experiencing a delicious lightness, until I could see from the cool heights far above the huge long meandering black mass of the swamp, and the lights of the big house shining as if it were a lantern on the smooth grass.

Towards New Orleans I willed myself, using this strangest of powers, the Cloud Gift, traversing the waters of Lake Pontchartrain and moving towards the infamous town house in the Rue Royale, which all Blood Hunters knew was the house of the invincible Lestat.

"One hell of a devil," my Maker had called him, "keeping his properties in his own name though the Talamasca is hounding him. He means to outlast them. He's more merciful than I."

Merciful; that was what I was counting on now. Lestat, wherever you are, be merciful. I don't come with disrespect. I need you, as my letter will show.

Slowly I descended, down, down, into the balmy air again, a fleeting shadow to prying eyes if there were any, until I stood in the rear courtyard of the town house, near to the murmuring fountain, looking up at the curving iron stairs that led to Lestat's rear door.

All right. I am here. So the rules have been broken. So I'm in the courtyard of the Brat Prince himself. Descriptions came to mind from the pages of the Chronicles, complex as the bougainvillea vine running rampant up the iron columns to the upstairs cast-iron railing. It was like being in a very shrine.

All around me I could hear the brash noises of the French Quarter: the clatter of restaurant kitchens, the happy voices of the inevitable tourists on the pavements. I heard the thinnest sound of the jazz blaring out of doors on Bourbon Street. I heard the creeping rumble of cars passing sluggishly in front.

The little courtyard itself was tight and beautiful; the sheer height of its brick walls caught me off guard. The glistening green banana trees were the biggest I'd ever seen, their waxy stalks buckling the purple flagstones here and there. But this was no abandoned place.

Someone had been here to clip the dead leaves from the banana groves. Someone had taken away the shriveled bananas that always wither in New Orleans before they ripen. Someone had cut back the abundant roses so that the patio itself was clear.

Even the water gurgling from the conch in the stone cherub's hand down into the basin of the fountain was fresh and clean.

All these sweet little details made me feel all the more like a trespasser, but I was too damned foolishly passionate to be afraid.

Then I saw a light shining through the rear windows above, a very dim light, as if from a lamp deep in the flat.

That did frighten me, but again the all-possessing madness in me mounted. Would I get to speak to Lestat himself? And what if, catching sight of me, he sent out the Fire Gift without hesitating? The letter, the onyx cameo, my own bitter pleas wouldn't have a chance.

I should have given Aunt Queen the new cameo. I should have grabbed her up and kissed her. I should have made a speech to her. I was about to die.

Only a perfect idiot could have been as exhilarated as I was. Lestat, I love you. Here comes Quinn to be your student and slave!

I hurried up the curving iron stairs, careful not to make a sound. And once I reached the rear balcony, I caught the distinct scent of a human being inside. A human being. What did this mean? I stopped and sent the Mind Gift before me to search out the rooms.

At once a confusing message reached me. There was a human there, no doubt of it, and he was furtive, this one, moving in haste, painfully conscious of the fact that he had no right to be where he was. And this someone, this human, knew that I was here as well.

For a moment, I didn't know what to do. Trespassing, I had caught an intruder in the act. A strange protective feeling flooded me. This person had invaded Lestat's property. How dare he? What sort of a bumbler was he? And how did he know that I was here, and that my mind had searched his?

In fact, this strange unwelcome being had a Mind Gift that was almost as strong as mine. I sounded for his name and he yielded it up to me: Stirling Oliver, my old friend, from the Talamasca. And at the same moment, as I detected his identity, I heard his mind recognize me.

Quinn, he said mentally, just as if he were addressing me. But what did he know of me? It had been years since I had set eyes on Stirling. Did he sense already the change that had been worked in me? Could he tell such a thing with his quick telepathy? Dear God, I had to banish it from my own mind. There was time to get out of this, time to go back to the Hermitage and leave Stirling to his furtive investigation, time to flee before he knew just what I'd become.

Yeah, leave—and now—and let him think I'd become a common mortal reader of the Chronicles, and come back when he's nowhere in sight.

But I couldn't leave. I was too lonely. I was too hell-bent on confrontation. That was the perfect truth. And here was Stirling, and here was the entranceway perhaps to Lestat's heart.

On impulse I did the most forbidden of all things. I opened the unlocked back door of the flat and I went inside. I paused for only a breathless second in the dark elegant rear parlor, glancing at its roaring Impressionist paintings, and then I went down the corridor past the obviously empty bedrooms and found Stirling in the front room—a most formal drawing room, crowded with gilded furniture, and with its lace-covered windows over the street.

Stirling stood at the tall bookcase to the left side, and there was an open book in his hand. He merely looked at me as I stepped into the light of the overhead chandelier.

What did he see? For the moment I didn't seek to find out. I was too busy looking at him, and realizing how much I loved him still for those times when I was the eighteen-year-old boy who saw spirits, and that he looked much the same as he had in those days—soft gray hair combed back loose from his high forehead and receding temples, large sympathetic gray eyes. He seemed no older than sixty-odd years, as if age hadn't touched him, his body still slender and healthy, tricked out in a white-and-blue seersucker suit.

Only gradually, though it must have been a matter of seconds, did I realize he was afraid. He was looking up at me—on account of my height just about everybody looks up at me—and for all his seeming dignity, and he did have plenty of that, he could see the changes in me, but he wasn't sure what had happened. He knew only that he felt instinctive and mindful fear.

Now, I am a Blood Hunter who can pass for human but not necessarily with someone as savvy as this man was. And then we had the question of telepathy, though I'd done my best to close up my mind the way my Maker had told me, that by simple will, it could be done.

"Quinn," said Stirling. "What's wrong with you?" The soft British accent took me back four and a half years in a finger snap.

"Everything's wrong with me, Stirling," I answered before I could rein myself in. "But why are you here?" Then I came right to the point like the blunderer I was. "Do you have Lestat's permission to be in this flat?"

"No," he said immediately. "I must confess I don't have it. And what about you, Quinn?" His voice was full of concern. "Why are you here?"

He shoved the book back into place on the shelf and took a step towards me, but I stepped back into the shadows of the hall.

I almost buckled on account of his kindness. But another inevitable element had come sharply into play. His sweet delectable human scent was strong, and suddenly I saw him divorced from all I knew of him. I saw him as prey.

In fact, I felt the immense impossible gulf that now divided us, and I was hungry for him, hungry as if his kindness would pour into me in his very blood.

But Stirling was no Evil Doer. Stirling wasn't game. I was losing my fledgling mind as I looked at him. My acute loneliness was driving me. My hunger was bedeviling me. I wanted both to feast on him and tell him all my woes and griefs.

"Don't come close to me, Stirling," I said, struggling to sound self-possessed. "You shouldn't be here. You have no right to be here. If you're so damned clever, why didn't you just come by day, when Lestat couldn't stop you?"

The scent of the blood was driving me crazy, that and my savage desire to close the gap between us, by murder or by love.

"I don't fully know the answer to that, Quinn," he said, his British accent formal and eloquent though his tone was not. "But you're the last person I expected to find here. Quinn, let me look at you, please."

Again, I said no. I was shaking. "Stirling, don't try to charm me with that old easy manner," I pressed on. "You might find someone else here who's a lot more dangerous to you than I am. Or don't you believe Lestat's stories? Don't tell me you think his vampires exist only in books."

"You're one of them," he said softly. He frowned but the frown cleared in a moment. "Is this Lestat's handiwork? He brought you over?"

I was amazed at his boldness, polite as it was. But then he was so much older than me, so used to a graceful authority, and I was painfully young. Again, in waves I felt the old love for him, the old need of him, and again it was fusing perfectly, and stupidly, with my thirst.

"It wasn't Lestat's doing," I said. "In fact, he had nothing to do with it. I came here looking for him, Stirling, and now this has happened, this little tragedy that I've run into you."

"A tragedy?"

"What else can it be, Stirling? You know who I am. You know where I live. You know all about my family at Blackwood Manor. How can I just walk out of here now that I've seen you and you've seen me?"

I felt the thirst thick in my throat. My vision was blurring. I heard myself speaking:

"Don't try to tell me that if I let you go, the Talamasca wouldn't come looking for me. Don't try to tell me that you and your cohorts wouldn't be prowling about in search of me. I know what would happen. This is god-awful, Stirling."

His fear quickened, but he was struggling not to give in to it. And my hunger was becoming uncontrollable. If I let it go, if I let it play itself out, the act would seem inevitable, and seeming inevitable was all that conscience needed; but that just couldn't happen, not to Stirling Oliver. I was hopelessly confused.

Before I realized what I was doing, I moved closer to him. I could see the blood in him now as well as smell it. And he made a fatal misstep. That is, he moved backwards, as if he couldn't stop himself from doing it, and he seemed in that gesture to be more the victim than ever. That backwards step caused me to advance.

"Stirling, you shouldn't have come here," I said. "You're an invader." But I could hear the flatness of my voice in my hunger, the meaningless-ness of the words. Invader, invader, invader.

"You can't harm me, Quinn," he said, his voice very level and reason-able, "you wouldn't do it. There's too much between us. I've always understood you. I've always understood Goblin. Are you going to betray all that now?"

"It's an old debt," I said, my voice having fallen to a whisper.

I knew I was in the bright light of the chandelier now, and he could see the subtle enhancement of the transformation. The transformation was very fancy, so very fancy. And it seemed to me in my demented state that the fear in him had increased to silent panic and that the panic was sharpening the fragrance of the blood.

Do dogs smell fear? Vampires smell it. Vampires count on it. Vam-pires find it savory. Vampires can't resist it.

"It's wrong," he said, but he too was whispering as though my very stare had weakened him, which it can certainly do to mortals, and he knew there was no point to a fight. "Don't do it, my boy," he said, the words barely audible.

I found myself reaching out for his shoulder, and when my fingers touched him I felt an electricity that shot through my limbs. Crush him. Crush his bones, but first and foremost swallow his soul in the blood.

"Don't you realize . . ." He trailed off, and out of his mind I sub-tracted the rest, that the Talamasca would be further inflamed, that it would be bad for everyone. The vampires, the Blood Hunters, the Chil-dren of the Millennia had all left New Orleans. Scattered in the dark were the vampires. It was a truce. And now I meant to shatter it!

"But they don't know me, you see," I said, "not in this form, they don't. Only you do, my old friend, and that's the horror. You know me, and that's why this has to come about."

I bent down, close to him, and kissed the side of his throat. My friend, my deepest friend in all the world once. And now we'll have this union. Lust old and new. The boy I'd been loving him. I felt the blood pushing through the artery. My left arm slid beneath his right arm. Don't hurt him. He couldn't get away from me. He didn't even try.

"This will be painless, Stirling," I whispered. I sank my teeth cleanly, and the blood filled my mouth very slowly, and with it there came the sudden course of his life and dreams.

Innocent. The word burned through the pleasure. In a luminous drift of figures and voices he emerged, pushing his way through the crowd; Stirling, the man, pleading with me in my mental vision, saying *Innocent.* There I was, the boy of that old time, and Stirling saying *Innocent.* I couldn't stop what had begun.

It was someone else who did that for me.

I felt an iron grip on my shoulder and I was whipped back away from Stirling, and Stirling staggered, almost falling, and then he tripped and sank down sideways into a chair at the desk.

I was slammed against the bookcase. I lapped at the blood on my lip and I tried to fight the dizziness. The chandelier appeared to be rocking, and the colors of the paintings on the wall were afire.

A firm hand was placed against my chest to steady me and to hold me back.

And then I realized I was looking at Lestat.

3

QUICKLY I REGAINED my balance. His eyes were on me and I didn't have the slightest intention of looking away. Nevertheless, I looked him up and down because I couldn't help it, and because he was as breathtaking as he has always described himself to be, and I had to see him, truly see him, even if he was to be the last thing I ever saw.

His skin was a pale golden that offset his violet blue eyes wonderfully, and his hair was a true mane of yellow, tousled and curling just above his shoulders. His colored glasses, almost the same violet tint as his eyes, were pushed up into his hair, and he was staring at me, golden eyebrows scowling slightly, waiting perhaps for me to regain my senses; I honestly didn't know.

Quickly I realized he was wearing the black velvet jacket with the cameo buttons that had been his costume in the Chronicle called *Merrick*, each little cameo almost certainly of sardonyx, the coat itself very fancy with its pinched waist and flaring skirt. His linen shirt was open at the throat; his gray pants weren't important and neither were his black boots.

What engraved itself into my consciousness was his face—square and taut, the eyes very big and the well-shaped mouth voluptuous, and the jaw somewhat hard, the whole more truly well proportioned and appealing than he could ever have claimed.

In fact, his own descriptions of himself didn't do him justice because his looks, though certainly a handful of obvious blessings, were ignited by a potent inner fire.

He wasn't staring at me with hatred. He wasn't steadying me anymore with his hand.

I cursed myself, from the pit of my heart, that I was taller than he was, that he was in fact looking up at me. Maybe he'd cheerfully obliterate me on that account alone.

"The letter," I stammered. "The letter!" I whispered, but though my hand groped, and my mind groped, I couldn't reach inside my coat for the letter. I was wobbling in fear.

And as I stood there shivering and sweating, he reached inside my jacket and withdrew the envelope. Flash of sparkling fingernails.

"This is for me, is it, Tarquin Blackwood?" he asked. His voice had a touch of the French accent, no more. He smiled suddenly and he looked as if he couldn't hurt anyone for the world. He was too attractive, too friendly, too young. But the smile vanished as quickly as it had come.

"Yes," I said. Or rather it was a stutter. "The letter, please read it." I faltered, then pressed on. "Before you . . . make up your mind."

He tucked the letter into his own inside pocket and then he turned to Stirling, who sat dazed and silent, eyes cloudy, his hands clinging to the back of the chair before the desk. The back was like a shield in front of him, though a useless one as I well knew.

Lestat's eyes fixed on me again:

"We don't feed on members of the Talamasca, Little Brother," he said. "But you"—he looked at Stirling—"you nearly got what you almost deserve."

Stirling stared forward, plainly unable to answer, and only shook his head.

"Why did you come here, Mr. Oliver?" Lestat asked him.

Again, Stirling merely shook his head. I saw the tiny drops of blood on his starched white collar. I felt an overwhelming shame, a shame so deep and painful it filled me completely, banishing even the faintest aftertaste of the attempted feast.

I went silently crazy.

Stirling had almost died, and for my thirst. Stirling was alive. Stirling was in danger now, danger from Lestat. Behold: Lestat, like a blaze in front of me. Yes, he could pass for human, but what a human—magnetic and charged with energy as he continued to take command.

"Mr. Oliver, I'm talking to you," Lestat said in a soft yet imperious tone. He picked up Stirling by the lapels and, moving him clumsily to the far corner of the parlor, he flung him down into a large satin upholstered wing chair.

Stirling looked the worse for it—who wouldn't?—still unable apparently to focus his gaze.

Lestat sat down on the velvet couch very near him. I was completely forgotten for the moment, or so I assumed.

"Mr. Oliver," said Lestat, "I'm asking you. What made you come into my house?"

"I don't know," said Stirling. He glanced up at me and then at the figure who was questioning him, and I struggled, because I couldn't help it, to see what he was seeing—this vampire whose skin still glowed though it was tanned, and whose eyes were prismatic and undeniably fierce.

The fabled beauty of Lestat seemed potent as a drug. And the crowning light of the chandelier was merciless or splendid depending entirely on one's point of view.

"Yes, you do know why you came here," said Lestat, his voice subdued, the French accent no more than a beguiling taste. "It wasn't enough for the Talamasca to drive me out of the city. You have to come into those places that belong to me?"

"I was wrong to do it," Stirling said. It was spoken in a sigh. He scowled and pressed his lips together hard. "I shouldn't have done it." For the first time he looked directly into Lestat's eyes.

Lestat glanced up at me.

Sitting forward he reached over and slipped his fingers behind Stirling's bloodstained collar, startling Stirling and glaring up at me.

"We don't spill blood when we feed, Little Brother," he said with a passing mischievous smile. "You have much to learn."

The words hit me rather like a wallop and I found myself speechless. Did this mean that I'd walk out of here alive?

Don't kill Stirling, that's what I was thinking; and then suddenly Lestat, as he still stared at me, made a short little laugh.

"Tarquin, turn that chair around," he said, gesturing to the desk, "and sit down. You make me nervous standing there. You're too damned tall. And you're making Stirling Oliver nervous as well."

I felt a great rush of relief, but as I tried to do what he'd told me to do my hands were shaking so badly that I was again full of shame. Finally, I managed to sit down facing the pair of them, but a polite distance away.

Stirling made a small frown as he looked at me, but it was entirely sympathetic and he was still obviously off base. I hadn't drunk enough blood to account for his dizziness. It was the act of it, the drawing on his heart. That, and the fact that Lestat had come, Lestat had interrupted us, Lestat was here and he was demanding again of Stirling, Why had Stirling come into the flat?

"You could have come here by day," said Lestat, addressing Stirling in an even voice. "I have human guards from sunup to sundown but the Talamasca is good at bribing guards. Why didn't you take the hint that I look after my properties myself once the sun has set? You disobeyed the directive of your own Superior General. You disobeyed your own common sense."

Stirling nodded, eyes veering off, as if he had no argument, and then in a weak but dignified voice he said:

"The door was unlocked."

"Don't insult me," said Lestat, his voice still patient and even. "It's my house."

Again, Stirling appeared to meet Lestat's gaze. He looked at him steadily and then he spoke in a more coherent voice.

"I was wrong to do it, and you've caught me. Yes, I've disobeyed the directive of the Superior General, that's true. I came because I couldn't resist it. I came because perhaps I didn't quite believe in you. I didn't believe in spite of all I'd read and been told."

Lestat shook his head disapprovingly and again there came that short little laugh.

"I expect that credulity of mortal readers of the Chronicles," he said. "I expect it even of fledglings like Little Brother here. But I don't expect it of the Talamasca, who have so ceremoniously declared war on us."

"For what it's worth," said Stirling, gathering his strength somewhat, "I was not for that war. I voted against it as soon as I heard of the declaration. I was for closing the Motherhouse here in Louisiana, if need be. But then . . . I was for accepting our losses and retreating to our libraries abroad."

"You drove me out of my own city," said Lestat. "You question my neighbors in these precincts. You rummage through all my public property titles and records. And now you trespass, and you say it was because you didn't believe? That's an excuse but not a reason."

"The reason was I wanted to see you," said Stirling, his voice growing stronger. "I wanted what others in the Order have had. I wanted to see you with my own eyes."

"And now that you have seen me," Lestat replied, "what precisely will you do?" He glanced at me again, a flash of brilliant eyes and a smile that was gone in an instant as he looked back to the man in the chair.

"What we always do," said Stirling. "Write about it, put it into a report to the Elders, copy it to the File on the Vampire Lestat—that is, if you let me leave here, if that's your choice."

"I haven't harmed any of you, have I?" Lestat asked. "Think on it. When have I harmed a true and active member of the Talamasca? Don't blame me for what others have done. And since your warlike declaration, since you sought to drive me right out of my home, I've shown remarkable restraint."

"No, you haven't," Stirling quietly replied.

I was shocked.

"What do you mean?" Lestat demanded. "What on earth can you mean? I think I've been a gentleman about it." He smiled at Stirling for the first time.

"Yes, you've been a gentleman," Stirling responded. "But I hardly think you've been restrained."

"Do you know how it affects me to be driven out of New Orleans?" Lestat asked, voice still tempered. "Do you know how it affects me to know I can't wander the French Quarter for fear of your spies in the Café du Monde, or wander the Rue Royale with the evening shoppers, just because one of your glorified gossips might be wandering about too? Do you know how it wounds me to leave behind the one city in the world with which I'm truly in love?"

Stirling roused himself at these words. "But haven't you always been too clever for us?" he asked.

"Well, of course," Lestat rejoined with a shrug.

"Besides," Stirling went on, "you haven't been driven out. You've been here. You've been seen by our members, sitting very boldly in the Café du Monde, I might add, presiding over a hot cup of useless café au lait."

I was stunned.

"Stirling!" I whispered. "For the love of Christ, don't argue."

Again Lestat looked at me, but not with anger. He returned to Stirling.

Stirling hadn't finished. He went on firmly: "You still feed off the riffraff," he said. "The authorities don't care, but we recognize the patterns. We know it's you."

I was mortified. How could Stirling talk like this?

Lestat broke into an irrepressible laugh.

"And even so, you came by night?" he demanded. "You dared to come, knowing I might find you here?"

"I think . . ." Stirling hesitated, then went on. "I think I wanted to challenge you. I think, as I said, that I committed a sin of pride."

Thank God for this confession, I thought. "Committed a sin"—

really good words. I was quaking, watching the two of them, appalled by Stirling's fearless tone.

"We respect you," said Stirling, "more than you deserve."

I gasped.

"Oh, do explain that to me!" said Lestat, smiling. "In what form comes this respect, I should like to know. If I'm truly in your debt, I should like to say thanks."

"St. Elizabeth's," said Stirling, his voice rolling gracefully now, "the building where you lay for so many years, sleeping on the chapel floor. We've never sought to enter it or discover what goes on there. And as you said we're very good at bribing guards. Your Chronicles made your sleep famous. And we knew that we could penetrate the building. We could glimpse you in the daylight hours, unprotected, lying on the marble. What a lure that was—the sleeping vampire who no longer bothered with the trappings of a coffin. A dark deadly inverse of the sleeping King Arthur, waiting for England to need him again. But we never crept into your enormous lodgings. As I said, I think we respected you more than you deserve."

I shut my eyes for an instant, certain of disaster.

But Lestat only broke into another fit of chuckling and laughing.

"Sheer nonsense," he said. "You and your members were afraid. You never came near St. Elizabeth's night or day because you were plainly afraid of the ancient ones among us who could have put out your light like a match. You were afraid too of the rogue vampires who came prowling, the ones who wouldn't respect the name Talamasca enough to give you a wide berth. As for the daylight hours, you had no clue what you'd find—what high-paid thugs might have terminated you and buried you under the concrete basement floor. It was a purely practical matter."

Stirling narrowed his eyes. "Yes, we did have to be careful," he conceded. "Nevertheless, there were times—."

"Foolishness," said Lestat. "In point of pure fact, my infamous sleep ended before your declaration of war on us was made. And what if I did show myself sitting 'very boldly' in the Café du Monde! How dare you use the word 'boldly'? You imply I don't have the right!"

"You feed on your fellow human beings," said Stirling calmly. "Have you seriously forgotten that?"

I was frantic. Only the smile on Lestat's face reassured me that Stirling wasn't headed for certain death.

"No, I never forget what I do," said Lestat equably. "But surely you don't mean to take on the whole question of what I do now for my own survival! And you must remember, I'm not a human being—far from it, and farther from it with every passing adventure and every passing year. I've been to Heaven and to Hell; let me ask you to remember that."

Lestat paused as though he himself were remembering this, and Stirling tried to answer but plainly could not. Lestat pressed on in a measured voice:

"I've been in a human body and recovered this body you see before you. I've been the consort of a creature whom others called a goddess. And yes, I feed off my fellow human beings because it's my nature, and you know it, and you know what care I take with every mortal morsel, that it be tainted and vicious and unfit for human life. The point I was trying to make is that your declaration against us was ill conceived."

"I agree with you; it was a foolish Declaration of Enmity. It should never have been put forth."

"Declaration of Enmity, is that what you called it?" Lestat asked.

"I think those are the official words," said Stirling. "We've always been an authoritarian order. In fact, we don't know much about democracy at all. When I spoke of my vote, I was speaking of a symbolic voice rather than a literal one. Declaration of Enmity, yes, those were the words. It was a rather misguided and naive thing."

"Ah, misguided and naive," Lestat repeated. "I like that. And it might do you good, all of you in the Talamasca, to remember that you're a pretentious bunch of meddlers, and your Elders are no better than the rest of you."

Stirling seemed to be relaxing, mildly fascinated, but I couldn't relax. I was too afraid of what might happen at any moment.

"I have a theory about the Declaration of Enmity," Stirling said.

"Which is?" asked Lestat.

"I think the Elders thought in their venerable minds, and God knows, I don't really know their venerable minds, that the Declaration would bring certain of our members back to us who had been inducted into your ranks."

"Oh, that's lovely." Lestat laughed. "Why are you mincing words like this? Is it on account of the boy?"

"Yes, perhaps I mince words because of him," Stirling answered, "but honestly, we members of the Talamasca think in language such as this."

"Well, for your records and your files," Lestat said, "we don't have ranks. In fact, I'd say that as a species we are given to rigidly individual

personalities and obdurate differences, and peculiar mobility as to matters of friendship and company and meeting of minds. We come together
in small covens and then are driven wildly apart again. We know little
lasting peace with each other. We have no ranks."

This was intriguing and my fear melted just a little as Stirling came
back in his careful polite voice.

"I understand that," he said. "But to return to the question at hand,
as to why the Elders made this warlike declaration, I think they honestly
believed that those vampires who had once been part of us might come
to try to reason with us, and we might benefit thereby in meeting with
actual beings such as yourself. We might carry our knowledge of you to
a higher realm."

"It was all scholastic is what you're saying," said Lestat.

"Yes. And surely you must realize what it has meant for us to lose
three members to your collective power, whatever the cause of it, and no
matter how it was accomplished. We were stunned by each defection,
and mystified as to the dialogue, if any, that might have preceded what
happened. We wanted to learn, you see. We wanted . . . to know."

"Well, it didn't work, did it?" said Lestat, his calm demeanor
unchanged. "And you weren't content with the Chronicles alone, were
you? They told you all about the dialogue. But you and the Elders
wanted this eye-to-eye view."

"No, it didn't work," said Stirling, and he seemed now to be possessed of his full dignity and strength. His gray eyes were clear. "On the
contrary, we provoked from you more audacity. You dared to publish a
Chronicle using the name Merrick Mayfair. You dared to do this even
though a great family by the name of Mayfair lives in this city and its
environs to this day. You had no care when you did that."

I felt a sharp stab in my heart. My own beloved Mayfair flashed
before my eyes. But here was Stirling being positively reckless again.

"Audacity!" said Lestat, his smile broadening as he glared at Stirling.
"You accuse me of audacity! You're living and breathing now entirely
because I want it."

"No doubt of it, but you are audacious," insisted Stirling.

I was about to faint.

"Audacious and proud of it," Lestat fired back. "But let's get one
thing straight. I am not the sole author of the Chronicles. Blame your
own versatile David Talbot for the Chronicle of Merrick Mayfair. It was
David's story to tell. Merrick wanted the Dark Gift. Merrick Mayfair

was a witch before she was ever a vampire. Who should know that better than you? There was no lie there. And it was David's choice to use her name, as well as the name of the Talamasca, I might add. What is all of this to me?"

"He wouldn't have done it without your blessing," said Stirling with astonishing confidence.

"You think not?" demanded Lestat. "And why should I care about some mortal family of witches? The Mayfairs, what are they to me? And what is a great family, pray tell, a rich family? Vampires loathe witches, whether they're rich or poor. Anyone who reads the story of Merrick Mayfair can see why. Not that Merrick isn't anything but a princess among us now. Besides, our eager readers think it's all fiction, and how do you know what's real and what's not?"

I wept inside thinking of my red-haired Mayfair! And on they talked.

"Thank God your readers think it's fiction," said Stirling, becoming faintly more heated, "and the Mayfair family is unaware of the truths you told; and a great family is one that has survived the ages, and treasures bonds of love. What else? You seek a family, always and everywhere. I see it in your Chronicles."

"Stop, I won't listen to you," said Lestat sharply but without raising his voice. "I'm not here to be judged by you. You've had corruption in your ranks. You know you have. And I know full well myself. And now I find that you're corrupt, disobeying your Elders to come here. You think I'd give you the Dark Blood?"

"I don't want it," said Stirling in suppressed amazement. "I don't seek it. I wanted to see you, and hear your voice."

"And now you have, and what will you do?"

"I told you. Write about it. Confess to the Elders. Describe it all."

"Oh, no you won't," said Lestat. "You'll leave out one key part."

"And what is that?" asked Stirling.

"You're such an admirable bunch," said Lestat, shaking his head. "You can't guess what part?"

"We try to be admirable," said Stirling. "I'll be condemned by the Elders. I might even be removed from Louisiana, though I doubt it. I have other important work to do."

Again, there came that stab in my heart. I thought of the "great family of Mayfair." I thought of my red-haired love, my Mayfair witch, whom I would never see again. Was that his important work? I wished with all my heart I could ask him.

Lestat appeared to be studying Stirling, who had fallen silent, staring at Lestat, perhaps doing that little mental trick of memorizing all the details about which he would write later on. Members of the Talamasca were especially trained to do it.

I tried to scan his mind, but I couldn't get in, and I didn't dare to try with Lestat. Lestat would know.

Lestat broke the silence.

"Revoke it, this Declaration of Enmity," he said.

Stirling was startled. He thought for a moment and then he said:

"I can't do that. I'm not one of the Elders. I can tell them that you asked me to revoke the Declaration. That's all I can do."

Lestat's eyes softened. They drifted over Stirling and then to me. For a long moment Lestat and I looked at each other, and then I weakened and looked politely away.

I had glimpsed something as we looked at each other.

It was something I'd never heard mentioned in the Chronicles—a shade of difference between Lestat's eyes. One eye was almost imperceptibly larger than the other, and colored by a little blood. I'm not sure that as a mortal I could have detected such a small difference. I was confused by having seen it now. If Lestat counted it as a flaw, he would hate me for seeing it.

Lestat was gazing at Stirling.

"We'll make a deal, you and I," he said.

"I'm relieved to hear it," Stirling said. It had the same gentle arrogance of his earlier remarks.

"It's a simple bargain," said Lestat, "but if you refuse me, or if you go against me, I'll go against you. I could have done that before now, I'm sure you know."

"David Talbot won't let you hurt us," said Stirling with quiet spunk. "And there's an old one, an ancient one, one of the grandest in your tales, and she, the great authority, won't let you harm us either, isn't that so?"

"Stirling!" I whispered before I could stop myself.

But Lestat seemed only to weigh this for a moment. Then:

"I could still hurt you," he said. "I don't play by anybody's rules but my own. As for the ancient ones, don't be so sure they want to govern. I think they want utter privacy and complete peace."

Stirling reflected, then said quickly, "I see your point."

"You despise me now, don't you?" Lestat asked with engaging sincerity.

"Not at all," was Stirling's quick reply. "On the contrary, I see your charm. You know I do. Tell me about this bargain. What do you want me to do?"

"First off, go back to your Elders and tell them that this Declaration of Enmity must be officially withdrawn. It doesn't matter that much to me but it matters to others, and besides, I know that if you swear honorably to be no more than observers in the future, then you won't annoy us, and with me that counts for a lot. I loathe being annoyed. It makes me feel angry and malicious."

"Very well."

"The second request stems from the first. Leave this boy completely alone. This boy is the key point which you must leave out of your report. Of course you can say that a nameless Blood Drinker assaulted you. You know, have it all make sense and do justice to whatever you think you may have learned here. I anticipate your inevitable fascination with all that. But this boy's anonymity must become a point of honor . . . and there's more."

Stirling was silent.

"You know his name," said Lestat, "you know where he lives, you know his family. All that was plain to me before I interrupted him in his bumbling attack on you. Now you know that he's one of us, as the expression goes. You must not only leave him out of your records, you must leave him completely and utterly alone."

Stirling held Lestat's gaze for a moment and then he nodded.

"You move against this boy," said Lestat, "you try to take up your combative posture where he is concerned, and as God is my witness, I'll wipe you out. I'll kill all of you. I'll leave you nothing but your empty libraries and your overflowing vaults. I'll start in the Motherhouse in Louisiana and then I'll move to the Motherhouses all over the world. It's a cinch for me to do it. I'll pick you off one at a time. Even if the ancients do rise to protect you, it won't happen immediately, and what I can do immediately is an enormous amount of harm."

I went from fear to astonishment.

"I understand you," said Stirling. "Of course you want him protected. Thank heaven for that."

"I pray that you do understand me," said Lestat. He glanced at me again. "This is a young one, an innocent one, and I'll make the decision as to whether he survives or not."

I think Stirling let out a little gasp.

As for me there came a flood of relief again, and then another wave of intelligent fear.

Lestat gestured to Stirling.

"Need I add that you're to get out of here now and never trespass on my property again?" he asked.

Stirling rose at once, and so did I. Stirling looked at me, and there came over me again the total realization that I'd almost ended his life tonight, and a recurrence of terrible shame.

"Good-bye, my friend," I said in as strong a voice as I could muster. I reached awkwardly for his hand and held it firmly. He looked at me and his face softened.

"Quinn," he said, "my brave Quinn."

He turned.

"Farewell, Lestat de Lioncourt," he said. "I think I understate my case when I say I'm deeply in your debt."

"You do but I find ingrates all around me eternally," said Lestat, smiling slyly. "Go on, Mr. Oliver. It's a good thing you have one of your prowling limousines waiting for you only a couple of blocks from here. I don't think you're up to walking far or driving a car by yourself."

"Right you are," said Stirling, and then with no further words he hurried down the hallway and out the back door, and I heard his heavy rapid steps on the iron stairs.

Lestat had also risen, and he came towards me and gestured for me to sit down again. He took my head in both his hands. There was no dreadful pressure; there was no pain. It was gentle, the manner in which he was holding me.

But I was too afraid to do anything but look up into his eyes quietly, and again I saw that small difference, that one eye was larger than the other by not even a fraction of an inch. I tried to repress the mere thought of it. I tried only to think *I will do whatever you want of me*, and without meaning for it to happen, I closed my eyes as if someone were about to hit me in the face.

"You think I'm going to kill you, don't you?" I heard him say.

"I hope not," I said shakily.

"Come on, Little Brother," he said, "it's time to leave this pretty lit-tle place to those who know so much about it. And you, my young friend, have to feed."

And then I felt his arm tight around me. The air was rushing past me. I was clinging to him, though I don't think I needed to, and we were out in the night, and we were moving towards the clouds.

4

I**T WAS LIKE TRAVELING** with my Maker—the speed, the altitude and the strong arms holding me. I gave it all of my trust.

And then came the sudden plunge.

I was shaken as he let me go, and I had to stop myself from stumbling until the dizziness passed.

We stood on a terrace. A partially open glass door separated us from a lighted room. It was tastefully furnished in rather routine modern furniture—beige velvet chairs and couches, with the inevitable large television, muted lamps and scattered tables of iron and glass.

Two very pretty young brunette women were inside, one busy with a suitcase on the coffee table, and the other in front of a nearby mirror, brushing her long hair. They wore skimpy silk dresses, both pretty fashionable, revealing a great deal of their dark olive skin.

Lestat put his arm around me again and gave my shoulder a gentle squeeze.

"What does your mind tell you?" he whispered.

I let the Mind Gift loose, casting for the one at the mirror, and caught the whisper of murder at once. The other was even more accustomed to it, and it seemed that both of the women were party to a crime that was actually happening now somewhere at a distance from this place.

It was an elegant hotel, this building. Through a door I saw the bedroom. I caught the scent from a gin drink on one of the tables, I caught the scent of fresh flowers, and of course I caught the overwhelming scent of Fair Game.

The thirst rose in me. The thirst clouded my eyes. I tasted blood as though I were already drinking it, and I felt the abysmal and desperate emptiness that I always feel before I feast. *Nothing will ever fill you. Nothing will ever make this abominable hunger go away.*

"Fair Game exactly," said Lestat in a low voice. "But we don't let them suffer, no matter how rough we want to get."

"No, Sir," I answered deferentially. "May I have the one in front of the mirror?"

"Why?" he asked.

"Because I can see her face in the mirror, and she's cruel."

He nodded.

He slipped the door open and we came into the cool refreshing air of the room. The thirst was too hot for it. The thirst was hopeless.

At once, the women cried out in protest. Where had we come from? Who were we? Vulgar words, threats.

With a remnant of my rational mind, I saw that the suitcase was filled with money, but what did it matter? How much more interesting was a huge vase of flowers near the far window, bursting with color. How much more interesting the blood.

Lestat drifted past me and caught the woman who ran to the right with both his arms. The rush of furious words from her came to an abrupt stop.

The other woman darted to the sofa, and I saw the gun there that she wanted so desperately to reach. I had her before she could lay her hand on it, and I crushed her against me, looking into her black eyes.

She gave me a string of curses in Spanish, and the thirst in me rose even more violently, as if her curses had drawn it out. I brushed her thick black hair back from her neck and ran my thumb over the artery. She was maddened, full of hatred.

Slowly, I bit into the fount of blood.

My Maker's lessons came back to me. *Love her sins, follow the path with her, make her evil your evil and you will do no evil.* I struggled to obey as her mind was broken open. I probed for the murders and I found them, rampant, savage and always over the white powder; and the wealth that had drawn her out of the deep filthy slums of her birth to finery and fortune, to those who toasted her beauty and her cunning; and murder after murder of those as covered in blood as herself. *Yes, love you,* I whispered, love the sheer will and the ever present anger; yes, give it to me, the rage in the warm sweet blood flowing, and suddenly there came, towards me, her unbounded love.

Without language, she said, *Surrender.* Without language, she said, *I see it!*, and *it* was all of her life, without pagination, and her ripened soul expanded, and there was a terrifying recognition of circumstance and inevitability, her crimes pulled up by the roots from her heart as though by the hand of Heaven.

But the hunger in me was sated, I was filled by her, I had had her, and I drew back, kissing the puncture wounds, lapping the tiny trickles of blood that I'd spilled, healing the evidence, even as the drowsiness overcame me and then gently, gently I set her down on one of the indifferent chairs. I kissed her lips.

I knelt down before her. I forced my tongue between her lips and, opening her mouth, I sucked on her tongue and sank my teeth into it delicately, and there came again a small rush of blood.

Finally there was no more.

I closed her large empty eyes with my left fingers. I felt her eyes through their lids as her blood washed through me. I bent and kissed her breasts. The blood sent shock after shock through me. I let her go.

In the usual daze, I turned and saw Lestat waiting, the royal figure, studying me, musing it seemed, his yellow hair looking almost white in the lamplight, his violet eyes wide.

"You did it right that time, Little Brother," he said. "You spilled not a single drop."

There was so much I wanted to say. I wanted to talk of her life, the great overreaching scope of it that I had so deeply tasted, the score she kept with fate; and how hard I'd tried to do what my Maker had told me to do, not merely to devour the blood but devour the evil, dip my tongue deep down into the evil, but she was beside the point.

She was a victim. She who had never been a Subject was now Past Tense.

The blood had me. The warmth had me. The room was a phantasm. Lestat's woman lay dead on the floor. And there was the suitcase of money, and it meant nothing, could buy nothing, could change nothing, could save no one. The flowers were bold and brilliant, pink lilies dripping with pollen, and dark red roses. The room was complete and final and still.

"No one will mourn them," said Lestat softly. His voice seemed distant, beyond my reach. "No need to find a hasty grave."

I thought of my Maker. I thought of the dark waters of Sugar Devil Swamp, the thick duckweed, the voice of the owls.

Something changed in the room, but Lestat didn't know it.

"Come back to me," said Lestat. "It's important, Little Brother, not to let the blood weaken you afterwards, no matter how sweet it is."

I nodded. But something was happening. We weren't alone.

I could see the dim figure of my double forming behind Lestat. I could see Goblin, designed as I was designed. I could see the crazed smile on his face.

Lestat pivoted. "Where is he?" he whispered.

"No, Goblin, I forbid it," I said. But there was no stopping him. The figure moved towards me with lightning speed, yet held itself together in human form. Right before my eyes he was seemingly as solid as I was; and then I felt the tingling all through my limbs as he merged with me, and the tiny stabs on my hands and my neck and my face. I struggled as if I were caught in a perfect net.

From deep inside me there came that orgasmic palpitation, that walloping sensation that I was one with him and nothing could part us, that I wanted it suddenly, yes, wanted him and me to be together always, yet I was saying something different.

"Get away from me, Goblin. Goblin, you must listen. I was the one, the one who brought you into being. Listen to me."

But it was useless. The electric shivers wouldn't stop, and I saw only images of the two of us as children, as boys, as men, all of it moving too fast for me to focus, to repudiate or confirm. Sunlight poured through an open doorway; I saw the flowered pattern of linoleum. I heard the laughter of toddlers, and I tasted milk.

I knew I was falling or about to fall, that Lestat's firm hands were holding me, because I wasn't in the room with the sunlight, but it was all that I could see, and there was Goblin, little Goblin frolicking and laughing, and I too was laughing. *Love you, all right, need you, of course, yours, us together.* I looked down and saw my chubby childish left hand, and I held a spoon in it and was banging with the spoon. And there was Goblin's hand on top of mine. And over and over came that bang of the spoon against wood, and the sunlight, how beautifully it came in the door, but the flowers on the linoleum were worn.

Then, as violently as Goblin had come, he withdrew. I glimpsed the humanoid shape for no more than a second, the eyes huge, the mouth open; then his image expanded, lost its conformity and vanished.

The draperies of the room swayed, and the vase of flowers suddenly toppled, and I heard dimly the dripping of the water, and then the vase itself hit the soft rug.

In a fog, I stared at the wounded bouquet of flowers. Pink-throated lilies. I wanted to pick them up. The tiny wounds all over me stung me and hurt me. I hated him that he had made the vase fall over, that the lilies were spilt now on the floor.

I looked at the women, first one and then the other. They appeared to be sleeping. There was no death.

My Goblin, my very own Goblin. That verbless thought stayed with me. My familiar spirit, my partner in all of life; you belong to me and I belong to you.

Lestat was holding me by the shoulders. I could barely stand. In fact, if he had let me go I would have fallen. I couldn't take my eyes off the pink-throated lilies.

"He didn't have to make the flowers fall," I said. "I taught him not to hurt things that were pretty. I taught him that when we were small."

"Quinn," said Lestat, "come back to me! I'm talking to you. Quinn!"

"You didn't see him," I said. I was shaking all over. I stared at the tiny wounds on my hands, but they were already healing. It was the same way with the pinpricks on my face. I wiped at my face. Faint traces of blood on my fingers.

"I saw the blood," said Lestat.

"How did you see it?" I asked. I was growing stronger. I struggled to clear my mind.

"In the shape of a man," Lestat said, "a man faintly sketched in blood, sketched in the air, just for an instant, and then there was a swirling cloud of tiny drops, and I saw it pass through the open door as rapidly as if it were being sucked out."

"Then you know why I came looking for you," I said. But I realized he couldn't really see the spirit that Goblin was. He'd seen the blood, yes, because the blood was visible, but the spirit who had always appeared to me was invisible to him.

"It can't really hurt you," he said, his voice tender and kind. "It can't take any real volume of blood from you. It took just a tiny taste of what you took from the woman."

"But he'll come again whenever he wants, and I can't fight him, and each time, I could swear, it's a little more."

I steadied myself, and he released me, stroking my hair with his right hand. That casual gesture of affection coupled with his dazzling appearance—the vibrant eyes, the exquisitely proportioned features— entranced me even as the trance induced by Goblin slowly wore away.

"He found me here," I said, "and I don't even know where I am. He found me here, and he can find me anywhere, and each time, as I told you, he takes a little more blood."

"Surely you can fight him," Lestat said, encouragingly.

His expression was concerned and protective, and I felt such an overwhelming need of him and love for him that I was about to cry. I held it back.

"Maybe I can learn to fight him," I said, "but is that enough?"

"Come, let's leave this graveyard," he answered. "You have to tell me about him. You have to tell me how this came about."

"I don't know that I have all the answers," I said. "But I have a story to tell."

I followed him out onto the terrace into the fresh air.

"Let's go to Blackwood Manor," I said. "I don't know of another place where we can talk in such peace. Only my aunt is there tonight and her lovable entourage, and maybe my mother, and they'll all leave us completely alone. They're utterly used to me."

"And Goblin?" he asked. "Will he be stronger there if he does come back?"

"He was as strong as ever only moments ago," I responded. "I think that I'll be stronger."

"Then Blackwood Manor it is," he said.

Again there came his firm arm around me and we were traveling upwards. The sky spread out, full of clouds, and then we broke through to the very stars.

5

WITHIN MOMENTS we found ourselves in front of the big house, and I experienced a flashing sense of embarrassment as I looked at its huge two-story columned portico.

Of course the garden lights were on, brilliantly illuminating the fluted columns to their full height, and all of the many rooms were aglow. In fact, I had a rule on this and had had since boyhood, that at four o'clock all chandeliers in the main house had to be lighted, and though I was no longer that boy in the grip of twilight depression, the chandeliers were illuminated by the same clock.

A quick chuckle from Lestat caught me off guard.

"And why are you so embarrassed?" he asked genially, having easily read my mind. "America destroys her big houses. Some of them don't even last a hundred years." His accent lessened. He sounded more intimate. "This place is magnificent," he said casually. "I like the big columns. The portico, the pediment, it's all rather glorious. Perfect Greek Revival style. How can you be ashamed of such things? You're a strange creature, very gentle I think, and out of kilter with your own time."

"Well, how can I belong to it now?" I asked. "Given the Dark Blood and all its wondrous attributes. What do you think?"

I was at once ashamed of having answered so directly, but he merely took it in stride.

"No, but I mean," he said, "you didn't belong to this time before the Dark Gift, did you? The threads of your life, they weren't woven into any certain fabric." His manner seemed simple and friendly.

"I suppose you're right," I responded. "In fact, you're very right."

"You're going to tell me all about it, aren't you?" he asked. His golden eyebrows were very clear against his tanned skin, and he frowned slightly while smiling at the same time. It made him look very clever and loving, though I wasn't sure why.

"You want me to?" I asked.

"Of course I do," he answered. "It's what you want to do and must do, besides." There came that mischievous smile and frown again. "Now, shall we go inside?"

"Of course, yes," I said, greatly relieved as much by his friendly manner as by what he said. I couldn't quite grasp that I had him with me, that not only had I found him but that he was wanting to hear my story; he was at my side.

We went up the six front steps to the marble porch and I opened the door, which, on account of our being out here in the country, was never locked.

The broad central hallway stretched out before us, with its diamond-shaped white-and-black marble tiles running to the rear door, which was identical to the door by which we had just entered.

Partially blocking our view was one of the greatest attributes of Blackwood Manor, the spiral stairway, and this drew from Lestat a look of pure delight.

The frigid air-conditioning felt good.

"How gorgeous this is," he said, gazing at the stairway with its graceful railing and delicate balusters. He stood in the well of it. "Why, it runs all the way to a third floor, doubling back on itself beautifully."

"The third floor's the attic," I said. "It's a treasure trove of trunks and old furniture. It's yielded some of its little secrets to me."

His eyes moved to the running mural on the hallway walls, a sunshine Italian pastoral giving way to a deep blue sky whose bright color dominated the entire long space and the hall above.

"Ah, now this is lovely," he said, looking up at the high ceiling. "And look at the plaster moldings. Done by hand, weren't they?"

I nodded. "New Orleans craftsmen," I said. "It was the 1880s, and my great-great-great-grandfather was fiercely romantic and partially insane."

"And this drawing room," he said, peering through the arched doorway to his right. "It's full of old furniture, fine furniture. What do you call it, Quinn? Rococo? It fills me with a dreamy sense of the past."

Again, I nodded. I had gone rapidly from embarrassment to an embarrassing sense of pride. All my life people had capitulated to Blackwood Manor. They had positively raved about it, and I wondered now that I had been so mortified. But this being, this strangely compelling and handsome individual into whose hands I'd put my very life, had grown up in a castle, and I had feared he would laugh at what he saw.

On the contrary, he seemed thrilled by the golden harp and the old Pleyel piano. He glanced at the huge somber portrait of Manfred Blackwood, my venerable ancestor. And then slowly he turned enthusiastically to the dining room on the other side of the hall.

I made a motion for him to enter.

The antique crystal chandelier was showering a wealth of light on the long table, a table which could seat some thirty people, made especially for the room. The gilded chairs had only recently been re-covered in green satin damask, and the green and gold was repeated in the wall-to-wall carpet, with a gold swirl on a green ground. Gilded sideboards, inset with green malachite, were ranged between the long windows on the far wall.

A need to apologize stole over me again, perhaps because Lestat seemed lost in his judgment of the place.

"It's so unnecessary, Blackwood Manor," I told him. "And with Aunt Queen and me its only regular inhabitants, I have the feeling that someone will come and make us turn it over for some more sensible use. Of course there are other members of the family—and then there's the staff, who are so damned rich in their own right that they don't have to work for anybody." I broke off, ashamed of rambling.

"And what would a more sensible use be?" he asked in the same comfortable manner he had adopted before. "Why should the house not be your gracious home?"

He was looking at the huge portrait of Aunt Queen when she was young—a smiling girl in a sleeveless white beaded evening gown that might have been made yesterday rather than seventy years ago, as it was; and at another portrait—of Virginia Lee Blackwood, Manfred's wife, the first lady ever to live in Blackwood Manor.

It was murky now, this portrait of Virginia Lee, but the style was robust and faintly emotional, and the woman herself, blond with eyes of blue, was very honest to look at, and modest, and smiling, with small features and an undeniably pretty face. She was dressed ornately in the style of the 1880s, in a high-necked dress of sky blue with long sleeves puckered at the shoulders, and her hair heaped on the top of her head. She had been the grandmother of Aunt Queen, and I always saw a certain likeness in these portraits, in the eyes and the shape of the faces, though others claimed they could not. But then . . .

And they had more than casual associations for me, these portraits, especially that of Virginia Lee. Aunt Queen I had still with me. But Virginia Lee . . . I shuddered but repressed those alien memories of ghosts and grotesqueries. Too much was taking my mind by storm.

"Yes, why not your home, and the repository of your ancestors' treasures?" Lestat remarked innocently. "I don't understand."

"Well, when I was growing up," I said in answer to his question, "my grandma and grandpa were living then, and this was a sort of hotel. A bed-and-breakfast was what they called it. But they served dinner down here in the dining room as well. Lots of tourists came up this way to spend some time in it. We still have the Christmas banquet every year, with singers who stand on the staircase for the final caroling, while the guests gather here in the hall. It all seems very useful at times like that. This last year I had a midnight Easter banquet as well, just so I could attend it."

A sense of the past shook me, frightening me with its vitality. I pressed on, guiltily trying to wring something from the earliest memories. What right had I to good times now, or memories?

"I love the singers," I said. "I used to cry with my grandparents when the soprano sang 'O Holy Night.' Blackwood Manor seems powerful at such times—a place to alter people's lives. You can tell I'm still very caught up in it."

"How does it alter people's lives?" he asked quickly, as if the idea had hooked him.

"Oh, there've been so many weddings here." My voice caught. Weddings. A hideous memory, a recent memory overshot all, a shameful awful memory—blood, her gown, the taste of it—but I forced it out of my mind. I went on:

"I remember lovely weddings, and anniversary banquets. I remember a picnic on the lawn for an elderly man who had just turned ninety. I remember people coming back to visit the site where they'd been married." Again came that stabbing recollection—a bride, a bride covered in blood. My head swam.

You little fool, you've killed her. You weren't supposed to kill her, and look at her white dress.

I wouldn't think of it yet. I couldn't be crippled with it yet. I'd confess it all to Lestat, but not yet.

I had to continue. I stammered. I managed.

"Somewhere there's an old guest book with a broken quill pen crushed in it, full of comments by those who came and went and came again. They're still coming. It's a flame that hasn't gone out."

He nodded and smiled faintly as though this pleased him. He looked again at the portrait of Virginia Lee.

A vague shimmer passed over me. Had the portrait changed? Vague imaginings that her lovely blue eyes looked down at me. But she would never come to life for me now, would she? Of course she wouldn't. Hers had been a famous virtue and magnanimity. What would she have to do with me now?

"And these days," I pressed on, fastening to my little narrative, "I find myself cherishing this house desperately, and cherishing as well all my mortal connections. My Aunt Queen I cherish above all. But there are others, others who must never know what I am."

He studied me patiently, as if pondering these things.

"Your conscience is tuned like a violin," he said pensively. "Do you really like having them here, the strangers, the Christmas and Easter guests, under your own roof?"

"It's cheerful," I admitted. "There's always light and movement. There are voices and the dull vibration of the busy stairs. Sometimes guests complain—the grits is watery or the gravy is lumpy—and in the old days, my grandmother Sweetheart would cry over those complaints, and my grandfather—Pops, we all called him—would privately slam his fist down on the kitchen table; but in the main, the guests love the place . . .

". . . And now and then it can be lonesome here, melancholy and dismal, no matter how bright the chandeliers. I think that when my grandparents died and that part of it was all over I felt a . . . a deep depression that seemed linked to Blackwood Manor, though I couldn't leave it, and wouldn't of my own accord."

He nodded at these words as though he understood them. He was looking at me as surely as I was looking at him. He was appraising me as surely as I appraised him.

I was thinking how very attractive he was, I couldn't stop myself, with his yellow hair so thick and long, turning so gracefully at the collar of his coat, and his large probing violet eyes. There are very few creatures on earth who have true violet eyes. The slight difference between his eyes meant nothing. His sun-browned skin was flawless. What he saw in me with his questioning gaze, I couldn't know.

"You know, you can roam about this house," I said, still vaguely shocked that I had his interest, the words spilling anxiously from me again. "You can roam from room to room, and there are ghosts. Sometimes even the tourists see the ghosts."

"Did that scare them?" he asked with genuine curiosity.

"Oh, no, they're too gung ho to be in a haunted house. They love it. They see things where there are no things. They ask to be left alone in haunted rooms."

He laughed silently.

"They claim to hear bells ring that aren't ringing," I went on, smiling back at him, "and they smell coffee when there is no coffee, and they catch the drift of exotic perfumes. Now and then there was a tourist or two who was genuinely frightened, in fact there were several in the bed-and-board days who packed up immediately, but in the main, the reputation of the place sold it. And then, of course, there were those who actually saw ghosts."

"And you, you do see the ghosts," he said.

"Yes," I answered. "Most of the ghosts are weak things, hardly more than vapor, but there are exceptions. . . ." I hesitated. I was lost for a moment. I felt my words might trigger some awful apparition, but I wanted so to confide in him. Stumbling, I went on:

"Yes, extraordinary exceptions . . ." I broke off.

"I want you to tell me," he said. "You have a room upstairs, don't you? A quiet place where we can talk. But I sense someone else in this house."

He glanced towards the hallway.

"Yes, Aunt Queen in the back bedroom," I said. "It won't take more than a moment for me to see her."

"That's a curious name, Aunt Queen," he remarked, his smile brightening again. "It's divinely southern, I think. Will you take me to see her as well?"

"Absolutely," I answered, without the hesitation of common sense. "Lorraine McQueen is her name, and everyone hereabouts calls her Miss Queen or Aunt Queen."

We went into the hallway together and once again he glanced up at the curving stairs.

I led him back past it, his boots sounding sharp on the marble, and I brought him to the open door of Aunt Queen's room.

There she was, my darling, quite resplendent, and very busy, and not in the least disturbed by our approach.

She sat at her marble table just to the right of her dressing table, the whole making the L in which she was most happy. The nearby floor lamp as well as the frilly lights on the dressing table illuminated her wonderfully, and she had her dozens of cameos out before her on the marble and her bone-handled magnifying glass in her right hand.

She seemed dreadfully frail in her white quilted satin robe, with its buckled belt around her tiny waist, her throat wrapped well in a white silk scarf tucked into her lapels, over which rested her favorite necklace of diamonds and pearls. Her soft gray hair was curled naturally around her face, and her small eyes were full of an exuberant spirit as she studied the cameos at hand. Under the table, and where her robe was parted, I could see that she wore her perilous pink-sequined high-heeled shoes. I wanted to lecture. Ever a danger, those spike-heeled shoes.

Aunt Queen seemed the perfect name for her, and I felt an instinctive pride in her, that she had been the guardian angel of my life. I had no fear of her recognizing anything abnormal in Lestat, what with his tanned skin, except perhaps his excessive beauty. And I was happy with the moment beyond words.

The whole room made a lovely picture as I tried to see it the way that Lestat must see it, what with the canopied bed to the far left. It had only recently been redone in scallops of rose-colored satin, ornamented with darker braid, and it was made up already, which wasn't always the case, with the heavy satin cover and pillow shams and other decorative pillows in a heap. The rose damask couch and scattered armchairs matched the hangings of the bed.

Jasmine was there in the shadows, our lifelong housekeeper, whose silky dark skin and fine features made her a special beauty, just as surely as Aunt Queen. She looked uncommonly sharp in her red sheath dress and high heels, with a string of pearls around her neck. I'd given her those pearls, hadn't I?

Jasmine gave me a little wave, and then went back to straightening small items on the bedside table, and as Aunt Queen looked up and greeted me, crying "Quinn!" with a little touch of ecstasy, Jasmine stopped her work and came forward, slipping right past us out of the room.

I wanted to hug Jasmine. It had been nights since I'd seen her. But I was afraid. Then I thought, no, I'm going to do it for as long as I can do it, and I've fed and I'm warm. A greedy sense of goodness overcame me, that I wasn't damned. I felt too much love. I stepped back and caught Jasmine in my arms.

She was beautifully built, and her skin was a lovely color of milk chocolate and her eyes were hazel and her hair extremely woolly, and always beautifully bleached yellow and close-cropped to her very round head.

"Ah, that's my Little Boss," she said as she hugged me in return. We were in the shadows of the hallway. "My mysterious Little Boss," she went on, pressing me tight against her bosom so that her head was against my chest. "My wandering Little Boy, whom I scarcely ever see at all."

"You're my girlfriend forever," I whispered, kissing the top of her head. In this close company, the blood of the dead was serving me well. And besides, I was hopeful and slightly crazy.

"You come in here, Quinn," called out Aunt Queen, and Jasmine softly let me go and she went towards the rear door.

"Ah, you have a friend with you," said Aunt Queen as I obeyed her, Lestat at my side. The room was warmer than the rest of the house.

Aunt Queen's voice was ageless, if not actually youthful, and she spoke with a clear commanding diction.

"I'm so pleased you have company," she said. "And what a fine strapling of a youth you are," she said to Lestat, satirizing herself ever so delightfully. "Come here so I can see you. Ah, but you are handsome. Come into the light."

"And you, my dear lady, are a vision," Lestat said, his French accent thickening just a tiny bit as if for emphasis, and, leaning over the marble table with its random cameos, he bent to kiss her hand.

She was a vision, there was no doubt of it, her face warm and pretty for all its years. It wasn't gaunt so much as naturally angular, and her thinning lips were neatly brightened with rose lipstick, and her eyes, in spite of the fine wrinkles around them, were still vividly blue. The diamonds and pearls on her breast were stunning, and she wore several rich diamond rings on her long hands.

The jewels as always seemed part of her power and dignity, as if age had given her strong advantage, and a sweet femininity seemed to characterize her as well.

"Over here, Little Boy," she said to me.

I went to her side and bent down to receive her kiss on my cheek. That had been my custom ever since I'd grown to the staggering height of six foot four, and she often took hold of my head and teasingly refused to let me go. This time, she didn't do it. She was too distracted by the alluring creature standing before her table, with his cordial smile.

"And look at your coat," she said to Lestat, "how marvelous. Why, it's a wide-skirted frock coat. Wherever did you get it, and the cameo buttons, how perfect. Will you come here this very minute and let me see them? You can see that I've a positive mania for cameos. And now as the years have gone by, I think of little else."

Lestat came round the table as I moved away. I was frightened suddenly, very frightened, that she would sense something about him, but no sooner had this thought gripped me than I realized he had the situation entirely under his command.

Hadn't another Blood Drinker, my Maker, charmed Aunt Queen in the same manner? Why the hell should I be so afraid?

As she examined the buttons, remarking that each was a different muse of the Grecian Nine Muses, Lestat was beaming down on her as if he were genuinely smitten, and I loved him for it. Because Aunt Queen was the person I loved most in all the world. Having the two of them together was a little more than I could bear.

"Yes, a real true frock coat," she said.

"Well, I'm a musician, Madam," Lestat said to her. "You know in this day and age a rock musician can wear a frock coat if he wishes, and so I indulge myself. I'm theatrical and incorrigible. A regular beast when it comes to the exaggerated and the eccentric. I like to clear all obstacles when I enter a room, and I have a perfect mania for antique things."

"Yes, you're so right to have it," she said, exulting in him obviously, as he stepped back and joined me where I stood before the table. "My two handsome boys," she remarked. "You do know that Quinn's mother is a singer, though what kind of a singer I'm not quite prepared to say."

Lestat didn't know, and he gave me a curious glance and a slight teasing smile.

"Country music," I said quickly. "Patsy Blackwood is her name. She's got a powerful voice."

"Very much diluted country music," said Aunt Queen with a vague tone of disapproval. "I think she calls it country pop, and that can account for a lot. She has a good voice, however, and she writes occasional lyrics that aren't too bad. She's good at a sort of mournful ballad, almost Celtic, though she doesn't know it—but you know, a little minor-key bluegrass sound is what she really likes to do, and if she did what she likes to do rather than what she thinks she ought to do she might have the very fame she so desires." Aunt Queen sighed.

I marveled, not only at the wisdom of what she'd said, but at the curious disloyalty, because Aunt Queen was never one to criticize her own flesh and blood. But something seemed to have been stirred inside her by Lestat's gaze. Perhaps he had worked a vague charm, and she was giving forth her deepest thoughts.

"But you, young man," she said, "I'm your Aunt Queen from now on and forever, certainly; but what is your name?"

"Lestat, Madam," he answered, pronouncing it "Les-*dot*," with the accent on the second syllable. "I'm not really very famous either. And I don't sing anymore at all actually, except to myself when I'm driving my black Porsche madly or riding my motorcycle at a raging speed on the roads. Then I'm a regular Pavarotti—."

"Oh, but you mustn't go speeding!" Aunt Queen declared with a sudden attack of pure seriousness. "That's how I lost my husband, John McQueen. It was a new Bugatti, you know what a Bugatti is" (Lestat nodded), "and he was so proud of it, his fine European sports car, and we were racing down the Pacific Coast Highway One, and on an unclouded summer day, screeching around the turns, down to Big Sur, and he lost control of the wheel and went right through the windshield. Dead like that. And I came to my senses with a crowd around me, only inches from a cliff that went sheer down into the sea."

"Appalling," said Lestat earnestly. "Was it very long ago?"

"Of course, decades ago, when I was foolish enough to do such things," said Aunt Queen, "and I never remarried; we Blackwoods, we don't remarry. And John McQueen left me a fortune, some consolation, I've never found another like him, with so much passion and so many happy delusions, but then I never much looked." She shook her head at the pity of it. "But that's a dreary subject, all that, he's buried in the Blackwood tomb in the Metairie Cemetery; we have a large tomb there, an inspiring little chapel of a tomb, and I'll soon be in it too."

"Oh, my God, no," I whispered, with a little too much fear.

"You hush now," she said, glancing up at me. "And Lestat, my darling Lestat, tell me about your clothes, your odd and bold taste. I love it. I must confess that to picture you in that frock coat, rushing along on a motorcycle, is quite amusing, to be sure."

"Well Madam," he said, laughing softly, "my longing for the stage and the microphone is gone, but I won't give up the fancy clothes. I can't give them up. I'm the prisoner of capricious fashion and am actually quite plain tonight. I think nothing of piling on the lace and the diamond cuff links, and I envy Quinn that snappy leather coat he's wearing. You could call me a Goth, I think." He glanced at me very naturally, as though we were both simple humans. "Don't they call us snappy antique dressers Goth now, Quinn?"

"I think they do," I said, trying to catch up.

This little speech of his made Aunt Queen laugh and laugh. She had forgotten John McQueen, who had in fact died a long time ago into stories. "What an unusual name, Lestat," she returned. "Does it have a meaning?"

"None whatsoever, Madam," Lestat answered. "If memory serves me right, and it does less and less, the name's compounded of the first letter of each of my six older brothers' names, all of whom—the brothers and their names—I grew up to cheerfully and vigorously despise."

Again, Aunt Queen laughed, plainly surprised and utterly seduced. "Seventh son," she said. "Now that confers a certain power and I'm deeply respecting of it. And you speak with a ready eloquence. You seem a fine and invigorating friend for Quinn."

"That's my ambition, to be his fine friend," said Lestat immediately and sincerely, "but don't let me intrude."

"Never even think of it," Aunt Queen offered. "You're welcome under my roof. I like you. I know I do. And you, Quinn, where have you been of late?"

"Round and about, Aunt Queen," I answered. "Bad as Patsy in my roamings, round and about—I don't know."

"And have you brought me a cameo?" she asked. "This is our custom, Lestat," she explained, and then: "It's been a week since you have been in this room, Tarquin Blackwood. I want my cameo. You must have one. I won't let you off the hook."

"Oh, yes, you know I almost forgot about it," I said. (And with reason!) I felt in my right-hand coat pocket for a little tissue-covered package that I'd put there nights ago. "It's from New York, this one, a lovely shell cameo."

I unwrapped the paper and put it before her in all its glory, one of the largest shell cameos that she would own. The image was from the white strata of the shell, naturally, and the background a dark pink. The cameo was a perfect oval with a particularly exquisite scalloped frame of heavy 24-carat gold.

"Medusa," she said, with obvious satisfaction, identifying the woman's profile at once by her winged head and the wild snakes for hair. "And so large and so sharply carved."

"Fearsome," I said. "The best Medusa I've ever seen. Note the height of the wing, and a bit of the orange strata on the wing tip. I meant to bring it sooner. I wish that I had."

"Oh, there's no point to that, my darling," she said. "Don't regret it when you don't come to see me. I think I'm timeless. You're here now and you've remembered me. That's what counts." She looked up to Lestat eagerly. "You know the story of Medusa, don't you?" she asked.

Lestat hesitated, only smiling, obviously wanting her to speak more than he wanted to speak himself. He looked rather radiant in his rapture with her, and she was beaming back.

"Once beautiful, then turned into a monster," said Aunt Queen, clearly enjoying the moment immensely. "With a face that could turn men to stone. Perseus sought her by her reflection in his polished shield, and once he'd slain her the winged horse Pegasus was born from the drops of blood that fell to earth from her severed head."

"And it was that head," said Lestat confidingly, "that Athena then emblazoned on her shield."

"You're so very right," said Aunt Queen.

"A charm against harm," said Lestat softly. "That's what she became once beheaded. Another wondrous transformation, I think—beauty to monster, monster to charm."

"Yes, you're right on all counts," said Aunt Queen. "A charm against harm," she repeated. "Here, come, Quinn, help me take off these heavy diamonds," she said, "and get a gold chain for me. I want to wear Medusa on my neck."

It was a simple matter to do as she asked. I came around directly to the dressing table and removed the diamonds from her, giving her a sly kiss on the cheek, and put the diamond necklace in its customary leather box. This always sat atop her dressing table on the right-hand side. The gold chains were in a box in the top drawer, each in its plastic pouch.

From these I chose a strong chain of bright 24-carat gold, and one that would give her a snug but good fit. I threaded it through the bail attached to the cameo, and then put the chain around her neck for her and snapped the clasp.

After another quick couple of kisses, very powdery and rather like kissing a person made of pure white confectioners' sugar, I came around in front of her again. The cameo was perfectly nested against the full gathered silk of the scarf and looked both imposing and rich.

"I have to admit," I said of my new purchase, "it is really quite a trophy. Medusa is her wicked self in this one, not just a pretty winged girl with snakes, and that's rare."

"Yes," said Lestat agreeably, "and so much stronger is the charm."

"You think so?" Aunt Queen asked him. For all her dignity, the cameo befitted her more than the roaring diamonds. "You're a curious young man," she went on to Lestat. "You speak slowly and reflectively, and the timbre of your voice is deep. I like it. Quinn was a bookworm and swallowed mythology by the mouthful, once he could read, and, mind you, that wasn't until very late. But you, how do you know about mythology, for surely you do? And obviously something about cameos, or so I judge by your coat."

"Knowledge drifts in and out of my mind," said Lestat with a little look of honest distress and a shake of his head. "I devour it and then I lose it and sometimes I can't reach for any knowledge that I ought to possess. I feel desolate, but then knowledge returns or I seek it out in a new source."

How they connected, the two of them, it was amazing to me. And then I felt a stab of bitter memory again, of my Maker, that appalling presence, that damnable presence, once connecting with Aunt Queen in this very room and in the very same easy way. The subject had been cameos then too. Cameos. But this was Lestat, not my Maker, this was not that loathsome being. This was my hero under my roof.

"But you love books, then," Aunt Queen was saying. I had to listen.

"Oh, yes," Lestat said. "Sometimes they're the only thing that keeps me alive."

"What a thing to say at your age," she laughed.

"No, but one can feel desperate at any age, don't you think? The young are eternally desperate," he said frankly. "And books, they offer one hope—that a whole universe might open up from between the covers, and falling into that new universe, one is saved."

"Oh, yes, I think so, I really do," Aunt Queen responded, almost gleefully. "It ought to be that way with people and sometimes it is. Imagine—each new person an entire universe. Do you think we can allow that? You're clever and keen."

"I think we don't want to allow it," Lestat responded. "We're too jealous, and fearful. But we should allow it, and then our existence would be wondrous as we went from soul to soul."

Aunt Queen laughed gaily.

"Oh, but you are a specimen," she said. "Wherever did you come from? Oh, I wish that Quinn's teacher Nash was here. He'd so enjoy you. Or that little Tommy wasn't away at school. Tommy is Quinn's uncle, which is slightly misleading since Tommy is only fourteen, and then there's Jerome. Where's little Jerome? Probably fast asleep. Ah, we'll have to make do with only me—."

"But tell me if you will, Miss Queen," asked Lestat, "why do you love the cameos so much? These buttons, I can't claim to have chosen them with much care, or to have been obsessed with them. I didn't know they were the Nine Muses until you told me, and for that I'm in your debt. But you have here a fine love affair. How did it come about?"

"Can't you see with your own eyes?" she asked. She offered him a shell cameo of the Three Graces and he held it up, inspecting it, and then he laid it down reverently before her again.

"They're works of art," said Aunt Queen, "of a special sort. They're pictures, complete little pictures, that's what matters. Small, intricate and intense. Let's use your metaphor of the entire universe again; that's what you find in many of these."

She was in a rapture.

"One can wear them," she said, "but it doesn't cheapen them to do it. You yourself just spoke of the charm." She touched the Medusa at her breast. "And of course I find something unique in every one I acquire. In fact, there's infinite variety in cameos. Here, look," she said, handing Lestat another example. "You see, it's a mythical scene of Hercules fighting a bull, and there is a goddess behind him and a graceful female figure in front. I've never seen another like it, though I have hundreds of mythological scenes."

"They are intense, yes," said Lestat. "I see your point completely, and it's truly divine, yes."

She looked about for a moment and then picked up another large shell cameo and offered it to him.

"Now that's Rebecca at the Well," she said. "A common scene depicted on cameos, and coming from the Bible, don't you know, from the book of Genesis, when Abraham sent a messenger to find a wife for his son Isaac, and Rebecca came out to greet this messenger at the village well."

"Yes, I know the story," Lestat said quietly. "And it's an excellent cameo too."

She looked at him eagerly, as much into his eyes as at his hands, with their lustrous fingernails.

"That was one of the first cameos I ever saw," she said, taking it back from him, "and it was with Rebecca at the Well that my collection began. I was given ten altogether of that exact same theme, Rebecca at the Well, though all were different in their carvings, and I have them all here. There's a story to it, to be sure."

He was obviously curious, and seemed to possess all the time in the world.

"Tell me," he said simply.

"Oh, but how I have behaved!" she suddenly remarked, "allowing you to stand there as if you were bad boys brought before the principal. Forgive me, you must sit down. Oh, but I am witless to be so remiss in my own boudoir! For shame!"

I was about to object, to declare it unnecessary, but I saw that Lestat wanted to know her, and she was having such a wonderful time.

"Quinn," she declared, "you bring those two chairs here. We'll make a cozy circle, Lestat, if I'm to tell a tale."

I knew there was no arguing. Besides, I was painfully stimulated that these two liked each other. I was crazy again.

As to the chairs, I did as I was told, crossing the room, taking up two of the straight-back chairs from Aunt Queen's round writing table between the back windows, and setting the chairs down right where we had stood so that we could face her again.

She took the plunge:

"It came about in this very room, my introduction to the passion for the cameo," she said, her eyes flitting over both of us and then fixing firmly on Lestat. "I was nine years old then and my grandfather was dying in here, a dreadful old man, Manfred Blackwood, the great monster of our history, the man who built this house, a man of whom everybody was afraid. My father, his only living son, William, tried to keep me away from him, but one day when the old beast was alone he saw me peeping in at that door.

"He ordered me to come inside and I was too afraid not to do it, and curious besides. He was sitting here where I am now, only there was no fancy dressing table here. Just his easy chair, and he sat in it, with a blanket over his lap, and both his hands on his silver-knobbed cane. His face was stubbly with his rough beard, and he wore a bib of sorts, and dribbled from the edge of his mouth.

"Oh, what a curse to live to that age to be slobbering as he was, like a bulldog. I think of a bulldog every time I think of him. And mind you, a sickroom in those days, no matter how well attended, wasn't what a sickroom is today! It reeked, I tell you. If I ever become that old and start to slobber, Quinn has my express permission to blow my brains out with my own pearl-handled gun, or to sink me with morphine! Remember that, Little Boy."

"Of course," I rejoined, winking at her.

"Oh, you little devil, I'm serious—you can't imagine how revolting it can be, and all I ask is permission to say my Rosary before you execute the sentence, and then I'll be gone." She looked at the cameos and then about herself and back to Lestat.

"The Old Man, yes, the Old Man," she said, "and he was staring blankly into nothing before he saw me, mumbling to himself until he started to mumble to me. There was a little chest of drawers beside him where it was rumored he kept his money, but how I knew this I don't now recall.

"As I was saying, the old reprobate told me to come in, and then he unlocked the top drawer of this chest and he took out a small velvet box and, letting his cane fall over on the floor, he put the box in my hands. 'Open that up and hurry,' he said. 'Because you're my only grand-daughter and I want you to have it, and your mother is too foolish to want it. I said hurry up.'

"Well, I did precisely what he told me, and inside were all these cameos, and I thought they were fascinating with all their tiny little people on them and their frames of gold.

" 'Rebecca at the Well,' he said. 'All of them of the same story, Rebecca at the Well.' And then, 'If they tell you I murdered her they're telling you the truth. She couldn't be satisfied with cameos and dia-monds and pearls, not that one. I killed her, or more truthfully, and it's time for the truth, I dragged her to her death.'

"Of course I was awestruck by his words," said Aunt Queen, "but instead of being suspicious and horrified, I was impressed that he was addressing these words to me. And he went on talking, the slobber com-ing down the side of his mouth to his chin. I should have helped him wipe his face, but I was too young to do anything as compassionate as that.

" 'Those were the old days,' he said to me, 'and she wore those high-collared lace blouses, and the cameos looked so very precious at her throat. She was so precious when I first brought her here. They're all so precious in the beginning and then they turn rotten. Except my poor dead Virginia Lee. My lovely, unforgettable Virginia Lee. Would she had lived forever, my own Virginia Lee. But the others, rotten, I tell you, greedy and rotten every time.

" 'But she was the worst of all my disappointments,' he told me, fix-ing me with his mean eyes. 'Rebecca, and Rebecca at the Well,' he said. 'It was *he* who gave me the first cameo for her, when he'd heard her name, telling me the story of it, and *he* that brought several more, all of Rebecca, all gifts for her, he said, *he* being the evil spy that he was, ever watching us; they all came from him, all these cameos, if truth be known, from *him*, though there's no taint on it, and you're just a child.' "

Aunt Queen paused, appealing to Lestat mutely to assure herself, I think, that she had an audience, and then when she saw that both of us were rapt, she went on.

"I remember all those words," she said, "and in my girl's heart I wanted the enchanting cameos, of course. I wanted them, the whole box! And so I held it tight as he went on, barking his words, or maybe even gnashing them out, it's hard to say. 'She grew to love the cameos,' the old beast said, 'as long as she could still dream and be content at the same time. But women aren't gifted with contentment. And it was *he* that killed her for me, a bloody sacrifice, that's what she was, an offering up to him, you might say and I would say, but I was the one who dragged her to it. And it wasn't the first time that I'd taken some poor misshapen soul to those bloody chains, to be sure.' "

I shivered. These words sounded a deep dark chord in me. I had a passel of secrets that weighed on me like so many stones. I couldn't do anything except listen in a vague spell as she went on.

"I remembered those words 'to those bloody chains,' " said Aunt Queen, "and all his other words as he yammered away: 'She gave me no choice, if the truth be known.' He was almost bellowing. 'Now you take those cameos and wear them, no matter what you think of me. I have something there sweet and costly to give you, and you're just a little girl and my grandchild, and that's what I wish it to be.'

"Of course, I didn't know how to answer him," Aunt Queen went on. "I don't think for a moment I believed he was a real murderer, and I certainly didn't know of this strange accomplice to whom he referred, this *he*, of whom he spoke with such mystery, and I never did find out who the man was, not to this very day. But he knew. And he continued as if I'd lanced a wound. 'You know, I confess it, over and over,' he said, 'to the priest and to the sheriff, and neither believes me, and the sheriff just says she's been gone some thirty-five years and I'm imagining, and as for *him*, what if his gold built this house; he's a liar and a cheat and he's left me this house as a prison, as a mausoleum, and I can't go any longer to him, though I know he's out there, he's out there on Sugar Devil Island, I can feel him, I can feel his eyes on me in the night when he comes near. I can't catch him. I never could. And I can't go out there anymore to curse him to his face, I'm too old now, and too weak.

"Oh, it was a powerful mystery," said Aunt Queen. " 'What if his gold built this house?' I kept it secret what he'd said. I didn't want my mother to take the cameos away. She wasn't a Blackwood, of course, and that's what they always said of her, 'She's not a Blackwood,' as though that explained her intelligence and common sense. But the point was, my room upstairs was full of clutter. It was an easy thing to hide the cameos away. I'd take them out at night and look at them and they bewitched me. And so my obsession began.

"Now, my grandfather did within a few months' time get right up out of this room and stagger down to the landing and put himself right into a pirogue and row off with a pole into Sugar Devil Swamp. Of course the farmhands were hollering at him to stop, but he went off and vanished. And no one ever saw him again, ever. He was forever gone."

A stealthy trembling had come over me, a trembling of the heart perhaps more than the body. I watched her, and her words ran as if written on ribbons being pulled through my mind.

She shook her head. She moved the cameo of Rebecca at the Well with her left hand. I could no more dare to read her mind than I would to strike her or say a cross word to her. I waited in love and full of old dread.

Lestat seemed quietly entranced, waiting on her to speak again, which she did:

"Of course eventually they declared him officially dead, and long before that, when they were still searching for him—though no one knew how to get to the island, no one ever even found the island—I told my mother all he'd said. She told my father. But they knew nothing of the old man's murder confession or his strange accomplice, the mysterious *he*, only that Grandfather left behind him plenty of money in numerous deposit boxes in various banks.

"Now maybe if my father had not been such a simple and practical man he would have looked into it, but he didn't and neither did my aunt, Manfred's only other child. They didn't see ghosts, those two." She made this remark as if Lestat would naturally regard this as peculiar. "And they had a strong sense, both of them, that Blackwood Farm should be worked and should pay. They passed that on to my brother Gravier, Quinn's great-grandfather, and he passed it on to Thomas, Quinn's grandfather, and that was what those men did, the three of them, work, work, work Blackwood Farm all the time, and so did their wives, always in the kitchen, always loving you with food, that's what they were like. My father, my brother and my nephew were all real countrymen.

"But there was always money, money from the Old Man, and everybody knew he'd left a fortune, and it wasn't the milk cows and the tung oil trees that made the house so splendid. It was the money that my grandfather had left. In those days people really didn't ask where you got your money. The government didn't care as they do in this day and age. When this house finally fell to me, I searched through all the records, but I couldn't find any mention of the mysterious *he*, or a partner of any sort, in my grandfather's affairs."

She sighed and then, glancing at Lestat's eager face, she continued, her voice tripping a little faster as the past opened up.

"Now, regarding the beautiful Rebecca, my father did have terrible memories of her, and so did my aunt. Rebecca had been a scandalous companion to my grandfather, brought into this very house, after his saint of a wife, Virginia Lee, had died. An evil stepmother if ever there was one, was this Rebecca, too young to be maternal, and violently mean to my father and my aunt, who were just little children, and mean as well to everyone else.

"They said that at the dinner table, to which she was allowed to come in all her obvious impropriety, she'd sing out my poor Aunt Camille's private verses just to show her she'd snuck into her room and read them, and one night, gentle though she was, Aunt Camille Blackwood rose up and threw an entire bowl of hot soup in Rebecca's face."

Aunt Queen paused to sigh at this old violence and then went on:

"They all hated Rebecca, or so the story went. My poor Aunt Camille. She might have been another Emily Dickinson or Emily Brontë if that evil Rebecca hadn't sung out her poetry. My poor Aunt Camille, she tore it all up after those eyes had seen it and those lips had spoken it and never wrote another verse again. She cut off her long hair for spite and burnt it up in the grate.

"But one day, after many another agonizing dinner-table struggle, this evil Rebecca did disappear. And, with no one loving her, no one wanted to know why or how. Her clothes were found in the attic, Jasmine says, and so says Quinn. Imagine it. A trunk or two of Rebecca's clothes. Quinn's examined them. Quinn's brought down more cameos from them. Quinn insists we keep them. I'd never have had them brought down. I'm too superstitious for that. And the chains! . . ."

She stole an intimate and meaningful glance at me. Rebecca's clothes. The shiver in me was relentless.

Aunt Queen sighed, and, looking down and then up at me again, she whispered:

"Forgive me, Quinn, that I talk as much as I do. And especially of

Rebecca. I don't mean to upset you with those old tales of Rebecca. We best have done with Rebecca perhaps. Why not make a bonfire of her clothes, Quinn? You think it's cold enough in this room, what with the air-conditioning, for us to light a real fire in the grate?" She laughed it off as soon as she'd uttered it.

"Does this talk upset you, Quinn?" Lestat asked in a small voice.

"Aunt Queen," I declared. "Nothing you say could ever sit wrong with me, don't be afraid of it. I talk all the time of ghosts and spirits," I continued. "Why should I be upset that anyone talks of real things, of Rebecca, when she was very much alive and cruel to everyone? Or of Aunt Camille and her lost poems. I don't think my friend here knows how much I came to know Rebecca. But I'll tell him if he wants to hear another tale or two later on."

Lestat nodded and made some small sound of assent. "I'm very ready for it," he said.

"It seems when a person sees ghosts, for whatever reason, he has to talk of it," said Aunt Queen. "And surely I should understand."

Something opened in me rather suddenly.

"Aunt Queen, you know my talk of ghosts and spirits more truly than anyone except Stirling Oliver," I said calmly. "I'm speaking of my old friend of the Talamasca because he did know too. And whatever your judgment of me, you've always been gentle and respecting, which I appreciate with all my heart—."

"Of course," she said quickly and decisively.

"But do you really believe what I told you of Rebecca's ghost?" I asked. "I can't tell even now. People find a million ways not to believe our ghost stories. And people vary in their fascination as to ghosts, and I have never been very sure of where you stand. Now's a good time to ask, isn't it, when I have you in the storytelling mood."

I was reddening, I knew it, and my voice had a break in it which I didn't like. Oh, the thunder of ghosts and their aftermath. Let it distract me from Stirling Oliver in my lethal arms and the bloody bride lying on the bed. Blunders, blunders!

"Where I stand," she said with a sigh, looking directly from Lestat to me and back again. "Why, your friend here is going to think he's entered a house of lunatics if we don't break off with this. But Quinn, tell me now that you haven't gone back to the Talamasca. Nothing will upset me so much as that. I'll rue the night I ever told such stories to you and your friend if it sends you back to them."

"No, Aunt Queen," I answered. But I knew I had reached my limit as to how much I could conceal if this painful conversation went on. I tried to rejoice again quietly in the fact that we were all together, but my mind was jumbled with frightening images. I was sitting very still, trying to keep all tight in my heart.

"Don't go into that swamp, Quinn," Aunt Queen said, abruptly appealing to me, as if from the core of her being. "Don't go to that accursed Sugar Devil Island. I know your adventuresome spirit, Quinn. Don't be proud of your discovery. Don't go. You must stay away from that place."

I was hurt through no fault of hers. I prayed I could soon confess to Lestat or someone in this world that her warnings were now too late. They had been timely once, but a veil had fallen over all the past, with its impetuosity and sense of invincibility. The mysterious *he* was no mystery whatsoever to me.

"Don't think about it, Aunt Queen," I said as gently as I could. "What did your father tell you? That there was no devil in Sugar Devil Swamp."

"Ah, yes, Quinn," she responded, "but then my father never set out in a pirogue in those dark waters to roam that island as you do. Nobody ever found that island before you, Quinn. That wasn't my father's nature, and it wasn't your grandfather's nature to do anything so impractical himself. Oh, he hunted near the banks and trapped the crawfish, and we do that now. But he never went in search of that island, and I want you to put it behind you now."

Keenly, I felt her need of me, as vividly as if I'd never felt it before.

"I love you too much to leave you," I said quickly, the words rolling from me before I thought of precisely what they meant. And then as suddenly: "I'll never leave you, I swear it."

"My dear, my lovely dear," she said, musing, her left hand playing with the cameos, lining up Rebecca at the Well, one, two, three, four and five.

"They have no taint, Aunt Queen," I said looking at those particular cameos, remembering discordantly but quite definitely that a ghost can wear a cameo. I wondered, Did a ghost have a choice? Did a ghost pillage its trunks in the attic?

Aunt Queen nodded and smiled. "My boy, my beautiful Little Boy," she said. Then she looked to Lestat again. His demeanor, his kindliness towards her had not changed one jot.

"You know, Lestat, I can't travel anymore," she said quite seriously, her words saddening me. "And sometimes I have the horrid thought that my life is finished. I must realize that I'm eighty-five. I can't wear my beloved high heels any longer, at least not out of this room."

She looked down at her feet, which we could still plainly see, at the vicious sequined shoes of which she was so proud.

"It's even an undertaking to go into New Orleans to the jewelers who know I'm a collector," she pressed on. "Though I have out back at all times the biggest stretch limousine imaginable, certainly the biggest limousine in the parish, and gentlemen to drive me and accompany me and Jasmine, darling Jasmine of course. But where are you these days, Quinn? It seems if I do wake at a civil hour and make some appointment you can't be found."

I was in a haze. It was a night for shame and more shame. I felt as cut off from her as I was near to her, and I thought of Stirling again, of the taste of his blood and how close I had come to swallowing his soul, and I wondered again if Lestat had worked some magic on both of us—Aunt Queen and me—to make us feel so totally without guile.

But I liked it. I trusted Lestat, and a sudden mad thought came to me, that if he was going to hurt me, he would never have gone so far in listening to Aunt Queen.

Aunt Queen went on with a lovely animation, her voice more pleasant though the words were still sad.

"And so I sit here with my little talismans," she said, "and I watch my old movies, hoping that Quinn will come, but understanding if he doesn't." She gestured to the large television to our left. "I try not to think bitterly about my weaknesses. Mine has been a rich, full life. And my cameos make me happy. The pure obsession with them makes me happy. It always has, really. I've collected cameos since that long-ago day. Can you see what I mean?"

"Yes," said Lestat, "I understand you perfectly. I'm glad that I met you. I'm glad to be received in your house."

"That's a quaint way to put it," she said, obviously charmed by him, and her smile brightened and so did her deep-set eyes. "But you are most graciously welcome here."

"Thank you, Madam," Lestat replied.

"Aunt Queen, my darling," she pressed.

"Aunt Queen, I love you," he responded warmly.

"You go now, both of you," she said. "Quinn, put the chairs back because you're big and strong, and Jasmine will have to drag them over the carpet, and you are free, both of you, my young ones, and I am so put out that I have ended this spirited conversation on a sad note."

"On a grand note," said Lestat, rising, as I took both the chairs easily and returned them to the writing table. "Don't think I haven't been honored by your confidences," he went on. "I've found you a grand lady, if you'll forgive me, an entrancing lady indeed."

She broke into a delighted riff of laughter, and as I came around in front of the table again and saw her shoes glittering there as if her feet were immortal and could carry her anywhere, I suddenly detached from all decorum and went down on my knees and bent my lips to kiss her shoes.

This I had done often with her; in fact, I had caressed her shoes and kissed them to tease her, and liked the feel of her arch in them, and I kissed that too, the thin nylon-covered skin, often and now, but for me to do it in front of Lestat was outrageously amusing to her. And on and on she laughed in a lovely soft high laugh that made me think of a crowded silver belfry against the blue sky gone quite wild.

As I climbed to my feet, she said:

"You go on now. I officially release you from attendance. Be off."

I went to kiss her again, and her hand on my neck felt so delicate. A ripping sense of mortality weakened me. The words she'd spoken about her age echoed in my ears. And I was aware of a hot mixture of emotions—that she had always made me feel safe, but now I didn't feel that she herself was safe, and so my sadness was strong.

Lestat made her a little bow, and we left the room.

Jasmine was waiting in the hallway, a warm patient shadow, and she asked where in the house I might be. Her sister, Lolly, and their grandmother Big Ramona, were in the kitchen, ready to prepare anything we might want.

I told her we didn't need anything just now. Not to worry. And that I was going up to my rooms.

She confirmed for me that Aunt Queen's nurse would come later, a ray of sunshine with a blood-pressure cup by the name of Cindy, with whom Aunt Queen would probably watch the movie of the night, which had already been announced as *Gladiator*, directed by Ridley Scott. Jasmine, Lolly and Big Ramona would of course watch the movie as well.

If Aunt Queen had her way, and there was no reason to think she couldn't, there might be another couple of nurses in the room for the movie too. It was her habit to make fast friends of her nurses, to inspect photographs of their children, and receive birthday cards from them, and to gather as many such young attendants around her as she could.

Naturally, she had her own friends, scattered about through the woods and up and down the country roads, in town and out of it, but they were as old as she was and could hardly come out to spend the night with her in her room. Those ladies and gentlemen she met at the country club for luncheon. The night belonged to her and her court.

That I had been a constant courtier before the Dark Blood was a fact. But since that time I'd come and gone irregularly, a monster among innocents, beleaguered and angered by the scent of blood.

And so Lestat and I left her, and the night—though I had almost murdered Stirling, and had fed without conscience on an anonymous woman, and had attended Aunt Queen in her storytelling—was actually quite young.

Lestat and I approached the staircase and he made a sign for me to lead the way.

For a moment I thought I heard the rustle of Goblin. I thought I felt his indefinable presence. I stood stock-still, wishing with all my heart for him to get away from me, as far away from me as if he were Satan.

Were the curtains of the parlor moving? I thought I heard the faint music of the baubles of the chandeliers. What a concert they could make if they all shivered together. And he had done such tricks, perhaps without deliberation, because he who had once been so silent now came and went with a bit of clumsiness, perhaps more than he could ever know.

Whatever the case, he was not near me now.

No spirits, no ghosts. Only the clean cooled air of the house as it came through the vents with the soft sound of a low breeze.

"He's not with us," said Lestat quietly.

"You know that for certain?" I asked.

"No, but you do," he replied.

He was right.

I led the way up the curving staircase. I felt sharply that for better or worse, I would now have Lestat to myself.

6

THE UPPER HALL HAD three doors on the right wall, and, due to the staircase rising against the left wall, only two on that side. The first door on the left led into my apartment, which was two rooms deep, and the last door on the left led to the bedroom on the rear of the house.

Lestat asked if he might see any rooms, and I told him that he could see most of them. Two of the three bedrooms on the right were uninhabited right now—one belonging to my little Uncle Tommy, who was away at boarding school in England, and the other always reserved for his sister Brittany—and were kind of fancy showpieces, each with its ornate nineteenth-century four-poster bed, ritual baldachin, velvet or taffeta hangings and comfortable though fancy chairs and couches, much like those in Aunt Queen's bedroom downstairs.

In the third room, which was off limits, there hovered my mother, Patsy, whom I hoped we would not see.

Each marble mantelpiece—one snow white and the other of black and gold—had its distinct detail, and there were gilded mirrors wherever one turned, and those huge proud portraits of ancestors—William and his wife, pretty Grace; Gravier and his wife, Blessed Alice; and Thomas, my Pops, and Sweetheart, my grandmother, whose real name had been Rose.

The ceiling lights were gasoliers, with brass arms and cut crystal cups for their bulbs, more ordinary yet more atmospheric than the sumptuous crystal chandeliers of the first floor.

As to the last bedroom on the left, it too was open and neatened and fine, but it belonged to my tutor, Nash Penfield, who was presently completing some work for his Ph.D. in English at a university on the

West Coast. He had always cooperated with the four-poster bed and its ruffles of blue silk, his desk was clean and bare and waiting for him and his walls, very much like mine, were lined with books. His fireplace, like mine, had a pair of damask chairs facing each other, elegant and well worn.

"The guests were always on the right side of the hallway," I explained, "in the old hotel days, and here in Nash's room, my grandparents slept—Sweetheart and Pops. Nash and I spent the last year or so reading Dickens to each other. I tread anxiously with him, but so far things have worked out."

"But you love this man, don't you?" Lestat asked. He followed me into the bedroom. He politely inspected the shelves of books.

"Of course I love him. But he may sooner or later know something's very wrong with me. So far I've had very good luck."

"These things depend a lot on nerve," said Lestat. "You'd be amazed what mortals will accept if you simply behave as if you're human. But then you know this, don't you?"

He returned to the bookshelves respectfully, removing nothing, only pointing.

"Dickens, Dickens and more Dickens," he said, smiling. "And every biography of the man ever written, it seems."

"Yes," I said, "and I read him aloud to Nash, novel after novel, some right there by the fireplace. We read them all through, and then I would just dip down into any book—*The Old Curiosity Shop* or *Little Dorrit* or *Great Expectations*—and the language, it was delicious, it would dazzle me, it was like you said to Aunt Queen. You said it so very right. It was like dipping into a universe, yes, you had it." I broke off. I realized I was still giddy from being with Aunt Queen, from the way he had been in attendance on her; and as for Nash, I missed him and wanted him so to come back.

"He was a superb teacher," ventured Lestat gently.

"He was my tutor in every subject," I confessed. "If I can be called a learned man, and I don't know that I can, it's on account of three teachers I've had—a woman named Lynelle and Nash and Aunt Queen. Nash taught me how to really read, and how to see films, and how to see a certain wonder even in science, which I in fact fear and detest. We seduced him away from his college career, with a high salary and a grand tour of Europe, and we're much better off for it. He used to read to Aunt Queen, which she just loved."

I went to the window, which looked out on the flagstone terrace behind the house and the distant two-story building that ran some two hundred feet across. A porch ran along the upper story of the building, with broadly positioned colonettes supporting it from the ground floor.

"Out there's the shed, as we call it," I explained, "and we call our beloved farmhands the Shed Men. They're the handymen and the errand men, the drivers, and the security men, and they hang out back there in their own den.

"There's Aunt Queen's big car, and my car—which I don't use anymore. I can hear the Shed Men now. I'm sure you can. There're always two on the property. They'll do anything in this world for Aunt Queen. They'll do anything in this world for me."

I continued:

"Upstairs, you see the doors, those are small bedrooms, small compared to these, I mean, though just as well furnished with the four-poster beds and antique chests and Aunt Queen's adored satin chairs. Guests used to stay out there too in the old days, for less of course than they paid to stay in the big house.

"And that's where my mother, Patsy, used to stay when I was growing up. Patsy lived out there ever since I could remember. Down below is where she first practiced her music, over to the left side, that was her garage—Patsy's studio—but she doesn't practice anymore and she's in the front bedroom now just down the hall. She's rather sick these days."

"You don't love her, do you?" Lestat asked.

"I'm very afraid of killing her," I said.

"Come again?" he asked.

"I'm very afraid of killing her," I said. "I despise her, and I want to kill her. I dream about it. I wish I didn't. It's just a bad thought that's come into my head."

"Then come, Little Brother, take me to where you want to talk," he said, and I felt the soft squeeze of his fingers on my arm.

"Why are you so kind to me?" I asked him.

"You're used to people being paid to do it, aren't you?" he asked. "You've never been too sure about Nash, have you? Whether he would love you half so much if he weren't paid?" His eyes swept the room as though the room were talking to him about Nash.

"A big salary and benefits can confuse a person," I said. "It doesn't always bring out the best, I don't think. But in Nash's case? I think it did. It's taken him four years to write his dissertation, but it's a fine one, and after he passes his examinations he'll be satisfied." My voice was quavering. I hated it. "He'll feel that he's independent of us, and that will be good. He'll come back and be Aunt Queen's companion and escort. He'll read to her again. You know she can't really read now. She'll adore it. I can't wait for it to happen for her sake. He'll take her anywhere she wants to go. It's all for her sake. He's a handsome man."

"You're facing mighty temptations," Lestat said, his eyes narrowing as he appraised me.

"Mighty temptations?" I asked. I was shocked and even a little revolted. "You don't think I'd feed off those I love, do you? I mean, I know I made this colossal mistake with Stirling, it was god-awful what I did; Stirling came within a hairsbreadth, but I was caught off guard and I was frightened, frightened that Stirling knew what I was, and knew me, you understand, and that Stirling understood—." *Off guard.* Bloody wedding dress, bloody bride. *You fool, you're not supposed to kill them when they're innocent, and on this her wedding night. She's the only bride you'll ever have.*

"That wasn't my meaning," Lestat replied. He brought me back to myself, out of my anguish.

"Come. To your room now, correct, Little Brother? Where we can talk. And you have a two-room apartment against the stairs."

A calm came over me along with a quiet happy expectation, as though he had enforced it.

He led the way and I came quietly behind.

We went into my sitting room, which was on the front of the house, and we had a good view of my bedroom through the open sliding double doors, and there was my enormous and regal bed, the baldachin padded in red satin, and the matching red chairs, thick and inviting, scattered from bedroom to sitting room, and between the front windows of the sitting room, my computer and desk. The giant television, to which I was as addicted as anybody, was catercorner, near the inside wall.

Beneath the gasolier stood the center table with its two chairs facing each other, and this was where I often sat, upright and very comfortable, to read. I wrote here in my diary while I was watching television with one eye. This was where I wanted to be with Lestat. Not in the two chairs by the fireplace, which was dead this time of year.

I saw at once that my computer had been turned on.

Lestat sensed that I was alarmed and then he too saw the message floating in green block type on the black monitor:

NO LESTAT.

The very sight of it sent a jolt through me, and I went at once to the machine and turned it off.

"From Goblin," said Lestat, and I nodded, as I stood sentinel waiting for the machine to be switched on again, but it was not.

A violent series of chills passed over me. I turned around. I was vaguely aware that Lestat stood on the opposite side of the center table and that he was watching me, but I could scarcely pay any attention. The heavy draperies of the front windows were swaying, and the gasolier above me had started to move. There was that faint tinkling music from the glass cups and their baubles. My vision was clouded.

"Get away from me," I whispered. "I won't see you, I'll shut my eyes, I swear it." And I did it, screwing my eyes tight as any little child pretending to sleep, but I lost my balance and I had to open my eyes before I fell.

I saw Goblin standing to my right, opaque, detailed, my duplicate—and the computer was on and the keyboard was clicking, and a series of nonsense syllables were jabbering across the monitor while a vague rumble came from the small computer speakers.

I tried to shut my eyes again, but I was too seduced by him, his total double of me, even to my leather coat and black pants, and his crazed expression which surely didn't reflect mine. His eyes were glittering viciously and triumphantly, and his smile was like that of a clown.

"I'm telling you, go, Goblin," I said, but this only redoubled his power, and then the image began to thin and to expand.

"Let me hurt him!" Lestat said urgently. "Give me the permission."

In confusion, I couldn't answer, even though I heard Lestat plead with me again. I felt the tight grip all around me, as though a boa constrictor had me, or so I imagined, and my vision had left me, melting into the violent chills that I couldn't shake. I felt the tiny pinpricks all over my face and the backs of my hands, and I tried to lift my hands to ward them off but my hands hurt. Every bit of my bare flesh hurt, even to the back of my neck.

A panic took hold of me, as if I'd been caught in a swarm of bees. Even my eyelids were attacked, and I knew that I'd fallen to the floor, but I couldn't orient myself. I could feel the carpet under my hand and I couldn't get up.

"Little Brother, let me hurt him," Lestat said again. And I heard my own voice as if it came from someone else.

"Damn him," I said, "hurt him."

But there had come that magnetic sense of union, Goblin and I, indivisible, and I saw the sunny room again in which a child stood in a wooden playpen scattered with toys, a curly headed toddler in little overalls whom I knew to be myself, and beside him his double, the two of us laughing together, without a single care—look at the red flowers in the linoleum, look at the sunshine, see the spoon flying end over end in an arc through the air—and fast after this there tumbled other images and random moments: laughter in the schoolroom and all the boys looking at me and pointing and murmuring, and me saying *He's right here, I tell you*, his hand on my left hand and my writing in crayon in that scrawl of his, love you, Goblin and Tarquin; and the pure electric shocks of pleasure left me without a body, without a soul. I was rolling on the floor, wasn't I?

"Goblin." I think I whispered. "The one to whom I belong and to whom I've always belonged. No one can understand, no one can fathom." Goblin, Goblin, Goblin.

The pleasure crested with unspeakable sweetness, and subsided into waves of certain bliss.

He was withdrawing, leaving me cold and hurt and lonely all over, fiercely, catastrophically lonely—he was deserting me.

"Hurt him!" I said the words with all my breath, terrified they weren't audible, and then my eyes opened, and above me I saw the great sprawling image of myself, face wavering and grotesque, and suddenly it was made up of pinpoints of fire!

Lestat had sent the Fire Gift to burn the blood he'd taken, and I heard Goblin's silent wail, his soundless raging scream.

Oh, no, it was wrong, not my Goblin, how could I have done it, how could I have betrayed him! His scream was like a siren. A rain of tiny ash descended on me, in fact it seemed flung at me, and his scream rose again, piercing my ears.

The air was full of the smell of the burning, like the smell of human hair burning, and the huge shapeless image hovered, drawing itself together into my solid double for one fateful and frightfully opaque moment, challenging me, cursing me—*Evil devil, Quinn, evil! Bad. Bad!*—and then it was gone, escaping through the door, leaving the gasolier creaking on its chain and the electric lights blinking, and sending a rippling wind through the lace panels on the windows as silence and stillness closed in.

I was on the floor. The blinking lights were unendurable. Lestat came to me and helped me to my feet, and ran his hands caressingly over my hair.

"I couldn't do it," he said, "until it was leaving you, because when it was with you the Fire might have burnt you too."

"I understand," I said. I was in a fever. "And I never thought to do it, to punish him with it, but think how he learns now. He's quick. He knows already what's obvious to me and to you, no doubt, that if I try to burn him, if either of us does again, he'll fuse with me again and make the fire burn me."

"Maybe he'll do that," said Lestat, guiding me to the straight-back chair at the table. "But do you think he wants for you to die?"

"No, he can't want that," I answered. I was out of breath, as though I'd been running. "He takes his life from me. Whatever he was before I came along, I can't imagine. But it's my focus, my love, that makes him strong now. And goddamn it, I can't stop loving him, feeling I'm betraying him, and he feeds off that!"

The blinking of the lights had stopped. The lace curtains were still. Chills ran up and down my spine. With a noise of static in the speakers, the computer suddenly went off.

Stammering, I told Lestat about the image I'd seen, of myself in the playpen, of the old linoleum that must have been in the kitchen, and of Goblin with me, and that it wasn't something I remembered but something I knew to be true.

"He's shown me those images before when he's attacked me, images of myself as an infant."

"And all this over the years?"

"No, only now after the Dark Gift—with these attacks, when I fuse with him as I would with a mortal victim. It's the Dark Blood. It's become the currency of memory, the vampiric blood. He wants me to know he has these memories of a time when I saw him and strengthened him with that vision even before I knew how to talk."

Lestat had settled in the chair on the other side of the table, and in a split second I developed a positive superstition about him having his back to the hallway door.

I went to the door and closed it, and then, coming back, I unplugged the computer entirely, and I asked if we could rearrange the chairs. Lestat caught me as I reached out to do this.

"Be patient, Little Brother," he said. "The creature's pushed you right out of your mind."

We sat down again, facing each other, Lestat with his back to the front of the house, and me with my back to my bedroom.

"He wants to be a Blood Hunter, don't you see?" I said. "I'm terrified of him and what he can do." I looked up at the gasolier to see if the electric bulbs were blinking. No. I looked at the computer to make sure that its screen was blank. Yes.

"There's no way that he can become a Blood Hunter," said Lestat calmly. "Stop shaking, Quinn. Look into my eyes. I'm here with you now. *I'm here to help you, Little Brother!* And he's gone, and after the burning I don't think he's going to come back, not for a long while."

"But can he feel physical pain?" I asked.

"Of course he can. He can feel blood and pleasure, can't he?"

"I don't know," I rattled on. "Oh, I hope you're right," I said. I was almost about to cry. "Little Brother," how I loved the words, how I cherished them, and how sweet it was, as sweet as Aunt Queen calling me forever Little Boy.

"Get a grip, Quinn," Lestat said. "You're sinking on me." He clasped my hands. I could feel the hardness of his flesh. I had some hint of his strength. But he was gentle, and his skin felt silky and his eyes were totally kind.

"But the old tale in the Chronicles," I said, "of the first vampires—of how they were humans until a spirit entered into them. What's to stop it from happening again?"

"It's never happened since, to my knowledge," said Lestat, "and we're speaking now of thousands of years ago, of a time before ancient Egypt. Many a Blood Hunter, as you call them, has seen spirits, and many a human as well. And how do we really know what happened in the beginning, except that we were told through tradition that it was a powerful spirit who entered its human host by many fatal wounds. You think your Goblin has the power or the cunning for such a perfect fusion?"

I had to admit that he did not.

"But who would have thought that he could drink from me?" I asked. "Who would have thought that he would? The night I was made, my Maker said that Goblin would leave me, that spirits had an aversion to Blood Hunters and I'd soon find myself alone. 'No more ghostly companions for you,' he said. He said it meanly. Because he couldn't see them, you see. Oh, what a demon he was!"

Lestat nodded. His eyes were filled with muted compassion.

"In the main, that's so," he said. "Ghosts shy away from Blood Drinkers, as though something about us, understandably, horrifies them. I don't know the full explanation of it. But you know it's not always so. There are many vampires who see spirits, though I'm not one of them, except on a very few remarkable occasions, I should openly confess."

"You mean you really can't see Goblin," I said.

"I told you the first time that I couldn't see him," Lestat said patiently. "Not until he had drunk the blood. Then I saw his image defined by the blood. It was the same this time, and I sent the Fire to that blood. Now, what if he had attacked you again? I don't think those minute flames could have ignited you. There wasn't thrust enough. But just in case, I'll use another power if he comes again, a power you have as well, and that's the Mind Gift, as some call it, not to read his mind but to push against him, to drive him away with a telekinetic strength until he's so weary with defending himself that he can't hold steady and has to flee."

"But how can I push against what is not material?" I asked.

"He is material," Lestat corrected me. "He's just made of a material we don't understand. Think clearly."

I nodded. "I've tried to push him away," I confessed. "But something happens, something happens in my reason, and he's on me, and the pleasure starts pounding, the guilty pleasure that he and I are together, and the chills are running rampant, as if my soul had chills, and there's a taunting rhythm to it, a thumping rhythm, and I'm his slave."

I felt a delicious numbness come over me even as I spoke of it, some last vagrant shiver of the union. I looked at my hands. All the tiny pinprick wounds had healed. I felt my face, and I could see the memories again. I felt a vast secret knowledge of Goblin, an unshakable dependence.

"He's become my vampire," I said. "He makes a meal of me, he locks into me. I'm . . . yes, I'm his slave."

"And a slave who wants to be rid of his master," said Lestat thoughtfully. "Has it been stronger with each attack, this guilty pleasure?" he asked.

"Yes, yes, it has," I confessed. "You know, there were years, important years, when he was my only friend. It was before Nash Penfield came. It was before my teacher Lynelle came. And even while Lynelle was here, it was me and Goblin together always. I never put up with anyone who didn't tolerate my talking to Goblin. Patsy hated it. Patsy's my mother, remember? It was at times a perfect comedy, but that's the way it was. Patsy would stomp her feet and scream, 'If you don't stop talking to that damned ghost, I'm leaving!' Now, Aunt Queen is perfectly patient, so patient that I could swear there have been times, though Aunt Queen won't admit it, that she saw Goblin herself."

"But why won't she admit it?" he asked.

"They all thought that Goblin was bad for me, don't you see? They all thought that they mustn't encourage it, don't you see? And that was why they didn't want me talking with the Talamasca, because they thought that Stirling and the Talamasca would nurture this damnable ability in me, of seeing ghosts and spirits, and so, if any of them saw Goblin, if my grandparents Sweetheart and Pops ever saw him, they didn't say."

Lestat appeared to ponder this for a moment. And once again, I noticed that very slight difference between his eyes. I tried to shut it out of my thoughts, but one eye was ever so much brighter than the other, and definitely tinged with blood.

He said, "I think it's time I read your letter to me, don't you?"

"Perhaps so," was all I could say.

He drew the envelope out of his inside coat pocket and he tore open the end of the envelope neatly, letting the onyx cameo slip out of it into his right hand, and then he smiled.

He looked rapidly several times from the deeply carved white image to me and back again, and then he rubbed the image very gently with his thumb.

"I may keep this?" he asked.

"It's my gift to you, if you want it," I said. "Yes, I meant it for you. It was when I thought we'd never meet face-to-face. But yes, keep it. It was made for Aunt Queen, let me confess it, but after the Dark Blood I didn't want to give it to her. But I don't know why I'm rambling on about such a point. I'm honored you ask to keep it. It's yours."

He slipped it into his side coat pocket, and then he opened the letter and read it carefully, or so it seemed to me.

There was my plea to help me destroy Goblin, and my begging for his patience that I dared to enter New Orleans in search of him, and my report of how I had known and loved the Talamasca, a confession that brought the blood teeming into my face when I thought of Stirling and what I had almost done this very night. There was my admission of how I loved Aunt Queen and how I wanted to take my leave of her, if Lestat chose to punish me by death for disobeying his only rules.

I realized now that much of the letter's contents had been revealed to him in every other way, and that what he held was only a formal document of what he already knew.

Very respectfully he refolded the pages and doubled them over and put them back in his pocket as though he wanted to save the letter, though why I didn't know. The envelope had been cast aside.

He regarded me for a long time in silence, his face rather open and generous, which seemed a natural expression for it, and then he spoke:

"You know, I was on the scent of Stirling Oliver when I came upon you. I knew that he was entering my flat—he's done it more than once—and I thought it was time that he should have a little scare. I wasn't certain how I meant to arrange that, though I had no intention of revealing myself to him, but then I came upon you about to make the little scare quite final for Mr. Oliver, and it was from your confused mind that I caught the reason you'd come."

I nodded, then said hastily, "He doesn't mean any harm, you saw that. I can't tell you how thankful I am that you stopped me. I don't think I could have survived my killing him. I'm sure of it. It would have been the finish for me, and I'm terrified of my own clumsiness, that a death like that—. But you must realize he won't do any harm to us, either of us—."

"Oh, yes, now you're out to save him from destruction. Stop worrying. The Talamasca's off limits, I told you. Besides, I gave them what they've wanted for some time, don't you see?"

"Yes, a sighting of you, a talk with you."

"Correct, and they'll mull that over, and letters will be sent to the Elders, but I know perfectly well they can't harm us. And he and his cohorts won't come out here looking for you. They're too damned honorable. But you must tell me now, in case I've underestimated them, do you lie by day in a safe place?"

"Very safe," I said quickly. "On Sugar Devil Island, which they could never conceivably find. But surely you're right, Stirling will keep his promise not to come looking for me or seek me out. I believe in him utterly. That's why it's so ghastly that I almost hurt him, I almost took his life."

"And would it have been to the finish with him?" he asked. "Have you no self-control once you've begun?"

I was full of misery.

"I don't know what self-control I have. On the night of my making I committed a blunder, taking an innocent life—."

"Then that was your Maker's blunder," he retorted. "He should have been with you, teaching you."

I nodded.

"Let me dream that I would have broken off with Stirling, but I wasn't just frightened of him, frightened of him knowing about me, I was hungry for his death. I'm not sure how it would have gone. He was fighting me with an elegance of mind. He has that, an elegance of mind. Yes, I think I would have taken his life. It was tangled with my love for him. I would have been damned for it forever, and I would have found some way to put an end to myself right away. I'm damned for almost doing it. I'm damned for everything. I live, I live in a fatal frame of mind."

"How so? What do you mean?" he asked, but he wasn't surprised by what I'd said.

"It's as if I'm forever in the grip of Last Rites or dictating a Last Will and Testament. I died the night my Maker brought me over; I'm like one of the pathetic ghosts of Blackwood Manor who doesn't know he or she is dead. I can't come back to life."

He nodded, raising one eyebrow and then relaxing. "Ah, well, you know that argues much better for a long existence rather than reckless-ness and devil-may-care behavior."

"No, I didn't know," I said quickly. "What I know is that I have you here and you helped me with Goblin, and you see what Goblin can do. You see that Goblin has to be . . . has to be destroyed. And maybe me too."

"You haven't the smallest idea of what you're saying," he returned quietly. "You don't want to be destroyed. You want to live forever. You just don't want to kill to do it, that's all."

Now I knew that I was going to cry.

I took out my pocket handkerchief and I wiped at my eyes and my nose. I didn't turn away to do this. That would have been too cowardly. But I did look about me without moving my head, and when I looked back at him I thought, what a staggeringly beautiful creature he was.

His eyes alone would have done the trick, but he'd been gifted with so much more, the thick massive blond hair, the large finely shaped mouth and an expression eloquent of comprehension as well as intelli-gence, and under the light of the gasolier he was the matinee idol drift-ing before me, carrying me out of myself into some unmeasured moment in which I relished his appearance as if he couldn't or didn't know.

"And you, my timeless one," he said in a soft sure voice with no hint of accusation in it, "I see you here in your exquisite setting of mirrors and gold, of human love and obvious patrimony, and robbed of it all in essence by some careless demon who's left you orphaned and uneasily, no, torturously, ensconced among the mortals you still so desperately need."

"No," I said. "I fled my Maker. But now I seek you out, and so I have you, even if just for this night, but I do love you, love you as surely as I love Aunt Queen, and Nash, and Goblin, yes, as much as I have loved Goblin, I love you. Forgive me. I can't keep it back."

"There is no forgiving," said Lestat. "Your head teems with images, and I catch them blinkering and crowding your brain as they seek a narrative, and so you must tell me, you must tell me all of your life, even what you think is not important, tell me all. Let it pour from you, and then we'll judge what's to be done with Goblin together."

"And me?" I asked. I was exuberant. I was crazed. "We'll judge what's to be done with me?"

"Don't let me scare you so much, Little Brother," he said in the kindest tone. "The worst thing I'd do to you is leave you—vanish on you as if we'd never met. And I don't think of that now. I think rather of knowing you, that I'm fond of you and have begun to treasure you, and your conscience shines rather bright for me. But tell me, haven't I failed you already? Surely you don't see me now as the hero you once imagined."

"How so?" I asked, amazed. "You're here, you're with me. You saved Stirling. You stopped a disaster."

"I wasn't able to destroy your beastly phantom," he said with an amiable shrug. "I can't even see him, and you've counted on me. And I threw the Fire at him with all I had."

"Oh, but we've only just started," I responded. "You'll help me with him, won't you? We'll figure it out together."

"Yes, that's precisely what we'll do," he responded. "The thing is strong enough to menace others, no doubt of it. If it can fight you as it did, it can attack others—that much I can tell, and that it responds to gravity, which for our purposes is a good sign."

"How so gravity?" I asked.

"It sucked the very air when it left you," he answered. "It's material. I told you. It has some chemistry in the physical world. All ghosts are material in probability. But there are those who know more of this than me. I only once saw a human ghost, talked to a human ghost, spent an hour with a ghost, and it terrified me quite out of my mind."

"Yes," I replied, "it was Roger, wasn't it, who came to you in the Chronicle called *Memnoch the Devil*. I read how you talked with him and how he persuaded you to care for his mortal daughter, Dora. I read every word. I believed it; I believed that you saw Roger and that you went to Heaven and Hell."

"And well you should," he rejoined. "I never lied in those pages, though it was another that took the dictation of it. I have been with Memnoch the Devil, though what he really was—devil or playful spirit—I still don't know." He paused. "It's more than plain to me," he said, "that you've noticed the difference between my eyes."

"I'm sorry, I couldn't help it," I said quickly. "It isn't a disfigurement."

He made a gesture of dismissal along with a kind smile.

"This right eye was torn from me," he said, "just as I described it, by those spirits who would have prevented me from fleeing Memnoch's Hell. And then it was returned to me, here on Earth, and sometimes I believe that this eye can see strange things."

"What strange things?"

"Angels," he said, musing, "or those who call themselves angels, or would have me conclude that they're angels; and they have come to me in the long years since I fled Memnoch. They've come to me as I lay like one in a coma on the chapel floor of St. Elizabeth's, the building in New Orleans which was bequeathed to me by Roger's daughter. It seems my stolen eye, my restored eye, my bloodshot eye, has established some link with these beings, and I could tell you a tale of them, but now is not the time."

"They harmed you, didn't they?" I asked, sensing it in his manner.

He nodded.

"They left my body there for my friends to watch over," he explained, and for the first time since I'd seen him, he looked troubled, indecisive, even faintly confused.

"But my spirit they took with them," he went on. "And in a realm as palpable as this very room they set me down to do their bidding, always threatening to snatch back this right eye, to take it forever if I didn't do what they bid me to do."

He hesitated, shaking his head.

"I think it was the eye," he said, "the eye which gave them the claim on me, the ability to reach down to me, in this realm, and take me—it was the eye, stolen in another dominion and then returned on Earth to its rightful socket. You might say that as they looked down from their lofty Heaven, if Heaven it is, they could see, through the mists of Earth, this bright and shining eye."

He sighed as if he were suddenly miserable. He looked at me searchingly.

"This wounded eye, this tarnished eye," he continued, "gave them their compass to find me, their opening, as it were, between the dominions, and down they came to enlist my spirit against my will."

"Where did they take you? What did they do?"

"Oh, if I only knew that they were Heavenly beings," he declared in a low passionate voice. "If I only knew that Memnoch the Devil and those who came after him had shown me truths! It would all be a different matter and I could somehow save my soul!"

"But you don't know. They never convinced you," I pushed.

"How can I accept a world full of injustice, along with their august designs?"

He shook his head again and looked off and then down, as though searching for some spot for his focus, and then back to me as he went on.

"I can't entirely accept what I learned from Memnoch and those who came afterwards. I've never told anyone of my last spiritual adventure, though the others, the Blood Drinkers who love me—you know, my lusty troop of beloveds, I call them that now, the Troop of Beloveds—they know that something happened, they sense it only too well. I don't even know which of my bodies was the true one—the body that lay on the floor of the chapel of St. Elizabeth's, or the body that roamed with the so-called angels. I was an unwilling trafficker in knowledge and illusions. The story of my last adventure, my secret unknown adventure, the adventure I haven't confided to anyone, weighs on my soul as if to make my spiritual breath die out."

"Can you tell me now of this adventure?" I asked.

It took a great sense of power in him, I thought, to look so readily abject, to show me such affliction.

"No," he said. "I haven't the strength for the telling of that story yet, that's the plain truth."

He shrugged and shook his head and then continued:

"I need more than strength. I need courage for that confession, and right now my heart's warm from being with you. You have a story to tell, yes, or we have a story to live together. Right now my greedy heart is fastened to you."

I was overcome. I cried like a silent baby. I blew my nose and tried to remain calm. Blood on the handkerchief. Body of Blood. Mind of Blood. Flash of his eyes on me. Violet.

"I should take my good fortune," I said, "and not question it, but I can't resist. What's kept you from destroying me, from punishing me for coming into your flat, for doing what I did to Stirling? I have to know."

"Why do you have to know?" he asked, laughing softly. "Why is it so very important to know?"

I shook my head and shrugged my shoulders. I wiped at my eyes again.

"Is it vanity in me to press the question?" I asked.

"Probably," he said, grinning. "But shouldn't I understand? I, the most vain of creatures?" He chuckled. "Didn't you see me preening for your aunt downstairs?"

I nodded.

"All right," he said. "Here comes the litany of reasons I didn't kill you. I like you. I like that you have a woman's lineaments and a man's body, a boy's curious eyes and a man's large easy gestures, a child's frank words and a man's voice, a blundering manner and an honest grace."

He smiled at me quite deliberately, and winked his right eye, and then went on.

"I like that you loved Stirling," he said. "I like that you honor your glorious Aunt Queen so candidly." He smiled mischievously. "Maybe I even like it that you went down on your knees and kissed her feet, though that gesture came rather late in the game of my deciding. I like that you love so many around you. I like it that you're more generous than I am. I like that you hate the Dark Blood, and that your Maker wronged you. Now—isn't that pretty? Isn't that enough?"

I was quietly delirious with gratitude.

"Don't think it so very unselfish of me to be here," he went on, eyes widening, voice gaining a little heat. "It's not. I need you or I wouldn't be here. I need your need of me. I need to help you, positively need it. Come, Little Brother, carry me deep into your world."

"My world," I whispered.

"Yes, Little Brother," he said. "Let's proceed together. Tell me the history you inherited and the life you've lived. Tell me about this beastly and beguiling Goblin and how he has gained his strength. I want to hear everything."

"I'm in love with you," I responded.

He laughed the most beguiling and gentle laugh.

"Of course you are," he replied. "I understand perfectly because I'm in love with myself. The fact that I'm not transfixed in front of the nearest mirror takes a great deal of self-control."

It was my turn to laugh.

"But your love for me," he went on, "is the reason why you'll tell me all about yourself and Blackwood Farm. Start with the family history and then go into your own."

I sighed. I pondered. I took the plunge.

7

"CHILDHOOD FOR ME INVOLVED two distinct polarities—being with Goblin, and listening to adults talk.

"Goblin and I were the only children here at Blackwood Manor because the tourists who came almost never brought children with them, and so I soon learned the vocabulary of adults and that it was fun to play in the kitchen and listen to their endless storytelling and arguing, or to tag after the tour guides—my great-grandfather Gravier and later my grandfather Pops—as they went through the house detailing its riches and its legends, including the gloomy tale of Manfred, the Great Old Man.

"Great-grandfather Gravier was truly the very best at this, having a deep sonorous voice and being a dignified man in a black suit with a white silk tie to match his white shirt, but he was very old when I was little and he went away to a hospital and died there, before I was five I think, and I have no clear memory of his funeral. I don't think I went to his funeral. But he had made an indelible impression upon me.

"And he at once became a famous family ghost apparently, on the sole authority of my having come down the stairs one morning and seen him standing by the front door, smiling at me placidly and waving his right hand. He was gone in an instant.

"Everybody told me to stop telling such stories, Great-grandfather Gravier was in Heaven, and I must certainly know that, and we ought to light a candle for him before the Blessed Virgin on the little altar in the kitchen, which we did—which made a total of ten-odd candles burning on the little altar for various ancestors, rather like the altars one sometimes sees in Chinese laundries. And furthermore, it was said I shouldn't try to scare people.

"Nevertheless, during every house tour ever given by anyone at Blackwood Manor, the whole world of our paying guests was told about my having seen Great-grandfather Gravier.

"Pops, Gravier's only son and my grandfather, took up the job of guide with gusto after Gravier's death, and though Pops was far more plain-spoken and rough at the edges, he was a grand storyteller, nevertheless.

"Gravier had been a man of considerable accomplishment, in that he had practiced law for years and even served on the bench as a local judge. But Pops was a rural man who had no ambition beyond Black-wood Manor, and if that meant he had to talk to the guests, he did it.

"My grandmother Sweetheart sometimes was recruited, much against her will, as she was always up to her elbows in flour and baking powder, but she knew all the family legends, and, heavy as she was, looked very pretty in a fine black gabardine dress with a purple orchid corsage on her left breast and a string of pearls around her neck. She was one of those women who, inclined to embonpoint, have round smooth wrinkleless faces until they die.

"And then there was Jasmine, our beloved black housekeeper, whom you've met, who could in a twinkling change from her kitchen clothes to a swanky black skirt and leopard-skin blouse, along with spike heels of which Aunt Queen would have been proud, to take everyone from room to room, very properly adding to the concoction of tales that she herself had seen Great-great-grandfather William's ghost in his bedroom, front right, or across the hall from us, as well as the ghost of Great-great-great-aunt Camille tiptoeing up the attic stairs.

"I don't know that you noticed Jasmine in her fancy red sheath tonight, but Jasmine has the figure of a model, rail thin with strong shoulders, and, with closets of loving cast-offs from Aunt Queen, she cuts a beautiful image as a tour guide, her pale green eyes positively flashing as she tells her earnest ghost stories and sighs before the portraits, or leads the expectant guests to the attic stairs.

"It was Jasmine's brilliant idea to include the attic in the usual tour, that is, to take the tourists right up and into it, instructing them to notice the delicious smell of the warm wooden rafters as they stood there, and to point out the fine steamer trunks and wardrobe trunks from earlier times, some open and heaped with furs and pearls rather like props for *A Streetcar Named Desire*, and the wicker wheelchair in which Great-great-grandfather William had spent his last days on the lawn. The attic was—before my own inevitable raid upon it—a wilderness of rare and antique wicker, and tales devolved around it all.

"Let me return to the big picture.

"The bed-and-board guests were always company and a bit of an inspiration to me, because they were often friendly and attractive— I tend to see most people as attractive until someone comes along and points out to me that they're not—and these people frequently invited me into their rooms, or wanted me to sit down at breakfast with them at the big table and chat about the Manor House, as we so pretentiously called it, and I warmed to all this friendship, and Goblin found it interesting because whenever I spoke to or of him, which was all the time, these guests thought Goblin the most intriguing thing in the world.

" 'So you have a little spirit friend!' one said triumphantly, as though she had discovered Confederate gold buried outside. 'Tell us about your little ghost,' said another, and when I petted or stroked Goblin while talking of him, he was very happy, indeed. He would flash on solid for a long time, and only sadly go transparent and then dissolve when he had to.

"I couldn't have done better had I been a paid performer whose sole occupation was to increase the mystery of Blackwood Farm. And I loved it. And then the guests kicked in their support of the mythology gratis, as I've explained, with all their sightings of the Old Man, Manfred, scowling in a mirror, or sweet Virginia Lee, roaming from room to room in search of her orphaned children.

"I learned from all this, from the endless variety with which the tales of our house were woven, and I learned from adults how to think and feel like an adult, and Goblin fed off the easy way in which he fitted into everything. And I came to think of myself from early on as being a maverick like the Old Man.

"Manfred, the Old Man, had come out to these parts in 1881 with a new bride, Virginia Lee. He had started out as a saloon keeper in the Irish Channel but gone on to make a fortune in merchandising in New Orleans, but could find no locale suitable to his visions of splendor and so was drawn north across Lake Pontchartrain to this open land.

"Here he found a parcel of real estate that is composed of high ground on which he could build a fabulous mansion, with servants' quarters, stables, terraces and pastures, plus two hundred acres of thick swamp in which he could hunt, and a charming abandoned cemetery with its shell of a stone church, a tribute to those whose families had long ago died out or decamped.

"Manfred sent his architects to the fine homes of Natchez to choose the very best of attributes for this mansion, and he supervised its Greek Revival style, circular stairs and hallway murals himself.

"All was for the love of Virginia Lee, who had a particular affection for the cemetery and sometimes went to the empty little stone church to pray.

"The four oak trees that guard the cemetery now were already well grown at that time, and the proximity of the old graveyard to the swamp with its greedy hideous cypress trees and endless tangles of Spanish moss no doubt added to, and adds to, the overall sense of melancholy.

"But she was no sappy Victorian girl, Virginia Lee. She had been an educated and devoted nurse to Manfred in a New Orleans hospital where he suffered a severe bout of Yellow Fever and, like many an Irishman, almost died of the disease. It was with great reluctance that she gave up her vocation to nurse the sick, but Manfred, being much older and very persuasive, successfully enchanted her.

"It was for Virginia Lee that Manfred had the portrait of himself painted, which is now hung in the parlor, and always was, as far as I know. He was in his forties when the portrait was painted, but he had already come to resemble a bulldog in some respects, with heavy jowls, an up-thrust obdurate mouth and large mournful blue eyes. He had thick gray hair by that time, circa 1885, and he still had a full head of it when Aunt Queen had her strange meeting with him some forty years later, when he gave her the cameos before he disappeared into the swamp.

"He doesn't look like a mean man in the portrait. In fact, I've always found the picture strongly compelling, and the man himself must have been lacking in vanity, that he allowed such an honest portrait of himself to be hung in his house.

"Virginia Lee was undeniably pretty, as you saw from her portrait in the dining room, a girlish woman with pale blond hair and intense blue eyes. She was said to have had a quick sense of humor and an eternal but gentle sense of irony, and to be utterly loving to William and Camille, the two surviving children she bore before she died. As to those which she lost to lockjaw and influenza, Isabel and Philip, nothing could ever take her mind off them.

"Galloping consumption is the disease that took Virginia Lee, who had also become quite sick from malaria, and only after a valiant struggle during which she dressed herself completely and independently every day, including the Saturday on which she died, at which time she had carried on amusing conversation, with her famous good cheer and self-deprecating humor, in the front parlor, lying on the sofa, until she took her last breath around noon.

"She was buried in the sky blue dress that she wears in her portrait. And if our house has a family saint, it's Virginia Lee. I'm not above praying to Virginia Lee.

"It was said that Manfred went out of his head when Virginia Lee died. He roared and mumbled. Not being able to endure the sight of a grave for Virginia Lee in the little cemetery—and it probably wasn't legal to bury her there in his own backyard anyway—he bought a huge crypt for the entire family in the new Metairie Cemetery in New Orleans, which is where our family are buried to this day.

"I've seen the mausoleum twice—when Sweetheart died and when Pops died. I presume little Isabel and Philip were uprooted to the crypt from wherever they'd been buried, but frankly I never asked.

"It's a small rectangular chapel of marble and granite, this Metairie Cemetery tomb, with two five-foot, well-carved granite guardian angels beside its bronze gates, and a stained-glass window in back. Three coffin slots lie on either side of the little aisle.

"You know how those tombs work, I'm sure. Coffins are placed in the slots until all the slots are full, and then when someone new dies, the oldest coffin is opened up, bones dumped in the vault below the ground, and the coffin smashed to pieces and discarded. The new coffin is given the place of honor above ground.

"It's where I always thought I'd be buried when I died, but now it doesn't seem that destiny will allow me that luxury or the long adventure I once contemplated to take me to that end. But who knows? Maybe my mortal remains could somehow be secreted into that crypt on some future occasion, after I have the courage to put an end to my own life.

"But let's return to Mad Manfred, as those around the parish began to call my unfortunate ancestor, who took to going out into Sugar Devil Swamp alone and muttering and cursing, and sometimes not returning for days at a time.

"There was a general commotion to it because all knew that Sugar Devil Swamp had never been logged and was damned near impenetrable for a pirogue, and legends already existed as to bears that habitually hunted there, and cougars and bobcats, and even worse creatures which howled in the night.

"That Manfred was snake-bit more than once and survived it was part of his growing reputation, and it was said he fired on a stranger he'd seen out there some distance from the house, and brought back the wounded poacher and heaved his body on the bank with oaths and vicious warnings to his workmen that this ought to be a lesson to anyone who dared to come into his swamp or onto his land.

"Soon it became known that there was an island out there, and it was to this island that Manfred went, pitching a tent for himself and shooting what he needed for food.

"You can just picture this guy tearing birds apart with his teeth.

"He made no secret of his island sanctuary, only warning again that no one must ever attempt to follow him to his 'lair,' as he called it, threatening open season on trespassers and boasting that he had shot and killed several bears.

"Rumor had it that the island was cursed and Manfred was cursed, and that his gold was ill-gotten from gambling, if not worse vices, and that his name, Manfred, he had taken from the play by Lord Byron, with the intent to signal other Demon Worshipers of his own ilk, and that he had sold his soul to the Devil long before he had ever laid eyes on the humble and sweet Virginia Lee, and that she had been his very last chance at salvation.

"As for their little children, William and Camille, it was Jasmine's ancestors who brought them up—Ora Lee and Jerome are the famous names—both of them Creole people of color with French accents, and something of a distinctive history, their parents having been free artisans before the Civil War.

"For Ora Lee and Jerome, Manfred built the bungalow out back to the far right, a real Creole-looking building, with a deep porch and rocking chairs, and two stories of good-sized rooms.

"Members of the clan have broken off all along to go to college and enter professions, but there are always some who stay in the bungalow, and they have their own vegetable and flower gardens and their own company whenever they choose.

"When I was a kid they still had their own cow and some chickens, but now it's too easy to go to market for anything a person needs.

"It's a charming house, a kind of tropical mansion in its own way, full of treasured antiques and various displays of needlework done by the women and furniture made by the men. It's also full of cast-offs from the big house, and Aunt Queen is famous for refurnishing the front room and giving all the old items to Jasmine, as if Jasmine had a warehouse rather than a family home. It's on a human scale, Jasmine's house. Blackwood Manor was built for 'giants in the earth.'

"Because African and Spanish and French and Anglo-Saxon genes were all scrambled in the lineage of Jasmine's people before they came, and down through the years by marriage to other people of all colors, Jasmine's family are all different shades of yellow, red, brown and black.

"Jasmine's dark, as you saw, with the fabulous green eyes. She bleaches that close-cropped Afro of hers and something happens with that yellow hair and those green eyes that's magic.

"Her older sister, Lolly, can pass for Spanish or Italian, and then there's Jasmine's brother, Clem, who has very dark skin and African features. He drives Aunt Queen's car and takes care of all the fleet, including the black Porsche I bought in imitation of you and your adventures in the Vampire Chronicles.

"Little Ida, Jasmine's mother, was very black with exquisitely fine features and tiny black eyes. She married a white man when she was pretty mature, and, after his death from cancer, she came back here with Jasmine and Lolly and Clem. She was my nurse or nanny till she died, Little Ida, sleeping with me till I was thirteen, and then dying in my bed.

"What I'm telling you now, this story of the Blackwood family, is what has come down to me from Jasmine and Lolly and Little Ida and Big Ramona, who is Little Ida's mother, as well as from Aunt Queen, or Pops or Sweetheart. Jasmine has an eye for ghosts, as I've said, and I'm always afraid she's going to realize I'm not really alive, but so far it hasn't happened. And I hang on to my family like a pit bull.

"But to return to my story, if it hadn't been for the fabled Ora Lee and Jerome, little William and Camille might have drowned in the swamp or starved from inattention.

"As to salaries for his hired help, Manfred couldn't be bothered with any such thing, only heaving fistfuls of money into a big bowl in the kitchen. Jerome had to see that the man wasn't robbed, and the keep of William and Camille and all the farmhands was provided for.

"The farm had its own chickens and cows in those days, and horses of course, and a fine carriage or two parked right beside the new automobiles in the back shed.

"But Manfred never bothered with anything but one black gelding, which he sometimes came ashore to ride back and forth across the broad lawns and pastures of Blackwood Farm, shouting and murmuring and cursing to himself, and declaring to his groom (most probably the versatile Jerome) that he was never going to die and join Virginia Lee, not until centuries had passed, that he would roam the earth, shivering from her death and honoring her memory.

"All this I learned by rote as you can tell.

"One spring day several years after Manfred had become a widower, carpenters and lumber were brought to the property, and the slow process of building the mysterious Hermitage on Sugar Devil Island began.

"Nothing but the finest kiln-dried cypress was seen to go off by pirogue into the swamp, in one small load at a time, along with a great quantity of other materials, including an iron stove and a great amount of coal, and only workmen from 'away' went out there to build, workmen who would go 'away' when the work was done, which is what those workmen did, solemnly afraid of uttering a word as to the location of the island, or what had been their specific tasks.

"Was there really such an island? Was there really a hermitage upon it? As I was growing up, who was to say that it was anything more than a legend? And why was there no swamp tour to take our tourists out to search for this mysterious Sugar Devil Island, for surely everyone wanted to see it. It was a regular feature of life to see the tourists down at the landing, hankering to wade in the bog. But the swamp, as stated, and it can't be stated enough, is almost impassable.

"The great silent groping cypress is everywhere, along with the wild palmetto and the rankest water. And one can still hear the roar of cougars and bears. It's no joke.

"Of course Pops and I fished in Sugar Devil Swamp and we hunted. And in my boyish ignorance I once killed a deer in the swamp, and lost my taste right there for all hunting as I watched it die.

"But in all our exploits, including trapping crawfish by the pound, we never went deeper in than some twenty feet from the shores. And even at that distance, it's hard to see one's way back.

"As for the legend of the Hermitage on Sugar Devil Island, Pops put no stock in it, reminding the curious tourists that even if such a building had existed, it might have long ago sunk into the muck.

"Then there are the stories of poachers who disappeared without a trace, of their wives gone crying to the local sheriff to please search, but what could the sheriff hope to find in a swamp infested by roaring bears and alligators?

"However, the most evil omen that hung over this odd, private jungle was the disappearance into the swamp of Mad Manfred himself in the year 1924, as Aunt Queen has already described to us, to which our tour guides would invariably add that the Old Man dressed in his tail-coat and white tie and boiled shirt and fine leather shoes before that last excursion, and ranted and raved at himself in the mirror for an hour before bolting out the door.

"Yes, people searched, as the Old Man had been convalescent for two years before this bizarre and desperate flight, but they never found any island, and they had to shoot many a gator just to survive, and came back with the gators to sell for their hides, but not with Manfred.

"And so it was that the idea took hold that there was no real island. And that the Old Man had simply drowned to put an end to his wheezing and choking misery, for he was surely at death's door when he bolted for the pirogue and headed out as if to cross the River Styx.

"Then, some seven years later, when his will was finally opened, there was found contained within the strong exhortation that no Blackwood or anyone belonging to the Blackwood household was ever to fish or hunt beyond the mud banks of Sugar Devil Swamp, and the admonition, in Manfred's own hand, that Sugar Devil Island was a danger not only to flesh and blood but to a being's immortal soul.

"A very good copy of these pages of Manfred's Last Will and Testament, all notarized in the year 1900, is framed and mounted on the living room wall. Guests adored it. I remember my teachers, Nash in particular, just howling with laughter when they read it. And it did certainly seem to me, as I was growing up, that the lawyer, the notary and Mad Manfred were all poets in Byronic cahoots with one another when they wrote this.

"But it doesn't seem that way to me now.

"Let me continue. Of William, Manfred's only surviving son, and Camille, his only surviving daughter, there are huge portraits in the parlor, very handsome paintings if nothing else, and the current tale that William has often appeared to family and guests, rummaging through a desk in the living room, is true.

"The desk is a beautiful piece, Louis XV, I believe, with inlaid wood, cabriole legs and ormolu—you know, the works—and I have myself glimpsed him once hovering near it.

"I have no doubt of what I've seen with my own eyes, but I will get to that when I return to the account of me and Goblin. It's enough to say right now that I never found anything in the desk. There are no secret compartments or documents.

"Camille's ghost is almost always seen on the attic stairs, a woman with tastefully coiffed gray hair, and in an old-lady black dress and old-lady thick-heeled shoes, with a double strand of pearls around her neck, ignoring those to whom she appears and vanishing at the attic doorway.

"And then there are the rushing feet of little children in the upstairs hall, these ascribed to Manfred's little daughter Isabel, who died when she was three, and his son Philip, who didn't live even that long.

"When it came to the rest of the family, it was simply a matter of elegantly painted portraits—Gravier's is especially fine, but then I did see Gravier, didn't I? But his wife, Blessed Alice, a lovely portrait subject, and Pops and Sweetheart, who reluctantly posed for their portraits, though it wasn't their nature, have never appeared to anyone. So far . . .

"Then there's the living legend of Aunt Queen—Miss Queen to all those of this parish—and of her heroic travels crisscrossing the globe. The guests were delighted to hear that she was 'presently in Bombay' or 'celebrating New Year's Eve in Rio' or 'resting in her villa on Santorini' or 'engaged in a major shopping spree in Rome.' It proved as exciting to them as any ghost story.

"That Aunt Queen was a great collector of cameos was also well known, and in those days, the public days, there was a dainty glass case in the parlor, perched on spindly legs in the corner, which held a display of her finest pieces.

"Bed-and-breakfast guests at Blackwood Manor never stole things, I'm relieved to report—I think they're far more interested in homemade biscuits, jam and architecture—and I was the one who periodically changed the display of Aunt Queen's cameos. I grew to like them. I could see the variations. Sweetheart had no real interest in them. And Pops was the outdoor man.

"Aunt Queen can be said to have been a living haunt, or a protective spirit, which was a remarkable thing to me when I was a child, because I felt safe merely thinking about her, and her visits were like the apparitions of a saint.

"Others died in this house. An infant born to Gravier and Blessed Alice; there are times when I swear I can hear a baby crying. Guests used to hear it too, and sometimes they would remark on it rather innocently.

"Gravier had a younger brother, Patrick, who fell from a horse and died of the concussion in the middle upstairs bedroom. His portrait hangs in there over the fireplace. His wife, Regina, lived out her life here, much beloved by the Kitchen Gang, of which she was a baking, frying, slicing, dicing bonafide member. Their only daughter, Nanette, moved away long years ago to New Orleans.

"There, in a cheap French Quarter boardinghouse, Nanette drank a whole bottle of bourbon and ate a whole bottle of aspirin and died of the result. I don't know any more of it than that. If her ghost walks, it doesn't do so at Blackwood Manor. Patrick too seems to be resting well in the family crypt. So is his wife, Regina.

"Professional ghost hunters came once and found evidence of multiple hauntings, and made a tantalizing presentation to the guests who had gathered for the Halloween weekend, and so the tradition of the Halloween Weekend came to be.

"The Halloween Weekend was always marvelous fun, with huge white tents on the terraces and on the far lawns, with chilled champagne and Bloody Marys. Tarot-card readers and palm readers, fortune-tellers and psychics were hired for the event, and the climax was a costume ball to which people came from all the parish around.

"If Aunt Queen happened to be at home, which was seldom, a great number of old friends of hers joined the festivities, and the costumes were wonderfully lavish, the place being full of princes and princesses of all description, elegant vampires, stereotypical black-hatted witches, sorceresses, Egyptian queens, moon goddesses and the occasional ambitious mummy, dripping with white gauze.

"I loved all of the Halloween Weekend, you can tell by the way I dote on it. And it won't surprise you to learn that the expert ghost hunters never once took notice of Goblin, even when Goblin danced around them in a circle and did the abominable trick of stretching his mouth.

"Of course Goblin isn't the ghost of a living person, but these experts were very good at declaring that poltergeists were working their subtle activities in the kitchen and pantry, accounting for pings and pongs of noise that one could scarce hear, or the sound of a radio devolving from music into static; and poltergeists are pure spirits as far as I know.

"This was my life growing up—this and the Christmas banquet of which I've already told you, with the caroling and the singing on the staircase and of course the huge dinner of roast turkey, goose and ham along with all the usual trimmings, and the weather outside being sometimes cold enough for the women to wear their old fur coats that smelled of moth balls, and the gentlemen joining in the singing with full hearts.

"It seemed at times that the men singing the Christmas carols made me cry. I expected the women to sing, it seemed natural, but for the men to join in, men of all ages, and to do it with such stout hearts, that seemed especially reassuring and wonderful. I cried every year. It was that and the purity of the soprano who sang 'O Holy Night,' and 'What Child Is This?' Of course I joined in the singing myself.

"And lest I overlook it, there was the Spring Festival, when the azaleas planted all around Blackwood Manor were blooming, in pink and white and red, and we would have a huge buffet, almost like that of a wedding, outside on the lawn. There was always an Easter Buffet as well.

"Then I suppose I should throw in all the weddings again and the commotion they brought, and the fascinating waiters I would meet in the kitchen, who to a one felt the 'vibrations' of spirits, and the brides becoming hysterical because their hair was not done right and the hairdresser had already gone, and Sweetheart, my darling Sweetheart, portly and ever solicitous, huffing and puffing up the stairs to the rescue and snatching up her electric curling iron and doing a few excellent tricks she knew to make everything right.

"There was Mardi Gras too, when, even though we're an hour and a half from New Orleans, we were booked solid, and we decorated in the traditional colors of purple, green and gold.

"Sometimes, a very few times, I went into the city to see some of the Mardi Gras parades. Sweetheart's sister, Aunt Ruthie, lived on St. Charles Avenue, which you know is the main parade route. But she wasn't a Blackwood, and her sons, though probably normal, appeared to me to be monsters with too much body hair and overly deep voices, and I felt uncomfortable there.

"So Mardi Gras didn't penetrate to me very much except for all the gaiety out here at the house, and the inevitable costume ball we held on the night of Fat Tuesday itself. It was amazing how many revelers came back at sunset from New Orleans, after hours of watching Zulu, Rex and the interminable truck parades, to drink themselves sick at our festive bar.

"Of course I did very occasionally encounter other children here—at the Halloween party and at the Christmas party in particular, and sometimes at the weddings—but I didn't take to them. They seemed to me to be freaky little people. I have to laugh at myself for thinking such a thing. But as I've said, my world was made up of spirits and adults, and I just didn't know what to do with children.

"I think I feared children as treacherous and even a little dangerous. I'm not sure why exactly, except that Goblin didn't like them, but Goblin really didn't like me to be with anyone very long.

"I hung with the adults by natural inclination and strong choice.

"I can't think about the weddings now, as we talk together, without thinking of something ghastly that I have to confess to you—something that happened far from Blackwood Manor, and on the night I was made a Blood Hunter. But the time will come for that, I know.

"That's the family history, as it came down to me when I was innocent and protected by the umbrella of Pops and Sweetheart, and Aunt Queen, who was ever like a fairy godmother, dipping down to Earth only now and then with her stacked heels and invisible wings.

"There are other family members—connections of William's wives—he had two, the first of whom was the mother of Gravier, and the second, the mother of Aunt Queen, and of Gravier's wife, and, of course, connections of Sweetheart's. But though I've seen such cousins from time to time, they are not part of this story, and they had no impact on me whatsoever, except perhaps a feeling on my part of being unordinary and hopelessly strange.

"It's time now for me to move on to the tale of me and Goblin, and the account of how I got educated.

"But before I do, let me trace the Blackwood lineage, for what it's worth. Manfred was the patriarch, and William was his son. William begat Gravier. Gravier begat Pops. And Pops, late in life when he and Sweetheart had despaired of having a child, begat Patsy. At age sixteen, Patsy gave birth to me and named me Tarquin Anthony Blackwood. As to my father, let me state now plainly and unequivocally that I don't have one.

"Patsy has no clear recollection of what was happening to her in the weeks during which I might have been conceived, except that she was singing with a band in New Orleans, with fake identification to get her into the club where the band was playing, and she and a whole mob of musicians and singers were hanging together in a flat on Esplanade Avenue, 'with plenty of weed and plenty of wine and plenty of company.'

"I've often wondered why Patsy didn't seek an abortion. She certainly could have managed it. And I'm tormented by the suspicion that Patsy thought that if she was a mother she would be an adult, and Pops and Sweetheart would give her freedom and money. She didn't get either one. And so there she was at sixteen, with a baby brother of a child, and obviously no notion of what to do with me, as she went on with her dreams of becoming a country-western singer and of having her own band.

"I have to remember all this when I think of her. I have to try not to hate her. I wish I could stop feeling pain every time I think of her. I'm ashamed to say it again but I would like to kill her.

"Now on to the story of me and Goblin and how I was educated and how I educated him."

8

"Y̲O̲U̲'V̲E̲ ̲H̲E̲A̲R̲D̲ ̲M̲E̲ say that Goblin is my double, and let me emphasize it, because the duplication of me is always perfect, and so I've had all my life a mirror held up to me in Goblin in which I could see, if not know, myself.

"As to Goblin's personality? His wishes? His temper? All this was wholly different in that he could be a perfect devil when it humiliated me and embarrassed me, and I could seldom control him, though I did learn early on that if I ignored him completely, which took an immense act of will, he might fade and disappear.

"There have been moments when I did nothing but inspect Goblin, the better to know how I myself looked, and when some alteration came in my appearance, such as the trimming of my hair, Goblin would clench his fists, make ugly faces and stomp his noiseless foot. For that reason I often wore my hair bushy. And as the years passed Goblin took an interest in our clothes, and sometimes threw down on the floor the pair of overalls he wanted me to wear, and the shirt as well.

"But I'm plunging too fast into the condition of things, and not telling memories as they are lodged.

"My first distinct memory is a third birthday party in the kitchen, with my grandma Sweetheart and Jasmine and her sister, Lolly, and their mother, Little Ida, and her mother, Big Ramona—and all of them on high stools or chairs at the white-enameled kitchen table, gazing down at me as I sat at my child's table, with Goblin right beside me, talking away with Goblin and telling him how to pick up his fork the way I'd been taught to do and eat his cake.

"He had his own little chair to the left of me and a place set for him, and milk and cake, the same as me. And at one point he grabbed my left hand—I'm left-handed and he's right-handed—and he made me smear my cake all over my plate.

"I started crying because I'd never known him to be so strong—he had truly made my hand move, though not perhaps as he wanted it to—and I didn't want my cake smeared, I wanted to eat it, and right away the kitchen was in a flying commotion, with everybody jumping up from the stools and Sweetheart trying to wipe my tears and at the same time tell me that I was 'making a mess.'

"Goblin was as solid as I was, both of us in navy blue sailor suits for the occasion, and I had some vague sense even then that he was at his strongest because of the heavy rain that was falling outside.

"I loved the kitchen on those rainy days, loved to stand at the back screen door and watch the rain come down in sheets, with the kitchen all warm and full of bright electric light behind me, the radio singing oldies, or Pops playing the harmonica, and all those beloved adults, and the smell of cooking from the stove.

"But let me return to my third birthday party.

"Now Goblin had ruined it and I was sobbing. And he, the little idiot, after crossing his eyes and rocking his head from side to side, took his two first fingers and stretched his mouth on both sides wide as he could, which made me scream.

"I know I would never have stretched my mouth like that, but he did it often with his mouth, just to get a rise out of me.

"Then he vanished, completely vanished, and I started to bellow his name.

"My last distinct picture of that event is of all the women trying to comfort me, the four black women who were as gentle as my grandmother Sweetheart, and even Pops coming in, drying the rain off himself with a towel and asking what was wrong.

"I was hollering, 'Goblin, Goblin,' over and over again, and Goblin wouldn't come back.

"A terror erupted in me as it always did when he would vanish, and how it was resolved then I don't know.

"It's dim, this memory, but it's fixed because I remember the giant number three on the birthday cake, and everybody saying so proudly that I was three years old, and then Goblin being so strong and so full of spite.

"Also Pops gave me a harmonica on that birthday and taught me how to blow in it, and I sat with him and we played together for a little while, and ever after we did that in the evenings right after supper before Pops headed up early to bed.

"What comes next is a series of memories of Goblin and me playing together alone in my room. Happy, happy memories. We played at blocks, with a marvelous set full of columns and arches, creating buildings of a vague classical bent to be sent crashing down, and for the purpose of crashing and banging we had fine little fire trucks and automobiles, but sometimes we just did the crashing with our hands or feet.

"Goblin didn't have the strength to do it on his own right away, but over time he acquired it, but before that he would take my left hand to do it, or to roll the fire truck into our marvelous structures, and then he'd smile, and break loose of me, and dance about.

"My memory of these rooms is pretty clear. Little Ida, Jasmine's mother, slept in the big bed with me, as I was already too old for a crib, and Goblin slept with us, and this room here was the playroom and filled with toys of all kinds.

"But I was easy with Goblin and he had no reason to be mean.

"And gradually, in spite of my young age, I began to see that Goblin didn't want to share me with the world, and was happiest, by far, when he had my full attention, which made him strong.

"Goblin didn't even want me to play the harmonica, because he lost me when I did, even though he loved to dance to the radio or to songs that the women in the kitchen sang. He had me laughing at him or dancing with him at those times. But when I played the harmonica, especially with Pops, I was in another world.

"Of course, I learned the knack of playing the harmonica especially for Goblin, nodding and winking at him (I could wink really early in life, with either eye) as he danced, and so he started to put up with it as the years passed.

"Most of the time, Goblin had what he wanted. We had our own table up here for crayons and drawing. And I let him guide me, his right hand on my left hand, but all he'd create was scribble scratch, whereas I wanted to draw stick figures, or figures made of circles, and faces with little circles for eyes. I taught him how to do the stick figures, or the egg people, as Little Ida called them, and how to make pictures of a garden with big round flowers that I liked to do.

"It was at this little nursery table that he first demonstrated his eternally feeble voice. No one could hear it but me and I caught it as so many bursts of fragmented thought brightening for an instant in my head. I talked out loud to him naturally, and sometimes in whispers which developed into murmurs, and I remember Little Ida and Big Ramona asking me all the time what I was saying, and telling me I wasn't talking right.

"Sometimes, when we were down in the kitchen and I was talking to Goblin, Pops or Sweetheart asked me the same thing, what on earth was I saying, and didn't I know how to talk better than that, would I please say whole words as I knew well enough how to do.

"I brought Goblin up to snuff on this, that we had to talk in whole words, but his voice was no more than broken telepathic suggestions, and out of sheer frustration he gave up on this means of speaking to me, and his voice only returned years later.

"But to continue with his infant development—he could nod or shake his head at my questions, and smile crazily when I said things or did things that he liked. He was dense when he first appeared to me each day and would become more translucent as his appearances, or lingering, increased. I had a sense of knowing when he was near, even if he was invisible, and during the night I could feel his embrace—a very light and distinct impression which I never tried, until this very moment, to describe to anyone else.

"It's more than fair to say that when he wasn't making faces and cavorting he impressed me with an engulfing love. It was stronger perhaps when he wasn't visible, but if he didn't appear to me at short intervals over the day and into the night, I began to cry for him and become severely distressed.

"Sometimes when I was running on the grass or climbing the oak tree outside, down by the cemetery, I could feel him clinging to me, piggybacking onto me, and I would all the time talk to him, whether he was visible or not.

"One very bright day, when I was in the kitchen, Sweetheart taught me to write some words—'good' and 'bad' and 'happy' and 'sad,' and I taught Goblin, with his hand on mine, to write these words as well. Of course nobody understood that Goblin was doing the writing some of the time, and when I tried to tell them they just laughed, except for Pops, who never liked Goblin and was always worried 'where all this talk of Goblin would lead.'

"No doubt Patsy had always been around, but I don't remember her distinctly until I was four or five. And even then I don't think I knew she was my mother. She certainly never came up here to my room, and when I did see her in the kitchen I was already afraid that a screaming fight between her and Pops was going to break out.

"I loved Pops, and with reason, because he loved me. He was a tall gaunt man with gray hair all the time I knew him, and always working, and most of the time with his hands. He was educated and he spoke very well, as did Sweetheart, but he wanted to be a country man. And just the way the kitchen had swallowed up Sweetheart, who had once been a debutante in New Orleans, so the farm swallowed Pops.

"Pops kept the books for the Blackwood Manor Bed-and-Breakfast on a computer in his room. And though he did put on a white shirt and suit to conduct the tours of the place now and then, he didn't like that part of things. He preferred to be riding the lawns on his beloved tractor lawn mower or doing any other kind of work outdoors.

"He was happiest when he had a 'project' and could work side by side with the Shed Men—Jasmine's great-uncles, brothers and so forth—until the sun went down, and I never saw him in any vehicle except a pickup truck until Sweetheart died, at which time he rode into town in a limousine like all the rest of us did.

"But I don't think, and it's hurtful to say it, that Pops loved his daughter, Patsy. I think he loved her as little as Patsy loves me.

"Patsy was a late child, I know that now, though I didn't then. And when I look back on it as I tell you this story, I realize there was no natural place for her. Had she gone debutante like Sweetheart, well, maybe it would have been a different story. But Patsy had gone country and wild at the same time, and this mixture Pops, for all his country ways, couldn't abide.

"Pops disapproved of everything about Patsy, from the way she teased her hair and curled it down her back and over her shoulders to the tiny short skirts that she wore. He hated her white cowboy boots and told her so, and said her singing was a bunch of foolishness, she'd never 'make it' with her band. He made her shut the garage doors when she practiced so her 'racket' wouldn't disturb the bed-and-breakfast guests. He couldn't endure her flashy makeup and her fringed leather jackets, and he told her she looked like common trash.

"She shot right back at him, saying she'd earn the money to get the hell out of here, and she broke a cookie jar once in a fight with him—a cookie jar full of Sweetheart's chocolate fudge, I might add—and whenever she left the kitchen, she never forgot to slam the screen door.

"Patsy was a good singer, I knew that much from the beginning because the Shed Men said it, and so did Jasmine and her mother, Little Ida, and even Big Ramona said it. And I liked the music myself, to tell the truth. But there was an endless procession of young men to the back garage to play guitar and drums for Patsy—and I knew Pops hated them—and when I played outside I crept close to the garage stealthily, not wanting Pops to see me, so I could hear Patsy wailing away with the band.

"Sometimes Goblin would get to dancing to Patsy's music, and, as happens with many spirits, Goblin can be caught up in dancing, and when he was dancing he rocked from side to side and made goofy, funny gestures with his arms, and did tricks with his feet that would have made a flesh-and-blood boy stumble and fall. He'd make like a bowling pin, rolling but never falling, and I would nearly die from laughing to see him carry on.

"I got to liking this dancing too, and being his partner, and trying to imitate his steps. And when Patsy came out of the shed to smoke a ciga-rette, and saw me, she'd swoop down and kiss me and call me 'darlin' ' and say I was a 'damned cute little boy.' She had a strange way of putting that last phrase, as if it were an admission over opposition, but no one would have opposed her in saying it, except her own self.

"I think I thought she was my cousin, until Patsy's screaming fights with Pops told me a different tale.

"Money was the cause of Patsy's screaming arguments with Pops because Pops never wanted to give her any, and of course I know now that there was plenty of money, always plenty plenty of money. But Pops made Patsy fight over every nickel; Pops wouldn't invest in Patsy, I see it now, and sometimes their quarreling made me cry.

"One time, when I was at my little table in the kitchen with Goblin, and one of these fights had broken out between Patsy and Pops, Goblin took my hand and guided my crayon to write the word 'bad.' I was happy when he did this, because it was right what he wrote, and then he sat real close to me and tried to put his arm around me, but his body was very stiff in those days. I knew that he didn't want me to cry. He tried so hard to comfort me that he became invisible, but I could feel him cling-ing to my left side.

"At other times when Patsy was battling for money, Goblin would pull me away, and he didn't have to try very hard. He and I ran up to my room where we couldn't hear them.

"Sweetheart was far too submissive to oppose Pops at the time of the kitchen quarrels, but Sweetheart did slip money to her daughter. I saw that, and Patsy would cover Sweetheart with kisses and say, 'Mamma, I don't know what I'd do if it weren't for you.' Then she'd ride off into town on the back of somebody's motorcycle, or in her own van, her much excoriated van which had 'Patsy Blackwood' written in spray paint on both sides of it beneath the windows, and we wouldn't see Patsy or hear any music from the studio for three days.

"The first time I realized that Patsy was intimately connected to me was a terrible night when she and Pops got to screaming at each other and he said, 'You don't love Quinn,' plain and simple, and 'You don't love your own little boy. There wouldn't be any Goblin in this house, he wouldn't need Goblin, if you'd be the mother you're supposed to be.'

"At that moment, I knew it was true, these words; she was my mother. They had an echo for me somewhere, and I felt a potent curiosity about Patsy, and I wanted to ask Pops what he meant. I also felt a hurt, a pain in my chest and stomach at the thought that Patsy didn't love me, whereas before I don't think that I had cared.

"At that moment, when Pops was saying, 'You're an unnatural mother, that's what you are, and a tramp on top of it,' Patsy grabbed up a big knife. She ran at Pops with it and Pops took ahold of both her wrists in one hand. The knife fell to the floor and Patsy told Pops that she hated him, that if she could she'd kill him, he'd better sleep with one eye open, and he was the one who didn't love his own child.

"Next thing I knew I was outside with the electric light pouring out of the shed, and Patsy was sitting in a wooden porch rocker before her open garage studio and she was crying, and I went to her and kissed her on the cheek, and she turned to me and hugged me and took me in her arms. I knew Goblin was trying to pull at me, I could feel him, but I wanted to hug Patsy, I didn't want her to be so unhappy. I told Goblin to kiss Patsy.

" 'Stop talkin' to that thing,' Patsy cried. She changed into a different person—rather, an all too familiar person—screaming at me. 'It kills me when you talk to that thing. I can't stand to be around you when you talk to that thing. And then they say I'm a bad mother!' And so I stopped talking to Goblin and gave all my kisses to Patsy for an hour or more. I liked being in her lap. I liked being rocked by her. She smelled good and so did her cigarette. And in my dim childlike mind, I knew it marked a change of sorts.

"But there was more to it than that. I felt a dark feeling when I clung to Patsy. I felt something like despair. I've been told I couldn't have felt such a thing at that age, but that's not true. I felt it. I clung to Patsy, and

I ignored Goblin even though he danced around and tugged on my sleeve.

"That night Patsy came up to watch television in here with Goblin and me and Little Ida, an unprecedented event, and we had a riot of laughter together, though what we actually watched I don't recall. The impression made upon me was that Patsy was my friend suddenly, and I thought she was very pretty, I always had thought she was very pretty, but I loved Pops too and could never choose between the two.

"From that day forward, it seemed that Patsy and I had more hugs and kisses for each other, if not anything else. Hugging and kissing have always been big on Blackwood Farm, and now Patsy was in the loop, as far as I was concerned.

"By age six or so I had the run of the property and knew well enough not to play too near the swamp that borders us to the west and southwest.

"If it hadn't been for Goblin, my favorite place would have been the old cemetery, which, as I've told you, was once beloved by my great-great-great-grandmother Virginia Lee.

"As I've described, the guests adored the place, and the tale of how Mad Manfred restored every tombstone just to quiet the conscience of Virginia Lee. The elaborate little cast-iron fence that surrounded the place had all been patched and was kept painted jet-black, and the small stone shell of a pointed-roof church was swept clear of leaves every day. It's an echo chamber, the little church, and I loved to go in there and say 'Goblin!' and hear it come back to me, and have him doubled over with silent giggles.

"Now the roots of the four oak trees down there have buckled some of the rectangular tombs as well as the little fence, but what can anyone do about an oak tree? No one kin to me would ever chop down any kind of tree, that's for certain, and these trees all had their name.

"Virginia Lee's Oak was the one on the far side of the cemetery, between it and the swamp, and Manfred's Oak was right beside it, while on this side there was William's Oak, and Ora Lee's Oak, all fantastically thick with huge heavy arms that dip down to the ground.

"I loved to play down there, until Goblin started his campaign.

"I must have been about seven years old when I saw the first ghosts in the cemetery, and I can see this very vividly now as I speak. Goblin and I were rollicking down there, and a long way off I could hear the thumping of Patsy's latest band. We had left the cemetery proper and I was struggling up one of the long armlike branches of Ora Lee's Oak that is closest to the house, though not really all that close to the house at all.

"I turned my head to the right for no apparent reason and I saw a small gathering of people, two women and a boy and a man, all drifting above the buckled and crowded community of graves. I was not frightened at all. In fact, I think I thought, 'Oh, so these are the ghosts that everybody talks about,' and I was silently stunned looking at them, at the way that all of them seemed to be made of the same translucent substance, and the way that they floated as though created mostly of air.

"Goblin saw them after I did, and for one moment he didn't move but only stared, the same as I was staring, and then he became frantic, gesturing wildly for me to get down out of the tree and come up to the house. I knew all his hand signals by now, so there was no question of it. But I had no intention of leaving.

"I stared at the cluster of people, wondering at their blank faces, their colorless matter, their simple clothes and the way that they all looked at me.

"I slid down the branch of the oak and went towards the cast-iron fence. The eyes of the ghostly gathering remained fastened to me, and as I see it now, as I gaze at them again in remembrance, I realize that they changed somewhat in their expression. They became intense and even demanding, though of course I didn't know those words then.

"Gradually, they began to fade, and to my severe disappointment they were no longer there. I could hear the silence that followed them, and a larger sense of the mysterious stole over me as my eyes moved over the graveyard itself and then the overpowering oaks. I had a peculiar and distinct feeling about the oaks—that they were watching me and had seen me see the spirits, and that they were sentient and vigilant and had a personality of their own.

"A real horror of the trees was conceived in me, and as I looked down the slope, towards the encroaching darkness of the swamp, I felt the giant cypress trees were possessed of the same secretive life, witnessing all around them with a deep slow respiration which only the trees themselves could see or hear.

"I became dizzy. I was almost sick. I saw the branches of the trees moving, and then very slowly there came into view the ghosts again, the very same collection, as pale and wretched as before. Their eyes searched my face, and I remained steadfast, refusing Goblin's frantic gestures, until suddenly I backed up, nearly stumbling, and took off running for the house.

"I went, as always, straight to the kitchen door, with Goblin skipping and racing beside me, and told Sweetheart all about it, which immediately put her in a state of alarm.

"Sweetheart was already very stout by that time, and a permanent fixture in the kitchen, as I've described to you, and she took me up in her arms. She told me point-blank that there were no ghosts down there and I should stay away from the place altogether from now on. I found the contradiction in that, young as I was, but I knew what I had seen, and no one could dislodge it from my mind.

"Pops was busy with the guests in the front part of the house, and I don't remember his ever responding.

"But Big Ramona, Jasmine's grandmother, who had been working in the kitchen with Sweetheart, was very curious about the ghosts and wanted me to tell everything about them down to the flower design of the women's dresses and that the men had no hats. She believed in the ghosts, I knew she did, and she launched into the famous story of how she saw the ghost of my great-great-grandfather William in the living room, going through the drawers of the Louis XV desk.

"But to return to the folks of the cemetery, the Lost Souls, as I've come to call them, Sweetheart was frightened at all this and said it was time I went to kindergarten, where I'd meet other children and have lots of fun.

"And so one morning, Pops took me in the pickup to a private school in Ruby River City. I was kicked out within two days. Much too much talking to Goblin, and mumbling and murmuring in half words, and not being able to cooperate with other kids. Besides, Goblin hated it. Goblin made faces at the teacher. Goblin took my left hand and broke my crayons.

"Back it was to where I wanted to be—either spying on Patsy and her music making, or working with Pops as he planted a row of beautiful pansies along the front of the house, or eating the cake icing mix that was left in the bowl in the kitchen, while Sweetheart and Big Ramona and Little Ida sang 'Go Tell Aunt Rodie' or 'I've Been Working on the Railroad' or songs I've long forgotten, songs I've lost, much to my shame.

"I saw the Lost Souls of the graveyard several times after that, and I've seen them in the past year. They don't change. They linger and they stare and nothing more. They do seem to be locked together, a floating mass from which no one spirit can detach itself. I'm not even certain they have personality, as we know the word. But the way that they follow me with their eyes argues that they do.

"I must have been asked to leave at least four schools when my Aunt Lorraine McQueen came home.

"It was the first time that I can remember ever laying eyes on her, though she had been home several times when I was a baby, and told me so with much enthusiasm and sweet embraces and fragrant lipstick kisses and proffering of the most delicious chocolate-covered cherry candies, which she gave to me from a large fancy white box.

"Her room was the same as it is now, in location, and I have no memory of ever noticing it until I was taken in to see her on that long-ago day and she put me on her lap.

"Even counting the guests who had passed through Blackwood Manor, Aunt Queen was the prettiest of the women I'd ever beheld. Her spike-heel ankle-strap shoes struck me as very lovely to look at, glamorous is my word now, and I very much enjoyed her heavy perfume and the feel of her soft white hair.

"I calculate she must have been near seventy around that time, but she looked younger than Pops, who was her grand nephew, or Sweetheart, and both of them were in their fifties, I think.

"Aunt Queen was dressed all in tailored white silk, which was her favorite style of dressing, and I remember I dripped some of the chocolate-covered cherry candy on her suit, and she said airily that I mustn't worry, she had a thousand suits of white silk, and she laughed in the most delightful manner and told me I was as 'brilliant' as she had once predicted I would be.

"Her room was all done in white, with lace and silk decorating the canopy of the bed, and long gossamer high-waisted white ruffle curtains on her windows, and she even had a white fox fur with real heads and tails, which she had tossed over a chair.

"She told me that she adored for things to be done in white, and showed me her fingernails, which were lacquered in white, and the cameo at the neck of her blouse, which was white on pale pink coral, and said that she had needed all things to be white for the last thirty years, or ever since John McQueen, her husband, had died.

" 'I think I am just getting tired of it,' she declared in the most dramatic and interesting manner. 'I did so love your Uncle John McQueen.

I never loved a man before him. And I never will marry again. But I'm ready to be drenched in color. Surely your Uncle John McQueen would approve. What do you think, Tarquin? Should I buy suits of different colors?'

"It was a positive landmark in my young life when she spoke these words. No one had ever asked me such a serious adult question before. In fact, she spoke to me entirely as if I were an adult. I adored her from those moments forward with a loyalty that has no limit.

"Within a week she was showing me swatches of colored damask and satin and asking me which I thought was the happiest and the sweetest color, and I had to confess, of all things, that yellow seemed to me to be the happiest, and I took her hand and led her to the kitchen to see the yellow curtains there, which made her laugh and laugh and say that yellow made her think of butter.

"But she did the room in yellow! It was all in light summery fabric, airy like the white she had used before, but the whole room was magical in yellow, and frankly I never liked it as much as I did with that first change.

"Over the years, she has done the room in many different colors, including bed hangings, draperies and chairs, and as for her clothes, she has done the same thing. But on that first day, she seemed a true royal personage of pure whiteness, and I remember reveling in her beauty and what seemed the purity of her manner and her words.

"As for the cameo, she told me all about it—that it was the mythical Hebe holding up a cup for Zeus, the king of the gods, who was in the form of an eagle, dipping his beak to drink.

"Now, Goblin had been sulking all this time by the doorway, hands in his overall pockets, until I turned to him and told him to come over and that I wanted to show him to Aunt Queen. I believe that I did my very best to describe him to her, since no one to my knowledge could ever see Goblin, except me, and I could swear that she looked at the space beside me, and I had an inkling, the barest inkling, that she did see him, at least for a moment, when she narrowed her eyes.

"She looked sharply to me again, as if snapping back, and demanded very gently, 'Does he make you happy?' and that too caught me off guard, as her earlier question had done.

"I think I stammered out something to the effect that Goblin was always around except when he was hiding, as if it wasn't a matter of whether he made me happy or not, and then Goblin began to tug on my hand to drag me from the room. I said 'Behave, Goblin!' just as Sweetheart sometimes said to me, 'Behave, Quinn!' and Goblin, pouting and making faces, disappeared.

"I started to cry. Aunt Queen was very distressed at this and asked the reason, and I told her that now Goblin would not come back for a long time. He'd wait and wait until I was crying and crying, and then he would come.

"Aunt Queen pondered this for a long time and said that I mustn't cry. 'You know what I think, Quinn?' she asked. 'I think if you remain quiet and pretend you don't need him, Goblin will come back.'

"It did the trick. As I was helping her and Big Ramona to unpack suitcases, as I was playing with Aunt Queen's cameos, which she set out on her famous marble table, along came Goblin, peeping around the door and then pouting and sulking and coming in.

"Aunt Queen didn't mind my murmuring to him as I explained who she was and that everybody called her Miss Queen but we were to call her Aunt Queen, and when Big Ramona went to correct me and tell me to hush, Aunt Queen said, No, let me go on.

" 'Now, Goblin, don't run off again,' Aunt Queen said, and once more I was certain she could see him, but she said that she couldn't, and was only taking my word for the fact that he was there.

"For the entirety of Aunt Queen's visit she spoke to me as if I were an adult, and I also slept in her bed with her. She sent into town for some men's white T-shirts, size large, and I wore these as my little white nightshirts. And I snuggled up to her spoon fashion as I did with Little Ida, and I slept so deeply not even Goblin could wake me before I heard Aunt Queen's call to get up.

"Little Ida was a tiny bit put out over this, as she and I had been bedfellows since I was a baby, but Aunt Queen soothed her so that she let it go. I liked the white canopy over our heads better than the satin-lined baldachin in my own room up here.

"Let me move to another recollection which must come from the same time. Aunt Queen and I drove into New Orleans in her big stretch limousine. I'd never been in a car like it, but I remember little of it, except that Goblin sat on my right side and Aunt Queen on my left. Goblin tried to stay solid, but he flashed transparent numerous times.

"What struck me that day most strongly was that we got out on a shady side street with a long brick sidewalk, and all over that sidewalk were pink petals, and it was one of the most beautiful sights I've ever seen. I wish I knew now where that street was. I've asked Aunt Queen but she doesn't recall.

"I don't know whether those pink petals had fallen from a long flank of crape myrtle trees or from Japanese magnolias. I tend to think it was crape myrtles after a rain. I'll never forget that stretch of sidewalk and that lovely path of flower petals, as though someone had strewn them especially for people to walk on and be transported out of reality and into dreams.

"Even now, when existence seems unendurable I think of that side-walk, I remember the drowsy light and the feeling of being unhurried, and the beauty of the pink petals. And I'm able to take a deep breath.

"It has nothing to do with my story, except perhaps to state that I had eyes to see such things, and a heart to be sensitive to them. But what is germane is that we went to the house of a very affected and artificial lady, much younger than Aunt Queen, who had a whole room full of toys, and the first dollhouse I'd ever seen. Not knowing that boys weren't supposed to like dollhouses, I was of course curious about it and wanted to play with it more than anything else.

"But the lady wanted to direct things, as I recall, and bombarded me with soft affected questions, in her phony baby voice, mostly pertaining to Goblin, who glared at her the whole while with a sullen and angry face. I didn't like her soft tone when she asked, 'Does Goblin do bad things?' and 'Do you feel sometimes that Goblin is doing something that you would like to do but can't?'

"Young as I was, I caught her drift, and I wasn't surprised afterwards when Aunt Queen made a phone call to Pops from the limousine and said, quite oblivious to Goblin and me beside her, 'It's just an imaginary playmate, Thomas. He'll outgrow Goblin. He's a brilliant child and he has no playmates. So we have Goblin. There's no point to be worried at all.'

"It was very soon after my encounter with the beautiful flower-strewn sidewalk—and the lady psychologist—that Pops drove me to a new school. I hated it passionately, as I had the others, talked to Goblin belligerently and without cease and was sent home before noon.

"The next week Pops made the long drive into New Orleans to take me to a fancier kindergarten in Uptown, but with the same result. Goblin made faces at the children and I hated them. And the teacher's voice grated on me, as she talked to me as if I were an idiot, and Pops was soon there in the pickup truck to take me back to exactly where I wanted to be.

"At this point, I have a vivid yet fragmented memory, very distorted and confused, of actually being incarcerated in some sort of hospital, of being in a small cubicle of a room and of sitting in one of those vast playrooms again, complete with a dollhouse, and of knowing that people were watching me through a mirror because Goblin made signs to me that they were. Goblin hated the place. The people who came in to question me talked to me as if they were great friends of mine, which of course they weren't.

" 'Where did you learn all the big words?' was one prize question, and, 'You talk of being happy to be independent. Do you know what "independent" means?' Of course I knew and I explained it: to be on one's own, to be not in school, to be not in this place; and out of there I soon went, with a sense that I had gotten my liberty through sheer stubbornness and the refusal to be nice. But I had been badly frightened by this experience. And I know that I cried hysterically when I rushed into Sweetheart's arms, and she sobbed and sobbed.

"It may have been the night of my return home—I don't know—but very soon after, Aunt Queen assured me I'd never be left in a place like that 'hospital' again. And in the days that followed I learnt that it was Aunt Queen's doing, because Patsy loudly criticized her for it in my presence and this confused me because I so badly needed to love Aunt Queen.

"When Aunt Queen shook her head and confirmed that she had done wrong with the hospital, I was very relieved. Aunt Queen saw this and she kissed me and she asked after Goblin, and I told her that he was right at my side.

"Again, I could have sworn that she saw him, and I even saw Goblin puff himself up and sort of preen for her. But she said only that if I loved Goblin, then she would love Goblin too. I burst into tears of happiness, and Goblin was soon in a paroxysm of tears as well.

"My next memory of Aunt Queen is of her sharing my little table with me in this room and teaching me more words to write with my crayon—in fact, a great list of nouns comprising the name of every item in the bedroom—and that she watched patiently as I taught all these words—bed, table, chair, window and so forth—to Goblin.

" 'Goblin helps you to remember,' she said gravely to me. 'I think Goblin is very clever himself. Does Goblin know a word we don't know, do you think? I mean a word you haven't learned so far?'

"It was a startling moment. I was about to say no, when Goblin put his hand on mine and wrote in his jagged way the word 'Stop' and the word 'Yield.' And the word 'School.'

"I laughed, I was so proud of him. But Goblin wasn't finished. He then wrote in short jerky movements the words 'Ruby River.'

"I heard Aunt Queen gasp. 'Explain each of those words to me, Quinn,' she said. But though I could explain 'stop' and 'yield' as signs we saw on the highway, I couldn't read 'school' or 'Ruby River.'

" 'Ask Goblin what they mean,' said Aunt Queen.

"I did as she asked, and Goblin explained everything silently by putting the thoughts in my head. Stop meant to stop the car, Yield meant to slow down the car, School meant to go slow when we were near the children, bah! ich! and Ruby River was the name of the water over which the car drove when we went to school or shopping.

"An unforgettable expression of seriousness came over Aunt Queen's face. 'Ask Goblin how he learned these things,' she said to me. But when I did this, Goblin just crossed his eyes, wagged his head from left to right and began dancing.

" 'I don't think he knows how,' I told her, 'but I think he learned them from watching and listening.'

"She seemed very much pleased with this answer, and I was immensely glad. Her solemn expression had frightened me. 'Ah, that makes a good deal of sense,' she said. 'And I'll tell you what. Why don't you have Goblin teach you several new words every day? Maybe he can start now with some more for us.'

"I had to explain to her that Goblin was through for the day. He never liked to do anything very long. He ran out of steam.

"Only now as I tell this do I realize that Goblin was talking coherently in my head. When did that start? I don't know.

"But in the months to come I did what Aunt Queen asked and Goblin taught me pages of common words. Everyone, even Pops and Sweetheart, thought it was a good thing. And the kitchen crowd watched in awe as this process unfolded.

"In jerky letters, I spelled out 'Rice,' 'Coca-Cola,' 'Flour,' 'Ice,' 'Rain,' 'Police,' 'Sheriff,' 'City Hall,' 'Post Office,' 'Ruby Town Theater,' 'Grand Hardware,' 'Grodin's Pharmacy,' 'Wal-Mart'—defining these words as Goblin defined them in my head, and this defining came not only with the pronunciation of the words, which Goblin gave me, but with pictures. I saw the City Hall. I saw the Post Office. I saw the Ruby Town Theater. And I made an immediate and seminal link between the audible syllables of the word and its meaning, and this was Goblin's doing.

"As I revisit this curious process, I realize what it meant. Goblin, whom I had always treated as grossly inferior to me and devilishly a troublemaker, had learned the phonetic code to written words and was ahead of me in this. And he stayed ahead of me for a long time. The explanation? Just what he had said. He watched and he listened, and given a small amount of indisputable raw material he was able to go quite far.

"This is what I mean when I say he is a fast learner, and I should add he's an unpredictable and uncontrollable learner because that's true.

"But let me make it clear that though the Kitchen Gang told me Goblin was a wonder for teaching me all these words, they still didn't believe in him.

"And one night when I was listening to the adults talk in Aunt Queen's room, I heard the word 'subconscious,' and again I heard it, and finally the third time I interrupted and asked what it meant.

"Aunt Queen explained that Goblin lived in my subconscious, and that as I grew older he would probably go away. I mustn't worry about it now. But later I wouldn't want so much to have Goblin and the 'situation' would take care of itself.

"I knew this was wrong, but I loved Aunt Queen too much to contradict her. And besides she was soon going away. Her travels were calling her. Friends of hers were gathered in Madrid at a palace for a special party, and I could only think of this with tears.

"Aunt Queen soon took her leave, but not before hiring a young lady to 'homeschool' me, which she did, coming up to Blackwood Manor every day.

"This teacher wasn't really a very effective person, and my conversations with Goblin scared her, and she was soon gone.

"The next and the next weren't much good either.

"Goblin hated these teachers as much as I did. They wanted me to color pictures that were boring and to paste strips of paper from magazines onto cardboard. And for the most part they had a dishonest manner of speaking which seems, I think in retrospect, to assume that a child's mind is different from that of adults. I couldn't bear it. I learned quickly how to horrify and frighten them. I did it lustily to break their power. I wanted them gone. With the fury of an only child with a spirit of his own, I wanted them gone.

"No matter how many came, I was soon alone with Goblin again.

"We had the run of the farm as always, and we hung out sometimes with the Shed Men, watching boxing on television, a sport I've always loved—in fact, the only sport that I love to watch and still do watch—and we saw the ghosts in the old cemetery several times.

"As for the ghost of William, Manfred's son, I saw him at least three times by the desk in the living room, and he seemed as oblivious to me as Aunt Camille on the attic stairs.

"Meanwhile Little Ida read lavishly illustrated children's books to me, not minding one bit that Goblin too was listening and looking, all of us crowded on the bed together against the headboard, and I learned to read a little with her, and Goblin could actually read a book to me if I had the patience to listen to him, to tune in to his silent voice inside my head. On rainy days, as I've mentioned, he was really strong. He could read a whole poem to me from an adult book. If we were running in the summer rain, he could stay perfectly solid for an hour.

"Sometime in these early years I realized that I had a treasure in Goblin, that his knack for understanding and spelling words was superior to mine, and I liked it, and I also trusted his opinion of the teachers, of course. Goblin was learning faster than I was. And then the inevitable happened.

"I must have been nine years old. Goblin, taking my left hand, began to write more sophisticated messages than I could have ever written. In the kitchen, where I sat at the big white-enameled table now with the adults, Goblin scrawled out in crayon on paper something like 'Quinn and I want to go riding in Pops' truck. We'd like to go to the cock fights again. We like to see the roosters go at it. We want to place bets.'

"Little Ida witnessed this and so did Jasmine, both of whom said nothing, and Sweetheart just shook her head, and Pops was silent too. Then Pops did a clever thing.

" 'Now, Quinn,' he said, 'you're telling us Goblin wrote this, but all I see is your left hand moving. Just to get this straight, you copy those words for us. Tell Goblin just to let you copy. I want to see how your hand is different from his.'

"Of course I had a difficult time copying, and the printing was much neater and squared off when I did it, the way Little Ida had taught me to print, and Pops drew back and was amazed.

"Then Goblin grabbed my left hand again and guided it as he wrote in his characteristic spidery scrawl, 'Don't be afraid of me. I love Quinn.'

"I became elated with these developments and I remember saying to all assembled that Goblin was the best teacher I had. But nobody was as happy about this as I was, and then Goblin grabbed my hand again, very tight, and scrawled out, nearly breaking the crayon, 'You don't believe in me. Quinn believes in me.'

"It seemed utterly plain to me that Goblin was a separate creature and everybody ought to know it, but no one was ready to say it in words.

"However, Pops and I went to the cock fights the very next weekend, and as we were driving over to Ruby River City, Pops asked if Goblin was with us in the car. I said Yes, Goblin was cleaving to me, invisible, saving his strength to dance around in the aisle at the cock fights, but not to worry, he was right there.

"Then when we got there, Pops asked, 'What's Goblin up to?' and I told him Goblin was there 'in living color,' by which I meant solid, and that he was running right alongside of me all over the arena to collect the bets that Pops won. Of course we had to pay off a few too that Pops lost.

"Just in case you've never seen a cock fight, let me briefly describe what happens. It's an air-conditioned building out in the country, with a crude lobby and concession stand in it selling hamburgers, hot dogs and soda. From the lobby you go into an arena that is round except for two entrances, the one through which you came and the one opposite through which the roosters and the handlers come in. In the center of this arena is a big round dirt-floor cage completely protected by chicken wire right up to the ceiling—where the birds fight.

"Two men enter the ring with their roosters, set them down on the floor and the roosters go at it, by their very nature, and as soon as one is bested the birds are taken out to continue the fight to the death out back. The handlers do everything they can to help their birds. They'll take them by the throat and suck the blood right out of their mouths to give them a second wind, and I think they blow in their hind ends too.

"Pops never went out back. It was dirty and dusty back there, which is why most of the people at the cock fights, no matter how well dressed, appear to be covered in dirt. Pops just liked the indoor portion of the battle, and he often stood up and hollered out his bets, and I did the running with the money as I described. There are some women at the cock fights, and lots of children, with a lot of children doing the collecting and the delivering, and it is a kind of American scene which is probably dying out.

"I personally loved it, and so did Goblin, as I've explained. We thought the cocks were gorgeous with their long colorful plumage, and when they leapt in the air to challenge their opponents, rising up some three feet or more, then dropping and rising again, it was a spectacle to behold.

"Pops knew everybody there. As I've said, he was a country man, and as I tell you this story I realize that he was deliberately country, throwing in his lot with the rural community when in fact he had a choice.

"He'd gotten his law degree from Loyola University in New Orleans, same as his father, Gravier. He could have been a different type of person. He chose to be who he was.

"He'd bred fighting cocks before I was born, and he told me all about it, how for two years they were fed on the best grain and let to grow their long plumes for the five minutes of glory in the ring. As for domestic poultry, he said they were miserably bred now and miserably treated and knew nothing of the grass or the fresh air. A fighting cock had a life.

"Well, that was Pops. He could come home from a cock fight, shower down, dress in his dark suit and go in and make sure that the Royal Doulton china had been properly set for dinner on the table, and call in Little Ida or Lolly to make the sterling silver settings more even and uniform all around. He played tapes of harmonica music in his truck and hired classical quartets and trios for the front rooms.

"He was a man between worlds, and he gave me the best of both of them, but why he hated Patsy when she had gone so totally country I don't understand. But then my mother did get knocked up at sixteen and refused to divulge the name of the father, if she ever knew it, so maybe that put her in a bad light.

"Let's fast-forward now to my tenth year when the best of the home teachers came, a nonpareil—a lovely woman named Lynelle Springer, who played the piano exquisitely and spoke several foreign languages, who 'adored' Goblin and often talked to him quite independently of me, even making me a little jealous.

"Of course I knew it was a game, but Goblin didn't and he frolicked and did tricks for Lynelle, which I described to her in a whisper. Everything that Lynelle taught me I taught to Goblin, or at least made the motions. And Goblin grew to love Lynelle so much that he jumped up and down when she arrived each evening at the house.

"Lynelle was tall and slender with long curly brown hair, which she pinned back casually from her face. She wore a perfume named Shalimar and what she called 'romantic' dresses with high waists and flowing skirts, suggestive of the time of King Arthur, she explained to me, and she adored the color sky blue. She was thrilled that my ancestor Virginia

Lee, for her portrait in the dining room, had chosen a gorgeous dress of sky blue.

Lynelle wore very high heels—Aunt Queen no doubt approved heartily—and had extremely full breasts and a tiny waist.

"Lynelle was enchanted by Blackwood Manor. She danced in circles in the big rooms. She explored everything with ebullient interest and was most gracious in her casual meetings with the guests.

"She pronounced me to be a 'rare intellect' at once. I opened my arms to her—and my world, as you can see, was very much influenced and punctuated by embraces and kisses, and Lynelle fell into this style with no inhibition at all.

"Lynelle bewitched me. I feared to lose her the way I'd deliberately lost all the other teachers, and experienced perhaps the greatest change of heart toward an aspect of my world that I'd ever known.

"Lynelle talked so fast that Pops and Sweetheart privately grumbled that they couldn't understand her. And I remember some deadly kibitzing that Aunt Queen was paying Lynelle three times what the other teachers had been paid, all because they had met in an English castle.

"So what? Lynelle was unique. Lynelle used Goblin's talents, inviting him to teach me new words and addressing her long cascades of lovely speech to both of us, her two 'elves.'

"That Lynelle had six young children, that she had been a French teacher, that she had returned to college to make up a pre-medical degree, that she was a scientific genius of sorts, as well as a sometime concert pianist—all this made Pops and Sweetheart all the more suspicious. But I knew Lynelle was a truly unique individual. I couldn't have been fooled.

"Lynelle came five evenings a week for four hours, and within a matter of a month, she conquered everybody on Blackwood Farm with her energy, her charm, her optimism and her effervescence, and she positively altered the course of my life.

"It was Lynelle who really taught me the basics—phonetic reading of big words and diagramming of sentences so I could grasp the scaffolding of grammar, and the only arithmetic I now confess to know.

"She took me through enough French to understand many of the subtitled movies we watched together, and she loaded me with history and geography, pretty much designing her fluid and wondrous lectures to me around historical personages, but sometimes romping through whole centuries in terms of what had been accomplished in art and war.

" 'It's all art and war, Quinn,' she said to me once as we were sitting cross-legged on the floor up here together, 'and it's a shocking fact but most great men were insane.' She was careful to address Goblin by name also as she explained that Alexander the Great was an egomaniac and Napoleon 'obsessive compulsive,' while Henry VIII was a poet, a writer and a despotic fiend.

"Irrepressibly resourceful, Lynelle came flying in with whole cartons of educational or documentary tapes for us to watch by VHS and also introduced into my head the idea that in the day and age of cable television nobody ought to be uneducated. Even a boy hermit on Blackwood Farm should know everything just from watching TV.

" 'People in trailer parks are getting these channels, Quinn, think of it—think of it, waitresses watching the biography of Beethoven and telephone linemen going home to watch documentaries of World War II.'

"I wasn't quite as convinced as she was on these points, but I saw the potential, and when she persuaded Pops to give me a giant-size television I was overjoyed.

"She insisted on the scientific documentaries which I, in the course of things, would have skipped, and she took me through the magnificent film *Immortal Beloved*, in which Gary Oldman plays Beethoven to such perfection that every time we watched it I cried. Then there was *Amadeus* with Tom Hulce as Mozart and F. Murray Abraham as Salieri, a masterpiece of a film that left me breathless, and she reached back into history for *Song to Remember* with Cornel Wilde as Chopin and Merle Oberon as George Sand, and *Tonight We Sing*, all about S. Hurok, the great impresario, and there were dozens of other films by which she opened my world.

"Of course she showed me *The Red Shoes*, which ignited me with fire to be around people of grace and culture, and then *The Tales of Hoffmann*, which transformed my dreams. Both of these movies caused real physical pain in me, so vibrant, so lofty, so exalted was their world. Ah, it hurts me now to think about them, to see images in my head from them. It hurts. They were like spells, those two movies.

"Picture me and Lynelle on the floor in this room with no light except the giant television, and those movies, those enchantments flooding our senses. And Goblin, Goblin staring at the screen, stultified by the patterns he must have been perceiving, Goblin quiet for all his struggle to understand why we were so stricken and so quiet.

"When I cried in pain, Lynelle said the kindest thing to me:

" 'Don't you understand, Quinn?' she said. 'You live in a gorgeous house and you're eccentric and gifted like the people in these films. Aunt Queen keeps inviting you to meet her in Europe and you won't do it. And that's wrong, Quinn. Don't make your world small.'

"In fact, Aunt Queen had never invited me to meet her in Europe, or, to put it more to the point, I had not known that Aunt Queen had invited me! No doubt Pops and Sweetheart knew. But I didn't confess this.

" 'You have to keep on teaching me, Lynelle,' I answered. 'Make me into somebody who can travel with Aunt Queen.'

" 'I'll do it, Quinn,' she said. 'It will be easy.'

"She almost made me believe it. And on she went, running rampant through archaeology and theories of evolution and dizzying lectures on black holes in space.

"She taught me to play some simple Chopin and a few exercises by Bach. She took me through the entire history of music, quizzing me until I could identify a period and a style and, even in Mozart's case, a composer.

"I was in heaven with Lynelle.

"She taught me many Latin words to show me that they were roots for English words. She taught me to waltz, to do the two-step and the tango, though the tango made me laugh so hard that I would fall down every time we tried.

"Lynelle also brought the first computer into my bedroom, along with the first printer, and though this was long before the days of the World Wide Web or the Internet, I learned to write on this computer and managed to become very fast at typing, using the first three fingers of each hand.

"Goblin was enthralled by the computer.

"At once he took my left hand and pecked out the words 'Ilove-Lynelle.' She was very pleased by this, and then, unable to free my left hand from him, I discovered myself typing all manner of words run together without spaces, and I gave Goblin an elbow in the chest and told him to get away. Of course Lynelle soothed his feelings with some kind words.

"It would be a long time before Goblin discovered that he could make words appear on the computer without my aid.

"But let me return to Lynelle. As soon as I could bat out a letter on the computer I wrote to Aunt Queen, who was on a religious pilgrimage of sorts in India, and I told her that Lynelle was a special emissary both from Heaven and from her. Aunt Queen was so pleased to hear from me that we began to exchange letters about twice a month.

"I had so many adventures with Lynelle.

"On Saturday, we went into the swamp together in a pirogue with a vow to find Sugar Devil Island, but at the first sight of a deadly snake, Lynelle positively freaked and screamed for us to head back to land. I had a gun and could have shot the snake if it had approached us, which it wasn't doing, but Lynelle was terrified and I did what she said.

"Neither of us had worn long sleeves, as Pops had told us to do, and we were covered in mosquito bites. So we never made an excursion like that again. But on cool spring evenings we often sat on one of the rectangular slab tombs in the cemetery and looked into the swamp, until full darkness and mosquitoes drove us inside.

"Of course we were going to venture out there one of these days and find that damned island, but there were always more pressing things to do.

"When Lynelle discovered I had never been to a museum in my life, we were off in her roaring Mazda sports car, the radio blaring techno-rock, going over the Lake and into New Orleans to see wonderful paintings at the New Orleans Museum of Art, and then on to the new Aquarium, and on to wander the Art District for galleries, and on to the French Quarter just for fun.

"Now understand, I knew something of New Orleans. We often drove an hour and half to go to Mass at the gorgeous St. Mary's Assumption Church on Josephine and Constance Streets, because this had been Sweetheart's parish and one of the priests stationed there was a cousin of Sweetheart's, and therefore a cousin of mine.

"And during the Mardi Gras season we sometimes drove in to watch the night parades from the front porch of Sweetheart's sister, Aunt Ruthie. And a few times we even visited Aunt Ruthie on Mardi Gras day.

"But with Lynelle, I really learned the city as we meandered in the Quarter or prowled about in secondhand bookstores on Magazine Street or visited the St. Louis Cathedral to light a candle and say a prayer.

"During this time Lynelle also educated me for my First Communion and for my Confirmation, and both these ceremonies took place on Holy Saturday night (the eve of Easter) at St. Mary's Assumption Church. All of Sweetheart's New Orleans people were there, including some fifty that I really didn't know. But I was very glad to be connected with the Church in a proper way and went through a mild period of fascination with the Church, watching any videos that pertained to the Vatican or Church history or the Lives of the Saints.

"It particularly intrigued me that saints had had visions, that some saints saw their guardian angels and even talked to them. I wondered if Goblin, not being an angel, had to be from Hell.

"Lynelle said no. I never had the courage, or the clear urge, to ask a priest about Goblin. I sensed that Goblin would be condemned as morbid imagination, and at times I thought of Goblin that way myself.

"Lynelle asked me if Goblin put me up to evil. I said no. 'Then you don't have to tell a priest about him,' she explained. 'He has no connection with sin. Use your brain and your conscience. A priest is no more likely to understand Goblin than anyone else.'

"That might sound ambiguous now, but it didn't then.

"I think, all in all, the six years I had with Lynelle were some of the happiest in my life.

"Naturally, I was drawn away from Pops and Sweetheart, but they were proud and relieved to see me learning things and didn't mind a bit. Besides, I still spent time with Pops, playing the harmonica after lunch and talking about 'old times,' though Pops was hardly an old man. He liked Lynelle.

"Even Patsy was drawn to Lynelle and joined us for some of our adventures, at which time I had to squeeze into the tiny backseat of the sports car while the two women chatted away up front. My most poignant memory of Patsy's joining us has to do with Goblin, to whom I talked all the time, and the shock of Lynelle when Patsy cursed at me to stop talking to that disgusting ghost.

"Lynelle softened and intimidated Patsy, and something else happened which I think I only understand now as I look back on those years. It is simply this: that Lynelle's respect for me, not only as Goblin's friend but as little Tarquin Blackwood, had the effect of causing Patsy to respect me and to talk to me more sincerely and often than she had in the past.

"It was as if my mother never 'saw' the person I was until Lynelle really drew her attention to me, and then a vague interest substituted for the condescending and arrogant pity—'You poor sweet darlin' '—that Patsy had felt before.

"Lynelle was a great watcher also of popular movies, particularly those which were 'gothic' or 'romantic,' as she called it, and she brought tapes of everything, from *Robocop* to *Ivanhoe*, to watch with me in the evenings, and sometimes this brought Patsy into the room. Patsy enjoyed *Dark Man* and *The Crow*, and even Jean Cocteau's *Beauty and the Beast*.

"More than once we all watched *Coal Miner's Daughter*, all about Loretta Lynn, the wonderful country-western star whom Patsy so admired. And I observed that Lynelle could talk 'country' pretty easily with Patsy. It made me jealous. I wanted my romantic and mysterious Lynelle to myself.

"However, I learned something about Patsy during these years, which I should have foreseen. Patsy felt stupid around Lynelle, and for that reason the connection petered away and at one point threatened to break. Patsy wouldn't stay around anyone who made her feel stupid, and she didn't have an open mind with which to learn.

"This turning away of Patsy didn't surprise me and didn't matter to me. (I think it was Ingmar Bergman's *The Seventh Seal* that proved the death knell of our little movie-watching triangle.) But something else good happened as regards to Patsy, and that was that Lynelle liked Patsy's music and asked if we could come in to listen, and then praised Patsy a lot for what she was doing with her one-man band, a 'friend' by the name of Seymour, who played harmonica and drums.

"(Seymour was an opportunistic jerk, or so I thought at the time. Fate had punishment in store for Seymour.)

"Patsy was obviously astonished by this, and jubilant, and we sat through quite a few concerts in the garage, which Lynelle enjoyed more than me. Naturally enough Goblin loved them and danced and danced until he flat-out dissolved.

"As I tell you this, I realize that Lynelle was quite deliberate in this design. She sensed that Patsy was afraid of her and backing off from us—'You're a couple of eggheads'—and so she took me out there to Patsy quite cleverly to forge a new link.

"In fact, she pushed the matter further. She took me to see Patsy perform at a county jamboree. It was in Mississippi somewhere, right across the border from where we lived, and part of the county fair. I had never seen my mother on the stage, and people hollering for her and clapping for her, and it opened my eyes.

"With her teased yellow hair and heavy face makeup Patsy looked plastic pretty, and her singing was strong and good. Her songs had a dark bluegrass tone to them, and she herself was playing the banjo, and another guy, whom I didn't know very well, was sawing away on a rapid, mournful violin. Seymour was a pretty stiff backup with the harmonica and drums.

"That was all very sweet and made a huge impression on me, but when Patsy launched into her next number, a real hard-edged 'You've been mean to me, you bastard!' type of song, the crowd went nuts. They couldn't get enough of my little mother, and people were flocking towards the stage from all over the fair. Patsy upped the ante with the next one, her priceless 'You Poisoned My Well, I'll Poison Yours.' I don't remember much else except thinking she was a hit, and her life wasn't in vain.

"But I didn't need Patsy. I'm not sure I've ever needed Patsy. Sure Patsy was a hit with the yokels, but I had Beethoven's Ninth.

"And I had Lynelle. It was when Lynelle and I drove into New Orleans alone together with Goblin that I was most overjoyed.

"I have never known a human being who drove faster than Lynelle, but she seemed to possess an instinct for avoiding policemen, and the one time we were stopped she told a tall story about us rushing to the bedside of a woman in labor, and not only did she not get the ticket, the policeman had to be discouraged from giving us a full escort to the fictitious hospital in town.

"Lynelle was beautiful. There is no more perfect way to say it. She had arrived here at Blackwood Manor to find me a country boy who couldn't write a sentence and left me some six years later, a dramatically well-educated young man.

"At sixteen I completed all the examinations for high school graduation, and ranked in the top percentile on the college entrance exams as well.

"In that last year that we would be together, Lynelle also taught me how to drive. Pops fully approved, and I was soon roving with the pickup truck on our land and on the backcountry roads all around. Lynelle took me to get my license, and Pops gave me an old pickup to call my own.

"I think Lynelle would have left me a real reader of books too if Goblin hadn't been so jealous of my reading, so intent upon being included, so intent upon me sounding every word to him out loud or listening to him sound it to me. But that skill—the skill of sinking into books—was to come to me with my second great teacher, Nash.

"Meanwhile, Goblin seemed to feed off Lynelle, even as he fed off me, though at the time I wouldn't have described it that way, and Goblin was getting physically stronger all the time.

"Big shocker. A Sunday. It was pouring down rain. I must have been twelve years old. I was working on the computer and Goblin cursed at me and the machine went dead. I checked all the connections, booted my program again, and there came Goblin, switching it off.

" 'You did that, didn't you?' I said, looking around for him, and there he was near the door, my perfect doppelgänger in jeans and a red-and-white checkered shirt, except that he had his arms folded and a smug smile on his face.

"He had my full attention. But I turned the computer back on without taking my eyes off him, and then he pointed to the gasolier. He made it blink.

" 'All right, that's excellent,' I said. (It was his favorite compliment and had been for years.) 'But don't you dare turn off the power in this house. Tell me what you want.' He made the motions to 'Let's go' and of the rain coming down.

" 'No, I'm too old for that,' I said. 'You come here and work with me.' At once I got a chair for him, and when he sat down beside me I explained that I was writing to Aunt Queen, and I read the letter out loud to him, though that wasn't necessary. I was telling Aunt Queen thank you for her recent offer that Lynelle could always use her bedroom if she needed to freshen up or change clothes or spend the night.

"When I got to the bottom and went to close, Goblin grabbed my left hand as always and typed without spaces, 'IamGoblinandQuinnisGoblin-andGoblinisQuinnandweloveAuntQueen.' He stopped. He dissolved.

"I knew without question that he'd exhausted himself in turning off the computer. That made me feel safe. The rest of the day and night was mine.

"Another time, very soon after, when Lynelle and I were dancing to a Tchaikovsky waltz—really cutting up in the parlor after all the guests were gone to bed—Goblin socked me in the stomach, which took the breath out of me, and then dissolved, not as if he wanted to but as if he had to—gone in a puff, leaving me crying and sick.

"Lynelle was quite astonished by this, but she never doubted me when I told her Goblin had done it, and then when we were sitting, talking in our intimate way, adult to adult, she confessed to me that she had several times felt Goblin pull her hair. She had tried to ignore it the first couple of times, but now she was certain he did it.

" 'This is a strong ghost you have,' she said. And no sooner had she spoken those words than the gasolier up above us began to move. I had never seen that trick before, this slight movement of those heavy brass arms and glass cups, but it was damn near undeniable. Lynelle laughed. Then she uttered a startled sound. She said she'd been pinched on her right arm. Again she laughed and then, though he wasn't visible to me, she spoke to Goblin in soothing terms, telling him that she was as fond of him as of me.

"I saw Goblin—now fourteen, you understand, because I was fourteen—standing by the bedroom door and looking proudly at me. I realized keenly that his face had more definition to it than it used to have in the past, principally because that slightly contemptuous expression was new. He was quick to dematerialize, and I was confirmed in my earlier opinion that when he affected matter physically he didn't have energy to 'appear' for very long.

"But he was getting stronger, no doubt of it.

"I vowed at once 'to kill' Goblin for hurting Lynelle, and after Lynelle took off in her shining Mazda, I wrote to Aunt Queen that Goblin was doing the 'unthinkable' by hurting other people. I told her about the sharp punch in the stomach as well. I sent the letter off by express so she'd get it in two or three days though she was in India at the time.

And to keep Goblin amused that weekend I read aloud to him by the hour from *Lost Worlds*, a wonderful book of archaeology that had been a gift from Aunt Queen.

"Aunt Queen called as soon as she'd received my letter and she told me that I must control Goblin, that I must find a way to stop him from his behavior by threatening not to look at him or talk to him, and that I had to make these declarations stick.

" 'You mean to tell me, Aunt Queen, you finally believe in him?' I asked.

" 'Quinn, I'm across the world from you right now,' she answered. 'I can't argue with you about what Goblin is. What I'm saying is you have to contain him, whether he's real and separate, or simply a part of you.'

"I agreed with her and I told her I knew how to control him. But I would concentrate on learning more than I knew.

"Meanwhile I was to keep her apprised of things.

"After that she raved about the coherence and style of my letter, which showed a vast improvement over earlier letters, and she attributed my progress correctly to Lynelle.

"I followed Aunt Queen's directions regarding Goblin, and Lynelle did too. If Goblin did something inappropriate, we lectured him and then refused to acknowledge him until his weak and puny assaults came to a halt. It worked.

"But Goblin wanted more than ever to write, and he moved into a new level of concentration, spelling out messages on the computer using my left hand.

"It gave me more than an eerie feeling, this takeover of my left hand, because Goblin didn't move my right hand, and so a strange rhythm of writing with one hand mastering the entire keyboard occurred. Lynelle would watch this with a mixture of trepidation and fascination, but she made an astounding discovery.

"And this astounding discovery was that she could communicate with me privately and secretly by typing out on the computer what she had to say using very big words. On that day she wrote something on the order of:

"'Our gallant and ever vigilant doppelgänger may not perceive the many perambulations that run through the cerebral organ of his much cherished and sometimes misused Tarquin Blackwood.'

"And it was plainly obvious from Goblin's nearby dumb appearance that Lynelle was perfectly right. Goblin, for all his early gains on me, couldn't interpret such messages. Lynelle typed out more, something like this:

"'Comprehend, beloved Tarquin, that your doppelgänger, though once he absorbed all that you absorbed, may have reached the limits of his power to master fine distinctions, and this allows you a luxurious measure of freedom from his demands and intentions when it is desired.'

"I took over the keyboard and, as Goblin watched suspiciously, being very solid and curious, I wrote that I comprehended all of this, and that we now had the computer for very rapid communication of two kinds.

"It could be used for Goblin's tapping out simple messages to me using my hand, and by Lynelle and me communicating with a larger vocabulary than Goblin could grasp.

"About this time in my adventures with Lynelle, she tried to explain these mechanisms to Patsy but met with a flat-out 'You're crazier than Quinn is, Lynelle; both of you ought to be locked up.' And when Lynelle approached Pops and Sweetheart they appeared not to understand the significance of Goblin not knowing everything that was in my mind.

"Because that was it: Goblin didn't necessarily read my thoughts! When I look back on it now it seems an earthshaking discovery, but one that I should have made a long time before.

"As for Pops and Sweetheart, I think they caught on that Lynelle believed in Goblin, which we'd withheld from them before, and they issued a couple of warnings that this 'side of my personality' oughtn't to be encouraged, and surely a high-quality teacher like Lynelle ought to agree. Pops got tough about it and Sweetheart started to cry.

"I took time alone with Sweetheart in the kitchen, helping her dry her tears on her apron and assuring her that I was not insane.

"The moment is deeply inscribed in my memory because Sweetheart, who was always pure kindness, said softly to me that 'things went terribly wrong with Patsy' and she didn't want for things to go badly for me.

" 'My daughter could have had a Sweet Sixteen Party in New Orleans,' Sweetheart said. 'She could have made her debut. She could have been a maid in the Mardi Gras krewes. She could have had all that—Ruthie and I could have managed everything—and instead she chose to be what she is.'

" 'Nothing's going wrong with me, Sweetheart,' I said. 'Don't misjudge Lynelle or me either.' I kissed her and kissed her. I lapped her tears and kissed her.

"I might have pointed out to her that she herself had abandoned all the refinements of New Orleans for the spell of Blackwood Manor, that she had spent her whole life in the kitchen, only leaving it for paid guests. But that would have been mean of me. And so I left it with assurances to her that Lynelle was teaching me more than anybody ever had.

"Lynelle and I gave up on the question of insight or commiseration with others as to Goblin—except for Aunt Queen—and Lynelle believed me when I complained of how difficult it was sometimes to stop Goblin's assaults.

"For instance, if I wanted to read for any length of time, I had to read aloud to Goblin. And that, I think, is why I am a slow reader to this day. I never learned how to speed through a text. I pronounce every word aloud or in my head. And in those times I shied away from what I couldn't pronounce.

"I got through Shakespeare thanks to Lynelle bringing the films of the plays for me to see—I particularly loved the films with the actor and director Kenneth Branagh—and she took me through a little Chaucer in the original Middle English, but I found it extremely hard all around and insisted we give it up.

"There are gaps in my education which no one could ever get me to fill. But they don't matter to me. I don't need to know science or algebra or geometry. Literature and music, painting and history—these are my passions. These are the things that still, somehow, in hours of quiet and lonesomeness, keep me alive.

"But let me close out the history of my love of Lynelle.

"A great high point came right before the end.

"Aunt Queen called from New York on one of her rare visits to the States and asked if Lynelle could bring me there, and both of us—along with Goblin—were delirious with joy. Sweetheart and Pops were glad for us and had no desire themselves to be away from the farm. They understood Aunt Queen's wishes not to come home just now, but they wanted her to know that they were having her room entirely redone, as she had requested, in Lynelle's favorite color blue.

"I explained to Goblin that we were going away, much farther away than New Orleans, and he had to cleave to me more closely than ever before. Of course I hoped that he'd stay at Blackwood Manor but I knew that wouldn't happen. How I knew I can't say. Perhaps because he was always with us in New Orleans. I don't know for sure.

"No matter what my hopes, I insisted that Goblin have his own seat beside me on my left on the plane. We flew first class—the three of us, with the stewardesses serving Goblin graciously—to join Aunt Queen at the Plaza on Central Park, and for a great ten days saw all that we could of wondrous sights, museums and the like. Though we had suites as big as Aunt Queen's, eternally filled with fresh flowers and boxes of Aunt Queen's beloved chocolate-covered cherries, Goblin and I bunked in with Aunt Queen as we had in the past.

"I was sixteen by this time, but it doesn't much matter to people like my people whether or not a teenager or even a grown man bunks in with his great-aunt or his granny; those are our ways. In fact, to be utterly frank, I was still sleeping with Jasmine's mother, Little Ida, at home, though she was now very old and feeble and sometimes dribbled a bit of urine in the bed.

"But where was I? Yes, in New York with my great-aunt, at the Plaza Hotel, cuddled in her arms as I slept.

"Goblin was with us for the entire trip, but something peculiar happened to Goblin. He became more and more transparent as the trip progressed. He seemed unable to be anything else. He lacked strength to move my hand, too. I learned this when I asked him to write for me how he liked New York. He could not. And this meant that there could be no pinching and no hair pulling either, though I had pretty much punished him—by silence and scorn—for those acts in the past.

"I pondered this, this uncommon transparency in a spirit who has always appeared to me to be three-dimensional and flesh and blood, but in truth I didn't want much to worry about Goblin. I wanted to see New York.

"The high point of our trip for me was the Metropolitan Museum, and I will never forget no matter how long I live Lynelle taking Goblin and me from painting to painting and explaining the relevant history, the relevant biography, and commenting on the wonders we beheld.

"After three days in the museum, Lynelle sat me down on a bench in a room full of the Impressionist paintings and asked me what I thought I'd learned from all I'd seen. I thought for a long time and then I told her that I thought color had died out in modern painting due to World War I and II. I told her that maybe now, and only now, since we had not had a Third World War, could color come back to painting. Lynelle was very surprised and thought this over and said perhaps it was true.

"There are many other things I remember from that trip—our visit to St. Patrick's Cathedral, in which I cried, our long walk through Central Park, our roaming Greenwich Village and SoHo, our little trek to obtain my passport just in case I might soon be drawn off to Europe—but they don't press in on this narrative, except in one respect. And that is that Goblin was utterly manageable all the time, and in spite of his transparency seemed to be as wildly stimulated as I was, appearing wide-eyed and happy, and of course New York is so crowded that when I talked to Goblin in midtown restaurants or on the street, no one even noticed.

"I half expected to have him show up beside me in my passport photo but he did not.

"When we returned, Goblin appeared solid again, and could make mischief, and danced himself into exhaustion and invisibility out of sheer joy.

"I felt an overwhelming relief. I had thought the trip to New York mortally wounded him—that my inattention to him had been the specific cause of his fading severely and perhaps approaching death. And now I had him back with me. And there were moments when I wanted to be with no one else.

"Just after I passed my seventeenth birthday, my days with Lynelle came to a close.

"She had been hired to work in research at Mayfair Medical in New Orleans. And it would henceforth be impossible to keep up with her work, and with tutoring me.

"I was in tears, but I knew what Mayfair Medical meant to Lynelle. It was a brand-new facility, endowed by the powerful Mayfair family of New Orleans—of which you know at least one member—and its laboratories and equipment were already the stuff of legend.

"Lynelle had dreamed of studying human growth hormone directly under the famous Dr. Rowan Mayfair and being accepted by the revolutionary Mayfair Medical was a triumph for her. But she couldn't be my teacher and boon companion anymore, it was simply impossible. I'd been lucky to have her as long as I did.

"The last time I saw Lynelle I told her I loved her. And I meant it with all my heart. I hope and pray that she understood how grateful I was for everything.

"She was on her way to Florida that day with two fellow female scientists, headed to Key West for a week of childless and husbandless relaxation.

"Lynelle died on the road.

"She, the speed demon, was not even at the wheel of the car. It was one of the others who was driving, and they were in a blinding rainstorm on Highway 10 when the car hydroplaned into an eighteen-wheeler truck. The driver was decapitated. Lynelle was pronounced dead at the scene, only to be revived and linger on life support for two weeks without ever regaining consciousness. Most of Lynelle's face had been crushed.

"I only learned of the accident when Lynelle's family called to tell us about the Memorial Mass that would be said for her in New Orleans. Lynelle had already been buried in Baton Rouge, where her parents lived.

"I walked up and down for hours, saying 'Lynelle' over and over. I was out of my mind. Goblin stared at me, obviously bewildered. I had no words. Just her name: 'Lynelle.'

"Pops and Sweetheart took me to the Mass—it was in a modern church in Metairie—and Goblin became very solid for the event, and I made space for him in the pew beside me, but he agitated me considerably, demanding to know what was going on. I could hear his voice in my head and he kept gesturing. He shrugged, turned his palms up, shook his head and kept mouthing the words 'Where is Lynelle?'

"The Mass was said by a very elderly priest and had a certain elegance to it, but for me it was a nightmare. When people went to the microphone to speak about Lynelle, I knew that I should step up, I should say all that she'd meant to me, but I couldn't overcome my fear that I would stumble or cry. All my mortal life I have regretted that I didn't speak at that Mass!

"I went to Communion, and as I always did after receiving Communion, I told Goblin flatly and furiously to shut up.

"Then came a frightening moment. As you might not expect, I believe strongly in the Catholic Church and in the miracle of the Transubstantiation—that the Priest in the Mass turns the wafers and the wine into the true Body and Blood of Christ.

"Well, as I knelt in the pew after having received Communion, and after telling Goblin to shut up, I turned and saw him kneeling right beside me, his shoulder not an inch from my shoulder, his face as vivid and ruddy as my face and his eyes sharply glaring at me; and for the first time in all my life, he frightened me.

"He appeared quickened and cunning, and he gave me the creeps.

"I turned away from him, trying not to feel the obvious press of his shoulder against mine and his right hand slinking over my left. I prayed. I wandered in my mind, and then, when I opened my eyes, I saw him again—dazzlingly solid—and I felt the coldest escalating fear.

"The fear did not pass. On the contrary, I became vividly aware of all the other people in the church, seeing those in the pews in front of me with extraordinary peculiarity, and even glancing to the sides at others and then turning boldly to look over my shoulder at all those behind. I had a sense of their normality. And then again I looked at this solid specter beside me; I looked into his brilliant eyes and at his sly smile, and a desperate panic seized me.

"I wanted to banish him. I wanted him dead. I wished that the journey to New York had killed him. And who could I tell this to? Who would understand? I felt murderous and abnormal. And Lynelle was dead.

"I sat in the pew. My heart went quiet. He continued his efforts to get my attention. He was just Goblin, and when he cleaved to me, when he gave up the solid image and wrapped his invisible self around me I felt myself relax in his embrace.

"Aunt Queen flew home for the Memorial, but, as she was coming from St. Petersburg, Russia, and there was a delay out of Newark, New Jersey, she did not make it in time. When she saw her room decorated in Lynelle's favorite blue, she cried. She threw herself on the blue satin comforter, turned over and stared up at the canopy, and looked like nothing so much as one of her own many slender flopping boudoir dolls, with her high heels and her cloche hat and her wet vacant weeping stare.

"I was so devastated by Lynelle's death that I fell into a state of silence, and though I knew that as the days passed those around me were concerned about me, I couldn't speak a single syllable to anyone. I sat in my room, in my reading chair by the fireplace, and I did nothing but think of Lynelle.

"Goblin went sort of mad on account of my state. He began to pinch me incessantly, and trying to lift my left hand, and rushing towards the computer and making gestures that he wanted to write.

"I remember staring at him as he stood over there at the desk, beckoning to me, and realizing for what it's worth that his pinches weren't any worse than they had ever been, and that he couldn't make the lights blink more than very little, and that when he pulled my hair I hardly felt it, and that I could ignore him without consequence if I chose.

"But I loved him. I didn't want to kill him. No, I didn't. And the moment had come to tell him what had happened. I dragged myself out of the chair and I went to the computer and I tapped out:

" 'Lynelle is dead.'

"For a long moment he read this message and then I said it out loud to him, but I received no response.

" 'Come on, Goblin, think. She's dead.' I said. 'You're a spirit and now she's a spirit.'

"But there was no response.

"Suddenly I felt the old pressure on my left hand, with the tight sensation of fingers curling around it, and then he tapped out:

" 'Lynelle. Lynelle is gone?'

"I nodded. I was crying and I wanted now to be left alone. I told him aloud that she was dead. But Goblin took my left hand again and I watched it claw the keyboard:

" 'What is dead?' "

"In a fit of annoyance and heightened grief, I hammered out:

" 'No longer here. Gone. Dead. Body has no Life. No Spirit in her body. Body left over. Body buried in the ground. Her Spirit is gone.'

"But he simply couldn't understand. He grabbed my hand again and tapped out, 'Where is Lynelle dead?' and 'Where is Lynelle gone?' and then finally, 'Why are you crying for Lynelle?'

"A cold apprehension came over me, a cold form of concentration.

"I typed in 'Sad. No more Lynelle. Sad. Crying. Yes.' But other thoughts were brewing in my mind.

"He snatched for my hand again, but he was weaker on account of his earlier efforts, and all he could type was her name.

"At that moment, as I stared at the black monitor and the green letters, I saw what looked like the reflection of a pinpoint of light in the monitor, and, wondering what it could be, I moved my head from side to side to block the light or get a clearer look at it. For one second it became distinctly the light of a candle. I saw the wick as well as the flame.

"At once I turned around and looked behind me. I saw nothing in my room that could have produced this reflection. Absolutely nothing. Needless to say, I had no candles. The only candles were on a hallway altar downstairs.

"I turned back to the monitor. There was no pinpoint of light. There was no candle flame. Again I moved my head from side to side and turned my eyes at every possible angle. No light. No reflected candle flame.

"I was astonished. I sat quiet for a long time, distrusting my senses, and then, unable to deny what I saw, I tapped out to Goblin the question, 'Did you see the candle flame?' Again there came his monotonous and panicky answers: 'Where Lynelle?' 'Lynelle gone.' 'What is gone?'

"I went back to my chair. Goblin appeared for a moment, in a vague flash, and there came the pinches and the hair pulling, but I lay indifferent to him thinking only, praying only in a bizarre way of praying backwards, that Lynelle had never really known how badly she was injured, that she hadn't suffered in her coma, that she hadn't known pain. What if she had seen the car careening into the truck? What if she had heard some insensitive person at her bedside saying that her face, her beautiful face, had been crushed?

"She never suffered. That was the story.

"She never suffered. Or so they said.

"I knew I had seen the light of that candle! I had seen it plainly in the monitor.

"I murmured to Goblin, 'You tell me where she is, Goblin. Tell me if her spirit went into the light.' There came no answer. He couldn't grasp it. He didn't know.

"I hammered at him. 'You're a spirit. You ought to know. We are made of bodies and souls. I am body and soul. Lynelle was body and soul. Soul is spirit. Where did Lynelle's spirit go?'

"He gave nothing back but his infantile answers. It was all he could do.

"Finally, I went to the computer. I wrote it out: 'I am body and soul.

The body is what you pinch. The soul is what speaks to you, what thinks, what looks at you through my eyes.'

"Silence. Then came the vague formation of the apparition again, translucent, face without detail; then it dissolved.

"I went on typing on the computer keyboard: 'The soul—that part of me which speaks to you and loves you and knows you—that part is sometimes called spirit. And when my body dies my spirit or my soul will leave my body. Do you understand?'

"I felt his hand clamp onto my left hand.

" 'Don't leave your body,' he wrote. 'Don't die. I will cry.'

"For a long moment I pondered. He had made the connection. Yes. But I wanted more from him, and a terrifying urgency gripped me, a feeling very near panic.

" 'You are a spirit,' I wrote. 'You have no body. You are pure spirit. Don't you know where Lynelle's spirit has gone? You must know. You should know. There must be a place where spirits live. A place where spirits are. You *do* know.'

"There was a long silence, but I knew he was right beside me.

"I felt him grip my hand. 'Don't leave your body,' he wrote again. 'I will cry and cry.'

" 'But where is the home of the spirits?' I wrote. 'Where is the place where spirits live, like I live in this house?'

"It was useless. I typed it out in two dozen different ways. He couldn't grasp it. And it was not long before he began to ask, 'Why did Lynelle's spirit leave her body?'

"I wrote out the description of the accident. Silence. And finally, his store of energy being exhausted and there being no rainfall to help him, he was absent.

"And alone, cold and frightened, I curled up in my chair and went to sleep.

"A great gulf had opened between me and Goblin.

"It had been widening for all the years that I knew Lynelle, and it was now immeasurable. My doppelgänger loved me and was as ever fastened to me but no longer knew my soul. And what was all the more ghastly to me was that he didn't know what he was himself. He couldn't speak of himself as a spirit. He would have done so if he could. He could not.

"As the days dragged on, Aunt Queen made plans to go off again to St. Petersburg, Russia, to rejoin two cousins she had left waiting there at the Grand Hotel. She prevailed upon me to go with her.

"I was amazed. St. Petersburg, Russia.

"She said in a very sweet and winning way that it was either go to college or see the world.

"I told her plainly I wasn't ready for either. I was still hurt by Lynelle's death.

"I said that I wanted to go, and in the future I would go with her if she called me, but for now I couldn't leave home. I needed a year off. I needed to read and absorb more fully many of the lessons that Lynelle had taught me (that really won the day for me!), and to hang around the house. I wanted to help Pops and Sweetheart with the guests. Mardi Gras was coming. I'd go with Sweetheart into New Orleans to see the parades from the house of her sister. And we always had a crowd at Blackwood Farm after that. And then there was the Azalea Festival, and the Easter crowd. And I needed to be home for the Christmas banquet. I couldn't think of seeing the world.

"When I look back on that time I realize now that I had slipped into a state of profound anxiety in which the simplest comforts seemed beyond reach. The gaiety of the guests seemed foreign. I felt afraid at twilight. Large vases of flowers frightened me. Goblin seemed accidental and unmysterious, an ignoramus of a spirit who could deliver me nothing of consolation or companionship. I was apprehensive on those inevitable gray days when there was no sun to be seen.

"Perhaps I had a premonition that there were terrible times to come."

9

"Not six months had passed before Little Ida died in my bed one night, and it was Jasmine who found her when she came to wake me for breakfast, wondering why her mother had not come down. I was hustled away from the bed with crazy gestures and summonses and blank looks from Goblin and finally Pops dragging me out of the bedroom. And I, a spoilt brat who had just woken up, was furious.

"Only an hour later, when the doctor and the funeral director came, did they tell me what had gone down. Little Ida was the angel of my youth as surely as Sweetheart was, and she had died so quiet, just like that.

"She looked tiny in the coffin, like a wizened child.

"The funeral was in New Orleans, where Little Ida was buried in a tomb in St. Louis no. 1, which her family had had for well over a hundred and fifty years. A host of colored and black relations were in attendance, and I was thankful that it was all right to cry, if not even wail out loud.

"Of course all the white people—and there were plenty from out our way—were a little more subdued than the black people, but a good commingling shed tears.

"As for my mattress back at home, Jasmine and Lolly flipped it over. And that was all there was to that.

"I framed the best picture there was of Little Ida, a photograph taken of her at Aunt Ruthie's house in New Orleans during Mardi Gras, and I hung that on the wall.

"In the kitchen now there was general crying, Jasmine and Lolly sobbing about their mother whenever the mood came on them, and Big

Ramona, Little Ida's mother, went silent and quit the big house altogether, sitting in her rocking chair all day for several weeks.

"I went out there again and again with soup for Big Ramona. I tried to talk to her. All she said was: 'A woman oughtn't have to bury her own child.'

"Crying came and went with me.

"I took to thinking of Lynelle constantly, and now Little Ida was mixed up with it too, and each day it seemed that Little Ida was more dead and gone than the day before.

"Goblin accepted that Little Ida was dead, but Goblin had never been too crazy about Little Ida—certainly he had loved Lynelle more—and so he took it rather well.

"One day when I sat at the kitchen table paging through a mail-order catalog, I saw that they had flannel nightshirts for men and flannel gowns for women.

"I ordered a whole slew of these, and when the goods arrived, I put on the nightshirt in the evening and went out to Big Ramona with one of the gowns.

"Now let me clarify here that Big Ramona is called Big Ramona not because she's big but because she is the grandmother on the property, just as Sweetheart might have been called Big Mama if she had ever allowed.

"So to go on with my story, I came out to this little mite of a woman, with her long white hair in its nighttime braid, and I said:

" 'You come on and sleep with me. I need you. I'm alone with Goblin and Little Ida's gone after all these years.'

"For a long time Big Ramona just looked at me. Her eyes were like two nickels. But then a little fire came into them, and she took the gown from me and looked it over, and, finding it proper, she came into the house.

"Thereafter we slept spoon fashion in that big bed, flannel to flannel, and she was my bedfellow as ever Little Ida had been.

"Big Ramona had the silkiest skin on the planet, and, having kept her hair long all her life, had a great wealth of it, which she always plaited as she sat on the side of the bed.

"I took to sitting with her as she went through the ritual, and we talked over all the trivia of the day, and then we said our prayers.

"Now Little Ida and I had pretty much let prayers go by the boards, but with Big Ramona we prayed for everybody in one fell swoop, reciting three Hail Marys and three Our Fathers and never failing to add for the deceased:

> *Let perpetual light shine upon them, O Lord,*
> *and may their souls and the souls of all*
> *the faithful departed rest in peace.*

"Then we'd chat about how it was a blessing Little Ida never knew real old age, or suffered illness, and that she was surely up there with God. Same with Lynelle.

"Finally, after all that, Big Ramona would ask if Goblin was with us, and then she said:

"'Well, you tell Goblin it's time to sleep now,' and Goblin settled down beside me and kind of merged with me, and off I went to sleep.

"Gradually, over a period of several months, a semi-calm came over me entirely due to Big Ramona, and I was astonished to discover that Pops and the Shed Men, and even Jasmine and Lolly, credited me with kindness to Big Ramona in her time of grief. It was all our grief. And Big Ramona was saving me from a kind of dark panic which had begun in me with Lynelle and was now creeping closer with the loss of Little Ida.

"I took to going out fishing in the swamp with Pops, something I'd never been all that crazy about before. I got to like it out there as we poked our way through in the pirogue, and sometimes we went deep into the swamps, beyond our usual territory, and I got a kind of fearless curiosity about the swamps, and whether we might find Manfred Blackwood's island, but that we did not do.

"One afternoon, late, we came upon a huge old cypress tree that had a rusted chain around it, grown into it in parts, and a mark carved on it that looked to me to be an arrow. It was an ancient tree, and the chain was made of large links. I was for pressing on in the direction of the arrow, but Pops said no, it was late, and there was nothing out there anyway, and we might get lost if we went any further.

"It was all the same with me because I didn't entirely believe all the stories about Manfred and the Hermitage, and I was sticky all over from the humid air, and so we went home.

"Then Mardi Gras came, which meant that Sweetheart had to go to her sister Ruthie's house, and this year she really didn't want to go. She claimed she was feeling poorly, she had no appetite, not even for

King cake, which was already arriving daily from New Orleans, and she thought she might be coming down with the flu.

"But at last she decided to go into the city for all the parades, because Ruthie was depending on her and she didn't want the crowd of her elderly aunts and uncles and all her cousins to be disappointed that she wasn't there.

"I didn't go with her, though she wanted me to, and though her cough worsened (she called Pops every day and I usually spoke to her too), she did stay for the entire time.

"On Ash Wednesday, the first day of Lent and the very day she returned, she went to the doctor without anybody prodding her to do it. Her cough was simply too bad.

"I think they knew it was cancer as soon as they saw the X rays, but they had to do the CAT scan, and then the bronchoscopy, and finally a biopsy by needle through Sweetheart's back. These meant uncomfortable days in the hospital, but before the final pathology report came in Sweetheart was already breathing with such difficulty that they had put her on 'full oxygen' and had given her morphine 'to lessen the sensation of gasping for breath.' She was in a half sleep all of the time.

"At last they broke the news to us in the corridor outside her room. It was lymphoma in both lungs and it had metastasized, meaning she had cancer all through her system, and they did not expect her to last more than a few days. She couldn't choose for herself whether she wanted an attempt at chemotherapy. She was in a deep coma, her breath and blood pressure getting fainter all the time.

"My eighteenth birthday came and went with nothing much to mark it, except that I got a new pickup truck and drove it back to the hospital as fast as I could to watch by the bed.

"Pops went into a protracted state of shock.

"This big and capable man who always seemed to be the one making the decisions was a shuddering wreck of his former self. As Sweetheart's sister and aunts and uncles and cousins came and went, Pops remained silent and inconsolable.

"He took turns with me in the room, and so did Jasmine and Lolly.

"Finally Sweetheart's eyes opened and would not be closed, and her breathing became mechanical as if she herself had nothing to do with the rhythmic heave of her chest.

"I ignored Goblin. Goblin seemed senseless to me, a part of childhood to be repudiated. I hated the mere sight of Goblin with his inane look of innocence and questioning eyes. I felt him hovering. Finally, when I could endure it no longer, I went down into the pickup truck and told Goblin that what was going on was sad. It was what had happened to Lynelle and to Little Ida, that Sweetheart was going away.

" 'Goblin, this is bad,' I told him. 'This is awful. Sweetheart's not going to wake up.' He looked grieved and I saw tears in his eyes, but maybe he was only imitating mine.

" 'Go away, Goblin,' I said. 'Be respectful and decent. Be quiet so that I can watch with Sweetheart as I should do.' This seemed to work some change in him and he ceased to torment me, but I could feel him near me day and night.

"When it came time to shut off the oxygen, which was by then the only thing keeping Sweetheart alive, Pops could not be in the room.

"I was in the room, and if Goblin was there I didn't know it. Aunt Ruthie and the nurse had the orders from the doctor. Jasmine was there and so was Lolly and so was Big Ramona.

"Big Ramona told me to stand close to the head of the bed and hold Sweetheart's hand.

"Off came the oxygen mask, and Sweetheart didn't gasp for breath. She just breathed with a bigger heave of her chest, and then her mouth opened just a little and blood poured down her chin.

"It was a horrible sight. Nobody expected it. I think Aunt Ruthie went to pieces and somebody was calming her. My focus was on Sweetheart. I grabbed a wad of paper tissues and went to blot the blood, saying, 'I've got it, Sweetheart.'

"But more and more blood came, sliding down her chin, and then Sweetheart's tongue appeared between her lips, pushing out more blood. Someone handed me a wet towel. I gathered up the blood, saying, 'It's all right, Sweetheart, I'm taking care of it.' Pretty soon I had all the blood. And then, after four or five widely spaced breaths, Sweetheart breathed no more. Big Ramona told me to close her eyes, which I did.

"After the doctor came in and pronounced her dead, really dead—I went out into the hall.

"I felt a dreadful elation, a horror that seemed manic when I look back upon it, a hideous safety from the consequences of Sweetheart's death due to the giant hospital enfolding us, the seamless fluorescent light and the nurses at their station very nearby. It was wild and pleasurable, this feeling. It was as if no other burden on earth existed. It was a great suspension, and I hardly felt the tiled floor beneath my feet.

"Patsy was standing there. She was leaning against the wall, looking all too typical with her huge yellow hair, wearing one of her fringed white leather outfits, her nails glittering with pearlescent polish, her feet in high white boots.

"Only then, as I stared at her, at her painted mask of a face, did I realize that Patsy had never come to the hospital once. I went into a silent stammer. Then I spoke.

" 'She's dead,' I said, and Patsy came back fiercely:

" 'I don't believe it! I just saw her on Mardi Gras Day.'

"I explained that the oxygen had been turned off and it had been very peaceful; Sweetheart had not gasped or suffered, she had never known of any danger, she had never known fear.

"Patsy suddenly flew into a rage. Dropping her furious voice into a loud hissing whisper (we were near the nurses' station) she demanded to know why we had not told her we were turning off the oxygen, and how could we do such a thing to her (meaning herself); Sweetheart was her mother, and who gave us the right?

"Pops appeared, coming round the corner from the visitors' waiting room, and I had never seen him so angry as he was then. He whipped Patsy around to face him and told her to get out of the hospital or he'd kill her, and then he turned to me, shaking all over, choked up and silent and trembling, and then he went into Sweetheart's room.

"Patsy made a move towards the door of the room, but she stopped and turned to me and said a stream of mean things. They were statements like, 'You're always the center of it. You were there, weren't you? Oh, yes, Tarquin, everything for Tarquin.' I can't clearly remember what her words were. Lots of Sweetheart's people were gathering. Patsy went away.

"I left the hospital, got in the pickup truck, vaguely aware that Jasmine was climbing in the seat next to me, drove over to the Cracker Barrel Restaurant, went in and ordered lots of pecan pancakes, slopped them with butter and ate them till I was nearly sick.

"Jasmine sat there opposite me, nursing a cup of black coffee and smoking cigarette after cigarette, her dark face very smooth and her manner calm, and then Jasmine said very distinctly:

" 'She suffered maybe about two weeks. Mardi Gras Day was February twenty-seventh. She was at the parades. And here it is March fourteenth. That's how long she really suffered, and that's not all that bad.'

"I couldn't speak. But when the waiter appeared I ordered more pecan pancakes, and I put so much butter on them they were swimming in butter. And Jasmine just went on smoking, and that's how it was.

"The undertaker in New Orleans did right by Sweetheart, as she looked exquisite against the satin in the coffin, with her makeup just the proper way. There was a little eyebrow pencil where she always wore it, and a shade of Revlon lipstick that she loved. She was in her beige gabardine dress, the one she wore in spring for the tours, and there was her white orchid on her lapel.

"Aunt Queen was inconsolable. We clung to each other through much of the proceedings.

"Before they shut the coffin, Pops took the pearls from around Sweetheart's neck and the wedding band from her hand. He said he wanted to save these things, and he heaved a sigh and he bent and kissed her—the last one of us to do it—and the coffin was shut.

"No sooner had that lid come down than Patsy broke into sobs. That painted mask of a face just broke into pieces. She just cut loose. It was the most heartrending chorus to hear, as she cried and cried and called out 'Mamma' as the pallbearers lifted the coffin to carry it out. 'Mamma, Mamma,' she kept crying, and that idiot Seymour held her, with a stupid face and a limp hug, saying 'Hush' of all things, as if he had the right.

"I took hold of Patsy and her arms came around me very tight. She cried all the way out to Metairie Cemetery, her body shaking violently as I held her, and then she said she couldn't get out of the car for the graveside ceremony. I didn't know what to do. I held her. I stayed there. I could hear and see the folks at the graveside, but I stayed with Patsy in the car.

"On the long drive back home, Patsy cried herself out. She fell asleep with her head against me, and when she woke up she looked up at me— I was already about six feet tall at that point—in a kind of sleepy way, and she said softly:

" 'Quinn, she's the only person who's ever been really interested in me.'

"That night, Patsy and Seymour played the most deafening music yet to come out of the back-shed studio, and Jasmine and Lolly were in a rage. As for Pops, he didn't seem to hear it or care.

"About two days later, after spreading out her suitcases to be packed once more, Aunt Queen told me that she wanted me to go to college. She was going to look for another teacher for me—someone as brilliant as Lynelle who could prepare me for the finest schools.

"I told her I never wanted to leave Blackwood Manor, and she only smiled at this and said I'd soon change.

" 'You don't have a beard yet, my baby,' she said, 'you're growing out of that dress shirt as we sit here talking, and your shoes must be size twelve, if I have any knack for guessing such things. Believe you me, there are exciting things to come.'

"I smiled at all this. I was still feeling the dazed elation, the cruel excitement that surrounded Sweetheart's funeral for me, and I didn't really care about growing up or anything else.

" 'When that testosterone really hits your blood,' Aunt Queen proceeded, 'you'll want to see the wide world, and Goblin won't seem the fascination that he is now.'

"The next morning she left for New York to catch a flight to Jerusalem, which she hadn't visited in many years. I don't remember where she went after that—only that she was gone a long while.

"About a week after the funeral, Pops produced a handwritten will from Sweetheart's dressing table drawer that left all her personal jewelry to Patsy along with all her clothes.

"We were gathered in the kitchen when he read out the words, 'For my only girl, my dearest, sweetest girl.' Pops then gave the will to Patsy and he looked away, and his eyes had that same flat metallic look which I had seen in Big Ramona right after Little Ida died.

"That look never went away.

"A trust fund was also left to Patsy, he mumbled, but there was a formal bank paper to deal with that. He produced an envelope of little Polaroid photographs which Sweetheart had made of her heirlooms, identifying each with writing on the front and back.

" 'Yeah, well that trust fund is next to nothing,' Patsy said, shoving the photographs and will in her purse. 'It's one thousand a month and that might have been big money thirty years ago but now it's small change. And I can tell you right now, I want my mother's things.'

"Pops took the pearl necklace out of his pants pocket and pushed it towards her, and she took it, but when he drew out the wedding ring, he said, 'I'm keeping this,' and Patsy just shrugged and left the room.

"For days and nights Pops did little or nothing but sit at the kitchen table and push away the plates of food set before him, and ignore the questions put to him, as Jasmine and Lolly and Clem took over the running of Blackwood Farm.

"I had a hand in the running of things also, and very gradually, as I conducted my first tours of Blackwood Farm and did my best to exert a charm over the guests, I realized that the crazy elation which had carried me through Sweetheart's vivid funeral was breaking up.

"A dark panic was reemerging. It was right behind me, ready to take over. I kept myself as busy as I could. I went over menus with Jasmine and Lolly, tasting hollandaise sauce and béarnaise sauce, and picking patterns of china, and chatting with guests who had come back to celebrate anniversaries, and even cleaning out bedrooms when the schedule demanded it, and driving the tractor mower over the lawns.

"As I watched the Shed Men lay in the late spring flowers—the impatiens and the zinnias and the hibiscus—a desperate sentimental fury possessed me. I clung tight to the vision of Blackwood Manor and all it meant.

"I went walking down the long avenue of pecan trees out front, looking back at the house to treasure the sight of it and imagine how it struck the new guests.

"I went from room to room, checking on toilet articles and throw pillows and porcelain statues on mantelpieces, and the portraits, most definitely the famous portraits, and when the inevitable portrait of Sweetheart arrived—done from a photograph by a painter in New Orleans—I took down the mirror in the back right-side bedroom for the portrait to go up in its place.

"I think, in retrospect, it was a cruelty to show that portrait to Pops, but he looked at it in the same dull way in which he regarded everything else.

"Then one day he said in a low voice, after clearing his throat, Would Jasmine and Lolly take all of Sweetheart's clothing and jewels out of their room and put them in Patsy's room above the shed? 'I don't want what belongs to Patsy in my room.'

"Now, Sweetheart's clothing included two ranch-mink coats and some beautiful ballgowns from the days when Sweetheart had been young and single and had gone to Mardi Gras balls. It included Sweetheart's wedding dress and other fashionable suits that were years out of date. As for the jewelry, there were many diamonds and some emeralds, and most of it had come down to Sweetheart from her own mother, or her grandmother before that. There were pieces that Sweetheart had worn when she hosted weddings at Blackwood Manor, and favorite pieces—pearls, mostly—that she had worn every day.

"One morning, early, while Pops was in his half slumber at the table over a cold bowl of oatmeal, Patsy quietly loaded all these possessions into her van and drove away. I didn't know what to make of it, except that I knew, as everyone did, that Seymour, Patsy's bum of a backup band and a sometime lover, had a crash pad in New Orleans, and I figured she meant to take these clothes there.

"Two weeks later, Patsy came home in a brand-new van. It was already painted with her name on it. She and Seymour (the bum) unloaded a new drum set and a new electric guitar. They shut the door of the studio and began practicing at full volume. New speakers too.

"Pops was aware of all this, because Jasmine and Lolly were at the screen door commenting on all of it, and when Patsy came through the kitchen after supper he grabbed her by the arm and demanded to know where she'd earned the money for all the new things.

"His voice was hoarse from not speaking and he looked sleepy and wild.

"What followed was the worst fight they had ever had.

"Patsy was up front about the fact that she'd sold everything Sweetheart left her, even the wedding dress and the heirloom jewelry and the keepsakes, and once again, when Pops came at her she grabbed up a big knife.

" 'You threw that stuff into my bedroom!' Patsy screamed. 'You had them cart it out and shove it into my closets like it was trash.'

" 'You sold your mother's wedding dress, you sold her diamonds!' Pops roared. 'You're a monster. You should never have been born.'

"I ran between them and pleaded with them to stop, claiming that the guests in the house could hear them; this had to come to an end. Pops shook his head. He went out the back door. He went towards the shed, and later I saw him out there in a rocking chair, just smoking and looking into the dark.

"As for Patsy, she moved some clothes of her own out of the upstairs front bedroom, where she stayed from time to time, demanding that I help her, and when I demurred—I didn't want to be seen with her—she called me a spoilt brat, a Little Lord Fauntleroy, a sissy and a queer.

" 'It wasn't my bright idea to have you,' she said, and then she headed for the spiral stairs. 'I should have gotten rid of you,' she hollered out over her shoulder. 'Damned sorry I didn't do what I wanted to do.'

"At that precise moment, she appeared to trip over her own feet. In a flash I saw Goblin near to her with his back to her, smiling at me. She let out a loud 'Ow!' The clothes fell down on the staircase, and with great difficulty she caught herself at the top step. I rushed to steady her. She turned and glared at me, and the dreadful realization came over me that Goblin had pushed her, or in some other manner made her trip.

"I was horror-struck. I picked up all the clothes quickly and I said, 'I'll go down with you.' The expression on her face, the combination of wariness and excitement, of morbid respect and detestation, is something I'll never forget. But what was in her heart I don't know.

"I was afraid of Goblin. Afraid of what he might do.

"I helped Patsy load all her things in the van so Goblin would know I meant her no ill will. And then Patsy was off, declaring that she was never coming back, but of course she was back in two weeks, demanding to stay in the big house because she ran out of money and there was no place to go but home.

"That night, as soon as Patsy was safely away, I demanded of Goblin, 'What did you do? You almost made her fall!' But I got no answer from Goblin; it was as though he was hiding, and when I went back upstairs to my room and sat down at the computer he at once grabbed my hand and typed out,

" 'Patsy hurt you. I don't like Patsy.'

" 'That doesn't mean you can hurt her,' I wrote, speaking the words aloud.

"At once my left hand was snatched up with extraordinary force.

" 'I made Patsy stop,' he answered.

" 'You almost killed Patsy!' I countered. 'Don't ever hurt anyone. It's not fun.'

" 'No fun,' he wrote. 'She stopped hurting you.'

" 'If you hurt other people,' I answered, 'I won't love you.'

"There came a silence and a chill in the room, and then by his power the computer was turned off. Then came the embrace, and with it a faint loving warmth. I felt a vague loathing of the pleasure this embrace produced in me, and a sudden fear that it would become erotic. I don't remember ever feeling that fear before.

"Patsy had called me a queer. Maybe I was one, I thought. Maybe I was steered in that direction. Maybe Goblin knew. Goblin and me together. Fear stole over me. It seemed like mortal sin.

" 'Don't be sad, Goblin,' I whispered. 'There's too much sadness as it is, at home. Go off, now, Goblin. Go off, and let me think by myself.'

"In the weeks that followed, Patsy never looked at me in quite a familiar way, but I did not want to admit to anything regarding the event on the staircase, so I couldn't ask her what she had felt.

"Meantime everybody knew that in her bathroom in the big house she was vomiting and retching in the morning, and she took to hanging about the kitchen, saying that all the food disgusted her, and Pops, driven away from the table, spent his long hours in the shed.

"He didn't talk to the men. He didn't talk to anyone. He watched the television and he drank Barq's Root Beer, but he wasn't seeing or hearing a thing.

"Then, one night when Patsy drove up late and came into the kitchen claiming she was sick and Jasmine had to make her some dinner, Pops sat down at the table opposite her and told me to get out of the room.

" 'No, you let him stay if you've got something to say to me,' Patsy said. 'Go on, out with it.'

"I didn't know quite what to do, so I stepped into the hallway and leaned against the back doors. I could see Patsy's face, and the back of Pops' head, and I could hear every word that was said.

" 'I'll give you fifty thousand dollars for it,' Pops said.

"Patsy stared at him for a full minute, and then she said, 'What are you talking about?'

" 'I know you're pregnant,' he said. 'Fifty thousand dollars. And you leave the baby here with us.'

" 'You crazy old man,' she said. 'You're sixty-five. What are you going to do with a baby? You think I'd go through all that again for fifty grand?'

" 'A hundred thousand dollars,' he said calmly. And then he said, 'Two hundred thousand dollars, Patsy Blackwood, on the day that it's born and you sign it over to me.'

"Patsy rose from the table. She shot up and backwards, glaring at him. 'Why the hell didn't you tell me that yesterday!' she shouted. 'Why the hell didn't you tell me that this morning!' She made her hands into fists and stomped her foot. 'You crazy old man!' she said. 'Damn you.' And she turned and flew out the kitchen. The screen door banged shut after her, and Pops bowed his head.

"I came into the kitchen and stood at his side.

" 'She's already gotten rid of it,' he said. He bowed his head. He looked utterly defeated. He never said another word about it. He went back to his silent ways.

"As for Patsy, she did lie sick in her room for a couple of days during which Jasmine cooked for her and took general care of her, and then she was up and off in her new van for a series of country jamborees.

"I was very curious. Would Patsy immediately get pregnant just to make two hundred thousand dollars? And what would it be like to have a baby sister or brother? I really wanted to know.

"Pops set himself to solitary tasks around the farm. He painted the white fences where they needed it; he clipped back the azaleas. He laid in more of the spring flowers. In fact, he enlarged the garden patches and made them more brilliant than they'd ever been before. Red geraniums were his favorite flower, and though they didn't last too long in the heat he set out plenty of them in the beds, and he stepped back often to get perspective on his schemes.

"For a while, a brief while, it seemed that somehow things would be all right. The joy had not quite fled Blackwood Manor. Goblin behaved himself, but Goblin's face mirrored my tension and my mounting conflict. The fear was winning over my mind.

"What was I afraid of? Death, I suppose. I longed to see Little Ida's ghost but it didn't happen, and then there was Big Ramona saying that people didn't appear to you once they'd gone to Heaven, unless they had a powerful reason for coming back. I wanted one last glimpse of Little Ida. I knew Sweetheart wasn't going to appear, but I had some peculiar faith in Little Ida. I wondered how long she'd been dead in my bed.

"Meantime, Blackwood Manor went on.

"Big Ramona, Jasmine and Lolly ran the kitchen to perfection as they had always done, handling the tours with equal aplomb, and Pops progressed to a rampage of repairs and renovations to keep himself exhausted all the time, so that he was in bed, out cold, by eight o'clock.

"Big Ramona did everything she could to cheer everyone, baking all her 'secret recipes' and even cajoling Patsy into staying with me for dinner a few times (when Pops was absent on errands), as if she felt that I needed Patsy, which frankly I did not.

"Some interesting guests came and went, Aunt Queen wrote loving letters, and Easter Sunday did see an enormous buffet with people from miles around and music on the lawn.

"Pops didn't help much with this Easter banquet and everyone understood why. He did appear, dressed in a fine white linen suit, but he mainly sat silent in a chair, watching the dancing and looking lifeless, as though his spirit had fled. His eyes were sunken. His skin had a yellowish tinge.

"He was like a man who'd seen a vision, and for whom normal life held no charm.

"When I looked at him, my throat tightened. I could feel my heart pounding. I could hear it in my ears. The sky was a perfect blue, the air was mild and the music of the little orchestra was lovely, but my teeth were chattering.

"Out in the center of the dance floor, Goblin danced. He was very solid, outfitted in a three-piece white suit just as I was. He didn't seem to care whether or not I saw him. He was winding his way in and out of the dancers. Then his eyes fixed on me and he became sad. He stood still and reached out to me with both arms. His face was marked with sorrow. And it was no mirror image, because I knew my face was blank with fear.

" 'No one can see you!' I whispered under my breath, and quite suddenly everyone there seemed alien to me, the way people had in the church at Lynelle's Memorial, or rather I felt myself to be a monster that I could see Goblin, a monster that he was my familiar, and there seemed no possibility of comfort or warmth in all the world.

"I thought of Sweetheart in the crypt in New Orleans. If I went to the gates of the crypt, would I smell formaldehyde? Or would I smell something worse?

"I drifted away. I went down to the old cemetery. There were quite a few guests hanging about down there, and Lolly was passing among them with a bottle of champagne. I saw no ghosts in the cemetery. I saw only the living. Cousins of Sweetheart's talked to me. I didn't hear them. I pictured going upstairs to Pops' bedroom, taking his pistol out of the drawer and putting it to my head and pulling the trigger. I thought:

" 'If you do that, this terror will end.'

"Then I felt Goblin's invisible arms around me. I felt him wrap himself around me. There came what seemed a heartbeat from Goblin and a spiritual warmth. It was not a new thing for me to feel this. It had lately made me feel guilty. Only just now it seemed desperately important.

"And the elation returned to me, the wild elation I felt when I left Sweetheart's hospital room, and tears rolled down my cheeks. I stood under the oak tree, wondering if the sad ghosts of the cemetery could see all these living people. I cried.

" 'You come inside with me,' Jasmine said. She took me by the shoulders. 'Come on, Taw-quin, you come on,' she said. She only called me by my full name, pronouncing it 'Taw-quin,' when she was very serious. I followed her in, and she told me to sit down in the kitchen and have a glass of champagne too.

"Now, being a country kid I had drunk wine and whiskey plenty of times, though never much in quantity—but very quietly, sitting at the kitchen table—after Jasmine left—I drank a whole bottle of champagne.

"That night I was violently sick, my head hurt as though it was going to burst, the Easter party was over and I was vomiting as Big Ramona stood over me declaring in no uncertain terms that Jasmine was never to set me to drinking wine again."

10

"I N THE WEEKS that followed I felt better. I don't think you can feel sheer panic continuously. Your mental system breaks down. It comes in waves, and you have to tell yourself, well, this will end.

"I went back to a leaden misery that was more easily manageable, and my mind was sometimes flooded with memories of Sweetheart, of her singing, and of her cooking, and of little things, unimportant and fragmentary things, that she had said, or would say, and then a terror would follow, as if someone had taken me bodily and put me out on a high window ledge nine stories up above a street.

"Meantime I hadn't forgotten what Patsy had called me—sissy, Little Lord Fauntleroy, queer. I knew perfectly well from the realm of television and movie watching, as well as books, what that meant, and I had a deepening inevitable adolescent suspicion that that characterization was true.

"Understand, I was too good a Catholic to experiment with sexual stimulation when I was alone, and no good opportunities had come up for experimenting romantically with anybody else. I didn't think people went blind from self-stimulation, but the contemplation of it filled me with a Catholic shame.

"But I had had wet dreams. And though I'd awakened disturbed and humiliated and cut them short, repressing the memory of what really drove them, I had a deep suspicion that they were about men.

"No wonder Pops had offered two hundred grand to Patsy for a baby. He thought I'd never marry, never have children. He knew from looking at me. He knew from the way I couldn't hammer a nail into wood that I was queer. What had he thought about me raving over supper about movies like *The Red Shoes* and *The Tales of Hoffmann*?

He knew I was queer. Hell, probably everybody who'd ever seen me knew.

"Goblin knew. Goblin was waiting. Goblin was a profound mystery of invisible tentacles and pulsing power. Goblin was queer!

"And what about the palpable embrace of Goblin, and the way that sometimes this embrace sent a cool delicious chill through all my skin, as though someone were stirring the hairs everywhere on my body and telling my body to wake up?

"There was something so eternally intimate about Goblin's attentions that they had to be sinful.

"Whatever the case, I did nothing but brood about it, and try to keep busy, and the panic grew in me, rising and falling, and it began to come at its very worst at twilight each day.

"Now that summer was coming and the days were longer, I knew the waves of panic longer—sometimes from about four p.m. till eight. There came that image to my mind of me putting a gun to my head and the thought that the bullet would make the pain end. Then I thought of what that would do to Pops and Aunt Queen and I put it out of my mind.

"It was around that period that I made everybody turn on certain lights at four o'clock, come hell or high water, and whether we had any guests at Blackwood Manor or not.

"I was becoming the Lord of Blackwood Manor—the Little Lord Fauntleroy, I suppose.

"Each evening, like a creature driven, I turned on classical music in the parlors and the dining room, and then I checked on the flower arrangements and the placement of furniture and went about straightening out all the pictures on the walls; and, as the panic went away a little, I sat in the kitchen with Pops.

"But Pops didn't talk anymore. He sat in a straight-back chair, staring out the screen door at nothing. It was awful to be with Pops. His eyes were more and more empty. He wasn't snapping back the way that Big Ramona had snapped back. There was no consolation I could give or take.

"Then one night, when the panic was on me heavy and it was mixed up with gloom and fear of being queer and mostly with gloom, I said to Pops:

" 'Do you think Patsy will get pregnant again just to sell you the baby?'

"This was a very uncommon kind of thing for me to say to Pops.

Pops and I spoke in rather formal terms with each other. And one of the things we had never done was discuss Patsy.

"He answered in a quiet flat voice, 'No. It was just something of the moment. I figured I could save that one. I thought that that was something to do, to bring up that one. But the truth is, I don't even think she could carry one to term if she wanted to. She's gotten rid of too many, and that makes a woman's womb weak.'

"I was amazed at his candor.

"I wondered why I was alive. Maybe he'd given her money to carry me. But I didn't say anything. I'd rather be afraid of it than know. And Pops' voice had sounded too dead and metallic. I wasn't easy with Pops. I felt sorrow for him. Neither of us said another word about it.

"And then at last—at last—it was eight o'clock and I could sit down on the bedside with Big Ramona and she'd brush her long white hair and slowly braid it and I'd be safe, safe in the shadows, and we would talk, and then lie down to sleep.

"One afternoon, around three p.m., I was sitting out on the front steps of the house, looking down the long avenue of pecan trees at the changing of the light. It was a Tuesday, I'm almost sure, and we had no company, the last of the weekend guests having gone away, and the guests for the coming weekend not yet arrived.

"I hated the stillness. I saw that image of the gun at my head. What could I do, I thought, to stop thinking of putting that pistol to my head? It was too late to go out fishing in the pirogue, and I didn't want to get all dirty in the swamps anyway, and everything—absolutely every single thing—was done in the house.

"Goblin was nowhere about. Goblin had learned to shy away from me when I got in these dark moods, when his influence to get me to do things was at its lowest. And though he would probably have come had I called him, I didn't want to see him. When I thought of putting the gun to my head, I wondered if one bullet would kill us both.

"No, I didn't want the company of Goblin.

"Then it occurred to me that I had not inflicted myself as Lord of the Manor on the attic; the attic was in fact an undiscovered territory, and I was too old to be forbidden to go up there, and I didn't need to ask anybody. So I went inside and up the stairs.

"Now, at three o'clock there was plenty of light coming in the dormer windows of the attic, and I could see all the wicker furniture—whole sets of it, it seemed to me, with couches, chairs, et cetera—and the various trunks.

"I inspected first a wardrobe trunk that had belonged to Gravier Blackwood and was now standing open with its little hangers and drawers all vacant and clean.

"Then there were suitcases with old clothes in them that did not seem to be all that fascinating, and more trunks, all stamped with the name of Lorraine McQueen. New things. What were they to me? Surely there was something older, something that had belonged perhaps to Manfred's sainted wife, Virginia Lee.

"Then I came upon a big canvas steamer trunk with leather straps to it, so big that the lid came almost to my waist, and I was already six feet tall. The lid was open a little, and the clothes were bulging out of it, the whole smelling strongly of mold, and the label on the top of the trunk read in faded ink 'Rebecca Stanford,' with the address of Blackwood Farm.

" 'Rebecca Stanford,' I said aloud. Who could this be? Very distinctly, I heard a rustling noise behind me, or was it ahead of me? I stopped and listened. It could have been rats, of course, but we really didn't have rats in Blackwood Manor. Then it seemed the rustling was a conversation between a man and a woman and someone arguing . . . *Just doesn't happen.* I heard those words very distinctly, and then the woman's voice . . . *Believe in him, he will do it!*

"She had pasted on the label, I thought. She'd packed her trunk and pasted on the label. She'd been waiting for him to come get her. Miss Rebecca Stanford.

"But where did all these thoughts come from?

"Then the noise came again. It had a rather deliberate sound to it. I felt the hair stand up on my neck. I liked the excitement. I loved it. It was infinitely better than depression and misery, than thoughts of guns and death.

"I thought, *A ghost is going to come.* Voices. No, a rustling. It will be stronger than the apparition of William. It will be stronger than the vaporous ghosts that hover over the cemetery. It's going to come because of this trunk. Maybe it will be Aunt Camille, who has been seen so often on the stairs, coming up to the attic.

" 'Who are you, Rebecca Stanford?' I whispered. Silence. I opened the trunk. A mess of clothing was inside it and mildew had grown all over it, and there were other articles all tumbled with the fabrics—an old silver-backed hairbrush, a silver-edged comb, bottles of perfume in which the contents had dried up and a silver-backed mirror, all splotched and darkened and no good anymore.

"I lifted up some of the mass of clothing so that the items tumbled down into the lower portion of the trunk, and there I unearthed a mass of jewelry—pearls and brooches and cameos—all thrown among the dresses as if no one had cared about them, which was a puzzle to me because I knew when I held them that the pearls were real; and as for the cameos, I lifted them out one by one and saw that they were fine little works, specimens Aunt Queen would like very much, and all of them— all three—had gold frames, and good contrast to them, being made out of dark shell.

"Why were they here, so neglected, so forgotten, I wondered. Who had just heaped them here amid dresses that were molding, and when had such a thing been done?

"The noise came again, a rustling sound, and another soft sound like a footstep that made me pivot and face the attic door.

"There stood Goblin, glaring at me with alarm in his face, and very emphatically he shook his head and mouthed the word No.

" 'But I want to know who she was,' I said to him. He disappeared rather slowly, as though he were weak and frightened, and I felt the air grow cool as it often did after his disappearances, and I wondered why he had been so weak.

"By now, you can guess that I was so used to Goblin that I wasn't all that interested in him anymore. I felt superior to him. At this moment, I didn't think much about him at all.

"I set to work laying out the entire contents of the trunk upon the top of another trunk beside it. It was clear that the contents had just been heaped inside, helter-skelter, and all except the cameos and the pearls was a total loss.

"There were beautiful old mutton-sleeve dresses, dresses that went back surely to the days of long skirts, and there were old rotted lace blouses, two or more with fine shell cameos attached at the throat, and what must have been silk gowns. Some items fell apart in my hands. Cameos, all 'Rebecca at the Well.'

" 'So you loved just that one theme,' I said out loud. 'Were you named for it?'

"I heard the rustling again, and I felt something brush me, soft, as if a cat had brushed my neck. Then nothing. Nothing but the quiet and the dying afternoon around us, and a kind of dread I had to escape.

"There was nothing better than to explore this trunk.

"There were slippers that were dried up now and gnarled as if they were driftwood. An open box of powder had been tossed into the contents, and it still had a bit of sweet fragrance after all this time. A couple of perfume bottles were broken, and there was a small leather book with lots of pages of writing, but all of the writing had almost faded away. It looked like purple cobwebs.

"The mildew had gotten to everything, ruining all this finery and in some places covering the wool garments with a slimy blackness, making them a total loss.

" 'But this is sheer waste,' I said out loud. I gathered up the pearl necklaces, of which there were three, and all of the five cameos, including two I had to take off the old blouses, and I went downstairs with these treasures and sought out Jasmine, who was washing some bell peppers for supper at the kitchen sink.

"I told her what I'd found and laid out the jewelry on the kitchen table.

" 'Well, you shouldn't have gone up there!' she declared. Much to my surprise, she got ferocious. 'You just run wild these days, you know it? Why didn't you ask me before you went up there, Taw-quin Blackwood?' And on and on she ranted in that vein.

"I was too busy looking at the cameos. 'All the same theme,' I said again, ' "Rebecca at the Well," and all so very pretty. Why did they get thrown up there in a trunk with all those things? Don't you think Aunt Queen would want these things?' Of course Aunt Queen had at least ten cameos of 'Rebecca at the Well,' I knew that much, though I didn't know how she had come by the first of them, and if I had known I would have been more engrossed than I already was.

"At supper I told Pops all about it and showed him the loot, but he was no more interested in this than in anything else, and while Jasmine read me the riot act about meddling where I didn't belong, Pops just said in his dead voice:

" 'You can have anything you find up there,' which made Jasmine quiet down at once.

"At bedtime, I gave the pearls to Big Ramona, but she said she didn't feel easy taking them, that there was a story to them and all the things that were in that trunk.

" 'You save them for some day when you get married,' she said. 'And you give those pearls to your new wife. You have them blessed by the priest first. Remember. Don't you give them away unless they're blessed by the priest.'

" 'I've never heard of such a thing,' I told her. 'A pearl necklace blessed by the priest?'

"I begged her to tell me the story—I knew she knew things—but she wouldn't, and she said she didn't remember it real well anyway, which I knew was a fib, and pretty soon she had me saying our evening prayers.

"It was her bright idea that night that we should say an entire Rosary, and we did it, meditating on the Sorrowful Mysteries, and then we made an Act of Contrition as well. All this we offered up for the Poor Souls in Purgatory, and then we said the famous prayer to the Archangel Michael to defend us in battle against the Evil One, and then we went to sleep.

"Next day, I wrote to Aunt Queen about the discovery, and I told her that I had put the cameos with her collection in the parlor showcase, and that the pearls were in her dressing table, if she should want them. I asked if she would please tell me the story that Big Ramona wouldn't tell. Who was Rebecca Stanford? How did her things get in our house?

"I went back up and searched all of the attic. Of course there were wonderful items—old art deco lamps and tables and overstuffed chairs and couches that were rotting, and even a couple of typewriters of the ancient black species that weigh a ton. Other bundles of old clothes appeared mundane and fit for the rag pile, and there was an ancient vacuum cleaner that ought to have been donated to a museum.

"As for the wicker furniture, I had all of it brought down to be restored, pending Pops' approval, which was granted with a silent nod. The Shed Men were happy to have a new project, so that went all right.

"I didn't find anything else that was really interesting. Rebecca Stanford was the mystery of the moment, and when I left the attic for the last time I took the leather-bound book I'd found in her things, and there came again that uneasy and exciting feeling. I saw Goblin in the doorway and again he shook his head.

"That it banished despair, this excited feeling—that's what I liked.

"The following day, Thursday, was another quiet one, an in-between day, and the panic started in on me, and after lunch I went outside to walk the avenue of the pecan trees and feel the crunch of the pea gravel under my feet.

"The light was golden and I hated it because it was already failing, and the dread was coming on me thick.

"When I reached the front steps I sat down with the leather-bound book I'd found in Rebecca Stanford's trunk, and tried to make out the writing inside.

"It didn't take long to decipher the name on the first page, and to my surprise it was Camille Blackwood. As for the rest of the writing, it was pretty near illegible but I could see that it was verse.

"A book of poems by Camille Blackwood! And it was Camille's ghost that was always seen going up the attic stairs! I ran to tell all this to Jasmine, who was having a cigarette on the back steps. And again, there came the tirade.

" 'Tarquin, you leave that stuff alone! You put that book of poems in Miss Queen's room until she comes home!'

" 'Now, listen, Jasmine, what do you think the ghost of Camille has been looking for? And you've seen her ghost same as I have. And why are you telling me to leave this book of poems alone? Don't you see, she lost it, or it got put in the wrong place, and you're acting like this isn't momentous when it is.'

" 'And for who is this momentous!' she fired back. 'For you? Did you see Camille's ghost on the stairs?'

" 'Twice I did and you know it,' I answered.

" 'So how are you going to tell her you found the book, I'd like to know. You going to tell your Guardian Angel when you say your night prayers?'

" 'Not a half-bad idea,' I said. 'You've seen that ghost, you know you have.'

" 'Now you listen to me,' she said, 'I never saw that ghost, I just said I did. I said it for the tourists. I've never seen a ghost in my life.'

" 'I know that's not true,' I declared. 'I think you've even seen Goblin. There are times when you just stare at him, and I know it. You know, Jasmine, you don't fool me one bit.'

" 'You watch your tone with me, boy,' she said, and I knew that there was nothing more to be got from her.

"She just told me again that I was to put the book away. But I had other plans for it. I knew that if I held up each page to a halogen light I could probably make out a little of the poem on it. But it was not enough. I didn't have the patience or the stamina for that kind of detail.

"I put the book upstairs on my desk and went back down to sit on the front steps again, hoping some guest would drive up and something would change in the morbid miserable spell of the late afternoon. The panic was coming on strongly, and I said bitterly, 'Dear God, I would do anything to prevent this! Anything.' And I closed my eyes.

" 'Where are you, Goblin?' I asked, but he didn't answer me any more than God had, and then it seemed to me that the heat of the spring day lifted somewhat and a cooling breeze seemed to come from the swamps. Now, cooling breezes never came from that way, or at least not usually, and I turned to look down there to the far right of the house, to the old cemetery and the hulking cypress trees beyond. The swamp looked as dark and as mysterious as ever, hovering over the cemetery and rising up black and featureless against the sky.

"A woman was coming up the sloping lawn from that direction, a petite woman, walking with big deliberate steps while with her right hand she gathered up the edge of her dark skirts.

" 'Very pretty,' I said out loud. 'I knew you would be.' And then the strangeness of my words struck me, Who was I talking to, and I felt Goblin pulling on my left hand. When I turned to look at him a sort of shock passed through me, and he flickered, shaking his head violently No, and then he was gone. It was like a lightbulb when it burns out.

"To my right, the pretty young woman was still coming on, and I could see her smiling now, and that she wore a lovely old-fashioned out-fit, a high-neck mutton-sleeve lace blouse with a cameo, and a tight-waisted skirt of dark taffeta to the ground. She had high-set breasts and full voluptuous hips, and they swayed as she walked. What a dish she was. Her brown hair was all pulled back from her face, revealing a serene hairline around her temples and forehead, and she had large cheerful dark eyes.

"She finally made it to the level part of the lawn where the house stands, and she gave a little sigh as if the walk all the way up from the edge of the swamp had been hard.

" 'But they didn't bury you down there in that cemetery, did they?' I asked her. We were the best of friends.

" 'No,' she answered in a soft sweet voice as she came on and sat beside me on the steps. She wore a pair of black-and-white cameo ear-rings dangling from her pierced lobes, and they shivered with the subtle motion of her head as she smiled.

" 'And you're as handsome as everybody said,' she told me. 'You're a man already. Why are you so worried?'—so gentle—'You need a pretty girl like me to show you what you can do?'

" 'But who told you I was worried?' I asked her.

"She was just gorgeous, or so it seemed to me, and she wasn't just endowed by nature with an admirable face and large eyes, she had a pertness to her, a freshness, a quick refinement. Surely there was a corset shaping her little waist, and the ruffles of her blouse were stiffly ironed and flawless. Her taffeta skirt was a rich chocolate brown color that glinted in the sunlight, and she had tiny feet in fancy lace-up boots.

" 'I just know you've been worried,' she answered. 'I know lots of things. You might say I know everything that goes on. Things don't really go in a straight line the way living people think. Everything is always happening all the time.' She reached over and clasped my right hand with both of hers, and I felt the shock again, electric, dangerous, and delicious chills ran all over me, and I bent forward and I went to kiss her lips.

"Teasingly, she drew back just a little, and then, with her breast pressed against my arm, she said, 'But let's go inside. I want you to light the lamps.'

"That made perfect sense. I hated the long shadows of the afternoon. Light the lamps. Light the world.

" 'I hate the shadows too,' she said.

"We rose together, though I was faintly dizzy and I didn't want her to know it. We went inside the cool and silence of the house. I could just barely hear the sound of running water in the kitchen. Four p.m. Dinner not for another two hours, and how curious the house looked! What a curious fragrance it had—of leather and crushed flowers, of moth balls and wax.

"The living room was full of different couches and chairs with frames that were somber and black and shiny, real Victorian furniture, I thought, and there stood another antique piano, far older than the one that had been there before. It was a square grand. The draperies were a heavy midnight blue velvet, and the lace panels were full of gracefully drawn peacocks. The windows were open. How pretty, the breeze against the lace peacocks. How perfect, I thought.

"A thrilling ecstasy took hold of me, a certainty of the pure beauty of what I saw and the irrelevance of all else.

"When I looked over at the dining room I realized that it too was altered, that the draperies were a peach silk with gold fringe on them, and that the table was oval, with a vase of flowers in the center. Fresh roses, natural garden roses on short stems, petals lying on the waxed table. Not cold magnificent florist roses. Just roses that could make your hands bleed. Drops of water on the round vase.

" 'Oh, but it's delightful, isn't it?' she said to me. 'I picked that fabric for the draperies myself. I've done so many things. Small things. Big things. I cut those roses from the back garden. I laid out the rose garden. There was no rose garden before I came. You want to see the rose garden?'

"A faint protest voiced itself in my mind that there was no rose garden on Blackwood Farm, that the rose garden was long gone for the swimming pool, but this seemed incomprehensible and unimportant, and to have mentioned such a thing seemed rude.

"I turned to tell her I couldn't hold off of kissing her, and I bent down and closed my mouth over hers. Ah. I never in my dreams felt that. I never tasted that. I never knew that. I felt the heat of her body through her clothes. It was so intense, I almost came. I put my arms around her and lifted her, and I put my knee against her skirts and pushed against her sex, and I put my tongue into her mouth.

"When she drew back, it took all my self-control to let her put her hand firmly on my chest. 'Light the lamps for me, Quinn,' she said. 'You know, the oil lamps. Light them. And then I'll make you the happiest young man there ever was.'

" 'Oh, yes,' I said. I knew right where they were. We always kept oil lamps at Blackwood Manor because, being out in the country like we were, we never knew when the electricity was going to go out, and so I found the oil lamp in the sideboard and I lifted it up and put it on the dining table. I raised the glass shade and lighted the wick with the cigarette lighter I always carried just for such things.

" 'Put it on the window, darling,' she said, 'yes, right there, on the sill, and let's go into the parlor and light the lamp there too.'

"I did what she told me, putting the lamp onto the windowsill. 'But that looks dangerous,' I said, 'with it under the lace panels and so near to the draperies.'

" 'Don't you worry, darling,' she said. She led me briskly across the hallway and into the parlor. I took the lamp out of the high Chinese chest between the two hall doorways. After it was lighted, I put it on the windowsill in the same manner as I had done across the hall. Now, that harp, that harp was the same, the big gold harp, I thought, but everything else was changed.

"This was the strangest dizziness. I didn't dare to think of having her, of her finding out that I didn't know how.

" 'You're my darling,' she said. 'Don't stare at the pretty furniture, it doesn't matter.' But I couldn't help it because only a moment ago—when I'd taken the lamp from the chest—it had been familiar and now it was different again, all those violet satin black-framed chairs, and there came a sudden chorus of voices, of people saying the Rosary!

"Candlelight flickered on the ceiling. Something was wrong, and terribly terribly sad.

"I was off balance. I was about to fall. I turned around. The sound of the voices was an inundation. And the room was full of people—people in black, seated on chairs and couches and in little gold folding chairs—and a man was sobbing.

"Others were crying. Who was the little girl who stared at me?

"There was a coffin lying before the front windows, an open coffin, and the air was heavy with flowers, drenched with flowers, the waxy smell of lilies, and then up out of this coffin there rose a blond-haired woman in a blue dress. In one swift gesture, as if she rode an invisible tide, she had come up out of the coffin and stepped down on the polished floor.

" 'Lynelle,' I cried out. But it wasn't. It was Virginia Lee. How could I not know the lovely little face of Virginia Lee! Our blessed Virginia Lee. The little girl let out a baleful cry, 'Mamma!' How could a woman rise from a coffin?

" 'You leave this house alone!' she cried, and she reached out in a perfect fury at the woman who stood with me, her white hands almost touching her, but the woman at my side drove her back with a great hissing sound, a flash and sputtering, and the figure of Virginia Lee, our blessed sweet Virginia Lee, our household saint, the figure of Virginia Lee, and the coffin, and the bawling child, the mourners—all of it blinkered and went out.

"The chorus of voices died away, as if it were a wave on the beach being sucked back into the ocean. Hail Mary Full of Grace and then nothing. Breeze and the flicker of the oil lamp in the shadows, and that smell of burning oil.

"I was too dizzy to stand. She clung to me.

"The silence crashed around us, and I wanted to say something, I wanted to ask something; I tried to form the thought, Virginia Lee had been here, but I was holding the woman again and kissing her—and I was so hard it was painful, I couldn't keep it back much longer, it was worse than waking from a wet dream—and saying, 'No, I won't let it go on, I can't do that. That's a mortal sin.' But she said,

" 'Quinn, my darling Quinn. Quinn, you are my destiny.' It was so inexpressibly tender. 'Take me to my room.'

"Smoke was rising behind the thick lace. A woman was crying softly, brokenheartedly. The child's sobs came like coughs. But the woman beside me was smiling.

" 'I'm light, I'm little,' she said. 'See my small waist? See how small I am. Carry me up the stairs.'

"Round and round and up and up. You can't fall down from dizziness if you are going up and up. Never in my life had I felt such exultation. Never had I felt so strong.

"We were in a bedroom, and though the configuration of the walls and the archway made it seem that it was my room, it wasn't, it was hers, and we were lying under her lace canopy and the bed was airy and the breeze was coming in from the windows and the lace was moving in the air.

" 'Now, my big boy,' she said as she opened my pants and pushed to get them down and lifted up her skirts. Her skin was hot. 'It's perfect now.' I slid inside of her! First time! The heat, the pressure, the tight sheath. I came in her, I flooded into her, I came, and felt her shivering and pushing her hips up against me, and her sex holding me, and then she was dying back, spent, with a short gasping laugh coming from her lips.

"I lay back. It didn't matter, the smell of smoke, the sight of it. It didn't matter, people rushing. She turned to me, and, rising up on her elbow, she said,

" 'Find what's left of me out there, Quinn. Find the island. Find what they did to me.' How passionate and exquisite she was, how wronged and frail. The cameo earrings shivered beside her delicate face. I touched her ear. I touched the place where the gold pierced it. I touched the handsome black-and-white cameo at her throat.

" 'Rebecca,' I said. Beyond her stood Goblin shaking his head No. Goblin was so vivid, Goblin was using all his power.

" 'Do that for me,' she said. 'Do that and I'll come back to you, Quinn. And it will be sweet, always so sweet. I was a creature born to make others happy. That's what I believe in, Quinn. I've given you your first time, Quinn. Don't ever forget me. To give pleasure. That's all I've ever tried to do.'

"The cameo at her throat, it was so like those in Aunt Queen's collection yet it was different. But all of this made sense. She'd died out there wearing this cameo. *Yes.* I reached out to touch her soft brown hair.

" 'Tawquin, Tawquin, Taw-quin,' Jasmine shouted. She was running up the steps. I could feel it, the vibration of the floorboards.

"I was alone.

"I sat up. My pants were open. The semen was all over my jeans and on the bedspread. I saw to myself immediately, and then, grabbing for a wad of paper tissue from the nightstand, I wiped up the evidence and stood staring at Jasmine as she came into the room.

" 'You crazy boy,' Jasmine cried. 'Why did you put those lamps on the windowsills? Are you stupid? You set the curtains on fire! What was going on in your mind?'

"I flew into action. On fire! Blackwood Manor! Never. But she grabbed my arm as I tried to pass her.

" 'We put it out!' she said. 'Why did you do it?'

"It could have been a disaster.

"As it was, Lolly and Big Ramona, with the help of the Shed Men, replaced the burnt lace panels that afternoon. The heavy draperies were all right. They hadn't caught.

"I was in a state of terror. I sat numb in my room. I hadn't answered a single question. Goblin had come around. Goblin sat in the other chair on the other side of the fireplace and wore a worried look on his face. The computer switched itself on. But I wouldn't go to it. I didn't want him to take my hand. I didn't have answers for him.

"Finally, in pure weariness of his being there and staring at me, I said, 'Why did she come? Where did she come from?'

"He couldn't answer. He was confused.

"I went to the computer and let him take my left hand. He tapped out: 'Rebecca was very bad. Burn down the house. Evil Rebecca.'

"I tapped out: 'Tell me something I don't know, like where did she come from?'

"Long silence. Nothing. I went back to brooding in my chair.

"Over supper, with Pops, Jasmine, Lolly and Big Ramona, I told them all pretty much what had happened. I told them the erotic part of it, that the ghost and I had been intimate. I tried to describe how very 'real' it had all seemed, and how reasonable to light those lamps as Rebecca had wanted, and I told them the things Rebecca said.

"I showed them a cameo that I had found in the attic trunk, one that I'd put in the case in the living room, one that had belonged to Rebecca Stanford, no doubt.

" 'Rebecca at the Well,' don't you see? And she was named Rebecca. Who was she, why did she come?'

"I felt a sudden dizziness. I looked down at the cameo on the kitchen table. It seemed I heard her saying something to me or I was remembering something. I tried to clear my head. I tried to remember. I strained to remember: *Died out there with the cameo on, died out there.* I shivered all over. *So many pretty lace blouses. That's what he had always liked, white lace.*

"I tried to talk clearly. I told them what she said about me finding the island, and the promise that she drew from me, that I would find 'what was left of her' out there.

"Pops looked as grave as ever when he spoke. His voice was listless. 'Don't go looking for that island. You can pretty damn well gauge that by now that island's gone. The swamp's swallowed it, and if you see this damned ghost again, you make the Sign of the Cross.'

" 'That's what you should have done, all right,' said Big Ramona, 'and she wouldn't have had any power because she came from Hell.'

" 'But how could she get out of Hell to come to me?' I asked.

" 'Those cameos of hers,' said Jasmine, 'you go put them back in the attic. Put everything back in that trunk just the way it was.'

" 'It's too late for that,' said Pops softly. 'Just don't let her get you again.'

"We sat there in silence. Then Big Ramona was boiling milk for our café au lait and it smelled good. I remember that, the smell of that hot milk.

"I just realized that Lolly was all dressed up because she was going out with her boyfriend, who was always trying to marry her and lure her away but never succeeded. She looked like a Hindu beauty, Lolly. And Jasmine, Jasmine in her plain shirtwaist dress of red silk was smoking in the kitchen, which was rare.

"The hot milk went into the coffee cups. I looked down into the steam.

" 'Everybody believes me,' I said. 'You all believe me.'

"Pops said to Jasmine, 'Tell him.'

" 'Tell me what?' I asked.

"Jasmine drew on her cigarette and crushed it out in her plate. Then she lit another one, just like that. 'It was Goblin,' she said, 'who came in here and pointed and carried on about the curtains burning. It was Goblin, in a flash'—she snapped her fingers—'as big as life.'

" 'Knocked the plate out of her hand,' said Lolly.

"Jasmine nodded. 'Knocked a plate off the drainboard there, too.'

"I was speechless. I was overwhelmed. All my life these very people had insisted Goblin didn't exist, or I shouldn't be talking to Goblin, or Goblin was my subconscious, or Goblin was just an imaginary playmate, and now they were saying these things. I had no answer. I felt amazement more than anything else.

" 'How could that creature knock that plate off the drainboard?' asked Pops.

" 'I'm telling you, it happened,' said Jasmine. 'I was rinsing the dishes in the sink, and that plate went crash, and then, when I turned, there he was, and he was pointing to the door, and he knocked the plate out of my hand.'"

"Everybody went quiet.

" 'And this is why you believe me?' I asked. 'Because you saw Goblin with your own eyes?'

" 'I'm not saying I believe one word of what you said,' Jasmine fired back. 'I'm just saying I saw Goblin. That's all I have to say.'

" 'You know who that Rebecca was, don't you?' I asked, glancing around at everyone. Nobody said a word.

" 'I'm going to have the priest out here,' said Pops in the same lifeless fashion in which he'd said everything else. 'I'm going to get Fr. Mayfair here. This is just too many ghosts, and I don't care if one of them was Virginia Lee.'

" 'And you, you idiot boy,' said Big Ramona, 'stop glorying in the fact that everybody believes you and get it straight in your head that you nearly burned down this house.'

" 'That's the damned truth,' said Jasmine. 'I'm not saying I don't believe you saw this creature, this thing, this woman, but Mamma's right, you damned near burnt down Blackwood Manor. You set the damned place on fire.'

" 'Look, I know that,' I said defensively. I got real defensive. 'But who was she? Why'd she want to burn down this house? Did she die out there on the island? That has to be it.'

"Pops raised his hand for silence. 'Doesn't matter who she was. If she did die out there, there's nothing left of her. And you do what I tell you about making the Sign of the Cross.'

" 'Don't you ever be caught up by her again,' said Lolly.

"And on and on it went for a half hour, them castigating me and excoriating me and everything else in the book.

"When I left the kitchen, I was in a sort of daze. Memories of being with her were coming back to me and I didn't dare tell the Kitchen Committee. I just wanted out.

"I went into the parlor, maybe to convince myself that it was the parlor I knew and not that strange apparition, and I found myself looking at the portrait of Manfred Blackwood. So distinguished. So much authority in his bulldog face. It is amazing, the varieties of beauty. His huge mournful eyes, his flattened nose, his jutting chin and turned-down mouth all seemed harmonious and silently grand. I found myself talking to him, murmuring to him that he knew who that Rebecca Stanford was, and I would find out.

" 'Why didn't you come to try to stop her?' I asked him, watching the play of light on the portrait. 'Why did it have to be Virginia Lee?'

"I went into the dining room and looked up at the portrait of Virginia Lee. I had seen her, vital, in motion, I had heard her voice, I had seen her small blue eyes blazing with anger and outrage. The dizziness came again. I welcomed it, straining to catch the mumbled voices that were maddeningly beyond my hearing: *Mean to my children.* Crying, brokenhearted. *I'm afraid I'll die and someone will be mean to my children.* The chorus of the Rosary came from the living room. She was crying. *So mean to my poor children.*

" 'Virginia Lee,' I said. 'I didn't mean to do it.' But only the silence came back at me, and her portrait was just a portrait, and there were no more prayers. I was struggling to remember things that hadn't happened. I was sleepy all over. I had to lie down.

"When I reached my room I was utterly exhausted. I cleaned up the bedspread as best I could with a wet washcloth, and then I flopped down and went into a strange half sleep. I felt myself falling out of consciousness.

"Rebecca was talking to me. The room was her room again, and she explained again that things did not happen in a straight line. Everything was happening all the time. She was always here. *I grow no older. I never escape.* I wanted to ask her what she meant, but some arbitrary darkness crept in, and I turned over and fell into a deep sweet state somewhere between sleep and wakefulness, in which my body enjoyed its exhaustion and knew it was exhausted from having spent itself sexually, and she and her strange talk were all gone.

"I was deliciously drowsy when suddenly I realized Pops was in this room. Pops was standing at the foot of the bed.

"Pops started to talk to me in his dull, flat voice:

" 'All your life you've talked of ghosts and spirits, of Goblin, and seeing shades down there in the cemetery, and now this thing has come either into our house or into your imagination, I honestly don't know which. But you have got to fight for your mind. You have got to fight for some direction of your brilliance, you, at the age of eighteen, have got to determine some ambition, and that ambition must never be clouded by these ghosts.'

"I sat up out of respect for him, and he went on.

" 'I'm angry,' he said. 'I'm real angry that you nearly burnt down this house. But I don't know what to make of what happened to you, and as angry as I am I'm convinced that something clouded your reason because you love Blackwood Farm as much as I do.'

"I said at once that this was true.

" 'Well, you get your mind in order, you hear me?' he went on. 'And in the meantime, put this woman's cameos back in her trunk. Close that trunk. Shut it up tight. That trunk is Pandora's Box. You let her spirit out when you opened it, so put everything you took out of it back.'

"He paused for a moment, and then he turned and stared at me with his wan expression and his pale face.

" 'I've given you all I can give you,' he said. 'I don't have anything more to teach you. Lynelle taught things that I could never teach you. She was better than school, I don't argue with it. But you're wasting your time now. You're wasting everything. And I know perfectly well that you won't go to any college right now, and maybe even at age eighteen that's not the right thing. But Aunt Queen has got to come home and she's got to find you a new teacher and she's got to take you on.'

"I nodded. Aunt Queen wasn't terribly far away at this time. She was attending a seminar in Barbados, and I knew that Pops would call her and that she'd be coming home. I hated it, hated that he would interrupt her, but after what had happened she'd definitely be called home.

"Pops stared at me for a long time, and then he went out of my room.

"I felt a dull shock because in all the years I had lived with Pops he had never spoken that many words to me at any one time. Also I had seen that he was weak and washed out, and no longer the hale and hearty individual that he had always been.

"That I had caused him worry upset me something fierce.

"I went down to the parlor and I got the cameos out of the display case which I had taken from the trunk. I brought them up to my room, and I resolved that tomorrow by daylight, I'd go up to the attic and put them back. Maybe. Maybe not. After all, the ghost hadn't said anything to me about opening her trunk.

"Again I fell into a doze, and there was a delightful wicked sense of Rebecca being there. *Just a thing for pleasure, that's all I ever was, Quinn. That's what I'll be to you, Quinn. This is the time, Quinn, just a thing of plea-*

sure, that's all I ever wanted to be. Somebody's jewel, somebody's ornament, somebody's pet, who knows?

"Sometime very late Big Ramona came and roused me and told me to dress for bed. I did what she told me, and when I came out of the bathroom in my long flannel nightshirt, she looked at me and said:

" 'You're too old for me to be sleeping with you.'

" 'That's not true,' I protested at once. 'I don't want that ghost coming back. I don't want that—what happened. If I need that, I'll take care of that somewhere else. I need you to sleep with me,' I said. 'Come on, let's say our prayers.'

"And we did, and we hugged each other close as we slept, and I slept so deep that there seemed no dreams to it, only deep deep rest until the morning light astonished me coming through the windows and spilling into the room.

"It was early, hours before my usual lazy adolescent time, but I got up quietly, taking great pains not to wake Big Ramona, and I dressed in my jeans and boots and got my heavy garden gloves and my rifle and my hunting knife, and, stopping silently in the kitchen to get a big knife— the very knife that Patsy had waved at Pops—I stole out of the house down towards the landing and the pirogue tied there.

"The little cemetery was bleak in the sunshine and overgrown with weeds, and somewhere in the back of my distracted mind I knew that Pops in the natural course of things would never have let it get that way, and that he was not himself anymore; that grief was bringing real harm to Pops, and I had to do something about those weeds. I had to clean up the tombs. I had to take care of more things. I had to take care of Pops too.

"I also knew that Goblin was near me but not showing himself, and I knew that Goblin was afraid.

"I didn't care about Goblin, and I thought perhaps that Goblin knew that too.

"As I look back on it now, I know that he knew it. He knew that once he had been the central mystery of my life and that he was that no longer—Rebecca had taken his place—and he was hanging back, weakened by my indifference and full of a panic which perhaps he had learned to feel from me.

"My heart was set on finding Sugar Devil Island, and so, with the pole in hand I pushed away from the bank and set out into the swamp."

11

"Now, I had been in the swamp plenty as a youngster. I knew how to fire the rifle. I knew how to fish. And Pops and I had ranged quite far from the banks of the farm. But there was a territory to which we adhered, and it had always seemed spacious enough for us because we caught lots of fish in it, and the swamp itself seemed so unvarying in its morass of cypress, tupelo gum and wild oak, its giant palmetto and endless snags of vine.

"But now, it was my single object to push beyond this territory and, in choosing a direction, I was guided only by my memory of the tree which had the arrow deeply carved into the bark, above its girdle of rusted chain.

"It took me longer to find than I would have liked, and the air was humid and heavy, but the water was at a good level for the pirogue, and so, taking out my compass, I did my best to chart a course in the direction to which the arrow pointed.

"If Pops and I had ever been this far, I wasn't conscious of it. What I was conscious of was that I could get dangerously lost. But I didn't care much about it. I was too sure of my mission, and when I began to experience feelings of dizziness I just pushed on.

"Again I heard voices speaking, just as if these whispers pushed at me and prodded me and broke my sense of balance, and once again a woman was crying, only it wasn't Virginia Lee.

"*You can't do this to me*, the woman sobbed. *You can't do it!* And there came a rolling rumble of deeper voices—*Engraved forever!* said the woman, and then I lost the thread of it.

"I could hear it but not understand it. It was submerged in a tangle of dreams and half impressions. I was desperate to follow, to remember, but I had to keep my balance in the pirogue, I had to not drop the pole.

"The pole could fall into the slimy water and I'd have to go after it. Now, I'd been up to my waist in swamp water before and I didn't like it one bit. The green light of the sun was flashing in my eyes.

"I thought I had caught more words, but then the memory was gone from me and nothing else came clear. I heard the birds crying, those strange seemingly isolated melancholy cries.

"Meanwhile the pirogue glided through the duckweed, and I was steering it steadily past the jungles of cypress knees, and I became aware of a huge tangle of blossoming wisteria to my right. The flowers were so vividly purple, so lusciously purple that I heard myself laugh out loud at them.

"The dizziness came again, and there was a luxury to it, a sweetness, like being slightly high on champagne. The light was dappled and the wisteria was so pure. I could hear the voices. I knew one of them belonged to Rebecca, and that Rebecca was in pain.

"*. . . they'll catch you, they'll find you out . . .* That fragment I caught like one trying to catch a falling leaf. And then a laughter came over her voice, drowning it out, and no more words were clear.

"Suddenly, there rose up on my right a giant cypress, surely one of the oldest I'd ever seen, and there was the girdle of iron chain, as fiercely rusted as before, and the arrow, deeply etched, instructing me to veer to the left. Now that was surely new territory, in the opposite direction from Blackwood Farm. And when I checked my compass I learned I was correct.

"The pirogue was traveling very easy now, and my pole was going down deep. I dreaded more than ever falling into the water, and on I sped, when another mass of gloriously blooming wisteria appeared.

"You understand how wild that vine is, I know you do, and how beautiful it can be. And now the sun was pouring down on it, in shafts, as it might through a cathedral window, and it was spreading out in all directions, except that there seemed a channel into which I'd found my way.

"On and on I went until the configuration of rusted chain and carved arrow appeared again. This time it was only to tell me to go on in the same direction, and I followed it, knowing that I was very far from Blackwood Farm, maybe an hour from any kind of help, and that is a lot in the swamp.

"I glanced at my watch and discovered that I was wrong by thirty minutes. I'd been gone an hour and a half. The excitement I'd felt on waking grew stronger inside me. And when another cypress appeared with its ancient chain and its jagged arrow I veered slightly to the left again, only to come upon another girded tree whose arrow told me to veer right.

"I was drifting along, in even deeper water, when, gazing upwards, I realized I was looking at a house.

"At that moment the pirogue struck a bank. I was jolted nearly out of it. I had to get my bearings. Wild blackberries swarmed over the front of the boat and reached out to scratch me, but with the kitchen knife I slashed at them and then pushed them back with my gloved hands.

"It wasn't an impossible situation. And in the meantime I could see that my first visual impression had been an accurate one. There was a big house looming up in front of me, a house of natural weathered cypress built on pilings, and it occurred to me that I had gone off our land and might have come to someone else's home.

"Well, I'd approach with respect, I figured, and, when I had cut through more of the wild blackberries and pulled the pirogue up onto the bank, I turned around to find myself in a forest of slapping palmetto and sickly blue-gum saplings rising up like the ghosts of trees beneath the desperate vicious arms of giant cypress trees on both sides of me and further on.

"I stopped, felt the dizziness again, and then I heard the humming of bees. I wiped at my face but my gloves were dirty and I probably got my face dirty, and though I had a linen handkerchief in my pocket, along with lots of paper tissue, it was no time for that.

"I walked on, making sure the land was solid, and realized I was climbing upwards onto a mound. At last a clearing broke in front of me, a very large clearing surrounded by immense cypress—in fact, it seemed then that the cypress had anchored the clearing and made an island out of it by their knees and their hateful sprawling roots.

"And in the midst of this clearing rose the house, some six to eight feet above ground atop its log foundations, a seemingly circular structure of two stories, each of connecting arches and in a rising succession of smaller sizes, like the two layers of a wedding cake. Adding to this impression was a cupola on the very top.

"A solid wooden stairs rose from the earth to the front doorway, and affixed above this front door was a rectangular sign with deeply etched and plainly readable letters:

PROPERTY OF
MANFRED BLACKWOOD
KEEP OUT

"If I'd ever felt as much triumph before, I didn't remember it. This was my house, this was my island; I had discovered what was only legend to other people, and it was all mine. I'd reclaimed Manfred's tale. I'd seen what William never saw, what Gravier never saw, what Pops never saw. I was here.

"In a heated delirium I surveyed the building, almost incapable of any true reasoning and not even remembering Rebecca's plea to me, or the deep simmering pain which I had just heard inside my head.

"The droning of the bees, the rattle and flapping of the giant palmetto leaves, the soft crush of gravel under my feet—all these things sort of embraced me and upheld me and seemed to wrap me in an incalculable fascination, as though I'd come into the paradise of another man's faith.

"I was also dimly aware, unwillingly aware, that though the ancient trees might have created this clearing, the clearing itself could not have remained free in any natural way. The swamp should have swallowed it up a long time ago. As it was the blackberries were eating at it, and the wicked, high-toned wisteria had a claim on it, sprawling out to shroud the undergrowth to the right of the house and to the back of it, coming up over the high two-story roof.

"But somebody was living here. Probably. But then maybe not. At the idea of squatters or trespassers I was incensed. I regretted that I hadn't brought a handgun. Should have. And might whenever I came back. It all depended upon what I discovered in the house.

"Meantime I had spied another structure, something seemingly solid and massive, well behind the house. The wisteria covered half of it. The sun was striking off the surface of the rest of it, positively sparkling on it and making a dazzle through the spindly trunks of the newborn trees.

"It was to this structure that I went first, very reluctantly passing by the inviting front steps of the house but determined to discover what this massive shape was.

"I could only explain it to myself as some sort of tomb. It stood as tall as me, was rectangular in shape and appeared to be made of granite, except for panels set into it front and rear and each side, which were made out of a metal which appeared to be gold.

"I yanked off the nest of wisteria as best I could.

"There were figures carved into this metal, Grecian figures who seemed to be engaged in a funeral procession, and the procession appeared continuous from panel to panel, enclosing the structure to which there was no back or front or door.

"I must have circled it some ten times, running my hands over the figures, touching the finely carved profiles and folds of garments, and realizing very slowly that the figures were more Roman than Greek. I made this judgment because the human beings were not idealized as the Greeks would have made them but were in fact slender and particular people of several groups. At one point it occurred to me that this was of pre-Raphaelite design, but I wasn't sure of myself on that score.

"Let me say simply, the figures were classical, and the procession was unending, and though some of the figures appeared to be weeping and others tearing their hair, there was no corpse or bier.

"After I'd surveyed it carefully I began to try to open the thing. But it was no luck. The gold panels—and by now I was convinced that they were gold—seemed firmly fixed into the granite pillars that marked the four corners of the structure, and the granite roof, peaked like those of so many New Orleans tombs, was very securely in place.

"To make certain that the substance of the panels was gold I chose a place on one of the panels very near the granite, and with the edge of my hunting knife I scratched there and discovered that not only did no base metal show through but that the gold itself was soft. Yes, it was gold. It was lots and lots of gold.

"I was totally baffled by this thing. It was august, it was beautiful, it was quite literally monumental. But to whom had this monument been made? Surely this wasn't Rebecca's tomb!

"Of course Mad Manfred had to be responsible for this thing. It befitted his Byronic image of the builder of Blackwood Manor, his fancy, his munificent dreams. Nobody else would come out here and make a gold tomb. Yet how could it be Mad Manfred's mausoleum? How could his interment have been achieved?

"My brain was crazy with questions.

"Mad Manfred had been past eighty when he made his Last Will and Testament. I had seen the dated document. And at the time of his wild escape from the sickroom to the landing he had been eighty-four.

"Who or what had awaited him on this island? And, of course, this tomb, if that is what it was, had no name or date or any writing on it. How utterly bizarre that one should make a mausoleum of solid gold and then leave it unmarked.

"I decided to take my time before going up into the house. I walked around the island. It wasn't very big. But over half of its banks were thoroughly blocked by the largest cypress trees I had ever seen. Choked in between where they could get the light were the wild tupelo gum and the black gum, making an impassable barrier, and then to the right of where I'd come ashore a mass of water oak and ironwood and the wisteria which I've already described.

"In fact, it was pretty evident that there was only a small place to come ashore, and I had done it properly by dint of sheer luck. Unless some other agency was involved.

"It was very still, except for the bees and a general pulsing drone that seemed to rise from the swamp itself.

" 'Goblin,' I called, but he didn't answer me, and then I felt him brush past me, soft as a cat against my neck, and I heard his voice in my mind:

"*Bad, Quinn. Go home. They worry about you at home.*

"The truth of that seemed very certain, but I had no intention of responding.

" 'What is this place, Goblin? Why did you say it was bad?' I asked. But he gave me no answer, and then, after a pause, he told me again to go home. He said, *Aunt Queen has come home.*

"I was powerfully intrigued by that statement. Goblin had never told me the whereabouts of others. But I was by no means ready to go back!

"I sat down on the stairs. It was solid, which was no surprise to me since it was built of cypress; the whole house was built of cypress, and cypress never rots.

" 'Rebecca,' I asked aloud, 'are you here?' There came that dizziness again, and, whereas I had been just a little afraid of it in the pirogue, I let myself slip deeper into it now, closing my eyes and lying back and looking up at the broken leafy light.

"There rose a wave of conversing voices, whispers, curses, a woman crying again, Rebecca crying, *Can't torture me like this,* and then a man muttering and saying, *Damnable,* and someone laughing. *What did you expect of me!* asked a voice. But the surging, driving conversation broke with no further clarification and washed away from me, leaving me almost sick.

"I felt a hatred for the voice that had spoken, the voice which had asked, 'What did you expect of me!' and it seemed a logical hate.

"I stood up and took a deep breath. I was sick. The damned heat had made me sick. I was also getting bitten by mosquitoes, and that was making me feel sick as well.

"I'd been too softened by staying indoors on hot days like this.

"I waited until my head cleared, and then I went up the stairs and through the open doorway, the door itself having been pushed aside.

" 'Fearless squatters,' I thought, and, as I noted that the door contained a big rectangle of leaded glass, glass that was clean, I was outraged. But I also had the strong sense that no one else was in this house.

"As for the room before me, it was perfectly circular and its unbroken surround of arched windows appeared to be bare of any covering at all. A stairway to the far left led to the floor above, and to the far right was a big heavily rusted iron fireplace, rectangular in shape with a rising chimney pipe and open folding iron doors. It was chock-full of half-burnt wood and ashes. The ashes were spilt out on the floor.

In the center of the room was the most surprising thing: a great marble desk upon an iron frame and a Roman-style chair of leather and gold. The style I mean here is what people today call a director's chair. But it's a style as old as Rome.

"Of course I went immediately to this configuration of marvelous furniture, and I discovered modern pens in a heavy gold cylinder, a nest of tall thick candles all melted together on a gold plate and a casual heap of paperback books.

"I fanned out the books and perused their covers. They ranged from what we so arrogantly call popular fiction to books on anthropology, sociology and modern philosophy. Camus, Sartre, de Sade, Kafka. There was a world atlas and a dictionary and several picture dictionaries for children, and also a pocket-size history of ancient Sumer.

"I checked the copyright dates in a few of these books. And I also glanced at the prices. This was all recent, though most were now swollen and soft from the humidity of the swamp.

"The wicks of the candles were black and the pool of wax that surrounded them on the gold plate argued that they had been burnt down quite a ways.

"I was shocked and intrigued. I had a squatter who came here to read. I had a squatter who warmed himself at a fireplace. And the gold chair, how handsome it was, with its soft brown leather seat and back, and its crossed legs, and its ornately carved arms. One little test with my knife assured me that its simple frame was genuine gold. Same with the plate and cylinder which held the pens.

" 'Same as the mausoleum outside,' I whispered. (I always talk out loud to myself when I'm confused.) 'I have a squatter who likes gold.'

"And then there was the dark multicolored marble of the desk, and the simple iron frame that bore the marble's weight.

"A squatter with taste, and intellectual interests! But how did he or she get here, and what had this to do with the attacks of dizziness I had felt as I proceeded? What had this to do with anything but trespassing, as far as I knew?

"I gazed about me at the open windows. I saw the stains of rain on the floor. I saw the flickering greenery. I felt faint again and batted at a mosquito that was trying to drive me mad.

" 'Just because this character has taste doesn't mean he's not upstairs waiting to kill you,' I reminded myself.

"Then, going to the interior stairs, I called out:

" 'Hello the house!'

"There was no sound above. I was convinced the place was deserted. If the mysterious reader had been here the books would not have been so swollen.

"Nevertheless, I called out again, 'Hello, Tarquin Blackwood here,' and I went up slowly, listening for any sound from above.

"The second floor was much smaller and tighter than the first, but it was made of the same firm planks, and light came in not only from the barren arched windows but through the cupola above.

"But those details I scarcely noticed. Because this room was markedly different from the one below it in that it contained a loathsome and hideous sight.

"This was a set of rusted chains attached to the wall opposite the chimney, chains which obviously had no other purpose than the chaining of a human being. There were handcuffs and ankle cuffs on these chains, and beneath these idle witnesses to some abomination there was a thick dark syrupy-looking substance and the remnants of a human skull.

"I was disgusted beyond imagining. I was almost violently sick. I steadied myself. I stared at the black residue, this seeming tar, and at the skull, and then I made out what seemed like the disintegrating whitish powder of other bones. There was also the evidence of rotting cloth in the morass, and something glinting brightly though it was caught in the dark viscid tar.

"I felt a cold stubborn rage. Something unspeakable had happened here. And the perpetrator was not on the premises, and hadn't been for several months, but might at any moment return.

"I approached this tarlike substance. I knelt down beside it and I picked out the glinting fragment and discovered it with no surprise to be one of the earrings which Rebecca had worn when she came to me. Within seconds my trembling fingers had found the mate. And there, in the nauseating substance, was the cameo Rebecca had worn at her throat. I collected this too.

"I was paralyzed with excitement, but that didn't keep me from seeing that a fifth chain, a chain quite separate from those which must have once bound wrists and ankles, also dangled from the wall, and at the end of it was a hook. This hook was caught in the dark filth, and the dark filth contained fragments of fabric and fragments of hair.

"It was this fifth chain that horrified me more than anything else.

"Chills ran over me. My head was swimming and I suffered a loss of balance, and a sense again of Rebecca speaking to me, Rebecca whispering to me, Rebecca crying; and then her voice rose, distinct in the buzzing silence of the house: *You can't do it, you can't!*

" 'Not Rebecca,' I whispered. But I knew that she had died here, I knew that for a century her bones had moldered here, I knew that even now, before my eyes, the tiny creatures of the swamp were eating at what was left of her—I could see them at work in the ugly residue—and soon there would be nothing at all.

"She had sent me here. I had a right to touch the skull, and as I did so it disintegrated before my eyes. It was no more now than a heap of white powder along with all the other bones. I should never have touched it! But it was too late.

"Quite suddenly I flew into action. I stood up. I secured the earrings and the brooch in my pocket. I pulled out my hunting knife—the kitchen knife was in the pirogue—and I spun round to face the stairs. No one had come, that was obvious, but at any moment someone might.

"And who were they, or who was he, I should say, who could sit at a desk and read by the light of candles when such a horror existed on the floor above?

"This had been a house of torture, this place, and surely it had been my great-great-great-grandfather Manfred who brought his victims here, I reasoned, and here it was that Rebecca had met her end.

"Who was it now who knew these things and did nothing about them? Who was it who had brought a fine marble desk here and a golden chair? Who was it that was buried in that doorless mausoleum? The whole pattern was overwhelming to me. I was shaking with sheer exhilaration. But I had to determine certain things.

"I went to the windows and was amazed to discover how well I could see over the swamp. And there, way far away, I saw Blackwood Manor very distinctly on its raised lawn.

"Whoever lived in this place, whoever visited it, could spy upon the house if he wanted to; he could see—among other things—my very windows and the windows of the kitchen as well. If he had a telescope or binoculars, and I saw neither one here, he could have studied us all very well.

"It was chilling to see this clear view of the house, but I used it to check my compass. I had to get home and fast.

"The voices threatened again. The dizziness came over me. I reeled. The wild cries of the birds seemed to mingle with Rebecca's voice. I was near to fainting. But I had to resist this.

"I went down the steps, through the big room and down onto the island and explored every inch of it that I could reach. Yes, the cypress trees had created it and anchored it, and from the west and the north they were so thick that the island itself must have been invisible. Only the eastern bank, where I had come ashore, was the way of access.

"Regarding the strange structure of granite and gold, I couldn't discover anything more about it, except that when I cut back the wisteria the graven figures were as beautiful there as anywhere else. The worth of the gold must have been staggering, I reasoned, but no one had ever stolen it; no one—it seemed—had ever tried.

"But I was so hot now, so coated in sweat, so bitten up by the mosquitoes and harassed by the lonesome cries of the birds and the way that they mingled with the half-heard voices that I had to get out of here. I had to get safe.

"I jumped into the pirogue, caught up the pole, pushed off the bank and headed for home."

1 2

"JASMINE WAS WAITING for me at the landing, in a perfect fit over the fact that I hadn't told anyone where I was going, and she was losing her mind with worry; and even Patsy was here and Patsy was worrying because Patsy had had a dream that I was in danger and she had driven in from New Orleans just to see if I was all right.

" 'Aunt Queen's here, isn't she?' I asked impatiently as I made my way to the kitchen with her. 'And as for Patsy coming in from New Orleans, it's probably because she needs money, and we'll be in for a big argument tonight. But I don't have time for this. I have to tell you what I found out there. We have to call the sheriff right away.'

" 'The sheriff? For what!' Jasmine demanded. 'And yes, your Aunt Queen is here. She arrived about an hour ago, and nobody could find you, and the pirogue was gone,' and so forth and so on for a straight three minutes.

"No sooner had she stopped her harangue than Aunt Queen appeared, and she threw her arms around me, dirty though I was from the swamp. She was her usual elegant self, right to the perfect curls of her white hair and her soft green silk dress. With Aunt Queen, it's silk or silk, that's about the extent of it, and I can't think of embracing her without thinking of silk.

"Patsy also came into the kitchen and sat down opposite me as I settled at the table, with Aunt Queen taking the chair to the right of me and Jasmine putting a beer down in front of me and then sitting to my left.

"I pulled off my dirty garden gloves and drank half the beer in one swallow, and Jasmine shook her head but got up to get me another.

" 'What is this about the sheriff?' Aunt Queen asked. 'Why do you want the sheriff?'

"I laid out the earrings and the brooch, and I told them all about everything I had seen. I told them about the skull just disintegrating, but that I knew the sheriff could get the DNA from the white powder left of it to prove it was Rebecca's, and that for a DNA match there was hair in the brush that Rebecca had used, upstairs in the trunk that bore her name. There was hair in her comb too.

"Aunt Queen looked at Jasmine and Jasmine shook her head.

" 'You think the sheriff of Ruby River Parish is going to run DNA tests on a pile of white powder!' Jasmine declared. 'You're going to tell this cockamamy story to the sheriff of Ruby River Parish? You, Tarquin Blackwood, dedicated buddy of Goblin, your spirit duplicate? You're going to call the sheriff? I don't want to be in this kitchen when that conversation takes place.'

" 'Listen to me,' I insisted. 'This woman was murdered. There's no statute of limitations on murder, and—'

"When Aunt Queen spoke, she was very soft and reasonable-sounding. 'Quinn, my darling, I don't think the sheriff will believe this story. And I don't think he will send anyone into the thick of the swamp.'

" 'All right,' I said, 'I see. No one cares about this. No one believes it.'

" 'It isn't that I don't believe it,' said Aunt Queen, 'it's that I don't think the outside world will believe it.'

" 'Yeah, that's it,' chimed in Patsy. 'The outside world is going to think you're a crackpot, Tarquin, if they don't already from all these years of your talking about that damned spook. Tarquin, the more you carry on about this, the crazier everybody thinks you are.'

"At some point while all this was going on—my valiant struggle to get them to believe and investigate and their pleading with me not to make a fool of myself—Pops walked in and I reiterated the whole story for him.

"He sat at the corner of the table listening with his dull eyes, and then said under his breath that he'd go back there to this island with me if I wanted, and when I said I did want this, that it was exactly what I wanted, he seemed surprised.

"All the while, Goblin stood over by the sink listening to this conversation and looking from one to another of the crowd at the table as this or that one spoke. Then he came over and started pulling on my right shoulder.

"I said, 'Goblin, get away, I've got no time for you now.' And with a profound will I pushed at him mentally, and to my amazement he was gone.

"Then Patsy imitated my voice and what I'd just said, making fun of me, and gave a low sneering laugh. 'Goblin, get away,' she repeated, 'and now you're telling us there's a marble table out there and a gold chair.'

"I fired back at her that those details were of the least importance and then I positively demanded to see the sheriff and tell him what I had seen.

"Pops said No, not until he'd gone out there with me, and that if this woman had been rotting for over a hundred years a day or two wouldn't matter now.

" 'But somebody's living there, Pops,' I said. 'Somebody who must know these chains are up there and must have seen the skull! We have a dangerous situation here.'

"Patsy snickered. 'It's a damned good thing that you believe yourself, Quinn, because nobody else does. You've been crazy since you were born.'

"Aunt Queen did not look at her. It struck me for the first time in my life that Aunt Queen didn't like Patsy any more than Pops did.

" 'So what was your dream, Patsy?' I asked, trying not to bristle at her insults. 'Jasmine told me you came home today because you had a dream.'

" 'Oh, it can't compare to your story,' she said ironically and coldly, her blue eyes hard as glass. 'I just woke up all scared for you. There was somebody who was going to hurt you, and Blackwood Manor was burning, and this group of people—they had you and they were going to hurt you, and Virginia Lee was in the dream and she told me, "Patsy, get him away." She was real clear, she was sitting with her embroidery, and you know all the embroidery we still have that she did, and there she was in the dream, embroidering, and she put it aside and told me what I just said. It's all fading now. But Blackwood Manor was on fire. I woke up scared.'

"I looked at Pops and Jasmine. They hadn't told her anything about Rebecca or the oil-lamp scare, I knew by their faces. I looked up at Goblin, who was standing in the corner to my far left, and Goblin was looking at Patsy, and he seemed thoughtful if not a little scared himself.

"At this point, Aunt Queen called for the end of the Kitchen Committee Confab. We did have guests coming in, supper had to be prepared, Lolly and Big Ramona were waiting for us to clear out, and Aunt Queen wanted to talk to me later in her room. We'd eat supper in there, just the two of us.

"Nobody was calling the sheriff until Pops had gone to the island with me. And Pops said he wasn't feeling very good, he had to go lie down. The heat was bad and he'd been working on the flower patches in the full sun; he didn't feel good at all.

"I insisted on placing the earrings and brooch in a plastic bag so that any residue of tissue clinging to them could be analyzed, and then I went up to my room to shower, realizing I was starving to death.

"It was maybe six o'clock when I sat down to supper with Aunt Queen. Her room had just been redone in golden yellow taffeta, and we were at the small round table against the back windows of the house at which she frequently took her meals.

"We devoured one of her favorite dishes—scrambled eggs with caviar and sour cream, along with her favorite champagne.

"She was wearing silver spike heels and a loose-fitting silk-and-lace dress. She had a cameo at her throat, centered perfectly on her collar—Jasmine must have helped her—and we had the earrings and the cameo brooch from the island with us.

"The brooch was 'Rebecca at the Well,' the earrings were tiny heads, as is usually the case with small cameos.

"I began by telling her all about Rebecca's trunk in the attic, and then Rebecca's ghost and what had happened, and then I went over again everything that was on the island and how perfectly strange it was out there, and that there was clear evidence of murder on the second floor of the house.

" 'All right,' she said. 'You've heard many a story of Manfred, and you know now that after Virginia Lee died and left him a widower he was considered a madman in these parts.'

"I nodded for her to go on. I also took note that Goblin was right behind her, some distance from her, just watching me with a kind of abstracted expression on his face. He was also leaning against the wall kind of casually, and something about that struck a bad note with me—that he would present such an image of comfort, but my mind was really not on Goblin but on Rebecca and Aunt Queen.

"Aunt Queen went on with her tale.

" 'But what you don't know,' she said, 'is that Manfred brought women here to Blackwood Manor, always claiming they were governesses for William and Camille, when in fact they were nothing more than playthings for him—starry-eyed Irish girls he got from Storyville, the red-light district in New Orleans—whom he kept for as long as it suited his purposes, and then from the picture they were abruptly erased.'

" 'God, you're telling me he killed more than one of them?' I asked.

" 'I don't know that he did any such thing,' said Aunt Queen. She went on. 'It's your story about this island that has put it in my mind that perhaps he did murder them. But no one knew what became of them, and it was an easy thing to get rid of a poor Irish girl in those days. You simply dropped her down in the middle of New Orleans. What more need be done?'

" 'But Rebecca, did you hear tell of Rebecca?'

" 'Yes, indeed, I did,' said Aunt Queen. 'You know I did. I heard plenty tell of her. And I'm telling you now. Now let me go on in my fashion. Some of these Irish girls were kind to little William and Camille, but in the main they didn't bother with them one way or another, and so they don't come down to us with any names or faces, or even mysterious trunks in the attic, though that would have been a significant clue.'

" 'No, there were no other suspicious trunks in the attic,' I interjected. 'But there are clothes, heaps of old clothes, clothes museums would pay for, I think. But only Rebecca's trunk.'

" 'Slow down and let me talk,' Aunt Queen said with a little graceful exasperation. 'Quinn, you're overexcited and it's a marvelous thing to see,' she said, smiling, 'but let me talk.'

"And talk she did.

" 'Now, while all of that was going on,' she said, 'Manfred was up to his famous tricks of riding his black gelding over the land, and disappearing into the swamp for weeks at a time.

" 'Then came Rebecca. Now Rebecca was not only more beautiful than the other women, she was also very refined and passed herself off for a lady with a gracious manner, which won everyone over to her side.

" 'But one night when Manfred was off in the swamps she got to cursing Manfred for his absence, and in the kitchen she got drunk on brandy with Ora Lee—that was Jasmine's great-great-grandmother—and she told Ora Lee her story, of how she, Rebecca, had been born in the Irish Channel in New Orleans and was as "common as dirt," as she put it, in a world "as narrow as the gutter," she declared, one of thirteen children, and how she had gotten raped in a Garden District mansion where she'd been working as a maid, and the whole Irish neighborhood knew about it, and when her family wanted her to go into the convent on account of it she went downtown to Storyville, instead, and they took her into a house of prostitution as she had hoped. Now, Rebecca was pregnant from the rape, but whether she lost the child or got rid of it, this part was unclear.

" 'To Ora Lee, she said flat out that being in an elegant and fine house in Storyville, with the piano always playing and the gentlemen being so gracious, was far superior to being at home in a miserable shot-gun house at St. Thomas and Washington by the river where her Irish father and her German grandmother used to beat her and her brothers and sisters with a strap.

" 'But Rebecca did not want to end her upward climb in Storyville, so she started to put on the airs of a lady and use what she knew of man-ners to make herself more refined. She also loved to do embroidery and crocheting, which had been beaten into her at home, and used her sewing abilities to make herself fine clothes.

" 'Wait a minute,' I interrupted her. 'Didn't Patsy say something about the embroidery in her dream, that Virginia Lee was embroi-dering? That's important. And you should see the embroidered things upstairs in that trunk. Yes, she knew embroidery, Rebecca—they're con-fused in Patsy's dream, but you know about the oil lamps and what I almost did.'

" 'I do know, of course I know,' said Aunt Queen. 'Why do you think I came home? But you need knowledge to arm you against this cozy lovemaking ghost. So listen to what the story was.

" 'The other prostitutes in the house in Storyville laughed at Rebecca, and they called her the Countess, but she knew that sooner or later a man would come who would see her attributes and take her out of that place. She sat right in the room where the women congregated for the man to make his choice, and she embroidered as if she was a great lady, and gave each gentleman her lovely smile.

" 'Well, Manfred Blackwood was the man of her dreams, and the tale came down in Jasmine's family that he had actually and truly loved Rebecca much in the same way that he had loved Virginia Lee. Indeed it was Rebecca, petite Rebecca with her brilliant smile and charming ways that finally took his mind off the grief.

" 'He was obsessed with giving her jewelry, and she loved it, and she was gracious and sweet to him and even sang old songs to him, which she had learned growing up.

" 'Of course, in her first weeks here she was all honey and spice to lit-tle William and Camille, but they didn't fall for it, or so the story says, just waiting for her to disappear like all the rest.

" 'Then Manfred and Rebecca went to Europe for a year, the two of them, and it was rumored they spent a very long time in Naples, because Rebecca loved it so, and they even had a villa for a while on the famous Amalfi coast. If you saw that coast, and you will someday, Quinn, you'll understand that it is one of the most beautiful places on earth.

" 'Imagine it, this poor girl from the Irish Channel in the dreamland of southern Italy, and think what it meant. It was there that Rebecca cultivated a love of cameos, apparently, as she had quite a collection when she returned, and it was then that she showed them off to Ora Lee and Jerome and their niece, Pepper, explaining all about "Rebecca at the Well," the theme that was named for her, she exclaimed—poor creature. And ever after that she wore a cameo at her neck and earrings such as those you've found out there.

" 'Now, speaking of out there—right after their return from Naples Manfred took to spending more time in the swamps than ever before. And within months there came all the workmen from New Orleans and the deliveries of lumber and metal and all manner of things to make the notorious Hermitage on Sugar Devil Island—this place you've now seen with your own eyes.

" 'But as you know, Manfred paid off the hirelings when the secret place was completed, and he took to spending weeks out there, leaving Rebecca at home to fret and cry and pace the floor while my poor father—William—watched the woman change from pretty girl to banshee, as he put it to me later on.

" 'Meanwhile, it had become the scandal of the parish that Manfred kept Rebecca in his own bedroom—and that was your room, Quinn, the room with the front parlor to it; it became your room as soon as you were born. Pops, as you know, wants the back room upstairs so he can see out the back windows and keep an eye on the shed and the garages and the men and the cars and all that. So you inherited that front room.

" 'But I digress, and it will probably happen more than once. Now, let me see. We left Rebecca, with a cameo at her neck, in her fancy clothes, pacing the floor up there crying and murmuring for Manfred, who was gone for as long, sometimes, as two weeks.

" 'And, happy with his new retreat, he often took expensive provisions with him, while at other times he said he would hunt for what he ate.

" 'Now, it couldn't have been a worse time for her to do it, but Rebecca wanted Manfred to marry her—make her an honest woman as they used to say in those days, you know—and she told everyone that he would. She even got the priest up here to accost him on one of his rare visits home and talk to him about it, how he ought to do it, and how Rebecca was a proper wife for Manfred no matter what her past.

" 'But you know, Quinn, in those days, what man was going to marry a prostitute from Storyville with whom he'd been living for over two years? Bringing the priest proved a terrible mistake, as Manfred was ashamed and annoyed. And the rumor spread that Manfred beat Rebecca for doing it, and Ora Lee had to interfere to make him stop.

" 'Somehow or other they made it up, and Manfred went back out into the swamp. Thereafter, when he came back from these forays into the depths of the bog he often had gifts not only for Rebecca, to whom he gave lovely cameos, but gifts of pearls and diamonds for Camille, and even fine stickpins and cuff links with diamonds for William to wear.'

" 'So he was meeting someone out there in the swamp,' I said. 'He had to be. How else could he come back with gifts?'

" 'Precisely, he was meeting someone. And his absences from the house grew longer and longer, and his conduct at home reclusive and peculiar, and when he was gone, William (my father) and Camille suffered downright meanness and heavy abuse from Rebecca, who grew to hate them for what they were—part of a family to which she did not legally belong.

" 'Imagine it, the poor children, now adolescents, at the pure mercy of this young stepmother, all left alone in this house with only the colored servants, the devoted and loving Jerome and Ora Lee and their niece, Pepper, trying to interfere.

" 'Rebecca would pyroot through their rooms whenever she wanted, and then came the incident of her finding Camille's poetry in a leather-bound book, and reciting the poems at dinner to taunt poor Camille, wounding Camille all but mortally so that Camille threw a hot bowl of soup in Rebecca's face.'

" 'I have Camille's book,' I told Aunt Queen. 'I found it in Rebecca's trunk. But why didn't someone else find it when the trunk was packed? Why were there cameos in the trunk? I know everything was thrown in there but still—?'

" 'Because the woman disappeared under violent circumstances, and it was Manfred who grabbed up her things and heaved them into the trunk. And besides, the old madman had been absent when the affair of the poetry took place, and who knew how much he knew? He didn't see the book, or care about it, that's plain enough, and he didn't bother to save the cameos you found in the trunk, either, though he did save five cameos as I'll explain.'

" 'How did Rebecca disappear? What were the violent circumstances?' I pushed.

" 'She tried to set fire to this house.'

" 'Ah, of course.'

" 'She did it with the oil lamps.'

"I gasped. 'So that's why everybody believed me!' I said. 'Jasmine and Lolly and Pops. They knew the story of what Rebecca had done in the past.'

"Aunt Queen nodded. 'Rebecca set the lamps on the windowsills of the front rooms. She had a blaze started in four places when Ora Lee and Jerome caught her in the act, and Jerome struck her and shouted for the farmhands to come in and put out the fire. Now you know what a risk that was for Jerome, a black man, to haul off and slap a white woman in those days, but this crazy Rebecca was trying to burn down this house.

" 'The gossip was that Jerome knocked her unconscious. And that she had almost succeeded in her mad designs, the fire really blazing before they caught it, and the repairs costing a mint.

" 'Now, imagine what a danger fire was in those times, Quinn. We didn't have the pumps on the banks of the swamp in those days, Quinn, we didn't have the water out here from town. This house could have really gone up. But it didn't. Blackwood Manor was saved.

" 'Of course Jerome kept Rebecca under close watch in the room without candles or lamps until Manfred came back from the swamp.

" 'You can imagine the tension, Quinn, with Jerome, a black man, taking on this responsibility, and Rebecca being locked up there in the dark, calling him a "nigger" and threatening to have him lynched and every other thing she could think of through the door. There were lynchings in those days, too. They didn't happen hereabouts that I know of, but they happened.

" 'The Irish poor were never great lovers of the black man, I can tell you, Quinn, and the threats Rebecca made, to bring her kin up here from New Orleans, were enough to scare Jerome and Ora Lee and Pepper and all their folks.

" 'But they couldn't let her out, and they wouldn't let her out, so scream and rant in the dark she did.

" 'Well finally Manfred came back, and when he saw the damage and the extent of the repairs, when he realized that the house had almost been lost, he went wild.

" 'He grabbed Rebecca up off the bed where she'd been moaning and crying, and he beat her with his hands and his fists. He slapped her back and forth and punched her until Jerome and Ora Lee screamed to make him stop.

" 'Jerome wasn't strong enough to hold Manfred, and he didn't dare hit him, but Ora Lee stopped the brawl simply by screaming over and over so that all the colored and white staff came flooding into the house and up into the room.

" 'Rebecca, being surely one of the most unwise human beings that ever lived, was roaring that Manfred had promised to marry her, that she would be his wife or die here, that she would never leave. Jasmine's family were all sort of holding her and reaching out to Manfred to please not hit her anymore.

" 'In his raging temper, Manfred sent for her trunk, and it was he, the man himself, who shoved every blessed thing that belonged to her into it, higgledy-piggledy, and told the men to drive her to the edge of the property and throw her off it with all that was hers. He threw fistsful of money at her, raining it down on her where she lay on the floor in a daze.

" 'But the wicked and unwise girl rose up and ran to him and wouldn't let go, screaming, "Manfred, I love you. Manfred, I can't live without you, Manfred, I won't live without you. Manfred, remember Naples." (Everyone remembered that "Remember Naples.") "Manfred, remember, Manfred, I'm your Rebecca at the Well, come out to be your bride. Look at the cameo at my neck, Manfred. Manfred, I've come to the well to be your bride."

" 'And it was then that he dragged her down the steps, out the doorway, across the lawn and past the cemetery to the landing, where he flung her into the pirogue and pushed away from the bank. When she tried to get up off the floor of the pirogue, he kicked her and she fell back.

" 'That was the last anybody saw of Rebecca Stanford alive or dead.

" 'Two weeks later—a fortnight as they called it in those days—Manfred came home. When he saw Rebecca's trunk in the middle of the room he was angry, and told Jerome to put it upstairs.

" 'Later, Ora Lee discovered a velvet box in the top drawer of Rebecca's bureau, and in it several cameos along with a note in Rebecca's hand. It said "First cameos given to me by Manfred. Naples." And the date. Now, Ora Lee kept these cameos for at least a year, not wanting them thrown away, as they were very pretty, and then she gave them to Manfred, who tried to give them to Camille.

" 'Now, Camille had not gotten over her hatred of Rebecca and frankly never did. She wouldn't touch the cameos, but Manfred kept them, and now and then he was seen taking them out and looking at them and mumbling to himself.

" 'When my father married my mother, Manfred offered her the cameos, but my father wouldn't let her take them because he remembered Rebecca with so much hatred, too.

" 'Then, when I was a little girl, Manfred gave the cameos to me. I was ten years old. The Old Man said strange things to me. Wild things, things I didn't understand.'

"—And here, Aunt Queen told me the story that she repeated to both of us tonight, of Manfred's wild ravings, only in that first telling, when I was a boy of eighteen, she included less detail—.

" 'I had no temerity about keeping the cameos,' she declared. 'I had never even heard the story of Rebecca, and wouldn't for many years.

" 'I had already begun collecting cameos by that time, and had a score of them when I finally told my father how Manfred had given me my first few. But it wasn't my father who told me the story of Rebecca. It was Ora Lee who told me—you know, it was kitchen-table talk—and to tell the truth, Ora Lee had felt a liking for Rebecca, an understanding of the poor Irish girl who had wanted to better herself, a girl who was afraid of her own vicious Irish father and German-Irish mother, a girl who had reached the faraway coast of Italy with Manfred, where Manfred at a candlelight dinner had pinned the first cameo of "Rebecca at the Well" to Rebecca's lace blouse himself.

" 'And, Ora Lee insisted, Rebecca hadn't started out being mean to the children, or mean to anybody; it was what came as the result of her dissatisfaction over time. It was what came of Manfred's downright meanness.

" 'And as Ora Lee put it, in old age she was more able to understand Rebecca, and make no mistake, Quinn, Ora Lee thought Rebecca was murdered out there—you can be sure of it—but the point I was making was that in old age, Ora Lee was more forgiving of Rebecca and what she had done, though she couldn't forgive Rebecca's meanness to Camille.

" 'Even as Ora Lee told me these things, she begged me never to mention Rebecca's name to my father or to my Aunt Camille.

" ' "Your Aunt Camille was done in by those days," Ora Lee told me.

"That poor child was always morbid, but she went deep into her shell and never came out anymore."

" 'To return to the history of your illustrious ancestor,' Aunt Queen went on, 'I didn't need Ora Lee to tell me that he had kept bringing his Irish girls to the house and keeping them in the front bedroom upstairs for many a year. I was a girl of twenty or so when my mother told me all about it—how just after my birth my father had begged the Old Man to please stop his bad behavior on account of his grandbaby coming into the world.

" 'The Old Man had cursed and fussed and slammed his fist down on the dining table so hard as to rattle the silver, but he agreed. For a daughter-in-law he hadn't bothered, but for a grandbaby, well, he would, and so he removed himself from the big upstairs best bedroom, in which you now reside, my blessed nephew, and he took this bedroom here on the back of the house. And even during my early years—before I was too young to remember—he slipped his women in by the back door.

" 'The changing of the room had a great significance for everyone. The priest of those days, Fr. Flarety, stopped calling on Manfred for his wicked ways, and by the time I was ten, by the time the Old Man gave me the cameos, he was pretty much just a pitiful slobbering old creature, raving at the empty air and trying to hail with his cane anyone who chanced to pass the door.

" 'My mother became the official lady of Blackwood Manor because Aunt Camille was a wounded being who could never take such a place.

" 'And as for the trunk, well, I suppose I forgot about it, and it just became one of many up there, full of uninteresting clothes. Oh, of course, I always meant to go and explore the attic, but thinking it a monumental chore to put a lot of chaos in order I never bothered, and neither has anyone else.

" 'And now, Quinn, you know more about what happened to Rebecca Stanford than anyone living, even me. Her ghost is a danger to you, Quinn, and to everyone around you.'

" 'Oh, but I don't know,' I answered. 'I found those chains out there, Aunt Queen. Rusted chains. But I don't really know what happened to her!'

" 'Quinn, the important thing is you don't call up this ghost again!'

" 'But I never really called her in the first place.'

" 'Yes, you did, Quinn. Not only did you find her things, you wanted to know her story.'

" 'Aunt Queen, if that's how I called her up, then why didn't she appear to you years ago when Ora Lee told you about her? Why didn't she appear to you when you were a little girl and Manfred gave you the cameos?'

" 'I don't have your gift for seeing ghosts, Quinn,' she came back fast. 'I've never seen a ghost, and you've seen plenty of them.'

"I sensed a hesitancy in her, a sudden sharp introspection. And I thought I knew what it was.

" 'You've seen Goblin, haven't you, Aunt Queen?' I asked her.

"And as I said these words, Goblin came and crouched down at the arm of her chair and peered at her. He was extremely vivid and solid. I was shocked by his proximity to her, and I loathed it, but she was definitely looking at him.

" 'Back off, Goblin!' I said crossly, and he at once obeyed, very sad and nonplussed to have made me so short with him. He withdrew, throwing beseeching looks at me, and then he vanished.

" 'What did you just see?' Aunt Queen asked me.

" 'What I always see,' I responded. 'My double. He's wearing my jeans, just as neat and pressed, and he's wearing a polo shirt same as me and he looks exactly like me.'

"She sat back, drinking her champagne slowly.

" 'What did you see, Aunt Queen?' I threw the question back at her.

" 'I see something, Quinn, but it's not like what you see. I see an agitation in the air; it's like the movement or the turbulence that rises above a hot road in front of one's car in the middle of summer. I see that and sometimes there's a vague shape to it, a human shape, a shape of your size, always. The whole apparition is no more than, perhaps, a second. And what's left is a feeling that something is lingering, that something unseen is there.'

"For the first time in my life, I was angry with Aunt Queen. 'Why did you never tell me this!' I demanded. 'How could you go year in and year out and not tell me that you saw that much of Goblin, that you knew—.' I was too out of sorts to go on.

" 'That's about the extent of what I see.' She went on as though I weren't frothing at the mouth, 'and I don't, by any means, see it very often. Only now and then when your spirit wants me to see him, I suspect.'

"I was not only angry—fit to be tied—I was amazed. I had been in a constant state of amazement since Rebecca appeared to me, reeling from one revelation after another, and now this, to discover that all these years Aunt Queen had been seeing Goblin.

" 'Is there anything else?' I asked with a hint of sarcasm, 'that you can confide at this time?'

" 'Quinn,' she said gravely, 'it's perhaps ridiculous of me to say that I've always done what I thought best for you. I've never denied the existence of Goblin. The path I chose was more careful and deliberate than that. It was not to ratify Goblin, not to reinforce him, one might say, because I've never known whether Goblin was a good creature or bad. But as we are laying it all out on the table, let me tell you that Big Ramona can see of Goblin about as much as I can—a turbulence in the air. No more, no less. And Jasmine can see that much too.'

"I was floored. I felt quite alone. My closest kith and kin had lied to me, as I saw it, and I wished with all my heart that Lynelle had not died. I prayed that somehow the spirit of Lynelle could come to me—since I possessed such a knack for ghosts and spirits—and I swore under my breath and to myself alone that I knew Lynelle could tell me what to make of all that had transpired.

" 'Beloved nephew,' Aunt Queen said—an expression she would use a lot as I got older, and she said it now with sweet formality and intimate devotion—'beloved nephew, you have to realize that I take your powers very seriously and always have. But I've never known if they were a good thing.'

"A sudden revelation came to me, a certainty based upon what she had said, if not everything else, that my powers weren't for good. I told her in a half whisper, the only manly voice I could manage, about the twilight panic, the thoughts of taking Pops' gun and putting an end to my life, and I told her about how on the afternoon of Rebecca's coming to me I had sat on the front steps, watching that golden light go down and saying to the powers that be, Please deliver me from this, please anything but this. I didn't remember my prayer. I don't remember it now. Perhaps I gave her a more nearly accurate version. I don't know.

"There came a tender silence, and when I looked up I saw the tears on her cheeks. Beyond her, by the post of her bed, stood Goblin, vivid once more, and he too was weeping and reaching out to me, as if he would like to cradle my head in his left hand.

" 'Go away, Goblin!' I said sharply. 'I don't want you here now!

Leave me. Go find Lynelle for me! Travel the spirit winds for me, but get away.'

"He flashed brilliant, at his most detailed, his most shining, and his face was full of hurt and insult and pouting lip, and then, snap, no more.

" 'If he's still in this room, I don't know it,' I confessed to Aunt Queen. 'And as for Rebecca, I have to find justice for her. I have to discover, if I can, what they did to her in that house.'

"Aunt Queen wiped her blue eyes with her napkin, and I felt more than a twinge of guilt that I had made her cry. I loved her, suddenly, no matter what she said or did, and I needed her and was so miserable at having been angry with her that I got up, came around, went down on my knees and embraced her and held her fragile form for some seconds in utter quiet.

"Then I looked at her shimmering, ankle-strap spike-heel shoes, and I laughed and I kissed her insteps. I kissed her toes. I gave her right foot an affectionate squeeze with my left hand.

" 'Tarquin Blackwood, you're certifiably insane, cease and desist,' she declared. 'Now sit down like a good boy, and pour me another glass of champagne.'

"We had finished one bottle, so I opened another, with the aplomb of a boy who has for years assisted in an elegant bed-and-breakfast hotel, and poured the foaming wine into her tulip glass.

"Of course she then poured out to me her horror at my having thoughts of putting a gun to my head, and I swore to her I would never do it, only think about it, not as long as she lived and Pops lived and Jasmine lived and Big Ramona lived and Lolly lived; and then I rattled off the names of all the farmhands and Shed Men, and I was being perfectly and convincingly sincere.

" 'But you see, what I'm trying to say to you,' I went on, now that we were both calmer and obviously a little drunker, 'is that spirits and ghosts must come from somewhere, and mine was a blasphemous prayer or a dangerous one and out of the darkness Rebecca came.'

" 'Now you're talking sense, my dear boy,' she responded.

" 'Of course, I know that, Aunt Queen. I've always known it. I'll never forget that she urged me to light the lamps. I'll never be her pawn again. It can't happen. I'm too wary, too in control of it when I see these creatures, I swear it, but I do have to find out what they did to her, and she alone can tell me, and that will be where she's strongest—on Sugar Devil Island in that strange house.'

" 'To which you will not go, Tarquin, unless Pops goes with you! Do you understand?'

"I didn't respond, then I spoke my mind: 'It's not good for Pops to go out in the swamp right now. Pops isn't himself. Pops isn't hale and hearty; Pops hasn't been eating for days, and the heat out there, and the mosquitoes—no, I can't take Pops—.'

" 'Who then, Tarquin? For as God is my witness, you shall not go alone.'

" 'Aunt Queen,' I said, 'nothing's going to stop me from going out there in the morning. I'd go now, if it wasn't pitch-dark.'

"She leaned across the table. 'Tarquin, I forbid it,' she said. 'Need I remind you that you've described a mausoleum made of gold, and signs of habitation in the Hermitage—a desk and a golden chair! Somebody's using the island. And why, pray tell, if this tomb is made of gold—.'

" 'I don't know all the answers, but I have to go back out there, and don't you see, I have to have the freedom to invoke this ghost, and to let her speak to me—.'

" 'A ghost that seduced you! A ghost that used her charm and sensuality so palpably that you actually lost your virginity with her? Is this what I'm hearing—and you mean to invoke her?'

" 'I have to go, Aunt Queen, and frankly, I think you know that if you were me, you would.'

" 'I'd speak to Fr. Kevin first, that's what I'd do and that's what I want you to do. Now, we'll call Father in the morning.'

" 'Father!' I scoffed. 'He just said his first Mass. He's a kid!'

"And I was exaggerating but I was right that Fr. Kevin Mayfair was young, meaning around thirty-five or so, and though I liked him enormously, I didn't think of him with the same respect I felt for the old gray-haired priests of the pre–Vatican II days who said Mass with so much more flair.

"She rose from the table in such a little huff that she knocked over her chair backwards and then went striding in her dazzling high heels to her dressing table where she rummaged through her top drawer.

"Then she turned and I saw a rosary swinging in the light. 'This isn't blessed, but it will have to do for now,' she said. 'I want you to put this around your neck, under your shirt, over your shirt, on your bare chest, I don't care, but you're to wear it from now on.'

"I didn't bother to put up a fight. The rosary was small with perfectly round gold beads, and I didn't mind having it, though it did disappear under my shirt.

" 'Aunt Queen,' I went on, 'Fr. Kevin isn't going to believe all this about Rebecca and her ghost any more than the sheriff will believe it. So why should we call him? After Mass he always laughs when he asks me about Goblin. I think he's seen me speaking to Goblin in church. No, I know I don't want to talk to Fr. Kevin. Just forget about that.'

"Aunt Queen was in no mood to give up. She'd told me that first thing in the morning she was heading for her favorite goldsmith in the French Quarter to get a gold crucifix on a chain for me, and then she'd head for the rectory at St. Mary's Assumption Church to have Fr. Kevin bless the crucifix, and then she would discuss the entire matter with Fr. Kevin and find out what he thought.

" 'And meantime,' she asked, 'what do we do about these earrings and this cameo brooch?'

" 'We're to save them. We have to. The DNA in this tissue can't be that degraded. We have to find out if she was the one who really died out there. That's what Rebecca wants of me; she wants recognition; she wants to be known.'

" 'And she wanted you to burn down this house, Quinn.'

" 'She'll never persuade me to do anything like that again,' I insisted. 'I'm wise to her.'

" 'But you care about what she wants,' said Aunt Queen, her tongue just a little bit thick from the champagne.

" 'It's justice, Aunt Queen,' I said. 'It's justice that I, a descendant of Manfred, have to carry out. Maybe it won't amount to much—say, just putting her cameos into the case in the living room with a special card explaining they belonged to a famous love of Manfred Blackwood. Maybe that will allow her spirit to rest. But for now, don't worry any-more about me. I'll do what I have to do, and I'll do what's best.'

"By that time I had pushed her past all patience, and after two more glasses of champagne I was humoring her, concealing my silent secret schemes.

"I loved her. I love her totally now. But I knew, knew for the first time that I had to deceive her, had in some way to protect her from pro-tecting me.

"Of course I was going out to the island, and of course I was going to invoke Rebecca, but just how and when I wasn't so sure."

13

"I WOKE UP very early, dressed in my hunting jeans and vest, and while Big Ramona still slept I sat down at my computer and wrote a letter to this strange invader of Sugar Devil Island, which went, sort of, as follows:

Dear Trespasser,

This communication is from Tarquin Blackwood and is to notify you that my family owns this island and this house, and that you must take your books and your furnishings and leave these premises without further delay.

The family has plans for this island and will be proceeding just as soon as you have vacated the Hermitage.

If you have any need to communicate with me, I reside at Blackwood Manor, and will be more than happy to talk with you by letter, by fax, or by phone, or in person—howsoever you desire,

Yours sincerely,
Tarquin Blackwood,
better known as Quinn

"Then, after supplying the relevant numbers for fax and phone, I hit the print button and, making four copies of the eviction notice, signed all of them and folded them and put them into my inside fishing-vest pocket.

"Then, I crept into Pops' room, and, not finding him thereabouts—he had probably gotten up at five a.m. and was already at work in the flower beds—I took his thirty-eight pistol, made sure it was loaded, put that into my pocket and then, stopping quickly in the kitchen pantry, got a card of thumbtacks, which were always in there, you know, for the family bulletin board, and I headed to the pier.

"Let me add that I also had my rifle, my hunting knife and the kitchen knife, and I thought I was completely ready until I found Jasmine in her bare feet down at the landing by the pirogue, smoking a cigarette.

" 'All right, you crazy boy, I know where you're going, and your Pops says to let you alone. So I put that cooler of drinks for you in the boat. And there's a couple of sandwiches in there too, wrapped in foil.'

" 'Oh, I love you for that,' I said, and I kissed her, feeling an awareness of her as a woman suddenly, a thing which caught my brain rather like a power surge, and most definitely a surprise. I'll never forget it, the way that kiss ignited something. And I think I very boastfully squeezed her arm.

"Whatever, I don't think it ignited anything for her. And as I went to push off, she called out:

" 'Tarquin Blackwood, are you an imbecile?'

" 'No ma'am,' I said sarcastically, 'you expect me to change my mind?'

" 'How you're going to get people to believe what you saw out there if you don't take pictures of it, genius!' She reached into her apron pocket and took out a small flash camera—the kind you can buy nowadays anywhere, in which the film is already loaded and ready to go.

" 'Oh, thank God you thought of it!' I said.

" 'You can say that prayer again, Little Boss. Don't forget to press the button for the flash.'

"I wanted to kiss her again, but I was already drifting away.

"As for Goblin, he came after me, vivid and yet transparent, pleading with me not to go, saying, 'Bad, Quinn, bad,' over and over, and once again I told him in polite terms to leave me alone. He vanished then, but I suspect he was with me as I went on.

"In fact, I figured that he had to be; because where else could Goblin go? I was thinking a lot of late as to where Goblin was and where Goblin wasn't, and I was more than impatient with him, as I've said.

"Back to the swamp:

"There was a mist crawling over the water, and at first the swamp looked inviting and beautiful, harmonious and embracing—the stuff of poetry and photograph captions—but within a very short time it was the evil bog of mosquitoes and chain-girded cypress trees with arrows carved into their bark. The rustling of creatures in the dark waters and the sight of more than one alligator gave me the creeps.

"The dizziness returned, which alarmed me considerably, and the voices came once more, too low for me to really understand what they said. What was I overhearing? Did these ghosts quarrel with each other forever? Is that what Rebecca had meant when she said things don't move in a straight line?

"You can't do it, you have to let me go. . . .

"Why wasn't this ghostly discourse loud enough for me to be sure of every word?

" 'I'm coming, Rebecca,' I said aloud. 'You be straight with me, now, Rebecca. I know your tricks, and yet I'm coming. You be straight.'

"On and on I went through this dense green hell of tormented gray trees and anguished vines, of rattling leaf and fetid water, feeling ever fainter and probing deeply with the pole and propelling myself forward as fast as I could.

"I'm begging you, God help me. . . .

"I knew it was Rebecca crying, Rebecca pleading, but with whom? Then came the inevitable sinister laughter and a man's voice speaking rapidly and angrily. Was it Manfred?

"A gator shot past me, his big slimy back visible for only a moment, and the pirogue rocked dangerously and then righted itself clumsily and on I went. I trembled, thinking about the gator, and I hated myself for it. I went on.

"Each time the dizziness came over me really heavily I slowed my pace, for fear of falling, and the high green thick of the swamp swallowed me treacherously, as I tried to make out what was being said: . . . *Loved you, always loved you, you promised, in Naples, forever, in the ruins* . . . And there came the deep voice, and the laughter rippling through it all.

"Were there three of them? Were there more?

"At last the weathered hulk of the Hermitage loomed in front of me, and the pirogue struck the bank amid the wild blackberries, and I was nearly knocked out of the boat. I quickly secured it to the nearest tree—a thing I had not done last time—laid the pole in it in intelligent fashion and then proceeded to explore the island once more.

"There had been gators on the island. I heard the plash as they went back into the swamp. What was I going to do if I encountered a mean gator? Well, it had never happened, and maybe it never would. I had no real fear of them, because they aren't generally vicious and they don't want trouble; nevertheless, this was the first time I had been in their august company without Pops or another man to take command.

"I stood listening. I could hear nothing but the mournful, broken cry of the birds. And that humming, that humming of bees and mosquitoes which I connected to the slime of sweat that now covered my skin.

"The house looked as empty as it had before. But that didn't mean a whole lot.

"Nevertheless, the mausoleum—or whatever it was—drew me, and I went back to it, studying it more carefully than I had the first time.

"No door of any kind, of that I was certain. So what in the name of God did it contain?

"As for the procession of figures graven in the gold, I was certain now they were Roman and that they were grieving; that the women were weeping and the men hammering on their foreheads with clenched fists.

"On an end panel which contained only a trio of weeping children there appeared some background engraving on a different plane from the figures—details that I hadn't noticed before at all.

"With my fingers I traced in one corner the image of a mountain, and the mountain had a high cone and was erupting, and above it streamed right and left a great heavy cloud. Far to the right, and somewhat below the position of the mountain, was the image of a small walled city, drawn in tiny detail, and it seemed more than obvious that the evil cloud from the erupting mountain was a threat to the little town.

" 'Volcano. Ancient Rome. A city. People in mourning.' It had to be Mount Vesuvius, this mountain, and the city had to be the fabled city of Pompeii.

"Even I who had traveled almost nowhere in my life knew the full story of the eruption of Vesuvius in A.D. 79 and how it had buried Herculaneum and Pompeii. Only in the eighteenth century had they been officially rediscovered, and if there was anywhere I wanted to travel— outside of Ruby River Parish—it was to the ruins of Pompeii.

"The tragedy of those buried cities had always enthralled me and sometimes in a painful way. Years ago I'd seen photographs of plaster casts made of those poor Romans struggling to escape the cinder rain falling on Pompeii and they had made me cry.

"Of course Pompeii and Herculaneum were on the Bay of Naples, and Manfred had taken Rebecca to Naples. Vesuvius loomed over Naples, and Rebecca had cried, 'Remember Naples' when Manfred had been beating her, when he had carried her or dragged her out of the house.

"Again, the dizziness came and there rose the simmer of voices. I tipped forward until my forehead touched the gold carving. I was aware of the perfume of flowers. Was that wisteria? My senses were scrambled. I was dry-mouthed and sweating. And I heard Rebecca sobbing, *What they did to me, Quinn, what they did.*

"With a supreme act of will, I threw off the dizziness. I was on my knees. And as I looked up I realized there was an inscription running in a band along the top of the gold plates, just beneath the granite roof of the tomb, an inscription I hadn't seen for the glare of the vagrant sun on the gold.

"I went round the mausoleum twice. The words were in Latin, and I couldn't translate, but I could pick out the name Petronia, and the words for sleep and for death.

"I cursed myself that I didn't have any paper with me, except my letters to the trespasser, so that I could copy this down. Then I realized I had four copies of my letter, for posting in four places, and all I needed to do was sacrifice one copy. So, taking out my pen, I scribbled down the entire inscription, circling the monument twice to make sure I had the words correct.

"By now I was thirsting and I went back to the pirogue, picked up the small plastic cooler that Jasmine had packed for me and went up the stairs into the house.

"All was the same as I had found it yesterday. I crept up the staircase and stared again at the iron chains. I noted with a faint twinge of horror that the fifth chain with the hook was somewhat shorter than the other chains but I didn't know what it meant. There were hooks in the wall also. I hadn't noticed those before either, and in the morass of blackish tarlike substance I thought I saw more of the shape of human bones.

"I took out the camera, and with trembling hands I snapped two pictures, and then I backed up and took a couple more. What would it show? I wasn't certain. All I could do was snap another two close-ups and hope that someone believed in what I saw.

"I knelt down and I touched what looked like the remnants of human hair. A jarring chill ran through me, and I heard the dreamlike laughter again, and then a scream that was so guttural it was almost a groan. It came again, a cry of pure agony, and I drew back, absolutely unable to come close again to the remains.

"I photographed the room and then I went downstairs and photographed the marble desk and the gold Roman-style chair. I photographed the fireplace with its heap of half-burnt wood and ash. I shot a close-up of the tumbled books on the desk.

"Next I went out of the Hermitage and photographed the whole place. I shot pictures of the mausoleum, and with my thumb over the flash so it wouldn't reflect in the gold I got close-ups of the figures, hoping there would be enough available light.

" 'Jasmine, I shall love you forever,' I said. I put the camera into my top vest pocket, zipped the pocket shut and resolved that I would now prove to all the world that, of Sugar Devil Island and Manfred's dark existence, I had spoken the truth.

"But what did it all mean? Was it some mad poet who made his way out here to sit in a golden chair in solitude, perhaps taking his work to and from with him, and only leaving behind those books which no longer mattered? Or was it a mere boy like me?

"And the time, what was it? Why it was just past noon, and I was hungry and getting sick.

"But I had to post my letters to the trespasser. I attended to that right away. I tacked up one such letter on the wooden door, placed another on the marble table, with books to anchor the four corners of it, and then tacked another on the wall near to the stairs.

"My duty was done, I figured, and now, to stop the nausea which was threatening, I brought the cooler over to the desk and sat down in the Roman chair. The leather sling seat was extremely comfortable, as it always is with such chairs, and I was overjoyed to discover that Jasmine had filled the cooler with six beers. Of course she had put some cola in there also, and there were the sandwiches, and even an apple nestled into the ice, but six beers!

"I don't think I will ever forget that moment. But there's no point in lingering on it. I have too much to tell. Let me only say that I whispered to the open air, 'Jasmine, can a woman of thirty-five find romance with a boy of eighteen? I'll meet you behind the big house at six.'

"By the time I finished that little ditty, I had swallowed half of the first beer. I tore open the sandwiches, which were thick with ham and cheese and butter—cold, delicious, visible butter—and devoured both of them in a few bites. Then I devoured the apple, finished the first beer and drank another one after that.

"I told myself that was plenty, that I had to keep my wits about me, but I was overexcited and instead of depressing me the beer had contributed to a kind of crazy elation, and with a third ice-cold can in hand

I went back upstairs again and I sat down as close to the chains and their dark legacy as I dared.

"The sun was lowering outside, and only feeble rays managed to get through the labyrinth of green that crowded most of the house. Some light came in through the cupola and as I lay back looking up there, watching the light twinkle and shift, I heard in my head a thin high-pitched scream.

"Was it a bird? Was it a human? My eyelids were closing. I reclined, one elbow on the dusty boards. I drank more of the beer. I finished it. And then I realized I had to sleep. My body was forcing me to it. I had to sleep. I lay back feeling comfortable and warm, and I said as I stared up into the cupola:

" 'Rebecca, come to me, tell me what they did.' I shut my eyes and I was dreaming, my body shapeless and vibrating in its half sleep. Her sobbing came to me clearly, and then before me, in a nighttime place of candles, I saw a leering face and I heard a low, vicious laugh. I tried to focus on the face but I couldn't see it, and then when I looked down I saw that I was a woman, and that someone was stripping away from me a beautiful burgundy dress. My breasts were bare. My whole body suddenly was naked, and I was screaming.

"I had to get away from those who tormented me, and there before me a hand gripped the rusted hook, the hook at the end of the chain. I screamed a woman's scream. I was a woman. I was Rebecca and yet I was Quinn and we two were one.

"Never had I known such pure terror as the hand with the hook approached, and then I felt an unendurable pain beneath my right breast, an agony as something thick yet sharp stabbed me and pushed against me, and then I heard the laughter again, chilling merciless laughter, and a man's voice murmuring—no, arguing, pleading disgustedly—but the laughter covered the argument, it covered the pleading. No one would stop this! I knew I was hanging by the hook, that the hook held me by the rib beneath my breast, and my whole weight now pulled on the chain and its hook!

"I cried out, I screamed. I was a woman and a man screaming, I was Rebecca helpless and in torment and near to fainting yet unable to faint, and I was Quinn, protective and horrified and yet desperately trying to see the evil ones who were doing this, and there were two of them, yes, definitely two of them, and I had to know if it was Manfred. And then I was Rebecca screaming and the pain went on, the unendurable pain that was endured—it went on and on, and then the scene, blessedly, started to shift.

" 'Oh, God, Rebecca,' I heard myself whispering. 'I know what they did—hung you by the hook beneath your rib and left you here to die.'

"Someone shook me awake. I looked up.

"It was Rebecca, and she was smiling, and she said, 'Quinn, you came. You didn't let me down. You came.'

"I was shocked. She was as real as she had been in the house, only she wore the gorgeous burgundy dress she'd worn in the dream.

" 'Oh, thank Heaven, you're all right!' I cried. 'It couldn't be going on forever.'

" 'Don't think about it now, my darling,' she said. 'Now you know it, and you know what the fifth chain was for. Just be with me, my darling.'

"As I sat up she sat down beside me and I turned to face her, and our lips met. I kissed her clumsily and she put her tongue into my mouth, and I was as aroused as I'd been in the house.

"I was pure male, quite divided from her and quite locked to her, enchanted by the low-cut burgundy dress and the pink nipples that had to be so close, and ah, how precious the cameo on its black ribbon around her naked throat.

"Her breasts were only half covered by the burgundy velvet, and I shoved my hand into her dress awkwardly, and when I felt her nipples I went a little bit mad.

" 'Love you, positively love you,' I said with gritted teeth, and then I pushed the cloth down and I kissed her nipples until she drew me back up.

"I looked into her eyes.

"I wanted her too much to talk, and she allowed it, taking my hand and putting it under her skirts. Real, all real, all savory and frenzied, and finally, her little sex gasping for me, closing on me, and then the moment of fulfillment—so sudden, so jarring, so total. So gone.

"I found myself staring down at her—I was actually lying on top of her—and the flush in her cheeks took my breath away. I muttered some obscenity, some crudity. But I was so purely satisfied, so blissful that I could question nothing in these moments. I kissed her in the same open-mouthed passionate way I had kissed her the very first time.

"I lay back, tired to the point of stupor, and she was the one now looking down at me.

" 'Be my vengeance, Quinn,' she said softly. 'Tell the world my story, yes, but be my vengeance, too.'

" 'But how, Rebecca? How can I do that when those who hurt you are gone?' I sat up, gently forcing her backwards.

"She looked urgent.

"We sat together. 'Tell me truly, Rebecca, what can I do to make your spirit rest?'

"The horror of the earlier scene came back to me, the grim picture of her hanging on the hook, naked and helpless, and of those two evil ones who had done it to her.

" 'It was Manfred himself, wasn't it?' I asked her. 'What can I do, Rebecca, to send your soul to peace?'

"She said nothing. She only kissed me again.

" 'You know you're gone too, Rebecca,' I said. 'Along with those who did the deed, however awful it was.' I had to say it. I had to tell her. 'Rebecca, there is no one alive now who can suffer for what is done.'

" 'No, Quinn, I'm here,' she said sweetly, 'I'm always here, I see you always, I see everything. Be my vengeance, Quinn. Fight for me.'

"I kissed her again. I covered her breasts with kisses. We lay tangled and I felt the velvet of her burgundy dress. Her hair came loose, tumbled disgracefully in our lovemaking, and then I sighed, and, kissing her cheeks, again I passed into a blackness that was cool and enveloping as if I had drifted bodiless into the sex act itself.

"Sleep. How long? Hours upon hours.

"Then suddenly I was awake. I knew the heat, the sweat.

"And the darkness! Good Lord, the darkness!

"Nighttime on Sugar Devil Island. Nighttime in Sugar Devil Swamp. Oh, of all the idiot mistakes to have made, to have fallen into a drunken sleep here one good hour from home, with all the swamp creatures waking and hungry. What good was a pistol? What good a rifle if a snake drops on you from an overhanging tree? I didn't mind poking at the gators to scare them off, but what about everything else, including the bobcats, that came out to feast after dark?

"I rose up, furious with myself. And I had been so sure that I wouldn't be tricked by her, that I knew her for the evil thing that she was.

"Then it all came crashing back to me, what they'd done to her, and I gasped aloud.

"Vengeance? Oh, it had been enough to make a vengeful spirit of a choirboy, what they'd done. And she had died like that, I knew it. She had died and rotted there, but did she mean her vengeance to be on me?

"I saw the sticky semen on the boards, glittering in the light of the moon, and, looking through the windows, I thanked God for that moon. I needed that moon. Maybe I could get the hell out of here with that moon.

"I made the Sign of the Cross. I felt for the rosary under my shirt. (This one's not blessed but it will have to do.) And hastily and shamefully I said a Hail Mary, telling the Blessed Virgin in my own words how sorry I was to call on her only when all seemed lost.

"Then I realized to my horror that my pants were still unzipped. I'd said a Hail Mary to the Virgin Mary while officially exposing myself. I put that to rights immediately and said another three prayers before I groped my way to the stairs and down to the first floor.

"I scooped up the gold plate with its little forest of wax candles, and, taking out my lighter, I quickly lighted every wick. Carrying my little tray of light, I went to the door of the Hermitage and looked out. Yes, the moon was up there all right, I could see it from this vantage point, but the swamp looked dead black, and once I pushed off from this clearing, once I tunneled into that blackness, the moon just might not do me any good.

"Of course, I didn't have a flashlight or a lantern. I hadn't planned on this! In fact, if anybody had said, 'Will you spend the night on Sugar Devil Island?' I would have answered, 'That's insane.'

" 'Wait till I get finished with this place,' I said aloud. 'I'll have electricity everywhere. And these windows will have properly fitted glass. Maybe they'll have screens as well. And these plank floors will be covered with marble tiles that the swamp can't consume with its infernal dampness. No, this shall be a small Roman palace, what with even more elaborate Roman furniture, and the stove, I shall get a new stove. And then if I'm trapped out here, I'll have delicious pillows on a couch on which to sleep, and plenty of books to read by fine lights.' It seemed I saw the vision of the place, and Rebecca's fate had no part in what I saw. It was as if her grisly death had been erased.

"But for now? For now I was in the damned jungle in a tree house!

"Okay, what if I stayed here and didn't try to find my way home in this abominable situation? What if I just read some of those old books by candlelight, and kept my pistol on hand for any emergency either man or beast might send my way?

"Well, the worst consequence of my doing that would be that everyone at Blackwood Manor would think something terrible had happened to me. Indeed, they might be looking for me right now. That was more than a good possibility. They might be out there in a pirogue with flashlights and lanterns.

"Didn't that argue for me staying where I was?

"I set the plate of light down on the desk, and I went out the front door, down the steps, and crossed the clearing before the Hermitage so that I stood near to the bank.

"It was quite amazing how the few candles illuminated the windows of the Hermitage. Indeed, nobody coming close in a pirogue could have missed it. Maybe it was best to sit tight.

"But if so, why did it seem such a cowardly decision? Why did I feel I should get back to reassure those who loved me that I was all right?

"I checked in the pirogue. No, I did not have a flashlight or lantern. Big surprise.

"Then I peered into the swamp. I tried to see what lay before me. I tried to make out the small channel by which I had come to this point. I could see nothing in the blackness.

"I walked around the island as best I could. Why precisely I wasn't sure. Maybe I wanted to feel that I was doing something, and I listened, listened very carefully in case anyone out there was calling my name.

"Of course I heard the countless night birds and low gurgling noises coming from the water, but there was no human voice.

"I came back to the point where I'd tied up the pirogue and there stood Goblin, my perfect mirror image, watching me intently, his figure apparently illuminated, just as if it was solid, by the candlelight that came from the house.

"What a marvelous spectacle, it seemed to me, that could create such an illusion, and I racked my brain to remember if he had ever done something so spectacular before.

"I had seen him in shadows, in darkness and in light, of course, but never had I seen light falling on him, outlining his shoulder and his face. He made a sudden gesture with his right hand, beckoning me to come closer to where he stood.

" 'What do you want?' I asked. 'You don't mean to tell me you're going to be useful.' I moved towards him and he reached out with his left arm to guide me in a turn. Then he pointed out into the swamp.

"For a moment I was only aware of a distant pool of moonlight—that is, an opening in the thick growth many yards from where we stood, where the water sparkled with clear radiance. Then I heard the sound of lapping. And Goblin's left hand tightened on my arm, and he made the symbol to me with his right index finger that I should be very quiet.

"Again he pointed to this distant spot of visibility, and into it glided a pirogue apparently helmed by one man. And quite distinctly I made out the figure of that man.

"He wore a jacket and trousers, perhaps jeans for all I could see, and as I watched with Goblin he lifted up a human body from the pirogue and slipped it into the water slowly with hardly a splash!

"I was confounded. Goblin hurt my shoulder he squeezed it so tight.

"The distant figure now appeared to do the same thing again. With inconceivable dexterity and strength he lifted another body and dropped it down into the muck.

"I stood stock-still. I was horrified. The thought of danger to myself didn't even occur to me. What filled my mind was the bitter sense that two dead bodies had just been fed to the swamp's lethal darkness, and no one, no one, would believe me when I returned home with this tale.

"Only gradually did I realize that the figure was now motionless and in all probability facing me, and that he looked on steadily and that Goblin and I were partially illuminated for the figure by the candles in the house.

"Across the black water there came a sound of laughter. It was low, simmering, as the voices of my visions had been simmering, but it was real, this laughter, it wasn't spectral. It came from the figure.

"And as I watched, as Goblin and I watched together, the figure guided his pirogue into the blackness and was gone.

"For some long agonizing moments Goblin and I stood together, and it was more than a comfort to feel Goblin's left arm around me, and to rest my weight against him in an intimacy I would never have shown with a human being.

"But I knew he couldn't keep up the solid shape for very long. I also knew that he could hear this individual, this character, who had just dumped the two bodies. Goblin would know when it was safe to leave.

"For the proverbial eternity we remained there, motionless and cautious, and then Goblin told me telepathically that we should escape the island as best we could.

" 'And what if I get lost, hopelessly lost?' I asked aloud in a whisper.

" 'I'll lead you,' Goblin answered. And then he disappeared. Within a second the candles in the house were extinguished, and my familiar was pushing at me and tugging me to make me go to the pirogue right now.

"All the way back to Blackwood Farm he guided me, sometimes in total darkness, other times by the light of the moon. In less than an hour I saw the lights of the house shining blessedly through the trees, and I shot straight for the pier.

"People were shouting. I heard someone scream. And then as I hurried up to the kitchen door, Pops came out to embrace me and say:

" 'Thank God, son. We didn't know what the hell had happened to you.'

"Aunt Queen came down the steps dabbing at her eyes.

"Sheriff Jeanfreau was there with one of his worthless, shiftless deputies, Ugly Henderson. All the Shed Men were hollering, 'He's home, he's okay.'

"Immediately I fired off at Jasmine, 'How come you put that beer in the cooler!' to which she answered that she wasn't the one who packed the damned cooler, her mother had done it, and then there was Big Ramona saying she wasn't even awake when I left (which was true), and Jasmine remembering that it was actually Clem. And where the hell was Clem?

"I didn't care. I wanted supper. I wanted everyone to gather round the kitchen table and listen so I'd only have to tell this story once.

"I demanded that Sheriff Jeanfreau stay. I even wanted worthless and annoying Ugly Henderson to stay. I told everybody that I wanted them to listen to me.

"Meantime, since it was only nine o'clock by my watch, I wanted one of the Shed Men to run the camera with its film over to the all-night drugstore in Ruby River City and get the pictures done in one hour, as the sign in the window always boasts.

" 'Where's Goblin?' I asked suddenly. I was in the kitchen. Big Ramona had just given me a wet washrag. 'Goblin, where are you?' and then I realized that after all he'd done, he didn't have the power to make me feel him or see him or hear him.

". . . And so mercifully, and gratefully, and with a new respect for him, and a new love, I let him alone."

14

"THEY DIDN'T BELIEVE a word I said. When I bubbled over crazily with the horrible dream of the piercing of Rebecca, Sheriff Jeanfreau just laughed at me, laughed at my references to myself as both man and woman in the dream, and only a sudden expostulation of

" 'Please!' from Aunt Queen shut him up.

"When it came to my depiction of the mysterious stranger dumping the two bodies, Sheriff Jeanfreau started laughing again and there even came some audible snickering from his worthless deputy Ugly Henderson.

"Patsy, who had come into the kitchen sometime during the proceedings, picked up on Ugly's snickering and started some snickering of her own.

"And when I described how Goblin had led me back out of the swamp, the sheriff, figuratively speaking, rolled on the floor.

"I ignored all this with first-rate patience, devoured two plates of pancakes made by Big Ramona from the Cracker Barrel pancake mix and looked to Aunt Queen.

" 'You know Rebecca was murdered out there, Aunt Queen. All I'm asking is that somebody go out there and collect the remains and test them for DNA!'

" 'Oh, Quinn, my precious darling,' " Aunt Queen sighed.

"As for Pops, it was well past his bedtime, and he looked like he'd been rode hard and put away wet. I knew what a worry I was to him.

"THEN the snapshots came back from the drugstore! THE SNAPSHOTS!

"And round the kitchen table I passed them like so many playing cards.

They were good shots too. You couldn't tell much about Rebecca's remains from the shots, but you could easily see the five rusted chains; and of course the outdoor shots of the Hermitage itself, and the mausoleum, were very good.

" 'Now you know damned good and well,' I said, 'that there's a house out there, you can't deny it; and if that metal there'—I jabbed my finger at the photograph—'isn't pure gold, then my name's not Blackwood.'

"The sheriff was in the midst of another belly-jiggling fit of laughter when Aunt Queen gestured for quiet.

" 'All right,' she declared. 'We've heard all Quinn has to say. Now, this island is real and he knows the way to it, and according to him these mysterious bodies were dumped at a spot some matter of yards beyond the banks of the island. In other words, he can take you to the very place from which he spied the dumping and a search of that small area would be entirely manageable.'

"The sheriff couldn't stop himself from laughing. 'Now, Miss Queen,' he said, 'you know how much I admire you, as does everybody in these parts. . . .'

" 'Thank you, Sheriff,' she at once responded. 'On New Year's Eve I shall expect a tribute of seven youths and seven maidens, handpicked of course.'

"Now it was my turn to die with laughter, because I knew this referred to the minotaur myth, but he hadn't a clue of that and only stared at me and then at her, and I was just stupid enough at eighteen to feel superior to him.

"Aunt Queen went on without missing a beat, ignoring my exultation.

" 'Now, I will personally pay,' said Aunt Queen, 'for the bagging and collecting of these chains and the black residue which Quinn has described. I will pay to have it thoroughly and completely analyzed as to its substance, and will go so far as to run DNA tests on it to determine, among other things, whether or not only one person perished in this spot, or more than one, and whether or not Rebecca Stanford—whose hair we have conveniently in a hairbrush in the attic—did indeed die in this place.' She paused for effect, her eyes narrowing.

" 'All I ask of you, Sheriff,' she continued in a high matriarchal fashion, 'is that you go back out there and you look for these mysterious bodies. I assume you and Pops can go by motorized pirogue in the morning.'

" 'The motors will never make it,' I piped up. 'We'll have to take the small pirogue, same as I did. The cypresses are just too dense.'

" 'Very well then, Pops knows how to handle the pole and I assume you do too, Sheriff Bobby Jeanfreau! So you take care of that, and consider yourself solemnly charged to find those bodies, while the labwork I will handle through my own personal physician, assuming that Ruby River City doesn't have a medical examiner on its payroll who is qualified in the field.'

"At this point, the sheriff, having been laughed at by me, very smoothly smiled and asked:

" 'And may I deputize Goblin, ma'am, so he can show Pops and me the way to the island?'

"Now it was Pops who became riled, though his tone was low and pretty much apathetic, given the state of things.

" 'We don't need for you to deputize Goblin,' he said. 'But I do think that you need a real team of people out there, not just to find those bodies but to examine this death scene with the chains, this residue as we're calling it; you need somebody to look to that in an official way.'

" 'Now, Pops, you know there's nothing to all this—' the sheriff countered. He was as stubborn as I'd ever seen him, and as ignorant, too.

"But Pops pressed on, his tone never changing except in terms of the contents of what he said. 'Now you listen to me, Sheriff,' he stated calmly. 'A body out there even on the second floor of a house could decompose within a few years. And it is possible that Quinn has stumbled upon the scene of a crime, and he might have stumbled on the criminal himself. I'm insisting you take a team of men out there, and if you don't I'll call in the FBI.'

"Why this struck utter terror into the sheriff I'm not sure, but given some of the rumors of what went on in Ruby River Parish, including the cock fighting (which isn't illegal in Louisiana, by the way), I guessed he didn't want the FBI snooping around, so he agreed to the terms.

"In spite of Pops trying to restrain me I followed the sheriff all the way to his car, hammering on him about those two bodies: 'You've got to check and see who's missing! I'm telling you, I saw it. Two bodies, just dumped out there. You've got to search.'

" 'One thing at a time,' Pops said finally. 'Let them check out the house. And then if you think you can pinpoint the place where this stranger dumped the bodies, then we'll insist on a search.'

"Finally the sheriff and his snickering deputy were gone from the property, and Aunt Queen and Pops had ahold of me and told everybody else to leave the kitchen so we could be alone.

"Patsy was pretty ticked off that she couldn't stay, but Pops gave her one of the worst glowering looks I've ever seen on his face, and she finally retreated, in a sulk, to her apartment over the shed.

"A bitter lecture came from Pops as to my having disobeyed Aunt Queen by going out there by myself, about my having 'stolen' his pistol, and some strong statements about how I was in real danger from myself now, and it was time for me to leave Blackwood Farm and go out into the world.

" 'What do you mean "out into the world"?' I asked. 'Can't you see these pictures! There's this gold tomb out there, Pops, I've got to find out what's in it, and then there's the house itself. I'm not going any-where. Pops, you know what I want to do,' I went on, full throttle. 'I want to run electricity out there to that house, you know, run the cables right through the swamp. I want to clean it up and make it livable again, a real Hermitage, but I can't do that until they collect and analyze Rebecca's remains. I can't do that until I've done right by Rebecca, even though if truth be told Rebecca doesn't always do right by me.'

"He looked sad and tired, moving slowly to exasperation.

"But I kept at him.

" 'And they have to catch this stranger,' I said, 'this murderer, this miscreant who is dumping bodies in our swamp.'

"There came a final change in Pops, a change I'd seen many times in the past. He became angry, angry with me, the way I'd seen him with Patsy.

" 'You're getting titched in the head, son,' he said. 'You need to get clear of here. You can enroll at LSU in Baton Rouge if you want to stay close to home, but I'm for you going up East to Harvard. Aunt Queen's looked over all the material given her by Lynelle on your schooling and your examinations, and you could easily get into an Ivy League school right now. You're going out of here.'

" 'My darling,' Aunt Queen said, 'Pops is absolutely right. You have to think now of your future in the world and not the mysteries and his-tories of those who once lived in this house. This house will be here for you all your life. But you are at an age now when impressions mean everything, and it's time for you to get away.'

"I went silent. I had met with total resistance. I wondered if the gators could eat those bodies so quickly that there would be nothing left. I wondered if I could pinpoint the place on the island where I'd been standing when I saw the dastardly deed.

" 'You go to bed, Quinn,' said Aunt Queen gently. 'I know you saw something out there. I don't doubt you. And clearly the Hermitage exists. You've brought back proof of it. But it's late, and nothing can be done until morning.'

"Upstairs, I found Big Ramona in my wing chair by the cold fireplace with her rosary beads in her hand. Her full white hair was already braided. She was in her best rose-flowered flannel nightgown. She gave me a big hug and I went in to shower and change.

"After we said our night prayers and I let it be known I was too damned tired for a whole Rosary, we were soon snuggling spoon fashion and I was remembering that mysterious stranger in the weak light of the broken moon.

"Then I heard the computer switched on. A low green light emanated from the monitor.

"What a nuisance, I thought. 'Goblin, why do you do these things?' I murmured, but then I heard a strange sound. It was the clicking of the computer keys.

"I shot up out of bed and came into this parlor and stared at the computer. He had most certainly typed out a message:

QUINN, DANGER EVERYWHERE; I'M AFRAID.

"I was stultified. Never had he done this before. Turn it on and off, yes, but to write on it without my hand? I sat down at the computer and I wrote out the words as I recited them aloud:

" 'Goblin, I love you. I couldn't have come home without you. Explain what you mean about danger.'

"I moved my hands away from the keyboard and watched the rapid, seemingly magical depression of the keys as he wrote out:

I SEE IT NEAR AND FAR. GO AWAY. I LOVE YOU. DON'T LOVE
REBECCA.

"I began to whisper my response to him, that is, to talk aloud to him as I had always done—that he needn't worry—when the keys started firing again, and I saw the writing on the screen:

THROUGH THE COMPUTER, QUINN. I AM STRONG IN THE
ELECTRICITY, NOT STRONG NOW IN ANY OTHER WAY. TOO
TIRED FROM SWAMP. QUINN, GO.

"This all but dumbfounded me, but it fitted with my growing understanding of him, and so I hammered out:

" 'Goblin, who was the stranger? Who were the bodies?'

" 'I don't know,' came his answers. 'The bodies were dead.'

"That was a typical example of Goblin's reasoning. For a long breathless moment I sat there, and then I typed out: 'Goblin, I love you. Don't ever think that I don't love you. Put up with me and my off-and-on ways.'

"There came no answer, and then, before I could hit the save button to preserve this little dialogue, the computer switched itself off. Or rather Goblin switched it off.

" 'What does that mean?' I said aloud, looking about me. But no answer came from the darkness. There was nothing to be done but to go back to bed. . . .

"And to lie there, awake, pondering all that had happened, including the fact that Goblin could now write on the computer without using my left hand to do so—a frightening discovery, though one which was all bound up in my head with the awareness that he had led me out of the swamp.

"In summary, what I mean is I felt guilty for how shabbily I'd treated Goblin.

"Goblin had my admiration again, the way he had gotten it when I was a little boy and he taught me to spell big words. Goblin and I were close again. Goblin knew I was telling the truth. Goblin understood everything.

"I felt it excitedly while at the same time rejecting totally his message. We were close, that's what mattered.

"But we were to come even closer.

"Sometime during the night, as Big Ramona snored and I dozed in a half sleep, dreaming of Rebecca, there came into the room a stranger.

"Goblin, with a hand on my shoulder, awakened and alerted me. Sleeping on the left side of the bed I was turned to my left, and I opened my eyes to see Goblin staring past me in the direction of the fireplace. There came the tight squeeze from Goblin which on the island had meant caution.

"I rolled over as if it were merely natural in my sleep.

"I could see the figure at the mantel, and measuring it by that marker I calculated it was a tall man—and I knew by its outline that it was no man I knew, but its shape conformed with the shape of the man I'd seen in the swamp in the moonlight.

"I could see the outline of a bold head, well squared-off shoulders, and the glint of a hand on the mantelpiece. I was certain it was the same man! There came a tapping sound from the mantelpiece. There was something white on the mantelpiece.

"And then there came a low utterance of laughter.

"I climbed out of bed lickety-split, though Goblin tried with all his effort to stop me. And as I rushed across the room in my bare feet I heard the sound of paper crumpled and I picked out of the shadows the sight of a white paper ball tossed into the fireplace.

"Before I took another step the man had vanished.

"My eyes searched the room. I rushed through the open doorway only to find the hallway empty. Attic and ground floor revealed nobody.

"All the guests of Blackwood Manor slept and so did its residents. And from the kitchen window I could see Clem, the night man, in the brightly lighted shed, sitting back with his feet up, watching the television.

"My heart was racing.

"What was the point of sounding an alarm? Who would believe me this time? I went back up to my room and I retrieved the crumpled paper from the fireplace. I knew what it was before I read it. It was my letter to the trespasser of Sugar Devil Island, warning him to get off the property.

"I straightened it out and turned it over. There was no response written on it. Then I remembered the tapping on the mantelpiece, and sure enough there was a letter there, or at least a piece of folded white paper.

"I was incalculably excited! Here was the smoking gun. I snatched up this paper with literally trembling hands and took it to my desk where I turned on my small halogen lamp in hopes of not awakening Big Ramona.

"The white paper was thick and fancy, and the writing was in script of a florid and large design. I could smell the India ink in which it had been written. This is an approximation of what it said:

Tarquin, my beloved boy,

I am not as amused by your notice as one might expect. On the contrary, I rather resent your intrusion into a portion of Sugar Devil Swamp to which I hold unwritten title, thanks to the generosity and foresight of your great-great-great-grandfather Manfred. If I had not set eyes on you tonight and not recognized you for the sensitive and serious young man which you are, I might take even greater umbrage than I do.

As it stands, allow me to explain that I want the island undisturbed by you, and it is my express wish that none of you or your family come there. I treasure my privacy, Tarquin, perhaps more than you treasure your life. Think on it, my boy.
The Resident of the Hermitage.

"I folded the letter, and, without bothering with a robe or slippers any more than I had during my earlier perambulation, I went downstairs to Aunt Queen's bedroom. I pushed open the door with a child's license.

"The light was on of course, and Aunt Queen was on her chaise lounge, swaddled in diamonds and satin covers, eating a pint of pink ice cream.

"Jasmine, who was bunking in with her, lay sound asleep in the bed.

"From the television there came the muted voices of Bette Davis and Olivia de Havilland.

" 'Tarquin,' Aunt Queen said at once, 'what is it?' She muted the murmuring television. 'You look like you've seen Banquo's ghost. Come here and kiss me.'

"I kissed her more than willingly.

" 'He's come into my room, Aunt Queen,' I said breathlessly, waving the letter in her face. 'And he's left me this note. I saw him, Aunt Queen. He stood at my fireplace. Goblin told me he was there. And this is the note which he's left me. Aunt Queen, I tell you something involving murder is afoot out there. And mad as it may sound it's some sort of secret Byronic society.'

" 'Let me see this letter,' she said. She set her ice cream aside. Meanwhile Jasmine had raised her head and was sliding out from under the blankets.

"I told them both what had transpired upstairs. Jasmine then read the note, and Aunt Queen read it a second time. I was too excited to do anything but pace.

" 'We've got to start locking the front and back doors,' Jasmine said, 'if people are going to come just walking right in without knocking.'

" 'We don't lock the front and back doors?!' I asked, appalled.

" 'No, you know we don't,' said Jasmine. 'The guests come back at all hours from New Orleans. You ever had a key to the front or back door, Tarquin Blackwood?'

" 'This guy laughed at me,' I said as calmly as I could, which wasn't calm at all. 'He laughed, I tell you. I heard him laugh and . . .' " I stopped. It was the laughter I heard in those dizzy spells. It was the laughter that had accompanied Rebecca's piteous pleas. Oh, but who would ever believe that!

" 'Tarquin, what is it!' Aunt Queen pressed. 'Don't stand there staring. Jasmine, go run and tell Clem to check the entire property. Tell Clem we've had an intruder. Hurry.'

"Jasmine headed out.

" 'Tarquin, stop staring like that,' said Aunt Queen. 'There has to be a reason for this, I mean something that makes sense here. Maybe you've hit it. It is a secret society that meets out there, you know, a sort of romantic clandestine thing, and one of them has come into this house, which you know is open at all times, you know, and he has dared to go upstairs. . . .' "

" 'There's nothing romantic about dumping dead bodies,' I said.

" 'Darling, maybe he was dumping something else, and it just looked that way.'

"I turned around in a small circle. I saw the faint outline of Goblin by one post of the fancy bed. Goblin nodded to me vigorously.

"I looked at her. She was looking past me to the place where Goblin stood.

" 'They were dead bodies, Aunt Queen,' I said. 'I know because Goblin knows and Goblin is afraid.'

"A deep silence fell over her, and then she looked up at me. 'My sweet boy,' she said. 'I shall have this investigated in every conceivable way, make no mistake on it. But I am going to get you out of here.' "

15

"ON THE FOLLOWING MORNING, Sugar Devil Island, which had always been the biggest secret of Blackwood Farm, became host to a dozen crime fighters, including not only the sheriff of Ruby River Parish and his deputies but two private investigators hired directly by Aunt Queen, two private laboratory technicians and two gentlemen from the Federal Bureau of Investigation.

"In this way, the Hermitage became public knowledge. And as I stood there on the banks, directing people to the locality where I saw the bodies dumped in the open swamp, I was treated to the semi-welcome sight of people trooping all over Manfred's sacred retreat.

"Pops had had real bad indigestion after breakfast and said that he just couldn't go with us. It made him feel really bad, but he just wasn't up to it.

"Aunt Queen, of course, could not be expected to make such a journey, but she did, handsomely turned out in khaki sportswear, which made her look like a nineteenth-century archaeologist. (I had forgotten that she had been to the Amazon only the year before for a retreat in the jungle.)

"And of course Jasmine was with us, in blue jeans, which she never wore, breasts poking through one of my hand-me-down checkered shirts, smoking Camel cigarettes and eyeing everybody with suspicion if not downright scorn.

"And I stood there, listening for anything that would lessen my feelings of being isolated and ridiculed.

"Of course, dead bodies in the swamp were nowhere to be found.

"But probing some six to ten feet of soft-bottomed muck was no easy task, and the alligators surrounding the island were particularly obtrusive and 'friendly,' which to me meant only one thing: they were expecting to be fed and they had probably just been fed on the bodies I'd seen given over to them.

"As for the remains, or the second-floor 'residue,' as it became officially called, a good sample of it was removed from the premises by the Federal Bureau of Investigation and by laboratory technicians from the private laboratory of Mayfair Medical, the giant private establishment only recently built by the famous Mayfair family of New Orleans, the family of which Fr. Kevin Mayfair was a Yankee member—which I've mentioned to you before.

"The FBI was there because they had the wherewithal to collect and test the residue, and because they had extensive files on missing persons which might just provide a DNA match to seal the story for some miserable victim's family.

"Mayfair Medical was there because they too had a state-of-the-art laboratory, and Aunt Queen had hired them to do the test on our behalf, the Hermitage being a dwelling on our property.

"The sheriff was there to traffic in platitudes and truisms and puffed-up stories about the practical jokes he played on his friends, and in general to be a source of comic relief.

"As for the letter which the mysterious stranger had given me, this had not been given to the FBI as I had requested, but to Mayfair Medical. Would that destroy a 'chain of evidence' if DNA from recent missing persons was found in the Hermitage? No. Because nothing linked the letter to the Hermitage except my meager testimony.

"Or so I understood the situation to be on the morning of this wholesale melee in which interstate officialdom and southern recalcitrance met head-on in a dense and reeking bog full of reptiles and insects.

"The men from the FBI were respectable and respecting, which is probably why the sheriff and his men would hardly acknowledge their existence. I gave my full statement to anyone who asked, and that included the technicians from Mayfair Medical, both of whom were tremendously curious about the task at hand, i.e., the collection of the data.

"Nobody fingerprinted the mysterious marble desk and Roman chair, but just about everybody sooner or later touched it.

"Everybody—even the sheriff—was impressed with the gold mausoleum, if that was what it was, and repeated efforts by various parties failed to discover any way to open it. The gold plates (the sheriff insisted they were brass), I repeat, the gold plates were so securely fitted into the granite framework that only a very destructive crowbar might have managed to loosen them, which we, the proud owners of the mausoleum, refused to allow.

"Finally, at midafternoon it was decided to call off the search for remains and the sheriff and his men made their way out, cursing their little pirogues and their poles and the cypress trees with their outrageous roots and knees, the wisteria and the blackberries and the heat and the mosquitoes. The FBI gentlemen went the same route, behaving altogether in a more reserved manner, as our local handyman, Jackson, was steering their boat and it did not seem to be the FBI style to curse at things.

"Aunt Queen, Jasmine and I, along with our Shed Men, Clem and Felix (both Jasmine's brothers, and one Aunt Queen's oftentimes chauffeur), not wishing to remain on the island alone—Jasmine had seen the letter—hurried behind the FBI right back to the landing.

"Once safe within the orbit of Blackwood Manor I told Clem and Felix that I wanted to wire the Hermitage for electricity in the near future, and to please not forget where they had just been. Aunt Queen gave her consent and so they paid attention to me.

"Also they were too kind to snicker. Also they were tired, and I gave them both a cash bonus, of which Jasmine expressed a certain refined jealousy. So I gave her a cash bonus too, which I was positive she wouldn't accept but she did, conspicuously stuffing it into her brassiere and winking at me.

"On that account I grabbed her and bent her way back and kissed her hard, to which she said in a whisper: 'Once you go black, you never go back.' And I nearly died laughing.

" 'Where did you hear that?' I asked.

" 'Forever and a long time ago,' she said. 'I'm surprised you never heard it. Watch your step, Little Boss.' Off she went, helping Aunt Queen up the slope, the two of them whispering suspiciously together.

"I don't know why I was so afraid. Everybody knew I'd told the truth about the existence of the island. Everybody had seen the marble desk and the golden chair. Everybody had seen the strange inscription on the mausoleum.

"Had I not gloried in those first few moments this morning when the chain of little pirogues came within sight of the island? Yes, I had! And had I not gloried in the moment of shock when everyone crowded onto the second floor of the Hermitage to see the evil rusted chains and the blackened morass on the floor? Yes, I had.

"But what did it mean now?

"It was four o'clock. The sun was lowering. The property, for all its vain magnificence, looked forlorn.

"I went low, very low.

"I stood out front, beyond Pops' close and beautiful flower beds, staring at the big columns of the house until Aunt Queen came out on the front porch and told me she'd been looking for me everywhere. I knew I ought to answer her but it seemed difficult for me to break the silence that surrounded me.

"I knew on some level that her genial, sweet face was just what I needed in my selfish little soul, but I couldn't speak. I thought of the mysterious stranger, I thought of the bodies slipping into the muck. I saw the moonlight as if it were shining on me now. I saw the dim figure who had stood at my bedroom fireplace. Glint of light on hand, on fore-head, on cheek. Terror. I felt mystery, yes, but cold panic.

"Aunt Queen came near to me. She said words but I didn't hear them. Then out of the silence I heard her voice . . . something about men being on the property to guard it. Men paid from an agency in New Orleans, excellent security men.

"Cerebrally I knew these words meant something. They meant something good, and I formed mental images of these men—of their being at the doors, and sitting in the parlor, the kitchen, the dining room. I pictured. When I can't think or register, I picture. I listened.

"But nothing could touch the cold panic I felt, and my only recourse seemed a motionlessness.

" 'Quinn!' she said. She put her hand on my neck, and I looked at her and I thought, *How long will it be before she dies?* And my throat was so tight I couldn't speak.

"Finally I came to the surface. I took her hand and kissed it, and I said, 'Let me help you up the steps, you always wear these impossible shoes, look at you, and what if you fall and you break a hip, what then, my beloved aunt, you won't be able to go to Katmandu or Timbuktu or Iceland.'

"She took my arm and into the house we went, and after seeing her to her room, and nodding to the security guard who sat in the far corner of the dining room, I went up the stairs.

"This memory's etched: but what isn't?

"The panic was still on me. Would it be washed away? I went into the bathroom, stripped off the dirty swamp clothes and stepped into the shower.

"I let the warm water splash over me, praying, if I was capable of praying, that this feeling of despair, this awful despair, would leave me. I tried to reach back to the excitement I'd felt when I first came upon the island. I tried to feel anything that would lift the awful despair from me. But excitement had turned to dread, and I was an expert on dread. Now it had other springs to feed it.

"I must have had my eyes closed. Because quite suddenly I realized Goblin was in the shower with me. And then I opened my eyes and saw him right in front of me.

"He was solid, so solid that the water washed over him, over his hair and his face and his shoulders. He was staring at me with big vital eyes.

" 'Go away, Goblin,' I said, which was what I always said when he came to interfere with my taking a bath or shower.

"But he showed no signs of backing off, and as I looked into his eyes I realized he was obdurately maintaining his stand and that the water was making him tremendously strong. I also realized that I had never seen the water washing down over him like this before. The water had at other times passed through him. He had volume here; he had new power.

"A sudden fear of him infected me. It was like the moment in the church at Lynelle's Memorial Mass, when he had knelt so very close to me after Communion.

"His cock was erect. So was mine.

"Never taking his eyes from mine for a moment, he reached for the soap on the small porcelain shelf, and he took this into his hands, and he lathered his hands thickly.

"*But how is this possible?* I thought. But he was doing it, he was holding the bar of soap, and as he put the soap back he reached under my scrotum and cupped it in his left hand and then put his right hand around my cock.

" 'No, don't do it, stop it, what are you doing?' I asked. But I was too far gone, and the motion of his right hand became rhythmical and my cock grew harder and harder and my willpower vanished.

"As I came he put his left arm tight around me and held me, and I felt his cock next to mine and I held his neck, unable to stand for a moment.

"When it was over, I rested back against the warm tiles, still savoring the pleasure, weak all over from the pleasure, the water softly thundering down, staring questioningly at him. His image—if I even thought of it as an image—was more vivid than ever.

"I closed my eyes. I was filled with both love and hatred. Most of all I was full of shame, and I thought of how all the world would say I had done this to myself, only making up the story of Goblin; but he had done it and I knew that he could do it again anytime that I wanted it. Or anytime that he wanted it. Again. Yes, again, forever. Me and Goblin forever.

"When I opened my eyes he was still grotesquely close to me, his eyes gleaming, his lips smiling. Am I this handsome? I thought. No. Something else shines from my eyes.

" 'Get away now!' I whispered furiously.

"He put his lips to my ear. I heard his telepathic voice in my head, a thin ribbon of words under the thunder of the shower: *Pops does this. Clem, Felix, men do this. Love me. Not love Rebecca. No Rebecca.*

"Again I felt his left arm around my shoulder, and when he drew back I kissed him openmouthed and lusty and closer to him than to any living thing, and then I shuddered.

"I pushed him with all my strength and of course my mental strength went behind that physical push, and he dissolved, and to my faint horror steam rose where he had been, as if a fissure had been opened in the floor to emit that steam, and then there was nothing.

"There came a pounding on the door. I heard Big Ramona say,

" 'Tarquin Blackwood, come out of there!'

"She knows, I thought, the whole world knows. Angry, I toweled dry and opened the door for her because she wouldn't stop pounding.

" 'Good Heavens,' I said. 'Is this house on fire again?'

"Then I saw the tears on her cheeks.

" 'It's Pops,' she said. 'He's been fighting with Patsy, out yonder by the gates. That damned Patsy. Come on, son! Come on, you're the man of the house now, they need you!' "

16

"THERE ARE two sets of gates to Blackwood Farm—the formal gates that lead to the lane of pecan trees which come up to the front porch, and the other larger gates, way off to the east, for the caterer trucks, deliveries and tractors.

"It was out there, beside the big gates, that Pops had planted two big oak trees in memory of Sweetheart.

"He had apparently driven out there, sometime in the afternoon, with a flat of multicolored impatiens to plant around the trees, a project he'd mentioned on and off for a while now. And the Shed Men said later that he seemed confused and strangely unconcerned about the goings on at Sugar Devil Island. One side of his face had not looked right, and they had meant to go check on him.

"Patsy had gone out there, in her new truck, to talk to Pops, cursing to the Shed Men that she had to ask Pops for money again and she hated it, it wasn't fair and all that. She'd left Seymour behind because he didn't want to see any more scenes. And he'd been drinking beer with the Shed Men.

"It was Patsy who came screaming back, having already called for emergency help on her car phone, and the Shed Men drove out with Patsy to find Pops dead right by the flower bed. His hands were caked with earth.

"Big Ramona and Jasmine and Aunt Queen and I got there about the same time as the medical team. They couldn't bring him around, and we all piled into our assorted vehicles, Aunt Queen in the ambulance with Pops, and headed for the small hospital in Ruby River City.

"But it was all up for Pops. We'd known that when we first saw him by the oak tree. Sobbing uncontrollably, Aunt Queen ordered an autopsy, saying she just had to know the cause, and we went on to make the funeral arrangements.

"Aunt Queen proved utterly incapable of doing it.

"So, quivering and incoherent, I went with Jasmine to McNeil's Funeral Parlor and arranged for the pickup of the body, the night of the wake, and the directions for the drive into New Orleans for the funeral Mass at St. Mary's Assumption Church and the burial at Metairie Cemetery.

"The nice people at the funeral home said I could put off all the rest—the autopsy would take two days—but I thought why not get it over now? And so I picked a beautiful dark hardwood coffin that I thought Pops would like, being the handyman that he was, and I chose a Biblical quotation for the program from the Book of Psalms, and I arranged for a singer to sing Pops' favorite hymns, some of which were Catholic and some of which were Protestant.

"When I reached home I found Aunt Queen broken and unable to do anything but sob, and I didn't blame her. She said over and over that a woman shouldn't have to bury her great-nephew, that it was all wrong, terribly wrong.

"We called her favorite nurse, Cindy, who said she'd come right over. Aunt Queen wasn't really sick, but she often had Cindy to do her blood pressure and collect her bloodwork before trips abroad, and so Cindy was the loving person to whom we turned now.

"As for myself I was in a cold panic, the same cold panic that had been coming over me since Lynelle's death, but I hadn't reached the worst stage of it yet. I was still in the elation state that immediately follows the miracle of death, and, in my ignorant youth, I had a 'take charge' attitude.

"I went into Pops' room and picked out his best Sunday suit, a good shirt, belt and a tie, and gave these to Clem to drive over to Ruby River City. I sent underwear too because I didn't know if it was needed. And I had the strange idea that Pops might want his underwear.

"After Clem had left me, and I was standing alone in Pops' room, Goblin appeared, and without a prompt he put his arms tight around me. He felt as real as I felt real. And I kissed his cheek, and I saw his tears. A rush of the most intimate love passed out of me into him.

"This was an extraordinary moment, a moment of confusion and contrition. And in the dark corners of my subconscious I knew it was a dangerous moment. But my heart was leading the band.

" 'Goblin, I loved Pops,' I said. 'You understand, you understand everything.'

" 'Patsy. Bad,' he responded in the telepathic voice. I could feel his kisses on my cheek and my neck. For a split second, I felt his hand on my cock.

"I reached down and gently moved his hand away. But the damage had been done. I had to nail down hard on myself. Then I spoke to him:

" 'No, it's not Patsy's fault,' I said out loud. 'She was just being Patsy, that's all. Now, you go and leave me alone now, Goblin. I have to go downstairs. I have to see to things.'

"He gave me a final hug and I was amazed at his strength. I could see nothing in him that appeared spectral or ephemeral. But he vanished as I had asked him to, and the baubles of the chandeliers moved as if he had evacuated the room at his departure.

"I stood staring at the chandelier. It hadn't hit me yet that nobody alive inhabited this back bedroom anymore. But it was trying to hit me. Things were trying to get through. Goblin had been the image of my weeping soul. Oh, I had so misjudged Goblin, but who would ever understand?

"When I came down to the kitchen, Patsy was sitting at the table just staring at me and Big Ramona was on one of the stools by the stove just staring at her. Lolly was there too, all dressed up for a date, her copper skin and rippling yellow hair just gorgeous, and there was Jasmine in her apron in the far corner by the back door.

"I could hear Aunt Queen crying in her bedroom. Her nurse, Cindy, had arrived, and I could hear Cindy's sympathetic tones as she tried to comfort her.

"Patsy's eyes were glassy and hard and she was chewing a piece of gum that made her jaw look hard. She put a cigarette on her lip and snapped her lighter. She had her huge poofed-up stage hairstyle, and her lips were thickly made-up with frosted pink lipstick.

" 'So everybody's going to want to know what we were talking about,' she said. There was a little tremor in her voice, a note I'd never heard before, but I wasn't sure anybody else heard it.

" 'Seymour says you wanted some money,' Jasmine said.

" 'Yeah, I wanted money,' said Patsy, in her hard voice, 'and it's not like he didn't have it to give. He had it. Just wait till they read his will.

He was loaded, and what did he ever do with it? But that's not what set him off to cursing and shouting at me and then grabbing for his chest and throwing up and dying.'

" 'So what did?' asked Jasmine.

" 'I told him I was sick,' said Patsy. 'I told him I was HIV-positive.'

"Silence. Then Big Ramona looked at me.

" 'What's she talking about?' she asked.

" 'AIDS, Ramona,' I said. 'She's HIV-positive. It means she's contracted the AIDS virus. She could come down with full-blown AIDS any time.'

" 'I'm the one that's sick,' Patsy said, 'and he's the one that up and dies because he was mad at me, mad that I got it. You ask me, he died of grief. Grief for Sweetheart.' She broke off and looked from one to the other of all of us.

" 'Grief's what killed him,' she went on. She shrugged. 'I didn't kill him. You should have seen what he was doing out there. He'd rolled over one row of pansies with his truck, and there he was laying another bed of them, like he didn't even know what he'd done with his truck. I said, "Look at what you've done, you sniveling crazy old man." He started in on all that, "You sold her wedding dress!" like that wasn't so over, sniveling crazy old fool, and he said he wasn't giving me a red cent, and then I told him. I told him I had medical bills to pay.'

"I was too stunned to think, but I heard myself ask her, 'How did you get it?'

" 'How should I know?' she replied, looking at me with those brittle glossy eyes. 'From some bastard who had it, probably a user, I don't know, I've got an idea and then I don't. It wasn't Seymour, don't you go blaming him. And don't you go telling him either. Don't you none of you tell anybody what I'm telling you. Don't you go telling Aunt Queen. Seymour and I have a gig tonight. But the thing is, I can't pay the rest of the pickers unless I have some money.'

"By pickers, she meant the guitar players who'd be backing her up.

" 'You expect one of us to go in there and ask Aunt Queen for money?' asked Big Ramona. 'Cancel your goddamned gig. You got no business playing music tonight when your father is stone dead at the mortuary in Ruby River City.'

"Patsy shook her head. 'I'm flat broke,' she said. 'Quinn, go in there and get some money for me.'

"I swallowed, I remember that, but I don't remember how long it was before I could answer her. Then I remembered that I had Pops' money clip in my jeans. They'd given it to me, along with his keys and his handkerchief, at the hospital.

"I took it out and I looked at it. It was a wad of twenty-dollar bills, but there were also more than several hundreds. He always saved those hundred-dollar bills just in case something came up. I counted it all out—one thousand dollars—and I gave it to her.

" 'You telling the truth about being HIV?' Jasmine asked.

" 'Yeah, and I see you're all crying buckets,' said Patsy. 'He blew his stack when he heard. You're just one big sympathetic family.'

" 'Anybody know outside of us?' Jasmine asked.

" 'No,' Patsy said. 'I just told you not to tell anybody, didn't I? And why are you asking me, you worried about your precious bed-and-breakfast? There's nobody left to run it, case you haven't noticed. Unless you all are taking over.' She shot a mean glance at each of us in turn. 'I guess Little Lord Tarquin here could become the youngest bed-and-breakfast owner in the South, now, couldn't he?'

" 'I'm very sorry, Patsy,' I said. 'But it's not a death sentence anymore, being HIV. There are drugs, lots of drugs.'

" 'Oh, save it, Little Lord Tarquin!' she shot at me.

" 'Is that going to be my name from now on? I don't like it,' I fired at her. 'I was trying to tell you about medicine, advances, hopes. They have a special clinic for research at Mayfair Medical, that's all I'm trying to say.'

" 'Oh, yeah, research, fine with your wonderful education, you know all about those things,' she hammered. 'Lynelle's little genius. You haven't seen her ghost lately, have you?'

" 'Patsy, you're not working any gig tonight,' declared Big Ramona.

" 'Are you getting decent treatment?' Jasmine asked. 'Just tell us that much.'

" 'Oh, yeah yeah, I know all about decent treatment,' Patsy said. 'I'm a musician, remember. You don't think I never shot up? That's probably how I got it, needles, not being tacked to the mattress. And all it takes is one time and all that, and I never shoot up except when I'm drunk, and so there we are, Miss Patsy Blackwood's not long for this world, 'cause she got drunk and shot up with somebody else's needle, but so far she's not symptomatic.'

"She shoved the money in her shoulder bag and stood up.

" 'Where are you going, girl!' Big Ramona said, standing up to block

Patsy from the back door. 'You're not working a gig with your father dead.'

" 'The hell I'm not, and I'm working it in Tennessee so I got to get on the road. Seymour's waiting.'

" 'You can't leave here,' I said. 'You can't not come to the funeral!'

" 'Watch me not come to it,' she sneered.

"The screen door banged shut behind her. I ran after her.

" 'Patsy, you'll regret this all your life,' I said. I ran along beside her to her van. 'Patsy, you're not thinking. It hasn't sunk in. You have to go through with this. Everybody will expect you to care enough to be there. Patsy, listen to me.'

" 'Like my life is going to be long, Quinn! My life? That old man. I told him I was HIV and he went crazy! You should have heard him cursing me and the crowd I run with; you wanna know what his final words were to me? "Damn the day you were born," and then he went down, gasping and throwing up his guts. I wouldn't come to his funeral if he was going to rise from the dead. If you see his ghost, you tell him I hate him. Now get away from me.'

"She and Seymour were off, screeching tires and all, and I just stood there, feeling the panic again, and within seconds the cold thought came over me that I didn't care whether Patsy came or not. It would do nothing to lessen the pain in me. Probably, it didn't matter to anyone.

"It would just be one of those things that people would talk about all over the parish.

"Only being near to my Jasmine or Big Ramona or Aunt Queen would help me.

"I made my way back inside. I could smell the pancakes Big Ramona was cooking up for me, and hunger seemed a reason to be alive, to put off for a little while telling Aunt Queen that Patsy would not be there for the funeral. In fact, maybe I'd never even mention it.

"The autopsy took only a day.

"Pops had suffered a massive heart attack.

"The funeral was enormous. It began with a long evening wake in Ruby River City to which all manner of people came, including shop owners, repairmen, carpenters, woodworkers—in summary, the many, many people in all walks of life whom Pops had known and who were devoted to him.

"I was staggered by the sheer number of young boys and young men who looked up to Pops and said he'd been like a father or uncle to them.

It seemed that everyone respected Pops and he was much more well known than I had ever imagined.

"Ugly Henderson and his whole clan were there, and so were the Dirty Hodges, all cleaned up, which had never happened before, their only bathtub being full of greasy auto parts. Sheriff Jeanfreau was crying.

"As for Patsy's absence, it was a total scandal. And the excuse that she had a show she had to work in Tennessee didn't cut her any slack with anybody. People had not only expected her to be at the funeral, they had expected her to sing.

"As it was, we hired an elderly woman who all but worshiped Pops for the handyman favors he'd done for her over the years, and she did just fine.

"Next morning when the procession set out for St. Mary's Assumption Church in New Orleans, the church in which Sweetheart and Pops had been married, people everywhere on the sidewalks of Ruby River City stopped out of respect.

"There was an old workman in a straw hat up on a ladder fixing something on the side of his house, and he stopped and took off his hat and held it to his chest as we passed. That single gesture will remain in my mind forever.

"Then to the Requiem Mass in St. Mary's there came another horde, many of them the country people who'd been at the wake, and hundreds of them being Sweetheart's side of the family, the New Orleans Mardi Gras crowd, and the procession had more cars than I could count when it went to the Metairie Cemetery to leave Pops' coffin with all the appropriate prayers at the open chapel vault.

"The sun was pounding down on us out there, in spite of the few lovely oaks that gave a little shade, but mercifully Fr. Kevin Mayfair was brief, and everything that he said, both at the church and at the cemetery, was heartfelt and fresh. I think when I heard him speak of it I believed again in eternal life, and I felt my panic was a sin against God, a sin of atheism.

"Optimism was a virtue; and the despair, the terror I often felt—it was a sin. As for the ghosts I saw, maybe that was somehow a gift from God. Maybe there would be a use for it.

"As for the mysterious stranger, he would be apprehended. Or he would move on, away from Sugar Devil Island to some other out-of-the-way place.

"I know how melodramatic that sounds, but I didn't fully understand my panic, and I don't now.

"Of course, Goblin was at the funeral—just as he had been at Sweetheart's funeral—he knelt beside me in church and he stood right at my side when others would permit, but I came to realize something as we stood before the little family mortuary chapel.

"What I came to understand was that Goblin's face was becoming more and more reflective of complex emotions. He had always made faces of sorts, but in general he looked blank and amazed. Only now, this was changing.

"What I remember from the funeral was that he seemed to have the face of a distinct character, a mingled confusion and wonder and a sharp attention to others present, his eyes roaming the crowd and frequently settling on Fr. Kevin Mayfair.

"Watching Goblin's eyes move, watching him take the measure of the crypt, all this had a hypnotic fascination for me. And when he looked back at me, to see that I watched, he smiled in a rather sad and sophisticated fashion.

"That's what it was—a sophisticated fashion. And when had Goblin ever seemed more than a clown? Out there in the Metairie Cemetery he didn't look like a clown at all, and he seemed also rather detached from me and my emotions.

"I didn't think too much more about it.

"But before we leave the funeral, let me dwell on Fr. Kevin Mayfair. Fr. Kevin Mayfair was superb. He was an inspiration. He looked too young to be a priest, as I've more or less already noted, and on that day he didn't look any older.

"And for the first time I noticed how really handsome he was. I felt awakened to his red hair and green eyes and his good build. I'd say he's six feet tall about. And his manner of speaking was utterly convincing. That he believed Pops had gone to Heaven was beyond doubt.

"And a young priest that strong—well, it's an inspiration. I felt drawn to him, I felt I could go to Confession to him and tell him some of the things that were wrong with me.

"After the funeral we returned to Blackwood Manor for a huge reception to which dozens of the country folk came. The buffets overflowed with casserole dishes of food which the neighbors had brought, and fabulous dishes which Big Ramona and Jasmine had cooked up, and the two paying guests we had on the premises were honored to be asked to join in with us.

"Big Ramona's two sons, who had gone out into the world, as we always said—George, a dentist in Shreveport, and Yancy, a lawyer in

New Orleans—were there with their wives, lending us all a hand with the food. And there were some half dozen or more of the black cousins there too.

"The security guards were everywhere, unobtrusively eyeing anyone or everyone and conferring with me repeatedly as to the 'mysterious stranger,' but I saw no one whom I could connect to that being.

"Repeatedly throughout the long ordeal Aunt Queen broke down and sobbed and said that nobody should have to bury a great-nephew and she didn't know why she had lived so long. I'd never seen her so broken. She made me think of a lily trod underfoot.

"At one point it seemed that everybody was talking about Patsy's absence but I was probably imagining it. I had just said too many times that Patsy couldn't possibly make it, and each time I found myself saying it I felt myself disliking Patsy a little more.

"As for the confession of her being HIV, I didn't know whether or not I believed her.

"At last the long funeral day was over.

"The paying guests checked out early, insisting that they were more than happy to do it and wanted to go off to gamble at the casinos on the Gulf Coast anyway.

"A quiet fell over Blackwood Manor. The armed guards took their positions, but the house and the land seem to swallow them.

"The dusk came on, with the grinding song of the cicadas in the oak trees and the rising of the evening star.

"Aunt Queen lay crying on her bed. Cindy, her nurse, sat beside her holding her hand. Jasmine lay behind her, rubbing her back.

"Big Ramona packed up food into the refrigerator in the kitchen.

"I went upstairs alone. I sat down in my reading chair, there, by the fireplace, and I fell into a doze. The panic was never bad enough to stop a doze. And hard as it had been, I was deliciously tired now and elated to be alone.

"At once, as sleep came down over me, Rebecca was with me and she said in my ear, 'I know how bad you feel.' Then the scene dissolved and I saw her being dragged by a shadowy figure towards the chains, I saw her lace-up shoe bouncing on the bare floorboards and I heard her scream.

"I woke with a start.

"The computer keys were clicking.

"I stared at the computer desk. The gooseneck lamp was on! I could see my double sitting there—see his back, the back of his head and his shoulders and arms as he worked, and there persisted: the clicking.

"Before I could rise the sound stopped, and he turned, turned as a human couldn't turn, and looked at me over his right shoulder. He wore no grin or mournful expression, only a vaguely startled look.

"As I rose from my chair he vanished.

"The message on the computer screen was long:

" 'I know all the words you know, words you type. Pops dead like Lynelle and Sweetheart. Dead, gone, not in the body. Sadness. Spirit gone. Body left. Body washed. Body painted. Body empty. Spirit is life. This life. Life gone. Why does life leave body? People say don't know. I don't know. Quinn sad. Quinn cry. Aunt Queen cry. I am sad. But danger is coming. Danger on island. I see danger. Don't forget. Rebecca is bad. Danger to Quinn. Quinn will leave Goblin.'

"Immediately I typed out the answer. 'Listen to me,' I said aloud as I wrote. 'I will never leave you. The only thing that could part us is for me to die, and then, yes, my spirit would leave my body and I would be gone, I don't know where. Now ask yourself again, Where did the spirit of Lynelle go? Where did the spirit of Sweetheart go? Where did the spirit of Pops go?'

"I sat waiting and there was no answer.

"Then the keys before me began to move. He typed out: 'Where did these spirits come from?'

"I felt a tightening, a keen sense that I had to be careful. I wrote: 'Bodies are born into the world. Remember when I was a newborn? A baby? Bodies are born into the world with the spirit in them, and when those bodies die the spirit leaves.'

"Silence.

"Then the keys moved again: 'Where did I come from?'

"I felt a dull fear. It was the panic breaking through, but it was something more as well. I typed out:

" 'Don't you know where you came from? Don't you know who you were before you became my Goblin?'

" 'No.'

" 'You must remember something,' I typed. 'You must have been somewhere.'

" 'Were you somewhere?' he asked. 'Before you were Quinn?'

" 'No. I had my beginnings when I was born,' I wrote. 'But you are a spirit. Where were you? Were you with somebody else? Why did you come to me?'

"There was a long pause, very long, so long that I almost rose from the desk and moved off, but then the clicking keys came again:

" 'I love Quinn,' the writing said. 'Quinn and Goblin one together.'

" 'Yes,' I said out loud. 'We are, one together.'

"The machine was clicked off. The gooseneck lamp flicked on and off twice and then went dark.

"My heart was pounding. What was happening to Goblin? And how could I confide to anyone in this world about him, what with Pops dead and everything at Blackwood Farm hanging in the balance? To whom could I go to say this spirit is taking on new strength?

"For some period of time I sat there, and then I turned on the machine and asked:

" 'Danger, this danger you speak of, is it from the stranger who came into this room?'

"No answer.

" 'What did you see when you saw the stranger? What did he look like to you? You must remember that to my eyes he was only a dark shape. Goblin, listen. Tell me.'

"A breeze sifted through the room, something chilling against my cheek—but no answer. He didn't have the strength. He had done enough for one day. Or he didn't want to answer. Whatever the case, there was only the silence now.

"I was no longer sleepy, only tired, and a deep sweet exhaustion swallowed up my grief and my panic. I wanted to fold down into my wing chair by the fireplace and sleep again, safe in the knowledge that there were armed guards around the property and the mysterious stranger couldn't harm me. But I couldn't do that.

"No, Little Lord Tarquin was the man of Blackwood Manor now.

"I went downstairs to see to Aunt Queen.

"Fr. Kevin Mayfair was in her room, seated by the bed, talking softly to her. He was wearing his severe and spotless clerical black along with his white Roman collar.

"And when I watched him from the door, I knew for the first time that I found both men and women erotically beautiful. Rebecca in the lace-trimmed bed, Goblin in the warm steamy thunderstorm of the shower. Fr. Kevin Mayfair with that dark curly red hair and those green eyes and not a freckle on his pale face. Men and women.

"I went out back and walked way over to the right to the bungalow in which Jasmine, Ramona, Clem and Lolly lived. Jasmine was in her green-painted rocking chair, just rocking and smoking.

"I was in a daze. I tried not to notice Jasmine's breasts in her tight shirt. I tried not to look at the front seam of her jeans. When she turned away from me to exhale I saw the light down the line of her throat to her breasts. Beautiful woman. Aged thirty-five. What were my chances? Like, maybe if I sold her a bill of goods that I doubted my manhood???

"Oh, that was a lovely thought. Wonderfully comforting. And where could we do it? Just go over to the shed, go up the steps and do it in Patsy's bed? I rolled that dream around for a moment. You don't get HIV from a bed. What if—and then—and so—and I felt the panic when I looked at the dim house—they had forgotten the four o'clock lights.

" 'What's going to happen now?' I asked.

" 'Come sit with me, little boy lost,' she said. 'I've been asking myself that very question.' "

17

"**F**OR THE NEXT WEEK I was under lock and key, or armed escort.

"I didn't find out about it until the morning after Pops' funeral, when I tried to leave my room and discovered I had a security guard with me, pledged to go where I would go.

"I didn't too terribly mind, since I alone knew how real the mysterious stranger had been and I didn't want to be shocked by him. But I made a nuisance of myself by warning everyone about the dangers of the island.

"Our investigations proceeded rapidly, and I know that I focused on them to escape the pure horror of Pops' death—the loss of the only man who had ever been my father. We had the reading of his will to attend to, and I was dreadfully concerned that he might have cut out Patsy altogether. If I had been left anything at all I resolved to split it with Patsy or at least to give her some of it.

"Meantime she was still out roaming the South, playing beer joints and small clubs, and Aunt Queen was desperately chasing after her by phone, trying to get her to come back so we could all face what Pops had done, whatever it was.

"Now let me return to the investigation.

"Regarding the mysterious letter, Mayfair Medical's laboratory could find no discernible fingerprints on it and reported that the brand of paper was rare, marketed in Europe and not in the United States, the ink was India ink and that the writing did not indicate any pathology and might have been done by a woman or a man. They noted further that the writer had used a quill pen, pressing down uncommonly hard for such an instrument, implying that the letter writer had been extremely sure of himself.

"In other words, they could tell almost nothing about the letter. And it had been passed on to a true graphologist with our happy permission.

"As to the rest of our concerns, we had better luck.

"Mayfair Medical confirmed in short order that the DNA collected from the residue in the Hermitage matched the DNA in the hair found in Rebecca's trunk. The materials were very old but there had been an abundance of both and the testing had been simple.

"Aunt Queen now felt certain that Rebecca had met her death at Manfred's hands, and that my dreams weren't entirely the work of a diseased mind, if she'd ever had any doubt in the matter.

"I cleaned all those cameos found in Rebecca's trunk and the cameos I'd taken from the island. These I placed in the china cabinet on the first floor with a display card, explaining they were gifts from Manfred Blackwood to a woman with whom he had been passionately in love. I explained the connection between Rebecca's name and the theme of the cameos, and I felt in so doing—in making this display for the public eye—I had done right by Rebecca.

"After long and intense discussion involving Aunt Queen, Jasmine and me (Aunt Queen had been bedridden since the night of Pops' burial), we agreed that we would include in the tour information that the Old Man, Manfred, was believed to have murdered a young woman with whom he was romantically involved, and her remains had only recently been discovered and properly interred.

"As to this interment, I was going to handle it, if and when allowed to do it. A small marble tombstone was ordered with the name Rebecca Stanford carved on it, and the tombstone guys had it delivered in one day. I put it down in the cemetery to wait until I could bring the remains to the spot.

"Meantime, the FBI could find no DNA material from the site which matched the material of any current missing person. Nevertheless, they were deeply courteous about having been called in, and they did confirm that the DNA of several persons was present in the evil morass and that the whole resembled an antiquated but gruesome crime scene.

"Finally, a full week after Pops' funeral, with Aunt Queen still in bed and refusing to take any nourishment, which had me and everyone else in near critical hysteria, I set out for Sugar Devil Island at dawn with all of the eight Shed Men coming in small pirogues behind me. We all had our guns—I now carried Pops' thirty-eight—and two security men brought up the rear. Clem was with us too, and Jasmine was at my side, in her skintight jeans, with her thirty-eight pistol, determined to have a front-row seat for everything.

"We brought with us plenty of tools to open the grand gold-and-granite tomb, and I had with me a small ornamental casket—a jewelry case, actually, which had been purchased from a gift shop—into which I meant to place whatever remained of Rebecca. The horrid collecting of her remains had to be done with a small spade. There was no way out of it.

"It was a convivial party, with Allen, the nominal leader of the Shed Men, referring to us as the Pirogue Posse, but beneath my smiles and laughter was an absolute dread as we set out to reclaim the Hermitage.

"What could I do but warn all the men of what was involved? The trespasser had had the gall to come into the house! How much they believed was a matter of conjecture.

"At last, after some forty minutes of pushing and pulling our way through the bog, we came to the bank overgrown with blackberries. There stood the house like a ship that had run aground, the violent thorny wisteria trying desperately to swallow it.

"I went onto the island, cracked open a beer and just watched as the men verified with their own eyes everything or almost everything that had been told to them. Allen and Clem, who had seen it all the first time around, also stood with me until the excitement was over.

"Then I said I would go and collect Rebecca's remains alone. I didn't want anybody trooping up there.

"There was immediate concern for my safety.

"Okay, Jasmine, you have your gun, you come with me," I said, but I went up first and I had my thirty-eight pistol raised.

"The sun was breaking pretty strong through the open windows of the second story. For a moment I was dazzled and then gradually I made out a living being before me: it was Rebecca, her dress torn off down her arms, her breasts naked, the hook snaring her rib bone as she hung by the hook, her face white, and the blood streaming from her mouth. She blinked her eyes but she couldn't talk. There was too much blood in her mouth.

" 'Good God, Rebecca,' I said, and I plunged at the figure, trying to get the hook out of her without hurting her more. She writhed and I could hear her gasping.

"This was absolutely happening. 'Rebecca, I'm here!' I declared as I tried to lift her.

"Then I heard Jasmine's voice, and I saw Jasmine's face, and the faces of Allen and Clem. We were all on the second floor of the house. I was lying on my back. And the sun was winking again in the cypresses.

"There was no more Rebecca. Only the rusted chains dangling and the dark slop there. I climbed to my feet.

"Jasmine said, 'Clem, you come here, please, brother, and hold this box while I shovel up what I can of this poor girl. Hold the lid back.'

"I went off down on the island and got sick to my stomach.

"Men were talking, talking about damaging 'gorgeous' gold plates to open the grave. I said, 'Do it. I have to know what's inside.'

"I sat on the steps of the house and I drank another beer, realizing that this woman might haunt me forever. What I'd done with the cameos was not enough, and the dreams were not enough, and coming here to do this, to gather her remains, was not enough; what would be enough? I didn't know. I couldn't think. I was sick and drinking too much beer and it was killing hot, and the mosquitoes were biting right through my shirt, and the men kept saying, 'Granite, solid granite.'

"Finally, at the first narrow side of the rectangular structure that they approached they found an opening beyond the gold plate, and they were able to push it back. It was a heavy door.

"They were all talking at once, groaning and fussing. Flashlights, who had the flashlights, here was a flashlight, well, will you look at that. I'm not opening that.

" 'Not opening what?' I said.

" 'A coffin.'

" 'Well, what the hell did you expect to find in a grave?' I asked. I was wildly stimulated. Ordinary things meant nothing to me.

" 'Now you mind your tone, Little Boss,' said Jasmine. She gave me another beer. What was this? Was I a mental patient she wanted to narcoticize? I said I was sorry. The beer was cold and good. I wasn't going to complain about an ice-cold beer.

" 'Have you packed up little Miss Stanford in her neat little box?' I asked.

" 'You're losing it, Little Boss,' she said. 'Now mind your manners. Don't talk to Allen and Clem the way you've been talking. You've always been Aunt Queen's gentleman, don't get rough now. Don't let this place make you contrary.'

" 'What the hell are you talking about?' I asked.

"She looked up thoughtfully at the Hermitage, and then at me, her face positively exquisite with its cacao skin and large pale eyes, eyes that were green or golden.

" 'Take after your Aunt Queen,' she said. 'That's the only point I'm trying to make, and yes, I have the remains of your ghost girlfriend in the casket. God only knows whatever else I have in this casket.'

" 'Make love to me when we get home,' I said. 'I'm no good for ordinary life. You don't see the ghosts I see. You didn't see that girl hanging by the hook. I've been having ghosts. They've been having me. I have to have somebody real. Make love to me when we get home, you and me, all right? Be my chocolate candy. I'm real unsure of my masculinity.'

" 'You are?' she shot back. 'Well, you could have fooled me.'

"Clem stood over me. 'Quinn, it's an empty coffin. You better come take a look at this for yourself. This is sort of your show, sonny boy.'

"I did. It was made of heavy iron, very ornate, and lightly rusted, with a window in it through which one could see the face of the deceased, I presume, though I'd never seen one like it. It had taken five of them with two crowbars to open it. It was lined with something. I thought it was lead. It was dry and soft to my touch. It was lead.

"And the coffin was in a vault of lead. Yeah, it was lead. And well sealed. Though the vault went down some three feet there was no sign that moisture had ever penetrated it.

"I stepped down into the vault, and for a long time I stood there, inside the mausoleum—in the vault—merely staring at the empty coffin. There was just room to walk around it, which I did.

"I climbed back up and out into the sunshine.

" 'Do you know how many of us it took to open that gold door?' Allen asked. 'What do you make of all this? What's that writing up there? You can read that, can't you, Quinn?'

"I shook my head. 'Manfred,' I said. 'Manfred had some plan to be buried out here, and those whom he trusted never fulfilled his dream. And so we have an empty coffin and an empty mausoleum. We have gold plates and an inscription in Latin. Look up there, that's Latin. I wrote that down. Manfred did all this. Manfred had this thing built when he built the Hermitage. Manfred did it all. And so we close it back up.'

" 'But what about all this solid gold!' Clem said. 'You can't just leave all this gold here for people to steal.'

" 'Do people still kill each other for gold these days?' I asked. 'Are any of you going to come back out here to steal this gold? Are we going to have a shoot-out over this gold? Let's go back where we came from. I can only take this place for so long. I don't like that a trespasser came into the house. Let's get out of here.'

"There was one more thing I wanted to check. I went back into the Hermitage.

"I was right!

"On the marble desk there were new books, books on philosophy and history, books on current events, novels. It was all new—a nice slap in the face. Even the candles were new, though the wicks were blackened. Oh, yes, the fearless one, my trespasser, had been here.

" 'So what are you going to do next, I wonder?' I said aloud. I flew into a rage. I grabbed up as many of the books as I could and threw them down the front steps of the Hermitage. I went back for the rest and threw them after the first. Then I hurried down the steps and pulled and tossed and kicked them all together.

"I took out my lighter. I set a small paperback volume aflame, and then another and another. It was going on its own now, with all the men just watching as if I was crazy, which I was.

" 'His books!' I said. 'He has no right on this property, and he leaves these books for me to see that he's been here again.'

" 'Lord God,' Jasmine said, as the flames rose and the fire crackled. 'We got a dead girl, a strange building, a bunch of weird books, and a regular tomb of gold with an empty iron coffin in it, and a crazy boy standing here!'

" 'Well put,' I said in her ear, 'and don't forget your promise to me, Milk Chocolate. It's you and me alone tonight.'

" 'I never made you any promise!' she said.

" 'I told you, I'm unsure of my masculinity,' I whispered. 'You've got to sacrifice yourself.' I kicked the fire to make it flare again. I hated burning books. I could hardly stand it to see a Merriam-Webster dictionary go up in smoke. But I had to do this.

"One or two more kicks and everything was incinerated. I turned and looked at Jasmine, expecting some wise remark, but all I saw was a sort of dreamy thoughtfulness in her face.

"Then she said:

" 'You know, boy, you really have me thinking about it. You should be more kind to a woman my age. You scamp. You think I don't have any feelings like that just 'cause I rocked your cradle?'

" 'How kind can I get?' I asked. 'You think I take up with just anybody?'

"Her expression never changed. She looked fine in her tight jeans. Her Afro was clipped close and the shape of her head and her face was beautiful.

"She lived like a nun. I knew that for a fact. There had been no men at all in her life since her husband died years ago. And her sister, Lolly, had had three husbands.

" 'I'm crazed,' I said, staring at her, staring at her buxom breasts and her small waist. 'I have these visions; what am I supposed to do about it, what does Rebecca want of me? I saw Rebecca up there. I don't understand. Maybe they'll find out I'm crazy. I know one thing though.'

" 'What's that?' she asked.

" 'That I've got you on my mind bad, Ms. Café au Lait. I don't want to sleep with the dead.'

"Silence from her and then a partial smile, an uncharacteristic smile. Very slowly she ran her eyes over me, from toe to head.

"I felt my cock getting hard.

"The fire had consumed just about everything.

"The men had closed the tomb. She had the little casket under her right arm. Everybody was hot and sick and cursing and batting at the bugs, and the sun was flashing in the trees, and the water stank of things rotted, things dying.

"That's what it was about the swamp. Of course things were being born and things were thriving and marvelous creatures lived in the treacherous slime, but more things were rotting and suffering for lack of sun, and it was death that had the upper hand, and death you smelled in the black water.

"We left the island.

" 'Better to drink this beer up home,' said Clem, 'where Mamma can cook us up some food. I'm starving.'

"We were all pretty damned drunk before we got home, and under the influence I'd made one or two bad turns which might have kept us lost for hours.

"As it was, we made it back before dark, and after I took the longest piss of my life I went down with the casket and the shovel to the little cemetery.

"I was fully tuned for the slightest chill, the finest frisson, but I was feeling nothing. And I didn't see the old troop of spirits that sometimes accosted me. But it was their style to be seen from a distance. I'd never been among them.

"I found a patch of soil that was clear and I dug easily through the moist earth. Pretty soon I had a hole about two feet deep, and the casket fitted easily there, and I filled in the earth around it and over it.

"I put the heavy marble tombstone firmly in place.

"I made the Sign of the Cross. I said three Hail Marys and two Our Fathers and then the old prayer:

Let perpetual light shine upon her, O Lord,
and may her soul and the souls of all
the faithful departed rest in peace. Amen.

"The new grave looked mighty little among the old coffin-sized concrete tombs, but it was still respectable and even fine.

"When I looked up I saw Goblin by the oak tree, watching me. I was drunk and he was cold sober. I was filthy dirty. He was immaculately clean. He wasn't just appearing to me. He was studying me. And only as I looked at him did I realize that I hadn't seen him all day. I hadn't even felt him near me. I hadn't thought about him. For the last few days, I'd seldom seen him. I hadn't talked to him.

" 'Yo, brother,' I said.

"I walked or staggered up the slope and reached out to embrace him. He vanished and left nothing there for me to hold, and a cold feeling crept over me. But I was drunk enough to cry about nothing.

"And Jasmine was shouting, 'Suppertime.' Red beans and rice, gravy thick with pork fat and pork chops simmered with it.

"It must have been around nine o'clock before I was showered and shaved, and sobered up. I came down to be with Aunt Queen and tell her what her nurse, Cindy, had been telling her for days, that she had to get up, get going and above all to take some nourishment.

"I found her sitting up in bed against a mass of white lace-covered pillows in one of her gorgeous feather-trimmed white negligees, her glasses down on her nose as she read what appeared to be a letter of several pages.

"Cindy, the nurse, with her usual very bright smile, was in attendance. She excused herself as I came in.

" 'Well, I have it, beautiful boy,' Aunt Queen said. 'Come here, pull up a chair.'

" 'Only if you eat something will I do that,' I said. 'What is it you have?'

" 'I'm way ahead of you, angel face,' she replied. 'I've drunk two cans of relatively innocuous lipids, as Cindy can verify, so I have had enough food to feed an entire Hindu village for one day. Now sit down. I have a translation here of the inscription on the island. This just arrived.'

"I wanted to snatch the pages out of her hand, but she wouldn't allow it and read out the words,

" 'Here sleeps Petronia, whose mortal hands once made the most beautiful of cameos, even for emperors and kings. Guard me, ye gods and goddesses whose images I rendered so well. A curse on those who attempt to disturb my resting place.'

"She gave me the page of the letter. I read it over and over. 'Petronia,' I whispered. 'What can all this mean?' I gave the page back to her. 'Who translated it, Aunt Queen?' I asked.

" 'A man I want you to meet, Quinn, a man who's going to change the course of your life the way Lynelle changed it, a man who's going to accompany you and me on the Grand Tour you should have had a long time ago. The man's name is Nash Penfield. He's an English professor from California, and I like him very much.'

" 'But what if I don't like him, Aunt Queen?' I asked. 'Aunt Queen, I don't want to go to Europe yet. I don't want to leave here. What's going to happen to this place? Aunt Queen, Pops just died. We can't be making plans.'

" 'We have to make plans, my dear boy,' she said. 'And Nash Penfield is flying here Friday. We'll have a nice dinner together and we'll see how you like him, and if you don't care for the man, which I truly cannot imagine, then we'll find someone else. But you need a tutor, Quinn, you need someone to take up where Lynelle left off.'

" 'All right. We'll make a bargain. You get up out of bed, eat three square meals tomorrow and I'll meet Mr. Penfield. How's that?'

" 'I'll go you one better,' she said. 'You check into Mayfair Medical tomorrow for a series of tests, and I'll get up, eat breakfast and go with you, how's that?'

" 'What tests?' I asked. But I already knew. They'd do brain scans on me, MRIs, electroencephalograms, whatever they called them. They'd be looking for lesions on the temporal lobe—something physical to account for what I claimed to see and hear. I wasn't surprised, even with all the verification that Rebecca Stanford had been real and had been murdered, I wasn't surprised.

"If anything, I was surprised that it hadn't come sooner. And I thought to myself, Well, we'll get this over with and I won't have to think about it anymore.

" 'All right, I'll check into Mayfair Medical,' I said. 'But I won't find myself on the psychiatric ward, will I?'

" 'My boy, I despise the idea of nuthouses as much as you do,' she replied. 'But I think I'd be remiss if I didn't request certain purely medical tests to be done. As for Mayfair Medical, it's a marvel, with the finest doctors and equipment in the South.'

" 'I know, Aunt Queen. You have to remember, Lynelle was going to work in research there. Who in the environs of New Orleans doesn't know all about Mayfair Medical? I've been there, beloved aunt, I walked those granite-tiled hallways with Lynelle. It was her dream come true, remember?'

"The fear came on me, it came on dark and strong when I thought of Lynelle in her breakneck high heels clicking on beside me through the hospital corridors, pointing out all the special features of this revolutionary clinic and hospital.

"I remembered the smallest, most special detail—that every ward in Mayfair Medical had broad comfortable benches along its walls, benches for the comfort of relatives and friends who were visiting with the patients. Every room was a private room. Every room had easy chairs for visitors.

" 'Oh, it's too sad to think of poor Lynelle,' Aunt Queen said, as if she were reading my mind or my wandering eyes. 'Lynelle, Sweetheart, Pops, it's too sad, too dreadful. But we cannot take our minds off the details of life, Quinn. The details will save us. We'll have these tests done and we'll discover if there's anything to be worried about.'

" 'Worried about? You have a letter from the stranger! You know I didn't write it or cook it up myself. I told you he was in my room, and he has been on the island since I warned him away. I burnt his books, I was so angry. And now this inscription. What can it mean? And the cameos. Why is it all connected?'

"She listened intently and affectionately.

"I told her the vision I had had of Rebecca hanging from the rusted hook, the hook having caught her rib. I told her how I had been unconscious on the floor afterwards.

" 'Jasmine said you fell down as if you'd been struck on the head. Your eyes never closed. And then you revived, just like that.'

" 'Did I have a seizure out there?' I asked. 'Is that what Jasmine really saw?'

" 'She didn't see it,' said Aunt Queen. 'But we can talk about all this tomorrow afternoon on our way to Mayfair Medical. As for the mysterious intruder, we have guards everywhere. The Shed Men are in their glory. But regarding tomorrow morning . . .'

" 'Patsy's been found and the will's going to be read,' I guessed.

" 'That's it exactly. Now brace yourself for a scene. But I have my hopes. And I have my plans. Your grandfather was Gravier's only living son. We'll see what happens. Now you go on up now, Big Ramona's probably waiting for you. Give me a sweet kiss. I love you.'

"I bent down to kiss her, to glory in her soft gray hair and her perfume. 'Good night, my love,' I said. 'Where's your bedfellow, Jasmine?'

" 'Oh, she is the most provoking creature. She's tired from her trip to the island. She's confused. She's soon to be our salvation, and she knows it. I think she's afraid of the challenge.'

" 'What do you mean?'

" 'Well, who's to run this place when you and I leave?' she said with a shrug. 'Jasmine can do it.'

"I'd never even thought of this, and it seemed so right suddenly. How many times had I gone into the bungalow to find Jasmine and come across her rapping on her computer. And who did the tours better than Jasmine?

" 'That's good, that's really good!' I said. 'I want to talk to her.'

" 'No, let me explain it to her,' Aunt Queen replied. 'She'll be coming later on. She's gone up to fuss in Pops' bedroom. I asked her to go through his jewelry, and she's making a night of it up there. Just tell the darling girl to stop her inventory and come down at a reasonable hour. I'll never go to sleep tonight if she's not here.'

"Something clicked in my mind. It clicked in my body, too. Jasmine alone in Pops' bedroom.

"I went up the stairs like a man going up to meet his bride. I looked in on Big Ramona and found her sound asleep. I went on to Pops' room.

"The door was open.

"His bed is a big heavy four-poster—you saw it—it's one of the oldest in the house. I saw Jasmine sitting on it, up against the velvet-covered pillows, and in her hand was a goblet of red wine. The bottle was on the nightstand.

"She was dressed all foxy, in one of her tightfitting leopard-skin tops that look brilliant with her mahogany skin, and close-cropped yellow hair, and a nothing of a leather skirt. One leg was up and the other stretched out. Spike heels. Flash of white panties. You never saw a more earnest invitation. And I was the only guest.

"I closed the door and locked it.

"She sighed and put the glass under the lamp on the nightstand. I sat beside her and then took her in my arms. I kissed her lips and felt the immediate fire. She pushed her breasts against me. I squeezed her breasts so desperately it was a wonder I didn't hurt her. *God, this is Heaven; you're in the wrong place.* I slipped my hand up her leg and touched her silk panties and the heat behind them.

" 'Pull'm down, tear'm off,' she said in my ear. 'Panties are cheap. Panties are nothing.' She was crying. I could hear it.

"I kissed her on the mouth again, and her tongue shot between my lips. Oh, Lord, God. I kissed her plenty, and I ripped her panties over her ankles and off her spike-heel shoes, and I cradled her foot in my hand and kissed her instep.

"Under her breath she cried. I gobbled her wet tears.

" 'Lord, it's wrong,' she whispered. 'I know it's so wrong. You, my baby Tarquin, but I need it so bad!'

" 'So do I, lady,' I said. 'You can't imagine!' "

18

"IT WAS what we call the middle of the night. One, two in the morning—something like that. All of Blackwood Manor slept. I slept. Big Ramona snored. I woke now and then. I had a vague sense of a conversation with Rebecca. We were on the lawn, in the antique wicker chairs from the attic, and she was explaining to me that all the old wicker had been hers, that Manfred had bought it for her.

"She was so happy that I'd taken it down and had it restored, that Pops had painted it white. How handsome it was.

" 'You are my world, Tarquin,' she said.

"But that was only part of what she tried to tell me. She was trying to talk of other things, things I must do, how justice would be achieved, and I was arguing with her.

"How thin and indistinct was all this. I woke and stared in front of me and all the fabric dissolved. Then I turned over again and I was talking to her.

"Suddenly, I was wrenched up out of the bed and dragged across the floor!

"I was fully awake in an instant.

"Into the bathroom I was forced by powerful hands that hurt my arms. My head was smacked against the wall. I was lifted off my feet and held that way, and by the thin light from the door through which I'd just been dragged I saw that it was a tall man who held me.

"His hair was cleanly brushed back from his high rounded temples, and his large dark eyes were fastened on me.

" 'Oh, so you burn my books, you little imp, do you!' he whispered to me, his breath warm and odorless against my face. 'You burn my books! You play with me!'

"I could feel my emotions coming together and I knew all of a sudden that what I felt wasn't terror after all, it was rage, the same rage I'd felt when I'd done the thing that had so angered him.

" 'Get away from me and get out of my house!' I cried. 'How dare you come into my very room! How dare you trespass again!'

"I struggled violently to get free. I pushed against his chest with all my might. He was immovable.

"His eyes were a glare in the shadows. Of the rest of him, all I saw was an open white shirt with white cuffs and a black coat. And he let me down on my feet slowly.

" 'You little fool,' he said, gripping my shoulders, and he smiled, and for the first time I saw his mouth, very finely shaped, with thick but perfectly sculpted lips.

"Again, I went wild in his grip. I pushed my knee against him, I kicked his shins. I gained nothing!

" 'Never go near the island again!' he hissed. 'Never touch what's mine, do you hear me?'

" 'You're a liar and a trespasser,' I said. 'Bring your claim in a court of law!'

" 'Don't you realize I could kill you?' he returned with blazing anger. 'I have no qualms about it whatsoever. Why do you protest? Why do you do foolish things? What's so precious to you?'

" 'What's rightfully mine!' I said. 'Get out of my house before I bring it down on you.'

"Of course I knew that no one could hear me. Ramona slept like the dead. The house was too big, the walls too thick, and here we were in a windowless tiled bathroom.

"Suddenly he released his grip. My shoulders ached. He didn't let me go, however. And then when he spoke it was more calmly:

" 'I'm not going to kill you. I don't want you dead. I have a theory about you. But you ever go near that island again and I will kill you, you understand me? You warn everyone away from that island forever. You make it off limits to the world, or I'll come back here and drag you out into that swamp and kill you slowly just the way Rebecca died, you impudent child.'

"He had scarcely finished the last two words when the big mirror to his right shattered and great dangerous pieces of glass fell with a loud noise all over the lavatory and the floor. I glimpsed Goblin behind him.

"Goblin's hands came up around the stranger's neck and I saw Goblin vanish as he obviously and fiercely exerted pressure.

"The man cursed in another language. He let me go, reaching for his own throat reflexively, and then the glass of the shower door broke and Goblin appeared again, tissue thin but visible to me and flashing a knife-like piece of glass at the stranger, which the stranger pushed away with his immense strength rather easily.

"Again the man cursed, looking hastily to the right and the left and then behind himself. I saw that his black hair was very long and worn in a slender wavy ponytail. He had sharply squared shoulders.

"He was maddened, pivoting and grabbing me again, but there came from Goblin another assault with both his fists, and more fine bits of glass hurled at the intruder, who let me go, backing up and twirling like a dancer.

"Glass was flying around the room. The stranger had to duck a fragment aimed right at his face. More glass clattered to the floor as the lower portion of the shower door broke into finer pieces.

" 'What is it?' he hissed, warding off the shards with thrusts of his hands that came so fast I couldn't follow them.

"Goblin bore down on him with his fists and then throttled him again. He threw off Goblin with visible effort, and furiously.

"The light flashed on, then off, then on again. I saw him fully illuminated, a young man with perfect skin and satin black hair, his black suit very fine and his face, even in its obvious hatred, no less than beautiful.

" 'What is it, damn you!' he snarled at me. Daggers of glass were raining upon him and he batted them off like insects. The lights continued to flash.

" 'You think I'm going to tell you!' I charged. 'You're in my house now, same as when you read your books on my island! Get out of it, or who knows what will happen? I can see the creature who fights you now. It's plain as day that you can't!'

"I was boiling with rage. I stood poised, lacking only the nerve to try to thrust a piece of glass right into his chest, and then he was gone, gone silently and swiftly as though he'd never been there, and I was alone in the bathroom, in the dark, amid all the broken glass, and Big Ramona in her bare feet and in her rose-print nightgown was staring at me.

" 'Lord, Child of Grace,' she said. 'What have you done!'

" 'It's not me, it was him, didn't you see him! Oh my God, didn't you see him?' I pleaded with her.

" 'I don't know what I saw. Don't you move, don't you walk in that glass! I was sound asleep and I hear all this glass breaking.'

"Goblin stood before the lavatory, and in a reserved manner, a wise manner, he smiled at me. I threw my arms around him. I felt his shape.

" 'Thank God for you,' I declared. I caressed his hair. I kissed him. 'You scared him off. You did it.'

"The whole house was waking up. I could hear feet pounding up the stairs. I heard Clem holler out to me from the hall. I heard an alarm go off, though how or where I didn't know.

"And as they crowded into the bedroom, I knew what they saw. They saw me standing alone amid all the broken glass, as barefoot as Big Ramona, and embracing a form they couldn't see—the empty air for all they knew or had ever known."

19

"Β γ τ η ε τ ι μ ε we reached Mayfair Medical I was a gibbering idiot in a bloody nightshirt. I was in the back of Aunt Queen's limo with her on one side and Clem on the other and Big Ramona in front of us, on the J seat, and Jasmine at the far end of the J, back to the driver, everybody begging me to calm down. Clem's fingers were biting into my arm and Aunt Queen was exerting as much pressure as she could. At one point, Big Ramona told Aunt Queen to move, and she took ahold of me like a professional wrestler.

"It was the old story. The more you tell people you're not insane the crazier they think you are. And they clearly thought I was crazy.

"How many times did I say that the intruder had been in the house? How many times did they tell me that was impossible? How many times did I tell them that Goblin broke the glass, Goblin saved my life, how many times did they exchange their urgent heartfelt glances?

"I was still raving when we pulled into the Emergency porte cochere, and they had a gurney ready for me. Of course I swore up and down that I didn't need it. Then I realized I was barefoot and my feet were scratched from the glass. All right. Hospital regulations.

"I could have dressed properly before we ever left home, if only people had listened.

"But off I went into the Emergency Room, where the nightshirt was unceremoniously cut off and topical medicines were applied to the cuts and scrapes all over me.

"As to my head, I told them that the pain was killing me. The stranger had slammed me against the wall. Give me something for my headache if you do nothing else. You can forget about the scratches and bruises.

"And bruises there were aplenty. And when I saw how bad they were, I started yelling for Aunt Queen and Jasmine to come. Oh, if only Pops were here! Oh, damn!

"They began to tie me down and I went truly crazy.

"All the time, Goblin was with me, very strong, very visible, his face full of concern, but I didn't dare try to speak to him and he knew it. After the energy he had used I couldn't understand why he still looked so dense and so powerful. He didn't like what was happening. He made no bones about it. And suddenly I became terrified that he would start breaking the glass and the whole scene would devolve into chaos.

" 'Goblin, don't do anything in here,' I said, staring at him. 'It will only make it worse. Let me just play it on out.'

"Then Dr. Winn Mayfair himself, proud scion of the legendary Mayfair family and working head of the whole complex, approached the gurney. It seemed a spell fell over the Emergency Room, doctors and nurses mesmerized by the mere presence of the guy.

"I calmed down too. I was quite literally bound hand and foot, and why should I object to this doctor examining me?

"Now, the only reason I knew anything about Dr. Winn Mayfair was that Lynelle had told me all about him. He had been born in New Orleans, reared in Boston and become a physician up North, coming South only when the family here contacted him and offered him a dream job at the new medical center.

"He had become the partner and confidant of Rowan Mayfair, the other M.D. member of the famous clan, the one who had created and endowed the center and designed all its special features.

"It was Dr. Winn who took over the actual day-to-day management of everything, whereas Dr. Rowan worked tirelessly in research having to do with human growth hormone, Lynelle's old dream.

"Somewhere behind the scenes was Dr. Winn's father, Dr. Elliott Mayfair, a cardiac surgeon, and he had also been persuaded to transplant back home, and Rowan, Elliott and Winn Mayfair were the backbone of the establishment.

"Dr. Winn had a reputation for having a very quiet voice and a very gentle touch. His field had been neurosurgery—the same field as that of Dr. Rowan Mayfair—and the two were said to be cousins who resembled each other in temperament and gifts, as well as physical looks, though they had only met recently, each quite astonished at the other.

"Lynelle had worshiped the guy.

"What I saw was a smooth, brilliant and attentive man, tall and lean, who had been roused from bed to meet Miss Lorraine McQueen and her legendary boy prodigy who communed with the Dead.

"He had beautifully groomed silver blond hair and cold blue eyes behind rectangular wire-rimmed glasses, and he talked to me under his breath, which tended to give his words a confidential tone, which I frankly welcomed. He also spoke slowly.

"At once he took my blood pressure himself, though a nurse had done it before, and then he looked into both my pupils. He put his stethoscope to my head, listening for the longest time, as though my brain were talking to him. Then he felt my glands and he inspected the bruises on my arms. His touch was reverent.

" 'I know your head hurts,' he said in a liquid voice, 'but we can't give you anything for the pain that might mask the symptoms of the head injury. As soon as they've finished with these lacerations, we're taking you for a CAT scan.'

" 'I didn't do this to myself,' I said. 'I'm not insane. You won't find any lesions in my temporal lobe. Mark my word. I'm miserable right now, but I'm not crazy.'

"He looked at me intently and for a long moment, and then he said, 'They told me you were eighteen, is that right?'

" 'Just about nineteen,' I said. 'Does eighteen and a half mean anything?'

"He smiled. 'Yes, I suppose it does,' he said. 'We won't be looking for seizures or lesions now. We're looking for bleeding from the wound that's causing your headache. We're going to be waking you up if you fall asleep. Now I'm going to get out of the way, and I'll see you after the CAT scan.'

" 'You're a neurosurgeon, right?' I said. I wanted to hold on to him. 'Well, I swear to you that what I saw didn't come from my brain and I don't want you to cut a piece out of it. I'd rather rave in a padded cell than have that happen.'

"Two orderlies, or at least that's what I thought they were, had come to take me away, but he gestured for them to wait.

" 'Tell me yourself,' he said, 'what happened to you.'

" 'This stranger, this man who'd been trespassing on a swamp hermitage on our property—he got into my bedroom in spite of the guards around our house, and he dragged me out of bed, pulled me into the bathroom, banged my head against the wall and cursed at me and threatened me.'

"I stopped. I didn't want to tell him about Goblin. Some deep instinct told me not to tell him about Goblin. But that instinct didn't stop me from silently summoning Goblin, and, quite suddenly, Goblin stood at the foot of the gurney, still looking extremely solid and vividly colored, which was amazing after his ordeal, and he shook his head in a firm negation.

" 'There was broken glass,' I said, 'from the lavatory mirror and the shower door. I think I got a few scrapes, nothing more than that.'

" 'How did this intruder drag you from bed?' Dr. Winn asked.

" 'By my arms.'

"Dr. Winn looked at both my arms. They were black and blue now. He studied them thoughtfully.

"Dr. Winn then asked me to lean forward so he could see the back of my head. I did, and I felt his amazingly gentle fingers touching a huge bump there. His touch sent a tingling all through me.

"Again, Goblin shook his head No. *Don't tell him about us. He will hurt me.*

" 'Do you believe me now?' I asked. 'That I didn't do this to myself?'

" 'Oh, yes, I believe you completely,' he said. 'None of your injuries are self-inflicted. For a variety of reasons it's quite impossible for them to have been self-inflicted. But we've got to get that CAT scan.'

"I was immensely relieved.

"The CAT scan was a relatively simple ordeal, which revealed that there was no bleeding inside of my head and that my brain was not swelling, and immediately after Dr. Mayfair confirmed these results I was wheeled to a fairly lavish suite consisting of a living room and two bedrooms. One bedroom was mine. Aunt Queen was setting up shop in the other one. Jasmine, who had gone home for her clothes, was already back but would soon have to leave again.

"I promised to leave the IV alone and to cooperate with everything if the restraints were removed, and Dr. Mayfair agreed to this readily.

" 'There are guards on the door, aren't there?' I asked.

"Aunt Queen confirmed that there were. A uniformed police officer was right down the hall. And Clem was in the parlor.

"I could see that Aunt Queen had been crying. But even more distressing to me was the fact that she still wore her feathered negligee. She hadn't had time to change. I felt bitterly angry and at the same time frightened.

" 'You know, this is a strange situation, my Little Boy,' she said as she came to sit by my bed. (Goblin was hovering in the corner.) 'We have two possible explanations for what happened tonight and either one is monstrous.'

" 'Believe me, there's only one explanation,' I said, 'and this man is a threat!' I then confessed to her how I had burnt the stranger's books and how this had provoked him. 'He's an eccentric, I can vouch for that by the cut of his handsome black clothes and his long hair, but he's strong as an ox, and Goblin gave him a terrific scare. He didn't know what was hitting him or where the glass was coming from.'

"I stopped. I realized I had told her all this in the car. I had told her over and over. Was she listening to me now because Dr. Winn had said my wounds weren't self-inflicted?

"She was deeply troubled. I wanted to be strong for her, not weak, not in a hospital bed. I picked up the small control pad for the bed and cranked it so that I could sit up.

"Dr. Winn came in to take his leave. 'The CAT scan's fine,' he repeated. 'And in the next few days we'll run some more tests. All you have to do, Quinn, is stay in bed. I'll be talking to you later this morning.'

" 'Doctor,' I said, 'would I try your patience if I asked you a question?'

" 'No, not at all, what is it?'

" 'There was a brilliant premed student; a friend of mine. She'd been accepted into a research project here. She died as the result of a traffic accident. I wonder if you knew her.'

"A change came into his calm face that was very eloquent of suffering. 'You're speaking of Lynelle Springer,' he said.

"I nodded.

" 'You're the boy she taught, the boy she talked so much about, aren't you?' he asked. 'Of course. Tarquin Blackwood, her pride and joy. She loved you the way she loved her own children.'

"I swallowed. I was about to cry. I hadn't expected this much of an answer. 'Is it true?' I asked, 'that after the accident she never regained consciousness? She never knew how badly she was hurt?'

" 'It's true,' he said. He spoke in a humble voice, a voice that was reverent. 'We had her here for two weeks. Her daughters came. They played tapes for her of music and poetry readings,' he said. 'But she was down too deep and her injuries were too great. Everything was done that could be done, and then she left us.'

"I felt immeasurable relief knowing all this. I felt like some key chapter in my life was finally closed so that it could remain with me in its entirety now without a host of little distractions. I also felt sure this man wouldn't lie to me—ever—about anything.

"Aunt Queen inundated me with kisses and told me she was going to get dressed.

"Fr. Kevin Mayfair came into the room and sat down beside me. Goblin, who still stood solidly at the end of the bed, eyed him suspiciously.

" 'So what do you want me to say?' I asked Fr. Kevin. 'They've probably told you all I told them. They've told you that Goblin rescued me. You know Goblin. Goblin comes to Mass with me every Sunday.'

" 'Don't be so scared of me, Quinn,' he said, his tone firmer and a little higher in timbre than that of Dr. Winn. 'I'm not the enemy. I'm not here to haul you up before the Spanish Inquisition. Your housekeeper, Ramona, she saw all this flying glass. If I'd seen it, maybe I'd never doubt Almighty God again. Maybe the Devil can do that for us.'

" 'It wasn't the Devil in that bathroom,' I said. 'It was an angry man, a tall, good-looking, vain man. He got past the guards and yanked me right out of sleep. And then Goblin, my Goblin'—I looked at him at the foot of the bed and saw him anxiously eyeing Fr. Kevin—'my Goblin, he broke the glass to drive the man away from me. He sent the glass flying at the man and the man couldn't see Goblin any more than you can. The man didn't know what was happening. You've got to understand, Goblin isn't from the Devil. There has to be some in-between kind of spirit that's neither devil nor angel. There has to be.'

"Fr. Kevin nodded. 'Maybe you're right,' he said, to my surprise. He looked off for a moment in an almost dreamy way, then back to me. I found him distractingly handsome. It wasn't just the true red hair and the green eyes, it was the alert expression and the excellent proportions of his face, the shortness of the nose and the length of his full mouth. His voice was kind.

" 'Two years ago,' he said, 'or maybe less, I wouldn't have believed you. But now? Since coming South I've heard so much of ghosts and family curses that I'm more flexible of mind and disposition.' He paused. 'But I'll tell you this. Whether they come from the Devil or inside our brains, whether they're ghosts or disembodied beings with no true origin, spirits don't do us any good. I'm sure of it.'

"Goblin was becoming agitated. He was staring at Fr. Kevin with a cold hate.

" 'No, Goblin,' I said. 'Don't do anything, Goblin.' In a sudden fit of alarm, I looked around. There was a mirror above the lavatory. What if he broke it into fragments? He knew he could do this now!

"Goblin, the Learner.

"Goblin looked at me with the strangest smile, as if to say, Don't you think I know better?

" 'Listen, he's here,' I said to Fr. Kevin. 'You can't see him but he's at the foot of the bed. And it's rude to him to speak in his presence as if he were evil. He isn't evil. How he became attached to me, I don't know. Maybe he was just drifting, drifting and looking for someone who could see him, and then I came along, a child who had the gift. And we made our little brotherhood, him and me. I have no answers. But he saved me tonight. He saved me with an extraordinary show of strength. He broke the glass, not me, and I don't want him to think for one moment that I am ungrateful.'

"Fr. Kevin studied me intently throughout this speech and then he nodded. 'Well, let's leave it at this. If you need to talk to me, you call me. I've given my number to your Aunt Queen, and I'm in and out of May-fair Medical doing rounds every day. I'm fast becoming the full-time chaplain here, and you'd be surprised what Dr. Rowan wants me to investigate. I'll stop back in later to see you.'

" 'What does she want you to investigate?' I asked. I was plenty intrigued. And I was simmering down, and I liked talking to him. He wasn't the cliché I'd expected him to be.

" 'Near-death experiences,' he said, 'that's what I'm investigating. You know, when people are pronounced dead and they see a bright light when they pass through a tunnel and greet a being of light—and then they're revived and they come back here to tell us about it.'

" 'Yes, I know. I read everything on that subject that I can find. I believe in it. I believe it happens.'

" 'Often those people aren't believed,' he said. 'I'm here to be-lieve, but never to ask a leading question or maybe make a suggestive statement.'

" 'I follow you,' I said. 'Have you talked to people who've had the experience?'

" 'Yes,' he said, 'I have. Of course I give the Sacrament for the Sick too. And I hear confessions, and I bring Communion.'

" 'Do you believe me—what I've just told you?'

" 'I believe you believe what you're saying,' he said. 'Now do you want the Sacrament for the Sick? You know it doesn't require much of one.'

" 'I'm not sick,' I replied, 'and as to my sexual sins, well, I'm not ready to give all that up. I can't go to Confession just now. I can't take Communion. Sex is brand-new to me.'

" 'Yes,' he said with a weary little smile, 'it's difficult at your time of life.' He shrugged. And then he flashed a brighter smile on me and said, 'I thought it was Hell when I was your age, and frankly I think so sometimes now. Priests go to Confession, you know. They go to other priests. It's not so easy.'

" 'I like you. I know that may not matter much—.'

" 'Oh, yes, it matters,' he said. 'But I have to get back to St. Mary's. I have my parish duties as well as some work later at the university. I'll see you this afternoon.'

"He stood up.

"Something flashed into my head. 'Father,' I said, 'what if you do see a ghost that's evil, a ghost that leads you into harm, a ghost who wants some kind of dark vengeance? What do you do? You make the Sign of the Cross and you pray? Is that your only weapon?'

"He looked at me for a long time before he answered. Then he said, 'Don't talk to it,' he said. 'Don't entertain it with talk or looks or any form of attention. Remember, it can't do much to you without your helping it. Just maybe it can't do *anything* to you without your helping it. Take the ghost of Hamlet's father, for instance. Suppose Hamlet had never gone to meet it and spoken to it. Suppose he had never given the ghost an opportunity to put a story of murder into his mind. The result was pure destruction for innocent and guilty. Think on it. What if Hamlet had refused to speak to that ghost?'

" 'You mean the ghost was evil?' I asked.

" 'The play tells us so,' he said. 'It could be named *The Damnation of Hamlet*.'

"I nodded.

"He left the room and I lay there, getting sleepy and woozy and thankful that Goblin now took the chair by the bed, and I took his hand in mine.

"I thought of the malicious stranger. 'Who was that bastard, Goblin?' I asked. 'How did he get in my room?'

"When I heard no telepathic answer I turned and looked at him, and I saw that same grave expression on his face that I had remarked down in the cemetery, after I'd buried the remains of Rebecca.

" 'Can't you talk to me, Goblin?' I said. 'Listen, I'll have them bring me paper and crayons tomorrow—a big sketchpad, you know—and we can write to each other.'

"He shook his head. He almost sneered. He did sneer. He looked cold and then angry. *Computer, Quinn, bring a computer here.*

" 'Of course,' I replied. 'Why didn't I think of that? I'll get a laptop, I'll tell them I have to have it.'

"I was getting sleepier and sleepier. He sat there, my guardian, and then he spoke to me telepathically again. *Anger makes me strong, Quinn.*

" 'Anger's bad,' I murmured. I was drifting off. I woke with a start, then reminded myself that I was safe. Aunt Queen came in. I heard her telling the nurse that I was falling asleep. They had to wake me up.

"I heard Jasmine at my ear:

" 'Little Boss, listen to me,' Jasmine said, 'we're booked solid at the Manor for the next two weeks. I have to go on back home again and so does Mamma. We have no choice. But Miss Queen is all set up. And the guards are outside. Don't you worry on that account. I'll be back when I can.'

" 'Kiss me,' I murmured. I was falling asleep.

"Was it sleep? Rebecca and I were on the lawn again in the big wicker peacock chairs and the sun was slanting down on the zinnias that Pops had planted all along the side of the house, and Rebecca said in a rippling, rhythmic voice, 'Oh, of course I'd like to live in a civilized fashion and pretend it all never took place, that he married me and made me mistress of this house and that my children would have been loved by him, and you know that you always had love, you always had love, you don't know what it means to not have love, to have nothing, simply nothing, and you, with Jasmine, you didn't taken any measures, and what if a child came from that union, would you love that child, the child you had with that colored bitch!'

"I tried to wake up. I had to ask Jasmine. Could she have gotten pregnant, but then it seemed dreamlike that I'd been with her, and I feared she'd be mean to me if I brought it up, and I knew she hadn't taken measures and neither had I, and maybe there could be a baby, and it almost made me happy.

"I couldn't move my hands.

"I opened my eyes. They had tied my hands to the bed! 'What are you doing?' I tried to say more but Rebecca was talking. They had tied my feet. I began to shout for help.

"Aunt Queen stood over me: 'Quinn, darling, you ripped out the IV.

You were talking out loud to someone. You were agitated. You pushed the intern away. He has to put the IV back.'

"This was too terrible, simply too terrible. I looked at the ceiling tiles. To get away, to get far away, I went into unconsciousness. And of course Rebecca was there, she was pouring coffee for me and smiling, and the marguerites were blooming with the zinnias, and I loved the marguerites so much, those little white-and-yellow daisies.

" 'You've got to find a way to get out of here,' I told Rebecca. 'You have got to find a way to escape this place and go into the Light. God's waiting for you. God knows what's happened to you, he knows about the hook, he knows what they did. Don't you understand that it's God who's going to give you justice?'

"('Wake up, Quinn. Quinn, wake up.')

" 'And why should I go when it's so nice here,' Rebecca said. 'Here, look, this is the blouse you found upstairs in the trunk. Big Ramona's been washing and ironing all my clothes just like you told her to do. I wore this specially for you, and you see my cameo? How pretty it is. It's Venus with the little cupid at her side. I took it from Aunt Queen's display. Oh, I just love being with you. Have some more coffee. What are you going to do with all my old clothes?'

"('Wake up, Quinn, come on, open your eyes.')

" 'What am I going to do with you is more the question,' I replied, 'and I'm telling you, you're going home to God. We all do. It's just a matter of time.' "

20

"IT TOOK three days for me to get the laptop computer. In fact, Nash Penfield, the out-of-town teacher, purchased it when he arrived, and though I wasn't to meet him until more favorable circumstances prevailed—my decision, not Aunt Queen's—I was grateful that he had had the wherewithal to get the appropriate machine and a long extension cord.

"During those three days they ran every conceivable medical test, and at the end of the ordeal it was plainly clear that I had no lesions on the temporal lobe, no indication of epilepsy and no brain tumors.

"I was not suffering an electrolyte imbalance and I wasn't anemic. I had no circulatory problems and I was clean of all narcotics.

"I had no thyroid problems or problems with my pituitary gland.

"The very minor swelling of my brain, as the result of the stranger slamming me at the wall, was quickly stopped. And my headaches vanished.

"We had a huge debate as to whether a spinal tap should be done, and I finally persuaded them to do it and get it over with. I survived the risk. They found no malignant cells in the fluid.

"In between my long journeys down the beautifully painted passageways of the hospital labyrinth I told the full story of the violent night to everyone who wanted to hear it.

"Dr. Winn Mayfair listened quietly and thoughtfully to my descriptions of Goblin and how Goblin had come to my defense, and Aunt Queen, who was in the room, did not interrupt, either to calm me when I became agitated or to add to what I had to say, though she was fast becoming an expert on the whole story.

"There was something deeply reserved about Dr. Winn. I didn't feel compelled to ask for his approval so much as his expertise, delicate though he was with all his remarks. And I wasn't surprised when he asked me to speak to a small select panel of psychiatrists.

"I said no. But Aunt Queen changed my mind. She had brought half her entire wardrobe to the hospital and was got up each day in one of her lovely sack-style dresses, with the appropriate cloche hat, and she sat at my bedside holding my hand warmly.

" 'Don't you see, I have to do this!' she pleaded. 'I have no choice. If I don't insist that you talk to these psychiatrists, we'll stand accused of simple negligence. Think it over, Quinn. We could both be accused. We have to get this out of the way and get back to life the way we want it to be.'

" 'And how's that, Aunt Queen? What's to happen with Black-wood Manor? Don't you realize that if you and I leave on one of your exotic junkets, there'll be no Blackwood on the premises? I'll meet this teacher, yes, I told you I would, but not here. I insist that it not be here.'

" 'I understand, absolutely,' she said. 'And don't you worry about Nash, he's happily ensconced in the middle guest room at Blackwood Manor, and even if the plan goes south, as they say, he will have had something of a delicious Creole vacation.'

" 'You may find this hard to imagine, but I could swear Jasmine is flirting with Nash. Something's come over Jasmine. And it's high time if you ask me. Jasmine was prancing around today in a fancy Chanel suit I gave her two years ago. She used to never wear the truly fine things that I gave her. I think Jasmine sees her destiny.'

" 'Which is what?' I asked.

" 'To run Blackwood Manor in our absence. She's completely capable, and Clem and Big Ramona will fully support her. I mean Jasmine has languished in domestic service all her life and she's sharp and well spoken and can certainly take on the responsibility for a portion of the profit.'

" 'I didn't know we made a profit,' I said. 'Pops said we operated at a loss perpetually.'

" 'Oh, Pops was pessimistic, bless his soul, and of course he was right. The guests pay for some of the maintenance and upkeep and that's the whole point, to keep Blackwood Manor in existence, isn't it? Maybe I should say earnings instead of profit. How does that sound to you? When Pops' will is read, everything will be easier.'

" 'When is that to happen?' I asked.

" 'Well, Patsy's home, she has been for two days. I imagine we could do it day after tomorrow.'

" 'All right,' I said. I was dazed by all this sudden information. I'd been so self-involved, so full of fear and strange dreams of Rebecca and glances from a Technicolor Goblin.

"This idea of Jasmine running Blackwood Manor began to excite me. It was perfect for Jasmine. Aunt Queen understood Jasmine as no one else did, not even Jasmine.

"Suddenly, and with surprising verve, I wanted to escape this place. If Jasmine was going to resist her 'destiny,' I wanted a chance to talk to her. The simple fact was that Jasmine *did* run Blackwood Manor to a large extent, and though I wasn't so all-fired sure of her brother Clem supporting her, he might become a second-string supervisor for the men—a job that Pops' helper, Allen, had done directly. I wanted desperately to get back.

"Besides, I wanted to see Jasmine all got up in a Chanel suit.

"(In my fiendish eighteen-year-old heart, I wanted a second shot at Jasmine.)

" 'All right, I'll see the panel of doctors,' I said. 'But I want my own clothes. I don't intend to run off. I just want my Armani duds, one of those handmade shirts you keep sending me from Europe, and my lucky Versace tie. Oh yeah, and my Johnston & Murphy shoes. I want to look sane if nothing else. And also Goblin likes those clothes. Whenever I dress up for an event at home, he's delirious.'

" 'That's very reassuring,' she said. 'I'll see to it at once. And really you should wear your Church's shoes. And can we expect Goblin to be with you at this meeting?'

" 'Of course,' I said. 'You think I'd cut him out? Besides, I can't always control what Goblin does. He's been quiet here in this place. He's put up with a great quantity of contemptuous dismissal.'

" 'I suppose so,' she said, and I saw that she was staring right at the spot where Goblin stood staring at her in the same cold remote fashion.

"What I couldn't tell her was that Goblin had been acting strangely throughout the hospital stay. Also his appearance was no longer a duplicate of mine, though it might be when I was outfitted for the psychiatric panel.

"On the contrary, he didn't wear the hospital gowns or flannel nightshirts that I wore. He wore the jeans and shirts that were back home—an amazing development.

"But it was the ever-shifting expressions on his face which most frightened me. I was definitely seeing his entire visage in greater detail. And there was a frigid quality to him and a despairing look at times, and it was rarely if ever a mirror of my feelings.

"After all, I hadn't felt the usual spells of panic in the hospital. I felt a cowardly sense of safety. There was too much going on, what with Aunt Queen ordering high tea to be served in my room and Big Ramona dropping in with fancy nightshirts for me and Sweetheart's beloved sister, Aunt Ruthie, coming by with gourmet chocolates, and guards poking their heads through the door and various cousins coming to pay their respects, though what they thought had happened to me, I don't know.

"Anyway, after innumerable delays I had the coveted laptop; I was seated in an easy chair beside the hospital bed and I wanted to draw Goblin out. My mind was a tangle of thoughts about Goblin.

" 'I need to work now, Aunt Queen,' I said very gently. 'Kiss me and go off to Commander's Palace for dinner. You haven't been there since this started.'

"She was suspicious. 'But you've no phone hookup here; what are you planning to do with the laptop? Write a novel?'

" 'I'm talking to Goblin through it. It's easier for him than telepathy. He feeds off the electricity. He asked for this.'

" 'Oh, my darling Quinn,' she said with a flamboyant gesture of confusion and anxiety.

" 'Aunt Queen, let me tell you again, he saved my life. That bastard would have killed me!'

" 'Darling, what would happen if you simply stopped speaking to Goblin altogether? And as for the island, what if we destroy the Hermitage, dismantle the strange mausoleum and move all of its gold panels back to the house and let the wisteria have the place?'

" 'You're shocking me,' I said. 'You're hurting me! I want the Hermitage. I've been inspired by that marble desk and golden chair. I want to paint the place, floor it in marble. Look, I know the grief I'm causing you. I know the pain you've been through with Pops' death, and I don't mean for this agony to go on, but I want that place, don't you see, and it belongs to us, not this interloper!'

"I glanced at Goblin. He was watching Aunt Queen in the most intense manner. And then he looked at me almost listlessly. It was as if he had acquired a taste for boredom. I had to talk to him. I had to make some judgment of what he now knew! I was the only person in the world who understood this problem.

" 'All right, precious dear,' said my beloved aunt. 'I'm going upstairs for supper.'

"She had previously made known to me, more than once, that there were four restaurants in this complex and the finest could rival any restaurant in New Orleans. This was all Rowan Mayfair's idea, to provide varying fare for relatives of the sick and the sick themselves. You could grab a quick meal in the generic cafeteria in the basement or mount to the rooftop Grand Lumière for the most succulent choices.

"Aunt Queen had become a regular at the Grand Lumière, and my meals came directly from their kitchen.

" 'I'm meeting Nash, you know,' she went on to say, 'and if you'd only just—'

" 'I'll meet him when I'm properly dressed,' I said. 'Not when I'm got up like Wee Willie Winkie.'

"She rose to go.

" 'And there's another thing,' I said.

" 'Yes?' she asked. She was so polite, standing over me, ready to plant her tender kiss, so solicitous.

" 'When *do* I get out of here?'

"Obviously this was a moment for a decision.

" 'Tomorrow, perhaps, after you talk to the panel of psychiatrists?' she proposed. 'It's scheduled for four p.m.'

"Already arranged, I thought, but I made no remark on it.

" 'All right,' I said. 'Then suppose you and I and Nash and Goblin have supper in the Grand Lumière after the appointment with the panel is over.'

" 'That sounds marvelous,' she said. 'You've made me very happy. Oh, so extremely happy. And you should see the restaurant. And you will! And I can't wait to tell Nash.' And after another wealth of kisses she was off with the fragrance of Lynelle's marvelous perfume lingering behind her.

"I looked at Goblin. He showed no inclination to move from his lazy position in the corner. He was wearing my lucky Versace tie. It was positively flaunting.

"I flicked on the computer. 'You haven't talked to me since that first night.' I said it as I typed it. 'What's up with you? What's the matter? I've told everyone what you did. I've given you credit.'

"He was gone, and the fact that he had been so vivid made it all the more startling. The computer keys started to move; he wrote:

" 'I like being angry.'

"I was stunned.

" 'That's wrong,' I typed as I spoke. 'The man who hurt me was angry. Did you see the bad things he did to me?'

" 'Use bigger words,' said the computer in a rapid fire of keys. 'I told you I know all the words you ever used on the computer. I listen. I know. I know words and things. And when I was angry it was for you.'

" 'I know it was for me,' I replied, speaking and tapping it out. 'Surely you've heard me tell everyone.'

" 'Don't you see what is happening to you here?' he asked. The keys were moving at terrific speed. 'They are trying to take me from you. They are trying to divide us and we are Quinn Goblin and they don't understand about us.'

" 'It doesn't matter what they think,' I said. I spoke softly. 'I love you. I am loyal to you. They can't part us. It's impossible. But you can't be angry. You can't be violent. If you're angry and violent I can't love you.'

" 'Unless it's for you, you mean,' he countered. 'If it's for you, then it's good, isn't it?'

"He had never phrased anything in this way. It was a tiny yet momentous twist of sophistication.

" 'That's true,' I said. 'I do want you to protect me. Protect Blackwood Manor. Protect all those I love.'

" 'You make me laugh,' he wrote.

" 'Why's that?' I asked with belligerent innocence.

"The computer was pushed out of my lap to the floor. Before I could rise from the chair he was beside me, fully realized, and he kissed me on the lips. Then he drew back until he was no more than a foot from me, and his arms slipped around me and they gripped me.

"He moved his lips, and for the first time I heard a true voice come out of him, slow, masculine in tone and without inflection.

" 'You're afraid of me now,' he said, his lips moving sluggishly.

" 'Is that what you want?' I asked.

"I was terrified. Never once in my brawl with the stranger had I felt this kind of fear.

" 'You want me to be afraid?' I asked. 'I can't love you and be afraid of you. I'll come to hate you if I'm afraid. Did you see how I hated the stranger? Make a choice.'

"Again, he came in for the kiss, and I felt his lips on mine, just as firmly as I had felt Jasmine's kisses. His hand went down between my legs. He ran his hand under my nightshirt.

" 'No, not here,' I said. 'Be patient.'

"Again he spoke to me. He *spoke*.

" 'But when you feel it, I feel it. I want it.'

"I felt his hand on my cock, and I gave in. I gave in quickly, and it was over within seconds.

"I sat back in the easy chair and closed my eyes. My body was lulled and humming. There was a time of silence. Perhaps five or more minutes. But he was still there. He was kneeling right beside me, but I couldn't look at him.

" 'Who *was* the stranger?' I asked. I opened my eyes. 'I've asked you over and over. Who was he?'

" 'I don't know,' he responded. The sound of the monotone voice was literally dreadful.

" 'Where is the stranger?' I asked.

" 'I don't know,' he responded again. 'If I knew, I would find him and hurt him. I don't know everything.' On it went, flat and low. 'I know lots more than you think I do.'

"I said nothing. I was too afraid. I tried to feel love, not because I wanted to love him but because I was going mad. By tomorrow I might be roaring mad.

" 'I want you to leave me now,' I said. I looked into his eyes. 'I want you to leave me to think, you understand me?'

" 'You think you can command me,' came that monotone voice. The lips were slightly disconnected from it. 'You can't command me,' he said. 'But for love, I'll leave you alone. Beware of what they do to you here.'

" 'Don't frighten me anymore,' I said.

" 'I don't want to frighten you,' said the voice. 'But you must understand they want to change you. They want to make you so you can't see or hear me.'

" 'That can't be done,' I whispered. 'Go now. I must be alone. Don't you ever want to be alone?'

"No answer.

" 'Where do you go when you're not with me?' I asked.

"No answer.

" 'Tell me,' I said. 'Where do you go when you leave? Or do you stay with me, invisible, just watching and learning?'

"No answer.

"I felt him leave. I felt a change of temperature in the room. I heard things stirring, the paper tissue ruffled in its box, the creak of the bed, the faint rattle of the Venetian blinds, then nothing.

"I made the Sign of the Cross. What was I going to do? Where was I going to go to find someone who would understand this? Hell, I needed someone to tell me what to do.

"I went into the bathroom and washed the slimy semen off my legs. I washed my hands. Then I came back, and I took my rosary out of the nightstand. Big Ramona had found it for me. It was a garnet rosary from my First Communion. Lynelle's gift. I started to say it.

"But I couldn't meditate on the mysteries. I thought of the stranger. What if he came back to Blackwood Manor? If the Hermitage was destroyed, what would he do? I pictured him, those fiery dark eyes. How perfectly furious he had been, pivoting wild as a dervish as the broken glass assaulted him.

"And if I went to sleep, I'd dream of Rebecca."

2 1

"GOBLIN WAS on time for the meeting with the panel of psychiatrists. He was my faithful duplicate again, and the look of contempt and boredom had vanished from his face. He put his arm around me and I could see that he was afraid of what was to happen with the panel.

"As we entered the room—Goblin, me and Aunt Queen—I felt for one moment: What could it be like if I were to trust these people? If I were really to make an appeal to them? Could they help me, not with some cooked-up psychiatric diagnosis but with an active assault on Rebecca and Goblin and on the panic that had driven me to the Hermitage? Could they be a party to my efforts to fight the trespasser?

"My own sheer disloyalty to Goblin, born out of a brand-new fear, put me to shame. But, not being able to read my mind, for all his new attainments, he had no clue of it.

"I quietly demanded that a chair be placed beside me for Goblin to sit, and I laid my hand on his knee and felt him relax. I glanced at his profile and found his eyes chilly as he looked at the panel. I told the panel that, though they couldn't see him, Goblin was sitting to my left and that he was looking at them and hearing everything being said by us.

"As for the panel, I was soon certain that it was impossible to expect anything exceptional from any member of it, and the examination was largely an uneventful half hour.

"Two of the doctors were young, sterile and heartless men, interns, I figure, and the one woman on the panel seemed tentative and overeager to please, and the chairman of the board was a big heavyset doctor who seemed himself to be suffering from terminal depression.

"Winn Mayfair was there and he studied me in dignified silence. His was by far the most interesting face.

"I told them quickly, and dryly, my whole story. I kept back nothing except the most recent and private details of my erotic relationship with Goblin. Of his heroics I made much. Of our sexual contact, I said nothing. When I described my love affair with Rebecca and the burial of her remains, the visits of the Mayfair Medical lab to the Hermitage and the attendance of the FBI, they looked to Aunt Queen, who confirmed what she could readily.

" 'You do realize,' said the heavyset head doctor, 'that no fingerprints whatsoever were found in the bathroom where you were supposedly attacked. Nothing on the walls, the lavatory or on the pieces of glass that could be examined.'

"I hadn't known, and I was bitterly disappointed that I had to be told such a thing in these circumstances.

" 'The trespasser didn't touch anything but me,' I said quietly, my face burning with restraint. 'The glass was in fragments.'

" 'You also know,' said the chairman of the panel, 'that your house-keeper Ramona didn't see this intruder, and none of the guards on your property saw him either.'

"Again, I was hurt that Aunt Queen had not told me these things before, but I swallowed hard on my anger and simply shrugged.

" 'Dr. Winn Mayfair can tell you,' I said. 'My injuries weren't self-inflicted.'

"We had come to an impasse.

"Then the doctors put the same routine questions to me that child psychiatrists had used years ago, with a few new wrinkles, such as, Did I hear voices? Did Goblin ever tell me what to do? Did I ever suffer blackouts? Did I know my own IQ? Had I no interest in attending college? I gave simple answers. I wanted it to be over.

"At last Winn Mayfair asked me in a very quiet and respectful voice whether or not he and the others could do anything for me. Did I perhaps have questions for those who'd been questioning me?

"I was completely taken aback by this. I never expected anything so friendly or reasonable. Common sense told me to stop and think this over. But then I heard myself responding:

" 'No, I think this has gone on long enough. I presume you will confer and send us word of your diagnosis?'

" 'We'll do that, if you like,' said Dr. Winn. 'We thank you for coming.'

" 'You talk like I'm a specimen,' I said, ignoring Aunt Queen's little gasp. 'Was I brought here for your sake or mine?'

"Dr. Winn was unfazed by the sharpness of my tone.

" 'This is a teaching hospital, Quinn,' he said. 'It's reciprocal what goes on. As for your diagnosis, let me tell you now it's perfectly obvious that you're not a manic-depressive, a schizophrenic or a sociopath. Those are the ones that worry people.'

"He rose to his feet—a signal to all those present—and this time he shook my hand and 'applauded' my patience.

"The two antiseptic young men vanished, the woman went with them, the huge, heavy, depressed captain of the team wished me good luck, and Aunt Queen said jubilantly that we could now go up to the rooftop Grand Lumière for a nice supper.

"Goblin remained locked to my side, and in the elevator going up to the roof, I felt his right arm tight around me.

"I was calculating; I was going to break in Mr. Nash Penfield right. I wasn't going to let him find out about all this in some delicate manner.

"The restaurant proved a marvelous surprise. Even Aunt Queen's glowing compliments had not fully captured it. We were quite high up over New Orleans, which was great, and huge arched windows were open everywhere to the glowing afternoon around us. There was a colonnade along the east side, where one could stroll in the open air, along a balustrade with Tuscan columns. And within the circular room itself, between the vast windows, there were rich paintings in heavy ornate frames—a sampling of art from all different centuries.

"I noticed the Dutch art right away. 'My God,' I said to Aunt Queen, 'we're surrounded by Rembrandts.'

" 'No, dear, they're all fakes, or reproductions, as Rowan Mayfair likes to put it. They were commissioned especially for the restaurant, but don't you worry. You'll be in Amsterdam soon enough, seeing some of the originals.'

" 'What a dazzling idea,' I said. 'Bringing it all here for people who don't want to go wandering.'

" 'Now, now, toots,' she said. 'Don't fret about wandering. There's Nash. He's already at the table. Please follow me.'

"I took the measure of the restaurant before I took the measure of the man, and saw that all manner of people in all manner of dress were seated at the white draped tables. Lots of patients in wheelchairs were dining with family members, it seemed, and many tables had people who appeared dressed for a night on the town, and then there were uniformed doctors and nurses.

"All the tables were round but they varied in size, and ours was set for four, which immediately delighted me.

"In summary, I knew it to be a boldly homogenized and democratic place, yet a place of genuine beauty and refinement, and my heart went out to the woman who had designed it.

"The windows were full of the sun-streaked sky, and I could see the twinkling lights of the two river bridges shining wonderfully in the dusk. I loved it.

"But now it was time to see Nash and to introduce him to Goblin.

"The man who was helping Aunt Queen with her chair was taller even than me (at that time), probably by about two inches. He had wavy black hair with a lot of gray at the sides, and he was dressed in a fine spring suit of blue-and-white seersucker.

"His eyes were pale blue and he had rather deep lines in his face, giving him a bit of a jowled look, but he was in fact slender. His expression was entirely wise and sympathetic, and he took my hand in his warmly.

" 'You're Nash,' I said. 'I thank you for helping with my computer.'

"His voice came with a depth and color that any man would envy. In fact, it had an effortless professional sound to it that was charming.

" 'I'm delighted to meet you, Quinn,' he said. 'I understand Goblin is with you?'

"We were getting off on the right foot. I presented Goblin to him immediately and I noted Goblin's cold stare as Nash tried his best to be courteous to something he couldn't see.

"We were immediately seated in a nice open circle, and when the waitress approached, I told her that an invisible personage was seated to my left, and that he would be having the same meal I would be having.

"She was horrified.

"Aunt Queen gave her immediate approval of the plan before the young woman could laugh or make some odd remark. And Nash immediately commented on the heavy silver of the table setting.

"I ordered a double vodka martini, with plenty of olive juice and olives, and that went over very well, too, thanks to Aunt Queen immediately ordering the same and one for Goblin, and asking to see the wine list.

"Nash asked for a glass of plain soda water, remarking that he had finished a lifetime of drinking earlier than one might have expected.

"The waitress departed in an anxious flurry.

"Then Nash began to introduce himself, his slow, careful sonorous voice telling of how he and Aunt Queen had met in Europe, where Nash had been shepherding a group of high school students on a tour of the Continent.

"This was apparently Nash's summer job throughout graduate school at Claremont College in California, but he was now finished with all course work for his Ph.D. and needed only to write his dissertation.

"Subject? A thorough investigation as to whether Charles Dickens had ever been edited, and what effect modern editing standards might have had on his work, with heavy reliance on an examination of how Dickens' writings had been abridged in England and America.

"I was immediately interested, and also attracted to this deep-voiced man with the gray at his temples, and I felt I could have listened to his easy eloquence for hours. In fact, I longed to do so. He had a natural wide-eyed expression when he spoke and an inveterate politeness that was totally disarming.

"But Aunt Queen quickly cut in to express her immediate desire: that as soon as Pops' will was read, we go on to Europe. Of course Nash agreed with her that I was the perfect age for the Grand Tour, and I believed Nash when he told me that I would never quite again be as impressionable as I was now. Then he turned to Goblin, and, trying to lock eyes with something parallel to me, asked Goblin what he thought of the travel proposal.

"I took Goblin's right hand, which felt heavy and warm, but he showed me nothing but that cold profile again and he was utterly silent.

" 'Goblin, what do you think? Do you remember our trip to New York?' The question came out of my mouth before I could realize that it was a blunder. Goblin had gotten weaker and weaker in New York, until he was scarcely more than a sheer phantom.

" 'Goblin, we won't do anything that's bad for us,' I said. 'Here, look at this martini.' I held up the glass for him. And then I took a swallow of it myself. 'Here's to you, Goblin. We're together. We're going home to the house tonight. We're through with this hospital and anybody and everybody that would have worked for our separation.'

"Of course this long speech was entirely audible to Nash and Aunt Queen, and Aunt Queen picked up the gist immediately.

" 'Come, Goblin,' said Aunt Queen, 'certainly you want to go to Europe. We'll have so much fun together.'

"Again, I tried to elicit some reaction from him, but I couldn't. He wasn't playing at eating his food or drinking his drink, and he stared at Nash as if he was the enemy.

" 'No, Goblin, he's not!' I leaned towards him. I whispered. 'He's good for us. Remember how Lynelle was good? That's how this man is. I knew it the moment he started talking to us.'

"Of course Nash and Aunt Queen could hear this, and Aunt Queen said at once: 'I'm so supremely overjoyed. Quinn, dear, don't drink that martini too fast. The wine I've chosen is excellent.'

"Goblin continued to stare forward.

" 'Never mind him for now,' I said. 'I think the hospital stay has exhausted him. Nash—I presume you do want me to call you Nash' ('Oh, absolutely,' he replied) '—we've just been through a peculiar ordeal upstairs and—.'

"Before I could say more I heard Goblin's ominous monotone: 'Europe, I can't,' he said. 'Too far for me. You remember New York. You talk like a fool. Goblin Quinn one person.'

"It was clear that no one else could hear him.

" 'I know,' I replied aloud. 'I understand. All right. We'll think on it.'

" 'I once thought,' he went on in the same chilling voice, 'Europe existed in pictures and stories. Then Aunt Queen called from Europe, we saw movies of Europe, Lynelle taught you about Europe. Europe is real and far away. No going to Europe. No. Do this and we split apart. Quinn Goblin one person.'

"My anxiety was cresting. Plates of steaming food were being set down, wineglasses filled, and all the world of this restaurant saw me whispering to empty space, but I had no intention of weakening.

" 'Just listen to this man,' I said. 'Listen to Aunt Queen. It doesn't mean we have to go.' I leaned closer to him, dropping my whispering even lower. 'I'm just humoring them, you see, I have to do it. Nash can be my teacher at Blackwood Farm. We'll be together. Goblin, look at me.'

" 'No, I don't want to look at you,' he replied. 'You are sly.'

" 'God in Heaven,' I declared in a louder voice. 'What do you want of me? I'm giving you my total loyalty. Nash, tell him that you can be my tutor at Blackwood Farm. It's possible, isn't it?'

"Nash stared intently at what he thought was Goblin's face, and he wasn't very far off, as I saw it.

" 'Of course, I'd be delighted to teach Quinn at Blackwood Farm.

The place is beautiful,' he said. 'Goblin, I'm new here. I want for you to approve of me. I know full well that Quinn will only accept me if you do.'

" 'Yes, that's it, that's why we're here!' I said forthrightly. 'Oh, if you could only see him,' I said to Nash. 'To me he's as solid as you.' I reached over and took Goblin's right hand. 'I love you, Goblin. It's love between us.' I kissed his cheek.

"I drew back, and in the small interval of silence I felt exposed in this crowded restaurant and maybe downright ridiculous. I had thought that Nash would be difficult to win over, but it was turning out to be Goblin. And I was out on a limb in this place, talking to what seemed to be nothing and no one, talking in fear because I knew what that invisible person could do and no one around me could even guess it. Not even Aunt Queen really had a guess at it.

"And then there came one of the rarest moments of my life.

"I was gazing from Nash to Aunt Queen when suddenly I noticed at the next table, behind them, a beautiful red-haired girl who was staring at me fixedly. It was as if Fr. Kevin Mayfair had been metamorphosed into his own divine sister.

"She had his same clear skin with a natural blush to the cheeks and the same rich red hair; and though she had breasts large enough to please any man, she wore ribbons on either side of her hair as if she were still something of a little girl in spirit.

"We locked eyes, the two of us, and then she looked from me to Goblin. *She could see Goblin!*

" 'Dull-witted Quinn,' he said to me in his icy loveless voice. 'She has been watching us from the beginning.'

"Of course. He had been staring at her, not at Nash, not at Aunt Queen; he had been staring past them at this person—the first person I had ever known, other than me—who seemed able to completely see him.

"The shock left me speechless. I knew Aunt Queen was asking me questions, and that Nash had just spoken up. But I made sense of nothing. And as I watched, a man who was seated beside this amazing young girl stood up and came towards us. He looked right at me as he approached.

"He was gray-haired, informal yet dignified in a blue blazer and slacks, and very vivacious of expression and of voice as he spoke to me.

" 'You'll forgive my intrusion, please,' he said. 'My name is Stirling Oliver. I'm a member of an organization. It's called the Talamasca. I want to introduce myself to you. We study the paranormal, you see, and I couldn't help but notice your companion.'

" 'You mean you can see him too?' I asked. But I saw at once he was telling the truth, and Goblin's eyes moved to his, but Goblin said nothing.

" 'Yes, I can see him very well,' said Mr. Oliver as he presented me with a little card. 'We're an old, old Order,' he went on. 'We've existed for perhaps a thousand years. We study ghosts and those who can see them. We offer assistance. We offer information. I am so very impressed with your friend. Do forgive me.'

" 'Goblin, talk to Mr. Oliver,' I said.

"Goblin neither moved nor spoke.

"Aunt Queen interjected. 'I really must ask you to stop,' she said with uncommon force. 'You see, my nephew in spite of his prodigious height is only eighteen, and you really must go through me if you want to establish any sort of relationship at all with him. I don't entirely approve of those who believe in the paranormal.'

" 'But Aunt Queen,' I said. 'How can you say this! All my life I've seen Goblin! Please, I beg you, let me talk to this man.' But it was to the red-haired girl I looked, and then abruptly I rose, excusing myself to nobody, and I went to her table.

"She looked up at me with Fr. Kevin's green eyes. The little ribbons held back beautiful tresses of her long thick wavy hair. She smiled. She beamed. She was exquisite.

" 'I want to marry you,' I said. 'I'm in love with you. You can see Goblin, can't you?'

" 'Yes, I can see him, and he's an egregious whopper of a spirit,' she said, 'but I don't think I can marry you.'

"I sat down, probably taking the chair which Stirling Oliver had vacated, barely casting a glance at him to discover he was in fast discussion with Aunt Queen, and only now did I realize that Fr. Kevin and Dr. Winn were both seated at the table facing us.

" 'My name's Mona Mayfair,' the girl said. She had the most crisp lively voice. 'These are my cousins—.'

" 'I know them both. Fr. Kev, please, properly introduce us.'

" 'Quinn, you are so strange,' said Fr. Kev with the flash of a warm smile. ' "Properly introduce." Next you'll want me to announce the banns on Sunday. Mona, this is Tarquin Blackwood, he's eighteen, and he takes his familiar with him everywhere.'

" 'That ghost is no familiar,' Mona said. 'He's much too strong for that designation.'

"Oh, I loved her voice, the lilt of it, the easy way she laughed.

" 'I want to marry you, Mona, I know it,' I said. I stammered. I had never beheld anyone as purely lovable as Mona, and I never would, I was totally aware of that. The world hung by a thread, and I had to seize the world and snap that thread. 'Mona, come away with me. Let's just talk together.'

" 'Slow down, Tarquin, please,' she said. 'You're really cut and cute, but I can't just go off with you. I've got so many people watching me you wouldn't believe it.'

" 'Oh, it's the same way with me, every decision is made by committee. Mona, I adore you.' I looked at my hands. What rings had I put on for the odious meeting with the psychiatrists? I had a diamond-studded band on my right ring finger. I pulled it off. I offered it to her.

" 'Quinn,' said Fr. Kevin, 'cease and desist. You can talk to Mona in normal fashion. You don't have to be offering her a ring. You don't even know her.'

" 'And look,' she said, pointing over at the table. 'Your ghost is standing up and staring at you. He knows I can see him and he doesn't know what he thinks about it. Look how he's looking down at Stirling.'

" 'Stirling, the Talamasca, that's what he said, right? I have to learn about it. You know this Talamasca, Fr. Kev?'

" 'About as much as a priest of the Church of Rome can ever know it,' he answered easily. 'Quinn, Stirling's a decent man. I can't endorse the organization, but he's been a good friend to Mona and to me.'

" 'You need somebody like him,' said Mona. 'Not me. I'm too ruined for you.'

" 'What on earth are you talking about?' I said. 'Ruined! You're gorgeous. I want to . . . I'm going mad. I knew I'd go mad today. First it's a panel of psychiatrists, and then it's Goblin acting sullen and weird, and now you're telling me you won't even think about marrying me! Let me just call on you, let me just bring you a bouquet of flowers and sit with you in your parlor with your mother, all right? I swear, I'll be a perfect gentleman.'

"Her smile broadened and I could see the most shadowy humor in her quick green eyes. I could see secrets, I could see cleverness and sweetness.

" 'I wish to God, if I wasn't who I am—' she said. 'Mayfairs like me always marry other Mayfairs. We have no choice. Nobody else understands us.' She sighed.

" 'I understand you. You've seen other ghosts, haven't you? You knew Goblin for what he was immediately.'

" 'I've seen plenty of ghosts,' she said soberly. 'Maybe you and I could just play for a while.'

" 'No, I don't think this is a good idea,' said Fr. Kev. 'Quinn, your Aunt Queen is getting pretty heated over there.' He rose to his feet. 'I think it's time for me to step in and restrain Stirling. I've never seen Stirling play it quite this way. I think Stirling thinks you need him, Quinn. And you come back with me now.'

" 'But I don't even know where you live!' I said to Mona.

"I stared at Dr. Winn. His cold blue eyes and impassive face told me nothing.

" 'Come on, Quinn,' said Fr. Kev.

" 'First and Chestnut Streets,' said Mona. 'Can you remember that? Riverside downtown corner. That's the Garden District—.'

" 'I know it totally,' I said. 'My grandma grew up on Coliseum Street. I'll come to see you.'

"I let Fr. Kev direct me back to my table. Stirling Oliver was in my chair talking heatedly to Aunt Queen.

" 'We only mean to help people,' he said. 'A person who sees spirits can feel very isolated.'

" 'You're right,' I said, 'you're so right.'

"And there stood Goblin staring down coldly on the proceedings and then looking over to the blossom of loveliness that was Mona.

"Stirling rose. He put a white card in my hand. 'Take this. Call me if you feel you need to talk to me. And if your aunt, Mrs. McQueen, will allow it.'

" 'I despise having to be rude,' said Aunt Queen, 'but I do not think this is a very good idea, Mr. Oliver, and I do prevail upon you to leave my nephew to his destiny.'

" 'His destiny,' said Mr. Oliver. 'Oh, but that has such a ring to it.'

" 'Yes, indeed it does,' I said. 'Aunt Queen, I'm in love. I'm in love with that girl. Turn your head. You won't believe your eyes.'

" 'Good Lord,' she said, 'it's a female Mayfair.'

" 'What kind of remark is that!' I said.

"Fr. Kevin chuckled under his breath. 'Now Miss Queen,' he said, smiling, 'you've always tolerated me very well. I know you've had your driver bring you all the way over the lake just to hear me say Mass at St. Mary's Assumption.'

" 'You do say Mass with a lovely flair, Fr. Kevin,' she responded, 'and you are a priest of God, as we well know, and a consecrated priest of the Roman Catholic Church, no dispute on that matter—but we are talking about your cousin Mona, if I'm not mistaken? Yes, Mona, and that is entirely another matter. Darlings, I think it's time for us to go home. Quinn, dear, you've been discharged and your room packed up. Nash, you don't mind too terribly—."

" 'Aunt Queen, what is happening?' I asked.

" 'We're leaving, darling. Mr. Oliver? I wish I could say that it has been a pleasure. Your good intentions have been acknowledged.'

" 'Please, keep this,' he said as he gave her his card again.

"I still held the one he'd given me. I put it in my pocket.

"I looked back at the radiant girl. And as our eyes connected I heard the message, clear as if Goblin had spoken it to me: *First and Chestnut*.

"Goblin vanished. I was being rushed out of the restaurant. Never had I felt such angry bewilderment!

"Only when we reached the car did I demand that we stop.

" 'Goblin,' I cried. 'Don't you see? He's off plaguing her now. Goblin, come back to me.'

"Then came the cold murmured reassurance I required, like a gnat at my ear. 'You are a fool, Quinn. I don't want to be with her. She doesn't love me. I'm not hers. I am with you. I am yours. Quinn and Goblin one person.'

" 'Thank God,' I whispered.

"The big stretch limousine pulled out of the porte cochere, and I started to cry like a little boy.

" 'You just don't understand,' I said. 'She saw Goblin. And I'm in love with her. She's the most radiant gemstone of a creature that I've ever seen.' "

22

"THAT NIGHT I connected with Nash as I have connected with few people in my life, and we forged a bond which lasted for my mortal lifetime and beyond it. He sat up with me for hours, comforting me as I poured out my soul, as I agonized over my fatal glimpse of Mona Mayfair.

"I made him privy to every nuance of the panic I'd been experiencing since Lynelle died, and I even dared to tell him in profound words and circuitous sentences of how I feared the recent shifts of emotional temperature in Goblin.

"Of course I told him about the stranger, the stranger in whom no one believed, apparently, and that I expected in short order to be accused of having actually written myself the stranger's letter to me.

"I positively raved about Lynelle's loss. I could do no less when I thought of it.

"Nash's deep voice, his strong arm around my shoulders, his gentle hand on my knee, it was beyond comforting. And there was something about him that was so proper yet relaxed, so inherently gentlemanly yet natural, that I felt I could trust him with my whole soul—even with the erotic adventures I'd had with my beloved Goblin and my terrifying Rebecca. I even told him about my sleeping with Jasmine.

"What did Nash really believe? Did he think I was insane? I didn't know. I only knew that he was being very honest with me in every word that he spoke and in every gesture. I knew that he respected me, and this respect counted for everything.

"I knew that he felt compassion for me just because I was young, yet he took me seriously, and he said time and again as the night wore on that he understood and remembered what it had been like for him at my age.

"We started our marathon conversation in the front parlor, thankfully deserted early by our few guests, and we ended at the kitchen table, drinking coffee like fuel, though I kept lacing mine with luscious amounts of cream and sugar.

"Only when Big Ramona ran us out did we walk down to the old cemetery, and I told him all about the spirits I'd seen. I told him the things I wanted to tell Mona.

"We were under the big oak when the dawn came with its soft silent and shimmering light, and it was there that I told him I would always love him.

" 'You know, whatever happens with us,' I said, 'as teacher and pupil, as friends, whatever comes to pass—whether we go to Europe eventually, or we study here—I'll never forget you listening to me tonight, I'll never forget your inveterate kindness.'

" 'Quinn, you're a battered soul,' he said to me. 'And probably the better for it. I can't deny how compelling you are to me, and the challenge that you present to me. Yes, I want to be your teacher. I'd be honored to be your teacher, and I do think there are things we could achieve together. But you don't know me yet, and you may come to change your mind about me when certain things become clear to you.'

" 'Nothing will ever change this love, Nash,' I responded. 'Any more than anything will change what I feel for Mona Mayfair.'

"He gave me the most reassuring smile.

" 'And now you need to go in and get dressed,' he said. 'The reading of your grandfather's will, remember?'

"How could I forget?

"I bolted down a huge breakfast in the kitchen and then went up to shower and change, half afraid of what I might find in the bathroom in the way of patchwork repairs, but everything was done to perfection.

"Feeling lightheaded and like a conquistador of grand emotions, I piled into the limousine with Aunt Queen and Patsy, who looked like deliberate and absolute trash in her red leather clothes, and Jasmine, dressed to the teeth in a gorgeous black suit and stiletto heels, and off we went to the lawyer's office in Ruby River City. Big Ramona and Felix were supposed to have come too, but there was no way the house could spare them. Clem, who was driving the limo, had also been alerted to come inside when we got there. And Lolly, who was up front with Clem, was also included.

"In short order, we settled down in one of those generic legal places of which I've seen several in my time, outfitted with blackberry leather chairs and a big glass-covered mahogany desk for the man who reads the document that is bound to make somebody feel rotten.

"Our pleasant-voiced lawyer, Grady Breen (Gravier's old and dear friend, and a relic of some eighty-five years in age), made all the appropriate offers of coffee or soft drinks, which we all in our anxiety declined, and then we were off and running.

"Last time it had been Patsy who was so brutally hurt with a trust-fund inheritance that didn't amount in her mind to a pittance. And everybody was silently betting it was Patsy again who would get scalded and leave the office yowling.

"But what unfolded surprised everyone. The smaller bequests—one hundred thousand dollars each to Clem, Felix, Ramona, Lolly and Jasmine—were no great shock. And that Pops had left them handsome annuities for retirement as well made everyone a little less nervous. In fact, I'm understating the case. This part of the will made Clem and Jasmine and Lolly jubilant. Jasmine started to cry, and Lolly held tight to her arm, tearing up as well, and Clem just shook his head at the marvel of it.

"But then there came the real meat of the feast and no one could have been more amazed than Patsy. It seemed that Great-grandfather Gravier had left a trust fund to Pops which was bound by its original terms to go in its entirety to Pops' only child, Patsy. The principal of the trust was in the high double-digit millions, and the income so handsome that Patsy positively screamed with astonished laughter.

"As to Pops' remaining trust funds, also enormous, one went to Aunt Queen until her death and then to me, and the other was mine immediately. It was a dizzying amount of income.

"In summary, Pops had disinherited Patsy, but it made no difference because he couldn't stop Grandpa Gravier's trust from going to her. And his frugal ways over the years, his paying himself a pittance of a salary and rolling back into the big trust its earnings, had even increased Patsy's fortune. Of course Patsy couldn't touch the principal of the big trust, and when she died I would inherit it.

"Patsy was so delirious that she threw her arms around Aunt Queen, squealing and giggling and stomping the floor with her red leather boots.

"And even I felt happy for her.

"Aunt Queen kissed her cheek and told her warmly that it was indeed wondrous news, and now Patsy could buy some new clothes with her newfound money.

" 'Oh, am I going to buy new clothes!' she declared. She ran out of the lawyer's office before anyone could stop her. How she found transportation without Clem I couldn't guess, except that she had her cell phone with her always these days, and Seymour was back at the house with her van. Whatever the case, never sensing the irony of Aunt Queen's gentle words, she vanished.

"I sat there absorbing the fact that I now had a substantial income in my own right, some one hundred thousand dollars a month immediately available to me, though it came with strict and nonbinding advice that I take Aunt Queen's guidance in everything.

"There was some fancy language pertaining to all that, something to do with Aunt Queen's advanced age, and my precocity, and I interpreted from it that I was being entrusted with my income now because of my obedient nature and the fact that my mother could not be relied upon to provide the proper guidance.

"I was given two credit cards on the spot, each with a line of credit of a hundred thousand, a checkbook for a checking account which would carry a rolling balance of twenty thousand dollars a month, a money market account into which would be deposited eighty thousand a month, and I filled out some important papers, signed bank forms and cards, signed the credit cards as well, slipped them into my wallet, pocketed the checkbook, and my part of the transaction was over. I was intoxicated with new-funded manhood.

"What followed had to do with the various other employees who were left handsome amounts, of which they would soon be apprised, as Aunt Queen, appointed executrix for these, had some six months to make them available to the designated persons. It was wonderful to hear of this. The men were going to be mighty pleased.

"Then came the description of the household trust, which had been established by the Old Man himself, Manfred. It had grown enormously over the years, and its sole beneficiary was Blackwood Farm. And try as I might I could not understand all its complications.

"That Blackwood Farm couldn't be divided, that its house could never be pulled down, that any architectural changes must be in keeping with its original designs, that all who were employed in the management and maintenance of Blackwood Manor and Blackwood Farm were to be well paid—all this was rolled out in complex language, spelling security for the estate that I loved, and making it very clear that the income we received from our paying guests meant absolutely nothing.

"There was also considerable language about the responsibilities for the farm trust now falling upon Aunt Queen, and then passing on to me, but this was also too complicated to follow. That Patsy would never own or control Blackwood Farm was the gist of this, and of course Patsy wouldn't give a damn about it.

"As for the present, the pure ownership of Blackwood Farm itself, including all buildings, swamp and land, passed from Pops to me, with a grant of usufruct to Aunt Queen, meaning she could live there throughout her lifetime.

"This left me astonished. But immediately Aunt Queen explained the wisdom of it. Were she to marry, she said, her husband might try to bring a claim of ownership against the land, and this was what Pops wanted to protect against. Of course, she was seventy-eight (or so she said) and she wasn't going to marry anyone, she remarked (Except perhaps the charming Nash Penfield. Laugh.), but Pops had to do it this way to protect me.

"But I couldn't help but note that Patsy didn't even have the right to live at the property, which Aunt Queen did. I kept quiet about it. Patsy would never know. And I certainly wasn't going to put her out on the porch with her bags packed.

"Besides, with her high monthly income—some half a million—she wasn't likely to be around much.

"What funded all of our trusts were enormous investments in such diversified instruments as railroads, international shipping, worldwide banking, precious metals and gems, foreign currencies, U.S. Treasury bills, pharmaceutical companies, mutual funds of every imaginable name and description and random stocks of all kinds, from the most conservative to the most speculative, the entire holding administered by the investment firm of Mayfair and Mayfair, in New Orleans, an arm of the law firm of Mayfair and Mayfair, which managed only a handful of very select private fortunes.

"It was quite impossible to find anyone superior to Mayfair and Mayfair when it came to investing, and it was also impossible to solicit their services today. The deal had been struck with them in 1880 between Manfred Blackwood and Julien Mayfair. And nothing but good luck and high profits had followed down to the present time.

"Since I was in love with Mona Mayfair, all this made a very favorable impression on me. But in the main it was over my head. I had always known I was well-off, and how well-off had never been a matter of concern.

"Now, when all this was complete and done, came the biggest shocker. Pops had confided to his lawyer something of which we didn't even dream. But before we were asked to hear it, Jasmine, Clem and Lolly were invited to excuse themselves.

"Aunt Queen, on what instinct I'm not sure, asked Jasmine to remain. Lolly and Clem seemed unperturbed by this and went out immediately to sit in the parlor. Jasmine moved closer to me as though to protect me from whatever was coming.

"Our lawyer, Grady Breen, laid aside the many documents he had before him and started to speak to us with a note of sympathy in his voice that seemed genuine.

" 'Thomas Blackwood' (this was Pops) 'confided in me a secret before he died,' he said, 'and he made a verbal request of me as to this secret, that I advise you of it and ask of you that you do right by it. Now, as you may or may not know, there is a young lady in the backwoods hereabouts, name of Terry Sue, who has about five or six children.' He glanced at his watch. 'Probably six children.'

" 'Who on earth hasn't heard of Terry Sue?' asked Aunt Queen with a faint smile. 'I'm ashamed to say every Shed Man on the property knows Terry Sue. She just had another baby—.' Now Aunt Queen looked at her watch. 'Didn't she? Yes, I believe she did.'

" 'Well, yes, she did,' said Grady, slipping off his wire-rimmed glasses and sitting back. 'And it's a well-known fact that Terry Sue is one beautiful young woman, and a young woman who likes to have babies. But it's not that new baby that I want to discuss now. It seems that Terry Sue had a child by Pops about nine years ago.'

" 'That's impossible!' I said. 'He would never have been unfaithful to Sweetheart!'

" 'It wasn't a thing he was proud of, Quinn,' said Grady. 'Indeed, he was not proud of it, and he was deeply concerned that the rumors about it would never disturb his family.'

" 'I don't believe it,' I said again.

" 'DNA has proved it, Quinn,' said Grady. 'And Terry Sue of course has always known it, and out of affection for Sweetheart, for whom Terry Sue did baking, you know—.'

" 'Those big Virginia hams,' I said. 'She'd soak them and scrub them and bake them.'

" 'What tenderness,' said Aunt Queen. 'Seems she soaked and scrubbed something else. But Grady, you have a point to make with this revelation, don't you, dear fellow?'

" 'Indeed, I do, Miss Queen,' said Grady. 'Pops was in the habit of taking an envelope of cash over there to Terry Sue every week or so, and though whatever man she's with tends to run off the old ones, no one was ever tempted to run off Pops with his envelope. It was about five hundred a week that he gave her. And this keeps the boy in a good Catholic school—St. Joseph's over in Mapleville—and that was the one term exacted for it, as far as I know. The boy's nine years old now, I believe. He's in the fourth grade.'

" 'We'll continue this, of course,' said Aunt Queen. 'Can we see this child?'

" 'I recommend you do,' said Grady, 'because he's a beautiful boy, handsome as you, Quinn, and he's bright too, and Terry Sue, for all her faults, is trying to bring him up right. His name is Tommy. One thing that might help, if you'll take my suggestion. Now Pops never would but . . .'

" 'But what is it?' I asked. I was flabbergasted by all this.

" 'Give her enough money to send all those children of hers to good schools,' said Grady. 'Equalize things, you know what I mean? If you take toys or video games or what have you out there, take it for all the children.'

" 'I see, yes, I understand,' said Aunt Queen. 'You'll have to give me a written report as to the size of the family and then we can arrange . . .'

" 'No, I wouldn't do it in writing, Miss Queen,' said Grady. 'I wouldn't put anything in writing at all. There's five little ones out there now, no, six as of this morning, and the latest boyfriend is a piece of trash, pure trailer trash, I should say, and in fact they do live in a trailer, the whole gang, and such a trailer you wouldn't believe, and there are the proverbial rusting cars up on blocks in the yard, it's just a classical situation out there, a regular motion picture set—.'

" 'Cut to the chase, my man,' said Aunt Queen.

" 'But there is that little boy whose father was rich, and he's growing up out there and Terry Sue is doing the best she can, and this new baby, this new baby makes six, I figure. I'll take the envelopes of cash for you, that much I can do, but don't put anything in writing.'

"Of course Aunt Queen and I both understood this. But we were eager and curious about this little boy, still unbelieving though I was emotionally. A little brother, no, a little uncle, named Tommy and with

Blackwood genes in him, and maybe a resemblance to the many portraits all over the household.

"It being agreed that we were finished, Aunt Queen had risen and so
had Jasmine, who had remained subdued throughout, and I was still sitting there, deeply preoccupied.

" 'Does the little boy know?' I asked.

" 'I'm not sure,' said Grady. He looked to Aunt Queen. 'You and I
can discuss this further.'

" 'Oh, indeed, we should; we're talking about a family of six children
living in one trailer. Good Lord, and she's so beautiful. The least I could
do would be to purchase the good woman a decent house, if it wouldn't
offend the pride of anyone squeezed into the trailer.'

" 'How come I never heard of her?' I asked. And to my bewilderment, they all went into peals of laughter.

" 'Then we'd have double trouble, wouldn't we?' said Jasmine. 'Men
just fall over flat at the feet of Terry Sue.'

" 'Well something stands up straight in those circumstances,' said
Aunt Queen.

" 'There's one last thing I should say,' said Grady, flushed with mer-
riment, 'and I am taking a bit of responsibility here.'

" 'Out with it, man,' said Aunt Queen gently. She didn't much care
for standing in her spike heels and sat down again.

" 'The man that's living with Terry Sue now,' said Grady. 'Sometimes he takes out his gun and waves it at the children.'

"We were aghast.

" 'And he did fling little Tommy up against the gas heater and burn
his hand pretty badly.'

" 'And you mean to tell me,' said Aunt Queen, 'that Pops knew of
this sort of thing and did nothing about it?'

" 'Pops tried to be an influence out there,' said Grady, 'but when
you're dealing with the likes of Terry Sue, it's pretty much hopeless.
Now she herself would never raise her hand to those children, but then
these men come in and she has to put food on the table.'

" 'Don't tell me another word,' said Aunt Queen. 'I have to go home
and think what to do about it.'

"I shook my head.

"Little Tommy? A son living in a trailer.

A gloom had come on me, a feeling of unrest, and I knew it was as
much from lack of sleep as it was from learning all this and how rich

Pops was, and thinking, though I didn't want to think of it, of those terrible arguments he would have with Patsy when she begged for money.

"Why, he could have set up the band. He could have bought the van. He could have hired the pickers. He could have given her a chance. And as it was, she begged and cursed and fought for every dime, and what did he do, this man whom I had so loved? What did he do with his powerful resources? He spent his days working on Blackwood Farm like a hired hand. He planted flower beds.

"And there was this child, this little boy, Tommy, no less, named after Pops, living on a pittance in the backwoods, with a passel of brothers and sisters in a trailer, a little boy with a psychotic stepfather.

"How had Pops seen his life? What had he wanted from it? My life had to be more. It had to be much, much greater. I would go mad if my life weren't more. I felt pursued by the pressure of life itself. I felt frantic.

" 'What's his full name?' I asked. 'You can tell me, can't you?'

" 'Please do tell us his full name,' asked Aunt Queen with a decisive nod.

" 'Tommy Harrison,' said Grady. 'Harrison is Terry Sue's last name. I believe the child is illegitimate. In fact, I know the child is illegitimate.'

"My mood grew even darker. Who was I to judge Pops, I thought. Who was I to judge the man who had just left me so much wealth and who might have done otherwise? Who was I to judge him that he had left little Tommy Harrison in such a situation? But it weighed on me. And it weighed on me that Patsy's character had perhaps been shaped by her lifelong struggle against a man who did not believe in her.

"Our farewells were being exchanged.

"I had to come to the surface. And off we went to lunch with Nash at Blackwood Manor.

"As we came out of the office Goblin appeared, attired as I was, my double again, but dour as he had been in the hospital, though not sneering, only solemn if not sad. He walked beside me to the car, and I felt that he knew my sadness, my disillusionment, and I turned to him and put my arm around him and he felt firm and good.

" 'It's changing, Quinn,' he said to me.

" 'No, old buddy, it can't change,' I said in his ear.

"But I knew he was right. I had things to do now. Places to go. And people to meet."

23

"WHAT BROUGHT ME out of my daze about the newfound uncle and Pops' wealth was the view of all the old wicker, painted white and grouped on the side flagstone terrace to the right of Blackwood Manor, just as it had been in my dreams of Rebecca. This was furniture I'd requisitioned from the attic, but the task of restoration had been completed while I lay in the hospital, and I marveled now to see the gathering of couches and chairs just as it had been when Rebecca served me her mythical coffee.

" 'Mona's going to understand,' I murmured aloud, 'and that man, that kindly man, Stirling Oliver, he'll understand, and then there's Nash, Nash who seemed as great and kind as a teacher could be, Nash who gave me hope that I would get through this strange time with some equanimity.'

"But when he entered the front hall I was stunned to see a pile of luggage by the door, and Nash, in a blue suit and tie, with a hand out for my shoulder.

" 'I can't stay, Quinn, but I must talk to your Aunt Queen before I talk to you. Let me have those moments with her now.'

"I was devastated. 'No,' I said, 'you have to tell me. It's what I said, wasn't it, all the things I told you, you think I'm insane, and you think it's going to be like this always, but I swear—.'

" 'No, Quinn, I don't think you're insane,' he said. 'But understand I must leave. Now let me speak with Miss Queen alone. I promise I won't leave without telling you.'

"I let them go into the front parlor together, and then I went into the kitchen for lunch, where Jasmine was just telling Big Ramona that they were rich. I hated to break up their happiness with my glum looks and I blamed it all on hunger. Besides, Jasmine had always been rich and so was Big Ramona. They just never wanted to leave Blackwood Manor, everybody knew.

"And since one thing I could always do was eat, I devoured a platter of Sunday chicken and dumplings.

"Finally, I could resist the suspense no longer. I went to the parlor door, and Aunt Queen beckoned for me.

" 'Now darling, Nash is under the impression that you'll be disturbed in time by the fact that he hasn't so much chosen a bachelor's life as been rather predisposed to it.'

" 'I have it all in a letter here, Quinn,' said Nash in his kindly but authoritative manner.

" 'Are you telling me you're gay?' I asked.

"Aunt Queen was shocked.

" 'Well, to be frank,' said Nash, 'that's exactly what I intended to tell you.'

" 'I knew that last night,' I said. 'Oh, don't worry that you gave it away with some obvious gesture or mannerism. You didn't. I just sensed it because I'm probably that way myself; at least, I'm bisexual, I have no doubt of that.'

"I was greeted by a stunned silence from Nash, and from Aunt Queen a low pleasant laughter. Of course I'd just made a little confession that might have hurt her, but I was very sure Nash would not be hurt at all.

" 'Oh my precocious one,' she said. 'You never fail to charm me. Bisexual is it, how Byronic and charming. Doesn't that double one's chances for love? I'm so delighted.'

"Nash continued to stare at me as if he could think of nothing whatsoever to say, and then I realized what had happened.

"Nash had resigned his post not because he was gay; he'd known he was gay long before he ever came here. He'd resigned his post because of what he'd seen in me and what I'd told him about my own predilections! Oh, it was so perfectly obvious and I'd been such a dolt not to catch on. I should have let him off the hook right away.

" 'Look, Nash,' I said, 'you've got to stay. You want to stay and I want you to stay. Now let's just take a vow that nothing erotic will ever pass between us. That it's, you know, inappropriate. You'll become the perfect teacher for me because I don't have to hide anything from you.'

" 'Now that's a potent argument,' said Aunt Queen, 'no pun intended. I do mean, really Nash, Quinn has a point there.' She made a pleasant airy laugh. 'Good Lord, in schools all over this country gay men and women make excellent and sympathetic teachers. The whole issue is settled.' She rose. 'Nash Penfield, you must unpack your bags, at least until we leave for New York, and Quinn, you have to get some sleep. Now everything's settled until suppertime.'

"Nash still seemed to be in a state of shock, but I shook his hand and elicited a wide-eyed and softly murmured statement that he would stay, and, not daring to take him in my arms, I headed up to my room to get three hundred dollars out of my bureau (I always had some money there) and to make certain that I had on the best suit of clothes I owned and the lucky Versace tie, which I had not worn to meet with our lawyer.

"As I came downstairs I felt something pull at me; I don't mean it was the hand of Goblin so much as it was a feeling or a mass of feelings. I had gone without sleep a long long time. And what I thought of now was Rebecca. In fact, it seemed for a moment Rebecca was with me, and then she wasn't.

Little redheaded bitch . . . black bitch!

"When I reached the side lawn I walked slowly over the flagstone terrace and through the new arrangement of wicker, and I had the feeling that Rebecca was very near. Rebecca was waiting for me to fall asleep. Rebecca was waiting to talk to me. Yes, I had been on this very couch with her, and she had sat on that chair, and the coffee had been on this table. A dizziness came and went as it had that day in the swamp, but I knew I had to fight it. *A life for my life. A death for my death . . .*

" 'What did you say?' I asked. 'A life for a life?' Who was I talking to? I battled the dizziness. 'Murderous ghost, get away from me!' I whispered.

"What was I doing out here on the side lawn? So they had refurbished the wicker as I told them to do.

"I had to be gone. I headed for the shed.

"And within minutes I was rolling out in Sweetheart's old Mercedes 450 sedan, the car I had always much admired, though I think it was as old as I was.

"I was on the highway in no time and flying towards Mona Mayfair. But there was time to swing by the florist on St. Charles and Third and buy Mona a beautiful bouquet of long-stemmed roses.

"Then I drove to my final destination: First and Chestnut, riverside downtown corner. Of course the house wasn't near the river. The river was a world away. The expression was just a way of orienting oneself in New Orleans.

"The house was quietly fabulous. It didn't have the arrogant splendor of Blackwood Manor. Rather it was a Greek Revival town house with a side-hall door, four columns up and down, its stucco walls painted a twilight lavender, and beyond to the far right a partially concealed side garden. The whole mansion was set about six steps off the ground and the steps were white marble.

"I parked the car across the intersection and I made the diagonal now on legs that didn't feel, they just guided, and with the huge bouquet in my arms, breathless to offer it to her.

"The iron fence wasn't high and there was the doorbell. I debated. What would I say to the person who answered? Mona, I'm desperate to see Mona.

"But I didn't have to face this complexity. One half second after I appeared at the gate, the big white front door opened, and out she came, quickly closing the door behind her and rushing down the steps to the gate. She had a key for it and turned it quickly, and then we stood facing each other outside the bounds of the fence and I thought I was dying.

"She was about one hundred times more lovely than I remembered her. Her green eyes were much larger and she had a naturally rouged mouth that I wanted to kiss immediately. Her hair was clear red, and to cap it off she wore an exquisite white cotton shirt, unbuttoned way low, and skintight white pants that showed off her small rounded thighs beautifully. I was even in love with her toes. She had on thick sandals and I could see all her red toenails. I adored her.

" 'My God, Mona,' I said, and I took the plunge, covering her mouth with mine and grabbing for her tiny wrists, but she broke away gently and said,

" 'Where's your car, Quinn? We have to get out of here quick.'

"We ran across the street like newlyweds running from a rice storm. We were driving out First Street towards the river in a twinkling.

" 'So where can we go? Oh, God, I don't know where we can go,' I said.

" 'I do,' she answered. 'You know how to get to the Quarter?'

" 'Absolutely.'

"She gave me an address. 'The LaFrenière Cottages,' she said. 'I called them this morning.'

" 'But how did you know I'd come? I mean I'm thrilled that you called them, but how did you know?'

" 'I'm a witch,' she said. 'I knew when you left Blackwood Farm just like I know that Goblin's in the car with us. He's right behind you. You don't even know it, do you? But I didn't mean that. I meant only, I wanted you to come.'

" 'You put a spell on me,' I said. 'I haven't slept since I saw you last, and half my night's ravings have been about you and wanting to come to you.' I could hardly keep my eyes on the road. 'Only lawyers and wills have kept me from you, tales of infidelity and orphan children and roaming in ghostly furniture and forging alliances as strong as the one I mean to forge with you.'

" 'God, you've got some vocabulary,' she answered. 'Or maybe it's just your delivery. It's meant that you should come to me. I'm Ophelia always, floating in the flowery stream. I need your rushing poetry. Can you drive if I unzip your pants!'

" 'No, don't do that. We'll have a wreck. I think all this is a hallucination.'

" 'No, it's not. Did you bring any condoms?'

" 'God, no,' I said. We had reached Canal Street. I knew where the LaFrenière Cottages were. Lynelle and I had eaten three times in their tasty little French bistro. 'Mona, Mona, Mona,' I said. 'We have to get condoms! Where?'

" 'No, we don't,' she said. 'I have tons of them in my purse.' "

24

"THE LaFrenière Cottages were nestled around a central brick courtyard crowded with the de rigueur palmetto and banana trees, and in the center of the courtyard was a wishing well that may once have served some purpose. Now it was merely decorative, and people had taken to pitching all manner of change into it.

"Mona handled our check-in as if it were nothing, even telling me to put away my money, the bill would go to her family.

"When I protested she whispered, 'Show your strength when we get in bed.'

"And off we went, into the little flag-paved cottage, to do just that, in a modern pewter ironwork bed with an enchanting canopy of metal leaves and grapes, and a light breezy fabric wound loosely around its four corners.

"As soon as the door was latched we both stripped off our clothes with the utter abandon of beasts, and when I beheld her naked, when I saw the pinkness of her nipples and the little blaze of red hair between her legs, I went appropriately crazy.

"It was Mona who helped me on with the condom and Mona who had the presence of mind to pull down the covers, so that we didn't stain them, and finally they wound up on the floor as we went at it like little jungle animals.

"Whatever was going on with my life, I figured, I had fulfilled one of my wildest dreams, no matter that it was newborn, it was wild and from the heart and I would never never forget it. I would never forget Mona's face as she blushed with the spasm that sent me into the final explosion of pure nirvana.

"When it was over we lay together, embraced, warm, contented and kissing each other playfully and gently.

" 'Oh, thank God,' she whispered into my ear. She helped me with the soiled condom. She went for the towel to clean me off. She kissed me again and she said, 'I wanted to put my mouth on it. Come, let me wash you in the bathroom and then I'll do it.'

"I protested gallantly. I required no such sacrificial adoration!

" 'Tarquin, I want to!' she said. 'I wanted to do it in the car. I just had an overwhelming desire to do it. And I never got to do it. Come on, out of bed!' and I was led like a slave into the tiled bath where she performed the arousing ablutions and then we were back amid the swirled sheets, only she had her mouth on my cock, stroking it hard, fast, and licking at the tip, and then I died when I came. All strength, all energy, all dreams went out of me.

" 'Nobody's ever done that before?' she purred in my ear as we lay there.

" 'No,' I said. It was all I could do to speak. 'Could we sleep, just like this, snuggled up together?'

"In answer I felt the warm weight of the covers and then her cool arm against my back and her lips kissing my eyes. There was a moist heat coming from her breasts and from between her legs. And the breeze of the air conditioner, chilling down the room, made the nestling all the more wonderful.

" 'Tarquin, you are one beautiful boy,' she whispered. 'And your ghost is here, and he's watching us.'

" 'Go away, Goblin,' I said. 'Leave me now, or I mean it, I won't speak to you for the longest time, I swear it.' Then I turned over and looked around the room. 'Can you see him?' I asked her.

" 'No,' she said. 'He's gone.' She lay back on the pillows next to me. 'I am Ophelia once again,' she said. 'I am floating in the water, with only "nettles, daisies and long purples" to hold me up, and I will never sink to "muddy death." You can't imagine how it is with me.'

" 'How so?' I asked. 'I see you borne along forever, vital, precious, oh, so sweet—.' I tried to stay awake, to listen to her.

" 'Go on, sleep. Men want to sleep when it's over. Women want to talk, at least sometimes. I am Ophelia drifting in "the weeping brook," so light, so sure, "or like a creature native and endued unto that element." They won't find me till tonight, and maybe not even then. I tip these hotels pretty high, I think I may have them won over.'

" 'You mean you've done this before? You've come here with others?'
Now I was wide awake. I rose up and propped myself on my elbow.

" 'Tarquin, I have a huge family,' she said, looking at me, her hair
exquisitely mussed on the pillow. 'And one time it was my goal to be
intimate with every one of my cousins. I succeeded with more than I can
count without the aid of a computer. Of course it wasn't always in a
hotel. It was more often in the cemetery at night—.'

" 'The cemetery!' I said. 'You're serious?'

" 'You have to understand that my life isn't normal. Most Mayfairs don't seek for a normal life. But my life isn't even normal for a
Mayfair. And this goal, this goal of sleeping with all my cousins, it's been
over for some time.' Her eyes looked suddenly sad, and she looked up at
me imploringly. 'But yeah, I've been here, I have to confess, I have
christened this room before with my cousin Pierce, but it doesn't
matter, Tarquin, it's all new with you, that's what matters. And I was
never Ophelia with Pierce. I'm going to marry Pierce but I'll never be
Ophelia.'

" 'You can't marry Pierce, you have to marry me. My life's not normal either, Mona,' I said. 'You have no idea how strange it is and you and
I are no doubt meant for each other.'

" 'Oh, yes, I do. I know your ghost goes everywhere with you. I know
you lived all your life among adults. You have no real knowledge of children. That's what Fr. Kev told me. At least that's what I could drag out
of him. I almost got Fr. Kev into bed, but in the final go-round he
proved to be immovable. He's what anybody would call a good priest,
but he's loosening up when it comes to gossip, though not, you understand, about anything he hears in the confessional.'

"Her eyes were so green that I could scarcely concentrate on what
she was saying.

" 'And did he warn you off of me?' I asked. 'Did he tell you I was
crazy?'

"She laughed a sweet laugh and she bit down on her lower lip as if
she was thinking. 'You've got it backwards. They're out to protect you
from me. Course they do want to keep me under lock and key. That's
why I was at the front door of the house waiting for you. I am now considered to be a raving slut. I had to see you before they did. And I'm not
the only witch in the family.'

" 'Mona, what do you mean when you say "witch"? What are you
talking about?'

" 'You mean you've never heard of us?'

" 'Yes, but only good things—like Dr. Rowan's dream of Mayfair Medical, and Fr. Kev and how he came South to revisit the Irish Channel where he was born, that sort of thing. We go to St. Mary's Assumption Church. We see Fr. Kev all the time.'

" 'I'll tell you why Fr. Kevin came South,' she said. 'He came South because we needed him. Oh, there's so much I wish I could tell you, but I can't. And when I saw you in the Grand Luminière, when I saw you talking to Goblin and embracing Goblin, I thought, God, you've answered my prayer, you've given me someone with secrets! Only now I realize it doesn't change things with me. It can't. Because I can't tell you everything.'

"She began to cry.

" 'Mona, you can tell me! Listen, you can confide in me completely.' I kissed her tears. 'Don't cry, Mona,' I pleaded. 'I can't stand it, seeing you cry.'

" 'I don't doubt you, Quinn,' she said. She sat up in the bed, and I sat with her. 'I'm not sure Ophelia actually cries in the play, does she? Maybe crying is what keeps people from going mad. It's just that there are things that can't be told,' she went on, 'and there are things that nobody can do anything about.'

" 'It's always been my way to tell,' I said. 'That's why you saw me embracing Goblin. It would have been very easy at a certain age for me to stop embracing Goblin. I could have maybe sent Goblin away to wherever he came from. But I never kept him a secret. There is a ghost who haunts me too, and then there is a stranger, the man who beat me up and put me in Mayfair Medical. I just let these things come out. I believe we have to do that.'

"I handed her the paper tissues from the bedside table. I took another and wiped at her tears.

" 'I know I'm going to marry you, Mona,' I said suddenly. 'I know it. I know it's my destiny.'

" 'Quinn,' she said, wiping her eyes, 'that isn't going to happen. We can have a little while, talk to each other, be with each other like this, but we can't ever really be together.'

" 'But why?' I demanded. I knew that if I lost her I would regret it always. I thought that Goblin knew it. That's why Goblin had gone away with no argument. He knew this was too strong, and he hadn't said a word to me.

"Yet I remembered what Goblin could do now. Goblin could break these windows if he wanted. Goblin had told me that he liked being angry. Could I tell Mona that? Should I tell anyone that? I felt a twinge of my panic, and I hated it as unmanly. With Mona, I wanted to be manly.

" 'Come back with me to Blackwood Manor,' I said. 'It's where I live. We can stay in my room, or I'll put you in my Pops' bedroom if you want the proprieties. Pops just died. The room's all cleaned and ready. He didn't die in the room. They packaged up his personal things right away. Where's the phone? I'll tell them to get it ready. Give me your size of clothes. Jasmine will go to Wal-Mart and get whatever you need to tide you over.'

" 'God, you're as mad as one of us,' she said with honest amazement. 'I thought we Mayfairs were the only ones who did things like that.'

" 'Just come. Nobody in my house is going to mess with us. My Aunt Queen may have some sage advice. She's pushing seventy-nine, or so she says; sage advice is to be expected. And I have a new private teacher, Nash, but he's a perfect gentleman.'

" 'So you don't go to school, either,' she said. 'Cool!'

" 'No, never have, going to school never worked with Goblin.'

"I flew into action. She watched with continued amazement as I spoke on the phone to Jasmine. Petite everything, white shirts, pants, cotton underwear, a few toiletries, and away we went.

"As soon as I got behind the wheel I realized I had been awake for over thirty-six hours. I began to laugh at the way everything looked, and at the way everything was working.

" 'Here, let me drive,' she said.

"I was glad to give in.

"She took over like a pro and off we sped, catapulting out of the narrow French Quarter streets and on to the interstate.

"I couldn't take my eyes off her, it was positively sexy the way she drove, that somebody so delectable could drive, and when she shot those green-eyed glances at me I felt weak and overjoyed, and in that mood, that crazy, elated mood, I spoke to Goblin.

" 'I love her, old boy, you understand, don't you?'

"I looked into the backseat and there he was, gazing at me with that cold contemptuous expression he had adopted in the hospital. It took the breath out of me. And then came his dark monotone voice:

" 'Yes, and I enjoyed her very much too, Tarquin.'

" 'You're lying, you bastard!' I said. I wanted to choke him. 'How dare you say that to me? I would have felt you if you'd been that close! You think you can sneak inside me!'

" 'Oh, he was there,' Mona said as she pushed the car past eighty-five miles an hour. 'I could feel him.' "

25

"Aunt Queen and Jasmine didn't let me down. Whatever Aunt Queen's misgivings about Mona, she would not hurt Mona's feelings. When we arrived, Aunt Queen, with open arms, welcomed Mona to the house, and when I announced that this was my future bride Aunt Queen received this information with sublime equanimity.

"Jasmine showed Mona up to Pops' room, where all her new clothes were waiting for her, and then we went off to my room, where we would really be during this visit, and we had a scrumptious meal at this very table where you and I are sitting.

"I don't remember what we actually ate. What I remember is that watching Mona eat was a trip, because I was so infatuated with her, and seeing her handle her knife and fork with such quick gestures and talk in an animated way the whole time made me more truly abandoned to her.

"I know what I am saying is crazy. But I was so in love with her. I had never known such feelings before, and for the time being they utterly erased the habitual panic I suffered, and they even took away my reasonable fear of the mysterious stranger, though I should add here that there were still plenty of armed security men around our house, even inside of it, and this did also give me some feeling of safety.

"Of course Aunt Queen wanted to see me alone, but I graciously declined. And when the lunch things were cleared away and Jasmine had polished up the table (and by the way, Jasmine was a stunner in a light navy blue suit and crisp white blouse), I was ready to lock the whole world outside if I could do it.

" 'Now you understand,' Mona explained. 'This cousin Pierce whom I'm probably going to marry is utterly boring, I mean this cousin is like a loaf of white bread, he has no paranormal powers whatsoever and he is a lawyer already in the firm of Mayfair and Mayfair, where his father, Ryan, is a partner, and Ryan, my beloved Ryan, he's a loaf of white bread too, and their life is just a direct line to conformity and security.'

" 'Then why the hell do you keep saying you're going to marry him?' I asked.

" 'Because I love him,' she said. 'I'm not in love, no, I could never feel that way with him, but I know him and he's beautiful to me—oh, not beautiful like you, not even tall like you, but beautiful in a calm kind of way, and with Pierce, I hate to say it, but with Pierce I'll probably be able to do what I want to do. I mean Pierce himself is not intense, and I have enough intensity for three people.'

" 'Exactly,' I said. 'So this is a safe marriage.'

" 'It's a Mayfair marriage,' she returned. 'And Mayfairs like me always marry other Mayfairs. Now it's a cinch that with his background and my background some of our children will be witches—.'

" 'There you go with that word again, Mona, what do you mean, "witches"? Does the whole family use that word? Does Fr. Kev use it?'

"She laughed the sweetest laugh. 'Yeah, the whole family does use it but that's probably on account of the Talamasca, and Aaron Lightner, a member of the Talamasca whom we all loved. We lost him. He died in a terrible accident. But Stirling is our friend now, and Stirling uses the word. You see, the Talamasca is this organization that for centuries watched our family without us ever knowing it. Well, no, that's not entirely true. Sometimes our ancestors knew it. But anyway, the Talamasca made what they call the File on the Mayfair Witches, and after we all read that material we had a better understanding of our history, and yeah, we do refer to some of us as witches.'

"I was too intrigued to put another question. She took a big gulp of her café au lait and went on talking.

"(Jasmine had left us a pot of coffee on a small candle warmer and the warm milk in a pitcher and plenty of sugar, and that was a good thing because we kept drinking it and the littleness of the china cups was annoying.)

" 'A witch to us is what a witch is to the Talamasca,' said Mona. 'It's a human being who can see and command spirits. You're born a witch and Stirling Oliver has the theory that it has its origins in the physical brain, rather like a person's ability to see fine gradations of color, for instance. But because we can't study those receptors in the brain, because they can't be isolated by science, it sounds mysterious.'

" 'In other words,' I said, 'Stirling thinks that someday one will be able to diagnose a witch in someone like you or me?'

" 'Exactly,' said Mona, 'and Rowan believes this too, and she is carrying out extensive research on this at Mayfair Medical. She has her own lab and she does pretty much what she pleases. I don't want to make her sound like Dr. Frankenstein. What I mean is the Mayfair legacy is so big that she doesn't need grant money, and so she doesn't have to answer to anyone. And she does secret and mysterious research. God only knows all Rowan's projects. I wish I knew what she was up to.'

" 'But what can she do if she can't cut into actual brain tissue?' I asked.

"Mona explained all the routine brain tests that could be run, and I explained that I had been through these and no abnormality had been found.

" 'I get it,' she said, 'but Rowan is searching with us, she's searching in ways that aren't routine.' Her face suddenly went dark, and she shook her head. 'There are other tests, blood tests on those of us who have abnormal genes. Yeah, abnormal genes, that's how you'd put it. Because you see, some of us do. That's why my marriage to Pierce will almost certainly happen. He doesn't have the abnormal genes but I do. So it's safe for me to marry Pierce. He's got the clean bill of health. But I wonder sometimes . . . maybe I shouldn't marry at all.'

" 'But I have safe genes, don't I?' I insisted. 'Why not forget utterly and totally about Pierce and marry me?'

"She stared at me for a long moment.

" 'What is it, Mona?' I asked.

" 'Nothing. I was just thinking of what it would be like to be married to you. It doesn't much matter about the clean bill of health. We'd surely have witch children. But I'm not too certain it would matter. But Quinn, you have to give up on that idea. It's just not going to happen. Besides, I'm only fifteen years old, Quinn.'

" 'Fifteen!' I was amazed. 'Well, I'm eighteen,' I said. 'We're both precocious. Our children will be geniuses.'

" 'Yeah, no doubt of that,' she said. 'And they'd have private teachers like I do now, and they'd travel the world.'

" 'We could travel the world with my Aunt Queen,' I said, 'and with Nash, and he would tell us about all the countries we would be visiting.'

"She had the most serene smile. 'It would be a dream,' she said. 'I've been to Europe—this last year I went all over with Ryan and Pierce—Ryan is Pierce's father. Ryan is the big lawyer in our lives, though we have a whole family firm of them actually. But anyway, what was I saying? Europe. I could go again and again and again.'

" 'Oh, think of it, Mona. You have your passport already, and I have mine. We could just steal you away. Aunt Queen's been pleading with me to go!'

" 'Your Aunt Queen would never let you steal me,' she laughed. 'I can see she has a venturesome spirit, but she wouldn't agree to kidnapping. Besides, the family would just come after me.'

" 'Would they really?' I asked. 'But why, Mona? You speak of your family as though it's a giant prison.'

" 'No, Quinn,' she said, 'it's really like a giant garden, but there are garden walls that separate us from the rest of the world.' She was getting abysmally sad. 'I'm going to cry again and I totally and egregiously hate it.'

" 'No, don't cry,' I said. I got the box of tissue for her and set it down before her. 'I totally can't bear the thought of you shedding one tear and if you do I'll swallow it, or I'll dry your eyes with these. Now tell me why they wouldn't let you go to Europe. I mean we'd have Aunt Queen as the perfect chaperone.'

" 'Quinn, I'm not just an ordinary Mayfair as I told you. I'm not just an ordinary witch. I'm what they call the Designée of the Legacy. And the Legacy is something that dates back hundreds of years. It's a great fortune that is inherited by a new woman in each generation.'

" 'How big a fortune?'

" 'It's in the billions,' she replied. 'That's why it could endow Mayfair Medical, and right now the Heiress is Rowan Mayfair. But Rowan can't have a child and I've already been named to succeed Rowan.'

" 'I see. They're grooming you and guarding you for the day when you have to take over.'

" 'Precisely,' she answered. 'That's why they want me to stop acting wild and sleeping with all my cousins. Since we got back from Europe I've listened pretty much. I don't know what it is with me and sex. I just love it. But you get the idea. I have to occupy a position of honor, if that doesn't sound too egregious. That's why they wanted me to go to Europe, to be educated and cultured and—.'

"Again her face went dark, and this time the tears came up to stand in her eyes.

" 'Mona, tell me,' I pleaded.

"She shook her head. 'Something bad happened to me,' she said. Her voice was breaking.

"I got up and I led her away from the table. I shoved back the bed-clothes and the two of us kicked off our shoes and we climbed in against the nest of down pillows. Never had I loved my fancy bed so much as when I was lying under that baldachin over there with her. And you have to picture that we were fully clothed, except for the fact that when I started kissing her I opened her blouse all the way down, feeling her breasts, but she didn't mind.

"But then we tapered off, principally because I was so tired, and then I brought her back to the subject.

" 'Something bad happened?' I asked her. 'Can you tell me what it was?'

"For a long time she was silent and then she started to cry again.

" 'Mona, if anybody hurt you, I'll hurt them,' I said. 'I mean it. Goblin could even—. Tell me what happened.'

" 'I had a child,' she said in a hoarse whisper.

"I said nothing but I could see that she wanted to go on.

" 'I had a child,' she said, 'and it wasn't what anyone would call a normal child. It was . . . it was different. Very precocious, yes, and perhaps what is best called a mutation. I loved it with my whole soul, it was a beautiful child. But . . . it was taken away.' She paused, then went on. 'It was taken far away, and I just can't come back from that. I can't stop thinking about that.'

" 'You mean they made you give up your baby! A family that size with all that money.' I was appalled.

" 'No.' She shook her head. 'It wasn't like that. It wasn't the family. Let's just say that the child was taken away, and I don't know what happened to it. It wasn't the family's doing.'

" 'The father's doing?' I asked.

" 'No. I told you this was something terrible. I can't tell you all of it. I can only say that at any time I might hear about that child.' She chose her words carefully. 'That child might be returned to me. Some news might come, good news or bad news. But for now there's nothing but silence.'

" 'Do you know where the child is?' I asked. 'Mona, I'll go get the child! I'll bring it back.'

" 'Quinn, you're so strong, so confident,' she said. 'It's really totally marvelous just being with you. But no, I don't know where the child is. I think the child is in England. But I don't know. And when we were in Europe I was sort of looking for it. There's no word from the man that took it.'

" 'Mona, this is ghastly.'

" 'No,' she said, shaking her head, the teardrops hanging in her lashes, 'it's not the way it sounds. The man was a loving man, and the child—the child was exceptional.' Her voice broke. 'I didn't want to give it up, but I had to. It had to go with this loving man, this gentle man that could care for it.'

"I was too perplexed to ask a sensible question.

" 'If you have an inkling where this man is, then I'll go to him.'

"She shook her head. 'We used to know how to reach him. Rowan and Michael—those are my cousins and foster parents now, they knew the man very well. But now we don't.'

" 'Mona, let me protect you in this, let me go after this man and let me go after the baby.'

" 'Quinn, my family has tried to do it. They've used the resources of the Mayfair Legacy to try to find both the child and the man and they can't do it. I don't need your vow that you'll try. I don't want you even to think about trying. I only need you to listen to me. I only need your vow that you won't ever tell another human being what I told you.'

"I kissed her.

" 'I understand,' I said. 'We'll have other children, you and I.'

" 'Oh, that would be so lovely,' she said. 'So very lovely.'

"We snuggled down into the covers, taking off each other's clothes, button by button and zipper by zipper, and then we were naked where I had always slept so chaste with Little Ida or Big Ramona. I felt the bed was being properly christened, and I was happy.

"Then I slept.

"In my dream Rebecca came knocking on the door. It was as if I was awake, but I knew that I wasn't. And in the dream I told her she had to go away. I told her I had done all that I could do for her. We fought, she and I. We fought at the head of the staircase. She went wild against me, and I forced her down the stairs, telling her she had to leave Blackwood Manor, that she was dead and gone and that she had to accept it.

"She sat down on the last step and began to cry piteously.

" 'You can't come anymore,' I told her. 'The Light's waiting for you. God's waiting for you. I believe in the Light.'

"The living room was full of mourners again, and I could hear the cadence of the Rosary rising like a tide, the Hail Mary, Full of Grace, and then I saw Virginia Lee sit up from her coffin again, her hands clasped, and at once she made her graceful ballet step to the floor, her skirts billowing, and she came to snatch up Rebecca, and together they were hurtling through the front door of the house, the two ghosts, Virginia Lee and Rebecca, and I heard Virginia Lee cry out, 'You come again to trouble my house, do you? You bring me down from the Light!'

"Rebecca screamed. *A life for my life. A death for my death.*

"All was silence. I sat on the steps in the dream, wishing I could wake up and be back upstairs in bed where I belonged, but I couldn't.

"*A life for my life*, she'd said. Did she want mine? Nothing I'd done had satisfied her. It wasn't enough.

"Someone tapped me on the shoulder. I looked up. It was Virginia Lee, very lively and pretty, though she wore her funeral blue dress.

" 'Get away from this place, Tarquin,' she said. Her voice had such tender resonance. 'Go on, Tarquin, leave this place. There is an evil here. That evil wants you.'

"I woke, sitting up, covered with sweat, staring forward. I saw Goblin in the corner near the computer merely watching me.

"Mona slept soundly beside me.

"I got into the shower and when I saw Goblin's shadow outside the glass I finished up and dried off and dressed quickly. He stood behind me looking at me in the mirror over my shoulder. His expression was not as mean as it had been before, and I prayed he couldn't sense my apprehension. He didn't seem as solid here, even with the moisture in the air, as he had been in New Orleans. I was grateful for that.

" 'You love Mona, too?' I asked as if I meant it.

" 'Mona is good. Mona is strong,' he said. 'But Mona will hurt you.'

" 'I know,' I said. 'You hurt me when you're unkind to me, when you say unkind things. We have to love each other.'

" 'You want to be with Mona alone,' he said.

" 'Wouldn't you if you were me?' I asked. I turned around and faced him.

"I had never seen such a face of trouble on him as I saw then. I had stung him and I was sorry for it.

" 'I *am* you,' he answered."

26

"THE LATE AFTERNOON WAS heavenly. To be that in love, to know that frenzy of the heart—even now, young as I still am, I look back on it as something that was part of the innocence of childhood. That it could come again, I don't even dream of, that I should ever know such consuming happiness is impossible.

"After Mona woke, had her bath and put on her fresh Wal-Mart white pants and shirt we went down to walk around Blackwood Farm, and it seemed our roaming is what kept me sane as I spilled out my soul to Mona. I told her all about Goblin, all about Lynelle, all about my strange life as I perceived it.

"She was an eager listener. Also she was charmed by the house and the long drive lined by the pecan trees. It didn't seem vulgar or over-done to her. She said she saw a symmetry and harmony in everything.

"Yes, it was bigger and more overbearing than a Garden District house, she conceded, but she could see why Manfred Blackwood didn't want to be constrained and so he had found his perfect spot in the country.

" 'Quinn,' she said, 'we live in houses that were built by people's dreams, and we have to accept that. We have to revere the dream and realize that someday the house will go to others after us. These houses are personalities in our lives. They have their roles to play.'

"She looked at the big columns. She liked the feeling of the place.

" 'Even the house I grew up in,' she said, 'poor as it was, it was a huge Victorian on St. Charles Avenue. It was chock-full of ghosts and people. You know, I didn't grow up rich. I was a poor kind of down-at-the-heel Mayfair when it comes right down to it. My parents were both spineless drunks. They gave their lives to the bottle. And now I'm the technical owner of a private plane and the designated heiress to billions of dollars. It makes me crazy sometimes, the switch, but there I go again talking about dreams, because I always dreamed I'd be the Designée of the Mayfair Legacy.'

"She started to look a little bit sad, which alarmed me.

" 'Someday I have to tell you all about our family,' she said. 'But right now I'm with you. Tell me about you.'

"I thought she was absolutely brilliant. I had never thought much about the kind of woman I'd marry, if any, and now it seemed perfectly right that she be brilliant as well as beautiful. And her beauty, it was natural. She wore no lipstick or eyebrow pencil. She had come out of the shower pure and young. I was totally captivated.

"It was getting dusk. The sky was streaked with amethyst and burning gold. I took her down to the old cemetery. I explained to her how the West Ruby River fed our lonely two hundred acres of Sugar Devil Swamp.

"I told her about Sugar Devil Island and the Hermitage, about the strange inscription on the mausoleum and about the strange trespasser breaking into the house, and that it was his attack which got me taken to Mayfair Medical.

" 'Can we go to the island, Quinn?' she asked. 'Can you show me? I have to see this place for myself. How can I be Ophelia forever if I fear to travel ever-flowing streams?'

" 'Well, not now, my precious immortal Ophelia,' I said. 'It's getting dark and I'm not macho enough to be going into the swamp in the dark. But I can take you there in the day. You saw the security guys all around? We'll take two of them with us. That way if the stranger shows his face we can blast him.'

"She was very curious. She wanted to know more about the Hermitage and its circular structure. Had there been a stairs up to the cupola?

" 'Yes, there is, and you know I never went up there. It was a circular iron stairs, and I hardly took notice of it, and I'm sure if you go up there you can have a better view over the swamp to Blackwood Manor.'

" 'I just have to see it,' she said. 'It's too grandly mysterious. And what do you plan to do about the trespasser?'

" 'I'm moving him out!' I said. 'He's already in a rage that I burnt his books. Well, when I get back out there with my men we're throwing out his marble table and his golden chair. He'll find them sunk in the muck where he dumped the bodies.'

" 'What bodies?' She was amazed.

"I doubled back and told her that part—of how I'd first seen him in the moonlight, dumping the bodies. She was very intrigued.

" 'But this is a killer, this person,' she said.

" 'I'm not afraid of him,' I countered. 'And after what happened when he attacked me upstairs, I know that Goblin can and will protect me.'

"I glanced back at Goblin who was coming behind us at a distance. I nodded at him. *My brave companion.*

"She looked at the darkening purple sky. The cicadas were singing everywhere. It seemed the Earth was purring. 'Boy, I wish there was time for us to go out there,' she said.

"I laughed. 'Neither of us has the sense to be afraid!' I admitted. She began laughing and then both of us were laughing, unable to stop it. I put my arms around her finally and just held her, happier than I'd ever been in my whole existence.

"We walked on together, but all I could think of was lying down with her on the grass and letting the gathering shadows be the bed curtains.

"I told her again that when we went out to the island tomorrow we'd take the armed guards. I had my thirty-eight. I asked if she knew how to shoot a gun. She said Yes, she'd been taught at a place called Gretna Gun by her cousin Pierce, just so she'd be able to protect herself if she ever had to. She was used to firing a three fifty-seven Magnum.

" 'This Pierce,' I said, 'I don't want to talk about him. The marriage plan is a dreadful miscarriage of fate. I feel like Romeo standing in the way of whatshisname.'

"She laughed in the most delightful manner. 'Oh, it's so good to be with you,' she said. 'And part of it is simply that you're not one of us.'

" 'You mean that I'm not a Mayfair?'

"She nodded. The tears were threatening. I put my arms around her and she laid her head on my chest and I could feel her crying.

" 'Mona, don't, please don't. Feel safe with me.'

" 'Oh, I do,' she said. 'I really do, but you know they're going to find me.'

" 'Then maybe we can just hide you behind those big columns,' I said. 'We can just bolt the door to my room and see if they can break it down.'

"She stopped. She was all right for the moment and she wiped her eyes with a paper tissue. She asked me to describe the stranger again, and I did, and she asked if he could have been some sort of ghost or spirit.

"It was the most surprising question. I had never thought of that.

" 'There are all kinds of ghosts, Tarquin,' she said. 'And they differ in the illusions they can create.'

" 'No, he wasn't a ghost,' I said. 'He was too outraged by the flying glass to be a ghost. And he couldn't see Goblin.'

"Goblin was still with us, trailing in a desultory fashion and unresponsive when I waved.

"Now, it was the time of day when I usually felt the panic most keenly, but I didn't feel it because I had to be strong for her, and frankly she just created some sustained excitement in me which had banished the panic and all my bad and sad thoughts.

"I told her about the phantoms I saw, here among the tombs. And how they didn't speak, and they seemed a coagulated mass, and we talked about the nature of ghosts in general.

"She said Stirling Oliver of the Talamasca was a kindhearted and profoundly honorable man, British to the core, like all the best of the Talamasca, and full of wonderful ideas about ghosts and spirits.

" 'Now, I don't know if there is such a thing as a true spirit,' she said as we were stepping respectfully among the gravestones and around the long-raised tombs. 'I tend to think that all spirits are the ghosts of something, even if they lived so long ago in the flesh they don't remember it.'

" 'Goblin's a pure spirit,' I said. 'He's not the ghost of anyone.' I looked back to see Goblin some distance away, with his hands in the pockets of his jeans, just watching us. I was afraid to say too much about him, about the speed with which he was learning, about his more dangerous aspects.

"But I turned and I waved at him, just a friendly wave, and I told him telepathically that I loved him. He didn't acknowledge me but his face wasn't mean, and all of a sudden I realized that he was again wearing my lucky Versace tie. Why was he doing that? Why was he all dressed up and wearing that tie? Maybe it meant nothing.

"I think Mona saw this—my noticing him. Well, I'm sure she did. But she went on. 'You never know with a spirit,' she said. 'It could be the ghost of something that wasn't human.'

" 'How on earth is that possible, Mona?' I asked. 'You mean it would be the ghost of an animal?'

" 'I'm saying things exist in this world that look human but aren't human, and there's no real telling how many species of these there are. There are beings walking the Earth fully disguised as humans, deliberately fooling us. So when it comes to a spirit, you never know what you're dealing with. It could be something good and loving, like Goblin.' She glanced at him. In fact, she smiled at him. 'Or it could be the ghost of something dreadful that secretly despises humankind and wants to hurt it. But the main thing is to understand that all spirits have a kind of organization.'

" 'How do you mean?'

" 'I mean that even though they're invisible to most people, they have a perceivable form and a nucleus of sorts in which the brain and the heart reside together.'

" 'But how do you know?' I said. 'And how is that possible?'

" 'Well, first off,' she said, 'it's what Stirling believes and he's been studying ghosts his entire lifetime. That's why he's spending so much time of late with me. I see ghosts constantly. And it's also what Rowan believes, you know, my cousin Dr. Rowan Mayfair.'

" 'But where is this nucleus? And how is it that a ghost can appear and disappear?'

" 'Science hasn't caught up with it yet,' she said, 'that's what Rowan is always telling me. But we have definite ideas about it. The nucleus and the particles that make up a ghost are simply too small to be seen by us and the force field that organizes them can pass effortlessly through the molecules that we can see. Think of tiny insects and how simple it is for them to pass through hardware cloth. Think of water passing through cotton or silk. That's the way ghosts pass through walls. It's all there to be known someday but right now we don't know it.'

" 'Yes, I see what you mean, as to how the ghost comes and goes through matter, but how does it appear to us?'

" 'It draws particles of matter to itself magnetically and organizes them into the illusion. The illusion can be so strong that it looks and feels solid. But it's always an illusion, and when the ghost wants to disappear, or has to disappear, the particles are diffused.'

"I was too entranced to argue with her. She took it very seriously, what she had to say, and all I had really were questions. But I knew that Goblin was listening too, and I would have been more frightened on that account if I hadn't known she knew it also.

" 'Now, some ghosts,' she said, 'those that are really strong, can make themselves so solid that they're visible not just to one or two receptive persons but to everybody. They're *there*,' she said. 'And God only knows how many of those ghosts are walking around among us.'

" 'My God, what a concept,' I said.

" 'Just think of it—something that looks human but it's a ghost, it's come back to have another go at life or something. But most of the time a ghost uses his organizing principles to appear to one receptive individual.'

" 'But how is it you and I both see Goblin?' I asked.

" 'It must be that we have the same kinds of receptors,' she said. 'I'm sure we do. And some of the ghosts I see? You probably could see them also.'

" 'That's why we have to get married, Mona,' I said. 'We'll only be lonely for understanding if we marry other people. We'll always remember this moment.'

"The comment startled her or in some milder way caught her off guard. Then she said a little testily:

" 'Quinn, stop talking about our wedding as if it's something that's going to happen. I told you. I'm going to marry Pierce. I have to marry Pierce. Now maybe we could have an affair afterwards, but I seriously don't think so, I think Pierce would be way devastated. That's the worst thing about marrying Pierce. When I marry him, my erotic adventures will be over.'

" 'That's a wretched thing to look forward to. I hate this guy Pierce. Maybe I'll kill him.'

" 'Don't talk like that, he's the sweetest Mayfair on the planet,' she replied, 'and he'll take care of me. Oh, let's not talk about Pierce. Sometimes I know Pierce deserves somebody better than me and there are so many unsullied virginal types in the family! Maybe you're right about Pierce. I mean for Pierce's own sake—. Now let's get back to the question of ghosts.'

" 'Yes,' I said, 'explain to me how the nucleus of a ghost is formed, assuming there is one. And let Pierce have one of the virgins, I think that's a fine idea.'

" 'Stirling says the nucleus is the soul, the soul that refused to move on when it was separated from its earthly body.'

" 'So the soul has matter to it!'

" 'Maybe more what we call electricity,' she said, 'or energy, at any rate. Let's think of it that way, something infinitesimal that is organized energy. It's all through our bodies when we're alive, but it contracts to a nucleus when we die, and that nucleus should go into the Light, as we well know. And instead of going out of our stratosphere, as it should when it disconnects from the body, it stays behind, earthbound, and generates for itself a spirit body, a body of energy imprinted by the shape of its lost human body, and that's how it acquires its characteristics as a ghost.'

" 'And you think that it can forget that it was ever human?'

" 'Oh, I think so definitely. There must be earthbound spirits which are a thousand years old. There's no ticking clock for them. There's no hunger. There's no thirst. Without us to make them focus and tighten, they simply drift. I'm not even certain what they see or know when they drift, but then along comes a person who can respond to them, and they begin to evolve as a ghost for that person.'

" 'And you call yourself a witch because you can see these spirits?'

" 'Yes, and because I can talk to them, but I can't just make them do what I want. I haven't experimented with that power. That's too danger-ous a power. The whole subject is dangerous, Tarquin.' She lowered her voice and she made a sly glance with her eyes at Goblin. 'Goblin proba-bly knows, don't you, Goblin?' she asked. 'He probably knows all of this.'

"I looked back at Goblin. Goblin's face was thoughtful. It had lost some of its meanness, and this relieved me somewhat.

" 'Mona, we have to be together, always,' I said. 'Who else will ever love me the way you can?'

"Goblin drew closer. I put my hand out to stop him.

" 'Be patient with me now, Goblin,' I said. 'It's a different kind of love.'

" 'I'd never seek to take your place, Goblin,' said Mona.

" 'But truly, Mona,' I addressed her again. 'Who else will ever love me the way you can?'

" 'What are you talking about?' she said. 'You're tall and gorgeous and you have the most honest blue eyes I've ever seen. You know it's really something when a man has both blue eyes and jet black hair, and that's what you've got. You're what girls call adorable.'

"Of course I loved hearing these compliments—I was very unsure of myself—but they only strengthened my hope that nothing could sepa-rate us.

" 'Marry me, Mona,' I said. 'I'm serious. You just have to.'

" 'I'm beginning to like the idea, but behave yourself,' she answered. 'Let's go on about ghosts and spirits. You need to know things. We were talking about earthbound spirits, how they fail to go into the Light.'

" 'Are you sure of the Light yourself, Mona?' I asked her.

" 'Well, you see, that's the very problem,' she answered. 'When these people die they aren't sure of it, and they may not recognize the Light for what it is. They may not trust it. They cling to the Earth; they cling to mortals whom they can still see and hear.'

" 'And so we have this theoretical spirit whose nucleus doesn't go into the Light,' I said, 'this soul that drifts—.'

" 'Yes,' she said, 'and it can start a whole adventure for itself, especially if it finds a receptive person like you or me, somebody who can see it even when its organizing powers are still weak. Then of course we help it focus by noticing it and talking to it, and paying attention to it, and its organization becomes stronger and stronger.'

" 'But what about a spirit like Goblin? He's not a ghost. He doesn't know where he came from.'

"She shot me a meaningful glance that said: Be careful. 'Goblin is pure spirit then,' she replied, 'but spirits are probably organized in exactly the same way—they have the nucleus and then a kind of loose body, a force field of a body, and it's this force field they use, just like a ghost, to gather particles to appear to someone.'

"We walked on out of the cemetery and towards the landing. The swamp looked dark and treacherous already—full of deadly things that want to kill. An evening song came from it that meant death. I tried to ignore it. Mona seemed to like it, to like the evening.

" 'Quinn, if only you could talk to Stirling,' she said. 'I think he would have so much to tell you. You know, it's so easy with Stirling. For centuries the Talamasca has given shelter to people who see ghosts. They welcome people like you and me, and not for selfish reasons. When I was in England I went to their Motherhouse there, and I even visited the Motherhouse in Rome.'

" 'Sounds religious, rather like the Trappist monks or the Carmelites.'

" 'Well, they are sort of that way,' she answered, 'but they aren't religious. They're good without being religious. Sometimes it's hard for Fr. Kevin to accept but he's getting used to it. You know how it is with us Catholics. Anything supernatural that isn't from God just has to be evil. And here you have the Talamasca studying the supernatural. But even Fr. Kevin is coming to like Stirling. Nobody could fail to be disarmed by Stirling.'

" 'Tell me about Fr. Kevin,' I said. 'What's his story?'

" 'He's a good priest,' she said. 'I ought to know. I tried hard to get him into bed, as I told you, but couldn't do it. He was born here in a big house on Magazine Street, the last of eight children. His eldest sister is a whole nother generation. We call them the Stainless Mayfairs because they are all very good and never get into any trouble. When he went into the priesthood they sent him up North, and now he's come back, principally because the family needs its own priest and also because he can teach here. He's quite the theologian when he wants to be.'

" 'Mona, why do you try to go to bed with so many people?' I asked. I knew that I sounded naive and childlike, but I had to ask her.

" 'Why do you do the same thing, Tarquin?'

" 'But I don't, not really. Aside from you, I've been to bed with one of the women on the property and that's all.'

" 'I know,' she said smiling. 'It's the gorgeous blond-haired quadroon, Jasmine.'

" 'How did you know?'

" 'We witches have a little bit of telepathic power,' she said with the same generous smile. 'I picked up on it, you might say. Didn't you feel that that was a road you had to travel?'

" 'Yeah, I guess I did. But compared to you, I'm kind of retarded. I'm almost nineteen and I've slept with one spirit, one ghost and two real women, you being the one with whom I am in love.'

" 'I can guess about the spirit,' she said, 'but tell me about the ghost.'

" 'I can't, not now. We're too near her grave.' I pointed to the little headstone in the cemetery. 'But let me say her name's Rebecca and she's beautiful, and she met her end in a cruel, unjust way and I lost my virginity with her. She has great charm when she comes. . . .

" '. . . And speaking of charm,' I said, 'I have a tutor who is like that and he's coming right towards us.'

"It was Nash come down from the house to invite us to supper. He looked elegant and handsome in his sharply cut blue denim three-piece suit and a white shirt open at the collar.

"Now, I have to achieve that style, I thought, and he comes by it so daringly and so naturally.

"At once I introduced him to Mona and told him I was going to marry her. He was faintly amazed but accepted it totally seriously.

" 'Congratulations, Quinn, and my dear'—he took her hand—'it's a pleasure.'

"I felt his mellow voice could level mountains. And his face was truly enhanced by its lines and its folds. It gave him the look of wisdom.

" 'Of course, we're still going to Europe, Nash,' I said. 'We're all going. We're stealing Mona.'

" 'Well, that makes things doubly exciting,' said Nash with just a twinge of a smile and a touch of gentle irony. He gave his arm to Mona graciously to help her up to the high ground, and I felt ashamed that I hadn't thought to do it.

"As for supper, we were all to join Aunt Queen on the other side of the house where the table was set on the flagstone patio using the newly refurbished wicker.

" 'Rebecca's wicker,' I explained to Mona. 'Rebecca and I—it was in a dream—we had coffee together and we were sitting in these wicker chairs. You'll see.'

"And I'll see too, I thought. I'll see if it matches the furnishings of my dream exactly, because I might have imagined it earlier when I'd wandered out there, so mystified and confused.

"As we walked on, past the front of the house, as I looked up at the reddened and darkening sky, I felt the panic again.

"But I drove it away. Time for something convivial and I was ready for it.

"Quickly I searched for Goblin. *Come with us, be with us.* I tried to smile at him, but I think he knew my multitude of fears. He could read my face if not my mind."

27

"A s soon as I saw the ensemble of white wicker tables and chairs I recognized them again as the setting in my dream. It sent the chills up me and the panic came again in a brilliant wave, almost causing my teeth to chatter.

"I could hear Rebecca's voice in my head and I was afraid I was going to get dizzy. When I had described these dizzy states to the doctors at Mayfair Medical they had spoken of small seizures.

"But how could such an explanation account for this—furniture duplicating that which I had only seen well in a dream? The fact was the seizure theory accommodated nothing.

" 'Mona, my darling love,' I said as we approached the table, 'I need you.'

" 'What you need more than anything in the world,' she said, 'is to be with Stirling Oliver.' But I could see the passion in her eyes; I could see that she was holding back. I could see the evidence of my progress with her.

" 'And what we all need is supper,' said Aunt Queen, who greeted me with a kiss and then planted one on Mona's cheek also.

" 'You know, dear,' said Aunt Queen, 'you really are quite beautiful.'

"Aunt Queen had decked herself out in a sack dress of beige satin, long strands of pearls, a shell cameo at her throat and the most glittering spike heels I'd seen ever. The band across her toes was studded with diamonds and the brilliantly wrought cameo of Apollo with his lyre at her neck was surrounded by tiny diamonds also.

"The entire supper arrangement was illuminated by soft floodlights attached to the side of the house and also by a ring of candles in hurricane lamps. The wicker was exceptionally detailed and well constructed—

what an antique dealer would have given a small fortune to have—and as I studied it the atmosphere of the dream returned to me. Rebecca said in my ear, *Red-haired bitch*. I tasted dream coffee. The chills were quietly passing over me. A wave of terror passed over me. *A life for my life. A death for my death.*

"We were seated at once in the newly painted peacock chairs, and yes, I realized, Goblin's place was there to my left as it always was, and I had not even thought to ask for it.

"My mind and body were aswim with sensations. Merely glancing at Mona on my right side made me want to carry her up to bed. And then a dull misery from Rebecca's dream kept breaking through. *Go into the Light*, I silently prayed. I tried hard to focus on what was around me. I had to be a man for Mona. And this was no place to become a centaur.

"Jasmine, got up exquisitely in a tiny-waisted violet suit with a frothy white blouse, brought the tarragon chicken and rice to us. Big Ramona, in her usual crisp white apron, was pouring the wine.

"I could see that Aunt Queen had been working some kind of magic with Jasmine. Jasmine was experiencing some change in status. Jasmine had a glamour to her, and surely I wasn't responsible for it.

" 'And look at the shoes on these lovely ladies, would you?' I said to Nash and Mona. 'It makes me want to kiss their feet.'

" 'Eat your supper, Little Boss,' said Jasmine in an under voice. 'You're not kissing my feet.'

"Mona laughed.

" 'Nothing succeeds,' Nash replied, 'like excess.' He smiled. 'I must say it is a pleasure being here in these glorious surroundings. I've never heard the cicadas sing like this except here in Louisiana.'

" 'And how have you spent today?' I asked. 'I feel that, having fallen in love with Mona, I'm neglecting you, but discovering one's future bride can be very distracting. I've become a happy madman.'

" 'And well it should distract you,' he replied. 'And you mustn't worry about me for a moment. This is all so new to me, so fascinating. I've been quite fine. I took a long early afternoon nap and then spent a wonderful time surveying your Aunt Queen's fabulous collection of cameos.'

" 'Cameos,' said Mona. 'You mean you have more than what we saw in the living room case?'

" 'Hundreds more,' said Aunt Queen. 'Spanning my whole life, and you can well imagine how long that is. But here, a toast to Mona Mayfair, our lovely young guest, and to Nash Penfield, who will soon guide us on the Grand Tour, and to my great-nephew, who this day came into part of his inheritance.'

" 'Mona's going with us to Europe, Aunt Queen,' I declared. 'Is there any way we could leave before midnight? Mona will be going as my bride.'

"Mona was clearly startled, but she didn't laugh. She only beamed at me, and then boldly she leaned over and kissed my cheek. 'You would really marry me tonight?' she asked. 'I think you're truly and egregiously in love with me.'

" 'Absolutely and forever,' I said. 'But we don't have to wait for the ceremony. We could fly out tonight, and get married in Paris. Aunt Queen does it all the time—just flying out. We'd need your passport of course, but I'd go back to the house with you—.'

" 'Darling,' said Aunt Queen, 'I don't think that's necessary. I think I see the Mayfairs coming up the drive now.'

"It was a giant black stretch limousine, just like Aunt Queen's car, crunching the gravel down as it lumbered to a stop before the front steps of the house.

"Mona turned around, then she turned back and she looked at me. The tears rose in her eyes. 'Tarquin,' she said, 'would you really take me with you tonight?'

" 'Yes, absolutely!' I said. 'Aunt Queen, you know it's what you want, that I go to Europe, that I be educated! Nash, you can guide and tutor all of us.' I would die for Mona, I knew it. I would fight everyone in that car.

" 'Nash,' said Aunt Queen, 'go and greet them for me, darling. I see the security man rising to his feet. Call him off. I'll never make it across the lawn in these shoes. Be the front man, will you, dear?'

"Mona quickly explained that it was Ryan Mayfair, the lawyer and father of Pierce, and Dr. Rowan Mayfair, and her husband, Michael Curry, who were now approaching the table. I stood up naturally, but Mona did not, and I moved behind her chair and I placed my hands on her shoulders. I had my back to those coming up the lawn. I was being rude. I was bracing for battle.

" 'Don't worry, my brave Ophelia,' I said under my breath, 'you shall not perish while this brave Laertes lives.'

"But the most curious aspect to all this for me was not my own pounding heart, it was the cautious and almost hostile expression on Aunt Queen's face as the little party came around to the left of me, with Nash quickly inviting them to sit down.

"They all declined a chair. They were very much 'in a hurry,' but were very thankful. 'We've come to pick up Mona,' said Dr. Rowan Mayfair in a very soft and polite voice. I believe it's what you call a whiskey voice. 'Mrs. McQueen,' she said with a little nod of her head, 'you have a magnificent house.'

" 'Well, I hope someday,' said Aunt Queen, 'you can come to visit.' But she was not her usual warm self when she said these words, and she was scrutinizing the group of them in a way I've never seen.

"Introductions were made all around, Ryan Mayfair looking as if he'd been born in his Brooks Brothers suit and Michael Curry, being the oldest and rough cut but a very handsome guy in his safari jacket, with his beautiful salt-and-pepper hair and a very easy manner. He had a very Irish look to him with his square face and blue eyes. The lawyer was uncomfortable and Dr. Rowan Mayfair wasn't exactly at ease either. Dr. Rowan had a high-cheeked, sleek beauty to her with bobbed hair. There was something undeniably frightening about her, though her manner was low-key.

" 'Come on, Mona,' said Dr. Rowan, 'we're here to take you home. You gave us a bit of scare slipping out this morning.'

" 'I want you to leave me alone!' Mona said. It was practically a cri de coeur.

"I could scarcely bear the sound of it, and I flew into action without even moving. I held her shoulders. My heart was racing.

"But suddenly Dr. Rowan adopted an ominous face and said, to my complete shock, 'Michael, take her.'

"Both Ryan Mayfair and Michael Curry moved towards Mona, and Mona screamed, backing up and overturning the chair, and I threw my arms tightly around her. She pivoted in my embrace and buried her face in my chest. She felt like the most fragile and precious little creature that I had ever known or loved, and I intended to fight for her.

" 'Come now, gentlemen,' said Nash in a gentle commanding voice, 'surely you're not trying to take this young lady by force! Mrs. McQueen, are you a neutral party in all of this?'

" 'Indeed not,' said Aunt Queen. 'Jasmine, run get the men.'

" 'Wait a minute,' said Michael Curry, and he made the universal gesture with both his hands for patience. He came on like the sweetest guy in the world. 'Mona, please stop the theatrics and come home, you know you have to. Mona, I don't want to be doing this. Nobody does, but you can't go off like this. Look at it from our point of view.'

" 'I'm going to marry her,' I said. 'And if you lay a finger on her, I'll break your face. Oh, I can see you've got brawn on your side, plenty of it, but I'm young and I'm meaner than I look, so don't try me.'

"As for Goblin, he had risen to his feet and I had whispered to him to do nothing. What he could have done I didn't know, but it frightened me and thrilled me at the same time.

"By now Clem and Allen were running towards the patio. And the security man had come from the front porch to stand by Aunt Queen, his hand on his gun.

"Aunt Queen motioned for Clem and Allen to come on and then stop.

" 'Aren't you all being a bit ridiculous about this?' Aunt Queen asked. 'This girl is having supper with us. I'll have my car bring her home this evening. I've never seen such hysterics before. Dr. Mayfair, I'm shocked.'

" 'I'm sorry, Mrs. McQueen,' said Dr. Mayfair. Her voice was still low and husky, and very sincere. Yet a terrible power enforced her words. 'Mona's fifteen years old. Her parents are both dead. Sometimes she does things that are impulsive. I'm her legal guardian. I want her to come home, and as you can see, she won't do it.'

"Michael Curry shook his head as if to say, The sadness of it, and then very gently he touched Mona's hair. He spoke to her in a soft soothing voice.

" 'Now come on, honey, I know how you feel.'

" 'No, you don't,' she sobbed against me. 'None of you do.'

" 'Mona, I love you,' he said, and then he went on tenderly. 'Let us take you back, sweetheart. You can see Quinn tomorrow. Quinn, you could come by the house, couldn't you? We'd be glad to have you. What about tomorrow afternoon? Come on, darling.'

"I grabbed her head and whispered in her ear, 'Go home and get your passport and be ready.'

"Dr. Mayfair shook her head as if she too hated this predicament. Or as if she'd heard my whisper. The lawyer, Ryan, the smoothie in the suit, never changed his pained expression. I think he was mortified but resigned. He was a good-looking son of a bitch, I had to give him that, and that probably meant his son, the infamous enemy Pierce, was also good-looking.

"Finally Mona turned around and, still clinging tight to my arm, she looked at them.

" 'I hate you that you did this to me,' she whispered. 'I hate you all. I don't trust you.'

" 'Dear God, child,' said Aunt Queen. 'What do you want us to do?'

"Nash looked totally alarmed. Allen and Clem were ready for battle. The security man was on full alert.

" 'She has to come home, Mrs. McQueen,' said Dr. Rowan patiently and courteously. Her face was too serene. 'Quinn, can you come see Mona tomorrow? I think Michael's suggestion was a good one.'

"Mona turned to face me again, and with her back to the evil three she mouthed the word 'passport.' 'You'll come at three o'clock, all right?' she said. But her fingers secretly pressed the number two against the inside of my arm.

" 'Yes, three o'clock, I'll come.'

" 'You can be our guest for dinner,' said Dr. Mayfair. 'Mrs. McQueen, Mr. Penfield, I'm sorry for all this. Truly I am.' She had such a frank simple manner that her words were almost believable. I mean by that that I couldn't hate her as much as I wanted to. But she was still scary in a secret way.

"Mona kissed me on the cheek. I took hold of her and kissed her on the mouth. 'I love you,' I said. 'I'm coming to get you.'

" 'Be careful of all the ghosts,' she whispered. 'Be very careful, and remember, if I somehow become unreachable, or they pull some trick, go to Stirling Oliver. Oak Haven is the southern Retreat House of the Talamasca. Everybody knows where it is. Oak Haven Plantation. It's on the River Road near Vacherie.'

" 'Got it,' I answered.

"She backed up. 'I'll see you tomorrow,' she said. 'Aunt Queen, thank you for the supper. Mr. Penfield, it was so nice talking with you.'

"Suddenly she paused, staring at Aunt Queen, whose own face was the picture of distress. And then Mona went to her and embraced her and kissed her.

" 'Oh, darling, sweet little darling,' said Aunt Queen. 'God bless you and keep you. And here'—Aunt Queen unhooked the diamond-studded cameo from her throat—'you take this.'

" 'Oh, no, I couldn't,' Mona said.

" 'No, you must. Always remember us by it.'

"Mona was going to break into tears again. Taking the cameo clenched in her hand she pivoted and went off fast, and the uncomfortable trio followed her, all of them piling into the awkward stretch limousine, which made a U-turn in the drive and soon vanished in the direction of the highway.

"Jasmine told our palace guard to go back to the kitchen. The security man seemed genuinely disappointed as he headed back to the front porch. Jasmine took my plate and gave me a hot helping of chicken and rice.

"I burst into tears. I just cried like a little kid. I cried and cried. I just sat there not caring who thought what and I cried. So what if I was eighteen. I cried.

"Nash came over to put his arm around me and Aunt Queen cooed to me and called me her poor darling.

" 'I never wanted anything so badly in all my life,' I said. 'I just love her.'

" 'Oh, my precious Little Boy,' said Aunt Queen. 'Why on earth does it have to be a Mayfair!'

" 'But what's wrong with them, Aunt Queen?' I asked. 'Good Lord, we went to their hospital! We go to their church. Fr. Kevin is a Mayfair. I don't get it.'

"Nash gave my neck a firm squeeze and went back to his chair.

" 'Jasmine, give Nash a fresh plate,' said Aunt Queen. 'And you, Little Boy, please eat something. How can you be six foot three and not eat something?'

" 'I'm only six foot one,' I explained, 'it's Nash that's six foot three. Nash, thank you for your moral support. Aunt Queen, I don't understand this.'

" 'Well, my boy,' she said, lifting her glass of white wine for Jasmine to refill, 'I'm not sure I understand it myself, but the Mayfair family has always been viewed with suspicion. Dr. Rowan Mayfair, the genius behind Mayfair Medical, is perhaps the most universally admired of the clan, and she has immersed herself in public life and public service.

" 'But even Dr. Rowan is a mysterious figure. At one point she was so severely injured that all hope was given up, and then she made a miraculous recovery.'

" 'Well, you can't blame her for that, surely,' I interjected.

" 'Can't I?' said Aunt Queen. 'I can tell you it wasn't through the intercession of a saint that she came back from the dead. That much is true.'

" 'But what are you saying?'

" 'As you saw, she's very restrained and sure of herself by nature,' Aunt Queen said. 'And perhaps she is a good person, perhaps she is a very good person. But the rest of the family is another matter.'

" 'But what do you mean? The lawyer was like a loaf of white bread.' (Of course I was stealing Mona's words, but so what?)

" 'He's quite well respected,' Aunt Queen admitted, 'though his practice is mostly dedicated to the family. I'm speaking of other things. And surely you haven't forgotten that he manages our money. But there has been talk for years of congenital madness in the female line. Well, and in the male line as well. Mayfairs were drugged, locked in padded cells, even let their house on First Street fall into ruin at one time, though now that Mr. Michael Curry has come it's wonderfully restored, or so they tell me. Then there's the matter of Michael himself, almost drowned once in the swimming pool.'

" 'But what could that mean?'

" 'I don't know, darling, I'm only trying to convey that they're shrouded in mystery. It's a family with its own law firm and its own priest. Rather like the Medici, don't you think, and you know how the people of Florence used to rise against them and throw all their art-works out of the palazzo windows!'

" 'As if the people of New Orleans would riot against the Mayfairs!' I scoffed. 'You're not telling me everything.'

" 'I don't know everything,' she replied. 'They're a haunted family and some say they're cursed.'

" 'You met Mona,' I said. 'You know she's lovable and brilliant. Besides, we're a haunted family, too.'

" 'Something's wrong,' said Aunt Queen. She hesitated.

"I saw her eyes veer off. She looked at the place where Goblin sat watching her very steadily. She knew he was there, and as I turned to him I saw that he was locked to her.

"She went on, eating tiny bits of chicken daintily as she talked:

" 'There are many old stories about Mayfair women having unusual powers—an ability to call spirits, an ability to read minds, to know the future. But more than anything else there is this question of hereditary madness.'

" 'Mona can see Goblin, Aunt Queen,' I said, glancing at him and then back to her. 'She has that power. Where in the world for the rest of my life will I find a beautiful brilliant woman who can see and love Goblin?'

"I glanced at him again. He stared coldly at Aunt Queen. And she was staring at the spot where he sat. I knew she was seeing something.

" 'You know anyone who marries me,' I went on, 'is marrying Goblin.' I took his right hand and squeezed it. But he didn't respond.

" 'Don't be sad, Goblin.'

"Aunt Queen shook her head. 'Jasmine, more wine, please, darling. I think I'm getting drunk. Be sure Clem's on alert to help me to my room later.'

" 'I'll help you to your room,' I said. 'Those breakneck shoes don't scare me. I'm about to be married.'

" 'Quinn,' said Aunt Queen, 'did you see how they have taken Mona home? Now please forgive my candor, but it seems to me that they are very afraid of Mona forming any alliance that can lead to her getting pregnant.'

"Nash asked if he should excuse himself. Aunt Queen said absolutely not, and I also nodded to it.

" 'Nash, if we're all going to Europe together,' I said, 'you have to know who we are.'

"He sat back nursing his soda quietly.

" 'Quinn, am I being unfair,' Aunt Queen asked, 'if I suggest that something intimate might have happened between you?'

"I was stunned. I couldn't answer them. I couldn't tell them all that Mona had told me—the story of the strange child, that it had been a mutation, that it had been taken away. I couldn't pass on these confidences.

" 'Maybe we are crazy,' I said, 'both of us. She being able to see Goblin, imagine that. And both of us seeing ghosts. She talked of it all from a scientific point of view. I felt like I wasn't a freak. I felt like she and I were of the same ilk. And now it seems this person, this precious person whom I so loved is being stolen from me.'

" 'Darling, it's only for one evening,' said Aunt Queen patiently. 'You've been invited there tomorrow afternoon.'

" 'And you're not dead set against my going?' I asked. I started cleaning up the chicken and rice on my plate. I was hungrier than ever. I wonder what trauma could have shaken my appetite. 'I thought you'd feel just the opposite.'

" 'Well, this may surprise you,' said Aunt Queen, 'but I think you might accept this invitation for a very good reason. Few people outside the family ever get to see the interior of that mysterious Mayfair house, and you ought to take advantage of the privilege. Also I have a hunch that when you see Mona again, some of this fire will burn itself out. Of course I may be wrong, the child's gorgeous, but it's what I'm hoping for.'

"I was plunged into misery but eating like a pig. 'Listen,' I said, 'if I can get her away from there, with her passport, can we set out for Europe immediately?'

"I could see the continued amazement in Nash's otherwise placid and dignified face, but Aunt Queen looked a bit provoked.

" 'Tarquin,' she said, 'we're not stealing the girl. Jasmine, more wine please. Jasmine, you're not yourself. When have I ever nagged you so much?'

" 'I'm sorry, Miss Queen,' she said. 'It's just those Mayfairs scared me. The stories people used to tell about their house, it was awful. I don't know if a boy Quinn's age—.'

" 'Bite your tongue, beautiful!' I said, 'and you can pour me some wine, too. I'm going tomorrow.'

" 'They had a ghost!' Jasmine said, quite belligerently. 'It used to scare off any workman who ever tried to work on that property. You remember my cousin Etienne, he was a plasterer, and they called him to that house, and the ghost pulled the ladder from under him.'

" 'Oh, stuff and nonsense,' I said. 'And Etienne used to tell fortunes in the cards.'

" 'I can do that too, Little Boss,' Jasmine sent back. 'I can read your cards, if you want, and tell you what your fate is.'

"She took my plate and heaped it with a second helping. The chicken was really delicious now, and the gravy was thick.

" 'Jasmine's telling you the truth, darling,' said Aunt Queen. 'They're a haunted family, as I said.' She paused. 'Before Dr. Rowan came out from California, no one would go near that house. Now they have big family get-togethers there. They are an immense clan, you know. And that's what I fear when I think of them. They're a clan, and a clan can do things to you.'

" 'The more you say, the more I love her,' I responded. 'Remember, I got my passport in New York, when I was there with you and Lynelle. I'm ready to rumble. But what do you mean, they're a haunted family?'

" 'For years,' she said, 'it was a dreadful ghost, just as Jasmine described. He did a lot more than push people off ladders. But he's gone now, this illustrious ghost. And what surrounds them is talk of genetic mutations.'

"I had to be quiet. But it didn't work. She went quiet too.

" 'What happened to the dreadful ghost?' I asked.

" 'Nobody knows except that something violent occurred. Dr. Rowan Mayfair almost lost her life, as I mentioned. But somehow or other the family got through it. Now Mona, Mona came down from an intensely inbred line of the family. That's why she's been named the

Designée of the Legacy. Can you imagine? Being chosen because you are inbred? If there are genetic problems, you might guess that Mona has them.'

" 'I don't care,' I said. 'I adore her.'

" 'Mona didn't grow up at the house at First and Chestnut. She grew up on St. Charles Avenue, not very far from Ruthie's house, and her people went back to a plantation house in the country. There was a murder. Mona wasn't a rich little girl, by any means.'

" 'Mona told me all this. So she wasn't rich. Do I have to love somebody rich? Besides—'

" 'You keep missing the point. The child is now in line to inherit the Mayfair fortune.'

" 'She told me that, herself.'

" 'But Quinn, don't you see?' she persisted. 'This child is under intense scrutiny. The Mayfair Legacy involves billions. It's like the capital of a small country. And here she's gone from an unstable family to inherit an unimaginable fortune. Nash, you explain it. The girl's rather like an heir to the throne of England.'

" 'Exactly,' said Nash in a very mild professorial manner. 'In the sixteenth century it was an act of treason to court young Elizabeth or Mary Tudor because they were in line for the royal crown. When Elizabeth finally became queen, the men who had dallied with her were executed.'

" 'You're implying the Mayfairs might kill me?' I asked.

" 'No, indeed not, what I'm trying to say,' Aunt Queen returned, 'is that they will reclaim Mona no matter where she goes or how. You saw for yourself. They were quite prepared to pick her up bodily and carry her to that limo.'

" 'We should never have let her go,' I said. 'I have a terrible feeling about it.'

"I glanced at Goblin. He looked solemn and remote, his eyes on those opposite me.

" 'When you see her tomorrow . . .' Aunt Queen began, but then she broke off.

" 'Tomorrow and tomorrow and tomorrow,' I murmured. 'How long must I endure until I see her? I want to go to the house now and climb the vines to her window.'

" 'No, darling, don't even contemplate such a thing. Oh, we never should have gone to Mayfair Medical, but how did I know that the little heiress would be in the Grand Luminière Café?'

"Jasmine refilled my plate with plenty more of the chicken and rice. I started eating again.

" 'I don't trust anybody now except Mona,' I said. 'I love you, you know that, but I'm in love with her, and I know, positively know, that I will never love anyone as I do her. I know it!'

" 'Quinn, dear, it's time for the worst tidbit of gossip.'

" 'I can take anything,' I said between forkfuls.

" 'They've already arranged a husband for Mona,' said Aunt Queen gently. 'It's her cousin Pierce.'

" 'She told me that, too,' I said, fudging just a little. I gestured to Jasmine for more wine.

" 'Did she tell you that Pierce is her first cousin?'

"Even I was shocked by that. But I didn't answer.

" 'Oh, darling,' Aunt Queen said with a sigh, 'I want to set our course for Europe right away, but we're not going to be able to take Mona Mayfair.'

" 'Well, I can assure you,' I said, 'I'm not getting on any plane for anywhere without her.' "

28

"THE NIGHT HAD too many hours, and surely the following morning would be an agony, or so I thought. Aunt Queen, Nash and I parted at about ten o'clock—after more insubstantial and agonizing conversation about the Mayfairs—with my promising to consider the European trip even if Mona's family wouldn't allow her to go, and my promising that if I remained behind, I would accept Nash as a new teacher.

"That part was easy for me. I liked Nash completely, and I believed his firm assurances that he would be entirely happy at Blackwood Manor if we were meant to stay there.

"When I went upstairs I found Big Ramona awake and the window open near the fireplace and a brisk breeze blowing through the room. Now, it was our custom to sleep with the air-conditioning on during warm nights such as these, so I was a bit surprised by this, and by the fact that Big Ramona climbed out of bed and came a-whispering to me as soon as I closed the door.

" 'It's Goblin!' she said. 'He opened that window! I'm telling you, it's the God's truth. I shut it twice and he opened it twice. He's down there! Look at the screen on your computer. See what he wrote!'

" 'You saw the keys move?' I asked her.

"The words were 'COME DOWN.'

" 'The keys move! Boy, I saw the window open and shut, are you listening to me! Do you see what's happening to you with Goblin? He's getting stronger and stronger, Quinn.'

"I went to the window and looked down over the east lawn. I saw him standing in the glow of the floodlights on the side of the house. He was dressed in a long flannel nightshirt, as was my custom by this hour, but I, of course, was still in my pants and shirt.

" 'Quinn, you go to Confession,' said Big Ramona. 'You tell the priest what you've done with this ghost! Don't you realize he's from the Devil? Now I know he was the one who broke all that glass.'

"I didn't bother to argue with her. I went downstairs and out to him by the cemetery where he was wandering barefoot like a lost soul.

" 'You go to Europe with Mona, you leave me,' he said. His lips were scarcely moving, but I could see his hair mussed in the breeze.

" 'I won't leave you. Come with me,' I said. 'Why can't you? I don't understand.'

"He didn't answer.

" 'I'm worried about you,' I said aloud and under my breath, 'worried about your feelings. You've become closer to me ever since you attacked the mysterious stranger. You've learned more things.' Again there came no response whatsoever.

"I tried to hide my fear, reminding myself that no matter how sophisticated he had become and how at odds with me he might be, he couldn't read my mind.

"As for me, I was restless and only partially focused on him. I was too in love with Mona to be focused on him. It was so wicked! After all these years. Did he know it?

" 'Come on, let's walk out of this light,' I said to him.

"I walked on back past the shed and onto the west side of the property, where the wicker patio lay in its own bath of electric light. He followed me, and when I glanced over to him, when I slipped my left arm around him, I saw that he had become my duplicate in clothing again. It seemed such a simpleton thing.

" 'Will you try to take me with you?' he asked. 'When you go to Europe? Will you hold my hand?'

" 'Yes,' I said. 'I'll do it. You'll be right next to me on the plane. I'll hold tight to your hand all the way.' With all my soul I meant it but I was speaking to a faded love when it was my blessed Ophelia to whom my soul belonged. I was her Hamlet and her Laertes and perhaps her Polonius as well. But I must not forget my Goblin, and it was not fear of him but loyalty that goaded me now.

"I had other things on my mind too. The Hermitage, for example, and how I meant to reclaim it from its wilderness neglect. I had already spoken to Allen, the supervisor of the craftsmen among the Shed Men, about running electricity out to it, and there were other things I meant to do.

"Of course the mysterious stranger was a real problem, more real than the Shed Men knew. But I was drawing pictures in my mind of how splendid I could make the place. And of how wonderful it would be to take Mona to the island, and how exciting it was that Mona wanted to see it and wasn't afraid.

"Dreaming of all this, conniving and planning, dreaming of Mona tomorrow and whether we could escape to Europe, I struggled to be true and faithful to Goblin, when quite suddenly he stiffened and, squeezing my hand, said in his telepathic voice:

"Be careful. He comes. He thinks I don't know him and he means harm.

"At once he vanished. Or at least he was gone from my vision, and at the same time the floodlights went out as if someone had tripped the switch. I found myself plunged into relative darkness.

"Instantly, an arm came up and hooked around my neck and a hand grasped my left arm behind my back tightly. I struggled but it was useless. My free right hand couldn't do a thing against either grip, and the voice of the stranger spoke in my ear softly.

" 'Call for help and I'll kill you. Turn your spirit friend loose on me and I'll kill you. You and all your dreams will be gone."

"I was in a rage. 'I fought you once,' I growled. 'I'll fight you again.'

" 'You're not listening.' His voice was low. It had no sound of menace. 'If your familiar strikes out at me again, you'll die here now.'

" 'So what's holding you back? Why don't you break my neck now?' I was furious.

" 'Really,' he said in my ear, 'you are the thinking man's victim.'

" 'I'm nobody's victim,' I responded.

" 'Of course not, because you're going to do what I want.'

" 'Which is what?' I asked. Remembering some advice from long ago, I tried to turn my head to one side so he wouldn't have full pressure on my larynx, but he only tightened his grasp on both my neck and my arm. I was in pain.

" 'Stop fighting me and listen,' he said in the same calm near-caressing voice. 'I'll leave you like a broken dove on the ground here for your Aunt Queen to find in the morning.' He went on in his reasonable way, just above a whisper. 'You know she comes out for a stroll before dawn, don't you? Old people don't sleep well. They don't need the full hours of the night. She comes with Jasmine and Jasmine is still dopey, but they make their little constitutional while the stars are still clear.'

" 'And you're watching,' I said. I was horrified. 'What do you want of us?'

" 'You're going to be enormously impressed with my generosity, but I have been eternally known for my generosity and my cleverness.'

" 'Try me,' I said. I was almost too angry to talk sense.

" 'Very well,' he said. 'I've done a great deal of thinking about you, and this island which we both claim. I've come to the conclusion that I want to share the Hermitage with you. That is, I'll allow you to use it by day and I shall use it by night as has been my custom.'

" 'By night? You come there only by night?' This was almost unendurable.

" 'Of course. Why do you think you found the candles, and the ashes in the fireplace? I have no use for it by day, but I don't want others troubling it ever. I'm to find no evidence of others when I come. Except for evidence of you. Your books, your papers, things like that. Now for the most important part of the bargain. You're to improve the Hermitage. You're to take it to a new level of excellence. Do you follow me?'

"He had loosened the grip just a little. I could breathe without it hurting. But he had me as firmly as ever, and my left arm, my good arm, was aching. I was paralyzed with fury.

" 'The improvements are key,' he said. 'You're to take care of them, and then we will both enjoy it happily. You'll never know I'm there perhaps. Oh we can share the books we read. We can grow to know each other. Who knows, we may come to be friends.'

" 'What improvements?' I said. Obviously the creature was insane.

" 'First off I want it thoroughly cleaned,' he said, 'and the gold on the sarcophagus, it has to be cleaned and polished.'

" 'Then it is gold,' I said.

" 'Most assuredly,' he responded. 'But you may tell your workmen it's brass if you like. Indeed, tell them anything about the entire island which will keep them away.'

" 'But who was the grave intended for?'

" 'You need never concern yourself with that, and never open it again either.' The voice came soft as breath. 'Now let's return to the Hermitage. You're to have electric wiring installed throughout the place.'

" 'You've been reading my mind, haven't you?' I asked.

" 'Then I want glass fitted in all the windows, glass that opens and closes. I'm not particular as to the design, just so that the night can be seen and felt and the rain kept out of the interior. The flooring should be laid both in the first and second story—something of marble tile like the tile in your entranceway would be most excellent, though I think that it should be all white with a dark grout.'

" 'Good God,' I said, 'you *have* been reading my mind. Who are you?'

" 'Have I? I do have a gift for it. And handsome lamps should be purchased as well as marble tables such as that which is there already. And fine gold chairs in the Roman style, and couches. You know. I leave it to you, the taste of such things—you've been born to and bred on fine things—and you shall see that it's all correct.'

" 'This is a game to you, isn't it?' I asked. I was breaking into a cold sweat.

" 'Not entirely,' he said. 'I want these improvements. And I want the privacy afterwards. I want it all from you.'

" 'And you're serious.'

" 'Well, of course I am,' came the low, hushed voice. 'Now what else do I propose? Ah yes, a better fireplace, don't you think, for the bitter cold Louisiana nights in winter of which outsiders know so little.'

" 'How did you manage to spy on me? From what vantage point?'

" 'Don't be so sure that I did. I'm cunning. You wanted to reclaim the place. I know the style in which you live. I want to be friends with you, don't you see? It's nice having my arms around you. I offer peace if you do these things. If you needed wealth for it, I'd oblige.'

" 'And your part of the bargain is to leave the place entirely alone by day?'

" 'Yes,' he said, 'and not to kill you. That's the most impressive part—that I'll let you live.'

" 'Who are you?' I demanded again. 'What are you? Were those human bodies I saw you dumping in the swamp? They were, weren't they, and the chains on the second floor. Did you never ask yourself what had happened with those chains?'

"I struggled. He tightened his grip.

"There came a dark slow laugh from him, a laugh I'd heard before though I couldn't place it. Or could I? Was it only in the swamp that night when I had seen him in the moonlight? I was too caught up in his strength and in my own sense of peril to know for certain.

" 'You can take away the chains if you like,' he said. 'Have it all cleaned as I told you. Have made a new stairs from first floor to second. Have it made of bronze. And caution your workmen not to speak of the place. Caution them to frighten others away. If and when they hire out-siders, let them choose from those at a distance rather than from those who are close at hand.'

" 'Like it was in Manfred's time,' I said.

" 'Like you tell it on your tours of the house and property,' said the voice. 'Now, I have a piece of advice for you.'

" 'What piece of advice?'

" 'You can see spirits and you've become enamored of a spirit named Rebecca.'

" 'How do you know?'

" 'Suffice it to say that I do know and I'm warning you against her. She wants a vengeance from you against those who have harmed her, and she'll settle for your life. You're a Blackwood and that's what matters to her. Your happiness fascinates her. It gives her strength. It causes her pain.'

" 'You've seen her yourself?'

" 'Let me humor you on this score. I have made myself privy to those dreams of yours in which she visits. And through those dreams I have come to know her tawdry desires.'

" 'She was tortured in the Hermitage,' I said. 'She was tortured with those chains.'

" 'You defend her to me? What is that to me? Allow me to suggest you remove the chains and put them with the casket of her remains which you've buried in the cemetery.'

" 'You spy on me night and day,' I said, my teeth clenched with anger.

" 'I wish I could,' he answered. 'Now I'm going to let you go and you can turn and you can look at me just as you please, and you keep your part of the bargain and I'll never hurt you or your family or your darling love with the red hair or her clan of witches.'

"His arms were removed. I spun around. He stood back.

"He was as I remembered. Six feet in height. Thick jet black hair pulled back from a square forehead with high temples and big black eyes with dark eyebrows that gave him a determined expression, and a long line of a smiling mouth, all very impressive, and a square jaw. Eyes positively flashing in the light. He was dressed in a fine black suit, and for one instant I saw all of him, and then he was turning, sporting the long thick black ponytail of hair—and gone as surely as if he'd dematerialized like Goblin.

"Goblin was immediately by my side, and Goblin said aloud, 'Evil, Quinn, evil. He doesn't disappear. He uses speed.'

" 'Hold my hand, Goblin!' I said to him. 'I knew you were near but you heard his threats.' I was shaking violently.

" 'Had I come between you, Quinn, he would have crushed you. He was too ready for me, Quinn. He wasn't afraid.'

"I turned, still trembling so badly that I could scarcely stand upright, and I saw the inevitable lights in Aunt Queen's window. It was the lurid flare of the television.

"I embraced Goblin and then told him we must go to Aunt Queen. I was crazed with excitement.

"I rushed into the kitchen, across the back hall, and banged on her door. I found her in her chaise lounge as usual with her champagne, and some champagne sherbert, concluding the marathon drinking bout that had begun at dinner. Jasmine was fast asleep under the covers. *The Scarlet Empress* with Marlene Dietrich was on TV.

" 'Listen to me,' I said, pulling up a chair. 'I know I'm fast losing my reputation with you as a sane person.'

"I pulled out my cotton handkerchief and mopped the sweat from my face.

" 'That's quite all right,' she rejoined. 'You have a powerful reputation as my great-nephew.'

" 'The stranger attacked again. It was just outside. He got me in a choke hold.'

" 'Good Lord, Jasmine—.'

" 'No, wait, don't call anyone. He's gone, but before he left he told me just what he wanted. He made a list of demands, all having to do with the refurbishing of the Hermitage, and he proposed that after the renovation we share the place—that he would use it by night and I would use it by day. And if I didn't agree to his plan he'd kill me.'

"She was aghast. She said nothing. Her small blue eyes gazed fixedly into mine.

" 'But Aunt Queen, this is the strange part—not that he crept onto our land, not that he made the floodlights go off on the west side of the property, not that he got me in a choke hold—all that's normal stuff more or less. It's what he wants done to the building!'

" 'What do you mean?'

" 'The refurbishing. It's all precisely what I want! It's as though he read it in my mind. He did read my mind. The electricity, the new marble floors, the glassed-in windows, the new bronze stairs inside. He asked for nothing that I hadn't already thought of. I'd even mentioned it to you, mentioned it to the men, that they should remember the route to the place because I wanted to put in electricity. He read my mind, I tell you. He played with me on it. The creature's not human. He's some sort of spirit or ghost like Goblin. Only he's a different species, Aunt Queen, and I have to go to Mona, because Mona will know and so will Stirling Oliver.'

" 'Quinn, stop, be still!' she said. 'You're raving! You're in a tirade. Jasmine, wake up.'

" 'Don't bring her into this, she'll be a nuisance,' I said.

"Jasmine was already awake and sitting there silently passing judgment.

" 'I'm going up to write out a complete plan for the renovations, then I'm going to rest before I go to Mona,' I said.

" 'Darling, it's midnight. You must talk to me before you leave to see Mona,' said Aunt Queen.

" 'Vow to me that you'll allocate the funds for the Hermitage. It's nothing compared to the money we spend all the time on Blackwood Manor. Oh, I can't wait to see the Hermitage redone. But then I myself have the money, don't I? I forgot that. I can afford it. How amazing.'

" 'And this splendid reinvention of a place you mean to share with a man who dumps bodies to alligators?' she responded.

" 'Maybe I was wrong. Maybe something else was happening. I only know that it won't hurt to carry out my own scheme for renovations and now he's no obstacle, don't you see? An hour ago he was a giant stumbling block to all I dreamt of for the Hermitage. He was an invader. Now he's part of the scheme. He asked for nothing that I didn't want already. Aunt Queen, he watches us. He knows you walk around the house in the morning. You need the guards with you. He's cunning.'

"The expression on her face was dreadful. I think I had taken all the bubbles out of the champagne and all the alcohol out of it also. Sober and miserable, she stared at me. Then she slowly ate a spoonful of sherbert as though it were the only thing keeping her alive.

" 'Oh, my darling boy,' she said. 'Jasmine, are you listening?'

" 'How could I not listen?' said Jasmine. 'Someday, when I'm old and gray, we'll have Quinn's portrait on the wall, and I'll be shuffling in front of the tourists talking about how he disappeared into the swamp and never came back—.'

" 'Jasmine, stop it!' I declared. 'Aunt Queen, I'm going up. I'll kiss you good-bye before I take off to see Mona. I won't go till tomorrow afternoon. I know I can't drive in this condition. Besides, I have work to do.'

"Goblin and I ran upstairs together.

"I turned on the computer, in spite of Big Ramona sound asleep in the bed, and fortunately, as I clicked away, she never woke up.

"Goblin took his chair beside me. His face was blank, and he didn't try to touch the keyboard. He watched the screen as I worked.

"I didn't speak to him. He knew that I loved him. But he knew as well that I was yielding to the blandishments of an ever broadening world.

"Yes, I feared the stranger, but now the very devil had potently excited me. I was going mad.

"I wrote up a total renovation proposal for the Hermitage, going into detail as to how everything was to be done and spelling out the fine points as best I could, depending on my memory. I assumed Allen and the Shed Men would be doing everything, bringing in outside contractors only when they had to, so I went into greater detail possibly than they would need.

"I chose Roman red paint for the exterior, with dark green for the trim on the window and doors, and the finest veined white marble tile with black grout for the interior floors and for the front stairs descending to a broad terrace of white marble which should go down to the landing—and indeed, they should build a proper landing—and ordered a new bronze stairway to go between the stories and up to the cupola as well. This would be a gorgeous and costly retreat when I finished. But it would be more in keeping now with the strange gold tomb.

"As for the furnishings, I would order them from the same catalogs we used for Blackwood Manor, and of course I'd go over to Hurwitz Mintz in New Orleans to check their fine stock for choice pieces. I wanted torchère lamps everywhere and marble-top tables galore, as I had dreamed and as my strange and cunning partner had directed.

"When I thought this over, when I caught myself in the very act of calling him a partner, I paused and reflected, and I remembered that moment in the moonlight, and I knew what I had seen. There was no mistaking it. And then there came back to me the memory of his earlier attack on me, and of the letter he had written. And how he had just held me helpless only a short time ago. He had told me that he would kill me if I didn't follow his instructions. Did I believe him?

"Of course I hated him. And I feared him. But not enough.

"I should have been far more cautious. I should have backed away from the venture. I should have loathed him. But what I had told Aunt

Queen was true. I wanted these renovations. I wanted this rebirth of the Hermitage, and one of my greatest problems had been solved, and that was how to deal with the mysterious stranger. I didn't have to battle the man for the place. We now had a partnership. And so I proceeded. Was I half in love with this monster? Was that the secret truth?

"I even remembered the man's advice to discourage hired workmen from going to the island, or rather to put a wreath of mystery about it, and I wrote this into the scheme.

"Lastly, I wrote about what must be done first—the cleaning and polishing of the mausoleum, and wrote out the solemn stricture that it must never be opened again.

"Finally I finished my written plan for the renovations.

"I printed out the requisite copies. Then I drew a clean design for a sumptuous granite bathroom to be built onto the back of the round Hermitage, occupying no more width than one window, and, copying this four times by means of my fax machine, I finished my official plans.

"At this point Goblin spoke: 'Evil, Quinn,' he said. 'Quinn Goblin will die in any direction.'

"I turned and looked at him and saw in his face a cold hard expression much as I'd often seen in him for the last few days. There was none of the old love or warmth or playfulness.

" 'How do you mean Quinn Goblin will die?' I asked. 'We won't let that happen, old buddy. We won't. I'm pledging that to you. Can you understand my words? They come from my heart.'

" 'They all want you,' he replied in his monotone. 'Mona wants you. Rebecca wants you. Aunt Queen wants you. Nash wants you. The stranger wants you. Any direction and Quinn Goblin dies.'

" 'We'll never be separated,' I said confidentially. 'Perhaps they simply don't know how strong the bond is between us. But we know.'

"His expression remained cold, and then very slowly he dissolved.

"I had the distinct impression that he had dissolved of his own accord, not because he had to, and that he wanted me to know this, that he had withdrawn, and indeed I did feel the sting of it.

" 'It's true what I told you,' I said. 'Only you can make us die, only you can divide us, and that would be by leaving me.'

"Whether he was near or far, whether he had heard what I said, I had no clue. And I was too madly excited to care about him.

"I hurried downstairs to place a copy of my scheme with Aunt Queen, who received the work agreeably enough, and then I went out to find Allen's mailbox in the shed, and I put a copy in there for him. Allen was the head of the craftsmen, as I've indicated. He'd see that the work was done. I put a copy in Clem's box as a courtesy, as Clem was actually the boss, and then I headed back to the house.

"As I crossed the back terrace a wave of giddiness came over me. And when I look back on that moment—when I remember the starlight and the warm air, and the light streaming out of the kitchen door to greet me, when I remember the feeling of charged excitement, I remember how very alive I felt, how in love with Mona and how foolishly excited I was by the mysterious stranger, and how I held myself to be invincible even in the face of strong evidence that I was not.

"Goblin's strange words meant nothing to me, absolutely nothing. In fact, I even suspected him of the most base jealousy, and all of his recent behavior seemed cause to doubt his love. Yes, I was drawing away from him. Yes, Goblin Quinn was going to die. It had to happen because Manhood was going to make it happen.

"And on the battlefield of Manhood, Mona was my Princess and the Mysterious Stranger a dark knight riding near me or even against me in a joust of which I was only just learning the rules.

"We would come to know each other, the dark knight and myself. We would talk together in the Hermitage. I would penetrate the illusion of the bodies being given over to the dark waters. I would discover that it had been a sort of dream. Anything so very bad had to be a dream. Take Rebecca for instance. Rebecca came in dreams.

"What more could I do for poor Rebecca? Of course I could not give her 'a life for a life, a death for a death.'

"I went back upstairs. The windows were closed. The air-conditioning hummed. No sign of Goblin. I went to the window and looked down on the west lawn. I could see in the distance the dim white shapes of the cemetery in the moonlight. I said a prayer for Rebecca, that her soul was in Heaven with God.

"Very reluctantly I lay down to sleep beside Big Ramona, and when I woke it was to the murky dawn, and I had the heavy tasks of Manhood upon me."

29

"MY FIRST MANLY TASK WAS to get to the Hermitage, and I wasn't fool enough to think I could collect those rusted chains alone. I took Allen with me. The Shed Men always arrived around six o'clock, so they could go home at three, and when I told him where we were headed he was convivial and all but hopped into the pirogue with me.

"It was and still is Allen's nature to find everything in life pleasurable. He's a big roundly built man with neat white hair combed to one side, and silver-rimmed glasses and a perpetual smile; he plays Santa Claus at Christmas parties with huge success.

"Anyway, when we reached the Hermitage it wasn't seven o'clock yet, and we went to our task with the best tools we had and soon gathered up all the rusted chains, dragging them down the steps after us.

"I had to force myself to set out for home, so strong was my fascination with the Hermitage, but I knew I had much to do this day and so after a little walk around, during which time I imagined my renovations with great approval and success, we were in the pirogue again.

"When we got back to the landing and I told Allen we were going to bury the chain with Rebecca's remains he went into a state of sustained hilarity.

"Nevertheless, I dug deep in the soil. I found the casket. I made the hole very very wide. I wreathed the chains around the casket. And then Allen helped me fill in the dirt and the headstone was replaced, and as I said my prayers Allen prayed with me.

"I felt no shimmer of Rebecca. I felt no dizziness. But as I stood there in the still morning I felt sorrow for all the ghosts I had seen in the cemetery over the years and wondered if I was fated to be a roaming spirit after my death.

"Nothing like that had ever occurred to me before. But I thought of it now. I said another long silent prayer for Rebecca and then I whispered, 'Go into the Light.'

"And so my first manly task had been completed.

"On to the second: of course Allen knew where Terry Sue lived, and to that spot we drove in the Mercedes. I told Allen I would go in alone, but even before entering the trailer I had a fair idea that Grady Breen, our attorney, had not exaggerated the state of ongoing disaster.

"There were the rusted ruined automobiles that he had described, one an old limousine and the other a pickup truck, neither with any tires, and two toddlers were roaming the yard, both with filthy faces and diapers.

"I knocked, then went in. Tucked at the very end of the trailer there was a voluptuous woman in the bed, a woman with the face of a big china doll, nursing a baby, and a little girl, perhaps ten years old and barefoot, was stirring a pot on the stove of what looked and smelled like grits. The little girl's arms were covered in bruises and she had a shy fearful manner to her. She had a pretty face and long black hair.

"The closeness of the place, the crowded damp feel of it was overwhelming. And so was the smell. I can best describe it as a mixture of urine, vomit and mildew. There might have been some rotten fruit in the recipe. And certainly there was excrement as well.

" 'I'm sorry to break in on you like this,' I said to the woman. I felt like a giant under the low ceiling. 'Congratulations on your new baby.'

" 'Did you bring any money?' she asked. Her face stayed lovely—she looked like a Renaissance Madonna—but her voice was full of meanness, or maybe it was just practicality. 'I'm broke and Charlie's walked out on me again,' she said. 'My stitches are torn and I'm running a fever.'

" 'Yeah, I have plenty money,' I said. I reached into my pockets and took out the thousand dollars I'd taken out of the kitchen petty cash box. She was appropriately flabbergasted. She took it with her left hand and shoved it in a pocket under the covers. Or just under the covers.

"The baby was miraculous. I had never seen one so tiny, so nearly newborn. Its little wrinkly new hands were marvelous. It already had a head of dark wispy hair. My heart went out to it.

" 'Brittany, hurry up with that grits,' said the woman, 'and go get

those kids, I'm going to need you to walk into town and get some groceries.' She looked up at me. 'You want some breakfast? This child
cooks the best breakfast. Brittany, put on the bacon. Go get those kids.'

" 'I'll take her into town,' I said. 'Where's Tommy?'

" 'Out in the woods,' she said in a sardonic tone. 'Like he always is.
Reading a picture book. I told him if he didn't take that book back to the
store he was going to go to jail. They're going to come get him. He stole
that book. And they knew he did. That woman at the store is as crazy
as he is. They're going to come get him. And they ought to take her to
jail too.'

" 'Does he have any other books?' I asked.

" 'Who's got money for books?' she asked. She was becoming
incensed. 'Look around this place. See that broken window? Look over
there. Look real good. See that little girl? She don't talk. Brittany, give
Bethany some grits. What happened to the coffee? Sit down here at the
table. Just move that stuff. This child makes the best coffee. I'm telling
you, I thank God every day that he sent me Brittany, and he sent her
first. Brittany, go get Matthew and Jonas. I done told you twice to do
that! This baby's wet. Hurry up about it. I don't have money for books.
My washing machine's been broken for two months. Pops never gave
me money for books.'

" 'All right,' I told her. 'I'll be back.' I went out into the woods. It
wasn't dense, just the spinally piney woods in these parts where there
aren't many live oaks. I could see this little boy sitting on a log and he
was reading.

"He had black curly hair like mine and he was lean yet well proportioned. He had sharp blue eyes when he looked at me. The book was
about art. It was open to Van Gogh's *Starry Night*.

"The boy had on a dirty polo shirt and jeans, and there was a huge
black-and-blue mark on his face and one on his arm. On the back of his
left hand was a visible burn.

" 'Did Charlie hit you?' I asked.

"He didn't answer me.

" 'Did he push your hand against the heater?' I asked.

"He didn't answer. He turned the page. A painting by Gauguin.

"I said, 'Everything's going to change. I'm your kin. I'm Pops' grandson and you're Pops' son, you know that, don't you?'

"He didn't say anything. Obdurately he looked back at his book and
again he turned the page. A painting by Seurat.

"I told him my name. I told him everything would be better. I was about to leave him when I said, 'One day you'll get to go to Amsterdam to see Van Gogh's work in person.'

" 'I'd settle for New York,' he fired back, 'so I could see all the Impressionists and the Expressionists at the Met.'

"I was stunned. His words were so clear, so crisp.

" 'You're some kind of genius,' I said.

" 'No, I'm not,' he said. 'I just read a lot. I read all I wanted to read in the branch library and now I'm working on the Books-a-Million store in Mapleville, where I go to school. My favorite books are about art. Couple of times, Pops brought me books on art.'

"That was an astounding revelation. Pops and books on art. Where would Pops get books on art? What did Pops know of books on art? Yet he had done it for this bastard son whom he allowed to live in squalor in this place.

"Thank God I still had some more money, about fifty dollars. 'Here,' I said. 'This will work wonders at the bargain table. Don't steal anymore.'

" 'I never stole,' he said. 'That's my mother talking. You listen to my mother and you'd think Charlie pushed my hand up against the heater.'

" 'Gotcha. The point is, you can buy some to own with that.'

" 'Who's your favorite painter in the whole world?' he asked.

" 'Hard to say,' I answered.

" 'Like if you could only save one painting from the Third World War,' he pushed, 'what would it be?'

" 'Have to be Renaissance. Have to be a Madonna,' I replied, 'but I'm not sure which one. Probably one by Botticelli, but then maybe Fra Filippo Lippi. But there are others. Just not sure.' I thought of the beautiful woman inside nursing the baby. I wanted to mention her in connection to a Madonna but I didn't.

"He nodded. 'I'd save Dürer,' he said. 'Salvador Mundi—you know, the face of Christ with the hair parted in the middle.'

" 'That's a good choice,' I said. 'Maybe much better than mine.' I hesitated. We'd come a lot further in this conversation than I'd thought possible when I drove out here. 'Listen to me,' I said. 'Would you like to go off to a good school, a boarding school, you know, get a fine education, get out of here?'

" 'I can't leave Brittany,' he said. 'Wouldn't be fair.'

" 'What about the others?'

" 'I don't know,' he answered. He sighed like a big man with a big burden. 'My mother, she doesn't really want us,' he said. 'She wasn't so bad when Brittany and I were little. But now that there's all the others, she hits us a lot. I have to get between her and Brittany and sometimes I can't do it. I don't let her hit the little ones at all. I just take the belt right out of her hand.'

"I was revolted, but I had no solution. I had all my life heard that there are real problems with the welfare system and with the foster care system, and I didn't know what to do.

" 'I understand,' I responded. 'You can't leave them behind.'

" 'That's right,' he said. 'I'm going to a better school now than Brittany but she's getting a good education. I can tell you that much. She does her homework and she's smart. I don't know the answer.'

" 'Well, listen to me,' I said. 'I'm not going to forget about you. I'll come back with more money. Maybe I can make everything better for your mother and all of you, and she won't want to hit the children.'

" 'How would you do that?'

" 'Let me think on it, but believe me. I will be back. Good-bye, Uncle Tommy.'

"That brought the first smile out of him, and as I waved he waved back.

"Then he jumped off the log and he ran after me. I stopped, of course, to let him catch up.

" 'Hey, do you believe in the lost kingdom of Atlantis?' he asked.

" 'Well, I do believe it's lost, but I don't know if I believe it's real,' I said.

"He laughed a real belly laugh.

" 'What do you think, Tommy? Do you believe in it?'

"He nodded. 'I hope to find the ruins actually,' he said. 'I want to lead a party to find it. You know, an underwater expedition.'

" 'Sounds wonderful,' I said. 'We'll talk about it as soon as I have time. I've got to go to work now.'

" 'Really? I thought you were so rich you didn't have to work or even go to school. That's what everybody says.'

" 'I mean work on my problems, Tommy, you know, special things that I feel ought to be done. I'll see you soon again. I promise. Can I give you a hug?' I leaned down and did it before he could commit himself. He was a solid, loving little creature. I really adored him.

"When I got to the car Allen was shaking his head.

" 'I hope you don't want us to clean up this place,' he said. 'That septic tank in back is overflowing something awful.'

" 'So that's what that smell is,' I said. 'I didn't know.'

"As soon as I reached Aunt Queen on the car phone I described the situation to her and asked if I might instruct Grady Breen to purchase a decent house for Terry Sue and her children. The title should be in our name with full insurance of every sort, and the woman would need furniture, appliances, new kitchenware, the works.

" 'You can't imagine this level of poverty,' I explained. 'And this woman hits her children and I haven't begun to figure what to do about that except it might stop if the house and the conditions were improved. At least I hope so. As for Tommy, he's brilliant.' I filled in all the relevant details.

"Of course she wanted to call Grady herself. But I said it was something I had to do. It was a job of maturity and it was important.

"Within half a minute I had Grady on the phone. We agreed that the woman's house had to be in a moderately priced new development outside of Ruby River City, Autumn Leaves being the ideal tract according to Grady, with all new construction, new appliances, new pots and pans, new everything, and that she had to have a full-time cleaning woman and a full-time nanny for the children.

"Grady would become her personal financial advisor and financial guardian. We'd pay the taxes, insurance, utilities, television cable and hired help direct. And of course Terry Sue had to have an income, and we decided upon one that was about equal to what she would have earned as a secretary in Grady's office. We thought that would give her a real spiritual lift.

" 'It's foolproof,' I said. 'The nanny and the cleaning woman will be working for you, and Terry Sue will have no call whatsoever to hit her kids. In front of those people she probably will be ashamed to hit her kids.'

"Meantime Brittany would switch over to the Catholic school that Tommy was attending, the only Catholic school in Mapleville and one with the cachet of a private prep school, and we'd get some medical help for the little girl Bethany, who didn't talk.

"As for the mysterious Charlie who had walked out of Terry Sue's life, according to Grady, he wasn't 'all that bad by any stretch,' but the baby in Terry Sue's arms wasn't his and he was a bit disgusted that the real father hadn't stepped up, and who that might be was open to question.

"I advised Grady to have a DNA test done to determine if this baby had been fathered by Pops. I felt it was only right to do so. I had a deep suspicion that Pops was the father, that the baby had been conceived in the aftermath of Sweetheart's death, and that Charlie didn't know what to do about it.

" 'Look, Grady,' I said, 'this is a situation that's never going to be perfect, but I think we can do these things to make it better. If men come and go in this new house there's nothing we can do about it. At least we have made Terry Sue independent. She doesn't have to put up with anybody whom she doesn't want. Just keep her income steady and what she does with it is her business. If she starves her children, then we give the housekeeper money for groceries. And the nanny cooks and serves. We'll fix it till it's not broken anymore.'

"What I didn't confide to Grady was that I had dreams that Tommy would come someday to live at Blackwood Manor. I had dreams that Tommy would someday travel the world with me and Mona and Aunt Queen and Nash. I had dreams that Tommy would someday become a brilliant scholar and, who knows, maybe even a brilliant painter. Maybe Tommy would find the lost kingdom of Atlantis. In essence I had dreams that someday Tommy would become an official Blackwood.

"I also didn't confide to Grady how much I judged Pops, though I tried not to do it, for leaving his son, Tommy, in this mess, and how loveless he had been to this woman Terry Sue. But then, maybe there was more to it than I in my youth could understand.

"Only after this was finished and I had almost reached home in the Mercedes did I remember my promise to take little Brittany to the grocery store. I told Allen he'd have to go back and take little Brittany to the grocery store and stock up the trailer.

"Of course he had a wisecrack or two, but in general he was agreeable and said he would go back in the pickup and take little Brittany wherever she wanted to go and buy them everything from soup to nuts.

"And so the second task of Manhood was done. Now for the third.

"I went home, showered and changed into my best Armani suit, pale violet shirt and lucky Versace tie, and with a passionate heart and a delirious head I went out to see my beloved Mona Mayfair, stopping only at a florist on St. Charles Avenue to buy her a big bouquet of daisies and other spring flowers. It seemed very fresh and soft and beautiful to me, this bouquet, and I wanted to put it tenderly into her arms. I dreamed of her soft kisses as the woman put the paper around the flowers, and driving towards the Mayfair house on First and Chestnut I counted the moments until two o'clock arrived."

30

"I**F EVER ANYBODY WAS** more in love than me that day I should like to speak to that person and hear it proved from his or her lips. I was floating with happiness. I parked half a block away, so as not to be espied by an evil opposing Mayfair, and then, bouquet in hand (I had pushed back the florist paper to make a mere cuff of it) I approached the gate, coming along the fence beneath a great shrub of crape myrtles that were already wildly and beautifully in bloom.

"In fact, the entire Garden District seemed fragrantly blooming and the streets so utterly deserted that I did not have to be subjected to ordinary individuals who weren't in love.

"As for Goblin, when he appeared beside me I told him firmly that I had to complete this mission alone, and he was to leave me now if he ever wanted a civil word from me again.

" 'I love you, I've told you that. Now give me my time with Mona,' I said crossly.

"To my astonishment he gave me loving kisses on my cheek and whispered 'Au revoir' to me and obediently disappeared. An aftertaste lingered, a shimmering feeling of good will and deliberate generosity that was as palpable as the breeze.

"Of course I had hoped that Mona would be waiting for me with backpack, suitcase and passport in hand.

"But soon as I reached the wrought-iron gate a tall, elegant individual came to meet me, shattering my hope of escape with Mona utterly, though he had a most compassionate look on his vibrant face.

"He was svelte, if not downright swanky, with prematurely white curly hair and quick inquisitive eyes. His clothes were positively dashing. They looked old-fashioned in cut, like something from a drama about the nineteenth century, but what part of that century I didn't know.

" 'Come in, Tarquin,' he said with a French accent. He turned the brass knob, whereas Mona had used a key. 'I've been waiting for you. You're most welcome. Come in. Please. I want to talk with you. Follow me into the garden, if you will.'

" 'But where's Mona?' I asked, being as civil as I knew how.

" 'Oh, no doubt combing her long red hair,' he said with the most exquisite intonation, 'so that she can throw it over yonder balcony,' he pointed upwards to the iron railings, 'and lure you like Rapunzel did her forbidden prince.'

" 'Am I forbidden?' I asked. I tried to resist his beguiling manner but it was difficult.

" 'Oh, who knows?' he said with a world-weary sigh, but his smile was brilliant. 'Come with me, and call me Oncle Julien, if you will; I'm your Oncle Julien as surely as your Aunt Queen gave her embrace to Mona last night. And, by the way, that was a stunning gift, the cameo. Mona will always treasure it. May I call you Tarquin? I have already, haven't I? Do I have that much of your trust?'

" 'You invited me in, didn't you?' I replied. 'I thank you very much for that.'

"We were walking now on a flagstone path beside the house, and to our right lay a great garden with an octagonal pattern of boxwood around its lawn. There were Grecian marble statues here and there—a Hebe, I think, and a bathing Venus—and beds of exquisite spring flowers and some small citrus trees, and one bearing a single lemon of monstrous size. I paused to look at it.

" 'Isn't it charming?' he said. 'The little tree puts all its heart into the one lemon. If it had many, no doubt they'd be of regular size. You might say the Mayfair clan does something very similar. Here, come let's walk on.'

" 'You mean with regard to the Legacy,' I said. 'They put everything into one Designée,' I continued, 'and she has to be guarded from intrigues with those who aren't marriageable and I've somehow been found wanting?'

" '*Mon fils,*' he said, 'you have been found too young! There's nothing in you that's unworthy. It's only that Mona is fifteen and you are not yet a man. And I must confess a little mystery surrounds you which I will explain.'

"We had gone up a few flagstone steps and were now walking past a huge octagonal swimming pool. Hadn't Aunt Queen said something about Michael Curry almost drowning in this pool? I was befuddled. Everywhere there was beauty. And it was so very quiet.

"Oncle Julien drew my attention to the fact that the shape of the pool was the same as that of the lawn. And in each of the short pillars of the balustrade that octagon was repeated.

" 'Patterns on top of patterns,' he said. 'Patterns attract spirits, spirits who are lost can see patterns, that's why they like old houses, grand houses, houses with big rooms filled with the touch of kindred spirits. I think sometimes that once a host of spirits have inhabited a house it's easier for other spirits to get in. It's an amazing thing. But come, let me take you into the rear garden. And we will escape the patterns to sit for a while beneath the trees.'

"It was exactly as he had said. As we passed from the flagstones around the pool through a large open double gateway we found ourselves moving out across a loose lawn to an iron table and chairs beneath a huge oak, where the grass grew sparse and the roots were visible, and other young trees to our right—willow, magnolia, maple—were fighting to make a grove.

"I could see the word 'Lasher' carved deep into the bark of the oak tree and there was a strange sweet fragrance in the garden, a perfume-like fragrance—something that I could not associate with flowers. I was shy of asking what the scent was.

"We sat down at the black iron table. It was set with cups and saucers for us and a tall thermal pitcher, which he lifted now to serve.

" 'Hot chocolate, *mon fils*, what do you say to that?'

" 'Oh, marvelous,' I said with a laugh. 'How absolutely delicious. I never expected it.' He filled my cup.

" 'Ah,' he said, as he filled his own, 'you have no idea what a treat it is for me.'

"We sipped, waiting for the temperature to become comfortable, and I saw there were animal crackers on the plate and the old poem by Christopher Morley came to me about this very repast:

> *Animal crackers, and cocoa to drink,*
> *That is the finest of suppers, I think;*

"Quite suddenly, Oncle Julien recited the next two lines:

'When I'm grown up and can have what I please
I think I shall always insist upon these.'

"We both laughed.

" 'Did you plan it on account of the poem?' I asked.

" 'Well, I suppose I did,' he responded. 'And because I thought you'd enjoy it.'

" 'Oh, I'm so thankful. What a thoughtful thing to do.'

"I felt high. I felt happy. This man wouldn't separate me from Mona. He would understand love. But I was forgetting something. I had heard the name Julien Mayfair, I was sure of it. It was in some connection, but I couldn't remember. . . . Surely not from Mona. No.

"I looked up and to the left at the long three-story flank of the May-fair house. It was immense and silent. I didn't want it to shut me out.

" 'Do you know of Blackwood Manor?' I asked suddenly. 'It was built in the 1880s. I know this house is far older. We live out in the country. But you have the charm and stillness of the country right here.' I felt foolish for my candor. What was I trying to prove?

" 'Yes, I know of the house,' he said, smiling agreeably. 'It's very beautiful. And my coming there was a macabre and romantic experience, which I wouldn't divulge to you in any detail, except that I must. It bears heavily upon your love for Mona. And so the light must shine in the dark.'

" 'How so?' I was suddenly alarmed.

"The chocolate was now at the perfect temperature. We both drank it at the same time. He sighed with pleasure, and then he filled our cups again. It was, as Mona would have said, perfectly egregiously delicious. But where was Mona?

" 'Oh, please tell everything,' I said. 'What does it have to do with my love of Mona?' I found myself trying to calculate his age. Was he older than Pops had been? Surely he was younger than Aunt Queen.

" 'It was in the time of your great-great-great-grandfather Manfred,' said Oncle Julien. 'He and I belonged to a gambling club here in New Orleans. It was secretive and fashionable and we played hands of poker for bets that did not involve money so much as secret tasks to please the man who won. It was in this very house that we played, I well remember, and your ancestor Manfred had at home his son William, who was a very young bridegroom, and rather afraid of Blackwood Manor and all the responsibilities that it involved. Can you imagine such a thing?'

" 'That he was intimidated? Yes,' I said, 'I can imagine it though I don't feel that way myself. I'm the young master there now and I love it.'

"He smiled gently. 'I believe you,' he said evenly. 'And I like you. I see travel in your future, great adventures, roaming the world.'

" 'Not alone, however,' I was quick to answer.

" 'Well, on this night in question,' he went on, 'when the gambling club was meeting here, it was Manfred Blackwood who won the hand and it was of Julien Mayfair whom he asked for the task to be done.

" 'We rode out at once in his automobile to Blackwood Manor and there I saw your marvelous home in all its moonlit glory, the columns the color of magnolia blossoms—one of those southern fantasies that nourish us perpetually in which northerners so seldom believe. Your great-great-great-grandfather Manfred took me inside and up the winding steps to an unoccupied bedroom and there he declared to me what I must do.

" 'He produced an artful Mardi Gras mask and a rich red velvet cloak lined in gold satin, and he said that, clothed in this apparel, I must deflower William's young bride, for William himself, who soon appeared, had been absolutely unable to do it, and both Manfred and William had seen such masked trickery in a recent opera in New Orleans and they felt it would work here.

" ' "But hasn't your wife seen the same opera with you?" I asked William, for I too had seen it at the opera house in New Orleans only a week before. "Yes," William responded. "Which is all the more reason why she will go along."

" '*Alors*. Never one to turn my back upon a virgin and having only respect and compassion for a young woman so far cheated of a gentle and loving wedding night, I donned the mask and the cloak and went about the enterprise, vowing that I should wring from the young woman tears of ecstasy or count myself a damned soul, and suffice it to say that I emerged from the bedroom some forty-five minutes later a victor on the Stairway to Heaven, having achieved my highest goals.

" 'Now from this union there came your great-grandfather Gravier. Do you follow my drift?'

"I was stunned into perfect silence.

" 'Now, within a few months after the birth of Gravier,' Julien continued in the same affable and ostensibly charming manner, 'William was able, at my suggestion, to commence his connubial duties by means of the mask and cape, and never was your great-great-grandmother ever the wiser as to the nature of the first encounter, and so on went their conjugal bliss, or so Manfred told me, the mild-mannered William very likely depending upon the mask and cape as long as fate required.

" 'Now in time the young woman in question went to her reward in heaven, as we say, and William took a second wife, only to discover that he could not deflower her any more than he'd been able to deflower his first wife, and once again Manfred called upon me to don the mask and cloak, and so I did, becoming the father of the noble lady whom you call your Aunt Queen. Ah, such a blessed daughter—.

" 'But my point is you are related to me and to mine by blood.'

"I was speechless.

"As I looked at him, as I sat there with the heat pumping in my cheeks, trying to fathom what he was saying to me, trying to evaluate what he was saying, some small voice inside said it was impossible, he couldn't be that old, he didn't look that old, the numbers weren't right for him to have been the father of Aunt Queen's older brother, Gravier, or of Aunt Queen herself, but maybe he was very young then, I didn't know.

"But far louder than any voice that troubled me about years or numbers was the voice that said, 'Both you and Mona see spirits, Tarquin, and you are hearing an explanation of how that tendency came about. Oncle Julien's blood gave you those genes, Tarquin. His blood gave you the receptors which Mona also enjoys.'

"As for the desk in the parlor of Blackwood Manor, the one round which William's ghost appeared to hover, I intended to go home and tear it apart.

"Right then I sat there in total shock. I decided to drink the second cup of chocolate and I did. I grabbed for the pitcher and refilled my cup. Quietly he drank from his own.

" 'It's not been my purpose to wound you, Tarquin,' said Oncle Julien, his voice very soft with affection. 'Far from it. Your youth and your sincerity appeal to me. And I see this lovely bouquet of flowers which you've brought to Mona, and this touches me that you want so desperately to love her.'

" 'I do love her,' I said.

" 'But we are a dangerously inbred family, Tarquin. And you cannot be with Mona. Even if you were both of age, my blood in your veins rules it out. Over time I have come to see that my genes in my offspring tended to dominate, and this has sometimes caused grief. When I was . . . when I was thoughtless and free and rebellious, when I hated time and was desperate, I didn't care about such things, but I care very much about them now. You could say I exist in a Purgatorial state of concern about them. That's why I must warn you that you can't be with Mona. You must leave Mona to her ghosts and you must go home to yours.'

" 'I won't do it, Julien,' I said. 'I want to respect you and I do respect you, even though you deceived my ancestor, this shivering virgin whom you seduced in the very bed in which I sleep now. But I have to hear rejection from Mona's own lips.'

"He took a deep swallow of his hot chocolate and looked away thoughtfully as though it comforted him to see the maple tree and the willow and the huge strapping magnolia that promised to dominate the little glen.

" 'Tell me something, young one,' he said. 'Do you pick up a strange fragrance in this yard?'

" 'Yes, it's overpowering,' I said. 'I didn't want to ask about it. But I can smell it. It's sweet.'

"There seemed a sudden change in his demeanor. He went from charming ease to fatality.

" 'Once again, I must say it, *mon fils*, that you must absolutely never be with Mona,' he said. 'And you will forgive me that I brought you to this spot.'

" 'What do you mean? Why do you say that to me? Who's to say that we won't be faithful to each other until we're grown? Three years from now, can't she make up her mind for herself? I'll hold her to my heart, I'll wear her hair in my locket of her and when the time comes I'll walk with her down the aisle.'

" 'No, that can never be. Please understand how much I love Mona and how much I respect you and know you to be of fine character. But you can see spirits, *mon fils*, and you can catch the scent of the dead. You know that buried here in this spot are mutations who should never have been born to this family. Take my confidence, *mon fils*, that if you marry Mona your children may be these mutations as well. That you can catch the scent is proof of it, I must confess.'

" 'Are you telling me you killed and buried Mona's child here?' I demanded.

" 'No. Mona's child is living,' he answered. 'Its destiny is a different matter, I can well say. But there must be no more of such creatures, not by the name of Mayfair, and Mona will never have any other name.'

" 'You're wrong!' I said.

" 'Don't despise me, Tarquin, for your own sake,' he said. He seemed endlessly patient. 'I thought if I explained things to you it would be easier. And maybe it will be in the course of time.'

" 'Tarquin!' I heard my name called. I turned to my left. In the broad gateway by the pool it was Michael Curry there who had called out to me and beside him stood Rowan Mayfair, and both were looking at me as though I had done something wrong.

"I rose immediately.

"They came towards me. They were both in casual, at-home dress. And Michael had a build on him in his blue work shirt that made my mouth water.

"Rowan spoke first. She was kindly. 'What are you doing here, Tarquin?' she asked.

" 'Well, I'm speaking to Julien,' I said. 'We were just having hot chocolate and visiting here.' I turned and gestured to the right but Julien wasn't there. I glanced at the table and then looked back to it. Except for my bouquet there was nothing there. No thermal silver pitcher, no cups, no animal crackers, nothing.

"The breath went out of me.

" 'My God,' I said. I made the Sign of the Cross. 'I tell you, I was speaking to him. I burnt my tongue on the second cup of hot chocolate. The pitcher, it was silver. He let me in at the front gate! He was telling me that I couldn't be with Mona, he said we were related. I . . .' I stopped. I sank down in the chair.

"Nobody knew better than me what had happened! Yet my eyes searched the garden for him. And again I stared at the empty table. I laid my hand on the bouquet. And where was Goblin? Why hadn't Goblin warned me? How impatient I'd been with Goblin, and Goblin had let me fend for myself!

"Dr. Rowan Mayfair came behind me and put her hands on my shoulders. I felt soothed immediately by the way that she massaged me. She actually bent down and kissed my cheek. Rampant, comforting chills went through me. Oh, the pure sweetness of it. Michael Curry sat opposite and he took my hand and held it firmly. He was like the uncle I never knew.

"God, how I loved them. How I wanted to be connected to them.

How I wanted to love Mona with their blessing. Desperately, I needed their comfort now.

" 'I'm going to be locked up,' I stammered. 'Julien Mayfair. Was he ever a real man?'

" 'He was real, all right,' said Rowan Mayfair in her patient and sincere husky voice. 'He's a legend in the Mayfair clan. He died in 1914.' "

31

"THEY BROUGHT me into the house. It was dim and magnificent. They showed me the shadowy double parlor with its carved archway and shining floors and they took me through the handsome dining room with its murals of Riverbend Plantation, long ago sacrificed to the curvature of the Mississippi River as it changed its fickle path.

"Rowan was the tour guide, pointing out details with a low-key simplicity, her voice warm, though her gray eyes were always cold. She was very shapely in her white shirt and pants and seemed at times to be ruminating in a dream.

"Then it was in the sunlit kitchen that we settled at a glass table with brass dolphins as a base to it, and we were ranged in comfortable brushed-steel chairs. There was a cozy back stairs in the corner and a small gas fireplace for cold days, but this wasn't one of them, and beyond the French doors we could see the rampant jasmine and the banana trees that grew around the wall of the rear garden where I had sat with Julien, so oblivious to the real world.

" 'But how do I know you're real?' I asked them logically. 'He seemed in those moments as real as anybody, except—.' And then I had to admit it, the things that were wrong, that he had been a friend to my ancestor Manfred, a sheer impossibility in terms of his appearance, and then there was the matter of his old-fashioned nineteenth-century clothes.

" 'Ghosts tip you off and then distract you,' I confessed.

"Michael Curry nodded his head. I knew instinctively that he had seen spirits, plenty of them. And he was such a genial man, almost humble. Yet he gave an impression of incredible strength. He had exceptionally large hands and they looked gentle.

" 'What did he tell you, son?' he asked. 'Can you share this information with us?'

" 'That he had sired my great-great-grandfather,' I said. I proceeded to recount for them the operatic drama and how it had been done. And that it seemed to mean that Mona and I both carried a sensitivity to see spirits and that was why we mustn't marry on any account.

"It may have been utterly self-defeating to repeat these things to Michael and Rowan but I had no intention of holding them back. I thought they should know everything. They should know why Oncle Julien had interfered.

"With my eyes opened now I told them of Oncle Julien's words, that he existed in a 'Purgatorial state of concern' about his genes dominating his offspring, and how he had asked me about the sweet scent in the backyard, and of how I could smell that scent and had not wanted to say anything until asked.

"Both Rowan and Michael seemed fascinated by these confessions, and I went on to tell them that Oncle Julien had said that mutations were buried in the earth of the rear garden, but not Mona's child, Mona's mutated child was living, and this seemed to enthrall them and they asked that I repeat it and I did.

"At this point I became so miserable, so certain that they would not let me see Mona, and so sure of failure in every regard that I began to cry. I begged them not to turn me away. I told them how much I wanted to be part of them. I had no shame in it. And perhaps in my own heart I felt I was worthy somehow.

" 'I don't come as a pauper,' I said. 'I don't come as a beggar. I don't offer Mona a small cottage in which to live.'

" 'We know that, son,' said Michael Curry. 'And forgive us if we seemed lacking in respect when we came to Blackwood Manor, but Mona has put us through some wild escapades and at times we forget our manners. Yesterday was one of those times. Believe me when I say we worry about Mona.'

" 'But what is so very wrong with Mona being with me? Do you believe it's that we both see spirits?'

" 'No, it's not that in itself,' said Michael. He sat back comfortably in his chair as he addressed me. 'The fact is, there are medical reasons, good medical reasons that have to do with Mona's health.'

" 'It's Mona who has the right to talk about the medical aspects of things,' Rowan said in her softly running husky voice, 'not us. But we can tell you that Mona isn't acting wisely and we are trying to guard Mona from herself.' She was soft and sincere.

"I wasn't sure what to say. 'I understand your problem,' I replied, 'because I can't divulge the things that Mona has said to me. But can't I see her? Can't you let her come down? Can't I tell her about the ghost of Oncle Julien? Can't I ask her what she has to say?'

" 'You do understand,' said Michael, 'that this was a powerful apparition. This ghost chose to intervene in a powerful way. Have you ever seen a ghost like this?'

" 'Yes,' I said, 'I have seen ghosts that strong.'

"I told them both the whole story of Rebecca. And as I did so I knew I was being my own worst enemy again. But there could be nothing under this roof but frankness, or so it seemed to me. My love for them ordained that frankness.

"I also told them about Goblin. As much as I thought right.

" 'Don't you see that I belong with her?' I said finally. 'She's the only one who will ever understand me, and I'm the only one who'll ever understand her?'

" 'Son, you have your own ghosts,' said Michael, 'and she has hers. You have to move away from each other. You have to seek a decent normality on your own.'

" 'Oh, God, that's impossible!' I said. 'We'll never achieve it. Besides, who's to say we can't achieve it better together if it's achievable at all?'

"I could see now they were pondering my words. I had made some incidental impression of intelligence on them if nothing else. They hadn't kicked me out of their house yet in any event, and now an overpowering urge to have hot chocolate came over me, a stupid, insidious desire to drink hot chocolate in large amounts.

"And to my utter amazement, Michael rose and said, 'I'll fix it for you. I'd like some myself.' I was stunned. They were a family of mind readers on top of everything else. I heard him laugh under his breath as he went to the pantry. Then came the noises and the deep delicious fragrance of the heated milk.

"Rowan sat there solemnly and pondering, and then, very softly, she spoke. Her voice as usual was much gentler than her angular face, with its high cheekbones and blunt-cut wavy hair.

" 'Tarquin, let me lay it out,' she said. 'Let me violate Mona's confidentiality. Let me make that judgment call. Mona has given me permission to do it, to tell you things about her, which really shouldn't be told.

She isn't really old enough to give that permission. But let me go on. Mona endangers herself every time she has intimate relations with a man. Do you follow me? She runs the risk of hurting herself severely. We're trying to keep Mona alive.'

" 'But we used protection, Dr. Mayfair,' I insisted. Nevertheless this was frightening news. I had dried my eyes by this time and was trying to behave like an adult.

" 'Of course you did,' said Dr. Mayfair, raising her eyebrows slightly, 'but even the best of precautions can fail. There's always the possibility that Mona will conceive. And just the smallest miscarriage weakens Mona in ways that a normal woman does not have to worry about. It's all because of the baby born to Mona, the baby whom Oncle Julien mentioned to you in the garden outside. It left Mona vulnerable. And we're trying to keep Mona alive. We're trying to discover how to fix what's wrong so Mona won't be so vulnerable, but for that we need time.'

" 'Dear God,' I whispered. 'That's why Mona was at Mayfair Medical the day I saw her.'

" 'Precisely,' said Rowan. She was becoming a little more heated, but she sounded compassionate at the same time. 'We're not insensitive monsters,' she said. 'Really we're not. We're trying to get her to stop seducing her cousins and to cooperate with our regimen of blood tests and nutritional supplements so we can find out what's going wrong inside of her and why she so often conceives. Now, I've told you more than I should, and by the way, let me add that she is in love with you and she's stopped roaming since she met you; you have every right to know that, but we can't countenance her being with you.'

" 'No,' I said, 'what you can't countenance is her being alone with me. Let me see her here with you present. Let me see her with a vow of celibacy. What could be wrong with that?'

"Michael came to the table with the very silver pitcher I had seen in the garden and cups for us all. It was the same damned china. The hot chocolate was as rich and delicious as it had been in the vision and I was ready for a second cup almost at once. I wanted to tell them about the pitcher and the china, but I wanted even more to talk about Mona.

" 'Thank you for humoring me on this score—I mean with this chocolate,' I said. 'I don't know what's the matter with me.'

"Michael refilled my cup for the second time. I drank deeply. It tasted better than anything known to man.

"I sat back. 'I've been level with you,' I said. 'Can't you be level with me? Tell her that I'm here—.'

" 'She knows that, Quinn,' said Michael. 'Her powers of clairvoyance are tremendous. She knew it when you came through the front gate. She's wrestling with the very things Rowan confided to you. The truth's coming full force on her. She's sick. And then there's the question of her lost offspring—the one that Julien told you was alive. She heard that news when you did, and she was the one who came to us and told us to come down and welcome you in.'

"I wanted to say this was a great consolation, which it was, but I wished they had told me before this time and I didn't want to complain. Also something else occurred to me. Why had they interrupted my conversation with Julien when they did? If they hadn't come, how much more would Julien have said?

" 'That's a question to which we don't have an answer,' said Michael, having read my thoughts again.

" 'But you stopped him. You stopped him from revealing family secrets,' I said. 'You thought it best.'

" 'We did,' said Dr. Mayfair. 'We thought it best.'

" 'Does it matter to you that I am one of you?' I asked in a sober voice.

"Neither of them had an answer for me. Then Rowan spoke in the most dejected manner. 'If only Mona wasn't ill,' she said. 'If only we could find a cure. Then everything would be different, Quinn. As it stands now, what is the point of asking you to cast your lot with us? What is the point of asking you to be genetically tested as all of us are? What is the point of you taking on the weight of our history and our curses and all we suffer and know?'

" 'Genetic testing?' I asked. 'To see if I have a susceptibility to see spirits?' I drank down the hot chocolate. Michael poured me another cup.

" 'No,' said Rowan, 'to see if you could produce the mutation in your offspring as Mona did.'

" 'I want it,' I said.

"She nodded. 'All right. I'll set it up at Mayfair Medical. You report in to Dr. Winn Mayfair. Call his secretary to arrange the time.'

" 'And now, where are you keeping my darling princess?'

"I heard her from the top of the back stairs: 'Quinn!'

"I rose at once and ran up to her, jogging left then left again with the little stairway, and then throwing my arms around her as we came together on the second floor.

" 'Remember my warnings,' came Rowan's voice from below.

" 'I promise, no penetration,' said Mona. 'Now leave us alone.'

"I picked her up off her feet.

" 'Oh, my egregious boy!' she declared, her breasts hot beneath her snow white shirt, her red hair everywhere in my eyes and against my heart, her naked legs smooth and beautiful to my touch.

"I carried her down the hallway. 'Where do we go, Princess Mona of Mayfair?' I asked. 'I have wrestled with angels and dragons to be with you!'

" 'To the very front of the house, Prince Tarquin of Blackwood,' she answered. 'There is my bower among the branches of the oaks.'

"We passed up a short few steps, out of a narrow hallway, to a big bedroom and through it into a large hallway and on past a regal staircase to the very front where my beloved, my red-haired beloved, signaled me to make a left turn.

"It was the very front bedroom, all right, and its two floor-length windows were open to the upper porch, and they seemed to be filled by the oak branches of the two trees which stood before the house.

"We fell onto the bed.

"I was all wound up with Mona's virginal white blouse and its volu-minous sleeves and lace, and we were tumbling in her white pillows, and I pressed my hand against her hot wet panties, and with the pressure of my palm brought her to the finish with divine blushes that made me come.

"Again we did it, and this time more slowly and playfully, and then again, and I was as always spent before she was, but I was in no mood to desert her in her need.

"It must have been an hour that we lay together, and all the while the door was partially open and there came no sound of any intruding per-son in the house.

"We were on our honor and on a small white lace baby quilt, which I had pretty much spoilt with my overspilled love. 'Entirely washable, and destined for the purpose,' said my Lady Love as she folded it and cast it away.

"Now it was the season for kisses and for snuggling and for lying back against the pillows and looking out of the windows at the oak branches in which the lithe little brown squirrels tripped among the clinging green ferns.

" 'I never want to leave you,' I told her. 'But awful things have hap-pened to me since we were together,' I confessed.

"I told her all about the stranger and his bizarre assault. I told her how he had read my very thoughts about the Hermitage. And how I had given the order for the renovations and he and I would be partners in it, but I was more sure than ever that I had seen him dumping bodies by the light of the moon.

"She was fascinated.

" 'Doesn't that scare you?' she asked.

" 'Of course not,' I said. 'I'm more scared of Oncle Julien.'

"She laughed.

" 'Does Oncle Julien come any time you want him?'

"She looked sad.

" 'No,' she said, 'it's more like he comes when he wants to come, and now you have to tell me everything that happened to you with him. I overheard your telling Rowan and Michael, I admit. I was an eavesdropper. But you have to tell me. Describe him. Describe how he acted. I have to know. I'm so ferociously jealous when Oncle Julien appears to anybody else.'

"I recounted the whole experience for her. I described Julien's dapper clothes, his gentle manner. I described the flowered china pattern. She knew it. She said it was Royal Antoinette. She wasn't sure they even had it in his time. She said he had snatched the image out of the pantry. He was a clever ghost.

"She was deeply affected by the fact that he had said her child was alive. That meant the world to her. I had a jewel there to give her in that simple intelligence.

" 'But doesn't a ghost ever lie?' I asked. I went, in my mind, back over my experience with Rebecca. Perhaps she never lied to me. She only deceived me and there can be a difference.

"I got up out of the bed. I went to the window and looked into the oak branches. It was so beautiful here. You'd never guess that you were in the middle of the city—that the waterfront lay a scant eight blocks from here to the left, that St. Charles Avenue with its legendary streetcars was only three blocks to the right.

" 'You know what I think?' I asked.

" 'What is it?' she said, sitting up. She pulled her knees up and wrapped her arms around her legs. Her hands looked beautiful in her big laced ruffles. Her hair fell down around her shoulders in a way I'll never forget.

" 'I think I need you much more than you need me,' I said.

" 'Quinn, that's not true,' she said. 'I love you. You're the first person I've ever fallen in love with. It came on me all last night after they brought me home. It hurts and it's splendid and it's real. I need you because you're fresh and vital and you're not part of us.'

"She sounded so earnest.

" 'But I am,' I protested. 'I told you what Julien told me. He took the place of my great-great-grandfather William, I told you.'

" 'But you weren't brought up a Mayfair,' she said. 'And you come with a strong name and tradition of your own. You live in a manor house with its own legends and grandeur! Besides, what does it matter? I need you and I love you, that's the point.'

" 'Mona, was it true what Dr. Rowan told me, that every time . . . ?'

" 'Yes, it's true. They don't know why. But I'm constantly ovulating, constantly fertile; I conceive constantly and I lose the offspring, and every time it happens I'm weakened. More calcium is pulled out of my bones. Now, it is extremely possible—totally possible actually—that if they performed a hysterectomy on me, the problem would be solved, but then I'd never have children, and they're hoping that somehow they can solve the problem without that step.'

"I was frightened by all this, frightened for her. That I had unknowingly hurt her terrified me.

" 'If it means your life, Mona, you have to let them do the hysterectomy,' I said. 'You can't keep risking your very life.'

" 'I know, Quinn, I think about it constantly,' she said. 'And so does everyone else. There will come a moment when they say that it's time to do it, and that time may be very soon. Think about that, Quinn. Does the Lord of Blackwood Manor want a bride that can never have a child?'

" 'I love you, Mona. I don't need children. In fact, I know of a child we can have.'

" 'Just have?' she said, laughing. 'You mean just like that?'

"I told her about Pops, about Terry Sue and Tommy. Brilliant little Tommy sitting on the log with the book of paintings in his hand, and the black-and-blue mark on his face.

" 'Wow, think of it!' she said. 'It would be like Cinderella! You could just change his entire life!'

" 'Yep. I intend to do that, no matter what happens. So don't think about me anymore when you think about this hysterectomy. I'm pretty sure that Terry Sue is open to bargaining where Tommy's ownership is concerned. I'm going to help Terry Sue with the whole passel of them, that's a done deal. But there's one thing I have to ask you.'

" 'You already sound like the man of the house,' she said matter-of-factly. 'I'll do my best.'

" 'No, I'm serious, Mona.'

"I sat on the bed next to her and I kissed her.

" 'Do Rowan and Michael know where your child is?' I asked.

" 'No,' she said, 'I don't think that they do. Sometimes I think that they might—Mayfair Medical is a world unto itself—but no, they couldn't—. I can't stand that idea. I can't stand that they wouldn't tell me. But let's not talk about it, Quinn. Rowan is a cold calculating scientist in many respects, but Rowan has a conscience made out of pure gold. Let's just talk about us.'

"I put my arms around her. Pure gold. The image struck me. Pure gold. I thought of the mausoleum and the mysterious stranger telling me that the mausoleum was made of gold.

" 'There's no way in the world you could run off to Europe with me,' I said. 'You need the treatment that Dr. Rowan is giving you at the medical center, don't you?'

"She sighed. She nodded. 'It was a dream, running away. They're giving me hormone treatments and all kinds of nutrients, I don't know. I'm in and out all during the week. I'm wired up for two and three hours at a stretch. I don't think there's much progress. I wanted to fly away. It was wrong of me to involve you in my dream, to let you believe it with me for a little while.'

" 'I don't mind,' I said. 'I don't have to go. In fact, I won't go. Not as long as we can see each other, and I think they trust us now. I think they know that I won't hurt you, and you know it too.'

"There came a rap at the door.

"Time for supper, and I was cordially invited to join them downstairs. In fact, they wouldn't hear of my not joining them, and after a quick call to Jasmine to report my whereabouts I appeared in the dining room to find Mona—attired in another gorgeous white shirt with billowing sleeves, this time over a tropical print miniskirt-shorts combination that was, if anything, more sexy than her bare panties had been earlier—and Michael and Rowan, somewhat formally attired.

"Michael looked quite the gentleman in his seersucker three-piece suit, and Rowan wore a lovely simple navy blue dress with a bold triple strand of pearls.

"Only on second glance did it register that Mona had put on Aunt Queen's cameo and that it looked beautiful at her throat.

"To my utter amazement Stirling Oliver of the Talamasca had come to join us and in keeping with the mild late spring weather he wore a white three-piece suit with a lemon yellow tie. I remember that tie for some reason. I don't know why. I remember men's ties. His gray hair was clipped short, combed straight back from his temples, and he looked like a man in his sixties of excellent health.

"They were all vivid impressive people and the house in no way overpowered them or diminished their easy charm.

"I was very glad to see Stirling again and had a strong sense that Aunt Queen would be disturbed if she knew. As it was I had little choice in the matter and that felt very comfortable for me.

" 'I saw your friend, Goblin, outside,' he said confidentially, as he shook my hand. 'He indicated you wished to be on your own.'

" 'Are you serious?' I asked. 'Did you really see him and talk to him?'

" 'Yes, he was right by the gate. He was very strong, but you must realize my talents for such perception are, if anything, rather over-developed. For me the world's a crowded place.'

" 'Was he angry or bitter?' I asked.

" 'Neither,' he said, 'but rather glad to be seen.'

"At this point Mona spoke up, taking our arms as she interposed, 'Why don't I invite him in? We'll make a place at the table for him?'

" 'No, not tonight,' I said. 'I want to be selfish. He has his moments. This is one of mine.'

"The dinner went on swimmingly, with lots of conversation about whether I should in fact go to Europe, and Michael felt that there comes in each person's life a perfect time to go to Europe and one can go either too early or too late. I agreed with that heartily and then dared to ask if it was at all possible for Mona to go if Aunt Queen would agree to bring another female chaperone dedicated entirely to Mona, and I made it clear in euphemisms, which the august dining room seemed to require, that I would never risk Mona's health or well-being for cheap lust.

"I hope I made half the potent figure that I tried to be. When only Mona consented to everything I said, Rowan went on to state matter-of-factly that Mona couldn't be away from Mayfair Medical at this time, it was simply out of the question, and that if it was at all possible she and Michael would take Mona to Europe so that Mona could have the experience again.

"In fact, Mona went on to explain that it had been on her trip to Europe that her 'condition' had been discovered and the tour had been cut short for that reason and she had come home to undergo intense study at the medical center, plus injections of hormones and nutrients and other drugs as well.

"Throughout, nobody mentioned Mona's mysterious child. And I didn't mention the mysterious stranger.

"We went into the double parlor after the supper and there I drank more brandy than I should. But I fixed the situation with a call to Clem to come get me in Aunt Queen's stretch limousine, with Allen to drive the Mercedes home, which worked out very well, since Aunt Queen was 'entertaining' in her room.

"Michael and Rowan showed no letup of interest in me, or if they did I was a perfect fool. Stirling Oliver was affable and curious as well. We talked about seeing ghosts and I told them all the entire story of Rebecca, again using all the appropriate euphemisms, which the parlor seemed to require. I had the feeling in my semidrunken pride that Mona was enjoying all of this.

"Her eyes were glistening and she never once interrupted me, which struck me as amazing given how very brilliant I found her to be. When she did talk it was to bring me out for Rowan and Michael and Stirling, or to bring them out to me. Of the three, Michael was by far the more talkative and the more given to laughing at himself, though Stirling had a great sense of humor, but Rowan was modest for a doctor, and, as I had found her in the afternoon, her husky voice was much warmer and sweeter than her finely angled face.

"She had the sharp gray eyes of a beauty, and one could believe she was a neurosurgeon by the look of her long tapering hands. Michael was the older one, the rugged one, the one who had worked on 'this house' with his hammer and nails. He spoke of feeling its embrace and of loving its shining floors and its creaks and groans in the small hours. And all of these three alluded modestly and naturally to having seen ghosts.

"Stirling talked of a childhood full of spirits in an English castle. And of discovering the Talamasca during his university years at Cambridge. Michael spoke of nearly drowning off the coast of San Francisco and being rescued by, of all people, Rowan, and of his having come through it with a power to know certain paranormal things through touch.

"Mona told them all laughingly that Oncle Julien had ransacked the pantry for Royal Antoinette to serve me the hot chocolate, and I told them about the poem by Christopher Morley which I had loved so as a child, and about the cocoa and animal crackers, which I had altogether forgotten to tell any of them until then, and they were impressed with it, and we speculated as to how spirits make up what they do.

" 'But it means God exists, doesn't it?' asked Mona. There was the most poignant tone in her voice.

" 'God or the Devil,' said Dr. Rowan.

" 'Oh, it would be too cruel if the Devil existed without God,' said Mona.

" 'I don't think so,' said Rowan. 'I think it's entirely possible.'

" 'Nonsense, Rowan,' said Michael. 'God exists and God is love.' And with a very deliberate nod to Mona he cautioned Rowan, and I saw at that moment that Mona was looking anxiously away. Then Mona spoke up.

" 'I guess I'll know soon,' she said, 'or I'll know nothing. That's the hard part. Blinking out like a burnt-out bulb.'

" 'That's not going to happen,' I said. 'When you have your treatments at Mayfair Medical, is it tiresome? Can I come and sit with you? Is it possible we could talk or I could read to you? What is it like?'

" 'That would be lovely,' said Rowan, 'until you get tired of it, which would happen at some point.'

" 'Rowan, for the love of Heaven,' said Michael. 'What's gotten into you?'

"Mona started to laugh. 'Yes, Quinn,' she said, laughing still, 'I have to be there for hours. I take the treatments intravenously, that's why I wear long sleeves, to hide the marks. It would be wonderful if you were with me. It doesn't have to be every time. And Rowan's right. When you get tired, I'll understand.'

" 'I'm ashamed that I've never asked if I could visit you during these treatments,' said Stirling. 'We've had so many suppers at the Grand Luminière Café. Why, it never crossed my mind.'

" 'And don't think that you have to,' said Mona. 'I watch the worst television imaginable. I'm hooked on vintage sitcoms. Don't give it another thought.'

"I wanted to vow that I would never get tired. I would bring flowers, and books of poetry to read. But I knew that the realist among us would think all this very lame, and so I let it go for the moment, thinking that later, when it came time to leave, I would ask when I could see Mona again.

" 'I know one thing,' Mona announced, quite suddenly. 'When it comes my time to die, I don't want it to be at Mayfair Medical. I still cherish my dream of going out like Ophelia, on a boat of flowers in a softly running stream.'

" 'I don't think it works very well,' said Michael. 'I think the flowers and the floating part of it are wonderful, but then comes the drowning and it's not so peaceful at all.'

" 'Well, then, I'll settle for a bed of flowers,' she said. 'But there has to be a lot of them, you know, and no tubes and needles and bottles of morphine and such things as that. I can imagine the water as long as I'm on a bed of flowers. And there are no doctors around.'

" 'I promise,' said Michael.

"Dr. Rowan said nothing.

"It was an extraordinary moment. I was horrified. But I didn't dare to speak.

" 'Come on, everybody, I'm so sorry I made it glum,' said Mona. 'Quinn, let me cheer you up. Have you ever read *Hamlet*? Will you read it to me sometime at Mayfair Medical?'

" 'I'd love to,' I responded.

"We had all seen Kenneth Branagh's landmark film of *Hamlet* and we'd loved it, and of course I knew the Ophelia underwater scene so very well. It had been a still shot after Gertrude's long description, all of it beautifully done, due to the fact that Branagh is a genius, we all agreed. I wanted to tell them all about Fr. Kevin's warning about speaking to ghosts, based on what happened to Hamlet, but I wasn't sure how I felt about it so I let it slide.

"The remainder of the evening was marvelous. We talked of so many things. Michael Curry loved books, the way that my old teacher Lynelle had loved them, and he thought it was fabulous that I had a new teacher in Nash Penfield, and he thought it perfectly fine that I had never gone to school.

"Rowan agreed wholeheartedly that I had probably missed nothing, that except for a certain margin of affluent American kids who occupy a tiny portion of the classes in ultrafine schools, 'organized educational experience' was more painful and unprofitable than anything else.

"Stirling Oliver thought it incredibly wonderful that I was getting such an intense education, wondering aloud what it would be like if so many others could have the same benefits. As for Tommy, whom I described to everyone, everyone believed that he and his brothers and sisters should be given 'every chance.' It wasn't playing God to show them another world.

"I was very surprised by all this, and in a very real way I did not want to go home. I wanted to live in this house with Michael and Rowan and Mona forever. I wanted to know Stirling forever. But in another way, I couldn't wait to go home. I couldn't wait to be 'me' again, because I had been so strongly accepted. I wanted to tell Nash and Aunt Queen about it. I wanted to set about my studies with Nash. I wanted to set up my visits with Mona. I wanted once more to postpone my trip abroad.

"Now as to that—postponing my trip—Michael had a suggestion. Why not go for a couple of weeks? 'One can see a lot of Europe in that time,' he told me. 'And if you have to choose one country then let me suggest either England or Italy. Either one will send you back transformed.'

"Everybody seemed to think it was a good idea. Stirling and Rowan also suggested Italy. I had to admit it was a good idea. It would quiet Aunt Queen's desires for me for a little while and Mona would be waiting, she vowed, to hear of all my adventures when I returned.

"Meantime, Clem had come for me, and though the conversation was moving along fiercely, with Michael describing his own visit to Italy, I knew it was time to go.

"Besides, I was really getting drunk.

"On the front porch I took Mona in my arms, vowing to call her the next day and get the times during which she would let me visit with her at Mayfair Medical.

" 'I spend my life there, egregious and beautiful boy,' she said. 'Pick a time, any time.'

" 'When do your spirits flag?'

" 'Four o'clock. I'm so tired of it. I begin to cry.'

" 'I'll come at two and stay with you as long as you allow.'

" 'That will be till six,' she said. 'Then we have dinner in the Grand Luminière Café.'

" 'You can dismiss me then or have my attendance, as you wish. I come with no strings attached.'

" 'You really do love me, don't you?'

" 'Passionately and undyingly.'

"Our final kisses were long and lingering, and drunkenly sweet.

"Then Michael Curry saw me to the gate, which did need a key to unlock it.

"He took me in his arms. He held me tight, and he kissed me, European-style, on each cheek. 'You're a good boy, Quinn,' he said.

" 'Thank you, Michael,' I said. 'I really adore her.'

"As soon as Goblin and I were securely in the back of the limousine I burst into tears.

"On and on we drove, and I couldn't stop crying. And as we crossed the black waters of Lake Pontchartrain, Goblin put his arms around me and he said in his low voice, rather like Ariel in *The Tempest*, 'I'm sorry, Quinn; if I were human, I would cry too.' "

32

"IT HAD BEEN some time since Aunt Queen had held Full Court in her bedroom, or boudoir, as we called it on such occasions, but when I entered the house I was informed by an exquisitely dressed Jasmine—read slinky black cocktail dress and murderous high heels—that this was a special night.

"She was entertaining Nash, of course, because the two were getting on far better than Aunt Queen had ever dreamed, but also a visitor had arrived with gifts of stunning cameos such as Aunt Queen had never beheld. Jasmine threw in a bit of mockery with a roll of her eyes and a lift of her eyebrows. 'All carved out of jewels,' she said.

"I was solemnly requested to go upstairs, freshen up, put on my best black Italian suit with handmade English shirt and Church's shoes and come down to meet the bearer of the stunning gifts. Since I was already pretty much dressed this didn't involve much inconvenience.

"As to the courtly life, I welcomed the distraction. The liquor I'd drunk had worn off and left me electrified with love and concern for Mona, and I could not possibly have fallen asleep. The night seemed my enemy, with my frightened Goblin no doubt hovering near, and I wanted the lights and cheerful conversation of Aunt Queen's room.

" 'Come, Goblin,' I said, 'let's do this together. We've been apart too much lately, you know it. Come with me.'

" 'Evil, Quinn,' he responded, with a sad face, which surprised me. Evil in Aunt Queen's room? But he was dressed as I was, down to the hand-stitching of his collar and the lacquer of his shoe leather, and he came with me down the stairs. I felt his right hand in my left. I felt a gentle pressure, and then I felt his soft lips against my cheek.

" 'I love you, Quinn,' he said.

" 'And I love you, Goblin,' I replied.

"All this was very unexpected, as was the invitation to visit with Aunt Queen. I hoped the night would continue to give me wonderful things. I hoped I wouldn't have to crash suddenly amid the knowledge that Mona was seriously sick and that she might not survive her illness, that that was exactly what she and her family had been trying to tell me all during the lively dinner, and Rowan Mayfair's one outbreak of pessimism had been a sharp admission of the truth.

"What had Mona said, 'blinking out like a dim bulb.'

"All was light and laughter in Blackwood Manor. A group of the guests were at the piano in the double parlor, and in the dining room yet another little group played cards.

"I passed all this with a cheerful smile and a wave and headed for the back bedroom, finding the door ajar and pushing it wide slowly to announce my presence to the convivial group inside.

"They made a circle, the company, with Aunt Queen in her glory, clothed in one of her priceless feathered white negligees, with a wide white ribbon and a glorious cameo on her bare throat. Her high heels were as always much in evidence, and right opposite her sat Nash, in black tie for the occasion, who stood up as I entered as if I merited such a thing, when I did not.

"Cindy, the nurse, was there in her crisp white uniform and she rose too, to deposit kisses on my cheek, which made me very happy.

"And then I saw, in full clarity, the guest of honor, the generous bringer of fine cameos, the newcomer to Blackwood Manor, who sat at the very opposite of me and did not rise and had no reason to rise as our eyes met.

"At first I simply could not identify what I saw. I knew but I did not know. I understood but I did not understand. All was abundantly clear. Nothing was clear at all. Then very gradually my mind absorbed the details, and do let me record them here so as to brand them into your mind, so as to make them plain to you as they came to be plain to me.

"That this was the mysterious stranger I had no doubt. I knew the shape of the head. I knew the shape and cut of the shoulders. I knew the high square forehead with its beautifully rounded temples, and the black eyebrows and the large black eyes. I knew the long mouth and the smile. I even knew the long black hair.

"But it wasn't tied back now, this hair. No, it was a wealth of gorgeous waves and curls, tumbled down over the stranger's shoulders. And it was perfectly obvious from the taut cut of the mysterious stranger's black satin vest that the mysterious stranger had large full breasts. But the rest of the black tie ensemble of dinner jacket and trousers indicated a man's body, and indeed the mysterious stranger, despite having glowing skin and rouged lips, was about six feet tall and did have a rather firm jaw.

"Was this a man? Was this a woman? I had no idea.

"And whatever it was, it sat there—sideways on the chair, with its right arm on the high back and its long legs comfortably in front of it and its left hand in its lap—challenging me with its silence, with its sly smile, as Aunt Queen reached for that slack hand, saying:

" 'Quinn darling, come here and meet Petronia. She's brought me the most exquisite cameos, and she made them herself.'

"Shock. Heart-pounding shock. Fury and delirium combined in me as never before.

" 'The pleasure's all mine, Petronia,' I said. I felt all the liquor I'd drunk rising in me again. 'But you are very beautiful, let me be so bold as to tell you. Having seen you twice or thrice by moonlight, before this moment, I could only guess.'

" 'How generous of you,' she answered me, and I heard exactly the voice I'd heard in my ear last night, hushed and soft. Of course it was female. Or was it? 'And you, just come from your red-haired vixen,' she went on. 'One would have expected to find you quite blinded by her light.'

" 'She's not a vixen in any sense,' I declared, my face burning. 'But don't let me be wearisome defending her. It's a pleasure that you and I are now properly introduced.'

"She turned, laughing under her breath to Aunt Queen.

" 'He is quite the versatile gentleman,' she said. She looked back at me, the eyes flashing. 'I rather thought I would like you if we came to really know each other. And do stop trying to determine if I am a man or a woman. The fact is I'm a good part both and therefore neither one. I was just explaining to your Aunt Queen. I was born endowed with the finest traits of both sexes and I drift this way and that as I choose.'

"Nash had brought a chair for me to join the circle. Jasmine had poured the champagne in my tulip glass. I sat down across from this spectacle, this creature, and I felt Goblin take hold of my shoulder.

" 'Caution, Quinn,' he said to me. And well he might because I was dangerously feverish of mind and soul and once again drunk. I was appalled by what was happening and monstrously exhilarated.

"I saw the mysterious stranger's eyes shoot to my left where Goblin stood, but she could not see Goblin. She only knew that Goblin was there.

" 'So you think of me as a woman,' she said to me now. 'Forgive me for reading your mind, it's a trait I can't seem to keep in harness. Once one is blessed with such a gift it runs rampant.'

" 'Really,' said Aunt Queen, 'you mean it's quite spontaneous? You simply hear people's thoughts.'

" 'Some people more than others,' she said. 'Quinn's thoughts come rather glaringly clear to me. And what a brilliant young man you are.'

" 'So people tell me,' I said. 'And how is it that the mausoleum on Sugar Devil Island bears your name?'

" 'It's the name of Petronia's great-great-grandmother, Quinn,' said Aunt Queen, obviously trying to take the sharp edge off my foray into the conversation. 'We've been talking about this very person, and about the subject of reincarnation. Petronia is a great believer in it, and that it happens over and over in her family, and of a time in ancient Pompeii, she has strange dreams.'

"A terrible sense of foreboding came over me. *Ancient Pompeii.*

"Goblin was squeezing my hand. The mysterious stranger was looking at me, and I could have sworn I saw Mount Vesuvius above the city as it roared and belched its fatal cloud Heavenward, pitching the city into panic far below. People ran screaming through the narrow streets. The earth moved. The cloud covered the sky. *I saw it.* Petronia was staring at me. We were there and we were here. Aunt Queen was talking. The rain of ash became a torrent.

"I was dizzy. Yes, dizzy, the fatal symptom.

" 'What are your strange dreams of ancient Pompeii?' asked Nash in his wonderful deep voice.

" 'Oh, they're truly tragic,' came her low voice in response. 'I see myself a slave girl in those times, a worker of cameos, the chief among a shop of such craftsmen, and my master has warned us all of the coming eruption, and I run through the streets trying to warn the citizens. Get out of the city. The mountain will bring disaster. But they don't believe. They don't heed.'

"I could see it as she spoke. I could see her, with her long full black hair, yet in a male's tunic, running through the narrow stone streets, banging on doors, grabbing people by the shoulders. 'Get out, get out now. The mountain's erupting. It will destroy the city. There's no time left.'

"I could see the buildings close around her, a little city of plastered walls, and she such a curious tall monstrous beauty. And no one listening. And finally, she took the slaves from their workbench. No. I didn't just see it. I was there!

"Into sacks they put the cameos. 'No time for that!' she said. 'Run!' We were all of us—slaves, free men, women screaming, children—running towards the shore. The roar of the mountain was monstrous and deafening. I saw the black cloud spread out over the sky. The day vanished. The night descended. We had climbed into a boat, and we were rowed out fast over the choppy waters of the bay. Crowded boats surrounded us. Again came the voice of the mountain. And then the flicker of fire in the darkness. Pompeii was soon to die.

"She sat in the boat. I was with her. She was crying. Huge rocks were rolling down the mountain. People were running from the huge rocks. Chaos on the heaving shores. The earth shook beneath those who tried to flee in their chariots. She wouldn't stop sobbing. The other cameo makers looked back in pure fascination. The rain of ash came down upon the city, upon the water. The waters of the bay were black. Boats were rocking. Boats were capsizing. The rowers went faster. We were moving out of the zone of danger. We were crossing the bay to safety. But the horror hovered over us. The mountain bellowed and spewed its deadly poisons. In the boat I held her trembling hand. She sobbed, she sobbed for those who wouldn't listen, who wouldn't run when she told them; she sobbed for the lost cameos, the lost treasures. She sobbed for the city fast disappearing in an evil mist of ashes and smoke.

" 'I'm not there!' I told myself. I tried to move my lips and speak aloud, tried to push against this vision, tried to come back from it, tried to know where I was, yet I didn't want to leave her sobbing in the boat, and all around were the other boats and people wailing and crying and shouting and pointing. My eyes were burning. And the night covered the day, as if forever, and without hope.

"Then came the electric shock of Goblin's hand. He had slipped his fingers into my left hand as he so often did, and I opened my eyes. I looked at her, and I saw her and heard her low voice running on like a low brook as she spoke to Aunt Queen.

" 'These strange dreams,' she said, 'they lead me to believe I once lived there, knew the people, suffered, died. I was as I am now, part male, part female; I loved nothing so much as making cameos. I was committed to it with a fascination that was total. I don't know how those who have no fascination live.'

"My heart beat wildly inside of me, but I couldn't shake the dizziness. I looked at Nash. I saw that his eyes were filmed over. Even Aunt Queen appeared dazed and wide-eyed as she stared at this being, this tall big-breasted creature with her raiment of long black hair.

"I shuddered. I would shake off this languor, this spell. I wouldn't be imprisoned by it, no. I did the most impulsive thing. I reached out, with Goblin's hand tucked over mine, and I motioned to clasp the hand of Petronia, and she, seeing this, accepted my hand and then pulled her hand back sharply, as sharply as if she'd been stung by a bee, all from Goblin's touch.

"I heard Goblin's secret laughter. 'Evil, Quinn,' he said to me. 'Evil!'

"Petronia's eyes searched for him but couldn't see him.

"I glanced at Goblin and saw him fully realized and saw him afraid. And then he said to me words that explained everything and nothing.

" 'Not alive.'

"What I had felt was even more baffling—a spirit thing like Goblin, electric, powerful, ready to form a current through Goblin to me. I couldn't grasp the principles of it really. But it was supercharged and terrifying. And the rage came back to me. How dare this being play with me? How dare he play with us all?

"Meantime, her voice was moving on in a hushed manner: 'And so I took up the art of making them because I loved them, and knowing of your love, I had to bring these few to you to keep with your others. It's been a long time since I visited the island, and of course the story came down to me of how my great-great-grandmother had wanted to be buried there, though it never did come to pass.'

" 'No, it never did, did it?' I said. 'And last night you caught me outside in a choke hold and you told me what you wanted done with the Hermitage, didn't you? And before that, you broke into my very room and dragged me from my bed!'

"I stood up, comfortably towering over her, as she looked up at me, smiling.

" 'I saw you dump those bodies,' I said. 'I know you did it. And you come here to be received by the person dearest to me in all the world!'

" 'Quinn, darling,' cried Aunt Queen, 'have you lost your mind!'

" 'Aunt Queen, this is the very person! I tell you this is the mysterious stranger. This is the one!'

"Nash was on his feet too and attempting to take me by the shoulders and turn me aside, and very slowly Petronia rose to her full height of over six feet, and with every inch over six feet grew out of femininity and into manhood, looking at me quietly with a gloating satisfaction in her pretty smile.

"Aunt Queen was frantic.

"Nash was begging me to be quiet.

" 'Deny it, I dare you,' I said. 'Say you didn't come into my very room and drag me from my bed.'

" 'Mrs. McQueen,' he answered. 'I did not come into this house at any time before tonight.'

" ' "My honored Lord, you know right well you did," ' I flashed on him from Ophelia in *Hamlet.* 'You came into my room. You accosted me outside. You made threats. You know you did. You come here to torment me. That has to be the reason. You play with me. It's a game that amuses you. It began with those bodies, dumped in the moonlight, when you knew I stood on the island and saw you there.'

" 'Quinn, silence!' Aunt Queen declared. Never had I heard such a cry from her, such a total command. 'I won't have it,' she said. She was shaking.

" 'Let me take my leave quietly,' said Petronia. She took Aunt Queen's hand.

" 'I am so sorry,' Aunt Queen said. 'So dreadfully, dreadfully sorry.'

" 'You've been very gracious to me,' she said in the same feminized voice. 'I'll never forget it.'

"He turned his pretty face to me, and I saw the woman in him, and then he was gone, with straight shoulders and big long strides, gorgeous hair flying, and I heard the heavy vibration of the big front door.

"All those around me were shocked. Cindy, the nurse, was full of concern. Nash didn't know what he should do or for whom to do it. And I sat down, knowing I was drunk and that I was going to be sick, and Aunt Queen stared at me with blazing anger and disappointment in her eyes. Jasmine was shaking her head.

"Finally, sinking down into her armchair, Aunt Queen spoke:

" 'Do you honestly expect anyone to believe the things you are saying?'

" 'It's all true,' I said. 'How in the world could you believe her instead of me? What did she tell you—that she was man and woman, so much of each that she was neither one? You believe that? And that she believes in reincarnation? You believe that? That she made the cameos she gave you? You believe that? And that the mausoleum on the island was made for her great-great-grandmother. You believe that? I'm telling you, she came at me. Or he came to me. And he has the strength of a man, that I can vouch for. And he does read minds and that's dangerous. And all the rest I've said—all along—is true.'

"Aunt Queen couldn't look at me. Cindy brought her a hot toddy. It sort of sat there in the cup. Aunt Queen asked:

" 'Where were you tonight?'

" 'I had dinner with the Mayfairs,' I said. 'I went over at two p.m.' I stopped. But what was the point of holding back? I had to tell Aunt Queen everything, didn't I? She had to know the full measure of what I felt. And so I blurted it out:

" 'I saw a ghost while I was there. I spoke with him. I talked with him for twenty minutes or more without knowing he was a ghost. It was the ghost of Julien Mayfair, and he told me he had conjugal knowledge of Grandfather William's wife, and I'm descended from him.'

"Aunt Queen sighed. 'You are stark raving mad.'

" 'Not raving,' I said. 'I became a bit heated, yes, at the effrontery of that creature, but not raving, not really raving. That's a far worse state, wouldn't you say?'

" 'What do I do?' she asked.

" 'Let me call Stirling Oliver. Maybe he can vouch for my sanity. He sees Goblin. He was at dinner tonight. I must see him and talk to him. I must tell him my feelings as regards that creature! I must talk to him. I don't feel safe. I don't feel anyone is safe from that creature. He'll help you to understand.'

" 'And you think I'm the one,' she asked, 'who needs the understanding?'

" 'I don't know, Aunt Queen. I want to kill that creature, that's all I can say. And there's something very vile and awful about the being. It isn't merely that it's a hermaphrodite, that I could well endure and find fascinating. It's something else. Goblin senses it. Goblin calls it evil. I tell you the creature frightens me. You must understand, at least that I believe what I'm saying even if you do not.'

"She wouldn't look at me.

"I went into the bathroom. I was sick. After a while I was able to drink a paper cup of water. And then I came out. They were all there, in the same state of shock as when I left them. I apologized to everyone.

" 'But you have to see it,' I said, 'from my point of view. You have to understand what my experience of this creature was. And then I come home and find him with my Aunt Queen.'

"Nash made the kind suggestion that perhaps I ought to go to bed. I looked very tired indeed. I agreed to it immediately, but I couldn't let it go without stating that the stranger, alias Petronia, was no great respecter of my being in or out of bed.

"But when I bent down to kiss Aunt Queen, she was loving to me, and I was as tender with her as ever, and I told her that I had really told the truth.

" 'We will call Mr. Oliver,' she said. 'We'll ask him to come here tomorrow. And we'll talk to him. How would that be?'

" 'I love you so much,' I whispered. 'And there's so much I want to tell you about Mona.'

" 'Tomorrow, my darling,' she said.

"I could hardly drag myself up the stairs. And as soon as I had the comfort of the soft flannel nightshirt I was dreaming of Mona, with my arm around Big Ramona, and thoughts of talking to Nash running randomly through my mind. Every now and then I'd wake with a start, fearing Petronia was on me, strange evil Petronia, bent on hurting me, bent on destroying me, but it was only drunken imagination and finally I went into a deep comforting sleep."

33

"I T WAS about nine a.m. when I called Stirling, and, unable to contain myself, spilled out all of the story of recent events, as I invited him to dinner to discuss them in greater detail. Perhaps I wanted him to know this was a loaded invitation. I thought it only fair.

"He surprised me. He insisted that we meet for lunch. He asked if it wouldn't be too inconvenient if we gathered at twelve noon. I went down to see Aunt Queen immediately. And finding her already awake, sitting up in her chaise lounge, watching a movie, saying her Rosary and eating strawberry ice cream, I was happy to have her agreement to lunch right away.

"Would Stirling come to Blackwood Manor? Of course.

"As Blackwood Manor was booked solid, we set up the small table in Aunt Queen's room, and her bed was dressed in its finest satin along with a broad collection of her red-cheeked boudoir dolls, all got up in the flapper attire that Aunt Queen herself so much adored.

"Stirling arrived promptly at five minutes before twelve, though his flowers, a huge vase of pink roses, arrived before him, and we gathered in Aunt Queen's room for Jasmine's finest veal scallopini and pasta and white wine. Nash, who offered several times to absent himself, joined us, and to my amazement Aunt Queen started right in with the 'strange tale' of Petronia and how she or he—it varied during the story because at times Aunt Queen had seen Petronia differently—had arrived at Blackwood Manor with the gift of the cameos, which were then produced for Stirling's inspection.

"Now this was the first time that I had seen these priceless pieces myself, and priceless they were. Because they were not cameos in the sense that we think of them, that is, ornaments carved from contrasting strata of shell or stone. They were portraits carved from gems, and in this case the gems were large amethysts and emeralds of Brazilian origin, and whereas amethysts are no longer very expensive gems, due to the discovery of such a supply of them in the New World, emeralds are expensive. And the carving of these small heads, each obviously of a particular Roman deity, was excellent if not absolutely magnificent.

"They were four in number, these gifts, and Aunt Queen had of course been incredibly grateful for this tribute, and then I had come home and pitched the gathering into confusion, as she was sure I was willing to explain.

"I did explain. I started at the beginning. I explained everything. I ate veal and pasta and guzzled white wine, forgetting to blot my lips before drinking and thereby going through two and three wineglasses before remembering, but I was passionately pouring out my tale, beginning with Rebecca and her visions and how they had driven me to the island, and what I had seen there in the moonlight, and how things had spun out from there, and how in a rage I had burnt the trespasser's books, and how he or she had come at me, and on it went. I left out nothing.

"Jasmine brought plate after plate of veal and pasta for me. I was happy to devour it.

" 'So there you see it,' I said. 'And then you have Goblin saying "Evil, Quinn," in my ear, and then that shock when I take Petronia's hand, that feeling of something like electricity that reaches out for Goblin and travels through Goblin to me! And this thing, this being, this creature, this interloper who threatens me, he can't see Goblin but he knows that Goblin is there. He knows Goblin can send showering glass at him, and for all his speed and strength, he doesn't want to be cut.'

"At last I came to a halt. I knew Aunt Queen and Nash were watching me. I knew they were watching Stirling as well.

" 'No,' said Stirling quietly. He had finished his meal in spite of many many pauses in which he had stared at me with rapt attention. 'It doesn't want to be cut.'

" 'Do you say "it," on account of her ambiguous sexuality?' asked Nash politely. There was some subtle tension between Nash and Stirling. I couldn't figure it.

" 'No, I don't think so,' said Stirling. 'I hope not. But who knows? Let me say, she does not want to be cut.'

" 'Do you believe my nephew?' Aunt Queen asked. 'Does all of this make any sense to you?' She was very kind in her tone. She sat to my right and pressed my shoulder softly as she spoke. 'My nephew is prepared for what you have to say.'

" 'Yes, I am prepared,' I said. 'I know you to be a frank and truthful person. Michael and Rowan respect you. Mona respects you. I know what I see in you. Tell me what you believe.'

" 'Very well,' said Stirling. He took another swallow of his wine and set the glass aside. 'Let me advise you first as if you were my son. Go away now. Take the trip with your Aunt Queen that she wants you to take. No, don't be upset with me. Let me explain. Mona Mayfair is sick. But she may get sicker. The time to leave Mona is now. You will obviously write to her, call her, stay in touch with her. And when and if she takes the turn for the worse, perhaps with your aunt's permission you can come home.'

" 'Oh, absolutely,' said Aunt Queen. 'I think that's a very sensible way of looking at it, and we can ascertain from Dr. Winn Mayfair whether or not he agrees. We can talk to Dr. Rowan Mayfair. And of course, Quinn, you'll speak to Mona herself.'

" 'Now, let me explain further,' said Stirling. 'I think you should leave on this trip at once. I think you should get away from Petronia. I think you should leave tonight if you can, and if not tonight then tomorrow, and if not tomorrow the day after that. But go. And go quickly, and in the meantime, have all the refurbishments done to the Hermitage on the island, exactly as the creature has insisted, but never, and I mean, never, have a workman on Sugar Devil Island after dark.'

" 'Well, that's no problem,' I said hastily. 'These guys come on at six a.m. and they want to be home in front of the television with a beer in hand by four o'clock in the afternoon.'

"But my speedy rejoinder hadn't taken the edge off Aunt Queen's response to this last remark on the part of Stirling, as I had hoped.

" 'You're saying that everything Quinn saw . . . happened?' she asked.

" 'Yes, I am saying that,' said Stirling. 'He's sane; if he testified in a court of law, I'd believe him. I believe him here and now.'

" 'Stirling Oliver,' said Aunt Queen, 'are you telling me that the swamps hereabouts are infested with vampires?'

" 'No, I'm not telling you that, Mrs. McQueen, because if I did, you'd think me mad and disregard everything else that I told you. Let's just say that Petronia is a creature of nocturnal habits and accustomed to having Sugar Devil Island to herself. Now, one night when she thought herself to be alone, she was caught up short by the landlord, and consequently began a game of cat and mouse with him, and has been his enemy ever since.'

" 'You do believe all this,' Aunt Queen said.

" 'Oh, definitely. But the important thing is this. Do what the creature wants right now. Refurbish the Hermitage. And remove Quinn from the vicinity. Take the trip to Europe. And expect to have big long-distance phone bills in every hotel. This young man is very much in love with Mona Mayfair, that I know full well from what I saw with my own eyes.'

" 'I don't know what to say to you, Mr. Oliver,' Aunt Queen responded. She was discouraged. But I was overwhelmingly glad to be believed, though not to leave Mona for a moment.

" 'Mrs. McQueen,' said Stirling. 'It is best that Quinn leave here with you now, you know that. The refurbishing of the island can well take place without him, and if he never sees Petronia again, all the better for him, surely you agree.'

" 'Yes, I do.'

" 'Then forgive me for this, but I'm going to say something to you which is going to make it simpler for Quinn to come to his decision. Please believe that I use this power respectfully.'

" 'Which power is this?'

" 'The same one Petronia claimed to have,' said Stirling, 'and when I came into this room today I used it, accidentally as always, unwillingly as always. But I couldn't help but know that your doctor had been here earlier, and he had told you that this trip to Europe would have to be your very last.'

" 'Oh, dear,' she sighed. 'I didn't want Quinn to know.'

" 'But I *should* know!' I said at once. I was chilled to the bone. 'Aunt Queen, we're going! I had no idea the doctor was here. I just have to discuss this with Mona; Mona will understand everything.' My heart ached.

"Jasmine appeared out of nowhere at this opportune moment and declared with full authority, 'That doctor said there should be no trip to Europe, that's what he said! And then Aunt Queen said she was going and then that doctor said this trip had to be her last, that's what happened here this morning, I know because I heard!'

" 'We'll go,' I declared. 'We'll all go together, and we'll stay as long as we can.' Oh my precious Mona, what else can I do?

" 'It's the best thing,' said Stirling. 'You asked me to come here, to listen to these stories, and I tell you, based on all I've heard, including this unforgivable little mental eavesdropping, that you should take Quinn away from here, away from Petronia's temper and whims and go. You have a great prize to give your nephew in this trip. Give it to him while you can. And give it to yourself. You deserve to have this great gift from him.'

" 'Yes, that's so true, Aunt Queen,' I said. 'Stirling, you're a magician with words. You've teased out the truth of it. We're going. I only need to talk to Mona.'

" 'Well, I think this is a marvelous resolution,' said Aunt Queen, 'but I'm still left with questions. Stirling, you speak as if you know of Petronia—.'

" 'No, I know nothing of her. I've never heard her name. I was judging from your story. All the elements were there to drive me to my conclusion that her tastes were nocturnal. Why else would she have agreed to split the usage of the Hermitage with Quinn, he for day, and she for night, were she not fond of the swamp after dark when few people like it save those who hunt for alligators, I suppose? As for the rest of her habits, she seems vicious and violent, and Quinn showed an enormous amount of courage in confronting her. I would imagine she left here very surprised last night.'

" 'She looked triumphant,' I said. 'She'd made me out to be a lunatic.'

" 'But you're not a lunatic,' said Stirling.

" 'No, you're not,' said Aunt Queen. 'I'm immensely relieved. You're not. But Stirling, you speak of her as though she's a species of creature.'

" 'I didn't mean to do that,' he said. 'That was unwise of me. I meant to disclose a feeling of impersonality by using that word, I suppose. As I said, I was trying to judge purely from the things you told me. I believe she's a menace to Quinn and she'll keep toying with him if you remain here. The important thing is to go away.'

" 'Nash, what do you think?' Aunt Queen asked.

"Of course Nash demurred. It wasn't really his place to comment, but Aunt Queen pressed him, as he had met Petronia and he had witnessed some of what had gone on.

" 'Quinn seems more than sane,' Nash explained in his deep commanding voice. 'I have to agree. As to the trip to Europe, I think it's a marvelous idea. Now, Petronia, I must say that her theories on reincarnation gave me pause. She claimed herself to have lived in ancient Pompeii as we have discussed, and she spoke of witnessing the eruption of Vesuvius, and I must confess that I experienced a faint, what would you call it, a faint . . .'

" 'Disorientation,' I said immediately.

" 'Yes, exactly, I experienced a disorientation while she was talking, as though she were a hypnotist. It wasn't entirely comfortable. And it left me with a feeling of confusion that I didn't much like. I would never have mentioned it, except that you've asked me. But I can say in conclusion that Petronia seemed otherwise to be charming and perhaps, perhaps a little sly.'

" 'How so sly?' asked Aunt Queen.

" 'When a person hypnotizes a whole room, yet never acknowledges it, there is a slyness there,' said Nash. 'Don't you think?'

"I was very impressed with these statements. I had expected Nash to claim neutrality, and I loved him now more than ever before.

"Lunch was concluded, but not before I had eaten all the veal and pasta on Goblin's plate, with his respectfully requested permission, and Jasmine and Big Ramona cleared away both dishes and table so that we could sit and talk.

"Aunt Queen made the necessary calls to set our plan in motion. Nash averred that his suitcase had never been unpacked. And tipsy as I was, I asked if I could drive Stirling around Blackwood Farm to show him the old pastures and a little bit of the swamp that one could see from the road. Before we would drive I would take him down to the cemetery to see the tombs and the old church.

"I could see that neither Nash nor Aunt Queen wanted me to be alone with him, but they couldn't very well object to it, and as soon as we were alone, headed down to the cemetery, I understood quite fully why.

" 'Listen to me,' Stirling said. 'I don't want to frighten your Aunt Queen or say things to her that will make her suspect my sanity as she now suspects yours. But I believe completely that you saw this creature dumping bodies in the swamp and I mean every word of it when I ask you to promise that you will never, never return to Sugar Devil Island at night.'

" 'You've got my promise,' I said. 'If it hadn't been for Rebecca's dream, I would never have been there in the first place.'

" 'That is a story unto itself,' he said, 'and for now I can't comment on it, but reaffirm your promise to me and never waver, and from now on, please keep in touch with me. Realize that I am your good friend.'

"We had reached the tombs and I showed him Rebecca's headstone. Of course he knew the full story. We went into the little chapel. I was distressed to see so many leaves. I would have to tell Allen to sweep it out.

" 'I'm the man of this place now,' I said, my voice echoing off the limestone walls. 'I'll have to run it from Europe. That won't be an easy feat.'

" 'I have another promise I want from you,' he said, looking out the door, as if to make certain no one was coming up on us. 'If you do see this creature again, try not to think of anything that she can read from your mind. I know this is obvious, but try to use definite techniques to cleanse your mind of anything important. You wouldn't want her finding out, for instance, as I have this very afternoon, that you have a new relation by the name of Tommy Harrison whom you've come to like—if not love—in a brief meeting yesterday morning.'

"I was shocked. I wasn't conscious of having thought of Tommy.

" 'You give that fodder to Petronia,' Stirling said, 'and she'll use it against you, the same way she might use Mona. And believe me when I tell you that it's a good thing Aunt Queen will soon be beyond her apparent reach as well.'

"I shuddered. 'Aunt Queen,' I whispered. Then I remembered the way that Petronia had taken her leave of Aunt Queen and the words she'd spoken: *You've been very gracious to me. I won't forget it.*

" 'I wish I had this gift for reading minds,' I said. 'I'd know what you're holding back.'

" 'It isn't such a great gift,' he said as we walked on up the slope towards the house again. 'You can't take Tommy to Europe with you, can you?' he asked.

" 'Oh, that would be splendid. I don't see why not. I bet Terry Sue would allow it. Not with Brittany of course. That's the little girl. She's the workhorse. But Tommy. Tommy's the dreamer who reads books in the woods. I'll talk to Aunt Queen about it.'

" 'Whatever you do, try not to do it after nightfall. If you must make plans, and certainly you must, do it in New Orleans. Do it perhaps at the Grand Luminière Café in Mayfair Medical. That ought to give you time to see Mona. She'll be in the center all day today and into the evening. I'm meeting her and Michael and Rowan there for dinner myself.'

" 'You know, I like your outspoken manner but it amazes me, the ease with which you make your suggestions. Again, I know you're hold-ing something back.'

" 'Know this, and I mean it from the heart. I hold back what I think I should hold back and nothing more than that. Take your Aunt Queen and Nash to dinner at the Grand Luminière Café tonight. Heed my advice on that.'

" 'But why is it so important?'

" 'Because creatures like Petronia don't like witches. And they never go where they are.'

"I was dumbstruck. I couldn't quite imagine what he meant.

" 'She's a mind reader, no? And a trickster on top of it, wouldn't you say?'

" 'Yes,' I answered.

" 'Take my word for it,' he replied. 'She'll never get within a hundred yards of Mayfair Medical. Rowan Mayfair would know she was prowling in an instant. So would Mona.'

" 'But what do you mean when you say they're witches, Stirling?'

"We walked on to the Mercedes, which was parked in the shed. I opened the door for him and then came around to the driver's side.

"He waited for me to back the car out and head down the road. I crossed in front of the house, turned right and went down the long pecan-tree drive.

" 'A witch to those of us in the Talamasca,' he explained, 'is a mortal man or woman who can see spirits and manipulate them, bring up spir-its and exorcise them, communicate with them and control them, talk to them and hear their talk.'

" 'Then I'm a witch,' I said, 'on account of Goblin.'

" 'Very much more than likely,' he said. 'Though I don't think you've experienced all the aspects I just explained.'

" 'No, I haven't. But I think that I could. And if Rebecca comes back, my powers of exorcism may be taxed.'

" 'I'll be here for you if you need me. I don't think Rebecca will tempt you anyplace but here.'

" 'Is that the way it is with ghosts?'

" 'Some of the time,' he said. 'It depends on the type of haunting. Sometimes a person is haunted, sometimes a place. Do you yourself know whether Goblin's a spirit or a ghost?'

" 'Oh, most surely a spirit,' I said. 'He knows nothing of where he came from or where he goes when he leaves me. There's no life for him except in my consciousness. He's probably with us right now.'

"I made an attempt to feel his presence, and I felt the answering grip of his hand on my shoulder and saw his face in the rearview mirror. He was very near me, of course.

" 'I love you, old buddy,' I said to him.

"I saw his poker face break into a childish grin.

" 'You don't know how much I've needed you, old buddy,' I said to Goblin. 'These last twenty-four hours have been mad.' It was marvelous seeing that grin.

"Stirling smiled.

"During the rest of our time alone Stirling told me about the Talamasca, pretty much reinforcing what Mona had explained to me—that they had existed for centuries, that they had vast libraries pertaining to the supernatural, that they had a huge history of Mona's family—confidential of course.

" 'Ah, but you see, I am a Mayfair,' I said, 'am I not? Oncle Julien told me I was, remember?'

" 'You have a good point there. But you don't have time for Mayfair history right now. You have your own adventures. You're going off on an odyssey. Have you made up your mind about little Tommy?'

" 'I'm totally for it. Can't wait to ask Aunt Queen. But I have a question for you,' I said. 'What is your honest opinion of Nash?'

" 'A wonderful man, brilliant, very well-read, very refined. He'll be a marvelous teacher and guide for you in Europe. Don't you think so yourself?'

" 'Yes, but I sensed something between you, that you didn't like each other. Was I wrong?'

" 'You were right to sense something,' he said. 'He doesn't like me. He suspects my motives. He doesn't understand the nature of the Talamasca, and not understanding our rules and our role he thinks me guilty of a brand of self-interest. When you come home, if you and I become friends as I hope we will, maybe he'll change his mind. For now, please don't trouble yourself about it. He's an extraordinarily nice man.'

" 'I know what you're talking about,' I said. 'He feels a lot of insecurity about being attracted to men. I don't really.'

" 'You don't?' he asked.

" 'I thought you could read minds,' I said. 'I hope that sounded agreeable. I meant it to sound agreeable. I've had an unusual life is what I ought to have said. I lost my virginity with Rebecca, then had fun in the shower with Goblin, then fell in love with Mona, and I'm not certain what's next. If Mona will marry me I'll be happy to my dying day.'

"He didn't answer me.

" 'What's wrong?' I asked. 'Do I sound too cavalier for your taste?'

" 'No, you don't at all,' he said. 'I was just thinking about Mona, and whether or not to say what came into my mind.'

" 'Oh, please do say it. I wish I could read it.'

" 'If you marry her, it's likely to be until her dying day before yours.'

" 'No,' I said. 'No. That's not true. That's not true. Dr. Rowan Mayfair knows that's not true. They're working on it night and day. They'll reverse Mona's condition. I mean they'll halt it. They'll fix it. It's not going to be that bad. She'll probably even—' I broke off. 'I'm sorry,' I said.

" 'You owe me no apology. I owe one to you. I shouldn't have said what I did. I thought last night you'd understood what they were talking about.'

" 'I didn't want to understand,' I said. 'But I knew.'

"We talked some more about the Talamasca.

"Anytime I wanted to visit Oak Haven I was welcome. Now it was time for parting and I drove Stirling back to his car. It was a handsome brown Rolls-Royce with cream-colored upholstery. He said the Talamasca spoilt all its members with fine cars and fine furniture.

" 'And what do we do in return for it?' he asked rhetorically. 'Live like celibates and work like dogs.'

" 'I like you very much,' I said. 'Thank you for coming to lunch and thank you for standing with me.'

" 'I had no choice,' he said. 'Please call me when you can. Let me know what's happening. Here's a card for your shirt pocket and one for your jacket and one for your inside pocket too, and here, put this somewhere also.'

" 'Don't worry about me, Stirling,' I said. 'I know I'm much better off on account of your advice. I'm never going back out there at night, and I'm going to do what I can to get everyone out of this house before nightfall.'

" 'Yes, and something else too, Quinn. It's very tricky, fighting a being like Petronia, but something tells me that you've been wise in putting up a fight, in using Goblin as you've done, and I wouldn't hesitate to do that in the future. I hope you enjoy your trip to Europe. I hope you enjoy it immensely.'

"Very reluctantly, I told him good-bye, and I watched until the car had made its long slow journey down the avenue of trees and turned towards the highway. He seemed a wise man. And I wonder now if everything would have been different if I had confided in him more, trusted him more, not gone against him and everybody else in my pride and impetuosity."

34

"I HURRIED inside. There was much to do and I meant to do it quickly—and was overjoyed to discover Aunt Queen and Nash already making plans for our European adventure.

" 'Can Tommy go too?' I asked. 'I can have him back here in an hour with his birth certificate and all his clothes.'

"Aunt Queen appeared to give it instant and deep thought for a long moment, and then, before I could make my legal case, inquired: 'Is he worthy of such a trip, Tarquin?'

" 'Just the word,' I declared. 'You have chosen it perfectly. He's worthy, and it will be so very right for him. You'll find him to be a delightful boy, I swear it to you. And if you don't, we'll line up a nanny for him, and he can be off on a day-by-day regimen of his own, but that won't happen.'

" 'Well, then, I say, by all means, let's take him with us.'

" 'Petty cash,' I replied. 'In case Terry Sue puts up an argument.'

" 'You mean she'd sell the boy!'

" 'Aunt Queen,' I replied, 'it's to sweeten the deal. The boy's worth the ransom. Terry Sue is the merely practical mother of six hungry kids.'

"I was soon furnished with the cash and rushing out the door. Goblin appeared at my side.

" 'We've got to win this one, old buddy,' I told him. 'You agree with me? The child's brilliant. I can't leave him behind.'

" 'You always know what to say, Tarquin,' said Goblin. 'But how can I go with you to Europe? Tarquin, I am afraid.'

"I felt a sudden stab of sympathetic fear.

" 'You're very happy, Tarquin,' he said. 'Don't forget me. Don't forget that I love you. Don't forget that I'm here.'

" 'No, I haven't forgotten,' I pledged. 'I'll hold your hand; remember, I told you. All the way to Europe, I'll hold your hand. That's how we'll do it. You'll sit next to me on the plane.'

"I doubled back into the house to make sure Aunt Queen understood this need for the extra first-class ticket for Goblin, to which she replied that she wouldn't dream of putting such an important member of our party in the coach section, and what sort of an aunt did I think she was?

"Once again I was headed for the trailer, but Goblin, riding beside me, was still insecure.

" 'Europe is far away, Tarquin,' he said.

" 'That doesn't matter, old buddy,' I said.

" 'Stirling said there were two kinds of hauntings,' said Goblin. 'Hauntings of a person and hauntings of a place.'

" 'God, you hear everything, don't you?' I asked him.

" 'Not everything, Tarquin,' he answered. 'I can't be in two places, and sometimes I wish that I could. I'd go to the Retreat House of the Talamasca, Tarquin, and learn from them about spirits, Tarquin, so that I'd be the finest spirit ever made. I know I need you to see me, Tarquin. I know that I love you. I know those things are true even when I hate you, Tarquin.'

" 'That's never, Goblin,' I said sharply. 'You have your moods, that's all. But be quiet for now. I have to do this all-important job.'

"I had reached the trailer and found that all was topsy-turvy, as Grady Breen's 'ladies' were moving 'everything' out to the new house in the Autumn Leaves development, on the outskirts of Ruby River City. How splendid that things were happening so fast! I had decreed it but not believed it. And who should come up to me but my nine-year-old self, with his black curly hair and in his navy blue Catholic school blazer?

" 'Do you want to go to Europe tomorrow night?' I asked. 'I'm not kidding you!'

"He was speechless. And then in a white-faced stammer he shook his head and said, 'I can't leave Brittany.'

" 'I'll make it up to her, I swear. And I'll tell her that myself. Okay? I can't take her from Terry Sue right now. You know that.'

"I caught Brittany's arm as she drew close. She had heard what we had to say. 'I will make it up to you, sugar plum, I promise,' I said. 'Let me take him now on this trip, and I swear by God I'll see you get to go too sometime real soon. Cross my heart. I'll see that good things happen.'

" 'Oh, that's okay,' she said. 'Tommy, you go on, you're the one that's always talking about books and things.'

" 'Brittany, you're going to have fun in the new house,' I went on. 'You're going to have new playmates and a new school, and there's going to be a maid to do the work and a nanny to help with the children.'

"She couldn't absorb it. I could see that plainly. But she was fascinated.

"Terry Sue was headed our way with the baby on her hip. She was dressed up in a pink polyester suit and pumps, and her hair was washed and combed, and she was sporting a brand-new set of drugstore fingernails.

" 'Why are you doing all this for us?' she asked. 'Pops never did it.'

" 'Never mind. Just let me take Tommy to Europe. Let me take him now. All I need is his clothes and his birth certificate. I have to make it to the federal passport office in New Orleans before it closes.'

" 'I don't have no birth certificate,' she said. 'Tommy, go get your clothes. Did you say "Europe," you mean, like in Europe?'

" 'Hurry up, Tommy,' I said. He ran for the trailer. 'I can get the birth certificate at the courthouse. Thank you, Terry Sue. Here's five thousand dollars.'

"She stared at the envelope. 'What's that for?' she asked.

" 'I was going to give you this if you argued. Seems you ought to get it since you didn't.'

" 'You're crazy, Quinn Blackwood, just as Pops always said you was. He said you'd never come to nothing, but I tell you, you're sure somebody in my book!'

" 'Well, thank you, Terry Sue,' I said. 'That's really consoling. Someday you'll have to tell me everything else Pops said. By the way, that's not his baby, is it?'

" 'You're not getting any complaints from me, are you?' she answered. 'I don't know whose baby it is, hush your mouth.'

"Tommy flew at me at a dead run, with all his books in one arm and a pillowcase of clothes over his shoulder. I backed up, laughing, and threw my arm around him.

" 'You mind Tarquin now, Tommy Harrison, you hear what I say,' said Terry Sue. 'And you do your homework, too.'

"I put my right arm around her and kissed her forehead. 'I'll take good care of him,' I said. 'I'll write the school board. Grady Breen will take care of everything just the way he said.'

"Off we went.

"Of course it was too late to make the passport office in New

Orleans, but I did get the birth certificate from the courthouse in Ruby River City.

"Then it was back to the house where I sat down with Allen and went over all the renovations that would be done to the Hermitage while I was gone. There was no doubt in my mind that I was doing this for myself. I loathed and despised the mysterious stranger! The vision of the Hermitage was mine.

"Thanks to last night's written request, Allen had already gotten me paint chips and samples of marble, and I was able to choose the most appealing colors and tile for the new floors. As to the bronze stairs, I drew pictures, and we agreed on a 'baroque' look to things and that he would call the local architects Busby, Bagot and Greene, who presided over all the antebellum restorations, and they could advise on the design of the windows and the construction of the bathroom, which was something I really couldn't do.

" 'Be fearless,' I said. 'You know my tastes, you see my drawings and my requests. Don't wait for my approval. It's more important to complete the task. And remember I'll be calling to talk to you. Forge ahead.'

"I could see that he was delighted to have something so interesting to do. Nevertheless, he shook his head and said it would be difficult, he wanted me to know that, hauling all that marble out there, but he did know how to lay it and he wouldn't trust anybody but himself. As to painting, well, the hard work was the preparation, and again, that was hard, really hard, but he didn't trust anybody but himself.

" 'You're my hero,' I said. 'You can get it done. Now comes the final warning: Never be there after dark.'

" 'Oh, you don't have to tell me that,' he said. 'We'll be out of there by three o'clock.'

" 'Promise me,' I said.

" 'You've got my promise.'

" 'All right, you'll get your first call from me next week.'

"And so the tasks of Manhood were done.

"Around four o'clock the twilight anxiety came over me with unprecedented ferocity. I thought that the swamp was creeping up towards the house—Birnam Wood coming to Dunsinane—and my desire to see Mona became absolutely uncontrollable.

"In all this time I had never for one second forgotten about her, and how agonizing it would be to tell her good-bye. Why, I had not even told her I was going. Such pain lay ahead.

"I tried to call her at Mayfair Medical but I couldn't get through. The switchboard said she couldn't take any calls, and my lack of knowledge of where she was and what was being done to her was unbearable.

"I put on the laser disc of Kenneth Branagh's *Hamlet,* and ran fast to the scene of Ophelia drowned under the glassy stream, and kept playing it back over and over again, switching between it and Gertrude's (Hamlet's mother's) description of how it had come about, haunted by the words:

> *Her clothes spread wide,*
> *And mermaid-like a while they bore her up;*
> *Which time she chanted snatches of old tunes,*
> *As one incapable of her own distress.*

"And then finally as the darkness thickened outside and Stirling Oliver's warnings came down heavy on me, as I thought of Rebecca and her wiles, as I thought of Petronia—I went downstairs to inform Aunt Queen, who was chatting away with Tommy and Nash, that we had to leave at once for New Orleans.

"Jasmine had already packed Aunt Queen's bags, Nash was packed, Big Ramona had finished with my luggage as well and Tommy's humble and entirely temporary wardrobe had been put into one of Aunt Queen's many spare suitcases.

"I announced that we must all head for the Windsor Court Hotel, book the finest suites available and then head for the Grand Lumière Café for supper. As I could not get Mona on the phone, I was more or less bound to go, as, surely, based on Stirling's promises, she was expecting me.

"Of course, I was hit with questions and objections. But I was adamant, and won out, finally, simply because everyone was so excited about our trip and the only thing preventing us from getting on the plane was the matter of Tommy's passport, which could be got with airline ticket in hand the following day.

"In truth there was one other very important matter. It was the matter of who was to run Blackwood Manor in our absence. And it was a very important matter indeed. And after much commiseration on the subject, it had already been decided that Jasmine was going to do it, but to alleviate her fears, it was also decided that she need take no new bookings and only fulfill those already made, and maintain the house for those drop-ins who came to see the site of their engagements or weddings, et cetera, or merely to visit the pretty house about which they had read in the guides.

"Now, Jasmine was very upset. She didn't feel up to it. But Aunt Queen knew that she could do it. And so did I, and most significantly, so did Big Ramona, and so did Clem. Jasmine had the education to do it. Jasmine had the smarts. Jasmine had the good English, and Jasmine also had the sophistication.

"What Jasmine lacked was the confidence.

"So we spent our last hour at Blackwood Manor trying to convince Jasmine that she was up to the task and once she got hold of it—she was already doing ninety-nine percent of the work—she would do fine. As to her pay, it was to be tripled. And Aunt Queen would have worked out a percentage of the profits, except that the percentage system frightened Jasmine, who didn't want to have to figure it out.

"At last it was decided that our attorney Grady Breen would take over the bookkeeping and that Jasmine could devote herself entirely to supervising and to hostess work, and Jasmine seemed a good deal more calm. That way Jasmine could get her percentage without fearing she'd signed some sort of pact with the Devil. Meantime, all of us told her how beautiful she was, how polished she was and how overqualified she was, which did not help as much as we had hoped.

"Clem and Big Ramona promised to back her up completely, and with kisses and embraces, as well as Jasmine's tearful farewell, we hit the road for New Orleans in Aunt Queen's stretch limousine.

"When after a brief stop at the hotel to approve our fabulous digs we reached the Grand Luminière Café, Mona rose from the table and flew into my arms, making me the envy of every man in the place. She was wearing one of her big white shirts, complete with white ruffles and bows at her wrists, but I could see the intravenous port with its evil carbuncle of tubing and tape on the back of her inflamed right hand.

"I sat down at the Mayfair table with her, and in an intimate voice told her of what the doctor had said to Aunt Queen, that this might be her last trip to Europe.

" 'Oh, I approve utterly and totally of your going,' Mona said. 'You must, you absolutely must. I'm doing fine. My condition is stable. Look, I have to be wired up again tonight.' She held up the bandaged hand. 'Do you want to come up to the room? It's not all that appetizing, I can assure you—.'

" 'I'm coming,' I said. 'I never made love to anybody who was wired up.'

" 'Good,' she said in a sweet whisper, 'because I have three or four baby quilts to ruin, and then we can read *Hamlet* to each other. I have a copy of Kenneth Branagh's version with all the screenplay directions, and we can pretend we're seeing it all over again. In fact, you can recite Gertrude's speech describing Ophelia's drowning, and I will lie as if dead on the pillow. I've already strewn flowers all over the bed. Oh, I am Ophelia forever,' she sighed.

" 'No, my Ophelia Immortal,' I said, 'and that's the name under which I'll write to you from Europe, and the name under which I'll E-mail you on the computer, my Ophelia Immortal. I think it is the most splendid name I ever heard.'

"I told her how that afternoon I'd put the film on the TV just to watch that scene of Ophelia underwater. 'I love you that you love it,' I said, 'but you'll be Ophelia Immortal because you'll never drown, you know that, don't you? We have to get that straight, don't we? That you're Ophelia in suspended animation, one most "capable of her own distress" and of her ecstasy, and born up forever on "her melodious lay." '

"She laughed and kissed me warmly. 'You really do know the words, don't you?' she said. 'Oh, I love you for it. And E-mails, why didn't I think of it? Of course, we'll E-mail each other from Europe, and write also. We have to print out our letters. Our correspondence will be as famous as that of Héloïse and Abelard.'

" 'Absolutely,' I said with a little shudder. 'But nothing so long and chaste, my beloved; I'll be home and you'll be cured and we'll soon be in each other's arms.' I laughed outright. 'By the way, you do know that for his love of Héloïse, Abelard was castrated, don't you? We don't want anything so dreadful to happen to me.'

" 'It's a metaphor for your restraint, Quinn, and that we can't merge into the same person as Ophelia would have done with Hamlet if only his father hadn't been killed.'

"I kissed her longingly and lovingly. ' "Oh, brave new world that hath such creatures in it," ' I quoted. 'What other fifteen-year-old in the world would know such things?'

" 'You ought to talk to me about the stock market,' she returned, her green eyes firing beautifully. 'It's perfectly egregious that Mayfair and Mayfair insists on managing my billions. I know more about stocks and bonds than anybody in the firm.'

"Stirling had just come to join the table. I realized I hadn't said hello to the graceful Rowan and the stalwart Michael. I corrected all that, glorying in the warmth with which we all greeted each other, and I explained to Stirling hastily that the family had checked out of Blackwood Manor, that if Petronia wanted to find us she'd have to come looking at the Windsor Court Hotel.

" 'And the little gentleman with the black hair over there, that's Tommy?'

" 'Precisely. Soon to become Tommy Blackwood. We're leaving for Europe as soon as we get his passport. I'll have his name changed at the passport office if I can get away with it. We'll see what a little persuasion does.'

" 'Let me know if you have trouble with that,' he said. 'The Talamasca can help.'

"We didn't join tables for dinner. I felt it was best. I wanted Nash and Aunt Queen to continue to get to know Tommy, and Tommy was doing splendidly well. He wasn't shy or overexcited, and just as I had surmised when I met him, he was extremely bright. Literature and history were his loves, thank God. Math he couldn't understand very well but he inched along. He'd benefited tremendously from his Catholic education so far, and Nash and Aunt Queen were both finding him fascinating, which was what I had hoped.

"After we had all had our 'egregious' desserts, I took Tommy over to be presented to the Mayfairs and to Stirling, and he comported himself with manners in keeping with the occasion, and then it was agreed my beloved family members would return to the hotel and I would go up with Mona to her room.

"I threw my arm around Goblin and I said in his ear, 'Go back to the family. Stay close to them. And come to me if Petronia comes.'

"He was surprised. But at once he nodded and disappeared.

"Mona's room was a luxury suite just like the one which I had occupied, with a parlor adjacent to it and a big double hospital bed. Mona had covered the bed with white eyelet baby quilts, as she had described to me. Only now she gathered up all the wilted lilies and daisies, and, choosing great handfuls of fresh ones from the baskets all around the room, she covered the bed afresh.

"Then she hopped up on the bed and leaned back on a huge nest of pillows, smiling playfully at me. And we both went into gales of laughter.

"Dr. Winn Mayfair stood by solemnly watching all these proceedings, and then he said in his soft respecting voice, a voice that always commanded respect in return:

" 'Very well now, Ophelia, are you ready for me to insert the line?'

" 'Go ahead, Doctor,' she answered. 'And be sure to understand, you can close that door afterwards. Quinn knows the line is the only thing that can be inserted, right, Quinn?'

"I think I blushed. 'Yes, Doctor,' I said.

" 'Do you fully understand the risk, Quinn?' asked Dr. Winn.

" 'I do, sir,' I replied.

"It was hard for me to look at the needle in the back of her hand, at the redness of her skin and the tape that overlay it, but I felt I had to, I had to experience it with her as best I could, and my eyes moved up the transparent tubing to the plastic sack of clear liquid which hung from its metallic hook at the top. At some uncertain juncture a tiny computer generated numbers and beeps. A larger machine sat near, ready for some more complex connection, but fortunately none seemed to be needed just now.

"There were so many questions I wanted to ask Dr. Winn Mayfair, but it wasn't my place to do it, and so I had to rely on Mona's assertion that her condition was indeed stable and I knew that I had to leave her the next morning with her word that Aunt Queen's health was what mattered at this juncture in my life.

"Within moments after the doctor had left we were in each other's arms, overly conscious of the sacred wiring, and I was kissing her with all the drama I could effortlessly muster, calling her my eternal love and seeking only to pleasure her as she pleasured me.

"It was a long night of tender kissing and lovemaking, and the quilts probably bear their testimony to this time.

"Dawn had come, vague and pink as twilight over the city, before I said my farewell to Mona, and if anyone had told me then that I would never see her again—this soft, drowsy child amid her lace and her flowers, and her gloriously disheveled hair—I wouldn't have believed it. But then there were many things I would not have believed then.

"And there were more good times to come.

"I went straight from her hospital room, where I left her sleepy and beautiful and fresh as the flowers all around her in their moist baskets, to obtain the airline tickets, and from there to obtaining Tommy's passport, where Aunt Queen and I were both able to 'claim that we knew him as Tommy Blackwood,' and then we were on our way by plane to Newark, with Goblin strong and visible and in his own expensive first-class seat, and from Newark we flew out to Rome."

35

"WHO CAN SAY how different my last few days in New
Orleans might have been had I known that we would be
gone on our European odyssey for a full three years?

"No one among our party knew that the festivities would go on so
long, and indeed it was the spirit of living moment to moment which
kept us going—forever checking Aunt Queen's blood pressure and general stamina with her favorite physicians of Paris, Rome, Zurich and
London—as we roved ever back and forth through the castles, museums, cathedrals and cities that Aunt Queen showed me with such love
and enthusiasm, and with Nash's wise instruction from which I drew
constant overwhelming stimulation; always yielding to Aunt Queen's
desire to travel 'a few more months,' to yet another 'little country' or
another great and grand 'ruin' that I should 'never forget.'

"Aunt Queen's health was failing, there was no doubt of it, or, to put
it more truly, she was simply getting too old to do what she was doing,
and that is what she would scarcely face.

"Cindy, our delightful nurse, was sent for and came to travel with us,
which put everyone's mind at ease somewhat, as Cindy could take vital
signs and administer appropriate pills at appropriate hours, and also she
was of that congenial brand of nurse who does not mind assisting with
all sorts of personal tasks, and so became Aunt Queen's secretary as well.

"Nash also fulfilled this function to a large extent for both of us,
delivering our faxes to the concierges of the various splendid hotels in
which we stayed, and taking care of all bills and gratuities so that we
had never to worry with such things. Nash, also being something of a
whizbang on his laptop computer, wrote out Aunt Queen's letters to her
friends.

"As to his commentary on all that we saw and visited, Nash took this very seriously, never failing to do his homework so that his observations were fresh and he could answer whatever questions we might have.

"He was a marvelous physical assistant to Aunt Queen, helping her in and out of limousines and up and down stairways, and was not above loosening and tightening the straps of her murderous shoes.

"But the point is, the more we traveled the more we enjoyed ourselves, the more Tommy and I visibly and joyfully marveled at everything—the little children of the group—the more I couldn't bear the thought of saying to Aunt Queen, 'Yes, you must terminate this, your last trip to all the wonderful places you have always loved. Yes, you will never see Paris or London or Rome again.'

"No, I could not bear it, no matter how much I loved Mona, no matter how much my heart yearned for her and no matter how much I feared that all her E-mails and faxes and letters to me asserting her 'stable condition' were not telling the truth.

"So for more than three years we meandered gloriously, and I will not try to recount our adventures, except for certain very specific things.

"Allow me to say for the record, if nothing more, that Tommy proved himself to be a genius, just as I had first believed him to be, in the precocity with which he absorbed all the beauty and knowledge around him; and, with no resistance to any adult authority, he gave back his written essays both to me and Nash with verve and appropriate pride.

"The fact that he so much physically resembled me obviously fed my vanity, I'm sure of it, but I would have loved him had he looked wholly different. What I found so purely virtuous in him was that he was curious. He had none of the sullen arrogance of ignorance and was forever asking questions of Nash, and purchasing cultural souvenirs of all sorts for his mother, brothers and sisters, which we sent off from every hotel by overnight express.

"Meantime, Grady Breen sent frequent packets of photographs of Terry Sue, her brood, her nanny, her maid, her yard man and the house, affirming that we had indeed preempted her doom.

"I knew, of course, without ever telling Tommy, that I would never surrender him to Terry Sue again, unless he himself madly insisted upon it, a condition I could hardly imagine and of which I got no inkling at all. On the contrary, by the second year he did not correct me or even go silent when I said, 'When you come to live with us at Blackwood Manor,' and that was good enough for me.

"Of course Aunt Queen made a total pet of him, buying him clothes he outgrew almost instantly, and nothing pleased her so much as to see people in the hotel lobbies or in the restaurants turning to look at him, the little gentleman in his black suit and tie, as we came in.

"As for me, I was so overwhelmed and so often in our travels that it would make tiresome reading here to recount it. It is enough to say that I drew intense enjoyment from everything I saw whether it was a tiny hamlet in England or the splendor of the Amalfi Coast.

"There is but one aspect of our Grand Tour that I want to recount, and that has to do with the ruins of Pompeii, outside of Naples.

"But let me first dispense with certain other matters, including the mystery of Goblin, because, as Goblin predicted, I lost him at some point on the first evening as we crossed the sea.

"I'm not even sure of how it happened or when. I sat beside him in the luxurious cabin of a newly designed model 800 jumbo jet , in which each seat swiveled and had its own private television set, and where a level of unparalleled privacy enabled me to talk to him and hold fast to his hand. And this I did, assuring him, against his fears, that I would do everything I could to keep him with me, and that I loved him. . . .

" . . . And then, quite slowly, he began to fade. I heard his voice grow faint and then become telepathic, and then it was gone altogether, but in those last moments I said, 'Goblin, wait for me. Goblin, I will return home. Goblin, guard the house for me against the mysterious stranger. I need you to do it. Make sure my beloved Jasmine and Big Ramona and Clem and Allen are all safe.'

"It was a song I had been singing to him ever since we took off, but now I put the case to him urgently, and then I saw him no more.

"The feeling of severance, the feeling of pure lonesome emptiness around me was shocking and awful, and it was as if someone had taken all my clothes from me and left me in a desert place. For a full hour, perhaps more, I said nothing to anyone. I lay back, hoping this feeling of misery would leave me, trying desperately to realize I was free of him, I mustn't complain of it, I was free to go on with the tasks of Manhood, to be Tommy's devoted nephew, to make Aunt Queen happy, to learn from Nash. All the world was quite literally waiting for me!

"But I was without Goblin. Utterly without. And I felt a quality of agony that I had never known.

"Strange that in this lengthening aftermath, as I lay back in the luxurious seat being served another glass of wine by the sweet stewardess, as the plane seemed enveloped in the silence of the engines, and I couldn't even hear the voices of Tommy and Aunt Queen, no, couldn't even see them, or Nash with his book—it was during this sudden long and cold interval that I realized I hadn't said farewell to Patsy.

"I hadn't even tried to find Patsy. None of us, to my knowledge, had tried to find Patsy. We hadn't even thought of her. Not even Clem had asked what he should do should she want the limousine. Nor had Big Ramona said, What do we do if she brings her singers and her drummers into the house?

"No one had given her a thought either negative or positive, and now I lamented it, that I hadn't tried to call her and say good-bye. A coldness stole over me. Did I miss her? No, I missed Goblin. I felt as if my skin had been peeled and the cold winds had me.

"Patsy, my Patsy. Would she have the sense to get the medical care she needed? I felt too weary suddenly to tackle the problem, and certainly too alienated and too far away.

"And then a fear gripped me, not just a fear but a certainty.

"And realizing that I couldn't possibly be reached by phone on this plane but that I could phone Blackwood Manor, I broke out my new credit card and phoned home.

"I could hear the glass breaking in the background before I heard Jasmine's voice.

" 'Thank God it's you,' she declared. 'Do you know what he's doing? He's breaking every pane of glass in this place. He's on a rampage!'

" 'Tell me exactly,' I said. 'Can you see him?'

" 'No, I can't see him. It's just the panes shattering. He went through the living room first. It was like a fist breaking them, one after another.'

" 'Listen to me. He's not as strong as you think he is. Whatever you do, don't look at the place where he's breaking the glass. You don't want to see him. That gives him power, and he's going to run out of power altogether, working the way he does.'

"I could hardly understand her as she continued. He had apparently broken all the glass in the dining room. Right this very minute he was in the kitchen, where Jasmine was, but he had just stopped there, and she could hear the glass breaking on the second floor and the guests were running down the stairs.

" 'He stopped in the kitchen?'

"She confirmed it.

" 'He didn't want to hurt you, then. You run get the guests out of the house. Let them go without a bill. Hurry. But don't go up to where he is, except to get the guests. And whatever you do, don't try to see him. That will only give him strength.'

"I hung on. It was hard to hear over the roar of the plane, yet the sound came to me over thousands of miles, the tinkling of that shattered glass as he worked his lonely fury. And I thought frantically, What do I do *before* I call Stirling. What do I do now at this minute as man of the house?

"After an eternity, Jasmine was back on the line. 'He's stopped,' she said. 'The guests have all gone. Boy, were they ever excited. They got their money's worth and didn't have to pay it! I'm telling you there'll be tales told in Ruby River City and Mapleville tonight.'

" 'Are you hurt? Is anybody hurt?'

" 'No, it just all fell to the floor,' she answered. 'Quinn, we've got to close this place down.'

" 'Like hell, Jasmine,' I said. 'You don't think he's got the stamina to keep this up, do you?' I asked her. 'He doesn't. Not without me to see him, don't you get it? He's run out. He took back what he could.'

" 'And who's to say he won't climb out of bed with a new bag of tricks tomorrow,' she asked. 'I wish you could see this place!'

"I held on while she had a big argument with Clem and Allen. One wanted all the glass replaced immediately, the other said Goblin would just break it. Then Big Ramona said it had to be fixed, as a thunderstorm was coming.

" 'Look, I'm the boss,' I chimed in from the plane. 'Fix the glass now. Tell them to get the best quality that the windows will hold. God knows we had some very weak glass in some of those windows.' (She told them what I said.) 'Now, Jasmine, I want you to put the phone on hold and go up to my room and pick it up at my computer desk.'

"It took her longer than I liked. I told her to switch on the computer.

" 'It's already on,' she told me. 'And I know you turned it off when you left.'

" 'What's on the screen?'

" ' "QUINN, COME HOME" in big letters,' she told me.

" 'All right, I want you to type in this response: "Goblin, I love you. But I can't leave Aunt Queen now. You know how I love Aunt Queen." ' I heard the keys clicking. Then I spoke some more. ' "Please protect those I love from Petronia." ' (I had to spell that for Jasmine.) ' "Goblin, wait for me. Love me. Love, Quinn." '

"I waited a moment as I listened to her type. I thought of something, something that just might work. Now, years later, I wonder if wasn't a disastrous thought. But all my love of Goblin seems now to have been full of disastrous thoughts.

" 'Jasmine, I want you to type another message,' I said. ' "Dear Goblin, I can write to you through the computer. I can send you E-mail. I will send it regularly to you care of my computer name, King Tarquin. I'll be using a new name to send. And you can send it to me as soon as I send that new name. You know the computer as well as I do, Goblin. Wait for my communication." '

"It took a good while for Jasmine to get this message straightened out, but it was typed in and then I instructed her from then on to leave the computer on. She was to put a note on it instructing everybody to keep hands off.

" 'Now we'll see if Goblin isn't happy,' I told her. 'And very soon you'll be able to reach us at the Hotel Hassler in Rome.'

"I rang off. As Lord of Blackwood Manor I saw no reason to tell the others that almost every window of the house had been broken. I lay back thinking that my new E-mail name should be Noble Abelard, and I should insist Mona use the name Ophelia Immortal, and perhaps Goblin should be Goblin.

"And so these things did come to pass.

"By the time we left the Eternal City, I and Mona and Goblin had established these links for computer correspondence, and it happened that all of my travels fed into my loving letters to my treasure, Ophelia Immortal, and only slightly edited versions of these same epistles went to my beloved Goblin, whilst from Mona I received passionate and highly humorous letters and from Goblin weaker and weaker transmissions largely only confessing his need of me and his love.

"Whenever we hit a hotel which had good computer equipment I printed out all this material, and it became my journal of the journey, and I was self-conscious enough not to write all of my erotic blandishments to Mona, and it was rather fun to try to speak in fractured Shakespearean tones.

"As for Goblin, his slow demise worried me intensely and ate at my soul as if a dark hand were scratching at my very heart, but I didn't know what to do about it other than what I had done.

"Meantime, there were no more disturbances at Blackwood Manor.

"But the legend of the breaking glass was now known throughout Ruby River Parish, and guests were calling for bookings day and night. My impression over the phone was that Jasmine was having a wonderful time, despite her protests of anxiety, and we again raised her salary and that of everybody on the staff.

"Jasmine, of her own volition, began to accept new bookings, and, as it turned out, the place was filled for the whole time that we were gone. Soon Big Ramona was cut in for a percentage of the profits, and I believe, though I'm not sure, that Clem was too. That took care of Jasmine's family. I drew the line when it came to Allen and the Shed Men, as they were making twice the wages of anybody similar in Ruby River Parish, with free drinks and lunch thrown in.

"Sugar Devil Island was giving rise to much gossip, as the marble tile for the floors was now being ferried through the swamps by slow motorless pirogue and people were asking over their coffee cups in Ruby River City and Mapleville whether or not Tarquin Blackwood had lost his mind.

"How glad I was to be in an ancient palazzo in Venice while all that was going on.

"It was some consolation to me that Sheriff Jeanfreau and his deputy Ugly Henderson had told everyone my tale of the man in the moonlight disposing of the two bodies. Because I hoped sincerely that people would take heed of it and not go boating around the island after dark.

"Sometime during the first year, while we were still in Italy, I wrote to Stirling Oliver at Oak Haven and told him what I had done. I told him that Goblin's abilities to write to me via the computer were apparently waning, and that I felt a great emptiness in spite of all the excitement of the Grand Tour.

"Stirling and I corresponded for a few months. He cautioned me not to rouse Goblin by letters that were either too short or too long, and he told me that according to his best guess, Goblin was a ghost connected in some way to the locality of Blackwood Manor, rather than to me personally, but of this Stirling wasn't perfectly sure.

" 'Try to experience your freedom from him,' he wrote. 'That is, try to enjoy it, and tell me whether or not you succeed. You might also ask those around you if they see any change in you. Mrs. McQueen, in particular, might illuminate you in some way.'

"I took his advice, and, indeed, Aunt Queen did have some reaction for me.

" 'You're really with us, my little darling,' she said. 'You're not distracted, talking to him. You're not fearful of what he might do. You're not always looking out of the corner of your eye.'

"She went on without any coaxing. 'You're much better this way, my sweet little boy. You're infinitely better. I see it so plainly because I know you as no one else does. It's time to put aside the things of childhood, and Goblin is of childhood.' She looked kindly on me as she spoke these words.

"And thus it was that my correspondence with Goblin trailed off into silence, and my beloved spirit, my counterpart, my doppelgänger disappeared beyond my reach. And believe me, it was beyond my reach. I tried with some desultory messages to summon him from the shadows, but they failed.

"And as Blackwood Manor prospered with every blessing under Jasmine's reign as Queen, as the carols were sung at Christmas, as the feasts were prepared at Easter, as the flowers bloomed in Pops' beloved flower beds, we traveled on our circuitous odyssey and Goblin drifted beyond the pale.

"Of course I didn't settle for only letters with Mona. Many a night I spent on the phone with her, and always we ended with passionate assurances that we lived only for each other—there was no question of it now, Ophelia Immortal and Noble Abelard would someday be in a chaste marriage (lust without penetration)—and our written correspondence became our fallback when odd hours kept us apart.

"Many times I got Michael or Rowan when I called, and I never failed to exact the confirmation that Mona's condition was stable, that she had no need of me, and many a time, much to my amazement, Michael volunteered that the relationship had been a godsend because Mona had stopped her erotic roaming and was now 'living' for my E-mails and phone calls and spending all the rest of her life hard at work on the Mayfair Legacy, seeking to understand and participate in the investments, and also working on the family tree.

" 'She's a bit scornful of her home teacher,' Michael said. 'I wish she'd read more books. But I do get her to watch classic films with me. That's one good thing, don't you think?'

" 'Oh, definitely,' I said. 'No one can move forward creatively until they've seen *The Red Shoes* and *The Tales of Hoffmann*. Am I not profoundly right?'

" 'Yes, you are,' he laughed. 'And she does have them under her belt. Last night I got her to watch *Black Narcissus*.'

" 'Now that's an eerie one,' I said. 'I bet she loved it.'

" 'Ask her,' he said. 'Here she is, Noble Abelard, give everyone there my love.'

"And so my life ran on for three blissful and action-packed years.

"I grew to be six feet four inches in height.

"I saw the world's most beautiful and wondrous sights. I went with my joyous company as far south as Abu Simbel in Egypt and Rio de Janeiro in Brazil, and as far north as Ireland and Scotland. I went as far east as St. Petersburg. As far west as Morocco and Spain.

"There was no great order and no great thrift to the manner in which we traveled. Back and forth we went often. It had something to do with the seasons. It had everything to do with desire and whim.

"Tommy and Nash worked intensely on homework for the school board of Ruby River City. But in the main, Tommy received his knowledge as I did—from Aunt Queen and Nash drawing our attention to things we might otherwise have missed, from Aunt Queen and Nash giving us the cultural background of the things we saw and telling us marvelous stories that had to do with the famous persons connected to monuments, countries, culture and time.

"There was such a richness to all of it that I felt a fool for not having yielded to Aunt Queen's requests that I travel made so many years before. It seemed the arrogance of ignorance that I had refused to join her. But as she said to comfort me, it was not a time for regretting things. It was a time for embracing the entire world.

"Let me also note that no matter how much we saw or how late in the day we toured, I still managed to read Dickens for Nash, and he greatly increased my appreciation of *Great Expectations, David Copperfield, The Old Curiosity Shop* and *Little Dorrit*. I also investigated the Brontë sisters with keen delight, swallowing *Wuthering Heights* and *Jane Eyre*. If only I had been a better reader I might have accomplished more. I tried hard with Milton, but I couldn't remember what I read of *Paradise Lost*, no matter how hard I tried, so I put it by for Keats, reading the odes aloud until I had them memorized.

"All was bliss for us as we roamed. But not so with everyone. In the middle of our second year, Jasmine called to let us know that Patsy had gone through her income entirely for that period (staggering), and had gotten Clem to invest his entire inheritance from Pops in a rock album which had flopped, and Clem was now blaming Patsy for having tricked him and wanted to sue her.

"At Aunt Queen's behest I got on the phone with our lawyer, Grady Breen, and ascertained that Patsy had spent all the money on a rock video, the making of which had cost a million dollars, what with a foreign director and cinematographer, and then all the big cable music networks had failed to give it airtime.

"Clem had not been wearing blinders when he sunk his hundred thousand into the deal, and he was, in Grady's words, no fool, but I told Grady to pay him off and be done with it. As for Patsy, if she wanted money, just give it to her. She did want money and he would give it to her.

"In closing, I asked Grady if Patsy was having any success at all with her music. He replied that she was very successful of late with the good clubs, playing House of Blues all over the country. Her album was selling about three hundred thousand copies. But that's nothing compared to the million copies she longed to sell, and which she needed to sell to attain the fame she wanted. She had simply overestimated her name-brand appeal with this video she had made. It had been a little too soon for her.

"I didn't dare to ask directly about her health. I put it simply: 'Have you recently seen her?'

" 'Yes,' said Grady. 'She was just on *Austin City Limits*. She's as pretty as ever. Your mother has always been a pretty gal. I'm old enough to say that much, don't you think?'

" 'Yes, sir,' I said.

"And so back at home, Patsy was still being Patsy.

"Now that I have said all the above—dispatching all subjects pertaining to this period—let me return to the matter of Pompeii.

"Of course I was eager to see the ruins, but I couldn't forget the spell which Petronia had cast over me when she had come to Blackwood Manor, and Aunt Queen had thoughts of her own about it, though they were far less alarmist than mine. We had discussed Petronia but only with some strain, Aunt Queen not quite forgiving me for my denouncing of Petronia and not quite believing that Petronia wasn't human and that Petronia had dumped two bodies in the swamp.

"As for me, I believed everything, and I wanted to see if the ruins of Pompeii—the excavations of an entire city once buried under ash and rubble—would bring to mind the images which Petronia had planted in my mind.

"I wasn't finished with Petronia.

"Back at home the renovations of the Hermitage were being completed to the tune of hundreds of thousands of dollars, and packets of color photographs had come to me revealing the stunning little house. Its interior rafters had been boldly gilded, Oriental rugs from my catalog collection were scattered over its shining marble and I had even ordered some ornate furnishings for it by long-distance from Hurwitz Mintz, in New Orleans. The place now sported velvet sofas and torchère lamps. It had a cluster of swan-backed chairs. All the comforts were connected in its spacious bathroom. Its new glass windows were kept shining clean.

"Allen had reported more than once that 'someone' was using the place in the evenings, that books were found on the desk (and never disturbed) and there were candles in evidence and ashes in the fireplace. So my partner was back in action. What did I expect? Had I not capitulated to every demand? But who had first thought of these efficacious designs? Was it not me?

"I was foolishly fascinated.

"And I was outraged. And too young perhaps to know the difference.

"And so I came to Pompeii on our third trip to Italy, not too far before the very end of our odyssey, in a bold and combative and curious frame of mind, ready at last to see the legendary spot.

"Aunt Queen probably did not even remember Petronia's spellbinding tale of that long-ago night. Nash spoke of it casually to me. Tommy and Cindy, the nurse, were merely happy to see one of the most famous ruins in the world.

"Coming by private car from our luxurious hotel in Naples, we visited the city early in the day. We had a leisurely stroll throughout the narrow rutted stone streets, knowing that we would come back tomorrow and tomorrow, and I felt everywhere the slight, thrilling frisson of Petronia's words. The sun was shining brilliantly, and Mount Vesuvius seemed safe and silent, a pale bluish sentinel of a mountain rather than anything that could have destroyed this little city, this small grid of multitudinous lives, in the space of half a day.

"We entered many of the partially restored houses, touching the walls only lightly with great reverence or not at all. There was a hush around us, even though tourists came and went, and it was hard for me to lift the veil of death that hung over the city so that I could imagine it alive again.

"Aunt Queen was intrepid as she led our little party to the House of the Faun and the Villa of the Mysteries. At last we came to the museum, and there I saw the natural white sculptures which had been made of those who had died in the ash and left nothing but the shape of their bodies behind. Poured plaster had immortalized their final moments, and I felt so moved by these featureless figures, drawn together in sudden death, that I was about to cry.

"Finally we went back to our rooms at the hotel. The night sky over the Bay of Naples was pregnant with a thousand stars. I opened the doors to the balcony and looked out over the bay and counted myself one of the happiest people alive. For a long while I stood at the stone balustrade. I felt pure contentment, as if I'd conquered Petronia and Goblin and Rebecca, and my future belonged only to me. Mona was doing wonderfully well. Even Aunt Queen seemed immortal—never to die as long as I did not die. Always to be with me.

"Finally I was tired and happy to be so. Putting on my customary nightshirt, though it was a bit warm for the lovely fragrant night, I lay down on the fresh pillow and drifted into sleep.

"Within seconds, it seemed, I was in Pompeii. I was running, pushing before me a reluctant group of slaves who wouldn't believe me that the mountain would soon rain down its fury on us, that it would demolish everything, including our lives. Through the gates of the city we ran and down to the seashore and into the waiting boat. Out to sea we went and then came the eruption, the dark spume rising, the sky darkening. A hideous roar came from the mountain. Everywhere boats rocked on the water. 'Keep going!' I shouted. People shrieked and screamed. 'Make the crossing,' I pleaded. Slaves jumped into the water. 'No, the boat's faster,' I insisted. The oars were dropped. The boat went over. I was drowning. The sea rose and fell. I swallowed water. Again came that unspeakable thunder.

"I woke up. I wouldn't dream this dream! I felt terror. I felt another body enveloping mine. And against the bright blue of the night sky I saw a figure on the balcony, a figure I knew to be Petronia.

" 'You devil!' I declared. I shot up from the bed and I ran at the figure, only the figure wasn't there. Shaking violently I stood at the balustrade and looked out into the darkness, as frightened as ever I'd been in my life, and as angry as well.

"I couldn't abide this terror, yet I couldn't put an end to it. Finally, grabbing my robe, I went out of the room and down the hall to Aunt Queen's suite. I pounded on her door.

"Cindy, our sweetheart of a nurse, answered.

" 'Aunt Queen, I have to sleep with you,' I said, charging towards her bed. 'It's a nightmare. It's that evil Petronia.'

" 'You come get in this bed with me right now, you poor little boy,' she said.

"And I did exactly that.

" 'Now, now, darling, don't fret,' she said. 'You are shaking! Now go to sleep. Tomorrow we'll go to Torre del Greco, and we'll buy lots of beautiful cameos, and you can help me as you always do.'

"Cindy climbed back into the other bed. The curtains blew out from the open windows. I felt safe with the two of them. I went to sleep again, dreaming of Blackwood Manor, dreaming of Tommy living with us, dreaming of Mona, dreaming of so many things, but never bad things, never ghosts, never evil spirits, never darkness, never disaster, never death.

"Had Petronia really been there? Was it a spell? I'll never know.

"But let me bring to a close the story of our happy wanderings. Because it did come time for us to go home.

"Aunt Queen could go no farther. She was simply too weak; her blood pressure was too high. She had sprained her wrist, and who knew when an ankle sprain would more severely hamper her? She was also battling some form of arthritis and her joints had begun to swell. Her exhaustion was defeating her. She could not keep up with her own pace. She was angry with her own weakness.

"Finally, Cindy, the nurse, became adamant. 'I love these grand hotels as much as anybody,' she said, 'but you belong at home, Aunt Queen! You're going to take a bad fall! You can't go on like this.'

"I joined my voice to Cindy's and so did little Tommy, who was by this time a pretty tall twelve years of age, and finally Nash chimed in with a solemn declaration: 'Mrs. McQueen, you've been valiant, but it is now time for you to retire to Blackwood Manor and reign in state as the irrepressibly entertaining steel magnolia which we all know you to be.'

"We were in Cairo when the decision was reached, and we flew on to Rome, where our adventure had begun, for a last few nights at the Hotel Hassler. I knew by this time that I had been negligent in not proposing the return because I had not wanted to be accused of self-interest in my love and longing for Mona.

"And I was anxious about Mona. She hadn't answered my E-mails for over two weeks.

"As soon as we were checked in—I was in a huge suite with a very long broad terrace, right below Aunt Queen, who had the penthouse with Cindy—I tried to reach Mona by phone and got a taciturn, somewhat solemn Rowan.

" 'She's in Mayfair Medical for some tests, Quinn,' she said. 'She's likely to be there for several months. She won't be able to see you.'

" 'My God, you mean she's taken a turn for the worse!' I said. 'Dr. Mayfair, tell me the truth. What's happening to her?'

" 'I don't know, Quinn,' she said in her beguiling husky voice. 'Those are hard words for a doctor to say, believe you me. But I don't. That's why we're testing her. Her immune system's compromised. She's been running a fever for months. Somebody sneezes in the same room with her and she comes down with double pneumonia.'

" 'Good God,' I responded. As usual Rowan's brand of truth was a little too harsh for me. Yet I told myself fiercely that I wanted it. 'Why can't I talk with her by phone?'

" 'I don't want her upset by anything now, Quinn,' said Rowan. 'And if she knew you were on your way home, she'd be upset that she couldn't see you. That's why she's in isolation. She's in a plastic bubble as far as the world's concerned, with a VCR and a monitor and a stack of vintage movies. She's eating popcorn and ice cream and chocolates and drinking milk. She knows you're having fun in Europe, and that's the way it has to stay for now.'

" 'But Rowan,' I pleaded. 'Surely she's getting my E-mails!'

" 'No, Quinn, she's resting. I took the computer away.'

"I was maddened. Just maddened. Here we were on our way home at last and she was beyond my reach. But the worst news was that she was sick! Too sick perhaps to even handle the computer!

" 'Rowan, listen, has she been sick all along? Has she been protecting me from it?'

"There was a long silence, and then she said in her characteristic straightforward fashion, 'Yes, Quinn, I'd say that's what she's been doing. But I think you knew that when you left. You knew she was undergoing a continuous treatment. She's been at various plateaus. But she's never really rallied.'

"I gasped. I didn't know if it was audible.

" 'I've got to see her when I come home,' I said.

" 'We'll arrange it,' she responded, 'as soon as it's possible. But it can't be right away.'

" 'Can you give her my love?' I asked. 'Can you tell her I called? Can you tell her I've sent her letters?'

" 'Yes, that I will do tonight,' she said, 'when I see her. And tomorrow and the day after.'

" 'Oh, thank you, Rowan, God love you, Rowan. Please, please tell her how much I love her.'

" 'Quinn, there's something else I want to say,' she said, surprising me. 'I know Michael's said it to you. Let me say it too. You really helped Mona. You got Mona to stop doing things that hurt her. You made her happy.'

" 'Rowan, you're frightening me,' I said. 'You're making it sound past tense.'

" 'I'm sorry. I didn't mean it to sound that way,' she said. 'I meant to say that during this time she's been deeply and totally in love with you. She's been writing to you, or talking to you by phone, instead of fighting us. She asks about you all the time.'

"I felt the chills come over me. My darling Mona. What had I done in leaving her? Had I fallen so in love with the letters and phone calls of Ophelia Immortal that I lost Mona herself?

" 'Thank you, Rowan,' I said. 'Thank you always.' There were so many more questions I wanted to ask, but I didn't dare to try it. I was so afraid.

"That night the champagne flowed in Aunt Queen's suite. Nash, who had drunk far too much of it, but with our liberal encouragement, proposed toast after toast to the lady he loved most in this world, Mrs. Lorraine McQueen; and young Tommy, now age thirteen by a matter of two whole days, stood up to read a poem he had written for the occasion, declaring himself to have become a man thanks to his guardian and inspiration, nephew Tarquin Blackwood. Only I failed to comport myself in keeping with the occasion. I could only smile and salute everyone with my glass and say how very happy I was that we were returning home at last, to take stock of all we'd learned, and to all those we had missed in our journeying.

"The fact was, a multitude of worries and apprehensions had a Byronic hold upon me. Not to see Mona was foremost among them. But I was also obsessed with Petronia, that she was occupying the Hermitage so boldly, and of course I was thinking of Goblin. Was I fool enough to believe that Goblin would not show himself to me as soon as I came within the orbit of Blackwood Manor? I was not.

"And so the three-and-a-half-year intermezzo was ended.

"The following morning we departed for Newark with a connecting flight to take us immediately to New Orleans."

36

"CLEM AND JASMINE BOTH GREETED us at the airport and I burst into tears embracing them, so glad was I to see them; and never before had Clem looked so handsome in his chauffeur's black suit and official hat, and never had Jasmine looked so lovely in her tailored suit of gray wool and her signature blouse of white ruffled silk, her blond Afro full and shaped and her tears flowing freely.

"Cheerful old Allen had also come to collect the luggage in the pickup and I fell to embracing and kissing him, but then came a moment of truth when Terry Sue appeared in a candy pink suit, much like the last one I had seen her wearing over three years ago, with a new baby on her hip (the last one had not been fathered by Pops); and Tommy ran to her, putting his arms around her and kissing her.

"It took a moment for me to recognize the slender and beautiful teenaged girl beside her, and then I realized it was Brittany.

"Tommy looked to us as to what to do, and I, drawing him aside, asked what I should have asked before we had come to this juncture: 'What do you want?' 'To stay with you,' was his answer.

" 'I then went to Terry Sue and put it to her that Tommy wanted to finish out the trip with a spell at Blackwood Manor if only she would allow it, and I told her and Brittany how wonderful it was that they had come to the airport. I slipped Terry Sue all the twenties I had in my wallet, and that was plenty.

" 'All right, you behave yourself, Tommy Harrison,' she said. And she gave him a big kiss.

" 'Brittany, I'll call you tonight,' he said to his sister.

" 'You've grown up to be a beautiful girl,' I told her.

"Of course Aunt Queen was showering her with compliments, and had even taken off her cameo—one of the new ones from the town of Torre del Greco—and given it to her.

"These tender emotions I had anticipated, and, tired as I was, I let them grip me, and was glad of them, but as we drove away in Aunt Queen's big car, as I sat back, exhausted from our long flight, and looked out the window, I was totally unprepared for the tremendous feeling that swept over me at the sight of the verdant grasses growing unkempt along the highway and the swaying oleanders in full bloom and the occasional oak trees, which meant we were truly home.

"I felt Louisiana all around me, and I loved it. And by the time we had reached the pecan tree drive before the house I was so choked up I could hardly speak into the intercom to ask Clem to stop the car.

"I got out and looked down the long vista at the house. It was inexplicable, the feeling in me. It wasn't happiness. It wasn't sorrow. Yet it was rendering me helpless and bringing only the sweetest tears.

"Nash helped Aunt Queen from the car and she stood beside me. We both looked at the distant white columns.

" 'That's your home,' she said. "It will be yours forever,' she continued. 'You must take care of it after I'm gone.'

"I put my arm around her and I bent down and kissed her, realizing perhaps for the first time how very tall I was, and feeling awkward in my somewhat new body. Then I let her go.

"As we continued up the drive, one aspect after another swept the same feelings of love and anguish over me, or maybe it was sorrow. I couldn't identify it. As the wash of childhood memories paralyzed me and humbled me, I only knew I was home.

"Of course I thought of Goblin, but I felt nothing of his presence. And of course I thought of Patsy and I expected to see her by and by. But it was the very landscape itself that evoked these titanic emotions in me—the sight of Pops' flower beds, the rolling lawns, the oaks leaning their dark elbows over the cemetery, the creeping swamp with its uneven wall of gnawing trees.

"Things happened very fast after this. And my extreme exhaustion made the events of the day fragmentary and disconnected yet bright and clear.

"I remember that there were no paying guests in the house because Jasmine had held all the bedrooms for Tommy and Nash and Patsy.

"I remember that I ate a monstrous breakfast cooked by a tearful Big Ramona who chastised all of us ferociously for having been gone three and one-half years. I remember that Tommy ate with me and that he seemed as impressed by Blackwood Manor as he had been by castles in England and palazzi in Rome.

"I remember that a darling little boy came in, a charming Anglo-African blending of blue eyes, distinguished African features and curly blond hair, who told me proudly his name was Jerome and that he was three years old, on both counts of which I congratulated him, wondering who in the world were his parents. I announced that I found him to be verbally very far advanced.

" 'That's because he lives in this kitchen the way you used to do,' said Big Ramona.

"I remember that Aunt Queen's doctor came and said she had to have bed rest for at least a week, and her nurses should be there round the clock. It was old age, he whispered to me. And once she properly recovered from her overexertions she should be right fine. Her blood pressure was a medical marvel.

"I remember that I spent a desperate half hour on the phone trying in vain to reach Mona. Mayfair Medical would not even acknowledge she was there. And servants at the First Street house would give me no information either. At last I reached Michael, who would tell me only that Mona was sick; pray for her, yes, but to see her was out of the question.

"It made me frantic. I was ready to go directly to Mayfair Medical and search for her, room to room, when Michael suddenly said, as if he could read my thoughts:

" 'Quinn, listen to me. Mona has asked that you not see her. She's made us promise repeatedly that we won't let you in. It will break her heart if we break our word. We can't do it. It would be selfish for you to come. Don't you understand what I'm saying?'

" 'Good heavens, you mean she looks sick as well as feels sick? She's deteriorated. She's—.' I was stymied.

" 'Yes, Quinn. But don't give up hope. We are a long way from doing that. We're trying to build her back up. Her appetite is good. She's holding her own. She's got her books on tape. She's got her films. She sleeps a lot. That's to be expected.'

" 'Does she know I'm back?'

" 'Yes, she does, and she loves you.'

" 'Can I send her flowers?'

" 'Yes, you can do that, but be sure you put Ophelia Immortal on the card, won't you?'

" 'Why can't I talk to her by phone? Why can't we use E-mail?'

"There was a long pause and then he said,

" 'She's too weak for it, Quinn. And she doesn't want to do it. She's sick to her stomach, son. But this won't go on forever. She'll get better.'

"As soon as I rang off I ordered tons of flowers, baskets and baskets of Casablanca lilies and marguerites and zinnias and everything I could think of. I hoped they would fill her isolation chamber. Every card was to be writ large, to my Ophelia Immortal.

"After that I remember that I drifted into the kitchen, light-headed with jet lag and grief, and I saw Tommy playing Scrabble with little Jerome and I thought how incredible that the little guy could play the game at the tender age of three, until I realized Tommy was actually just teaching him words like 'red' and 'bed' and 'web' and 'do' and 'say' and 'go.'

"I remember drifting into the pantry and thinking the child was one of Jasmine's little nieces or nephews and asking her, 'Who are his parents?' and hearing her say, 'You and I are.' I remember nearly fainting. But that's a figure of speech. She also said to me, 'His middle name is Tarquin.'

"I remember going back out, feeling I was floating, and staring at my son and at my adopted thirteen-year-old uncle, and feeling myself utterly and totally privileged with these two generations, and when Jasmine appeared I put my arm around her and kissed her and she pushed me away, saying under her breath that there had been enough of that, and I ought to know it.

"I was positively groggy as I made my way to Aunt Queen's bedroom, and she looked up at me from her chaise lounge, where she was already under one of her white satin quilts with her feathered negligee stirring hither and thither with the motion of the overhead fan, and said:

" 'Darling boy, go to sleep. You're white as a sheet. I slept on the plane, but you didn't. You're staggering.'

" 'Are you drinking champagne?' I exclaimed. 'You must, for we have something to celebrate.'

" 'You come here to me!' Jasmine called out as she chased after me. But I wouldn't be deterred.

" 'Champagne it is!' I said, discovering the chilled bottle in the ice, and an extra glass, and that Aunt Queen was already happily swilling.

"What time was it? Who cared? I drank and then I told her all about Jerome, even as Jasmine dug her finely buffed fingernails into my arm and whispered curses into my ears to which I responded not one syllable.

"Aunt Queen was overcome with happiness! 'Why, splendid!' she declared. 'And all this time, Tarquin, I thought you were a virgin! Bring this child to me. And Jasmine, you amaze me. Why on earth didn't you write to us and tell us! This calls for child support among other things.'

"And so the handsome little infant was brought into the presence of the Queen, and groggily and happily I drank two more glasses of champagne before becoming totally incoherent. By then my son had been told that I was his father. And Tommy had received the news too, being advised by Aunt Queen that in this house we kept no secrets, a fact which would work to the betterment of all of us.

"I remember staggering to Aunt Queen's bed, and someone, some very blessed individual, sweeping away her many fancy quilts and boudoir dolls so that I could fall facedown into the immaculate pillows, and that same someone, no doubt, pulled off my shoes, and I was soon under the heavenly weight of the quilts and in the chill of the air conditioner, fast asleep.

"I dreamed a dream of Goblin. It was an awful dream that he was suffering and couldn't come to me. I saw him incomplete, a gaseous and hideous being, struggling to be solid, but without my will he was indistinct and loose and miserable. I knew myself in the dream as cold and cruel to him.

"I danced with Rebecca. She said, 'I would not take you for my vengeance. You have been too good.' 'Who then would you have?' I asked, and she answered me only with laughter. She went away and the music went with her. I opened my eyes.

"Aunt Queen lay beside me. She wore her silver-rimmed glasses. She was reading her paperback *The Old Curiosity Shop*, which I had given her on the plane, and she said to me:

" 'Quinn, Dickens is a madman.'

" 'Oh to be sure,' I said. 'It becomes wilder and wilder, all the darkness surrounding Little Nell; just keep going.'

" 'Oh, I will,' she said.

" 'She snuggled up to me. The feathers of her negligee tickled my nose but I loved it. I loved her frail arm so close to mine. I could read the book in her hands if I wanted to. I smelled her sweet perfume. She could buy anything in the world and she wore drugstore Chantilly, and a sweeter scent in all the world there is not.

"I remember seeing the violet sky through the windows.

" 'Lord, it's almost dark,' I said. 'I have to go to the Hermitage! I have to see my Petrine masterpiece.'

" 'Tarquin Blackwood, you will not go out in that swamp at this hour.'

" 'Nonsense, I have to,' I said, kissing her forehead and then her soft powdered cheek. 'Both Mona and Goblin are denied to me, and of Goblin's loss I have nothing to lament, I confess it, but I must go out there and claim what I've done.'

"I remember further protest, but I was deaf to it.

"I hurried up the stairs and into my room and into my closet, and I knew myself to be light-headed still as I pulled on a new pair of jeans and a new shirt and new boots (all purchased for my new size by Big Ramona as soon as she knew we were coming home) and then I took my thirty-eight pistol from the nightstand and headed down and out of the house. From the kitchen I took a bottle of water and a big knife, and from the shed a flashlight, and then I went down towards the swamp.

"Of course I was disregarding the terms of my bold and savage partner, but I had never agreed to them, had I? It was for myself that I had done the refurbishment and the renovation of the Hermitage. It was for me the fine furnishings that I would soon see. I had no fear of him, and if anything I felt a brooding curiosity to see him again and contend with him—perhaps to have a decent conversation with him. Perhaps to discuss 'our' little house and to discover whether we did indeed have a bargain, since I had achieved all of the splendid renovations, not he.

"That Goblin was not with me to help me did not matter to me. I would handle it. The Hermitage was mine.

"As I passed the little cemetery going down to the landing I stopped for a moment near Rebecca's grave. I shone the flashlight on her tombstone. A frisson of the dream came back to me, and I heard her voice again in my memory as though she was near to me. 'Not your life,' she said. 'Whose life then?' I asked. And I felt a sense of foreboding, a dreadful sense of it—as though life itself were full of nothing but misery.

"Wasn't Mona sick unto death, nauseated and miserable, and here I was going out to the Hermitage with no thought of her? Mona wanted so badly to see the Hermitage. But what could I do but pray for Mona?

"The sky was darkening. I had to go.

"When I returned I'd go to Mayfair Medical. I'd search the wards. What hospital room doesn't have a window for nurses to peep inside? I'd get as close to Mona as I could. Nobody would stop me, but for now it was the Hermitage that beckoned. I had to go.

"Into the pirogue I piled my gear, and, double-checking my gun for bullets, I set out. There was just enough light from the reddening sky to see the trees clearly and I knew the way now, and it soon became evident that the many pirogues of the renovation had plainly marked a trail.

They had worn the way, one might put it. And I was soon speeding along.

"In less than half an hour I saw the lights of the Hermitage! And as I pulled up to its new landing and tethered the pirogue, I saw the brilliantly lighted windows and the gleam of the white marble stairs. All around the little house were neat beds of flowers, and the wisteria vine came crawling splendidly over its high roof. The little building resembled a small Coptic church with its many arches.

"In the doorway, facing me, indeed watching me, was the stranger, in his male attire, hair full and loose, neither beckoning me to come closer nor putting up his hand to forbid my coming ashore.

"How was I to know this was the last day of my mortal life? How was I to know that all those random little things which I have described to you would mark the end of my history—that Jerome's father, Tommy's nephew, Aunt Queen's Little Boy, Jasmine's Little Boss and Mona's Noble Abelard were about to die?"

37

"I FOUND a paved path to the foot of the stairs. Allen had mentioned it to me on the phone but I had forgotten it. I had forgotten the flowers as well, and how tranquil and sweet they looked in the light from the windows.

"I came to the bottom of the marble steps. He was up there, merely looking down at me.

" 'Need I ask your permission to come up?' I asked.

" 'Oh, I have great plans for you,' he replied. 'Come up and I shall put them into execution.'

" 'Is that cordial?' I asked. 'Your voice puts me in doubt. I'm curious to see the place but wouldn't inconvenience you.'

" 'Then come up, by all means. Perhaps tonight is not the night for me to torment you.'

" 'Now you surprise me with your agreeable tone,' I said. I came up the stairs. 'But is it certain that you do mean to torment me?'

"He stood back, in the bath of light, and at once I saw that he was more definitely a she this evening. She had darkened her lips with red and worked a line of black kohl around each eye to make herself more bewitching. Her gleaming black hair was a raiment. And the actual garments she wore were a simple long-sleeve tunic shirt of red velvet and red velvet pants as featureless and simple. Around her small waist was a belt of onyx cameos, clasped in front, a real prize of a thing, each cameo being some two inches in size.

"She was barefoot, and her feet were beautiful with gold painted nails. Her fingernails were painted gold too.

" 'You're beautiful, my friend,' I said, feeling wonderful with excitement. 'Is it permitted to tell you this?' I bit my tongue before I said, I hadn't expected to find it so. What I remembered from that long ago night was something harsher and more dreadful.

"She gestured for me to enter the house.

" 'Of course it's permitted,' she responded in her low voice as I moved past her, which might have done well for a man or a woman, and as she smiled now her face was radiant. 'Look around your fine house, Little Gentleman,' she said.

" 'Ah, "little," ' I quoted it back to her. 'Why does everyone refer to me as little?' I asked.

" 'No doubt because you're so very tall,' she replied amiably, 'and because your face is so very innocent. I told you once I had a theory about you. My theory has proved correct. You've learnt more and you've grown to a great height. Both developments are splendid.'

" 'Then you approve of me.'

" 'How could I not?' she replied. 'But take your time. Look around at your handiwork.'

"It was difficult for me to look at anything but her. However, I did as she had asked and found the room stunning. Its white marble floor was brilliantly clean. And the deep green velvet couches I'd purchased from afar were sumptuous, as I'd hoped. The gilded torchères, positioned between the many windows, shone their light up on the outrageous gilded rafters. There were low marble tables before the couches and their accompanying Grecian swan-backed chairs.

"And then there was her desk and her chair, same as they were before, only polished up a bit it seemed.

"And the new fireplace, a black iron Franklin stove of great proportions, with only a heap of gray ash in it tonight, thanks to the warm weather.

"The curving stairs to the second floor was a heavily carved bronze created with pivots, and very handsome too. Beneath it was the only bookcase in the place, small, of heavily carved wood, neat and crammed with thin paperback volumes.

"There was nothing here that wasn't lovely in its own right.

"At the same time, there was something completely wrong with it, something grotesque, impure, out of keeping with the night noises of the swamp. Had my adolescent madness done this or her total insanity?

"Even the cup on her desk was a golden chalice with jewels embedded in it. It looked rather like the ciborium used by the priest at Mass for the wafers of the Blessed Sacrament.

" 'And so it was,' she remarked, 'before a little thief sold it to me in the streets of New Orleans. It's still consecrated, don't you suppose?'

" 'Really,' I replied, taking note that she had read my thoughts. I saw two bottles of red wine, already uncorked, sitting beside the ciborium.

" 'Those are for you, King Tarquin,' she said. She gestured for me to walk about more if I wanted to. I did so.

" 'Ah, you know the derivation of my name,' I said. 'Not many people do.' Clumsily I tried to match her eloquence.

" 'King Tarquin of ancient Rome,' she said, smiling. 'He ruled before the beginning of the Republic.'

" 'And do you think he was real or merely a legend?' I asked.

" 'Oh, most real in old poetry,' she replied, 'and most real in my mind in that over these three years I have so often thought of you. You have done well by my fantasies. I don't entirely know why I crave this remote paradise, but crave it I do, and you have restored my little house and made it splendid. I slip away from other palaces where I'm too uncomfortably known and come here with no loss of comfort. Why, your men even come to clean this house by day. They mop the marble and polish it afterwards. They clean the windows. I never expected this much attention.'

" 'Yes, I told them to do these things. They think me quite the madman, I must tell you.' Was this me talking?

" 'I'm sure they do, but that's the common price of all wild eccentricity, and small eccentricity isn't worth a damn, is it?'

" 'I don't know,' I said, laughing. 'I haven't settled that one yet.'

"I saw a big long heap of dark mink thrown over one of the couches—a bedspread, a wrap, something like that it had to be.

" 'Is that for cold nights?' I asked.

" 'Oh, yes,' she said, 'and also for flying. It's fiercely cold in the clouds.'

" 'You fly?' I asked, wanting to play along.

" 'Indeed, I do,' she responded with a straight face. 'How do you think I get here?'

"I laughed but not too loudly. It seemed an absurd fantasy to espouse.

"She was distractingly beautiful now, with the light of the torchères making a soft wreath of illumination behind us. Her breasts were prominent under the soft red velvet tunic, and there was something positively unsettling about her gorgeous bare feet with her golden toenails. As I looked down at them, indeed I couldn't stop myself from looking at them, I saw they were small feet, and that I found rather fetching. Also she wore a gold ring on her left big toe, and there seemed something deliciously evil about singling out that toe for this adornment.

"My three and one-half years of Catholic abstinence weighed heavily upon me suddenly, especially since there seemed something 'makeable' about her, maybe the fact that she seemed genuinely wild.

"I also found it beguiling that she was shorter than me now—no longer the six-foot devil who had borne down on me in the shower so long ago, fiercely threatening my life until Goblin had sent the shower of glass at her.

" 'And while we're on the subject of Goblin,' she said in the most agreeable tone, 'I can tell that the demon isn't with you. What a loss. Do you expect him to return and proffer his affections soon enough like a loyal dog, or do you think he's gone forever?'

" 'You puzzle me,' I said, 'taking such a sweet voice to speak such a hostile thing. I don't know whether or not I've lost him forever. Could be. Could be that he's found another soul with whom he's made a better communion. I gave him eighteen years of my life. Then distance divided us. I don't claim anymore to understand his nature.'

" 'I didn't mean to sound hostile,' she said. 'The truth is, and I do like to speak the truth when I can, that I never expected to find you so sanguine.'

"I didn't know what 'sanguine' meant. She moved towards the table, uncorked one of the bottles and filled the ciborium.

" 'Three and a half years has mellowed me, somewhat,' I said. 'And I never expected you to invite me in tonight. On the contrary, I expected to find you jealous of your nighttime hours. I thought you'd turn me away.'

" 'And why would that be, do you think?' she asked. She brought the cup to me and extended it. And only then did I see the giant sapphire carbuncle on her finger. 'Oh yes, this,' she said as I took the cup. 'I carved this likeness of the god Mars. I was consecrated to him once, but it was in jest. I've been the victim of so many jests.'

" 'I can't imagine why,' I said. I looked at the wine. 'Am I to drink alone?'

"She laughed softly. 'For the moment,' she said. 'Please go ahead. You'll make me unhappy if you don't.'

"My breeding was such that I couldn't refuse the drink on that account, and so I drank, noticing a strange flavoring in the wine, though it wasn't unpleasant. I drank deeply again. I was excited.

" 'You really mean what you say, don't you?' she asked. 'You don't see why people laugh at me. Or ever have, do you?'

" 'No,' I said. In my typical fashion I drank even more of the wine, loving the taste of it suddenly and letting it hit my hungry heart immediately. Nothing for lunch. Nothing for supper. Awake on the plane. Awake round the clock. I had to watch myself.

" 'They laughed and they still laugh,' she said, 'because I'm both man and woman. But you see nothing to jest at there, do you?'

" 'I told you no. I think you're rather magnificent. I thought you were before. My, but this wine is strong! Is it wine?' I realized that the bottles carried no labels. I felt the floor moving beneath me. 'Would you mind if I sat down?' I asked. I looked about me for a chair.

" 'No, you must,' she said. She drew up one of the swan-back chairs for me. It was a graceful thing, like the chairs on Grecian urns. I remembered having ordered it. And Allen had teased me over the phone about all the swans in my house of marble and gold.

" 'Yes, your workmen laugh at your taste,' she said, reading my thoughts, 'but your taste is excellent, have no doubt.'

" 'Oh, I don't have any doubts,' I said, more sure of myself now that I was seated. I laid the cup on the edge of the desk. My hand rested beside it. I think I had almost dropped it.

" 'Drink some more,' she said. 'It's a special brew. You might say I blended it myself.'

" 'Oh, I can't,' I said. I looked up into her eyes. What powerful eyes. People with big eyes have such a gift. And hers were so enormous. So white and black.

"She sat on the desk looking down at me. She smiled reassuringly. 'It seems I don't know quite what to do with you when you're so polite,' she said. 'You made an annoying enemy once, and now I want you to love me. Perhaps when all is said and done, you will.'

" 'That's entirely possible,' I said, 'but there're so·many species of love, aren't there? I'm religious still, and something tells me you live freely.'

" 'Catholic,' she said. 'Of course. The grand Church. Nothing less would be worthy of you and Mrs. McQueen, would it? It seems one evening in Naples that I saw you and your party at Mass. No. It was in the catacombs of San Gennaro. Your family had booked a private tour.

Why, I'm almost sure of it.' She lifted the ciborium and filled it from the bottle. She gave me the cup.

" 'You saw us in Naples?' I asked. My head was spinning. I drank the wine, thinking that just a little bit more might eliminate this precarious feeling. That happened sometimes, didn't it? Of course it didn't. 'How utterly remarkable,' I said. 'Because I could have sworn I saw you in Naples as well.'

" 'And where was that?' she asked.

" 'Are you my enemy?' I asked.

" 'Not at all,' she said. 'If I could, I'd deliver you from old age and death, from aches and pains, from the blandishments of ghosts, from the torment of your familiar, Goblin. I'd deliver you from heat and cold and from the arid dullness of the noonday sun. I'd deliver you into the placid light of the moon and into the domain of the Milky Way forever.'

" 'Those are strange words,' I said. 'I can't make sense out of them. I could have sworn I saw you in Naples, that I saw you on my balcony at the Excelsior Hotel, that I had a nightmare sent from you. Isn't that madness? Surely you'll tell me it was.'

" 'Nightmare?' she asked softly, sweetly. 'You call a fragment of my soul a nightmare? Oh, but who would want a fragment of another person's soul? You think you want Mona Mayfair's soul. You don't know what it would mean to see her now.'

" 'Don't play with her name,' I said. I was startled. Suddenly it seemed to me that everything that was happening was wrong. Mona, my beloved Mona. Don't speak of Mona. The wine was not wine. The house was overwhelming. Petronia herself was too large and grand for a woman. I was too drunk to be where I was.

" 'When I am finished with you, you won't want Mona Mayfair,' she said quickly, almost angrily, though her voice remained soft. She purred like a cat. 'And of my soul you'll know no more. My soul will be locked as though a key, a golden key, were turned inside it. It will all be silence between us, the silence you know now.'

" 'I have to get away from here,' I said weakly. I knew I couldn't stand. I tried. My muscles wouldn't work. 'I have to get back to the boat. If you have a modicum of honor, you'll help me.'

" 'I have none, so rest where you are,' she said. 'We'll part soon enough in my time, though not in yours, and then you may have this house as your Hermitage, and I even bequeath the tomb to you. Yes, you may have that, and you may take your chances with it, and you may crave this dark, lively swamp as I so often craved it. I think I've been waiting for you these long three and a half years, knowing I would relinquish everything to you when I saw you. Yes, waiting. Why is it that this must be done I can't answer—.'

" 'What? What must be done? What are you saying?' I pleaded. 'I don't understand you.'

" 'It's as though the evil builds up,' she said, 'and then it must be siphoned off into a new one, and I give birth as I never could in life.'

" 'I can't follow you.'

"She turned and looked down at me, and there spread across her face the most transcendent smile.

" 'Why do I get the feeling that you're a giant cat?' I asked suddenly, 'even to your lovely eyes, and I'm some luckless prey that you've randomly selected?'

" 'Never random,' she said, her face exquisitely serious. 'No, never random. But carefully, out of circumstance, and on merit, and out of loneliness. But never random, no, never that. You are much loved. You have been long awaited.'

"A wave of sheer drunkenness passed over me. I was about to slip into unconsciousness.

"The figure before me started flashing on and off, as if someone had ahold of the light switch and meant to drive me mad. I tried to stand up but I couldn't.

"I put the ciborium on the edge of the desk and pushed it back with my right fingers. I saw her fill it again with wine. No more, I thought, but then she lifted it and put it to my lips. I took it. I tried to decline. She tipped it and I drank it as it spilled down my neck and into my shirt. It was delicious, much more so now than in the beginning. I fell back. I saw the ciborium lying on the floor. I saw the red wine on the marble.

" 'No, not on the beautiful white marble,' I said. 'It's too like blood, look at it.' Again, I tried to stand up. I couldn't.

"She knelt down in front of me.

" 'I have cruelty in me,' she said. 'I have cruelty in me which will be answered. Don't expect anything else from me. You'll have the gifts I choose to give and those only, and I'll make no mewling bastards such as others make, fodder for the old ones, but I'll leave you strong when I leave you, and with all the gifts you need.'

"I couldn't answer her. My lips would no longer move.

"Suddenly I saw Goblin behind her! He was indistinct, all force, not illusion, and she rose in a fury, trying to throw him off. He had pulled the choke hold on her, the very move she had once pulled on me, and she stomped her foot on the floor as she threw her elbow back at him. He dissolved yet came at her again, infuriating her.

"Again the light was flickering. My muscles were paralyzed. I saw her in the flicker as she darted across the room. She gathered up the huge wrap of mink and came towards me, and again he tried to stifle her, but she would have none of it. Slapping him away from her, she reached for me. And with one slender arm she snatched me bodily from the chair, and in the mink wrapped my entire body as though such a gesture was nothing to her, and then she enveloped me in her arms.

"She cursed at Goblin. 'Say farewell to your lover!'

"We were in the open air. I saw Goblin clinging to us. I saw his face, his open mouth as he howled. He slipped down, down as though he were drowning.

"We were rising, and I saw the clouds below me. And I felt the wind against my cheek, and my skin was chilled, but it didn't matter because all around me were the glorious stars.

"She pressed her lips to my ear. And just before consciousness left me entirely, I heard her speak.

" 'Pay heed to these cold beacons,' she said, 'for in all your long life, you may never find warmer friends than these.' "

38

"I AWOKE once during daylight. I lay on a soft bed on a terrace, and all around me were flowers. There were potted geraniums along the balustrade, and beyond those were white-and-pink oleanders, and I thought in my dizziness and my madness that I could see a distant mountain to my right, which I knew certainly by its shape to be Vesuvius, and when I rose, sick and aching, I staggered to the edge of the oleanders and I looked down on the tile roofs of the town way far below me and saw that I couldn't escape in that way.

"Far to my left the road wound on with the cars like tiny beetles speeding along it. It was the coast of Italy in all its rugged glory, and beyond the road was the sizzling sea. The sun was high and blinding and it burnt down upon me, and there was no escape from it on this terrace.

"As for the house, it was locked against me. The dark green shuttered doors had nothing that I could even grasp. I fell back down on the bed and my eyes closed, though I willed them to stay open.

"My fevered mind said, *You must escape here. You must go down the slope somehow. You have to drop to the roofs below.* That this creature, Petronia, meant to murder me, I had no doubt.

"I felt unconsciousness creep over me again, hot and dark and full of desperation. Some drug was working in me still that I couldn't fight.

"Then, against the blue sky I saw the shadowy outline of a woman and I heard her talking low and fast in Italian and I felt a sharp stab in my arm. I saw the outline of the syringe in her hand as she held it up with a dainty gesture, and I wanted to protest but I couldn't. And next I knew, she was shaving my face with a small electric razor that was like a noisy little animal running all over my upper lip and my chin.

"She was speaking to another woman in Italian, and though I spoke a little Italian I couldn't tell what it was she was saying, only that she complained. Finally she moved to one side, and I could see her, and she was young and brunette and with an upturn to her eyes.

" 'Why you, I would like to know,' she said to me with a thick accent. 'Why not me after all this time? I serve and I serve, and she brings you to me and says make him ready. I am nothing but a slave.'

" 'Help me to get out of here,' I said, 'and I'll make you rich.'

"She laughed. 'You don't even want it, and they're giving it to you!' she said scoffing. 'And why? Because she has a whim.' Her voice was soft but insistent. 'Everything is a whim with her. To come. To go. To live in this palazzo. To live in that palazzo.' She laid down the syringe. I heard the clink of metal. She lifted a long scissors. She cut a lock from my hair.

" 'What did you put into me?' I asked. 'Why did you shave my face? Where is Petronia?'

"She laughed, and so did another young woman who appeared on the left side of me, opposite. She was also slender, fashionable-looking and pretty of face, just like the one who was trimming my hair. She stood with her back to the light, her shadow falling over me.

" 'We should kill you,' said the other woman, the new one, 'so that she can't do it. We could tell her that you died.'

"They both laughed at this joke uproariously.

" 'Why do you wish me harm?' I asked.

" 'Because she chose you instead of us!' said the one who had injected me. She was angry but she didn't raise her voice. 'Do you know how long we've waited? We've been teased by her since we were children. Always she has an excuse, except when she is angry, and then she offers no excuse for anything, and God help those who ask her for one!' She took a comb to my hair. 'You're ready as far as I can see.'

" 'Don't worry,' said the other one. She stood with folded arms. Her face was cold. She had beautiful sneering lips. 'We won't hurt you. She would know when she comes. And then she would kill us for certain.'

" 'Are you talking about Petronia?'

" 'You don't know anything,' said the one who had been combing my hair. 'She's just playing with you. She's going to kill you like all the rest.'

"I could feel the drug working in me, or was it my imagination? I was so hot, so miserable. I was neither drugged nor conscious.

" 'Don't try to get up,' said the woman with the comb. But I did try and I pushed her away from me.

"She fell back, murmuring in Italian. I think she was cursing. 'I hope she tortures you!' she said.

"I was flat on my back. I imagined myself crawling to the balustrade. I should have dropped down, no matter how low it was. I had been a fool not to try it. My eyes closed. I could hear their voices, their cheap, cruel laughter. I hated them.

" 'Listen to me,' I said. 'Help me to the balustrade. I'll go over it myself. You can tell her that I jumped. I'll probably die, and you'll be happy and free of me, just like . . . just like . . .' I couldn't make my mouth form the words. I wasn't sure I had said even what I thought I had said.

"I was swooning. I could no longer see.

"The bed was moving, and at first I thought it was my disorientation, but then I heard the squeak of the wheels. A coolness came over me and I felt my clothes being ripped from me, and then, down into a pool of warm water, my body was slipped.

"Thank God for it, I thought. The sweat and the heat were gone. Someone was bathing me and I didn't hear the voices of the young women anymore.

" 'Listen to me,' said a voice right close to my ear.

"I tried to open my eyes. In a flash I saw the ceiling painted with murals—a great blue sky with flying gods and goddesses: Bacchus in his chariot and satyrs around him with wreaths and trails of green ivy, and the maenads with their hair ripped and their clothes in tatters following behind. Brand-new. Too bright.

"Then I saw the boy who was bathing me. He was one of those extraordinary young Italian beauties with a halo of black curls for hair, and a gorgeous naked chest and muscular arms.

" 'I'm talking to you,' he said with a thick accent. 'Can you understand me?'

" 'The water feels good,' I tried to say, but I'm not sure I managed the words.

" 'Can you understand me?' he asked again.

"I tried to nod but my head was against a rim of porcelain. I said, 'Yes.'

" 'She'll test you,' he said. He went on bathing me, lifting the water in his hands and letting it flow over me. 'If you fail her tests, she'll kill you. That's always her way with those who fail her. There is nothing to be gained from fighting her. Remember what I say.'

" 'Help me to get away from here,' I said.

" 'I can't help you.'

" 'Do you believe me?' I struggled to articulate it. 'When I say that I can reward you? I have plenty of money.'

"His eyes widened and he shook his head. 'Doesn't matter if I believe you,' he said. 'She would find me, no matter where we went or what you gave me. She's too powerful for me ever to escape her. My life was finished the night that she saw me waiting tables in a café in Venezia.' He made a short bitter laugh. 'I wish to God that I had never brought her that little glass of wine, that useless little glass of wine.'

" 'There has to be a way,' I said. 'She's not God, this woman.' I was losing consciousness again. I fought it. I remembered the cold air and the stars around me. What was she? What kind of monster?

" 'No, not God,' he said smiling bitterly. 'Just powerful and very cruel.'

" 'What does she want with me?' I asked.

" 'Try to stand up to her tests,' he said. 'Try to please her. Otherwise you die. She never does anything else with those who fail her. She gives them to us, and we rid the world of the bodies, and for that we are allowed to continue to live. That's our existence. Can you imagine the place the Devil has for us in his inferno? Now, if you believe in God, use this time to say your prayers.'

"I couldn't speak anymore.

"I felt him raise my arms, one at a time, and shave the hair beneath them. It was a strange ritual, and I couldn't understand the desire of anyone for such a thing to be done.

"He seemed to sense my discomfort.

" 'I don't know what it means,' he said to me softly, 'but for you she has ordered us to take great care.' He shook his head sadly. 'Maybe it means nothing, maybe it means something. Only in time will we know.'

"I think I laid my hand over his and patted him to console him because he sounded so sad.

"All the while the water of the bath was warm and moving, and then he told me in my ear that he was taking me to a place where I would wake from the drugs I'd been given, but I mustn't make noise.

"I slept.

"When I woke, I knew that I was alone. I could hear the silence and stillness around me, and I found myself on a couch and surrounded by golden bars.

" 'How my friend loves gold,' I whispered, 'but then I have always loved it myself.'

"Within seconds I realized I was in a glorified round cage. The door was securely locked, and I wore no boot or even a sandal with which to kick at it, and my fist did little good.

"As for my clothes, I'd been dressed in a pair of black pants. No shirt.

"Now, outside of this cage there was a great marble room, precisely what one would expect in a hillside palazzo, and it had its large square floor-length windows open to a long terrace, as one might also expect, and there was the sunset streaking the sky with red, and the violet light simmering as the sun sank into the sea.

"Italy, so glorious, on the flank of the great mountain, and not very far no doubt from the ruins of tragic cities it had destroyed.

"I sat back on the couch, watching the windows fill up with early stars and the room darken before me, which only proved to put it in a gentler light.

"There was something so very decadent and perverse about the cage in which I was imprisoned that I loathed it intensely, yet it had an odd calming effect on me because I knew that in a monstrous game with Petronia I might have some chance. That had been the implication of the boy who had bathed me. At least that had been the inference which I drew. Nevertheless, I was revolted by everything around me. This was a completely new emotion for me.

"The lights came up slowly, revealing scattered lamps along the inner walls of the room and murals which somewhat mimicked those of Pompeii—that is, rectangular paintings framing in Roman red various goddesses who danced with their backs turned to the room.

"And as these lights filled the space with a golden illumination there entered not the proud arrogant Petronia whom I expected but two other creatures equally strange.

"One was a black man, so black indeed that he looked like polished onyx, and though he was at the very far end of the marble room, away from me, I could see the gold earrings in his ears.

"He had very delicate features and he had yellow eyes. His hair was very curly and short-cropped and not totally unlike my own.

"The other man was a puzzle. He appeared old. Indeed, he had heavy jowls and receding temples and his hair was silver, but he appeared to be without blemish, as if he were made not from old flesh and blood but from wax. His eyes sagged slightly at the outside edges as if they were going to slide down his face, and his chin jutted, which gave him a firm look.

"This one, the old one, reminded me of someone, but I couldn't think who it was.

"Neither of these creatures looked human and there settled over me the certainty that they weren't.

"I flashed on the stars I'd seen last night, or whenever it had been as we'd risen into the air, and I felt a dreadful fatality—indeed, an awful sense that everything I'd known and loved was about to be taken from me and there was little really that I could do to prevent it. The test, the fight, the contest, whatever, would be a matter of form.

"I was mutely horrified and I sought to adjust my emotions. To be tantalized was my only hope. There was no time for wonder or curiosity.

"These two men came towards me but purely by accident. Though they looked at me, they seated themselves at a table in the center of the room. And there they began to play chess and to talk to each other, their profiles turned to me, which meant that the silver-haired man with the waxy jowls had his back to the star-studded sky and the black man looked out.

"Both of these creatures wore immaculate evening dress of a sort. They had on shining black dinner jackets and trousers and patent leather shoes. But they wore white turtlenecks of some very glossy material rather than shirts and black ties.

"They were soon laughing and joking with each other, and the language was Italian, so I couldn't follow what they said. But when I'd had a bellyful of it, I spoke up.

" 'So neither of you will enlighten me,' I asked, 'as to why I'm held captive here? You don't think I'd be in this predicament of my own free will?'

"It was the elderly-looking gentleman who answered me, his chin jutting even more as he did so. 'Well, now,' he said in clear English, 'you know you did something to be here. Now, what did you do to Petronia? She wouldn't have brought you here if you were innocent. Don't claim to be that with us.'

" 'That's exactly what I claim,' I said. 'I was brought here out of her caprice, and I ought to be released.'

"The black man spoke to the other. 'I do tire of her games, I swear it.' His voice was mellow and sweet, as though he was used to power.

" 'Oh, come, you know you enjoy it as much as I do,' said the elderly one. His voice was deep. 'Why else would you be here now? You knew she had this boy.'

" 'All I ask is to be released,' I said sharply. 'I can't send the authorities after you because I don't know who you are, and as for Petronia, all attempts in the past by me to have her discovered or arrested have failed, and they'll fail in the future. I won't attempt any such thing. What I ask is to be let go!'

"The black man rose from his armchair and he came towards me. He was the taller of the two. I didn't stand up to measure my height against his. He reached through the bars and laid his cool hand on my head. He looked into my eyes. I hated him. It took all my self-control to remain still.

" 'You've done no wrong to anyone,' he said under his breath, as though he had read it from my mind. 'And across the world she brings you for her blood sport.' He sighed. 'Oh, Petronia, why the cruelty, always the cruelty? Why, my beautiful pupil? When will you ever learn?'

" 'You'll let me go?' I asked. I looked up at him. What a splendid being he was. His features were sublimely chiseled and his face looked kind.

" 'I can't do that, my child,' he said in an even voice. 'I wish that I could, but I believe your fate is decided. I'll try to make your agony short.'

" 'Why does my life mean so little to you?' I asked. 'I come from a world where every life is precious. Why is it so different for you?'

"The old man had approached by this time, walking in a sprightly manner completely out of keeping with the appearances of age in him, and he was peering through the bars at me too.

" 'No, you're not innocent, don't tell us that,' he chortled. 'You're the Evil Doer in some guise,' he protested. 'She wouldn't bring you here otherwise. I know her too well.'

" 'Not well enough,' said the coal black one. 'She does what she pleases and it's never enough for her.'

"I stared at the old man. 'The old man,' I said aloud, and then I realized it. 'The Old Man,' I said again. 'It's you. The portrait on the living room wall! It's Manfred Blackwood, that's who you are.'

" 'And who are you to say my name so boldly to me?' he demanded. He puffed himself up.

" 'You're demons, all of you. God, this is Hell.' I laughed. I felt the drug in me again. There was no escape. My words came in a rush. 'If it weren't for Julien Mayfair, you'd be my ancestor. I'm Tarquin Blackwood, that's who I am. She took me from the Hermitage, the Hermitage you built for her, and that I refurbished for her. Blackwood Manor's in my hands now. Your granddaughter, Lorraine, is still living, living to mourn for me and tear out her hair that I've disappeared from Blackwood Farm. Didn't Petronia tell you what she was up to?'

"He went into a fury. He tried to shake the bars but he couldn't. He pounded upon the lock. Now he was an old man in all his parts, his jaw trembling, his eyes tearing. 'Abomination!' he roared.

"The black one tried to calm him. 'Now, let this matter be in my hands,' he said. 'We have an order here of authority.'

" 'Do you see what she means to do?' the Old Man shouted. His jowls trembled. All of him trembled. His eyes were inflamed as he gazed at me. 'Who told you about Julien?' he demanded, as if such a thing were important now.

" 'Julien himself told me. I'm a seer of spirits,' I retorted. 'But what does it matter? Get me out of this place. Your granddaughter Lorraine needs me. Blackwood Farm needs me. I have flesh and blood that need me.'

"Suddenly Petronia herself appeared. Clad in a black velvet tunic and pants with a belt of cameos, she came striding across the long room and up to the two men, declaring as she did:

" 'What is this, the convocation of the cage?'

"As Manfred tried to seize her by the throat she threw him backwards, so that his body went yards across the marble floor and slammed into the wall, his head snapped back in a blow that would have killed an ordinary human and out of his throat came a deep and terrible roar.

" 'Don't dare to question me,' she said.

"The black one, as though nothing could perturb him, reached out for her and slipped his arm around her neck. He was taller than her by some inches. Probably he was my height. He brought her head down onto his shoulder and I saw her hand tremble as she let him do it, and he whispered to her,

" 'Petronia, my dearest, why, why always the rage?'

"He held her and she allowed herself to be held, and the Old Man wept as he collected himself, came forward, wounded, furious, helpless, shaking his head.

" 'My own,' wept the Old Man, 'and your pledges to me are worthless, your bond is worthless—.'

" 'Leave me alone, you fool,' she said, raising her eyes and turning her head to look at him. 'I've kept my pledges to you ten times over. I've given you immortality! What in hell do you want? And then on top of it riches undreamt of. This boy is nothing to you but something senti-mental, like the photographs you keep of your precious Virginia Lee and your son William and your daughter Camille, as if these people were anything to you in the dust of time. They are not.'

"The Old Man sobbed. Then he spoke, blubbering.

" 'Stop her, Arion,' he said. 'Don't let her go on. Stop her.'

" 'Wretched, miserable, old man,' Petronia said. 'Old forever. Noth-ing could give you youth. I despise you.'

" 'And that's your reason for what you've done to me?' I asked. It would have been wiser perhaps to say nothing, but in some way this case was being tried before Arion, the black one, and I had to make some effort or die full of regret.

"Petronia looked at me, and, as if seeing me for the first time, she smiled. And as always happened when she smiled, she looked serene and lovely. She was still in the arms of Arion, and Arion was stroking her loose full hair. It was utterly loving the way that Arion held her. Her breasts were against him, and he seemed to adore her.

" 'Don't you want to live forever, Quinn?' she asked me.

"She slipped gently out of the embrace of Arion, and she took from underneath her black velvet tunic a gold chain, and on the end of this chain was a key, and with this she unlocked my handsome prison.

"She opened the door. With the meanest fingers imaginable she grabbed my left arm and yanked me from the couch and out into the room, slamming me up against the bars. It sent a shudder of pain through me.

"Arion remained close, staring at me, and the Old Man was some distance away. He had taken a small picture from his coat and he looked at it piteously. I wondered if it was of Virginia Lee. He was whispering to himself insanely.

" 'Are you prepared to fight for immortality?' Petronia asked of me.

" 'Not at all, not one wit,' I said, 'nor for my life. Not against the bully that I know you to be.'

" 'Bully!' She mocked me. 'You call me that? After you had your familiar attack me with flying shards of glass?'

" 'He did what he could to protect me. You were in Blackwood Manor. You meant to do me harm.'

" 'And why isn't he here?' she asked.

" 'Because he can't be. You know this,' I said. 'I'm no match for you. I saw what you did to Manfred a moment ago. You play an unfair game with me. You always have.'

" 'Stubborn,' she said as she smiled, cruelly this time, and shook her head. 'Always your way. Pride, that's your sin.'

"Arion reached out for me and took my head in both his hands, and I felt his soft silky thumbs against my cheeks. 'Why don't you let him go?' he asked. 'He's innocent.'

" 'But that's the best kind,' said Petronia.

" 'Then you mean truly to do it,' said Arion, stepping back, 'not merely to kill him?'

" 'I mean to do it,' she said nodding, 'if I find him fit for it, if I find him strong.'

"Before I could protest, before I could mock, before I could sneer or plead or whatever might have come into my head, she picked me up and threw me, as she had done with Manfred, against the far wall. The blow to my head was terrific, and I thought, This death is not going to take very long.

"At the same time I became enraged as I always do by such hurt, and, falling down on the floor, I sought to get up immediately, and I flew at her, missing her and falling on my knees.

"I heard her cruel laughter. I heard Manfred weeping. Where was Arion? I looked up and caught a glimpse of the two men seated in their chairs at the table. And where was she?

"She slipped her hand under my shoulder and yanked me to my feet and slapped me hard on the left side of my face and then threw me across the floor. I went sprawling. It was pointless to try to fight. It was everything to keep to my word. To give her no sport at all. But I couldn't keep to it. Again, I tried to get up.

"Now, I knew nothing of fighting. Or I should say all I knew of it was what I had watched in boxing, which was my favorite spectator sport. And there was no way to apply what I knew in this situation, and I had never acquired any skill at fighting myself.

"But as I rose to my feet this time I saw Petronia standing right before me, and it seemed commonsensical that if I ran low at her I could topple her, and so I did this, tackling her right below the knees, and over me she went.

"The men laughed at this, which was unfortunate. I would rather have had cheers. But spinning round I came down on her before she could rise, and I tried to put my thumbs into her eyes. She caught me around the throat with both her hands, and now, fully enraged, she threw me over and back on the floor and then dragged me across it until she had come to the balcony, at which point she grabbed both my wrists in one hand and slung me over the white railing and asked me if I would like to be dropped to my death.

"I could see the lights of the traffic far below on the winding road. I could also see the ocean boiling on the rocks just beyond it. I gave her no answer. I was dazed. I also thought I was doomed. I knew Manfred didn't have the power to stop her. And I didn't think that Arion would.

"That I had thrown her over only made things worse.

"Next I knew she had drawn me up and thrown me onto the floor again and was kicking me and dragging me about the room. I thought of her as a giant cat again, as I had in the Hermitage, and of myself as her prey.

" 'This is not the way to do such a thing,' Arion said to her. I heard it near me as though he had come up to her, but where we were in the room, I didn't know.

"Petronia said, 'We choose our own way, don't we? We must do it the way we want to do it. In a fraction of a second, all his wounds will heal. He'll know the power of the Blood when that happens, and it will be all the finer for him. Let me have what I need.'

" 'But why, my darling, why do you need it?' Arion said. 'I don't understand, my precious one, why the rage, always the rage?'

"They went on talking but they had switched back into Italian. I sensed that he was talking about the passage of time and that she had once been different, but that was all I could divine. The Old Man continued to cry.

"I tried to move and then I felt Petronia's foot on my throat. I was choking. She let up on the pressure and I saw her face above mine, her hair pouring down and tickling me as she drew me up to her with both her hands. My weight meant nothing to her. She came in close to me as though she meant to kiss me on the throat.

"I lay back on a couch, and she had her arms behind my back, and her mouth was open against my skin, and then I felt two sharp pinpricks on the side of my throat, and the world and all my pain went dim. I heard her heart beat.

"*Teach me*, she said. *I will not have my kiss be quiet.*

"That she was sucking my blood from me I knew, and that I was getting weaker and weaker I knew as well. And it did seem that all my life fled from me, that image after image of childhood, young manhood and the last few years of love and ecstasy and wonder fled from me with my blood—uncontrollably, unstinting and pure. What this intimacy meant in the greater scheme of things I was helpless to understand, and then she drew back and I went limp in her arms. I sank down, free, onto the floor.

"Petronia had hold of my arm. She was dragging me again. I felt the sharp kick of her foot in my ribs. I could no longer see. I could hear the Old Man cry out. I knew it was for me that he cried. But she merely cursed under her breath. The marble felt cold beneath me. I lay sprawled against it.

"Suddenly the scene changed. I was no longer in my body but looking down on it, and down on all the occupants of the room. I was at the entrance to a long dark tunnel, and a roaring wind surrounded me, a frightening wind, and at the end of the tunnel there appeared a wondrous light, a light truly beyond description, and in that light, huge gold-and-white light, I could see the figures of Pops and Sweetheart gazing at me. Lynelle was also with them. I wanted desperately to join them, but I couldn't move. Some hideous fascination with Petronia and Manfred and Arion prevented me from moving. Some putrid ambition kept me from turning and reaching out for those I so loved. There was no clarity in me. There was only turbulence. Then, as suddenly as this vision had come, it was gone. I had made no decision.

"I was back in my aching and bruised body. I was on the marble floor again.

" 'You're dying,' Petronia said. 'But I know you now, I know you from the Blood, and I won't let it happen, Tarquin Blackwood. I claim you as my own.' Again, her arms lifted me.

" 'Ask him what he wills,' said the black one named Arion.

" 'What do you will?' she demanded. She held me up on my knees in front of her. I could feel her velvet pants against me. 'Speak to me,' she said. 'What do you will?'

"Helpless and clumsy I fell against her crotch, grabbing for her leg and then recoiling, and near collapsing, as she jerked my shoulder and held me on my knees.

" 'What do you want!' she demanded again. What was I to say? To die? In this place, around the world from Aunt Queen, from Mona, from all I loved, to die without a trace?

"I raised my fist, trying to hurt her. I hit her but my fist had nothing behind it. I clawed at her velvet clothes. I tried to hit her again. I struck at her private parts.

" 'Oh, you want to see it, do you? You want to see what they all laughed at!' she said. 'Come now, pay me homage,' she said. I heard the snap opening, and then my hand was placed upon the short, very thick stub of her erect cock, then down lower, between two pendulous labia, the shallow crevice that was her vagina, then back again to her cock. 'Take it in your mouth,' she said to me angrily. I felt the pressure against my lips. 'Take it!' she demanded.

"I did the only thing I could do. I opened my mouth, and when she shoved her cock into it I bit down with all my might and main. I heard her howl but I hung on. And there came into my mouth a copious flow of electrifying blood such as I never expected—and madly I hung on.

"I bore down with my teeth and the blood, this liquid fire, streamed into me. It poured down my throat. I swallowed without meaning to swallow. It was as if my body, once drained by her, could not resist it, and suddenly I realized that her hands were cradling my head and her howling was laughter and that the blood was not blood as I knew it but a great rush of stimulating fluid that seemed to come from her heart and her brain.

"*Know me. Know who I am!* This she said to me, and there came a rush of knowledge into me which I couldn't deny. I would have turned away from it if I could. I hated her that much. But I couldn't turn away, and now I couldn't let go.

"Long, long centuries ago she had been born to an actress mother and a gladiator father in the Rome of Caesar, a freakish child, half male, half female, a thing to be destroyed by ordinary parents but kept by hers for the theater, in which she grew to be a gladiator of great strength by the age of fourteen.

"Before that point, a thousand times she'd been shown privately to those who could pay for it, for those who wanted to touch her and have her touch them. Never had she known love for her own sake, or privacy, or a moment of delicacy, or a scrap of clothing that wasn't for show.

"In the arena she was fierce and murderous. I saw the spectacle—the huge crowds roaring for her. I saw the sand red with the blood she shed. She won every match, no matter how heavy or great her opponent. I saw her in her shining armor, her sword at her side, her hair tied back, her eyes on Caesar as she made her regal bow!

"Years passed during which she fought, her parents commanding ever higher and higher fees. At last, when she was still a girl, she was sold to a merciless master for a fortune, and he sent her into the ring against the fiercest of wild beasts. Even these could not defeat her. Nimble and fearless she danced against lions and tigers, thrusting her spear deep and true to the mark.

"But she grew tired in her heart, tired of combat, tired of lovelessness, tired of misery. The crowd was her lover, but the crowd was nowhere in the dark of night when she slept chained to her bed.

"Then Arion had come, Arion had paid to see her as had so many. Arion had paid to touch her, as had so many. Arion had bought dresses to pose her. Arion had embraced her. Arion had liked to comb her long black hair. Then Arion had bought her and set her free. Arion had given her a heavy purse and said, 'Go where you please.' But where could she go? What could she do? She couldn't bear the sounds of the circus during the games. She couldn't bear the thought of the gladiatorial schools. What was there for her? Was she to be pimp and whore at the same time? She had tagged after Arion, loving him.

" 'You are my life now,' she had told him. 'Don't turn your back on me.' 'But I gave you the world,' he had answered her. Unable to bear her tears, he had given her more money, a house in which to live. But still she came to him weeping.

"And finally he took her under his wing. He brought her to his city. He brought her to beautiful Pompeii. His was the cameo trade, he told her. He had three shops of cameo makers, the finest in all of the empire. 'Can you learn this art for me?' he asked her. 'Yes,' she said. 'For you I would learn anything. Anything at all.' She set to work with a passion she'd never known. She wasn't fighting for multitudes, she wasn't fighting for her own worthless life. She was fighting to please Arion, a fragile and total thing. Her enemies were clumsiness, impatience, anger. She studied with all the masters in his shops. She watched. She imitated. She worked in shell, in stone, in precious jewels. She mastered the chisel, the small drill. She learned all that she could.

"Finally, at the end of two years, she had her specimens to show Arion, fine and perfect things. She had done gatherings of gods and goddesses like unto the friezes on the temples. She had done portraits like unto the finest in the Forum. She had made art out of a craft. Never had he seen such work, he told her. He loved her. And such happiness she'd never known.

"Then came the terrible days of Vesuvius, the eruption of the mountain and the death of the idyllic little city where they had all known such happiness. Arion had fled the night before to the far side of the Bay of Naples. He'd sensed early on the evening before the eruption what was to happen. It had been her duty to see that the slaves of the shops escaped. But only a few would listen to her.

"And when it was all over and the air was full of ash and poison and the sea was full of bodies, when nothing remained where Pompeii had once stood, she had come to Arion's villa—the very place where we were now—weeping and with only a handful of followers, to tell him that she had failed.

" 'No, my beloved,' he said. 'You have saved my finest prize, you have saved your own life when I thought that all was lost. What can I give you for this, my sweet Petronia?' And in time he had given her the Blood that she was giving me. In time he had made her immortal as she was making me.

"She let me go. My lips stroked her cock as I withdrew.

"I fell back on the floor. But I could see with new eyes all around me. And I felt the bruises all over my body healing. I felt the pain leave my head. I sat up as though waking from a dream and I looked out the open window over the railing, and the pure azure of the evening sky caught me and held me and I didn't hear the voices of the room.

"Arion came. He took hold of me and lifted me just the way she had done it, without effort, and then he reached up to his throat, and he said to me to Drink.

" 'No, wait please,' I whispered. 'Let me savor what she taught me of herself. If you will.' I meant it reverently.

"But she flew at me and knocked me to the floor again and there came her foot against my ribs. 'Trash!' she said. 'You dare answer that way to the Master, and who are you to savor what you know of me!'

" 'Petronia!' said Arion to her. 'Enough.'

"He picked me up. 'My blood will give you added strength,' he said. 'Take it. It's far older than hers, and you won't be bound to her so very much.'

"I could have cried at her savagery. I had so loved her in the Blood, and I had been a fool for it, such a fool, but as he said now to drink, I ran my tongue over my teeth, why I didn't know. And I discovered the eye-teeth were fangs, and with them I kissed his throat, as he had directed me, and there came a new stream of images and blood.

"These images I can't claim to remember. I think that somehow, through some skill, he guarded his generous and older heart. I think he gave me the Blood and its strengthening power without all his secrets. But what he did give me was inexpressibly glorious and it filled my hurt soul after her rebuff.

"I saw Athens in him. I saw the famed Acropolis thronged and thriving. I saw it with temples and images brilliantly painted as I had been taught it was painted, not as we now see Greek art, as white and pure, but done in vivid blues and reds and flesh tones, oh, the marvel of it! I saw the Agora filled with people! I saw the whole town spread on the gentle slopes of the mountain. My head teemed with priceless visions, and where he was in all this I couldn't guess. I felt the language of the people all around me, and I saw the hard stone street beneath my sandals, and felt his blood pumping into me, washing my heart and my soul.

" 'Only the Evil Doer, my child,' he said to me as the Blood pounded. 'Feed only on the Evil Doer. When you hunt, unless you take only the Little Drink, pass by the innocent heart. Use the power you will have from me to read the minds and hearts of men and women and ferret out the Evil Doer everywhere, and only from him take the blood.'

"Finally, he pulled me back. I licked the blood from my lips. I sighed. This was to be my only nourishment. I knew it. The knowledge had come to me instinctively. And much as I had loved the taste of his blood and the taste of Petronia's blood, I hungered for a base human so that I would know that taste as well.

"He stroked my forehead and hair with his silky hands and he looked into my eyes.

" 'Only the Evil Doer, you understand me, young one? Oh, the innocent beckon. They do it unwittingly. And how savory they seem. But mark my word, they'll lead you straight to madness whether you have an educated soul or no. You'll come to love them and to despise yourself. Mark my words, it's the tragedy of Petronia. For her there is no innocence and therefore no conscience and therefore no happiness. And so in misery she goes on.'

" 'I follow your rules,' Petronia said. I heard her nearby.

" 'You did not with this one,' said Arion emphatically.

" 'My grandson, my very grandson,' cried the Old Man to himself in his misery. 'You blaspheming wretch.'

" 'And so he will live forever,' said Petronia solemnly. She laughed. 'What more can I do? What more can I give?'

"I turned to look at her. With these precious eyes I saw her harsh loveliness as though it were a miracle.

"And I knew what had been done to me. Of its history, of its commonness, of its rules, of its limits I knew nothing. But I knew what had been done. *Immortality*. I knew it but couldn't grasp it. Where was

God? Where was my faith? Had the whole edifice collapsed in this monstrosity?

"I began to feel a wrenching pain. Was I deluded?

"Arion said:

" 'This is human death. It'll take a few short moments. Go with the attendants into the bath. They'll dress you afterwards, and then you'll learn how to hunt.'

" 'So we are vampires,' I said. 'We are the legend.' The pain in my gut was intolerable. I saw the male attendant I had known before. He was waiting.

" 'Blood Hunters,' said Arion. 'Defer to me with these words, and I'll love you all the more.'

" 'But why do you love me at all?' I asked.

"Placing his hand on my shoulder, he said,

" 'How could I not?' "

39

"ALL MY LIFE I'd believed in Heaven and Hell. Did Heaven look down upon this metamorphosis?

"I was a drunk man at the height of his folly, regretting nothing. I lay in the bath, naked, as the dark fluids poured out of me. At last the pain stopped and the streams of fresh water ran pure. The human death was over.

"I looked at the three servants—the Adonis and the two sharp-featured young girls. They were either horrified or perfectly astonished.

"As I washed in the fresh water, as I scrubbed with the sponge, it was the young Adonis who brought the soap to me, and the towel, and helped me out of the bath and into fresh clothes—the same fancy garments as the others wore—black dinner jacket, trousers and white satin turtleneck, so that I would look like my new companions who I was now to join, or so I imagined.

"I felt a sharp unconscionable hunger for the blood of these young servants, born of the very sight of the blood moving under their flesh and the strong smell of it in the air around us. I wasn't one of them. I wasn't their brother. They couldn't feel what I felt. They couldn't know what I knew.

"Arion's admonitions came back to me. Evil Doers. I realized I was looking into the eyes of the roughest of the girls, who had most assuredly expected me to be murdered, and as I did so I could see into her mind: I could see her anger, see her bitterness, see her heated temper. And as I stared at her, with the tender Adonis adjusting my clothes, there came from her the nastiest voice.

" 'Why you?' she demanded. 'Why you instead of one of us? Who are you that it should be you?'

" 'Hush, no,' said the boy quickly. 'Don't be so foolish.'

"The other girl affected a cold, cynical air, but she felt the same sentiment. She felt cheated and angry. Hatred emanated from both women, and I realized it was angering me, and I detested them, detested them that they would have dumped my body this very night with no thought more than that it was a cumbersome task for them.

" 'We work, we wait,' said the brash one, 'and then you're brought here, and she chooses you. Why!'

" 'No, quiet,' said the boy again. He had finished adjusting my turtleneck and the lapels of my coat. He looked pleadingly into my eyes, wondering, adoring. He seemed to feel some mammoth sympathy for me that I hadn't died. He seemed to think it marvelous.

" 'How many others has she brought here?' I asked him.

"He had no time to answer. The two doors to the bath were shut with a snap. And before the two girls or the boy could turn around, another two doors were also shut. No exit now remained except the terrace, and I knew the drop that existed beneath it.

"I turned around. I found Petronia against the doors behind me.

" 'Very well then,' she said, 'so you've finished dying, and you'll never know it again unless you choose to know it. Now you'll make another choice. You'll choose your first kill. And that will be one of these. Be swift about it. I don't care who it is. No. I do care. I'm curious. Go on!'

" 'The girls gasped and screamed and, reaching for each other, backed up against the marble-tiled wall. The boy merely looked at Petronia and did nothing. He seemed to feel a profound disappointment but never made a sound.

" 'I can't do it,' I said.

" 'You can and you will,' said Petronia. 'Choose one of these or I'll choose for you. They're Evil Doers par excellence. They would have hauled you away tonight, a mere carcass to them, had you died.'

"She came up beside me. Her face softened and she put her arm up over my shoulder and she looked up at me tenderly. She spoke in a gentle voice as the girls still shivered and whimpered in panic and the boy stood his ground, frozen.

" 'Quinn, Quinn, my pupil,' she said in her loving voice, a voice I'd heard before so seldom from her. 'I want you to go forth strong and on your own. So take my harsh lessons. Read their minds. Use the Spell Gift to charm. You're hungry for them. Yes, yes, there, my pupil. Use your gifts and take the scent of their blood as your guiding genius.'

"I found myself staring at the hard-speaking one. Into her mind I did look. I saw her evil, her casual and vicious disconnect from the human herd, her brittle, cheap egocentricity. And as I drew close to her, her face was smooth, her eyes large and empty, as if I had put out my hand to her and stilled her. Her partner in crime had slunk away and with the boy moved across the room. She was all mine, deserted, enthralled, unprotesting. There was nothing but peace in her now.

" 'Devour the evil,' said Petronia, near to me like my Bad Angel. 'Eat it and make it into your clean and everlasting blood.'

"The girl had gone limp. She tumbled, silky and hot into my arms. Her head went to one side. Her mind was broken like the stem of a thorny rose. I kissed her throat. And then I sank my teeth and I felt her rich delicious blood pour forth, saltier than that of my vampire teachers, somehow more pungent, and there came the wretched story of her life, putrid, common, indecent. I sought the lush taste of the blood only. I sought the rich thick flow of the blood alone. I repudiated the images. I turned my heart away from her heart. I turned my senses only to the thick seasoned blood, and then Petronia was pulling me back, and the girl was lying at my feet, a crumpled corpse with large empty black eyes, such lovely eyes, and blood all over her neck, and Petronia said,

" 'You've spilt the blood, look at it. Bend down now and catch all of it on your tongue. Clean the wound until nothing remains.'

"I knelt down and lifted her. I did as I was told.

" 'Make a cut in your own tongue,' said Petronia, 'and with a drop of your own blood seal the wound until it disappears.'

"I was intent as I did this. I watched the tiny punctures vanish, and then the girl, pale-faced and purplish, fell limp to the tiles as I let her go.

"I rose groggily. Again, I was the drunk man. The most common object or surface seemed to pump with life.

"In a daze I reached out for Adonis. I said, 'I thank you for your kindnesses to me.' He was too afraid to answer. He paused, merely staring at me as though I'd forced him to do it, and then I turned away.

"Was I walking out of the bath with Petronia? Were we going up a great staircase? The evening seemed a mist rather than a thing of light. The stars seemed to move in the night sky as we walked along a roofed terrace. I could hear and smell the sea.

"We came into the room where Manfred sat at his chessboard still with Arion, and both of them appeared magnificent to me, infinitely more glorious than the two girls and the boy.

" 'And so we have this charged vision,' I murmured. 'We see all things as though they were quietly on fire in all their parts.'

" 'I knew you would understand,' Petronia responded. 'I like your words. Don't ever be afraid to speak up to me. I watched you for years before I chose you—you and your spirits. It was language that drew me as truly as beauty.'

" 'I love you,' I said. 'Isn't that what you wanted?'

"She laughed a mild helpless laugh. Her warm arm was around my waist, and for the moment her beauty could touch my heart. She even had about her a gentle majesty. I felt that I adored her.

"We went out on the terrace and looked down at the sea. It was a clear green and blue below. I could see this in the dark, see it subtracting its color from the moonlighted sky. And see the stars above moving as if they meant to embrace us. Far away, there came marching down the slope a town of white buildings, so perilously perched it seemed unreal, and beyond, the snowcapped mountain.

" 'Want you to love me?' she repeated my question. 'I don't know,' she said. 'Maybe I wanted you to love me for a while. Maybe I want it still. How do I know what I want? If ever I knew, I might have been content. But why do I tell such lies? Or more to the point, why do I believe them? I wanted you thus from the very first moment I saw you. I marked you for myself. And only for this night or a handful of nights after. And I resolved to leave you strong, I told you so, and so we go back to Arion, and he will leave you hungry again, won't you? Sweet Master?'

" 'Dare I talk of the things I saw in the blood?' I asked her.

" 'Try me,' she said in her new kindly manner, 'and if I detest what you say, who knows what I will do? Not even I know. What did you see in the blood?'

" 'When you fought in the arena, was it to the death?'

" 'Oh, always,' she said. 'Now weren't you a student of old Rome? There were countless women gladiators. I was only one of the finest, and always a favorite of the crowd. I was as you know me now, vicious. I stayed alive in those years by viciousness. It was natural. It was expected. And I took to it with a raging simplicity.'

"She beamed as she looked at me.

" 'It was Arion who tamed my heart,' she went on. 'It was Arion who turned me from vicious pursuits, from mockery and meanness into the making of cameos. Oh, you've never seen the fine things I made for Arion. Arion gave me rubies and emeralds, and I made whole stories for

Arion in shell—the victories of emperors, the progress of legions. My work was famous throughout the empire. All day I bent over my workbench, dressed carelessly as a boy, my hair tied back with a rawhide string, nothing before me but that work, that all-important work, whatever it might be. Then night would come and so would Arion. Then I became the woman for him. I became something soft, something decent, something fine for Arion.'

" 'What is decent?' I asked.

" 'You know, you've always known.'

" 'But what is it now?' I asked. 'I knew what it was before, yes, but now I don't know what it is. I killed that wretched girl, that murderous girl. That wasn't decent. Tell me.'

" 'Oh, come now, it's much too early for such questions. We have hunting to do. Your night's going to be long. As I told you, I'll make no mewling fledglings. You'll be very strong when I'm finished with you.'

" 'Will I be decent?' I asked. 'Will I be honorable?'

" 'See that you are,' she said. Her face grew sad. 'Use your intellect for that,' she said quietly. 'Don't imitate me. Imitate those who are better than me. Imitate Arion.'

"We went into the big room again, where Manfred rose to meet us and to look at me and embrace me and to be separated from me only by the loving arms of Arion, whose fine black face utterly charmed me. How lean and caring he seemed, a creature of such miraculous contours and expressiveness.

" 'Drain him, Master,' said Petronia in the tone of a request, and now the Master took me into his arms, and, pressing his teeth to my throat, did as Petronia had requested.

"Again, I felt the images of my life passing with the blood. I felt the sorrow I knew, the untold sorrow of being lost forever from Mona, from my son, Jerome, from Aunt Queen, from Nash, from Jasmine, my beloved milk chocolate Jasmine, from my beloved little Tommy, I felt all of this passing from me with the blood, but not leaving me forever, only revealed, opened like a fierce and terrible wound in me—*You have died, Quinn*—and I felt Arion taking it into himself as if he would relieve me, and a swoon of weakness came over me.

"I awoke seated in a chair, and for a moment the pain was more than I could bear. It was so terrible that it seemed the thing to do was to go to the railing and throw myself down on the rocks there to be smashed and truly dead. But I wondered, and wisely so, would such a thing accomplish death for me?

"Then pure hunger consumed me. I had never hungered so much, and blood was my only desire. I wanted Arion's blood. I wanted Petronia's blood. I stared at Manfred, as he peered keenly back at me.

" 'And so for our lessons,' said Arion. He stretched out his arms to me. 'Now, come, and to my throat, and take from me the Little Drink, only one fraction of what you want, and spill nothing when you do it. You learn to do the Little Drink, and you can feed from the innocent. You can feed from them gently without biting off a soul. You can leave them only dazed after your kiss.'

"I went directly to obey. The blood was so thick! And there again, the flash of sunny Athens! It was an agony, but I drew back at the appropriate moment as he had directed me, and with my tongue I lapped the few drops that threatened the whiteness of his satin shirt. He held me until I was steady on my feet, and then, covering my lips with his, he kissed me. He slipped his tongue into my mouth. He forced it up against my fang teeth. The blood came again. I reeled. I danced backwards.

" 'What is my life to be now?' I whispered, after he'd withdrawn. 'Ecstasy?'

" 'Ecstasy and control,' he said to me softly. 'Now drink from Manfred in the same way. Call your son to you, Manfred.'

"The Old Man stretched out his arms.

"I went to him.

" 'Come, child of my house, child of my legacy,' he said in his deep voice. 'Beloved child of my heritage. Drink from me the blood. It was Petronia in her wickedness who built Blackwood Manor with her gold, her miserable gold. I give you my love, luckless boy! I give you my blood. Take from me the image of the only pure thing I ever loved!'

" 'Short, and neat,' said Petronia near to me.

"I sank my teeth in his bull neck, as his large hand held my shoulder. But it was not Virginia Lee whom I saw, it was Rebecca, Rebecca hanging hideously on the rusted hook, and Manfred cursing Petronia as she howled with laughter, and Rebecca too tormented, the dark blood that means death pouring out of her naked torso, the hook deep in her body, deep, run through her very heart for all I knew.

"Suddenly, Rebecca laughed! She stood alone, pointing at me, sneering. Laughing.

" 'Good God!' I shouted. I was pulled back. I staggered. The Old Man had clapped a handkerchief to his neck, and how miserable he looked. Arion had ahold of my shoulders.

" 'Aw, such pain,' said the Old Man. 'And why did you reach for her, Quinn, why that shrew? Why reach for such a thing?'

" 'Control, my child,' said Arion. 'Control. So that you can move through a room crowded with mortals, picking the ones you want, giving the fatal kiss and leaving with no one any the wiser.'

" 'But why did I see Rebecca?' I gasped. 'What was the reason?' I demanded. 'You meant for me to see Virginia Lee.'

" 'Aye, but how can I hide the guilt inside my soul?' asked the Old Man. 'You reached for it, you found it, you possess it.'

"I heard her hissing whisper: *And they howl and weep for you on your precious Blackwood Farm. When will they put your name on a gravestone?*

" 'Get away from me, luckless ghost,' I said. 'So you have in me a life for your life. Leave me.'

"There came no answer.

"And so my learning went on for hours amongst them.

"They schooled me until I could take the Little Drink, but never was I filled, and they laughed at my hunger when I complained of the pain, and if Petronia became sullen or impatient, Arion shamed her with his kindness.

" 'Now we go to hunt, the four of us,' said Arion. 'And you will search out the Evil Doer, using the power to read minds, and we'll watch over you.'

" 'It's a wedding,' said the Old Man in his bass voice. 'A rich American come to Napoli for his daughter's nuptials. You'll find the Evil Doer everywhere you turn. You lure him, you take him in such a way that no one's the wiser and from your tongue the drops of your own blood will seal up the wound. Are you ready, son, to be one of us? Truly one of us?'

" 'Picture it before we leave here,' said Arion. 'They've been drinking for hours. You want to move amongst them quietly. Anonymously. You want to leave your victims as if they're drunk. You want to take the Little Drink from the innocents as you desire it.'

"I nodded. 'Yes,' I declared. I was thirsting. And my heart was inflamed. I wanted with all my wretched soul to be one of them. I was one of them!

"Suddenly, Petronia lifted me and flung me out from her, out beyond the open terrace doors and into the night, and I fell down, down all the way to the beach below, and I landed quietly on the rocks, standing, just on the edge of the foaming green sea, still and quiet, gazing all around me.

"I looked up. How very far away she was, and from the terrace I could scarcely see as she beckoned me. I heard her whisper as though she was near my ear, 'Come up to me, Quinn.'

"I willed my body to rise, and I did rise, and faster and faster I moved until I drifted near her and over the railing of the terrace and then I stood beside her.

"She slipped her arm around me, her dark eyes flashing as she looked up at me, and whispered in my ear. 'And so you see,' she said, 'we move by speed, not magic. I have you in my grip. And don't you spill a drop when you drink. We expect perfection of you.'

" 'But do we kill?' I asked.

"Arion shrugged. 'If you wish,' he answered. "If the evil is ripe for it and you are graceful and sly.' "

40

"A blue haze of cigarette smoke hung over the rooms. The faces came at me as if I were a camera lens. All were beautiful. All were imperfect. The voices were a senseless and deafening babble, the thoughts of so many minds a chaotic hubbub. I lost my sense of balance. I wanted to retreat, but I pressed forward.

"The smell of the food was revolting, the smell of the liquor strangely acrid and foreign, as if my body had never drunk it. The scent of blood rose from every inch of flesh pressed against me as I worked my way through the labyrinth.

"I saw the bride beneath the heavily laden pergola. Wraith thin. Pretty. Her bridal gown had long white lace sleeves, and she was smoking a cigarette which she held in her left hand, and when she saw me she beckoned urgently as if she knew me, and I saw in her mind: invitation, but what did she want?

"I couldn't take my eyes off her as I pushed towards her, and her free arm hooked around my left arm as we came together, and I caught the scent of her blood, strong and pumping alive beneath her olive skin.

"She pulled me into a large bedroom and shut and locked the door behind her. Her big low-set black eyes looked at me imploringly. Smudged mascara. Pouting red mouth.

" 'You saw him, that bastard,' she seethed, cursing. 'On my wedding night, he does that to me!' Her face was a breathtaking snarl of rage. She ripped at my coat and pulled me towards the bed. Her black hair was falling loose from its diamond-studded combs. 'Come on, now, let's do it, hurry, I want him to try to break that door down, damn him, the pig.'

"I caught her chin in my right hand and turned her face up to me. I kissed her mouth. What was that to me? The blood scent overwhelmed me. I went for her throat. I bit down hard and the artery exploded, the blood gushing down over her wedding dress as I tried to pull away; it was a positive fountain springing from her. She gasped. I closed my mouth over it, cursing myself, my clumsiness, my hunger, my luck. Oh, God in Heaven. I drank and drank. She was limp, in a brand of ecstasy, a litany of banal innocence thudding out of her, no evil, no design, no malice, no knowledge, no pain.

"On and on I drank the salted blood. I belonged to it, was a slave to it. Wanted nothing more than it. Except that she somehow not die, that there not be blood all over her white dress, her splendid white dress.

"Her heart went out like a match or a candle. No way to bring it back. I held her, shook her. Come back. Mistake. Awful mistake. I drank again, like a fool, until there was no more to drink. I cringed. I moaned. She had no more life in her, no more blood to give. I tossed her like a doll. A broken bride doll. She was so dead! Look at the diamonds in her ruined hair.

"Someone took me by the hair of my head and swung me back against the wall. I hit it so hard that I went blind and senseless for a moment, and then in the blinkering light I saw her dead there, sliding off the foot of the bed onto the floor, the blood all over her dress, her pretty lace dress, her lovely white lace dress with its webs and circles of lustrous pearls, her hair fallen from her diamond combs, her face so sweet, no more anger, no more hate.

"It was Petronia who had flung me back and now she dragged me out the window under the pergola and threw me against the wall again. This time I felt the blood flow from the back of my head. I was in a shock of pain. She pitched me over the railing. I dropped down, down towards the sea. I felt I was dying. I was full of innocent blood and I was dying. I was weeping and I was dying, and the bride, the poor bride, she was dead, and I had left her covered in her own blood, all the brides of Blackwood Farm betrayed, Ophelia Immortal never to be my bride betrayed, blood on her white dress, Rebecca never to be Manfred's bride laughing.

"We were back in the palazzo and Petronia struck me over and over again, cursing me and herself that she had made me.

" 'Imbecile, you killed her. Imbecile, she was nothing but a tart, and for that you killed her! In a wilderness of killers, you killed her. She was nothing but a tart. You fool.' Again and again, there came the blows to my face—pain, but pain isn't death—then the kicks to my ribs. I clung to the floor.

" 'Stop her,' roared the Old Man. 'Stop her, stop her, stop her.'

" 'I take you to hunt a wedding, thick with killers, and you kill the bride!' she seethed. She kicked at my face. I rolled over onto my back. She kicked at my groin. 'Stupid, clumsy, fledgling, idiot, clumsy!'

"The Old Man roared: 'Make her stop!'

" 'And the blood on her dress, how you did it! Moron, idiot, fool! Where did you think you were? What did you think you were?'

"Finally Arion pulled her off me.

" 'It was our doing,' he said. 'We left him alone. He was too young. We should have been with him.'

"She was crying. She was in Arion's arms and she was actually crying.

"The Old Man sobbed.

"I lay there and dreamt of death.

"Oh, Lord, how could I have come to this? How could my senses have so richly misled me? How could my greed have led me to this abysmal pass? I am in a place of darkness beyond panic and beyond anxiety. Lord, this is anguish. Yet I cling to what I am. I cling to all that I am.

"And somewhere very far away, others were searching for me. Rebecca was right. And they must have been saying, 'The gators got him, had to be. Poor Quinn. He's dead.'

"And I was."

41

"BEFORE THE SUNRISE Arion took me to the cellar beneath the house and showed me the crypt in which I would sleep. He told me simply that, young as I was, the sun could destroy me, and that even when I had attained a great age, such as he had, it would still render me powerless and unconscious. He told me also that fire could mean my death. But that no other injury could kill me.

"I felt, unwisely, no doubt, that I understood these things. He told me as well that all the wounds inflicted on me by Petronia in her rage would heal over the day's time, as they weren't very serious for one of my strength, and that he would come for me when the sun had set, and I should wait for him.

" 'Don't be afraid of the narrow box, my child,' he said. 'Make it your refuge. And don't be afraid of your dreams. You are an immortal now, and all your faculties are enhanced. Accept it and rejoice in it.'

" 'I lay down then in the crypt, and I did suffer the most unspeakable horror of it, but there was nothing to be done about it, the granite lid was closed over me, and very soon, weeping quietly, I lost consciousness.

"I dreamed a dream of Patsy. She smelled like cotton candy. Her lips tasted like candy apples. I dreamed I was a little child, and I sat on her lap, and she pushed me off, and I grew to be a man in a twinkling and I killed her. I drank her blood. It tasted like maple syrup. Her diseases and her meanness could not contaminate me. I tried to wake up. I dreamed this over and over and I woke once, or so I dreamed, with her body in my arms. A Barbie. I pushed her down into the green water of the swamp and as I watched her sink below the surface I felt horror. But she was gone and dead, and blood came up. It was too late to save her. Bye Patsy. Rebecca laughed. *A death for my death.* 'Oh yes,' I scoffed, 'you think you planned everything.' 'The Damnation of Quinn,' said Fr. Kevin.

"When I opened my eyes the next time Arion was there looking down at me. The sun had only just set and the sky was still red and the golden light filled the crypt, and he was pleased to see that I was conscious. He led me up the stairs and to the terrace.

"The stars drifted in the purple sky. The gold hung behind the clouds. It was magnificent.

" 'Some Blood Hunters don't wake till the sky is full dark,' he said, 'and they never know this quiet glory. I see you shade your eyes, but it doesn't hurt you.'

"In fact it didn't and it was only with difficulty that I absorbed the reality that I would never see 'the light of day' again.

"He saw the trouble in my face. He said, 'Look back on nothing. I'll take you out to hunt now. You're my apprentice for the evening.'

" 'And so I've disappointed her,' I asked, 'and she'll have nothing further to do with me?'

" 'No,' he said with a short honest laugh. 'She's eager to see you. But it happens that she's a miserable teacher. And so I've told her no, and that I'll take you out, and so we'll hunt the cafés and the clubs of Napoli.'

"He was dressed informally tonight in a black silk shirt open at the neck and a finely cut jacket of dark red silk and a pair of sleek trousers.

"He took me to a room where the young mortal boy waited to help me select a similar suit of clothes, which I did hastily. Once again, I thanked him for his kindness.

" 'If I had any money,' I said, 'I'd give it to you.'

"He smiled at me. And I patted his shoulder.

"Then we were off to the cafés and bars for more lessons.

"We moved through all manner of crowds, taking the Little Drink over and over until I was very skilled at it, and then, cornering for ourselves two 'perfect killers,' we had our fill of them in a back alley in the oldest part of Naples. We left their bodies because Arion said it didn't matter there, but there would be other times when it did and the bodies had to be disposed of. As it was, he slashed the throats of the two so it would seem they had bled to death.

" 'To thrive without killing,' he said, 'that is everything. If you can live without bringing death, you will endure. But now and then the urge to kill will overrule—you'll want the burning bitter heart—and so I've taught you how to do it.'

"I was exhilarated all this while, and the elegant figure of Arion constantly thrilled me. I imitated his grace. I wanted him for my model in everything. And in some ways he is my model to this very moment. He had a feline way of moving and speaking in a hushed tone that commanded respect and loyalty of me.

"His skin was so black that under the lights of the cafés and bars it had a bluish tinge to it, and his deep yellow eyes had tiny flecks of brown and green in them. His teeth were powerfully white, and his lips small for his face, and his smile very smooth and loving.

"Finally, after we had hunted perhaps more than was required, we settled in a somewhat quiet café where he could talk to me and educate me, and this thrilled me almost as much as our hunting.

"But as soon as the stillness settled over me, as soon as I had the coffee in my hands, which I couldn't and didn't want to drink, I found myself in a state of shock and I began to shiver violently.

"He reached over and laid his hand on mine, and then, kissing his fingers, he repeated the gesture. Then he drew back.

" 'Understand the gift you've been given, as best you can,' he said. 'Don't forswear it in the first years. Too many perish in that way. Of course you despise Petronia for giving it to you—all this is natural and right. When she drained you, when she almost killed you, you saw a vision of those who'd gone to Paradise before you. And you turned away.'

" 'How did you know?' I asked.

" 'I could read your mind then. It's not the same now. We've exchanged too much blood. It's the same with her too. Don't let her fool you. She's mercilessly clever and eternally whimsical and persistently unhappy. But for whatever it's worth, she loves you and she can't read your mind any longer.'

" 'Is she always a woman for you? Do you ever see her as a man?'

"He laughed. 'She made her choice in life early on to be the woman with me. When she fought in the arena centuries ago, it was as a woman. Those who came up against her marveled at her musculature and her stamina. But they thought her a woman. She switches back and forth. She's truly both. But we don't need to talk of her now. Let's talk of you.'

" 'And what is there to say about me?' I asked. 'Did I will myself into this? I did not. And yet I blame myself that it happened. I turned away from my grandparents in that vision of Paradise, you're right, and can you tell me now, even if the answer torments me—was what I saw real?'

" 'I can't tell you,' he said with an easy graceful shrug. 'I don't know. I only know what you saw. It's the same with my victims. Often they see the light of Paradise and those they once loved call to them, and so they leave my embrace, in spirit, and I am left with the corpse.'

"That answer rattled me. And I sat quietly for a long moment. I even picked up the cup of coffee and then set it down. The café was half empty. The street outside was noisy with passersby. There was a night-club opposite. The music was throbbing beyond the neon sign. I wondered if I had been in this street when I was alive. I didn't remember it. But Nash and I had gone a-wandering in Naples. It was possible. And now, how would I see Nash again? How would I even go home?

" 'Now let me take up the point again,' said Arion. 'Don't be destroyed in the first years. It happens with too many. There's so much danger all around you. It's easy to despair. It's easy to succumb to bitter hatred of yourself. It's easy to feel that the world no longer belongs to you, when nothing is further from the truth. It's all yours and the passage of the years is yours. And now you must simply and plainly live up to it.'

" 'How long do we have?' I asked.

"He was surprised by the question. 'Forever,' he said with another shrug. 'There is no lifetime for us. When I gave you my blood I tried to hide my life from you, but you saw the place of my mortal happiness. You knew it was Athens. You knew the Acropolis. You recognized it immediately. You saw the Temple of Athena in all its grandeur. I couldn't keep from you the secret of the sheer brilliance of that time, and the Athenian sunshine, so harsh, so hot, so merciless and wonderful. You breathed this knowledge from me. And you must certainly know how long I have been alive, how long I've walked the Earth as we say, how many centuries I've wandered.'

" 'What sustains you? What supports you? Surely not Petronia and the Old Man.'

" 'Don't be so quick to judge,' he said gently. 'Some night far distant from now—if you survive—you'll laugh when you remember asking me such a question. Besides, I love Petronia, and I can control her. You wonder perhaps why I didn't stop her from making you, as we call it, why I didn't call upon my authority to stop her from defiling you? Because you must understand I saw her as giving you immortality.'

"He paused, smiling at me faintly and touching my hand again with his hand, which was warm.

" 'Were there other reasons? I don't honestly know,' he went on. 'Perhaps I harbored a heated desire to see you transformed. You are so very admirable. So young. So splendid in all your parts. And with the sole exception of Manfred, it's been centuries since she worked the Dark

Trick, as some of us call it. Centuries. And she has an idea that the desire builds in us and then must be discharged, and so she brings someone into our midst and makes of that one a Blood Hunter.'

" 'But the girls who prepared me, and the boy—they spoke as if there had been others.'

" 'She plays with others, and then she destroys them. The servants? What do they know? They're told that the postulant is being prepared for great gifts, and then fails. That's all. Now the girl, I don't know about her. She's ignorant and greedy. But there is some spark in the boy. Perhaps Petronia will bring him to us.'

" 'And has it been well done?' I asked.

" 'Oh, yes, of course it's been well done,' he said, almost as if I'd insulted him with my question, 'not without much more cursing and kicking I think than was ever necessary, but in the main well done; I saw to it that it was well done, though I have more to tell you.'

"He made a little gesture with the coffee, playing with it, as though he liked to see it move in the cup and savor the aroma of it, which was dark and thick and alien to me. Then he spoke.

" 'I'm watching you, of course,' he said. 'When you drink from the evil ones you have to revel in it, not cringe from the evil. It's your chance to be evil as the one you kill. Follow your victim's evil as you empty his soul. Make it your adventure into crimes you yourself would never wantonly commit. When you've finished, you take your soul back with what you've learned and you're clean again.'

" 'I feel anything but clean,' I said.

" 'Then feel powerful,' he said. 'Disease can't touch you. Neither can age. Any wound you receive will heal. Cut your hair and it will grow back within the space of a night. Forever you will look just as you are now, my Caravaggio Christ. Remember, only fire and the sun can harm you.'

"I listened intently as he continued.

" 'Fire you must avoid at all costs,' he said, 'for your blood will burn, and terrible suffering may result, which you may survive, healing slowly over centuries. As for the sun—one day of it cannot kill me. But in these early years, either can destroy you. Don't yield to the desire for death. It claims too many of the young in their impetuosity and grand emotions.'

"I smiled. I knew what he meant—grand emotions.

" 'You needn't find a crypt every day of your life,' he said. 'You're strong from me and Petronia combined, and even the Old Man's blood has been good for you. A room that is shut up and sealed away from the sun, a hiding place, that will suffice, but eventually you should choose a refuge to which you can retire, a place that is yours where no one can find you. Remember when you do this that you are some ten times stronger than mortals now.'

" 'Ten times,' I marveled.

" 'Oh, yes,' he said. 'When you took the pretty bride you broke her neck in the final moments. You weren't even conscious of it. It was the same with the killer in the alley. You snapped his spine. You have to learn to be careful.'

" 'I'm drenched with murder,' I said. I looked at my hands. I knew I would never see Mona again, because I knew that a witch like Mona would see blood all over them.

" 'You feed from mortals now,' said Arion in his usual graceful manner. 'It's your nature. Blood Hunters have existed since the beginning of time, and probably before that. Old myths are told and written that we once had among us parents from whom the primal fount poured forth to us all, and that whatever happened to them happened to us and so they must be kept forever inviolate. But I'll give you the books to read which tell these tales. . . .'

"He paused, looking around the café. I wondered what he saw. I saw blood in every face. I heard blood in every voice. At will I could receive the thoughts of any mind like so much static. He went on.

" 'Suffice it to say that the Mother rose from her slumber of thousands of years and on a rampage destroyed many of her children. It was at random that she moved. And I thank the gods that she passed over us. I could have done nothing against her power, because she had the Mind Gift—that is, to destroy by will—and the Fire Gift—that is, to burn by will—and she burnt those Blood Hunters whom she found, and they numbered in the hundreds.

" 'At last she herself was destroyed, and the sacred nucleus—the primal blood from which we all come—was passed into another, otherwise we would all have withered as so many flowers upon a dead vine. But that root has been preserved without interruption.'

" 'This one, this one who has the nucleus or the root, is he very old?'

" 'It's a woman,' he replied, 'and she is ancient, as old as the Mother was, and she has no desire to rule, only to keep the root safe and to live as a witness to time, in a place apart from the world and its worries. With that kind of age comes a peace from the blood. She no longer needs to drink it.'

" 'When will that peace come for me?' I asked.

"He laughed softly, gently. 'Not for thousands of years,' he said. 'Though with the blood I gave you, you can go many nights with just the Little Drink or even nothing. You'll suffer but you won't become weak unto dying. That's the trick, remember. Don't become so weak that you can't hunt. That you must never do. Promise me.'

" 'It matters to you what happens to me?'

" 'Of course,' he said. 'I wouldn't be with you here if it didn't. I gave you my blood, did I not?' He laughed but it was kindly. 'You don't know what a gift it was, my blood. I've lived for so long. In the parlance of our kind, I'm a Child of the Millennia, and my blood is considered too strong for the young and unwise, but I hold you to be wise and so I gave it. Live up to it.'

" 'What do you expect of me now? I know that I'm to kill those who are evil and no others, yes, and the Little Drink must be done with stealth and grace, but what else do you expect?'

" 'Nothing, really,' he said. 'You go where you wish to go and do what you wish to do. What will sustain you, how you will live, these are things you must figure out for yourself.'

" 'How did you do it?' I asked.

" 'Oh, you ask me to go back so many years,' he said. 'My Master and my Maker were one, a great writer of the Greek tragedy just before and during the time of Aeschylus. He had been something of a roamer before he set to work in Athens writing for the theater, and he had traveled into India, where he bought me from a man I scarcely remember who kept me for his bed, and had educated me for his library, and who sold me for a dear price to the Athenian who brought me home to Athens to copy for him and be his bed slave. I loved it. The world of the stage delighted me. We worked hard on the scenery, the training of the chorus and of the solitary actor whom Thespis had introduced into the mix of the early theater as it was then.

" 'My Master wrote scores of plays—satires, comedies, tragedies. He wrote odes to celebrate victorious athletes. He wrote long epic poems. He wrote lyrics for his own pleasure. He was always waking me in the middle of the night to copy or merely to listen. "Wake up, Arion, wake up, you won't believe what I've done here!" he would say, shaking me and shoving a cup of water into my hands. You know that meter and rhythm were much more important to the Greeks back then. He was the past master of it all. He made me laugh with his pure cleverness.

" 'He wrote for every festival, every contest, every conceivable excuse, and was ever busy on every detail of the performance down to the procession that might precede it or the painting of the masks to be used. It was his life. That is, when we weren't traveling.

" 'It was his joy to go to other Greek colonies and there participate in the theater as well, and it was here in Italy that he encountered the sorceress who gave him the Power. We were living then in the Etruscan city that would later become Pompeii, and he had been involved in putting on a theatrical in the festival of Dionysus for the Greeks.

" 'I can still remember the night he came back to me, and how at first he would have nothing to do with me, and then he brought me into his presence and clumsily he drank from me, and when it seemed that I would die, when I was sure of it, he gave me the Blood in a blundering terrible moment, weeping and desperate and pleading with me to understand that he didn't know what had happened to him.

" 'We were neophytes together. We were Children in the Blood together. He burnt his plays, all of them. He said that all he had written was worthless. He was no more among humankind. To the end of his existence he sought sorcerers and witches to try to find some way to cure the Evil Blood in himself. And he perished before my very eyes, immolating himself when scarcely twenty-five years had passed. He left me a hardened orphan.

" 'But I have always been a resourceful soul, and, never wanting death, have not been tempted by it. I saw Greece fall to Rome. I saw my Master's plays in the bookshops and the marketplaces for a very long time—centuries. I saw my Master's personal poetry read and studied by young Roman boys, and then I saw the rise of Christianity and the loss of thousands of works—poetry, the drama, yes, even plays of Aeschylus, Sophocles and Euripides lost—history, letters—and with them the loss of my Master's name, and the salvage of a precious few from those days when I had known so many.

" 'I am content. I am resourceful still. I deal in diamonds and pearls. I use the Mind Gift to make me rich. I cheat no one. I am clever beyond what I need. And I keep Petronia always with me. I love the company of Manfred. He and I play chess and cards and we talk and we roam the streets of Naples together. I remember so vividly the night that she brought him here, cursing that she had had to keep a bargain.

" 'They had met here in Naples, she and he, and she had taken a fancy to visiting the swamps where he lived, and having there a hideaway. It had seemed to her an appropriate wilderness from which she could hunt the drifters and the drinkers and gamblers of New Orleans and all the Southland. And eventually, he built her a domicile and a fancy tomb such as she desired, and she loved to retreat to that place whenever she was angry with me, or whenever she wanted what was new and raw, and would be away from Italy, where everything had been done a hundred times over.

" 'But in time she'd come to promise Manfred that she would give him the Blood, because she had told him what she was, and at last she had had to keep her word, or so I told her, and do it she did, and brought him here, so that those he loved would think he had died in the swampland.

" 'Now it will be the same with you. They will imagine that you died in the swamp. Is that not so?'

"I didn't answer him.

"Then I said:

" 'Thank you for all you told to me, and for all you've taught me. I'm humble in your presence. I'd be a fool if I claimed to fully understand your age, the value of your perspective, your patience. I can only offer gratitude. May I put one more question to you?'

" 'Of course you may. Put any question.' He smiled.

" 'You've lived over two thousand years, perhaps closer to three,' I said.

"He paused, then he nodded.

" 'What have you given back to the world on account of this?' I asked.

"He stared at me. His face became thoughtful but it remained warm and cordial. And then he said gently, 'Nothing.'

" 'Why?' I asked.

" 'What should I give?' he asked.

" 'I don't know,' I said. 'I feel as though I'm going mad. I feel as though if I'm to live forever I have to give something back.'

" 'But we're not part of it, don't you see?'

" 'Yes,' I said with a gasp. 'I see only too clearly.'

" 'Don't torment yourself. Think on this matter for a while. Think. You have time, all the time in the world.'

"I was near to weeping. But I swallowed it back down.

" 'Let me ask you,' he said. 'When you were alive, did you feel you had to give back something for life?'

" 'Yes,' I said. 'I did.'

" 'I see. And so you are like my old Master with his poetry. But you mustn't follow his example! Imagine it, Quinn, what I have seen. And there are small things to do. There are loving things.'

" 'You think so?' I asked.

" 'I know so,' he said. 'But come, let's go back to the palazzo. I know Petronia is waiting for you.'

"I laughed a short ironic little laugh. 'That's comforting,' I said.

"As we stood to leave the café I stopped and looked at myself intently in the mirrored wall. I looked human enough even to my enhanced vision. And no one in the café had so much as stared at us, except for an occasional pair of pretty girls who had come and gone after their espresso. Human enough. Yes. I was pleased with it. I was magnificently pleased with it."

42

"WHEN WE RETURNED to the palazzo, which we did by ordinary means, that is, walking, we were told by the young serving girl, who was now frightened out of her wits, that Petronia was in her dressing room and wanted to see me there.

"I found the room entrancing. The entire wall was covered in mirrors, and Petronia sat at a great curve of granite, on a bench that appeared made of the same material, with a velvet cushion on it, while the young Adonis finished her hair.

"She was clad as a man in a buff-colored velvet coat and pants, with a ruffled white shirt that would have looked good in the eighteenth century, I well imagined, and at her throat was a huge rectangular cameo that was crowded with little figures, the whole thing surrounded by diamonds.

"Her hair was pulled straight back from her face, and the boy was plaiting it for her. She had two threads of diamonds running over her head, which as I've mentioned was beautifully shaped for this kind of severity, and the two threads of diamonds were being plaited into her hair.

"The room was open to the sea like all the rooms of the palazzo which I had seen, though I think I forgot to mention it with the bath.

"The sky appeared violet to me in spite of the hour, and once again the stars seemed to be moving; in fact the sky appeared to be moving into the room.

"My breath was quite literally taken away from me, not merely by the stars and their various patterns but by the sheer beauty of Petronia in her sharp male clothing, with her bold head once again revealed by the austerity of her pulled-back hair.

"I stood for a long few moments gazing at her as she looked back at me, and then the young Adonis told her softly that the plait was complete and the diamond clasp applied to the end.

"She turned around and gave him what appeared to be a very large amount of money and said, 'Go out, enjoy yourself, you've done well.' He bowed and backed out of the room, as though he'd been dismissed by the Queen of England, and then he was gone.

" 'So you find him beautiful, do you?' she asked.

" 'Do I? I don't know,' I said. 'Everything charms me. As a human being I was an enthusiast. Now I think I'm losing my mind.'

"She rose from the cushioned bench and came towards me, and then she took me in her arms. 'All the wounds I inflicted, they've healed. Am I right?'

" 'Yes, you're right,' I said. 'Except the wound no one can heal, the one I inflicted on myself, that I killed the innocent young woman, that I murdered her at her own wedding. No one can heal that. And no time will heal it either, and I don't suppose it should.'

"She laughed. 'Come, let's join the others,' she said. 'All your grandfather knows is how to play chess. He was a raving poker player when I first met him. He beat me at it, if you can believe it, and that Rebecca, she was cagey too, I tell you, and don't go moping after her, but I must tell you—about the bride, I've had the most splendid night.'

"Within moments we were in the big room with the ominous and empty gold cage at the end of it. I pictured a giant bird inside it. Certainly I hadn't looked like a bird. I thought of Caravaggio's *Victorious Cupid.* Had I looked a little like that?

" 'I must tell you what happened,' Petronia went on, drawing the attention of Arion. 'It was the best luck. The bride's father and husband, you know, were first-rate killers, and of course the little minx knew it, so salve your conscience with that if you wish, Quinn. But they sent an armed guard here tonight, some four bravos as we used to call them, because we were recognized, it seems, and you can imagine the fun I had with them. Now it doesn't please me to bully mortals, no matter what you think to the contrary, Quinn, but there were four of them.'

" 'And where are they now?' said Arion. He sat at the table with the Old Man, who was looking at the chessboard. I sat between them.

"Petronia walked up and down in front of us.

" 'Gone, into the sea,' she responded. 'In their car, over the cliff. Like that. It was nothing. But the fighting here before I disposed of the bodies, now that was a class act.'

" 'I'm sure,' said Arion with faint disgust. 'And that's made you happy.'

" 'Supremely happy. I drank my fill from the last one, and that was the finest part of it. No. I take that back. The fight was the finest part of it, killing them before they could draw their weapons and make a nasty hole in my body! It was divinely exciting. It made me think I should fight more often, that it's not enough to kill.'

"Arion shook his head wearily. 'You should talk more elegantly for your fledgling. Tell him a few rules.'

" 'What rules?' she inquired. She continued to stride back and forth, almost to the windows and then again to the murals, her eyes sweeping the room around her and then seeming to drift over the stars.

" 'Oh, all right. Rules,' she said. 'You never disclose to any mortal what you are or what we are. How's that for a rule? You never kill one of our kind. Is that enough for you, Arion? I don't know that I remember anything else.'

" 'You know you do,' he said. He too was looking at the chessboard. He made a move with his queen.

" 'You cover up the kill as to bring no notice to yourself,' she said with a flair, 'and always, always!' she stopped and stared at me, pointing her finger in a declarative manner. 'Always, you respect your Maker as your Master, and to strike out at your Maker, your Master, is to merit destruction at his or her hands. How's that?'

" 'That's all very good,' said the Old Man in his deep bass with his jowls trembling. He squeezed my shoulder and smiled at me with his big loose mouth. 'Now give him the warnings. He needs warnings.'

" 'Such as what!' said Petronia disgustedly. 'Don't be scared of your own shadow!' she said pointedly. 'Don't act like you're old when you're immortal! What else?'

" 'The Talamasca, tell him about the Talamasca,' said the Old Man, nodding at me, mouth turned up in the manner of a fish. 'They know about us, they do!' he said with an emphatic nod. 'And you mustn't ever fall for their blandishments. Do you know that word, my son? They flatter you with their curiosity, which is what they do to everyone! Flattery is their calling card. But you must never yield to them. They're a secret order of psychics and magicians, and they want us! They want to lock us up in their castles here in Europe and study us in their laboratories as though we were rats!'

"I was speechless. I tried to wipe my mind clean of all thought of Stirling. But the Old Man was peering at me in a probing fashion.

" 'Ah, what do I see but that you've known them? They've already invited themselves into your life because you were a seer of spirits! Oh, this is most dangerous. What is this? A plantation house? You must never risk being in the vicinity of them again.'

" 'It was all broken off a long time ago,' I said. 'I saw spirits, yes. I'll probably continue to see them.'

"Arion shook his head no. 'Ghosts don't come to our kind, Quinn,' he said quietly.

" 'No, indeed not,' said Petronia, walking and walking. 'You'll find that your familiar has vanished should ever you go back to spy perhaps on those you used to know and love.'

"I said nothing.

"I looked at the chessboard. I watched the Old Man put Arion's queen in check.

" 'What other rules are there?' I asked.

" 'Don't make others,' said Arion, 'without the permission of your Maker, or the eldest of those who make up the group in which you live.'

" 'You mean I can make another?' I asked.

" 'Of course you can,' said Arion, 'but you must resist the temptation. As I told you, you can do it only with the permission of Petronia, or in reality, my permission, as you are in my house.'

"Petronia made a contemptuous scoffing sound.

" 'That may come to be your worst temptation,' said Arion. 'But you're too young and too weak to make the transformation. Remember it, what I'm telling you. Don't be a fool in this. Don't share eternity with someone you may come to despise or even hate.'

"I nodded.

"There was a long silence during which time Petronia stopped at the window and looked out at the stars.

" 'There is one other warning,' she said. She turned back and looked at me. 'If you go back to the swampland, and some night you might, just to spy on your beloved aunt, that great lady, or for some other simple reason, don't be tempted to hunt New Orleans. The Talamasca keeps a tight watch for us there, and though they're bumbling mortals they can do us harm. But there is one other danger and that is a powerful Blood Hunter who styles himself the Vampire Lestat. He rules New Orleans and he destroys young Blood Hunters. He's ruthless, iconoclastic and self-centered. He's written books about us which pass as fiction. A lot of the stories in those books are true.'

"I was quiet for a long time.

"She came over to the table, and, drawing up a chair, she put her arm around Arion and she watched the game. Arion had saved his queen, but just barely, and was now about to be checkmated in a very sly way. I saw it coming but I saw he didn't by the pieces he was moving and what his eyes were doing, and then quite suddenly there came the Old Man's surprise move, and Arion sat back, amazed and then smiling and shaking his head.

" 'Another game!' he said. He started laughing. 'I demand it.'

" 'And so you shall have it!' said the Old Man, his face all atremble.

"As the Old Man was setting up the pieces I slowly rose to my feet.

" 'I'm going to leave you, gentlemen,' I said. 'I thank you for your hospitality and your gifts.'

" 'What are you talking about?' said Petronia.

" 'I'm going home,' I said. 'I want my family.'

" 'What do you mean, you're going home!' she demanded. 'Have you taken leave of your senses?'

" 'No, I haven't. And I wish now to abolish our bargain. The Hermitage is mine. I reclaim it as of now. I need the mausoleum for my hiding place by day, and I need the rest of it for a getaway in the night. Now, I'll leave you to your chess, and again I thank you—.'

"Arion rose to his feet.

" 'But how will you get home?' he asked gently. 'You can defy gravity very well over short distances, and with great speed, perhaps more than you know. But you can't travel halfway around the world. It will be years before you have that skill.'

" 'I'm going the way any mortal would go,' I responded.

" 'And what will you do when you get there!' demanded Petronia, looking up at me.

" 'Live in my house as I've always done,' I said. 'Live in my room where I've always lived. Be with my family as I've always been. I'll do that as long as I can. I won't give them up.'

"Petronia rose slowly. 'But you don't know how to pretend to be human. You don't have the faintest idea.'

" 'Yes, I do,' I said. 'I watched you do it, and you're ancient by your stories and yet you managed in a roomful of people. Why should it be so hard for me? Besides, I'm determined to do it. I won't relinquish the life I had.'

" 'Won't you realize,' Petronia said, 'that if you take those mortals into your secret, you'll destroy them?'

" 'I'll protect them from it with my whole heart,' I said. 'You won't make me lose my nerve.'

" 'You can't just leave here and do this, Quinn,' said Arion gently. 'Besides, why would you? You don't belong with humans now.'

" 'Must I ask your permission?' I countered, looking him directly in the eye.

"He shrugged gracefully, just as I knew he would.

" 'No, you don't have to ask me.'

" 'I don't give a damn what you do!' said Petronia, just as I knew she would.

"I smiled. 'Then the Hermitage is now mine?' I asked.

" 'Take it as a present from me,' she said venomously.

"I looked down at the Old Man. 'Manfred, we'll meet another night.'

" 'Be careful, my son,' he said.

"I left the room, and, finding the grand stairs of the palazzo, was soon out, walking down a narrow winding path to the city below.

"Within twenty minutes I walked into the lobby of the Hotel Excelsior, where we had stayed on three occasions on our trips to Naples, and went to the desk of the concierge. He remembered me and immediately asked after Aunt Queen.

" 'I've been robbed. Everything's gone,' I said. 'I need to make a collect call to my aunt.'

"The phone was at once placed at my disposal. And a suite was being prepared.

"It was Jasmine who answered. She began to sob. When Aunt Queen came on the line, she was damn near hysterical.

" 'Listen,' I said. 'I can't explain this, but I'm in Naples, Italy. I need my passport, and I need funds badly.' I told her over and over again how much I loved her and how unexpected this was, even for me, and that I would never be able to explain, but the thing now was for me to spend a decent night in the hotel and then start the flight home tomorrow evening.

"Finally Nash came on the line to give all the appropriate numbers to the cashier, and I was officially set up with every convenience, and I was told that airline tickets would be delivered to me. I explained to Nash that I would only travel at night—that I wanted to fly from here to Milan on an evening flight, then from Milan to London on another evening flight, and from thence to New York in one evening. From there, of course, I'd return to New Orleans.

"When I shut the door of the suite, I went into a state of shock.

"It seemed my life had been a series of escalating fears, and this fear I knew now was the worst. It was quiet and cold and worse than panic, and I felt my heart throbbing in my throat. It seemed there would never be any relief from this fear, never any relief from this pain.

"Tarquin Blackwood was dead, this I knew perfectly well. But a great remnant of me existed still, and that remnant, dazzled as I was by so many unwelcome gifts, longed only to be with Aunt Queen, with Tommy, with Jasmine, with all my beloved witnesses, my irreplaceable and adored kith and kin.

"No, I wouldn't let go of my family. No, I wouldn't go quietly from my place at Blackwood Manor and from all those whom I so loved!

"No—not without a struggle would I leave them, not without the noblest attempt to remain with them for as long as I could.

"As for Mona, my beloved witch, I would never, never see her again or let her hear my voice over a phone. Never would my evil touch her, never would my true fate be known to her. Never would my pain be mixed with her pain.

"An hour must have passed as I stood there, my back to the door, unable to move. I tried to breathe deeply. I tried not to clench my fists. I tried not to be afraid. I tried not to be in a rage.

"It was over and done with, this transformation. And I must go on. I must go home. I must do everything gently and with great conviction and love those who loved me with all my heart.

"Finally, I lay down on the bed, my throat tight, and my body full of tremors and I felt a sudden overwhelming exhaustion, and fell into a mortal sleep.

"It must have been dreamless. No Patsy, no Rebecca, though it did seem that I heard Rebecca laughing again, and that I didn't care.

"The early light awakened me like scalding water.

"At once I pulled all the draperies and their under curtains, and was soon in a sweet chilled darkness. Then I crawled under the bed, and soon lost consciousness.

"The following evening I had a temporary passport, money in my pockets, a new American Express card and the tickets to commence the journey. As soon as I reached London I realized I had to chart a different course for home, so I made stops in Nova Scotia, Canada, and finally Newark. Then at last I was bound for New Orleans.

"During all this time, I practiced, fearfully, my skill at the Little Drink in airports, prowling the big crowds like a swamp cat, stalking this or that victim for hours before the opportune moment, that sweet moment, loving it and loathing it at the same time. There was no doubt in my mind that I looked human to people. I even looked agreeable. And in my hunting, I made no blunders. I made no kills. I never spilt a drop.

"Oh, it was an agony of fear and pleasure, drifting through a humanity I could only penetrate as a monster. And the swarming airports became hellish, like vast sets for some existential drama. But I was fast becoming as addicted to the hunt as to the blood.

"Finally, I came down the concourse in New Orleans and Aunt Queen opened her arms and then Nash did the same and then my lovely Jasmine and my little son, Jerome, whom I picked up and kissed, crushing him to me totally. And then there was Tommy, my reserved thirteen-year-old uncle, whom I so adored. I had to hug Tommy.

"If any of them found anything strange about me it was totally overwhelmed by my enthusiasm. As for how I had gotten to Italy, I promised only that someday I would tell them. Of course they raised bloody hell, but that was all I would say.

"As we piled into the limousine to go home, they broke the news to me that Patsy had full-blown AIDS but was responding well to the medicines; however, Seymour was suing her. He had it too, and he claimed she had never told him she had it and that she had given it to him. I didn't know what to say. I thought of that dream I had, that awful dream. I couldn't get the images of the dream out of my head.

" 'How's she feel?' I asked. They said fine.

" 'How's she look?' I asked. They said fine.

" 'How's the band?' I asked. They said fine.

"That was the end of it.

"As soon as I reached the house I hugged Big Ramona and I told her I was too old to be sleeping with her anymore, and she said it was about high time for me to be saying that, that she was just waiting. She couldn't believe it when I turned down her pancakes.

"When I finally reached my room and shut and locked the door, I felt faint and mad. But I had fooled them. I had fooled them and I was back with them. I was with them and I had their love. I began to cry.

"I cried and cried. I went into the bathroom and I saw the blood streaming down my face, and that's how I learned that we cry blood tears, and I wiped away the blood with a paper handkerchief, and I finally stopped crying, and then I realized Goblin was there.

"Goblin was sitting in my desk chair, facing me, and Goblin was a full duplicate of me right to the blood in his eyes and the blood tears streaming down his face.

"I almost cried out in terror, it was such a sight. My heart stopped beating for a moment and then caught up.

"I wiped and wiped at my face. I ran at him.

" 'Look,' I said, 'I'm wiping them away, can't you see? I'm wiping them away! Look, they're gone, the blood is gone, can't you see?' I was shouting at him, I was thundering. I had to lower my voice. 'Don't you see! The blood's gone. I wiped it away!'

"He just sat there with the blood in his eyes and the blood dripping down his cheeks and then he ran at me. He ran into me. He merged with me, and I felt myself pushed backwards against the round table and then to the side and to the foot of the bed, and I couldn't fight him off, he was in me, he was merged with me, and it felt like a pure fatal electric shock, and when he withdrew I saw him huge and filled with tiny droplets of blood, and I collapsed."

43

"Now you have my story. You know my greatest shame, that I killed the innocent bride. You know how Goblin began his attacks on me.

"You can guess the events that happened after my homecoming. You know from this story how much I love my family. You know how much my life is enmeshed with theirs.

"I felt a great and terrible hatred for Petronia and what she had done to me! With a passion that can only be called vengeance I pitched myself back into my human life, my mortal world, my family existence. I would not have it otherwise, unless proved to me that all suspected me and shunned me. But nothing of that sort happened.

"On the contrary, people needed me and I knew it. My strange disappearance had severely wounded Aunt Queen, Tommy, Jerome, Jasmine and even Clem and Big Ramona. I made amends with my endless apologies, though I couldn't and wouldn't explain how my disappearance had come about.

"All I could do is what I did—promise that I would never disappear again, that though I had become something of a secretive bachelor and a night creature, and though I might from time to time be off for a night or two or even three, I would always be home afterwards. And no one should ever fear for me.

"And so 'Quinn is going through a phase,' they said with laughter. But Quinn was around a lot.

"I had my room outfitted as you see it, with heavy velvet draperies, so that the light can be shut out, and there's a heavy lock on the door; but usually I spend the daylight hours in the mausoleum on Sugar Devil Island, where I feel completely safe from prying eyes, since I alone can open the crypt with ease, it having taken some five men to open it on the long-ago exciting day when we examined it.

"In a house where Aunt Queen is accustomed to rising at three p.m. and taking her six a.m. constitutional before going to bed, my habits proved normal, and so everyone has come to assume.

"Now, Aunt Queen has admitted that she's actually eighty-five years old, not eighty, a nice little secret she kept from us when we stumbled through the ruins of Pompeii with her, but she's spry and curious and full of the capacity to enjoy life in all its richness, as you saw for yourself, and she holds court in her room every night with Cindy, the nurse, and Jasmine and various other assorted attendants, including me, especially if it's earlier in the evening, as I usually do not disappear on my nightly errands until the stroke of twelve.

"As far as the bed-and-breakfast is concerned, Jasmine was plum tuckered out, as we say around here, and simply did not want to go on with the running of it. And once we gave Tommy one of the bedrooms upstairs, and set up another one for Brittany when she came to visit, and put Nash in Pops' old room, that left only one room for a guest, so it seemed pointless to be renting it.

"And then Patsy, who is on the frail side now, took to staying in that last front bedroom. So the bed-and-breakfast was therefore crowded right out.

"But the parish all around couldn't do without the big Christmas banquet and the Easter buffet and the azalea festival and an occasional wedding, so Jasmine still sees to that with a tremendous amount of pride, though she complains about it as if she were the local saint.

"I was in the background when the carols were sung this last year, not daring to weep, but weeping in my soul as the soprano sang 'O Holy Night' twice just for me.

"Being a madman, I also instigated a midnight dinner on Holy Saturday—Easter Sunday morning, just because I couldn't attend the Easter buffet, and that went splendidly this year, right along with the usual afternoon buffet, drawing a whole different body of after-church guests. And I've been conniving to instigate some other late-night charity affairs and fund-raisers, it's just my brain has been a bit distracted of late.

"Tommy astonished all of us by asking of his own free will to be sent off to boarding school in England, to Eton no less, and Nash took him over and got him established, and when he calls us we all marvel that he is acquiring a British accent, and we are overjoyed. I miss him terribly. He will be coming home for the holidays sometime soon. He's now fourteen and growing tall. He still wants to lead an expedition to find the lost continent of Atlantis. I clip every article I read on the subject and mail it to him. And Nash does the same.

"Terry Sue and her children are doing well. The nanny and the housekeeper have made all the difference in their lives and things run smoothly there. Brittany and the other children are in good schools, and they will have a real chance in life. Terry Sue herself is happy. As soon as she gets her check every two weeks she goes to Wal-Mart to buy clothes and artificial flowers. Her house is absolutely chock-full of artificial flowers. It's a virtual rain forest of artificial flowers. You can't find a spot in her house to put another artificial flower. As soon as you walk in she tries to give you some old artificial flowers so she can get some new artificial flowers. She has had an operation to prevent the birth of any more children. Charlie, her gun-wielding boyfriend, after holding the entire family and the sheriff at bay with a three fifty-seven Magnum, finally shot himself in the head.

"Aunt Queen has decided that she's to be a finishing school for Terry Sue, and about twice a week Terry Sue comes over to discuss clothing purchases with Aunt Queen, and Aunt Queen gives her advice on her nail polish and how to have her hair done. Brittany has also become the pet of Aunt Queen and now has a doll collection as the result of it.

"Jasmine, after a knock-down drag-out fight, allowed me to give Jerome my name, and even to have him call me Dad, but she wasn't happy about it. And then she gave in on having him driven every day into New Orleans to go to Trinity School. Jerome is very bright. Aunt Queen loves to read to him. Nash spent considerable time tutoring him. He's already making up stories of his own, which he dictates into a little tape recorder. He does it like a radio broadcast with all the sound effects.

"It deeply moves me that he's my son, and the only one I'll ever have, but I also feel a similar affection for Tommy, and I think back to what Petronia said to me in Napoli, that I could do honorable or decent things. I don't know whether or not she was thinking of such things as being the patron of mortals, but I think of it, and I feel that my work is just begun. I dream of being the patron of a pianist—you know, buying him sheet music, and paying for his records, and helping with his tuition and lessons, and things of this sort. It's a dream, but I think I can do it. I don't see why not.

"But I'm becoming distracted. Let me continue. The epilogue, yes.

"For nine months, Nash and I read Dickens together. We spent the early part of every evening at it, before I went to hunt, and while I was still safe from Goblin's attacks. We occupied the two chairs by the fireplace in Nash's room and traded off reading out loud to one another. We went back through *Great Expectations, David Copperfield* and *The Old Curiosity Shop*. We also read *Hamlet*, which set me to secretly weeping about Mona, and *Macbeth, King Lear* and *Othello*. We usually parted company by eleven p.m. and on those few days when Aunt Queen forced herself to endure daylight in order to shop for cameos or clothes, Nash accompanied her.

"Other nights Nash watched films with Aunt Queen, Jasmine, and Cindy, the nurse, and other assorted folks. Even Big Ramona got into the spirit of it.

"Then Nash went back out to California to finish his Ph.D. and when he returns he'll be Aunt Queen's escort again. She sorely misses him, and, as she's told you herself, she has no one just now and it hurts her.

"Patsy is doing well on the drug cocktail they're giving her for AIDS and she's been able to do a little work with her band. We settled out of court with Seymour for a huge sum of money, but he died shortly after receiving it. Patsy's sworn she doesn't infect people. Two more lawsuits have been brought against her by former members of her band.

"All this has worn out Patsy. She likes being in the big house in the front bedroom across the hall. I don't talk to her very much because every time that I come up those steps I have the overpowering urge to kill her. Every night. I can read her mind without wanting to, and I know she has negligently run the risk of infecting numerous people with AIDS and even now she would do it except that everyone is wise to her. I feel the urge so strongly to take her life that I stay away from her.

"But let me go on.

"From the first night of my return, I have tried to increase my skill and learn my powers.

"I control my telepathy around my family, and around everyone but my victims, really, because it feels obscene to me, and also it feels like noise.

"I have traveled through the air, I have practiced speed. I have come and gone from the Hermitage to far-flung taverns and highway beer joints to hunt for drifters and Evil Doers, or to make a staple of the Little Drink, and I've been successful. Even when I've drunk my fill I've almost always left the victim alive. I've learned, as Arion said, to go with the evil, to make it part of myself for those important moments.

"I never go to hunt before midnight, and of course Goblin always attacks right afterwards. I usually don't come back to the house until his attack is over. I don't want the family in any way disturbed by what Goblin means to do. But sometimes I miscalculate.

"There have been no moral blunders on my part until tonight when I almost killed Stirling Oliver.

"But Goblin's attacks have grown ever more virulent, and as for communication with him, it is nil. He will say nothing to me. He seems to feel that in becoming what I am I have in some massive way betrayed him, and he will take from me what he wants—the blood. And no affection or conversation is needed.

"Of course, he may also feel that he was betrayed by my long absence in Europe.

"I've tried to talk to him, but to no avail. He seldom appears. He is present only right after I feed.

"And during this last year, as I proved to myself that I could hunt, that I could survive, that I could live with Aunt Queen and Nash and with Jasmine, that I could be with my son, that I could sneak into the human world every night of my life and then pass out of it into my grave, Goblin has grown far stronger and far more vicious, and so at last I've come to you to beg your help, and I think I've come to you out of loneliness.

"As I believe I've indicated, I know how to go back to Petronia but I don't want to do it. I don't want her sneering coldness. I don't want even the softer indifference of Arion. As for the Old Man, though he would open his heart to me, he seems locked in his dotage. What do any of them know of a spirit like Goblin? I've come to you to help me. You've been with the spirits. I risked my life to do it.

"I believe that Goblin is a menace not only to me but to others, and one characteristic is now certain—that he can travel with me wherever I go, no matter how far it is from Blackwood Farm.

"He is attached to me in some new way, and perhaps it has to do with the Blood. In fact, I'm sure it has to do with the Blood. The Blood has given him a link to me that is stronger than his link to this place.

"There very well may be a limit to the distance he can travel, but I myself can't give up Blackwood Farm, that's the rub. I can't be away from those who need me. I don't want to be away from them. And as a consequence I must battle Goblin here for my home, and for my life, if I'm to live it.

"And I feel a great responsibility for Goblin. I feel that I created

Goblin and that I nourished him and made him what he is. What if he should hurt someone else?

"I have one last detail and my story is closed.

"I have seen Petronia once since I left Naples. I was sitting in the Hermitage, amid all the shining marble and torchères, dreaming, thinking, brooding, I don't know what exactly, feeling my unhappiness in a sort of spectacular way, when she came up the stairs, all dressed in a white three-piece suit with her hair loose and flying and full of chains of diamonds, and she gave me your books, which she had in a little dark green velvet sack.

" 'These are the Vampire Chronicles,' she said. 'You need to read these and know these. We told you about them, but we don't know if you listened. Remember. Don't hunt New Orleans.'

" 'Get out of here, I loathe and detest you,' I said to her. 'I told you our bargain is off. This place is mine!' I stood up and ran at her and struck her hard across the face before she could get her wits about her. The blood flowed from her mouth where her fangs had cut her lip, and it soiled her white vest and she was furious. She slapped me hard this way and that before I could get back and be ready for it, and then she knocked me down and went to her trick of kicking me.

" 'What a charming greeting,' she said, ramming the toe of her boot over and over right between my ribs. 'You are the epitome of the grateful child.'

"I climbed to my knees, pretending to stagger and to be hurt, and then rose up and grabbed her hair and hung on to a hank of it with both hands so that she couldn't shake me off, cursing her all the while. 'Some night, I'll make you pay,' I said. 'I'll make you suffer for all your hateful blows, for the way that you did it, for the way you brought this curse on me.'

"She clawed at me as I pulled her hair with both hands; she clawed at my head and dragged me off herself, so that I had hair in my fingers, and then she slammed me down on the floor and she kicked me across the room and against the wall. Then she sat down at the desk and with her face in her hands she sobbed. She sobbed and sobbed.

"I climbed to my feet and slowly made my way towards her. I felt that tingling in all my limbs that meant the bruises she'd inflicted were healing. I saw bits and pieces of the diamond chains from her hair on the floor, and I gathered them all up, and I came to the desk where she cried and I laid them down where she might see them.

"She had her face buried in her hands, and her hands were stained with blood.

" 'I'm sorry,' I said.

"She took her handkerchief out and wiped her face and her hands. Then she looked up at me, prettily.

" 'Why should you be sorry?' she asked. 'It's only natural for you to hate a creature like me. Why shouldn't you?'

" 'How so?' I asked. I expected her at any moment to fly at me again.

" 'Who should be made into creatures like us?' she asked. 'The wounded, the slave, the destitute, the dying. But you were a prince, a mortal prince. And I didn't think twice about it.'

" 'That's true,' I said.

" 'And so you . . . you fool the fools?' she asked gesturing with her right hand in a roving motion. 'You live with your mortals lovingly around you?'

" 'Yes, for now,' I said.

" 'Don't be tempted to bring them over,' she said.

" 'I'm not tempted,' I said. 'I'd rather go straight to Hell than do it that way.'

"She looked at the diamonds. I didn't know what to do about them. I looked around. I had gotten them all. She picked up the strands and put them in one of her pockets. Her hair was mussed. I took out my comb. I gestured, Would she let me comb it? She said Yes, and so I did it. Her hair was thick and silky.

"Finally she stood up to go. She took me in her arms and she kissed me.

" 'Don't run afoul of the Vampire Lestat,' she said. 'He won't think twice about burning you to a cinder. And then I'd have to fight him and I'm not strong enough.'

" 'That's really true?'

" 'I told you in Napoli to read the books,' she said. 'He's drunk the blood of the Mother. He lay in the sands of the Gobi Desert for three days. Nothing can kill him. It wouldn't even be fun to fight him. But just stay out of New Orleans and you don't need to worry about him. There's something ignoble about one as powerful as Lestat picking on one as young as you. He won't come here to do it.'

" 'Thank you,' I said.

"She walked towards the door as though she was making a graceful exit. I didn't know whether or not she knew there was blood on her clothing. I didn't know whether or not to tell her. Finally I did.

" 'On your suit,' I said, 'blood.'

" 'You just can't resist white clothes, can you?' she asked, but she didn't seem angry. 'Let me ask you something. And answer me truthfully or not at all. Why did you leave us?'

"I thought for a long moment. Then I said, 'I wanted to be with my aunt. I had no real choice in the matter. And there were others. You know this already.'

" 'But weren't we interesting to you?' she asked. 'After all, you might have asked me to bring you home now and then. Surely you know my powers are very great.'

"I shook my head.

" 'I don't blame you for turning your back on me,' she said, 'but to turn your back on one as wise as Arion? That seems rash to me.'

" 'You're probably right, but for now I have to be here. Then later perhaps I can bring my suit to Arion.'

"She smiled. She shrugged. 'Very well. I leave you the Hermitage, my boy,' she said. And she was gone just as if she had vanished. And so our one brief visit ended.

"And so my story is at an end."

44

I SAT THERE in silence. We had perhaps two hours before dawn, and I felt that all my life was pressed against my heart, and, though I was a sinner, I had not sinned in holding anything back. It was all laid out before me. I wondered if Goblin was near me in any form. I wondered whether or not he could have been listening.

Lestat, who had been quiet this whole time, waited for a long moment in silence. Then he spoke up.

"Your epilogue was very thorough, but you haven't mentioned one person. What has become of Mona Mayfair?"

I winced.

"I have never received another E-mail or phone call from Mona, and for that I thank God. However, periodically Michael or Rowan will call. I find myself trembling as I listen. Will these powerful witches pick up something from the timbre of my voice? But it doesn't seem so. They tell me the latest. Mona is in isolation. Mona is on dialysis. Mona is not in any pain.

"About six months ago, maybe more, I received a typewritten letter from Rowan, written on behalf of Mona, explaining that Mona had had a hysterectomy, and that Mona wanted me to know. 'Beloved Abelard, I release you from any and all promises,' Mona had dictated to Rowan. They had hoped the operation would help Mona, but it hadn't. Mona needed dialysis more and more often. There were still medications they could try.

"My answer was to raid every flower shop in New Orleans, sending sprays and baskets and vases of flowers with notes that pledged my undying love, notes which I could dictate over the phone. I didn't dare to send anything touched by my own hands. Mona could lay her hands on such a note and sense the evil in me. Just couldn't take such a risk.

"As it stands now, I still send the flowers almost daily. Now and then I break down and call. It's always the same. Mona can't see anyone just now. Mona is holding her own.

"I think I actually dread the moment when they might say, 'Come see her.' I'm afraid I won't be able to resist it and I won't be able to fool Mona, and in those precious moments, perhaps our last precious moments, Mona's mind will be clouded with some dim fear of what I've become. At the very least I'll seem cold and passionless though my heart's breaking. I dread it. I dread it with my whole soul.

"But more than anything I dread the final call—the message that Mona has lost the fight, the word that Mona is gone."

Lestat nodded. He leaned on his elbow, his hair somewhat mussed, his large blue eyes looking at me compassionately as they had throughout the long hours of my storytelling.

"What do you think is the point of the tale you've told?" he asked. "Aside from the fact that we must protect Aunt Queen from all harmful knowledge of what's happened to you, and we must destroy Goblin?"

"That I had a rich life," I said. "As Petronia herself said it. And she didn't care about that life. She took it capriciously and viciously."

Again he nodded. "But Quinn, immortality, no matter how one comes by it, is a gift, and you must lose your hatred of her. It poisons you."

"It's like my hatred of Patsy," I said quietly. "I need to lose my hatred of both of them. I need to lose all hatred, but right now it's Goblin who needs destroying, and I've tried, out of fairness to him, to make it plain to you how much I'm responsible for what he is, and even for the vengeance he wishes on me."

"That's clear," said Lestat, "but I don't know that I alone can help stop him. I may need help. In fact, I think I do. I think I need it from a Blood Drinker whose prowess with spirits is a legend." He raked his hair back from his forehead. "I think I can persuade her to come and help me with this. I'm speaking of Merrick Mayfair. She doesn't know your fair Mona, at least not as far as I know, and even if she did at one time there's no connection now in any event. But Merrick knows spirits in a way that most vampires don't. She was a powerful witch before she ever became a vampire."

"Then the Dark Blood didn't take away her powers with spirits?" I asked.

"No," he said, shaking his head. "She's far too complex for that. And besides, it's a lie that spirits shun us. As you said yourself, I'm a seer of spirits. I wish to God I weren't. I'll need tomorrow evening to find Merrick Mayfair. Merrick is almost as young in the Blood as you are. She's suffering. But I think I can bring her here, perhaps at one or two in the morning. I can't imagine her refusing to come, but we'll see. In either case, I'll return. You have my firm pledge on it."

"Ah, I thank you with all my heart," I said.

"Then let me make a little confession," he said with a warm, irresistible smile.

"Of course," I said, "what is it?"

"I've fallen in love with you," he said in a low voice. "You might find that in the nights to come I'm a bit of a nuisance."

I was so amazed I was speechless. To say that he looked exquisite to me was an understatement. He was savory and elegant and all night as I had talked I had been so locked to him that I had felt myself under his spell, opening up, as if there were no boundary between us.

"Good," he said suddenly as though he was reading my mind. "Now perhaps I'll leave you early so that I can try to find Merrick right away. We have some time left before morning—."

A loud scream suddenly interrupted both of us. It was Jasmine, and I heard another scream right after it.

"Quinn, Quinn, it's Goblin!" she was roaring from the foot of the stairs.

I had to hold myself back and force myself to run like a mortal man as I descended with Lestat behind me.

Screams came from Aunt Queen's room. I could hear Cindy, the nurse, crying. Big Ramona was sobbing. Jasmine rushed towards me. She grabbed me by both arms and said:

"It was Goblin, Quinn! I saw him!"

We ran back through the hall together, I once again suppressing my speed, trying desperately to keep to a mortal pace.

As soon as I saw Aunt Queen lying on the floor by the marble table I knew she was dead.

I knew by her eyes.

I didn't have to see the blood streaming from her head, or the blood on the marble table. I knew, and when I looked at her bare stocking feet, when I looked at her humble stocking feet, I began to sob, covering my face with my handkerchief.

And there was the beautiful cameo of Medusa at her throat, the charm against harm, and it had done her no good, it hadn't saved her. She was dead; she was lost. She was gone.

She and her majesty and her goodness were gone forever.

What else was there? People were making frantic phone calls. Sirens were soon screaming. What did it matter?

How many times did they explain it before dawn?

She had taken off her treacherous shoes. That's why no one was holding her arm. She had taken off her terrible shoes. That's why Jasmine didn't have her by the arm. She had taken off her dangerous shoes. That's why Cindy wasn't at her side. She had gone over to the table to look at her cameos. She had wanted to find one in particular for Cindy's daughter.

On and on they said it, and the Coroner listened and Sheriff Jeanfreau listened and Ugly Henderson listened, and Jasmine and Cindy both said it had been Goblin who made her fall, it had been Goblin whirling in the air, Goblin like a small tornado in the room, and Aunt Queen had cried out twice "Goblin!" and thrown up her arms, and then gone down, her head crashing into the marble.

Cindy and Jasmine had seen it! They had seen the commotion in the air! They knew what it was. They heard her say it twice: "Goblin, Goblin!" and in her stocking feet on the carpet she fell, she fell and hit the marble table with the side of her head, and she was dead before she reached the carpet.

Oh, God in Heaven help me.

"Now, are you two ladies telling me that a ghost killed Mrs. McQueen?" asked the Coroner.

"Sheriff, for the love of Heaven," I said. "She fell! Surely you don't believe that either Cindy or Jasmine had anything to do with it!"

And so on it went, round and round, until I had to go, and I took Jasmine aside and told her to make all the arrangements with Lonigan and Sons in New Orleans. The wake should be tomorrow night, starting at seven. And I would see her then, and I told her to try as she might to arrange for an evening interment. Of course that would be highly irregular but maybe money could manage it.

"And for the love of Heaven," I said, "beware of Goblin."

"What are you going to do about him, Quinn?" she asked. She was trembling and her face was puffy from crying.

"I'm going to destroy him, Jasmine. But it will take just a little time. Until I can get it done, beware of him. Tell all the others. Beware of him. He's swollen with power—."

"You can't leave here now, Quinn," she said.

"I have to, Jasmine," I said. "I'll see you at the funeral parlor in New Orleans at seven tomorrow."

She was horrified, and I didn't blame her.

Lestat stepped in front of me and he gently took her by the shoulders, looking intently into her eyes. "Jasmine," he said in a low tone, "we have to go and find the woman who can put an end to Goblin. It's imperative that we do that. Do you understand?"

She nodded. She was still crying and she licked the tears from her lips as they fell. But she couldn't take her eyes off his.

"Keep little Jerome close to you," said Lestat, his voice soft and persuasive. "This creature wants to hurt everyone dear to Quinn. See that everybody is on guard."

He kissed her forehead.

Quietly, we withdrew.

At last, Lestat and I were alone on Sugar Devil Island and I gave vent to my grief, sobbing like a child. "I can't imagine the world without her, I don't want the world without her, I hate him with my whole soul that he did it, how in the name of God did he get the power, she was too old, too fragile, how can we make him suffer, how can we make him suffer so much that he'll want to die, how can we send him to whatever Hell exists for him?"

On and on I raved. And then we went to our rest together.

45

A T SUNSET I rose hungry and miserable, but I understood that Lestat had to leave me to my mortal commitments so that he could contact Merrick Mayfair and see if she would render me support.

As soon as I reached the big house I realized that Nash and Tommy were both there. Tommy had flown all day and some of the evening to get home from England, and Nash had just arrived much earlier from the West Coast. The look of grief on both their faces was dreadful, and I could scarcely hold back my tears.

In truth, I didn't want to hold them back but the fear of the blood made it absolutely essential, so I gave myself up to hugs and kisses and saw to it that I had at least three linen handkerchiefs, and, saying next to nothing, for what was there to say, we all piled into Aunt Queen's luxurious limousine and headed into New Orleans for Lonigan and Sons in the Irish Channel—back to the turf where Manfred Blackwood had owned his first saloon.

The crowd at the wake was already enormous when we arrived. Patsy was at the open door and very soberly dressed in black—which amazed me, as she was a great one for skipping funerals—and it was plain that she'd been crying.

She flashed a small square of folded pages at me.

"Photocopy of her will," she said in a tremulous voice. "She instructed Grady a long time ago not to keep us in suspense. She left me plenty. It was a damn nice thing for her to do. He has a copy in his pocket for you."

I merely nodded. It was all too typical of Aunt Queen to have done this last little generous gesture, and over the evening I was to see Grady passing the little folded photocopy packets to Terry Sue and Nash, among others.

Patsy went on out to smoke a cigarette and didn't seem to want to talk.

Jasmine, lovely in her blue suit and signature white blouse, and lamentably exhausted from the long day of picking out the coffin, the vault and the dress for Aunt Queen, was near to collapse.

"I brought her fingernail polish," she repeated to me three times. "They did a nice job. I told them to wipe off some of the rouge, but it was nice. A nice job. You want to bury her with the pearls? Those are her pearls." Over and over she asked.

I said Yes.

Nash finally collected Jasmine and escorted her to one of the many little French chairs that lined the walls of the front parlor. Big Ramona was sitting in a chair simply crying, and Clem, having parked the limo, came in to stand over his mother and looked perfectly wretched.

Terry Sue was crying too as she held on to Tommy, who was sobbing. I wanted to comfort Tommy but I was so rattled by my own grief, and, holding back the blood tears, I couldn't do it. Brittany was white-faced and miserable.

Rowan Mayfair was there, which amazed me, looking softly delicate in her tailored suit with her carefully bobbed hair flattering her high cheekbones as always, and there was Michael Curry at her side, with a little more gray in his curly hair than I remembered, the two of them sharing a common radiance which alarmed me. Witches, yes. The Blood told me and they both nodded respectfully at me, suspecting nothing, and I veered away from them, wary of their power, with only a nod, as if I was too stricken to talk, which in fact was true.

There was no avoiding it: I had to approach the coffin. I had to look into it. I had to do it. And so I did.

There lay Aunt Queen in satin splendor, with ropes of pearls on her breast and a large rectangular cameo at her throat which I had never seen in her collection, and which for the moment I couldn't place. Then I recalled it. I had seen it on Petronia. Petronia had worn it when last I saw her at the Hermitage. And when last I saw her in Naples.

How did it get here? I had only to look up to see. There stood Petronia at the foot of the coffin, dressed all in dark blue with her glorious hair pulled back, looking sad and forlorn. In a swift motion that seemed no more than a blink of my eye she was beside me, and, curling her fingers gently around my upper arm, she whispered into my ear that Jasmine had allowed her to place the cameo on Aunt Queen and she had done it, and if I would allow it, it should remain.

"That way, you can keep her special treasures," she said, "yet know she was buried with something worthy of her, something she would have admired."

"Very well and good," I said. Then Petronia was gone. I knew it without looking. I felt it. I felt it and I felt a strangeness at having seen her among so many mortals, and I felt a new confidence in my own abilities to dissemble, but more than anything I felt an overwhelming misery as I looked down at my beloved Aunt Queen.

Lonigan was an undertaker par excellence as everybody knew, but he had really outdone himself in capturing the pleasant, almost gay expression of Aunt Queen. She was almost smiling. And her gray hair was in perfect soft curls around her face. The rouge on her cheeks was subtle and the coral lipstick on her lips was perfect. She would have been most happy with all that had been done. Of course Jasmine had helped. But Lonigan had wrought the masterpiece, and Aunt Queen's generosity shone forth from his work.

As to the salmon-colored dress and the pearls which Jasmine had chosen, they were lovely, and the rosary in Aunt Queen's hands—it was the crystal rosary from her First Communion, which she had carried with her all through the great world.

I was so stricken with anguish that I couldn't move or speak. In desperation I wished that Petronia had lingered, and I found myself staring at the large rectangular cameo, with its little mythological figures—Hebe, Zeus, the raised cup—and the blood tears started to fill my eyes. I wiped furiously with the linen handkerchief.

Then quickly I withdrew. I went hurriedly through the crowded parlors and out into the hot evening and stood alone at the curb of the corner, looking up at the stars. Nothing would ever assuage the grief I felt now. I knew it. I would carry it with me all my nights until whatever I was now had disintegrated, until Quinn Blackwood had become somebody or something other than what he was now.

My time of privacy lasted only a few seconds. Jasmine came to me and told me that many people wanted to express their condolences and were hesitant because I seemed so upset.

"I can't talk to them, Jasmine, you have to do it for me," I told her. "I have to go now. I know it seems hard and I seem the coward to you. But it's what I have to do."

"Is it Goblin?" she asked.

"It's the fear of him, yes," I said, lying just a little, more to console her than to cover my own shame. "When is the Mass? When is the interment?"

"The Mass is at eight p.m. tomorrow at St. Mary's, and then we go to Metairie Cemetery."

I kissed her. I told her I would see her at the church, and then I turned to go.

But as I glanced back at the crowd leaking out of the doorways onto the street, I saw yet another figure who astonished me—the figure of Julien Mayfair, in his fine gray suit, the suit he had worn the day he so regally entertained me with hot cocoa, standing as if he was merely taking the warm air with all the others, his eyes fixed casually on me.

He seemed as solid as every other person present, except that he was a faintly different color than everyone else, as though he had been painted in by another artist, and all the tones of his clothes and skin and hair were done in darker hues. Oh, such a fine and elegant ghost, come from who knows where, and who in the world thought that as a Blood Drinker I wouldn't see my spirits?

"Ah, yes, she was your daughter, of course," I said, and though there was a great distance between us, and Jasmine was looking up at me uncomprehending, he nodded and he made a very sad little smile.

"What are you saying, you crazy Little Boss?" said Jasmine. "You punchy as I am?"

"I don't know, darling," I answered. "I just see things, always have. Seems the living and the dead have turned out for Aunt Queen. Don't expect me to explain it. But it's fitting, all things considered, don't you think?"

As I watched him, Julien's expression gradually changed, sharpening and strengthening and then becoming almost bitter. I felt the chills coming up my neck. He shook his head in a subtle but stern negation. I felt the words coming from him soundlessly over the distance. *Never my beloved Mona.*

I drew in my breath. A flood of assurances came from that part of me which could reach him without words.

"Come around, Little Boss," said Jasmine. I felt her lips on my cheek and the hard press of her vigilant fingers.

I couldn't take my eyes off Julien, but his face was softening. It went blank.

He began to fade. And then dissolve just as Rowan and Michael, along with Dr. Winn Mayfair, came out of the nearest doorway. And who should be with them now but Stirling Oliver, Stirling who knew what I was, Stirling whom I had almost killed the night before, Stirling— gazing at me as if he accepted me when that was utterly morally impossible, Stirling whom I had so loved as my friend. I couldn't bear their scrutiny—any of them. I couldn't talk common talk of Mona, as if my soul didn't hunger for her, as if I didn't know that I could never see her again, even if they thought that I could, as if Julien's ghost hadn't just threatened me. I had to make a hasty exit.

And I did.

It was a night for a special killing. I pounded the hot pavements. I left the great trees of the Garden District behind me. I crossed the Avenue. I knew where to go.

I wanted a drug dealer, a wanton killer, a fine repast, and I knew where to find one; I had passed his door on gentler nights. I knew his habits. I had saved him for a time of vengeance. I had saved him for now.

It was a big two-story house on Carondolet Street, shabby to the world and rich inside with his electronic gadgets and wall-to-wall carpets, a padded cell from which he ordered executions and purchases and even put the mark on children who refused to run deliveries for him, having their tennis shoes tied together and thrown up over the electric wires to let others know that they had been killed.

I didn't care what the world thought; I broke in on him and slaughtered his two drugged-up stumbling companions with rapid blows to the head. He scrambled for his gun. I had him by the throat, broke him open like a stem. At once I had the sweet sap of his monstrous self-love, poison plant in the garden of hate, lifting his symbolic fist against any assassin, believing to the last drop of blood that he would triumph, that somehow consciousness wouldn't betray him, until finally he was just spilling out the child soul, the early prayers, the images of mother and kindergarten, sunshine, and his heart stopped, and I drew back, licking my lips, glutted, angry, full.

I took his gun, the gun he had reached for to shoot me, and, taking the pillow from off his couch, I pressed pillow and gun to his head and put two bullets in him, and then I did the same to each of his companions. That would give the Coroner something he could understand. I wiped off the gun and left it there.

In a flash I saw Goblin, eyes full of blood, hands red with blood, then he shot towards me as if to grab my throat.

Burn, you devil, burn! I sent the fire into him as he surrounded me, as he sought to merge with me, and I felt the heat singe me, singe my hair, my clothes. *You murdered Aunt Queen, you devil, burn! Burn if I have to burn with you.* I fell to the floor, or rather the floor came up to take me, full of dust and filth, and I was sprawled out flat on the stinking carpet with him inside me, his heart thudding against my heart, and then the swoon—we were children, we were infants, we were in the cradle and someone was singing, and Little Ida said, Doesn't that baby have the most beautiful curly hair, oh so sweet to be with Little Ida, to hear her voice again, so sweet, so safe. Aunt Queen let the screen door bang behind her. "Ida, you darling, help me with this clasp. I swear I'm going to lose these pearls!" *You devil, you murdering spirit, I won't look at her, I won't feel it; I won't know it.* And I was with Goblin and loved Goblin and nothing else mattered—not even the tiny wounds all over me and the tug on my heart. "Get off me, you devil! I swear it, I'll put an end to you. I'll take you into the fire with me. Don't count me a liar!"

I rose to my hands and knees.

A gust of wind wrapped itself around me and then swept past the broken door. The panes of glass in the window shattered and clattered.

I was so full of hate I could taste it and it didn't taste like blood.

He was gone.

I was in the lair of the drug king, amid the rotting bodies. I had to get out.

And Aunt Queen was dead. She was absolutely dead. She was laid out on cream-colored satin with ropes of pearls. Someone remembered her little eyeglasses with their sterling silver chain. And her Chantilly perfume. Just a little Chantilly perfume.

She is dead.

And there is nothing, absolutely nothing, that I can do about it.

46

THERE CAME into my heart some wild dream that Mona would be at the funeral Mass, but no such thing happened, though Fr. Kevin Mayfair was the celebrant, and though all the Mayfairs I knew—Rowan, Michael and Dr. Winn—were there as they had been at the wake the night before. They all shared that eerie glow which so unsettled me. Stirling Oliver was also with them, and they gave me their polite nods when our eyes met.

The same immense crowd was there, filling the central nave of St. Mary's Assumption Church in a way I'd never witnessed at weekly Mass. In fact there were more people present because McQueens had flown in from far and wide who had not been able to reach New Orleans in time for the wake the night before.

It chilled me mercilessly to see the closed coffin lying on its bier in the main aisle, and since it was only just dark when I reached the church, I had been unable to see Aunt Queen before they shut her up for all time.

But I did not have to bear this misery alone, because both Lestat and Merrick Mayfair appeared at my side just as I was making my way past the Mayfairs and into the pew with Jasmine, Tommy and Nash.

This was so unexpected that for a moment I was shaken and had to be supported by Lestat, who took my arm firmly. He had trimmed his hair quite short, was wearing a pair of pale sunglasses to blunt the effect of his iridescent eyes and was dressed very conservatively in a double-breasted blue jacket and khaki pants.

Merrick Mayfair, in a crisp white linen shirtwaist dress, had a white scarf wrapped around her face and neck and a large pair of sunglasses that almost masked her face. But I was certain that it was she, and I wasn't surprised when Stirling Oliver, who was in the pew behind us, came up and spoke to her, whispering that he was glad to see her and hoped he might later have a word with her.

I could hear her plainly when she said she had many things on her mind but she would try to do what he wanted. It seemed then that she kissed Stirling on both cheeks, but I wasn't certain as her back was turned. I knew only that for Stirling this was a moment of incredible magnitude.

Fr. Kevin Mayfair commenced the Requiem Mass with two altar boys. I hadn't been to church since the transformation and I was unprepared for the fact that he reminded me so very much of my red-haired Mona. I felt an ache just looking at him as he greeted us all and we returned the greeting. And then I realized I ached for him as I always had.

He believed completely in the sacred words he spoke. He was an ordained priest of God and the awareness of this permeated his entire being. The Blood revealed this to me. But even as a mortal I had never doubted it.

That Lestat and Merrick actually knelt beside me, making the Sign of the Cross and apparently praying in whispers, answering the anthems of the Mass, just as I did, was a shock but a pleasant one, as if the mad world in which I was lost could form its own flexible connective tissue.

When it came time to read a passage from the Bible and to speak of Aunt Queen, Nash made a very solemn and proper speech about nobility existing in Aunt Queen's eternal consideration of others, and Jasmine came forth shaking badly and spoke of Aunt Queen having been the guiding star of her life, and then others spoke—people I hardly knew—all saying kind things. And finally there was silence.

I remembered vividly how I had failed to speak at all the funerals of my life, in spite of my love for Lynelle and for Pops and for Sweetheart, and I found myself rising and coming forward to the microphone at the lectern just behind the altar rail. It seemed unthinkable that being what I was I would do this, but I was doing it and I knew that nothing would keep me from it.

Adjusting my voice for the microphone, I said that Aunt Queen had been the wisest person that I had ever known and that being possessed of true wisdom she had been gifted with perfect charity, and that to be in her presence was to be in the presence of goodness. Then I recited from the Book of Wisdom the description of the gift of wisdom, which I felt Aunt Queen possessed:

"For wisdom is more active than all active things: and reacheth everywhere by reason of her purity.

For she is a vapour of the power of God, and a certain pure emanation of the glory of the almighty God: and therefore no defiled thing cometh into her.

For she is the brightness of eternal light, and the unspotted mirror of God's majesty, and the image of his goodness.

And being but one, she can do all things: and remaining in herself the same, she reneweth all things. . . ."

I broke off there. "No finer language can be used to describe Aunt Queen," I said. "And that she lived among us to be eighty-five years of age was a gift to all of us, a precious gift, and that death took her so abruptly must be seen as a mercy if we are to remain sane, and to think of her and what decrepitude might have meant to her. She is gone. She, the childless one who was a mother to all of us. The rest is silence."

Then, scarcely believing that I had stepped up to the sanctuary of the church to deliver these words before a human crowd at a Requiem Mass, I was about to return when suddenly Tommy rose and anxiously gestured for me to wait.

He came to speak, shaking violently, and he put his arm around me to steady himself, and I put my hand on his shoulder, and he said into the microphone:

"She gave me the world. I traveled it with her. And everywhere we went, from Calcutta to Aswan to Rio to Rome to London, she gave me those places—in her words, in her enthusiasm, in her passion, and in . . . in . . . showing me and telling me what I could make of my life. I'll never forget her. And though I hope to love other people as she taught me to love people, I'll never love anyone the way I loved her."

Looking up at me to indicate he was finished, he clung to me as we made our way out of the sanctuary and back to the pew.

I was very proud of him and he took my mind off my own sins completely, and, as I sat down right beside Lestat I held Tommy's hand with my left hand and Lestat took my right.

When it came time to receive Communion, a great many people were moving out of the pews to get in line, and of course Tommy and Jasmine were going to do it. And on impulse I rose and went before them to get in line.

And to my utter shock, so did Merrick, and so did Lestat, following my example perhaps, or doing what they would have done in any case.

The three of us received the sacrament.

I took it in my hand as was my custom, then put it in my mouth. I don't know how they took it—whether in their hands or directly into their mouths. But they took it. I felt it dissolve on my tongue as always—such a tiny morsel of food not being repulsed by my body—and I prayed to the God who had come into me to forgive me everything I was. I prayed to Christ to redeem me from what I was. I prayed to know what I must do—if there was any way, honorable or decent or moral—for me to live.

Was Christ inside me? Of course. Why should one miracle cease just because another one had taken hold of me? Was I guilty of sacrilege? Yes. But what is a murderer to do? I wanted God to be inside me. And my Act of Contrition, my renunciation of all sin, was for the moment pure. I knelt with my eyes closed and I thought the strangest thoughts.

I thought of the omniscient God becoming Man and it seemed such a remarkable gesture! It was as if I'd never heard the story before! And it seemed that the omniscient God had to do it to fully understand His Creation because He had created something that could offend Him so deeply as humankind had done. How tangled it was. How bizarre. Angels hadn't offended Him so deeply. No. But human beings had. My head was so full of ideas, and my heart for the moment was full of Christ, and my soul wept its own bloodless tears, and I felt innocent just for this little while.

Fast-forward: the cemetery:

Lonigan and Sons had provided us all with small candles, each with its round paper shield so the wax wouldn't burn our hands. Fr. Kevin Mayfair finished the graveside ceremony with dash and charm. He wept for Aunt Queen. Many people were crying. Terry Sue was still crying. Flowers were heaped all around the coffin on its bier. We were invited to file past and touch the wood for the last time. The gates to the tall granite tomb stood open. The coffin would be interred on one of the shelves after we left.

Patsy broke into hysterical sobbing.

"How could you bring us out here at night!" she shouted at me, her eyes wet and streaming. "You, always you, Tarquin. I hate this place, and you have to bring us at night. You, always you, Tarquin."

I felt sorry for her that she was so unhappy and that everyone was staring at her, and not knowing how sick she was, and how insane she was in general.

Big Ramona tried to quiet her. Merrick Mayfair stood at my elbow watching her intently. I could feel Lestat watching her as well. I felt humiliated for her, but what did it matter to them, her strange theatrics? And why had she come?

She had not come to the gravesides of her own parents. But she had loved Aunt Queen. Everybody had.

And then Big Ramona guided her towards the car. Our lawyer, Grady Breen, tried to pet her and quiet her.

"Damn you, Quinn!" she shouted as they forced her into the limousine. "Damn you to Hell!" I wondered if she had some divining power to call out such perfect curses.

"We should meet tonight," said Merrick in a low voice. "Your spirit friend is dangerous. I can sense his presence. He isn't eager to be seen by me or by Lestat. But he's here. There's no time to lose."

"We'll meet at the house?" I asked.

"Yes, you go with your family," said Lestat. "We'll be waiting for you when you arrive."

"Your mother, she's headed there also," said Merrick. "She wants to leave, however. Try to keep her. We have to talk to her. Tell her that we have to talk to her. Use any means you can to keep her there."

"But why?" I asked.

"When we get together," said Merrick, "you'll understand."

The limousine was waiting for me. And so were Tommy, Patsy, Big Ramona, Nash, Jasmine and Clem.

I glanced back once at the coffin and the mortuary personnel and the cemetery workers as they prepared the crypt—just what they had not wanted us to see—and then I went back to take two red roses from the bank of flowers, and, glancing up, I saw Goblin.

He stood at the very door of the mausoleum. He was dressed as I was, in a black suit, and his hair was like mine, full but trimmed, and he stared at me with wild, sparkling eyes, and all through him, solid though he was, I could see an intricate web of blood, as it infected all that made up the illusion. The image remained for one second, perhaps two, and then winked out as though it had been a flame.

I shuddered. I felt the breeze. The emptiness.

Taking the two roses with me, I got into the car and we headed for Blackwood Manor.

Patsy cried all the way. "I haven't been right up to that damn tomb in all these years," she kept saying. "And we have to come in the middle of the night on account of Quinn, little Quinn, how fitting, little Quinn!"

"You didn't have to come," said Big Ramona. "Now shush, you're making yourself sick."

"Oh, damn you, damn you all, what do you know about sick?"

And so on it went for the long ride home.

By the time we reached the house my anxious hands had involuntarily crushed both roses into wanton petals.

47

PATSY WAS in the front bedroom across from mine, and as soon as we reached home, Cindy, our beloved nurse, went up to attend to her, to make certain she had taken her medicines and to give her some sort of mild tranquilizer. She was soon in an official Blackwood Manor flannel nightgown with no intentions of going anywhere, though when she saw me pass the door to my room she screamed at me that I had made her nauseated by dragging us all to the cemetery "at midnight."

It was not yet midnight.

As for Goblin, everyone knew the danger. I did not have to tell Jasmine and Clem to look after Jerome, or tell Nash to keep his eye close on Tommy. Everyone knew what Goblin had done to Aunt Queen. Even Patsy believed it and Big Ramona was now her companion and guardian.

No one was to climb the staircase alone. No one was to react with panic to the breaking of glass. Everybody was to remain within the house, in pairs or threes, including me, who had my "two friends" visiting in my private parlor.

And they were waiting for me just as they had promised. We clustered around the center table, Merrick, Lestat and I, and Merrick, a tall, very lean woman with almond-colored skin and full dark hair, who had taken off her white scarf and her big glasses, immediately began to talk.

"This creature, this ghost that's haunting you, he's related to you by blood, and the connection is more than important."

"But how can that be?" I said. "I've always believed him to be a spirit. I've been haunted by ghosts. They declare who they are. They have histories; they have patterns."

"He has a history and a pattern too, believe me."

"But what is it?" I asked.

"You have no idea?" she probed, looking me in the eye as if I was concealing something from myself perhaps.

"None whatsoever," I replied. I found it easy to talk to her. I felt she would understand. "He was always with me," I said, "from the beginning. I thought that I created him almost. That I drew him to myself, out of the void, and developed him in my own image. Oh, I know he's made of something. Ether. Astral particles—some form of matter. Something, yes, something that obeys natural laws. Mona Mayfair explained to me once that such spirits have a nucleus, a kind of heart, and a circulatory system, and I understand that my blood feeds that system now, and that he's becoming stronger and stronger as he draws blood from me after I feed. But I've never had an inkling that he was the ghost of somebody."

"I saw him in the cemetery," she responded. "Just as you did."

"You saw him before our crypt? When I went to take the roses?"

"I saw him before that," she said. "He was very strong there. Tarquin, he's your twin."

"Yes, I know, my absolute doppelgänger."

"No, Tarquin, I mean he's the ghost of your twin brother, your identical twin brother."

"That's impossible, Merrick," I said. "Believe me, I appreciate your wanting to attack this problem head-on, but there's a very simple reason why that can't be so. There are two reasons, actually."

"Which are?" she asked.

"Well, first off, if I'd had a twin, I'd know. Somebody would have told me. But far more important, Goblin writes with his right hand. And I've always been left-handed."

"Tarquin," she said, "he's a mirror twin. Haven't you ever heard of them? They mirror each other exactly. And there's an old legend that argues that every left-handed person is the survivor of mirror twins, one of whom perished in the womb, but your twin didn't perish that way. Tarquin, I think we need to talk to Patsy. I think Patsy wants you to know. She's weary of the silence."

I was too shocked to speak.

I made a little gesture for patience and then I stood up and beckoned for them to come with me.

We crossed the hall. Patsy's door was open. Her room didn't have a parlor like mine, but it was spacious and beautiful, with a regal bed done up in blue-and-white ruffles, and a blue silk couch and chairs before it. She was sitting on the couch with Cindy, our nurse, watching the television while Big Ramona sat with her embroidering ring in one of the chairs. The volume of the television was so low it seemed unimportant. Big Ramona rose to go as we entered. So did Cindy.

"What kind of invasion is this?" Patsy asked. "Hey, Cindy, don't you go without giving me another shot. I'm sick. And you, Tarquin Blackwood, half the time you don't know I'm alive. When I die, are you going to drag everybody to Metairie Cemetery at the stroke of twelve?"

"I don't know, Patsy," I said. "Maybe I'll just strangle you and dump you in the swamp. I dream about that sometimes, murdering you and dumping you in the swamp. I dream I did it. You tasted like cotton candy and candy apples, and you sank deep down in the green water."

She laughed and shook her head as she looked at me and at my two friends. In her long white flannel nightgown she looked particularly thin, which worried me for her. And her blond hair, so often teased, was brushed out and hung down in waves, making her look young. Her eyes were big and hard.

"You're so crazy, Tarquin Blackwood," she sneered. "You should have been drowned when you were born. You don't know how much I hate you."

"Now, Patsy, you don't mean that," said Cindy, the nurse. "I'll be up to give you another shot in an hour."

"I'm sick right now," said Patsy.

"You're loaded right now is what you are," said Big Ramona.

"Can we talk to you for a little while?" asked Lestat. He gestured gently and she motioned for him to sit beside her. He settled there and actually put his arm along the back of the couch behind her.

"Sure, I'm glad to talk to friends of Quinn's," Patsy said. "You sit down, all of you. It's never happened before. Nash is so stuck-up, he calls me Miss Blackwood most of the time. Jasmine can't stand the sight of me. She thinks I don't know that black bastard of hers is your child. Like Hell I don't know. Everyone in the parish knows. And she runs around saying, 'He is my son' like he came from a virgin birth, can you imagine? I tell you if that child's father had been anybody but you, Quinn, it would have been out with the trash, but it was little Quinn who got into Jasmine's panties and so it's just fine, according to Aunt Queen, just fine, let the little bastard have the run of the house, it's just—"

"Come on, Patsy, stop it," I said. "If anybody hurt that child's feelings, you'd be the first to stick up for him."

"I'm not trying to hurt him, Quinn, I'm trying to hurt you, 'cause I hate you."

"Well, I'll give you some real good opportunities to hurt me. You just need to talk to me and my friends."

"Well, that will be a pleasure."

Merrick had taken the chair in which Big Ramona had been sitting, and all this while she had been studying Patsy, and now in a low voice she introduced herself by her first name and she introduced Lestat also.

I sat down beside Merrick.

Patsy nodded to these introductions and said with a searingly vicious smile, "I'm Tarquin's mother."

"Patsy, did he have a twin?" Merrick asked. "A twin that was born at the same time he was or moments after?"

Utter silence fell over Patsy. I had never seen such an expression on her face. It went blank, yes, with a combination of stupefaction and dread, and then she screamed for Cindy. "Cindy, I need you, Cindy, I'm panicky! Cindy!"

She turned this way and that, until Lestat placed his hand firmly on her shoulder. He spoke her name in a whisper. She appeared to look into his eyes and to lose her hysteria as if it were being drained out of her.

Cindy appeared in the door with the syringe poised.

"Now, Patsy, you just hang on," she said, and then she came forward and, sitting on Patsy's left, she very modestly lifted the gown and gave Patsy a shot of the sedative in her left hip, and then stood there waiting.

Patsy was still looking into Lestat's eyes.

"You understand," Patsy said. "It was the most pitifulest, terriblest thing—." She shuddered. "You can't imagine."

Without taking his eyes off Patsy, Lestat told Cindy that Patsy was fine now.

Patsy turned her eyes to the Oriental rug and she appeared to be tracing its patterns. Then she looked up at me.

"I hated you so much," she said. "I hate you now. I always hated you. You killed it."

"Killed it! How—?" I was stunned.

"Yes," she said. "You did it."

"What are you saying?" I asked. "How did I do that?" I wanted to probe her mind, but I'd never used that power with her and some profound inveterate distaste kept me from doing it.

"You were so big," she said. "You were so healthy, so normal. Ten pounds, eleven ounces. Even your bones were big. And then that other little one, my little Garwain, only three pounds, and they said he had given you all his blood in my womb, all his blood. You were like a vampire baby drinking up all his blood! It was so awful, and he was so small. Just three pounds. Oh, he was the most terriblest, pitifulest creature you ever saw in your life."

I was too amazed to speak.

The tears were rolling down her cheeks. Cindy took out a clean Kleenex and wiped them away.

"I wanted so badly to hold him, but they wouldn't let me," Patsy went on. "They said he was the donor twin, that's what they called him. The donor twin. He gave everything. And there he was, too tiny hardly to live. They put him in an incubator. They wouldn't even let me touch him. I sat there in that hospital day and night, day and night. And Aunt Queen kept calling me and telling me, 'This baby at home needs you!' What a thing to say to me! Like this tiny little baby in the hospital didn't need me! Like this little pitiful creature in the hospital didn't need me! She wanted me to come home and give my milk to a ten-pound monster of a baby. I couldn't even look at you! I didn't want to be in the same house with you! That's why I moved out back."

She wiped angrily at her tears. Her voice was so soft. I don't think human beings could have heard her. I'm not sure Cindy who sat right beside her could hear her.

"I sat there in that hospital day and night," she said. "I begged them to let me touch that tiny little baby, and don't you know he died in that machine with all those tubes and wires, and monitors and numbers clicking. He died! That little baby, that poor little Garwain, my Little Knight, that's what I called him, Garwain, my Little Knight, and then they let me hold him, when he was dead, that poor tiny infant, I held him in my arms."

I had never seen her like this, never seen her cry such tears, never seen her in such abject sadness. On she went:

"And we had a tiny coffin for him, a white coffin, with him in a white christening gown, all nestled in it, poor little thing, and we went to the Metairie Cemetery, all of us, and Aunt Queen, for the love of God, why on earth did she bring you out there, and you were screaming and hollering and carrying on, and I hated her for bringing you, and she kept saying that you knew that your twin had died, you felt it, that I should hold you, can you imagine, that I should hold you, and there was my little Garwain in the teensy white coffin, and they put him in the grave and I had it carved on the stone, 'Garwain, My Little Knight,' and he's in there now, in his own little place."

The tears flowed down her cheeks. She shook her head.

"Don't you think they moved him for Pops' and Sweetheart's coffins, or Aunt Queen's. No, sir. They did not." She shook her head resolutely. "There are eight slots in that mausoleum, and they did not move him. I saw to that. And I never, never went back to that crypt since the day we buried him until tonight and only because Aunt Queen left it in Grady Breen's hands that I was to get a bonus check if I attended her pitiful stupid funeral. And Grady Breen tipped me off. He gave me a photocopy of the will last night, like I told you, because Aunt Queen said he could do it.

"Now talk about a bribe. If that isn't the limit. And she knew how I felt about that place, she knew, it was her who made me vow I'd never breathe a word to you, that nobody would ever tell you that you had sucked all the blood out of that child, that little three-pound donor child. Like you were the one who had to be protected. Poor Quinn. God help you that you did that, you damn son of a bitch. You don't know what hate is, unless you know how I hate you."

She sobbed into her paper tissue. Cindy was distraught. She rose to go, but Patsy pulled her down. Patsy's trembling fingers clung to her. Lestat's hand closed over Patsy's left shoulder and gently held it.

"Garwain," said Lestat. "And when Goblin began to appear, did it ever seem to you that it might be the ghost of Garwain?"

"No," she said sullenly. "If it had been Garwain's ghost, it would have come to *me* because I loved it! It would never have come to Quinn! Quinn killed it! Quinn took all Garwain's blood. Goblin was just Tarquin wanting a twin because he knew he should have had one, and he killed one, and so he made up Goblin out of nothing, and he used all his craziness to do it. He was crazy from the start."

"No one thought it might be the little one's ghost?" Merrick asked very gently.

"No," said Patsy in the same sullen voice. "Garwain, my Little Knight—that's what's written on the stone." She looked up at me. "And how you screamed at that funeral! How you screamed and screamed! I didn't even look at you for a whole year. I couldn't stand it. I only finally did because Aunt Queen paid me to do it. Pops wouldn't give me a nickel. Aunt Queen paid me all the time you were growing up. It was a clean deal. Don't tell you about the twin, don't make you feel guilty about the twin, don't tell you you killed the little twin, and she'd take care of me, and she did."

She shrugged. She raised her eyebrows and then her face relaxed somewhat, but the tears still fell.

"Aunt Queen gave me fifty thousand dollars," she said. "It wasn't what I wanted, but she gave me that to get started, and to hold you, and so I did. Just one time. And she got Pops and Sweetheart and everybody on her side. You were the one they cared about. Don't ever tell Quinn he had a little brother who died. Like I didn't have a son? Don't ever tell Quinn about little Garwain. Don't ever let him know that he drained all the blood from that helpless little baby. Don't ever tell Quinn that awful story, like it was your story. And so now you come in here and you ask me, did you have a twin. You want to know, and Aunt Queen's dead, and thanks to Grady tipping me off about the bonus and what was in her will, I know it's got nothing to do with telling you anything. So there you have it. And I guess you know now. You know why I've hated you all these years. I guess you can figure it out finally."

I rose to my feet. As far as I was concerned we had discovered what we wanted to know. And I was too shocked and exhausted to say a word to Patsy. I hated her as much as she hated me. I hated her so much I couldn't look at her.

I think I uttered my thanks, and with my two friends I started to leave the room.

"Don't you have something to say to me?" Patsy asked as I reached the door.

Cindy looked so miserable.

"What?" I inquired.

"Can you imagine what I went through?" Pasty asked. "I was sixteen years old when that happened."

"Ah," I replied, "but you're not sixteen years old now, that's what matters."

"And I'm dying," Patsy said. "And no one in all my life has ever loved me the way that people love you."

"You know, that's really true," I responded, "but I'm afraid I hate you the way that you hate me."

"Oh, no, Quinn, no," said Cindy.

"Get away from me," Patsy said.

"That's what I was doing when you stopped me," I answered.

48

BEFORE I COULD so much as think about what I'd heard I had to hear it from Big Ramona and from Jasmine as well, and so I went down the stairs and found them in the kitchen with Jerome and Tommy and Nash. They were around the oak table having a late supper of red beans and rice, and of course invited me to join them.

"I have to know something," I said, not accepting the chair that was offered. "Patsy just told me I had a twin brother who was buried in the Metairie Cemetery. Is this true?"

Immediately I received my answer. I could see it in their faces and read it from their minds. Then Big Ramona said,

"Patsy's got no call to be telling you that now. She's got no call at all." She started to get up.

I gestured for her to sit down.

"And Goblin," I said. "Did you never think Goblin could have been the ghost of that little twin brother, Garwain?" I asked.

"Well, yes, we thought it," said Big Ramona, "but what would have been the good of saying that to a little child, and then to a growing boy, and then to a young man who was off in Europe having a fine time, with Goblin disappeared and not making any more trouble, and then to a fine man come home to a peaceful household?"

I nodded. "I understand," I said. "And it was a smaller twin? A little tiny one?"

"She's got no call for worrying you with all of that," said Jasmine sharply. "Everything's an excuse with that girl. An excuse or a lie. Only reason she carried on about that tiny twin is she wanted everybody to feel sorry for her."

Nash rose to take Tommy out, but I gestured for them to go on with their supper. I could see that Tommy was curious but I didn't see the harm in it. Why keep the secret a moment longer? Nash looked concerned, as he so often did.

"And nobody did feel sorry for Patsy?" I asked.

There was silence all around. Then Big Ramona said,

"That Patsy, she's a liar. Sure, she cried over that little twin. She knew it was going to die. It's easy to feel sorry for something that doesn't have a chance, something that's not going to live a week. It's a lot harder to be a real mother. And Aunt Queen did feel sorry for her and gave her money to start her band. And then she didn't stick around to—."

"I understand," I said. "I just wanted to know."

"Aunt Queen never wanted you to know," said Big Ramona gently. "Like I said, there was no call for anybody to tell you. Pops and Sweetheart didn't want you to know either. Pops always said it was best forgotten. That it was morbid, and he used another word too. What was that other word?"

"Grotesque," said Jasmine. "He said it was morbid and grotesque and he wasn't telling you about it."

"He just never found a good time to tell you," said Big Ramona.

"Sure we thought Goblin was that twin's ghost," said Jasmine, "some of the time, at least, and some of the time we didn't. And I guess, most of the time, we didn't think it mattered."

Big Ramona got up to stir the pot of beans on the stove. She heaped some onto Tommy's plate. My son, Jerome, had peach cobbler all over his face and his plate.

"Now, if when you'd come home from Europe," Big Ramona said, "Goblin had been a big nuisance again, maybe we would have told you about that little twin—you know, to have some sort of exorcism. But you never mentioned Goblin again."

"And then out of nowhere he came," said Jasmine with a catch in her throat, "and he made Aunt Queen fall." She started crying.

"Now don't you start with that," said Big Ramona.

"It's my fault what happened," I responded. "I'm the one who brought him up and made him strong. Whether he was a ghost or spirit doesn't have a whole lot to do with it."

"Then it's not your fault either," said Big Ramona. "And now we have to get rid of him."

I felt a faint breeze in the air. The blades of the overhead fan started to whirl though the fan had been turned off. Jasmine and Big Ramona both felt it.

"Stick together," I said, "and don't look at him, or at any of his tricks. Now I have to go and talk to my friends. I have to talk to them about getting rid of him."

A plate came off the pantry shelf and was smashed on the floor. Jasmine moved shakily to get the broom. Big Ramona made the Sign of the Cross. So did I.

Nash put his arm around Tommy. Tommy seemed thrilled. Little Jerome ate his peach cobbler as if nothing was happening.

I turned and left the room.

He was making his doleful music in the chandeliers.

Big Ramona rushed past me up the steps murmuring that she had to be with Patsy and Cindy. I could hear Patsy's hysterical crying.

I stood outside her closed door listening to her for a long time, unable to make out the syllables, wondering what drug Cindy had injected into her hip that she was still so miserable, and I realized I felt chilled all over. Of course I had always known that she hated me, but she had never said it quite so clearly, quite so convincingly; and now I had my self-hatred to add to the mix, and for the moment it was almost too much for me.

I went into my room and shut the door.

Lestat and Merrick sat at the table, two elegant and high-toned creatures facing one another. I took the chair with my back to the door. The computer was immediately switched on. The windows were rattling. A convulsion moved through the heavy velvet draperies. The trimming of the baldachin over the bed undulated in the breeze.

Merrick rose from the table, looking about, her mahogany hair a thick mass down her back. Lestat watched her keenly.

"Show yourself, spirit," she said in a low breath. "Come, show yourself to those who can see you." Her green eyes probed the room. She turned around, gazing at the gasolier, at the ceiling. "I know you're here, Goblin," she said, "and I know your name, your true name, the name your mother gave you."

At once, the windowpanes closest to us were shattered. The glass flew against the lace curtains but could not pierce them and fell, tangled and splintering and loudly clattering to the floor. The hot breeze of the night gusted into the room.

"Cowardly, foolish trick," said Merrick under her breath, as if she were whispering in his ear. "I could do that myself. Don't you want me to say your true name? Are you afraid to hear it?"

The keys of the computer fired like crazy. I saw nonsense marching across the screen. I drew near to it.

MAKEMERRICKANDLESTATLEAVENOWORIWILLCUTUPALLOF
BLACKWOODMANORWITHGLASSIHATEYOUQUINN

Suddenly a huge amorphous cloud spread itself out beneath the ceiling, the billowing hideous shape of a human form made only of filaments of blood, with a huge and silently screaming face, the entire shape abruptly contracting and thrashing as it surrounded Merrick and whipped her with its tentacles as she fell over backwards onto the carpet.

She threw up her arms. She cried out to us. "Let it be!" And then to Goblin, "Yes, come into my arms, let me know you, come into me, be with me, yes, drink my blood, know me, yes, I know you, yes. . . ." Her eyes appeared to roll up in her head, and then she lay as one unconscious.

At last, when I was just at the point where I could endure it no longer, he rose, a wind full of blood rising, thrashing wildly once more before the ceiling and then gusting through the broken window, more tiny bits of glass flying into the lace curtains, which he left stained with bits of blood and gore, as he left her bare arms and hands and face and legs covered with it.

Lestat helped her to her feet. He kissed her on the mouth and stroked her long brown hair. He helped her into the chair.

"I wanted to burn him!" he said. "God, I was seething to do it."

"So was I," I said. I straightened her white skirt. I took out my handkerchief and began to blot the bloody scratches he had left all over her.

"No, it was too soon for the Fire," she said, "and our meeting had to come. I had to be sure of everything."

"And he is the ghost of my twin? It's true?" I asked.

"Yes, it's true," she said quietly. She motioned for me to stop with my handkerchief, taking my hand gently and kissing it. "He's the ghost of the baby buried in Metairie Cemetery, and that's why he's always been strongest here," she explained. "It's why you couldn't take him with you to Europe, as Lestat told me. It's why he was transparent and weak when you went as far as New York. It's why he was even stronger when you went into New Orleans. It's why he appeared so very strongly by the mausoleum tonight. His remains are inside of it."

"But he doesn't really understand, does he?" I asked. "He doesn't know where he comes from or what his real name is?"

"No, he doesn't know," said Merrick.

I could see the little wounds vanishing, leaving her again the alluring woman she had been before. Her long wavy brown hair was gorgeously mussed, and her green eyes were bloodshot still, and she appeared overall to still be shaken.

"But he can be made to know," she continued, "and this is our most powerful weapon. Because a ghost, unlike a pure spirit, is connected to his remains, and this ghost is most connected. He is connected to you by blood, and that is why, don't you see, he feels he has always had a right to what you have."

"Of course," I said, "oh, of course!" Only now was it hitting me. "He thinks it's his right. We were in the womb together." I felt a deep rivet of pain in my heart.

"Yes, and try to imagine for a moment what death was like for this spirit. First off, he was a twin, and we know of twins that they feel the loss of the other terribly. Patsy speaks of your crying at his funeral. Of Aunt Queen begging her to console you. Aunt Queen knew that you were feeling Garwain's death. Well, Garwain had felt this separation from you in the incubator as well, and at death, undoubtedly his spirit was confused and had not gone on into the Light as it should have gone."

"I see," I responded. "And now for the first time in all these months I feel pity for him again. I feel . . . mercy."

"Feel mercy for yourself," said Merrick kindly. Her entire manner was gracious. In fact, she reminded me very much of Stirling Oliver. "But when you were brought to that funeral for him," she went on, "when you were carried there on the day of his interment, his poor miserable little spirit, cast adrift, found its living twin in you, Tarquin, and became your doppelgänger. Indeed, he became something far stronger than a mere doppelgänger. He became a companion and a lover, a true twin who felt he had a right to your patrimony."

"Yes, and we began our long journey together," I said, "two genuine twins, two genuine brothers." I tried my damndest to remember that I had once loved him. I wondered if she could see into my soul and sense the animosity I now felt for him, the enslavement which had been so vicious for me all during this long year since Petronia had so rudely made me. And the loss of Aunt Queen—the unspeakable loss of Aunt Queen.

"And now that you've been given the Dark Blood," said Lestat in a cross voice, "he wants what he sees as his share of it."

"But that's not all that's happening," said Merrick, continuing in her subdued fashion. She looked intently at me. "I want you to describe for me, if you will, what goes on when he attacks you."

I considered for a moment, then I spoke, my eyes moving from Merrick to Lestat and back again.

"It's like a fusion, a fusion I never felt when I was alive. Oh, he was inside me at times. Mona Mayfair told me that he was. She said when we made love that he was in me and she knew he was there. She could feel this. Mona considers herself a witch on account of the way she feels spirits."

"You love Mona Mayfair?" Merrick asked gently.

"Very much," I managed to reply. "But I'll never see her again. She'd know me for what I am the minute she looked at me. I avoided Rowan Mayfair desperately at the wake and the Mass. Her husband, Michael, too. They're both what the Talamasca calls witches. And then there was the ghost of Julien Mayfair at the wake. Aunt Queen was his child. I'm his descendant."

"You have Mayfair blood?" Merrick asked. "And you saw Julien?"

"My precious darling, I had hot cocoa with Oncle Julien in the days when I could drink it," I said. "He served me animal crackers with it on a china plate, all of which later vanished just as he did."

Very hastily I told her the whole tale, including the affair of the mask and the cape, and saw her lips spread in a generous and beautiful smile.

"Oh, our Oncle Julien," she said with a winsome sigh. "The beds he left unmade and warm, what a man he was. It's a wonder there's anyone in the city of New Orleans who doesn't share some genetic inheritance from him!" She beamed at me. "He came to my Great Nananne in a dream when I was eleven years old and told her to send me to the Talamasca. They were my salvation."

"Oh, God in Heaven," I declared. "You don't know what I almost did to Stirling Oliver."

"Forget that!" said Lestat. "I mean it! That's over and done." He raised his hand and made the Sign of the Cross. "In the name of the Father, and of the Son, and of the Holy Ghost, I absolve you from all sin. Stirling Oliver is alive! Now that matter's closed as long as I'm Coven Master here."

Merrick broke into a soft, sweet laugh. Her dark skin made her green eyes all the more brilliant.

"And you are the Coven Master, aren't you?" she said, with a flirtatious flashing glance at Lestat. "You become that automatically wherever you go."

Lestat shrugged. "But of course," he said, exactly as if he meant it.

"We could argue about that, my magnificently feathered friend," she replied, "but we need this time while Goblin is exhausted. And must get back to the matter at hand. So Goblin is your twin, Tarquin, and you were going to tell me what it's like when the two of you are together now. Describe the fusion."

"It's positively electric," I said. "It's as if his particles, assuming he's made of them—"

"He is," she interjected.

"—are fused with mine, and I lose my equilibrium completely. I'm lost as well in memories, which he either engenders or falls prey to, I don't know which, but we travel back to moments in the crib or the playpen, and I feel only love for him as I must have felt as an infant or a toddler. It's a laughing bliss that I feel. And it's often wordless except for expressions of love, which are rudimentary."

"How long does this last?"

"Moments, seconds," said Lestat for me.

"Yes, and each time is stronger than the one before it," I added. "The last time—it came last night—there was a tug on my heart as well as tiny slashing wounds, much worse than I've felt before, and he exited through the window, shattering all the glass much the same as he did tonight. He's never been so destructive before."

"He has to be destructive now," she said. "He's foolishly increased the material makeup of his being. Whereas once he was almost entirely energy, he now has considerable matter as well, and he can't pass through solid walls as he once did. On the contrary, he needs a doorway or a window."

"That's exactly right," I said. "I've been witnessing it. I've been feeling the air change, feeling him leave."

She nodded. "It's in our favor that he's subject to gravity, but it's always so with ghosts. It's only more so now with him because he's developed an appetite for blood, and so encumbered himself. Can you tell me anything else about this fusion?"

I hesitated, then confessed. "It's very pleasurable. It's like . . . like an orgasm. It's like . . . it's like our contact with our victims. It's like the fusion with them, only it's much much milder."

"Milder?" she asked. "Do you lose your equilibrium when you take your victims?"

"No, no I don't," I answered. "I see your point. But the pleasure isn't as strong with Goblin. I'd admit it if it was. It's confusion I feel, along with mild pleasure."

"Very well. Is there anything more that you can tell me?"

I thought for a long time. "I feel sad," I said, "terribly sad because he's my brother, and he died, and he never had any life except the life I gave him. And now this has occurred, and he can't go on. And I think— I know—I should die with him."

She studied me for several minutes, and so did Lestat, and then Lestat spoke up, his French accent rather sharp as he looked at me:

"That's not required, Quinn, and besides, even if you did try to take him with you into death, there's no guarantee that he would go."

"Precisely," said Merrick. "He might well let you go on and remain here to plague someone else. After all, he chose to be with you because you were his brother. But he could move to someone else. As you told Lestat, he's very cunning and he learns quickly."

Lestat said,

"I don't want you to die, Little Brother."

Merrick smiled. She said,

"The Coven Master won't let you die, Little Brother."

"So what do we do?" I asked. I sighed. "What is to be the fate of Little Brother's Little Brother?"

"In a moment I'll explain that," she said, "but let me explain what is happening now when you fuse with him. He is binding not just with you but with the spirit of the vampire inside you. Now, you know the old tales, that we are all the descendants of one parent in whom a pure spirit fused with a mortal, and that all of us to this very day are part of that one pure spirit, carrying in our preternatural bodies the immortal spirit which animates us and gives us our thirst for blood and our ability to live on it."

"Yes," I said.

"Well, your demon brother, being a ghost himself, is very like a spirit, and when he fuses with you now, he fuses with that spirit in you, and he knows a pleasure far greater than any he knew when you were mortal."

"Ah, I see," I said. "Of course."

"He doesn't understand it. He only knows it's like a sweet drug to him, and he drinks of the vampiric blood to experience the supernatural as long and as completely as he can, and only when his endurance is at an end does he release you and vanish into invisibility and weakness again, lulled and dreaming with the blood he's taken."

"Where does he go?"

She shook her head. "I don't know. He spreads out, losing his shape and his organization. Compare him to a great sea creature who is composed largely of seawater, only with him it's air, and he enjoys the blood as best he can until his energy burns it off, and he must wait for another opportunity, and all this takes time for him, just as appearances and communication have always taken time, as is so with all spirits."

She stopped for a moment and watched me closely, as if to see if I understood. Then she continued.

"The better you understand him, the better it will be for us when I try to send him out of the Earthly Realm, because I can't do it, I don't think, without your full cooperation."

"You have my cooperation," I said. "As for my understanding, I'm trying."

"Are you ready to let him go?" she asked.

"Let him go! Merrick, he killed Aunt Queen. I loathe and despise him! I hate him! I hate myself that I ever nourished him and fostered him! He's betrayed the womb we shared!"

She nodded to this.

The tears rose up in my eyes. I took out my handkerchief, but I had half a mind to let them flow. I was with the two people in the world who wouldn't be stunned by the sight of them.

"So how do we get rid of him?" I asked. "How do we get him out of the Earthly Realm?"

"I'll tell you," Merrick responded. "But first let me ask. When we arrived tonight, I saw a very old cemetery down by the swamp. Lestat said it belonged to you. He said you'd seen spirits there."

"Yes," I replied. "Dumb spirits, spirits that give you nothing." I wiped at my eyes. I felt a little more calm.

"But there are two or three raised tombs there, maybe three feet high."

"There's one that's about that height. The letters are all worn away."

"It's broad? Long?"

"Both. A rectangle."

"That's good. I want you to lay out wood and coal for a big fire on that tomb. You need plenty of fuel. The fire has to burn really hot and for some time. Then throughout the rest of the cemetery, I want candles. Candles on every grave. You know the kind of candles I mean, thick church candles." (I nodded.) "I'll light the candles. I'll light the fire. Just have these things ready for me. You can have your people do this part if you like, it's not important who does it."

"But surely you don't want them around," said Lestat.

"No, I don't. They have to go away from Blackwood Farm. Everybody."

"What do I tell them?" I asked.

"Tell them the truth," said Merrick. "Tell them that we are holding an exorcism to get rid of Goblin. The ritual is a dangerous one. Goblin in his fury might try to hurt anyone."

"Of course," I said. "But there's one problem. Patsy. Patsy is the only one who might not go."

"Patsy herself has given you the key to her character," said Lestat. "Here." He reached into his pocket and he took out a gold money clip bulging with thousand-dollar bills. "Give her this. Send her with her nurse to a fine hotel in New Orleans."

"Of course," I said again.

"Big Ramona will see that she goes," said Merrick. "You yourself see that everyone else is gone, and sending them to the Windsor Court or the Ritz-Carlton Hotel is a fine idea. I'm sorry I didn't think of it."

"I'll take care of it," I said. "But tell me—the actual exorcism. How are you going to do it?"

"The best way I know how," she said. "My loving friends, the Troop of Beloveds, don't call me a witch for nothing."

49

I THIRSTED and I was alone.

I stood beneath the oak tree at the edge of the cemetery. I looked at the tomb which would be our altar tomorrow night.

Clem had known just where he would get our firewood—an old dead oak on the very boundary of the pasture. Tomorrow he'd come back and cut it with the chain saw, and the coal he'd buy in Mapleville. I wasn't to worry about a thing.

And for now he was gone with the rest of them. They had been glad to be going. There had been a positive excitement to their packing and laughter and talking, and rushing out to the limousine with suitcases, and hollering in the middle of the night.

Tommy had pleaded desperately to be allowed to watch the exorcism. Nash had finally guided him to the car.

Only Patsy had refused to go. Only Patsy had cursed at me and told me she wouldn't go along with my self-centered schemes to get rid of Goblin, only Patsy had remained behind. Finally I had sent Cindy the nurse away.

"I'll take care of her," I had said.

And so the moment had come. It had been so quiet, actually, with the closing of the door of her room.

"What are you doing in here?" she had asked me. "You spoilt brat."

Like a little child she looked in her cream-colored flannel nightgown, with her beauty parlor blond hair in rivulets down each side of her face.

"Get out of here," she had said, "I don't want you here. Get going. I won't leave this house no matter what you do, you little bastard."

And from her mind came the pure stream of animosity and jealousy, the pure hate she had so keenly expressed.

"I told you I don't want your money! I hate you."

And then behind her, the filmy figure of Rebecca, my long-ago ghost. Hateful ghost, vengeful ghost. Why had she been there?— Rebecca, in her pert lace blouse and full taffeta skirt, smiling. Get away from me, vengeful ghost. Why had she dared to be there? *A life for my life.* I will not hear you!

I had picked up Patsy and snapped her neck before she had even become frightened. Killed my mother, my own mother. Big empty eyes. Lipstick. Dead Patsy.

Not a drop of her blood had I drunk.

Did anyone see me carry her over the threshold like a bride? No one, except for Rebecca, vengeful, hateful Rebecca hovering near the grave-yard, Rebecca, just a vapor, smiling, exultant, in her pretty dress. *A death for my death.*

And no one else saw me lay Patsy down in the pirogue. No one saw me go with her limp body out into the deepest waters of the swamp. And there she went down, down beneath the slimy green water—Cotton Candy Patsy no more. Barbie no more. My mother no more.

No one but me felt the shimmer of Rebecca. No one but me heard Rebecca's voice: "Now I count that a real fine vengeance: the life of Patsy for my life." Laughter.

"Get thee behind me, Satan," I had said. "I didn't do this for thee but for me."

And then no more Rebecca, just as there was no more Patsy.

It had been so startling, the ghost gone, and Patsy gone, and the dense deadful swamp so empty. Mothergone.

The gators had moved in the water. Eat up Mother.

I had gone back alone to the empty cemetery.

Hours had passed.

And the blood of my mother was on my hands though there was no blood. And I would lie when I had to tell about her leaving, as I had lied about so much else, Quinn the killer of his own mother, Quinn the killer of the womb that bore him, Quinn the killer of so many, Quinn the killer of the bride, Quinn who had carried his mother over the threshold, Quinn who had sunk Patsy in the waters of the swamp.

I was alone now on Blackwood Farm.

And such a thing had never, ever happened, my being alone on this my land. And I stood beneath the oak looking at the tomb on which the altar would be laid, and wondering if the evil creature Goblin whom my little brother had become, the killer of Aunt Queen, could really be forced into the Light.

I closed my eyes. How I thirsted. But it was almost morning. I couldn't hunt. I hadn't the stamina. And tomorrow night, how could I do such a thing? Yet I had to do it before we began. How foolish had been my planning that I hadn't put aside my sorrow and my murdering hate, and gone before now.

Why did I linger by the little cemetery? What was I trying to remember? Where were the mute ones who had long ago gazed on me in my innocent years? Why did they not come this morning as the sky turned purple and pink to tell me that I belonged with the dead?

Maybe the sun wasn't as painful as the fire. But how could I do my part in destroying Goblin by merely walking into the morning? I needed courage. I needed strength.

I have it for you. Come into my arms.

I turned around. It was Lestat. I obeyed his command. I felt his arms tighten as he closed them. I felt his hand on the back of my head.

Kiss me, young one. Take what you need. It's mine to give.

I pressed my teeth to his skin. I felt the surface give and the boiling blood fill my mouth and flood down my throat. I felt it, potent and divine. For a long moment the pure physical power of it overcame all imagery, but then there rose a deluge of pictures, vivid and high tempo and neon brilliant, a roaring carousel of life, the shuffling of centuries, the panoply without end of magnificent sensations, and at last, a jungle of myriad colors and flowers and the tender, pulsing core of his heart, his pure heart, his heart for me, his heart and nothing more could ever be wanted, nothing evermore.

50

SUMMER NIGHT. The sun didn't set until six-thirty. Quiet lay over Blackwood Farm.

Clem had banked the firewood high around the entire tomb, and wood and coal were layered on top of it. And everywhere stood the candles.

Merrick was there in a lovely full-skirted dress of black cotton with long sleeves, and beads of jet around her throat. Her hair was free. And she carried with her a very large bag covered with fancy and glittering beadwork with two grips for handles, which she carefully set beside one of the tombs, and she made the Sign of the Cross and laid her hand respectfully on that grave, which was to be the altar.

With a lighter she ignited the first candle. Then from the bag she took a long taper, and, once it was lighted, went to the other candles one by one. Slowly the little cemetery filled with light.

Lestat stood at my side with his hand in the small of my back. I was shivering as if I was cold.

At last the entire graveyard was illuminated, and as Clem had put several rows of candles in the little church, which I had forgotten altogether, they were lighted by Merrick as well, and a flickering light came from the church windows.

I felt a cold trepidation as Merrick lifted the can of kerosene and poured it over the coals and the wood lavishly, and then applied the taper and stepped back. I had never seen a freestanding fire of this size.

"Come here to me, both of you," she called out. "And be my helpers, and repeat what I tell you to repeat and do as I say. What you've believed in the past is not important. Believe with me now. That is everything.

And you must put your faith in what I do and say to make this exorcism strong."

We both gave her our consent.

"Quinn, don't fear it," she said.

The fire was blazing and crackling. I stepped back, instinctively, and Merrick and Lestat moved back as well. Lestat seemed particularly to hate it. Merrick seemed in some way fascinated. Too fascinated, I thought, but then what did I know?

"Tell me the true names of Garwain's parents and ancestors, as you know them," said Merrick.

"Julien and Grace; Gravier and Alice; Thomas and Rose; Patsy—that's all."

"Very well. Now remember what I've said to you," she told us. And, stepping back, she reached into the large black bag again and took from it a golden knife. With the knife she slashed at her wrist, and, drawing as close to the fire as she could, she let her blood splash into it.

Then Lestat, fearing for her, yanked her back from the scorching flames.

She drew in her breath as though she had been in danger and even frightened herself. Then she brought out a chalice from the bag, and she told me to hold it, and she slashed her wrist again, deeply and roughly, and the blood flowed into the cup, and she took it from me, and she heaved the blood into the flames.

The heat of the fire was dreadful now, and it frightened me and I hated it. I hated it with a Blood Hunter's instinct and a human's instinct. I was relieved when Merrick took the chalice from my hands.

Suddenly Merrick threw back her head and raised her arms, forcing us both to step away from her and give her room. She cried out:

"Lord God, Who made all things, seen and unseen, bring your servant Garwain to me, for he still roams the Earthly Realm and is lost to your Wisdom and your Protection! Bring him here to me, Lord, that I may guide him to you. Lord, hear my cry. Lord, let my cry come unto you. Hear your servant Merrick. Look not on my sins, but on my cause! Join your voices with me, Lestat and Tarquin! Now."

"Hear us, O Lord," I said immediately, hearing Lestat murmuring a similar prayer. "O Lord, hear us. Bring Garwain here."

Frightened as I was, I found myself suddenly locked to the ceremony, and as Merrick continued, Lestat and I murmured some of the more familiar chants.

"Lord, look with mercy on your servant Garwain," called out Merrick, "who from infancy has roamed in confusion among other mortals, lost from the Light and no doubt hungering for it. Lord, hear our prayer. Lord, look down on Garwain, Lord, send Garwain to us!"

All of a sudden, a huge gust of wind swept the nearby oak trees, and a shower of leaves came down on the fire, which sent up a roar of crackling, and the wind greatly excited it and increased it, and I saw above it, as best as I could, the figure of Goblin as my double, his eyes red in the light of the fire.

"You think a spirit doesn't know the tricks of a witch, Merrick," said Goblin in his low flat voice, which carried over the noise of the fire—a voice I hadn't heard in over four years. "You think I don't know you want to kill me, Merrick? You hate me, Merrick."

At once the figure began to thin out and grow immense and come down with full force upon Merrick, but she cried out:

"Burn now, burn!"

And we all cut loose with our force against him, crying out the single word, "burn," as we sent the power, and as he rose over the flames we saw him, a thing of myriad tiny flames, paralyzed above the fire and retracting and howling in a soundless and ghastly confusion, and then turning in on himself and coiling so that he became a formed wind assaulting the altar, and then a funnel as he bore down on Merrick once again.

The noise was intolerable. The leaves were a hurricane upon us and the blaze flared. Merrick staggered backwards, but we kept up the force, crying out:

"Burn, Garwain, burn!"

"Burn till all of you is pure ghost as it should be!" cried Merrick, "and you can pass into the Light as God wills, Garwain!"

And then she turned and from the large black bag she snatched a small bundle, and, peeling back the white blankets that covered it, she revealed the small shriveled corpse of a child!

"This is you, Garwain!" she cried out. "This is you, brought from your grave, the body from which you departed, wandering astray, confounded and confused! This is your mortal body, your infant self, and from this self you have roamed lost and feeding upon Quinn! See this tiny form, this is your form, Goblin!"

"Liar!" came his voice, and he rose up on this side of the altar, right before us, my doppelgänger down to the buttons, raging at her and trying to snatch the tiny black shriveled infant out of her arms, but she wouldn't let it go and she roared at him:

"You are smoke and mirrors, you are air and will and theft and terror. Go where God will send you! Lord, I beg you, take this servant, take him as you will!"

His image wavered. He was trying to fuse with her. She was resisting him with all her power. I could see him faltering and fading. He grew pale and large and billowing in the firelight. What did the fire feel like to him?

Once again, he rose high above us, spread out above us like a canopy.

I raised my voice: "Dear God, who made Julien, Gravier, Patsy, take him, take this orphan! Grace, Alice, Rose, come for this doomed wanderer. Add your prayers to ours."

"Yes," cried Merrick, clutching the infant corpse tight to her breast, "Julien, Gravier, Thomas—I beg you, come from your eternal rest and take this child into the Light, take him!"

"I repudiate you, Goblin, now and forever!" I called out. "I do so before God! Before Pops, before all my ancestors, before the angels and the saints! O Lord hear my prayer!"

"O Lord, hear our cry!" pleaded Merrick.

She lifted the baby up, and I saw with my own eyes a living child! I saw its limbs move, I heard its mewling! I heard its crying!

"Yes, Goblin!" she cried out. "Your infant self, yes! Come into this form. Come into your rightful flesh! I adjure you, come as I command you."

High above the fire the giant image of Goblin shivered, horrific and weak and confused, and then plunged, plunged into the crying infant. I saw it. I felt it. I said in my heart: *Amen, brother, amen.*

There came a terrible wailing and once again the branches of the oak trees thrashed in the wind.

And then there was utter stillness except for the fire. There was a stillness so total that it seemed the Earth had stopped turning.

Only the fire roared.

I realized I was on the ground. An invisible force had knocked me down.

I was seeing a brilliant light but it wasn't hurting my eyes. It was nothing short of magnificent and it was falling down on the fire, and yet something terrible was happening in the fire.

Merrick had gone into the fire. Merrick had climbed up on the altar and had gone into the fire with the baby and they were both burning. They were burning—unspeakable, irrevocable—but in the pure celestial Light I saw figures moving, thin figures—the gaunt unmistakable figure of Pops in the Light, and with him an infant, a tiny infant toddling along, and there also was Merrick, Merrick and a small old woman, and I saw Merrick turn and raise her hand as if to say farewell.

I lay transfixed by the Light, by its immensity and the undeniable sense of love that seemed part of its nature.

I think that I cried.

Then slowly the great wealth of blessed Light faded. Its warmth and its glory went away. The heat of the night closed around me. The Earth was the lonely Earth again.

Rediscovering my limbs and how to use them I rose to my feet and realized Lestat had pulled Merrick's body from the fire and was sobbing and trying to put out the flames that were consuming her, beating at her burning figure with his coat.

"She's gone, I saw her go," I said.

But he was frantic. He wouldn't listen to me. The flames were finally smothered, but half her face was burnt away and most of her torso and her right arm. It was a dreadful sight. He slit his wrist, he let the thick, viscid blood pour down on her body, but nothing happened. I knew what he wanted to happen. I knew the lore.

"She's gone," I said again. "I saw her go. I saw her in the Light. She waved farewell."

Lestat stood up. He wiped at his blood tears and at the soot on his face. He couldn't stop crying. I loved him.

We lifted her remains and put them on the altar together. We built up the fire and it wasn't long before the body was ashes, and we scattered them. And the fire and Merrick's body were no more.

The humid night was quiet and calm and the cemetery lay in darkness.

Lestat cried.

"She was so young among us," he said. "It's always the young ones who end it. The ones for whom mortality holds magic. As we grow older it's eternity that is our boon."

51

LESTAT WAS still covered in soot. He didn't much care about it. We rang the front doorbell of Oak Haven, and it was Stirling himself who answered, in his heavy quilted robe, and perfectly astonished to see the pair of us right there at the Retreat House of the Talamasca—two wanderers in the night.

Of course he invited us into the library and we accepted the invitation, and we settled into the big leather wing chairs that were so comfortably arranged everywhere, and Stirling told the agreeable little housekeeper that we didn't require anything, and then we were alone.

Slowly, in a broken voice, Lestat told Stirling what had happened to Merrick. He described the ceremony and how Merrick had climbed onto the altar, and what he had seen—the baby come alive, and Goblin descending into it.

And then I told Stirling what I had seen—the Light and the figures moving in the Light. Lestat had not seen this Light but he never doubted me.

"May I put this into our records?" Stirling asked. He took out his handkerchief and wiped at his nose. He was crying inside for Merrick. And then the tears came and he let them flow for a moment and then he wiped them away.

"That's why I'm telling you," said Lestat. "So you can close your file on Merrick Mayfair, and know what became of her. So it doesn't end in silence and confusion, so you don't mourn for her forever without ever knowing where she wandered or what she became. She was a gentle soul. She preyed upon the Evil Doer only. No innocent blood ever stained her hands. And it was very deliberate what she did. And why she chose this moment I don't really know."

"I think I know," I said. "But I don't want to be presumptuous. She chose this moment because she wasn't alone. She had Garwain."

"And how do you feel now that he's gone?" asked Stirling.

"Free of him," I responded, "and rather shocked by all that's happened. Shocked that Garwain killed Aunt Queen. You knew he did that, didn't you? He frightened her and made her fall. Everyone knew it."

"Yes," Stirling said, "there was much talk about it at the wake. What will you do now?"

"I'm shocked that Merrick died," I said. "Merrick freed me of Garwain. Lestat loved Merrick. I loved Merrick. I don't know what I will do or where I will go. There are people who need me. There have always been people who need me, people who matter to me. I'm enmeshed in human life."

I thought in silence of the murder of Patsy. I wanted desperately to confess it, but I loathed myself so much for it that I didn't speak of it at all.

"That's a good way to put it," Lestat said bitterly, " 'enmeshed in human life.' "

Stirling nodded to this.

"Why don't you ask *me* what I'll do?" asked Lestat archly, with a raised eyebrow and a wink.

"Would you tell me?" asked Stirling with a little laugh.

"Of course not," said Lestat. "But I'm in love with Tarquin, you can put that in your file, if you like. That doesn't mean you can entrap me at Blackwood Manor, and you do remember your promise to me to leave Tarquin alone, don't you?"

"Absolutely," said Stirling. "I'm a man who keeps his promises."

"I have a question for you," I said shyly. "I've talked to Michael Curry and Rowan Mayfair several times in the last few months, but they only put me off with vague answers. They won't really tell me much about Mona except that she can't see me, that she's undergoing a special therapy, that she's in intensive care. They say she can die from any kind of infection. I can't even talk to her on the phone—."

"She's dying," Stirling said. He sat staring at me.

Silence.

Then Lestat spoke:

"Why are you telling him this?"

Stirling was still looking at me.

"Because he wants to know," Stirling responded.

"Very well," said Lestat. "Come on, Little Brother, let's hunt. I know of two Evil Doers in Boca Raton who are alone in a magnificent waterfront mansion. It will be such fun, you wouldn't believe. Good night, Stirling. Good night to the Talamasca. Let's go."

52

THE SKY WAS still a deep lavender when I walked into the house the following night. Lestat was lingering in the cemetery saying some last prayer for Merrick, or to Merrick, I wasn't sure which.

Our hunting last night in Boca Raton had been marvelous and he had once again given me the gift of his all-powerful blood and I was exhilarated and confused and praying in my own way for some sign of what to do about Mona, wondering if I could just see her and talk to her; if I went to Mayfair Medical and insisted, could I perhaps use some spellbinding power to get to where she was? One last glimpse . . . one last talk.

But suddenly Jasmine and Clem both came rushing up to me at the foot of the stairs.

"There's a crazy woman in your bedroom," said Jasmine. "There was nothing we could do to stop her, Quinn. It's Mona Mayfair, you remember her? She's up there, Quinn. She drove here in a limousine full of flowers, Quinn, and she's a living skeleton, you're gonna die when you see her. Quinn, wait, we couldn't stop her. Only reason we helped her with all those flowers is she was so weak."

"Jasmine, lemme go!" I shouted. "I love her, don't you understand?"

"Quinn, she's got something wrong with her! Be careful!"

I ran up the stairs as fast as any mortal man dared and rushed into my bedroom and slammed the door shut and locked it.

She rose up to greet me. A living skeleton! Oh yes! And the bed was covered with her flowers. I stood there shocked to the core of my being, shocked and so glad to see her, so glad to rush to her and take her fragile form in my arms! My Mona, my frail and withering Mona, my pale and magnificent Mona, oh, my God, don't let me hurt you.

"I love you, my beloved Ophelia," I said, "my Ophelia Immortal, and mine always . . ."

Oh, look at the roses, the marguerites, the zinnias, the lilies.

"Noble Abelard," she whispered. "I've come to ask the ultimate sacrifice; I've come to ask, let me die here, let me die with you here, let me die here instead of there with their needles and their tubes, let me die in your bed."

I drew back. I could see the entire outline of her skull beneath her skin, and the bones of her shoulders underneath the spotted hospital gown that she wore. Only her full red hair had been spared. Her arms were like sticks, and her hands were the same. It was ghastly, the sight. She suffered with every breath.

"Oh, my darling, my sweetheart, thank God you came to me," I told her, "but can't you see what's happened to me? Can't your witch's eyes see? I'm not human anymore. I'm not your Noble Abelard. I don't sleep where the rays of the sun can reach me. Look at me, Mona, look at me. Do you want to be what I am?" What was I saying? I was mad. I couldn't stop myself. "Do you want to be what I am?" I asked again. "Because you won't die if you want to be what I am! If you'll live off the blood of others forever. You'll be immortal with me."

I heard the lock of my door turn. I was outraged, then silenced. It was Lestat who entered.

Mona stared in astonishment. He had removed his sunglasses, and he stood under the gasolier as if he was bathing in its light.

"Let me work the Dark Trick, Quinn," he said. "That way, you'll be much closer to your princess. Let me take her for you with my strong blood, and that way your minds won't be closed to each other. I'm a past master at such Dark Tricks, Quinn. Mona, would you know our secrets?" He came to her. "Make your choice, pretty girl. You can always choose the Light some other night, *cherie*. Ask Quinn if you doubt it. He's seen it. He's seen the Light of Heaven with his own eyes."

She clung to me while he talked to her, pacing the floor, back and forth, telling her so many things—how it was with us, the rules, the limitations, the way he violated the rules and the limitations, the way the strong and the old survived, the way the new ones went into the flames. On and on he talked, and she clung to me, my Ophelia in her nest of flowers, with her legs so fragile and her whole little body trembling, oh, sweet Ophelia Immortal.

"Yes. I want it," she said.

A NOTE ON THE TYPE

This book was set in Janson, a typeface long thought to have been made by the Dutchman Anton Janson, who was a practicing typefounder in Leipzig during the years 1668–1687. However, it has been conclusively demonstrated that these types are actually the work of Nicholas Kis (1650–1702), a Hungarian, who most probably learned his trade from the master Dutch typefounder Dirk Voskens. The type is an excellent example of the influential and sturdy Dutch types that prevailed in England up to the time William Caslon (1692–1766) developed his own incomparable designs from them.

Composed by Creative Graphics, Allentown, Pennsylvania
Printed and bound by R. R. Donnelley & Sons, Harrisonburg, Virginia
Designed by Virginia Tan